SUPERSTRING

VICTOR CABINTA

Superstring

Victor Cabinta, Regan Westergard

For

Rhoana, Justin, Kierr, Gladys, and Junior.

Thank you for living in my world with me.

To my best friend,

Jesruel Segovia.

Your unending love and support got me through it.

Contents

Prologue

October 4, 2007

The meadow stretches out before me, a world too perfect to be real. Every blade of grass glistens in the soft golden light, swaying as a breeze whispers through, carrying the scent of something sweet—it reminds me of honey but sharper, more alive. The sky hangs in a mesmerizing blend of deep purples and soft amber, as if dawn and dusk have collided in an endless moment.

High above, birds—or what I *think* are birds—glide silently. Their wings shimmer, catching the light in a way that makes them flicker, almost like they aren't really there at all. Their song is faint, a distant hum, like a lullaby meant to soothe the earth. It should feel peaceful, but it doesn't. It's *too* perfect, *too* still.

At the far edge of the meadow, a towering tree looms above, its branches stretching toward the sky. Its bark, twisted and ancient, radiates a soft glow, and its leaves are a deep ocher hue, catching every last ray of light. They shimmer and chime faintly, like the wind itself is playing a quiet tune through them. Around the tree, golden dust swirls in constant motion, pulsing with life. It dances in loops around the branches, never settling—charged with something beyond my understanding.

The sun dips lower, casting shadows that stretch across the meadow, yet the tree remains untouched, bathed in its own golden glow. The dust keeps spiraling, vibrant and alive, adding to the feeling that this tree isn't just *part* of the world, but *beyond* it. A pull stirs deep in my chest, an instinct to reach out, to step closer. But I don't. My feet stay frozen, and I just watch.

The air thickens, heavy with something I can't name. Silence deepens. I feel this world holding its breath.

"Psst, Rictor, wake up."

And just like that, it snaps away.

"Pa?"

One eye cracks open, his voice pulling me back into the waking world. His hand rests firm on my shoulder. The glow of the tree, the swirling gold dust—it's all gone, slipping away like it was never there.

He's already in his jumpsuit, ready for work. "Happy birthday, *anak*," he says, sitting on the edge of my mattress. He's huge, broad-shouldered, his light brown eyes crinkling as he smiles. It always makes me feel safe, like no matter what, everything will be okay.

"Thanks, Pa," I mumble, rubbing my eyes as I sit up.

"Twelve already, huh?"

"Yeah, Pa, I'm a man now," I grin.

He laughs and pinches my cheeks. The overpowering scent of Axe tickles my nose, and I sneeze.

"I showered; I promise," he protests.

"It's your body spray, Pa. It *stinks*," I say, wrinkling my nose.

"Hey, your Mama loves it."

"Gross."

The bubble of brief happiness deflates in my chest. My stomach twists, and I drop my gaze.

"What's wrong, *nak*?" Pa's brows furrow as he lays a hand on my knee. "It's your birthday, you should be happy."

"Do you really have to go, Pa?" My voice cracks, tears pricking at my eyes. "Can't you stay for my party? You're never around anymore."

He hesitates for a moment. Then, as if finding the right time to say it, he exhales. "I promise, when I come back, I'll quit."

My head snaps up. "*Really?*"

"Yes. So don't be sad." He presses a kiss to my forehead. "Now, you wanna see your gift or what?"

I try to hide the greedy expression that crosses my face.

"Do you remember when I told you about the white hole that appeared by the moon?" he asks softly. Of course, I remember. It was a NASA secret, but Pa had trusted *me* with it. It was the most important thing I had ever learned.

"I haven't told anyone, not even my friends," I whisper back.

He smiles. "That's good, *nak*. You remember what a white hole is?"

"Yeah. It's like the opposite of a black hole. It doesn't suck things up, it vomits them out."

Pa nods. "And what did the white hole on the moon spit out?"

"Space rocks!" I whisper excitedly. "Am I getting graded for this test, Pa?"

He chuckles. "No, no." Reaching into his pocket, he pulls out a small gray box and lifts the cover. "These are for you."

"Are—"

"The white hole's vomit." He hands me the box. Inside, six meteorite shards rest like clumps of white, hardened sand, metallic gold crisscrossing the glittering surface. I pick one up between my fingers, and a soft glow pulses through my palm—gentle, like silent heartbeats. I glance up at Pa.

His face has gone pale, like he's seen a ghost.

"Is it supposed to do that?" I ask nervously.

His eyes widen, as if seeing the golden glow for the first time. He inhales sharply and nods. "Yeah, they're supposed to... do that."

"Cool. They're all mine?"

Instead of answering, he snatches the stone from my hand, inspecting it closely. The glow vanishes the moment it leaves my skin.

My brows furrow. "Is it broken?"

"No, uh—the light... disappears after a few seconds." He hesitates before placing it back in my palm. The stone is warm now, its weight comforting despite its alienness.

"Can I share them with my friends?" I ask suddenly, looking up from the cosmic shard. My closest friends have grown up right alongside me—they're more like siblings than anything.

Pa studies me for a moment. "Do you trust them?"

I laugh. It's a ridiculous question. "Almost as much as I trust you."

"Then okay. But it has to be a secret."

I close the gray box, clasping my hand tightly around the space rock. Its jagged edges press into my palm. "Thank you, Pa!" I throw my arms around him, hugging him as hard as I can.

He lets out the breath he's been holding and returns the hug. "I have to go now, *anak.*" He gives me one last squeeze, kissing my forehead. "I'll be back, okay? Then we can look at those together."

"I love you, Pa!"

"I love you, *anak.*"

He stands, moving toward the darkened doorway before glancing back at me. He smiles.

"Astralis."

"Astralis," I echo.

BOOK ONE:

AFTER ALL THESE YEARS

September 26th, 2024

Dear Rictor,

I've been sitting at this table for what feels like hours now, trying to find the right words to say to you. But I don't think there are any. Maybe an apology is a good start. I'm sorry that it took this long for me to contact you. Your Auntie Ina would have written this herself, but in all honesty, Rick, she hasn't been herself lately. But she has been thinking about all of you. I can't believe how successful you've become.

It says here on Google you are the Head Game Developer of Flemming Corporations. I am an old man now. I don't know what that means, but you sound really important. I'm so proud of you. I'm sure Jhoanalyn would be too.

From time to time, I think back to the wonderful group of friends that my baby girl was so grateful to be a part of. All the adventures your little squad had in our backyard, like you were all living in a different world. It brings me to tears all the time. Those are my favorite memories of her and all of you. I took pride in watching your friendships blossom into something so unbreakable, just like what your Auntie Ina and I have with all your parents. I wish I had checked up on all of you a little sooner or even kept some semblance of a relationship with you.

I have always considered all of you my children. I hope you understand why your Auntie and I did not stay in touch, and how hard it has been these past several years. Please forgive me, because you are all so important to Jhoanalyn.

I don't know how to tell you this.

I wish I could do it in person, but I don't have what it takes. Your Auntie Ina and I have finally come to a decision. After a few months of hard thinking and with heavy hearts, we've decided to end our little girl's suffering. I never wanted to lose hope, but it's been far too long. I don't think I have any fight left in me, and neither does your auntie.

Jhoanalyn's not coming back to us, and it's time we let her go. We will host a vigil in our house from September 30th to October 6th. We invited everyone in town to come and pay their final respects. I know I'm asking a lot, but she needs her best friends now more than ever, to say her final goodbye. Please. I beg you, come home.

Sincerely, Uncle Kit

Naputi

RICTOR

My head spins. A sharp ringing fills my ears, blotting out all sound. I can't catch my breath. The letter slips from my fingers.

Two days...

Cold pins shoot through my legs, twisting my stomach into knots. I glance at the glass walls—is anyone watching? I lunge for the door, lock it, and swipe my hand down to activate privacy mode. The glass clouds over. My legs give out, but the rolling chair catches me before I hit the ground. I grip the edge of the table, my pulse racing like it's trying to escape.

They're killing Jhoana? The weight of this letter lures a portion of memory inside my brain's cortex, and I am twelve years old once again. The echoes of my own screams resound in my ears. There are trees, a forest, I think, but it's vague. An overwhelming sense of fear clouds the vision. *Bitch... It's happening again.*

I'm not able to see anything past that memory because my brain protects me from it. Dissociative amnesia, my therapist calls it. I stabilize my breathing and glance at the letter lying on the floor.

"Uncle Kit..." I haven't heard from him or his family since I left after high school. He was such a kind man, truly the Squad's dad when all our parents were busy with work. He always ensured we were fed—cooked most of our meals when we stayed at their house—and walked us home when our parents couldn't pick us up. He always loved being a stay-at-home dad to his two kids.

My throat tightens. None of them deserve this—least of all Jhoana. The last time I saw her is a vivid and unchanging memory. She had those adorable chubby cheeks that always made her smile so warm and inviting. I still see her signature look: that Dora the Explorer haircut, the blue headband, and her teal jacket she wore from October to March. It was so perfectly her.

Despite being the softest one in our Squad, she was always clinging to Emierr, who was the complete opposite. Jhoana had a timid nature, but she was the glue that brought us all back together whenever we had our little fights.

In the most challenging year of my life, she was the one who carried me through. Ma couldn't be there for me, neither physically nor emotionally, and I get it. She was hurting too, but I was just a kid. It felt like the pain of losing Pa would never fade, but Jhoana never left my side. She believed in me and pushed me to become stronger. I wipe away a tear. All I can see now is her gentle smile and the warmth that came with it.

The room starts closing in on me. It's an all-too-familiar sensation. My chest constricts, and I struggle to catch my breath. I rush towards the door, fumbling with the knob and desperately unlocking it. As my field of vision shrinks, I flee the room, aware of the stares from every booth on the floor. I need to escape. Finally reaching the hallway, I lean against the wall, resting my forearms and forehead on it for support.

Breathe, Ricky, breathe! "No... It's our fault. It's our fault. It's our fault." The ringing starts in my ears again, and my twelve-year-old self's screams return. I can see my own face through fronds of near-black. The face. . . It isn't right.

"Rick?" a muffled voice calls out, and I instinctively shrug the comforting hand off my shoulder. The ringing in my ears intensifies, overwhelming my senses. With a raised index finger, I signal for them to wait as I focus on taking slow, deep breaths. "Take it easy, Rick," Bonnie's familiar voice reassures me. I finally look at her, seeing genuine concern etched on her face.

"Sorry," I mutter, still trying to regulate my oxygen levels.

"What's happening? I've never seen you like this," she asks. Her worry fills the narrow space, carried by her tone and lined in her face.

I hesitate, searching for the right words. How do I explain the fact that I'm hallucinating due to inexplicable childhood trauma? How do I tell her that my childhood best friend is on the brink of death, and I can't shake off the feeling that I played a part in it?

"I want—Well, something from my childhood just reappeared in my life, and I don't know how to handle it," I confess, my voice steadier now. I've opted for the simplest explanation.

Bonnie's dark eyes flick across my face, calculating. "You've never really talked about your childhood with me, but I'll do whatever I can to help. Not as your assistant but as your friend, I'm here for you." Her words bring a sense of reassurance, calming my racing thoughts. "And come on, you're the guy who can handle anything, right? Where's that confident spirit?" She gives me a playful nudge.

I take a deep breath, gathering my courage. "Bonnie. . . I really. .
. " I breathe out, reaching out to hold her hand, my grip tight.

Her expression shifts. "What happened?"

"Holy shit." Bonnie places the letter on the table.

A tiny robot barista arrives with our drinks. "Matcha green tea
frappe and a soy latte," it beeps. The little Starbucks apron is the
perfect touch.

"That's his." Bonnie takes the matcha green tea frappe and places
it in front of me. "And that is mine." She grabs the soy latte.

"Thank you, enjoy your beverages," the robot chirps. I watch
it roll away, back behind the unmanned counter. The Starbucks
around the corner from Flemming Corporations looks like every
other Starbucks; dark wood, big windows, and kelly green accents
everywhere. At least the view of Central Park is nice.

"Where were we?" Bonnie taps the plastic lid of her cup. "Oh
right, holy shit."

"Right? I don't even remember what happened." I drop my straw
into the glorified milkshake and take a sip. "Honestly, I don't remember anything from my hometown. I get pieces here and there,
but genuinely, I can't remember anything about the accident. All I
know is we woke up, but Jho didn't."

"And you haven't spoken to her parents in...?"

"Ten years."

"Ten years!" Bonnie falls back against the backrest behind us.
"That means Jho's been in a coma for... sixteen years. Jesus, I don't
think I could handle that if I were a parent." She raises her drink to
her lips, eyes distant. "I mean, going through that must be tough..."
she amends hastily.

"No, you're right. Sixteen years is too long. I would have given up
years ago if I were them," I agree, though the words puncture my
lungs.

"Damn."

"The timing couldn't be more *perfect*." I rub my temples. "The
showcase is in two weeks; everything has to go smoothly, or we can
kiss the grant goodbye."

"Okay, we're not done talking about this childhood friend thing,
but you need to relax. We're going to get that grant. This new

technology you came up with will change the gaming world forever, so confidence up." Bonnie's small, warm hand comes to rest on mine.

I glance at her curly bangs dangling above her light brown eyes. Now that I think about it, Bonnie physically resembles Jhoana a lot, down to the bangs. They have the same round face and soft shape. Maybe that's why I felt drawn to her when we first met in college.

"You have too much faith in me." I suppress a smile.

"Yeah, stupid, I believe in the work you're doing. Even if you can get a little nit-picky with the things you want." She side-eyes me.

"What does that mean?"

"All I'm saying is, you've had crazier projects, but you never acted like *this*. Do you even notice how your programmers are around you? They scatter like cockroaches when you enter the floor."

"Fair point. Everyone hates me." I fling myself backward into the padded bench.

"They don't hate you; they're afraid of you. Remember the outburst you had with that intern, Kevin?"

"Oh no, not Kevin." Humiliation heats my face and I half-bury it in my hands. "In my defense, he should have known the difference between developer and programmer."

Bonnie clicks her tongue. "Okay, he should have known but don't be *that* boss. Pull your head out of your ass before it gets stuck up there."

"Ugh, you're right, I know, I know. What is wrong with me?"

"You have your period."

"Shut up." I drop my hands and snatch up my drink.

"Okay, pep talk time. Did you know most people chose to work in the company because of you?"

That gives me pause. "Really?" I don't know whether to feel embarrassed or flattered.

"Yes. I did the hiring. I think you need to remember your roots, who you are, and where you came from." She nudges me.

"Bitch." I smile at her. "You really know how to make me feel better."

"What good would I be if I didn't? And besides, who else is going to set you straight? Nobody else will ever be this honest with you." She laughs.

You're wrong. I had four true friends who always spoke their minds, even when I didn't want to hear it. They knew me better than I knew myself—the siblings I never had. And now, one of us is going to die... because of me.

"Rick?"

"Huh?

"You drifted." She scoots in closer to me. Her warm, pillowy arm anchors me. "Where did you go?"

"I don't know," I mutter, feeling a heavy weight in my chest. I let out a frustrated groan. "I have to see my mom, too."

"That's something, at least. You still have her," Bonnie responds optimistically.

I shake my head. "No, it's not that simple. Our relationship was strained after my dad passed away. Hell, I left home without even saying goodbye to her. She's reached out, but I thought it was best to leave the past behind, so we haven't spoken since."

Bonnie murmurs sympathetically.

"I know I have to go... right?" I say quietly. "I owe Jho that much..."

"But?"

"I don't want to," I confess, my voice filled with a mix of resentment and fear. "I don't ever want to go back there. Fuck, even remembering that place makes my skin crawl. I'm scared of a memory I can't even remember." I let out a bitter chuckle. "How fucked up is that?

"Rick, I may not know what happened, but I do know it's not your fault," Bonnie takes hold of my arm. "You were just kids."

"I can't help but feel guilty. The shaking, the panic attacks... Some part of me must know that I'm the reason she's about to be *euthanized*, the reason she never got to grow up—"

"You're not responsible for her condition," Bonnie insists. " Jhoana *chose* to be there with you and your friends."

"You don't know what you're talking about," I reply, my tone sharper than I meant it to be. I'm not even sure of what I'm doing. Hell, I can't remember anyway so who am I to deny what Bonnie's saying?

"No, I don't," Bonnie agrees. "But I also don't see it as your fault. Unless you deliberately made sure Jhoana wouldn't wake up—"

"Of course not!"

"Exactly. You didn't do that. Deep down, you know you didn't mean to cause her harm."

I heave a massive sigh. *Why can't I just* remember? My phone dings, cutting our discussion short. "Hold that thought." I dig into my pocket.

"I can't believe you're still using a regular phone," Bonnie remarks, showing off her Holo-phone bracelet with a smirk.

I imitate her in a high-pitched voice as I read the message on my phone. "Crap. Oscar wants to see me." The CEO rarely bothered to meet face to face with his underlings. So, either this was really good or really bad.

"What do you think it's about?" Bonnie asks, raising her eyebrows.

"I have no idea. The message just says, 'Please head to my office

ASAP.' I wasn't expecting to hear from him until next week."

"Could it be about the game?"

"I hope so, and I hope it's good news." I reply, quickly putting my phone back in my pocket. "Ready to go?" In my peripheral vision, a figure in a white button-up shirt catches my attention, and my head snaps in their direction.

Oh shit, it's them again.

A man stands outside the glass wall, his eyes bulging, lips pressed into a thin line. They remind me of the Mormon missionaries back home, but they never try to proselytize. They just... watch. Since I moved here, I've spotted them occasionally, but it's been a few years since the last encounter. Their timing is impeccable—they show up just when my world is about to fall apart. They used to freak me the hell out, but I guess I just got used to them.

Bonnie lets out a sigh. "I was enjoying our impromptu day off."

Ignoring the man, I turn back to Bonnie and say, "Hey uh—thanks—Bon. You know—um—for being here with me. I appreciate this a lot." I glance up at her awkwardly, trying to smile. The creepy man behind her slowly lifts an arm and waves it. The motion is stilted, wrong, like he's underwater. There's no way he can see me through the sun's reflection on the glass... Right?

"Stop being weird." Bonnie smacks my arm, oblivious to the scene at her back. "I know you would have done the same for me if the roles were reversed." She leans in for a hug, and I accept it. "Just breathe, okay? You'll be alright."

We unlock our embrace. The man over her shoulder doesn't appear to have blinked. I shudder.

"And I'll support any decision you make. Do you remember our oath in college?" she presses. I wrench my gaze from the man and focus on Bonnie's warm brown eyes.

"Yeah. To the moon and back."

"Exactly, do what you have to do."

In front of me stands a monumental sign, proudly declaring "Flemming Corporations". Even after five years of working here, the sight never fails to amaze me. The sheer spectacle of this place leaves my jaw hanging open every time. Twin towers intertwined in a double helix structure, defying all expectations of modern architecture. It sounded crazy when the idea was first proposed, but they actually pulled it off.

At ground level, a ring-shaped structure encircles the building. As we step inside, I spot the redheaded receptionist, Arlene, playing tour guide to a group of middle schoolers. Just beyond her are the elevators. Instead of moving straight up and down, they follow the spiral pattern of the towers themselves. It's mind-blowing, really. But beyond the impressive architecture, the corporation's most groundbreaking invention so far is "Translucency"—the ability to make things invisible. It's right up there with the new game I'm developing, both products pushing the boundaries of innovation.

I've never actually met Oscar in person. Our interactions have always been through nerve-wracking video calls, and even those were short and to the point. Standing in front of the elevator that leads to his office feels surreal. Bonnie confidently presses the button, summoning the elevator, inspiring heads of curious onlookers to turn our way. It's always a spectacle when someone is called up to Oscar's office. A whirl of anxiety and excitement courses through me. This is big, especially since the game department isn't exactly considered a high priority.

Bonnie scoffs. "People can't mind their own business."

"You know how the word gets around here, only the top of the food chain gets an invite, and we're at the bottom."

"Yeah, so get your A-game on." Her elbow bumps my arm comfortingly just as the doors slide open. I take one last deep breath before walking in and punching the only other button available.

"Don't mess things up," Bonnie says, giving me a saccharine smile.

I grin at her, quickly checking to make sure no one can see me, and then raise both middle fingers at her.

She raises both her own back, and the doors shut.

The higher I get, the more Central Park reveals itself. I now see why the CEO's office is on the highest floor—it's a bird's eye view of the entire city.

Gleaming skyscrapers punctuate the skyline, adorned with vibrant holographic displays. The streets hum with the silent glide of electric vehicles, surrounded by smart, energy-efficient infrastructure. Above, drones dart through the air, delivering packages with precision.

Sustainability is front and center, with vertical gardens capturing carbon emissions and breathing new life into the city. Here, nature and technology blend seamlessly, weaving green spaces into the urban fabric.

Central Park is especially captivating from this vantage point.

Amidst all the modernization, the park remains a serene oasis, untouched by the encroaching cityscape. Towering skyscrapers loom like sentinels, guarding their verdant kingdom. Sunlight dances on the translucent solar panels, casting an ethereal glow that only heightens the park's almost magical atmosphere. Yet its beauty does nothing to assuage the nauseating anxiety churning inside me.

Once out of the elevator, I find myself on a floor tiled with pristine white marble. It leads down a narrow hallway to a grand, sliding wooden door. It's probably mahogany. Oscar's perfectly polished secretary smiles at me from behind her desk while a sturdy security guard stands by the entrance with his arms folded. I approach the friendly-looking woman and try not to make eye contact with the guard. I can see a giant scorpion tattoo on his forearm.

"Hello," I say, voice wavering. "Uh, Mister Wilder called for me."

She looks at me for a moment, picks up a tablet, and raises it to me. I hastily dig in my pockets for my badge and tap it. My employee profile pops up.

"You're good to go. He's waiting for you," she says with a reassuring smile. I nod and move toward the doors, but the security guard stops me in my tracks.

"Didn't you hear the lady give me the pass?" I joke weakly, hoping to lighten the grim expression on his face.

"Spread your arms and legs, sir," he instructs, ignoring me.

I comply and wait as he scans me with a metal detector. When he reaches my pocket, the detector goes off.

"Just my phone," I explain, mentally double checking that I don't have a knife concealed in my jeans without my knowledge.

"Empty your pockets, sir."

Letting out a sigh, I retrieve my phone from my pocket. No surprise knife.

"Okay, you can proceed," he says, stepping aside.

I take a deep breath, trying to steady my trembling hand as I muster the courage to knock on the door three times.

"Step right in!" Oscar's voice carries through the door.

The door glides open before I can even reach for the handle.

"O—Os—Mr. Wilder, you asked for me—" My clumsy greeting is cut off by absolute terror. The floor is completely translucent, as if it's not there at all. All my nerve endings seem to react at once, sending a howling danger signal through my body. I've always had a paralyzing fear of heights, and seeing the park hundreds of feet below churns my stomach.

"Rictor! Please have a seat."

I keep my eyes fixed on the floor, my knees wobbling as I take my first step.

"It's perfectly safe," he chuckles. "No need to worry."

"I know that rationally." I take back everything I said about the translucent floors being a marvel because this is definitely not it. I look to the ceiling and glue my eyes to the crystal chandelier. It flings rainbows across the spacious office. I manage to make it to the chair and half-fall into the linen cushions. My fingers curl around smooth, polished oak arms. *How embarrassing is this?*

"Are you alright?" Oscar's tone seems genuine rather than mocking.

"Yep," I grit out. "Just peachy." Once my adrenaline levels have lowered, I get a good look at Oscar. I can't believe how wrong my expectations of him were. First of all, he looks amazing for his early sixties. It's clear he takes care of himself, and his muscles are defined despite being concealed under a perfectly tailored suit. He appears much more relaxed in person than he seems over the phone which is a small relief. In meetings, he always seemed so uptight, never even cracking a smile.

Wait, is that how my employees see me? Am I the drama?

Then, out of nowhere, Oscar sighs, "You look so much like your father." His words bring my thoughts to a screeching halt. I can feel my pulse begin to quicken.

"You knew my dad?"

"Yes, more than you realize. He was like a brother to me," Oscar murmurs. "Weren't you aware that I originally worked for NASA?"

I'm taken aback. "He never mentioned you when he was alive."

He scoffs, shaking his head. "I'm not surprised. I made a mistake in the past that caused us to drift apart—My apologies, Rictor. This is inappropriate of me. We can discuss your father outside of work. But right now, I brought you here because I finally had the chance to review your project proposal." He clenches his hand once again, triggering the Holo-phone interface. With a few practiced motions, he retrieves a document and places it on the desk. It looks nearly tangible until you inspect it closely. Holo-docs always have a shimmer to them.

But the project proposal is the last thing on my mind right now.

"Were you there?" I hear myself say. "When he died?"

Oscar pauses and looks up at me. "No. I was in a different lab. Now, I'd like to talk about this." He pushes the Holo-doc toward me.

He's clearly not going to say more, but the sudden reminder of my father and his death has tied a secondary knot in my stomach. I cast my eyes down at the document, willing myself to focus. *Why does he even have this?* Oscar has a team of reviewers at his disposal specifically for this kind of thing.

"I took the liberty of reviewing your proposal myself, and I must say, it's quite a hefty grant you're seeking." Oscar places the tips of his fingers together.

I swallow hard. "Yes, sir, but if you consider—"

He raises a finger, cutting me off. "That's precisely what I'm doing. I understand your scheduled presentation to the board is in two weeks, but I believe that's unnecessary. You can present it to me right now."

"Huh?" My stomach, which had just been twisted into a pretzel of anxiety, now plummeted approximately to the level of my colon. *Present it now? To Oscar?*

"Present your proposal to me, and by the end of it, I'll provide you with a decision." His tone is light but the challenge behind his words is clear.

I hesitate, completely stymied. Accept, and deliver a presentation I'm unprepared for, or refuse, and have my project tossed unceremoniously out one of his stupid translucent windows?

"Is there a problem?" Oscar asks. I can see a grin tugging at the corners of his mouth.

Fuck yeah, there is! "No, sir. I actually left my smartpen in the office. I'll need it for the presentation. If you can give me just five minutes, I'll be able to start," I say, fighting to keep the panic out of my voice. *Decision made, I guess.*

"Perfect, I'll take this opportunity to call my wife and let her know I'll be home soon," he says genially, already raising his hand to his ear.

I leap up from my seat, forgetting to be afraid of the drop below. *Should I thank him?* My body short-circuits and I bow my head. "Th—thank you, sir." *What the fuck was that?*

Before I can embarrass myself further, I make a swift exit from his office.

I retrieve my phone from my pocket and dial Bonnie's number, my voice hissing with urgency as I relay the situation.

"What! Are you even ready for that?" Bonnie's voice crackles through the speaker.

"Obviously not but this is our only chance." My legs carry me numbly to the elevator doors, pacing across the small reception area.

"Okay, what do you need?"

"I left my pen on my desk," I reply, voice barely above a whisper. "The gold one." The receptionist is watching me with amusement. I guess I'm not Oscar's first victim.

"Got it! I'm coming!" I can hear wind rushing across her microphone as she sprints for my office "I'm going to throw up!"

"Me too!" I laugh, though it sounds suspiciously like a sob.

We hang up, and I anxiously wait by the elevator doors, stealing glances at the guard and the receptionist. This is really happening. I have to believe in myself. I have to believe that I can do this, even though my hands won't stop shaking. The elevator doors open, and Bonnie hands me the golden pen, just as shiny and impressive as it was when Emierr had presented it to me on my twelfth birthday. Of course, it has undergone some modifications since then.

"Good luck!" she whispers, giving me a tight hug. "Go for it!"

"Thanks!"

My hands continue to tremble, and a cold sweat breaks out over my palms. The pen quickly grows slick in my grasp. *Come on, please stop shaking.* I clench my hands into tight fists and take slow breaths. I'm standing in front of the sliding mahogany door now, trying to ignore the security guard standing a few feet away.

"Fake it till you make it. You've got this, Ricky." The office door slides open, and Oscar's eyes meet mine.

"You ready?" he asks, his voice calm and reassuring.

"Yes, sir," I say with newfound assurance. I step forward, pushing past my fear of heights and focusing on the weight of the pen in my hand. *I can do this.*

Oscar gestures to the center of the room. "The floor is yours."

With a surprisingly steady voice, I reply, "Thank you." I inhale and exhale one last time before launching into action.

I set my phone on the chair and tap the hologram button. The camera activates, projecting a floating folder in the air. A small beep tells me my pen has connected. I swipe through the hologram, suddenly thankful I just cleared out all my old files, and open a folder entitled "Superposition." Years of blood, sweat, and tears contained within a single folder. As the interface vanishes, stylish black-rimmed sunglasses with yellow lenses materialize.

"Five years ago, we released the AMOS VR, transforming not just gaming but technology itself," I begin. "Our talented developers pioneered the cutting-edge AMOS chip, revolutionizing immersive gameplay worldwide." I press the pen's push button twice, zooming in on the lenses in the hologram. "We were the first to integrate augmented reality into a virtual reality device, selling a staggering 2.8 billion units and counting." I've fallen into a groove now, the script rolling off my tongue, rehearsed a thousand times. "But what if I told you we've created an even more mind-blowing device that will reshape technology forever? Allow me to introduce..." I click the button, and the glasses explode into a mesmerizing array of pixels before seamlessly reconstructing into the new device. "The Augmented Macro Operating System: Superposition."

"Wow, it's incredibly tiny." Oscar leans forward, inspecting the small, circular object shimmering just a few feet away. From the look on his face, my proposal is off to a good start.

I nod. "Yes, that's intentional. We designed it to be portable—perfect for long flights or any extended travel. Would you like to see it?"

"Absolutely." Oscar stretches out an expectant hand.

I sweep the holograms out of the air and pass them to Oscar. They hover above his palm, each resembling a penny in size and appearance.

"Amazing," he marvels, using his thumb and index finger to examine one of the devices.

"The Superposition, true to its name, combines augmented and virtual reality in an entirely new way. In collaboration with NASA and their VR technology, we've taken what we achieved with AMOS VR and integrated Neurolink capabilities."

I aim my pen at him, causing the hologram to zoom in on the device, displaying pulsating waves on a human head model. "Superposition will scan the user, transmit signals to the Neurolink, and stimulate the brain to experience touch, taste, and smell."

Oscar lets out a whistle, leaning back in his chair. "What about pain?"

I shake my head. "Pain is the one aspect of touch we deliberately omitted. We don't believe in causing harm to our players. Our goal is to create an intensely immersive experience, and pain detracts from that. By excluding it, players can fully immerse themselves in the journey." I click the pen, feeling excitement rise in my chest. This is the moment I've been building up to for five years. "Introducing Supernova, the first and only game designed for the Superposition." The hologram shifts, transforming into a portal, revealing a sprawling landscape filled with towering trees and fantastical creatures straight out of myths.

"It looks so real." Oscar's eyes glitter in the holographic sunlight, and pride swells in my chest.

"For the past decade, open-world games have reigned as the favored genre, and Supernova is no exception," I continue, catching my breath. Everything I've worked for is culminating right here. I have to keep pushing. "But we've taken it to the next level. Our creation is a world so immense, it rivals Earth itself."

The hologram floats between us, the landscapes glowing. My heart pounds—*is it enough?* I force myself to stay still, my pulse hammering in my ears. Oscar's eyes narrow as he studies the projection, and for a moment, I can't read him.

"Rictor..." Oscar rises from his seat and walks over to the hologram, his gaze fixed on the myriad of landscapes and civilizations awaiting him. "This will change the world. How did you come up with all of this?"

"The only way to achieve greatness is if you—" I begin, feeling my face heat up as I regurgitate my well-rehearsed brown-nosing.

"You become your greatest self," Oscar finishes.

"Sir, you have instilled that motto in each and every one of us. We have achieved greatness because you are the greatest. We believed in your vision, and you supported us wholeheartedly. Flemming Corp is all about pushing boundaries, and with your continued support, Mr. Wilder, we can achieve even more. Together." *Damn, even I believed that.*

"Well done." I'm fairly certain I can see each and every one of his heavily whitened teeth. "All of this is truly impressive. You've earned your grant."

Any air remaining in my lungs vanishes. *Did he really just say that?*

"Thank you, sir!" I manage, gripping his hand tightly while fighting to regain control of my airways. This cannot be real.

A jovial smile forms on his face as he releases my hand. I wince slightly, feeling pins and needles. "Do you have someone on your team I can communicate with regarding the grant?" he asks, walking back to his desk.

"Someone on my team?" *Me? Delegate? As if.*

"Rictor, your life is about to change in the coming weeks." Oscar's face is still stretched in a grin. He's starting to remind me of the creepy man I'd seen that morning. "Go home and spend time with your friends and family. Take a week off. You deserve it."

I'm taken aback. *Does he know about Jhoana?*

"I'll be expecting updates. Stay in touch," he says, raising his hand to toggle his phone's interface. It was a subtle yet clear dismissal.

"Thank you, Mr. Wilder. I won't let you down." I tuck the gold pen behind my right ear and grab my phone from the chair. Without glancing back, I rush out to the elevator, step inside, and press the second of the two buttons on the panel. My mind is in turmoil. Today, I have received both the best and the worst news of my life. How can I celebrate when I know what is about to happen to Jhoana?

I contemplate what to text Bonnie. Finally, all my hard work is coming to fruition. "We did it," I type. The elevator dings open, but my eyes remain fixed on my phone, waiting for the incoming flurry of exuberant messages.

"Ricky."

I lift my head and there he is, staring at me with an envelope in his hand. After ten years, Emierr is standing right in front of me.

"Security!" I roar.

EMIERR

"**S**hit." I put the letter down on the table.

I thought I had until summer to get the Squad together. *A letter? Why didn't he just call me?* My left hand clenches then opens, the home screen of my Holo-phone popping up. I bend my thumb and index finger, opening the contacts app. I scroll until I find Uncle Kit's name and tap on it.

My finger hovers over the phone icon. *A damn letter? Why couldn't he just—Wait—A letter...* My hand closes again. This could be the opening I need. I flip my hand over and a hologram of the time and date appears on my wrist. September 28, 8:06 a.m. The letter is dated the 26th. If Uncle Kit wrote to all four of us, I must have gotten mine first, since I'm in the same state as him. Hell, the same *town* as him. The others should get theirs tomorrow.

I breathe in deeply and exhale. "It's really happening." I twist the rolling chair to my left and push toward the tiny cubby jammed full of my things. My beaten-up mini-gym bag has seen better days, but it's time to come out of retirement. I roll back to the desk. "Okay, what am I bringing?" My eyes scan the messy table. Definitely no schoolwork.

The polaroid picture frame of Ma and Dad is coming with me for sure. I've barely spoken with them these past several years, but I love having them with me. The letter, too, of course. I look at the door window to see if the coast is clear and open the desk drawer. I'm a little hesitant, but I grab the golden flask Dustin sent me for my twenty-first birthday and throw it inside the bag. I'm definitely going to need it. I lift the pile of papers scattered all over the desk and reveal a battered composition notebook, scotch-taped with construction paper on its covers.

Rictor's scribbles and doodles of space fill nearly every square inch.

The day after Jhoana didn't wake up, I kept it, hoping to understand what had happened to us. There has to be something I missed, some explanation in the cramped pages of notes. I didn't want to admit it before, but recently I've come to accept that I can't figure this out on my own. My mind drifts to the others; Dustin, Jadis, and Rictor. I haven't spoken to them in nearly a decade. I get calls from Dustin from time to time, but even then, it's been three years since we last talked. I'd like to think they think of me, too, even if they remember me as a coward.

I look around my tight, dingy cupboard of an office—a storage room if we're being truthful—and reminisce about the day Farmington High offered me a faculty position seven years ago. I was confused as to why I wasn't offered the position of agricultural sciences teacher when I majored in botany. But regardless, there was relief at the offer. I was fresh out of college and not yet ready to leave Farmington behind, not ready to leave my comatose cousin, and most definitely not ready to forget the world we created together. My hands rest on the desk, and I look at the rack of balls by the window. The all-encompassing smell of dried sweat on the wrestling mats is something I won't miss. I don't like dwelling on the what-ifs, but there could have once been a path which led me to the Amazon rainforest.

I could have spent the last decade discovering new flora and living amongst the endless swathes of canopy. That was my dream, but I think people like me can only have the what-ifs.

I know what the next few days are going to mean. Things will never be the same, but I'm happy I got a chance to have a life. Maybe it wasn't exciting, or even what I wanted. But at least it was simple and easy.

I zip the bag and get up. It looks like I'll be gone for a week. Or indefinitely. I switch the lights off. Since the renovations in 2018, the school has gotten bigger, more expensive, and more tech-friendly.

My office is one of the few structures that stayed the same. Even when they tried moving me to a bigger area, I chose not to. Change is weird. I'd rather stay in my storage room.

As I make for the field, I begin to hear a gratingly familiar voice. Coach Danny stands in the field, arms crossed, legs spread apart, and wearing those tacky Oakley shades he took from the lost and found years ago. Coach Danny has been a football coach for almost thirty years. He was my and Dustin's coach in middle school, then followed us when we joined the football team freshman year.

When I was hired, he recognized me. On my second day, he complained about the last person who had my job because he wasn't "man enough" to work with him. I always knew he was condescending, but an asshole? That was new to me. He is a great coach, but that's the only positive thing I can say about him.

"Coach," I say, coming to a halt beside him.

"Come on! Keep the pace going! It's morning. You all should have energy!" he shouts at the miserable students running laps.

"Coach," I say a little louder.

"Oh." He glances at me. "Naputi, did you get me my coffee?"

"What?"

"I'm messing with you." He smacks my stomach. "But next time, I'd like one."

"Coach, I wanted to talk to you about the game in two days. I ca—"

"Keep those legs up! I see you rolling your eyes at me, missy. Keep it up, and everyone gets an extra two laps!" he threatens. "What did you say?"

"Sir, I can't coach the game." That catches his attention.

"And why is that?" He frowns and lowers his head, his cold eyes darting to mine.

"I—ther—sir, uh—"

"Spit it out, Naputi."

"I'm going away for a week."

"Oh… Did you finally find a girl to go on that weekend trip I've been telling you about?" He grins.

"No, Coach, my cousin is—"

"Okay. I'll take over the game for you." His attention is back on the track, eyes narrowing at the stragglers falling behind. "The others won't take it if you ask them. Nobody wants a losing team. And you owe me a big one." He makes eye contact with a boy near the back and motions *hurry up*. "By the way, I'm going on my own trip to Thailand if you catch my drift, so on Wednesday, you have to take my teams to their games, got it?"

I stare at him. "Sir, you don't understand. I won't be here for that."

"Good talk, Naputi." He raises his fist, eyes trained on the field. He's clearly not listening to a word I say.

Douchebag. "Okay, Coach, I'll do it." I fist-bump him. I can already imagine the fit he's going to throw when he realizes I'm not back.

"Come on! Faster! I gotta eat!" he hollers at the final three students.

I wish Jadis were here. She'd tell him to suck it.

I shake my head and walk across the field, taking the well-worn shortcut to the main building. The school has gotten the Flemming Corp. treatment. Ever since they announced their new building design, the world has wanted to be like them. Our school looks more like a university now than it did during my time, though that's not saying much. I remember back when the sleek walls were laid with red brick. The halls aren't even school halls anymore, with their higher ceilings, LED lights in the pillars, marbled tiles, and robots. It feels as though I work at a science museum with significantly more, half-assed graffiti.

I get to the main office and ask the front desk lady to see Principal Brackett. His office door creaks under her overlong, manicured fingers and she murmurs something through the crack. She glances at me and signals me to go.

"Mr. Naputi, what can I help you with this morning?" Principal Brackett says, voice somewhat muffled by a McMuffin.

"Good morning, sir." I lower myself into a plush chair in front of the wood laminate desk. "I am requesting a week off from work."

The principal doesn't respond, jaw working through an enormous bite of the sandwich. I try not to stare at the blob of ketchup dangling tremulously from his mustache. *Who puts ketchup on their McMuffin?*

When I can no longer handle the awkward silence, I elaborate. "My cousin is... She's going to—"

"Approved. Thank you, have a great day," he says, finally having managed to swallow.

I blink. "Just like that?" I'd worked through an entire mental debate in preparation for this meeting.

Principal Brackett drops his breakfast and puts his greasy fingertips together. "Mr. Naputi, frankly, I don't care what you do. You're a PE instructor. There are plenty of slackers out there who can do your job for a week. The school won't fall apart in your absence."

Fuck this guy too. "Okay, thank you. I'll be leaving now."

"Have a great day, Mr. Naputi." I can hear the sound of his chewing resume as I slip out the office door.

I shake my head and make my way to the parking lot. This is really happening. I get inside my truck—Dad's old truck, the one he's had since before I was born—Betsy, he called her. A wave of nostalgia flows through me, flashes of him teaching me to drive, and those late nights I saw him drive it home after hanging out with his old mailman buddies. And then it hits me: that promise I made to Sólel all those years ago—I'm finally going to see it through. My knuckles go pale on the steering wheel.

"I'm coming. Wait for me," I murmur, looking at the gym bag.

A sudden knock on my car window startles me.

"Jesus," I blurt out as I see a woman in a white blouse standing by my door. Oh great, they're out again. These people—Mormon 2.0, as I've come to call them—have been getting weirder and weirder lately. At first I thought they were the standard missionaries but I quickly realized I was wrong. My new theory was some kind of

Mormon offshoot cult. It would explain why they're so ghoulish.

This one is more off than usual. It's not just her creepy smile; it's her eyes, dark and empty, like there's no one home. I turn the ancient hand crank to roll down the window just a bit, enough for her to hear me. "Yes, ma'am?"

She doesn't say a thing at first. She just smiles and leans in, her eyes slowly widening. She has a strange pattern in her irises, like a coppery starburst around the pupil. They might have been beautiful if they weren't set in the face of a banshee.

"Are you going to save us?" Her voice is barely a whisper.

"Sorry?" I lean in closer, surely, I've misheard. Aren't they supposed to be selling some god that's going to save me?

"*Are you going to save us?*" she shrieks, specks of saliva splattering on my window.

I quickly roll up the window and start the engine. "Geez, lady. Back the fuck off. I hear meth's bad for your teeth."

"We know!" Her fists bang on my window.

"Fuck this." I put the truck into gear and speed out of the parking lot.

"*Take us home!*" she screams behind me. I glance in the rearview mirror to see her standing frozen, hands in the air, and dry, black hair whipping in the wind.

"Fucking crazy bitch." I mutter. Her creepy smile is hitched back into place. I wrench my gaze back to the road. If they're a cult, she's doing a real shit job at recruiting.

It takes about twenty minutes for me to get to my apartment. It would've been a five-minute drive to my parents' house, but I don't think I can face them after our last encounter. I'd yelled that they were good parents to everyone but me then stormed out the front door. Just thinking about it brings a flush of shame to my face.

I try to focus on the drive. The town has undergone some changes, but in reality, it hasn't changed all that much. Despite the massive school renovation, this town hardly looks any different from when I was a kid all those years ago.

We have holograms now, but not enough to take over the town. I guess, strangely, I relate to Farmington. We're both too stubborn to fully change. I even got the Holo-phone only because Brunner forced me to finally update past my high school flip phone.

When I arrive at the Oak Groves apartment complex, I park my car and head upstairs. The apartment is small, but it works. I don't have guests over anyway; when I do, it's just Brunner. Brunner... I wonder if he got a letter, too.

My wrist dings, and the bracelet blinks. "*Brunner Fischer calling...*" I raise my hand to my ear, extending my pinky and thumb. "Rune."

"Holy shit! Did you get a letter?" His voice crackles as it pushes my speaker to its maximum capacity. I pull my hand away, wincing. "Yeah, this morning."

"I thought you said during summer. Why is it happening now?"

Great fucking question. "Rune. I'm home."

"What, aren't you at work?"

"We don't have summer anymore. It's starting."

"Oh... Shit." I can practically hear him processing.

"When you can, come over. We need to talk about the plan."

"I'll be there tonight. And Meer..." Brunner pauses. There's something tense in his breathing.

"What?" I ask, nonplussed.

"I'll just tell you later, don't worry about it."

The line cuts.

I stand there for a few seconds. I can't bring myself to be curious about whatever Brunner wasn't telling me. My thoughts were several neighborhoods down, in an upstairs bedroom at my aunt and uncle's house.

"Oh, Jho." I breathe out.

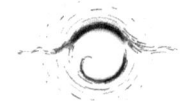

"Take us home!"

The alarm goes off, waking me from my subconscious's horrific rendition of the Mormon 2.0 encounter this morning. I grab the blaring Holo-phone bracelet from its charger and slide it on my wrist. The alarm silences with two quick clenches of my fist. It's 7:22 p.m. Brunner should be coming any minute. Sleeping it off didn't change anything. The emotional turmoil boiling in my gut is very much unmoved. I still can't believe it's finally happening.

A knock comes from the door. 7:30 p.m., right at his usual time. I open the door and see Brunner with both arms raised, holding two plastic bags.

"I brought food, compliments from Mrs. Mason."

"Ricky's mom?" I'm vaguely surprised. I hadn't had much contact with Auntie Luna in the past few years, beyond the occasional food deliveries.

"She cooked for Jho's family," Brunner explains, pushing past me and into the living room. "It looks like the town knows about the... You know." Brunner drops down on the beat-up couch that he gave me years ago and places the food on the coffee table.

"How did you even run into her?" I call over my shoulder from the kitchen. The drawer in front of me is filled to the brim with plastic utensils.

"Our parents, they're all doing this united front stuff. And I really mean all of them."

"And how does that explain the food?" I toss a paper plate at him like a frisbee and watch with satisfaction as it whacks him in the chest.

Graciously ignoring me, he sets the plate on the table and continues, "I dropped my parents off at Jho's. Mrs. Mason was there, and so were your parents. Your Squad's parents were all there, actually." He takes out the Tupperware filled with Filipino spaghetti, hotlinks, fried chicken, and my favorite, lumpia. "She knew I'd see you, so she packed extra."

My stomach grumbles.

Brunner nods in agreement with the sound. "As always, Mrs. Mason was right. Sainthood, that lady."

"Dude, I was attacked by a Mormon 2.0 today," I say. "She was batshit crazy. I mean Halloween is around the corner, so I guess... could have been a prank." I pop the lids off all the Tupperware containers and carefully form a mountain on my plate. Rictor's mom always cooks the best food.

"Bruh, I think they've been awakened or something because when I was leaving Jho's house, there were like three of them standing across the street, just staring blankly." Brunner starts shoveling food as if he hasn't seen a meal in years. He probably didn't eat today, either. I had certainly lost my appetite after opening that letter.

"Man, Rictor had it good, huh? This food is uh-mazing!" he says through a mouthful of spaghetti.

All I can do is nod, savoring the taste of heaven in my mouth. The nearest Filipino food joint is in downtown Salt Lake City. Who wants to try to find downtown parking just for that? I'm grateful Auntie Luna cares enough to drop food at my door every now and then.

"Should we be worried about them? It's starting to go beyond coincidence, isn't it?" Brunner finishes his plate at an alarming pace and gets up to grab a drink from the kitchen. I shake my head in resignation. Brunner might as well live here. He stuffs his plate into the overflowing kitchen trash and opens the fridge.

Sorry, bro, that's all I have. I smirk.

"Seriously, Pepsi? Not even a Coke?"

I grin, ignoring his complaints. "Nah, no need to worry about the Mormon 2.0s. They're creepy but not exactly dangerous. I still think it's some kind of weird cult."

I look down at the remaining spaghetti on the paper plate in my lap. I recall Rictor, his face smeared with sauce, joyfully devouring a similar dish on his twelfth birthday. Ma told me that Auntie Luna was determined to recreate Jollibee's beloved Filipino spaghetti and sought advice from any Jollibee's cook who would give her the time of day. With a blend of sweet tomato sauce, juicy hotdogs, and creamy cheese, she concocted a masterpiece, capturing the essence of "mom's cooking." At least, it was mom's cooking for Rictor.

"Meer." Brunner snaps me back to reality.

"Huh?"

"I said, what's the plan? You alright? Don't tell me you're thinking of backing out?" His eyes are accusatory.

"No, what the hell. I was just—Ricky loves this spaghetti."

With a snort, Brunner hands me a can and drops down next to me. "I bet. That was the best spaghetti I ever had."

"Yeah." I'm still a bit preoccupied with my memories of the past as my fingers automatically crack the can open. Soda fizzes down my thumb.

"Meer, we can't back out on this," Brunner says, twisting his body to fully face me on the peeling pleather cushions. "Jho needs us."

"I know, that's why we need to think fast. We don't have time anymore." I sigh.

"Okay then, well, to spaghetti." Brunner raises his can to mine. I clink, and we both drink deeply, as if the Pepsi contained something more potent than high fructose corn syrup. He burps. "What's our plan B now?"

"The plan..." *What is the fucking plan?* Brunner watches me intently while my brain spins hamster wheel circles. "Dustin," I say suddenly. "He'll listen to me. He'll follow along."

Brunner presses his lips together, brows furrowing.

"What?" I demand.

"Maybe you should go see Rictor first."

"What? Why him? I kept in contact with Dusty. If anything, he'll understand more."

"I'm not trying to question your relationship," Brunner says quickly, leaning forward, "but wasn't Rictor like... the leader?"

"No..." I try to deny it with conviction, but do I even believe what I'm saying?

"Well, from what I remember, he made all the moves, and you guys always followed."

"Shut up. You don't know anything." I take another sip of soda for something to occupy my mouth. *That was mean, fuck.*

"All I'm saying is, Rictor is the best shot. If he follows you, the rest will." Brunner was always too frank. He never sugarcoats anything. I hate and respect that about him. The others always agreed with my plans, but maybe he's right. They haven't been around in so long. Brunner has, though. I glance at him.

Growing up, I knew things about his background, like that he's half German from his dad's side and half Chuukese from his mom. Both his parents are from Guam, too, and they knew Uncle Kit and Auntie Ina when they lived there. Soon after, they followed Brunner's parents here to Utah.

But over the years, I started to get to know him more deeply. I know he likes his hair short because he can't be bothered to maintain the curls. He definitely got that from his mom's side. I vaguely envy the way his light brown complexion compliments his eyes. There's something about that deep shade of blue that exudes confidence.

I mean, he's no game developer like Rictor, no NFL player like Dustin, nor is he traveling the world like Jadis. He's just the supervisor of Barnes and Noble. But I guess, even at that, Brunner is up there with them. He may have stayed in Farmington, too, but he's made something for himself. And he enjoys doing it.

Brunner drops his gaze, probably thinking of something to say, but doesn't. Once he notices he said something to irk you, he doesn't push. This is what I appreciate about him. I cave.

"Fine."

He looks back up at me.

"I'll go to Ricky first."

An exhale of relief sweeps past his lips.

"I haven't spoken to him since he left without a word after graduation," I admit, hunching into the sofa. "I don't know what he's thinking. Or if he'll even give me a chance. Not after what I said to him."

"Then what about me?" Brunner straightens. "What will he think about me if he won't even listen to you?"

"No, you'll change their minds, just like you changed mine."

"But they're not like you—Meer, you don't have anybody else. You only forgave me because I was Jho's best friend and probably the only person who understands you."

"That's not true." It isn't, although it had been a major reason in the beginning.

"Is it not? I bullied you guys for years because of what happened. I've said and done a lot of fucked up things during high school, especially." His face reddens with shame. "I wouldn't even forgive myself."

"Well, you're wrong, alright?" I punch his arm. "I forgave you because you changed. And you proved you changed. Period."

"I just—This has to work. Jho cannot die." His voice cracks.

"And she won't. We're gonna save her together." I grab his hand and squeeze it.

He nods, wiping tears away, and grasps my hand back. "Okay, what should I do?"

"Prep your basement?" I suggest with a shrug. "If I get Ricky to come, like you said, Dusty should follow without a doubt, and Jads... That one I really don't know... Anyway, maybe we'll need the basement to have meetings. We'd have a hell of a time fitting in this shoebox. I don't even own six forks."

"Alright, I'll clean up. My parents would love to have you guys over anyway. When will I come into the picture? Are you telling them right away?"

"No, they'll be weird about it. I'll message you; I just have to get them here first."

I get up and place the Tupperware into the sink.

"How about Jadis? Do you know where she is?" Brunner asks.

"Last I saw, she was in Alaska. I think Ricky has her number."

Brunner nods absently, tapping at the display before him. "Okay, you're set. Your flight to New York is 6:30 a.m., and you'll arrive there at 9:46 a.m."

I pause. "You're booking my flights? You don't have to—"

"Next flight to Detroit is at 5:42 p.m., same day. Dustin has a game there that night, so you should catch him. Your flight coming back home is at 2:18 p.m. the next day, just in time for the first day of the wake."

"Man, thanks." I may not like owing favors, but I definitely hate planning air travel more.

"Don't mention it." Brunner rises to his feet and stretches. "I'm gonna head home. Safe travels, okay?" He reaches out for a fist bump.

I look at his fist and shake my head. "Get in here." I open my arms, and crush him in a hug. "Thanks. I'll see you soon."

He claps me hard on the back. "Thanks, Meer, for giving me a chance, and Jho."

"Always, man." I release him.

"Okay, shoot." He turns to the door.

"Please clean that basement, like scrubby-dub it all. Ideally with a toothbrush. Your toothbrush."

He raises a middle finger toward me without looking and the door clicks shut behind him. So it begins.

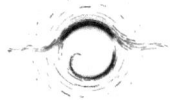

I sit down on row 51, seat A, with my mini-gym bag on my lap. I know New York is New York, but what is up with the fully booked plane? I lift the window cover and see it's a good day today. I honestly prefer the aisle seat, but who am I to be picky? This is a free ride.

"Excuse me, dear," a frail old lady says, sitting in the middle seat.

"I'm going to see my husband." Her quivery voice makes me wonder if there's an age limit on flights.

"Oh, that's lovely." I say politely.

"His grave, I meant."

"Oh."

A man, a little on the bigger side, sits in the aisle seat. This is going to be a long flight. I open my bag and pull out the Squad's notebook, placing my bag under the seat in front of me. The old composition notebook looks rough. I smile softly at the thought of all the stuff this thing has been through. A flight attendant walks down my aisle, closing the overhead baggage door.

"Excuse me, miss," I say with a little wave at the attendant. "Can you please get me three shots of Tequila? I'm afraid of flying." I'm lying but she doesn't need to know that. My seatmates gape at me.

"Oh, I understand," she says sympathetically. "I'll get them to you once we're up in the air. We should be on the runway in about two minutes."

I glance at the two next to me as the attendant walks off. Their heads are resting on their chairs, avoiding my eyes. *Judgers.*

I need to fill up the flask I'd brought. I think I'm going to need the liquid courage to see Rictor. He probably got the letter already and is on his way back home. Oh my god, what if he's already home? I didn't think this through. He and Jhoana were really close.

My anxiety is now in full force. I need to distract myself. I open the book, and the plane starts moving. Too late to get off now. I shove the book in the back pocket of the seat in front of me and hold onto the arms of my chair. There is some partial truth to my fear of flying.

I lean my head back on the chair and close my eyes. The tingly sensations of liftoff bring me back to my childhood. The memory of us flying through space fills the darkness of my eyelids. I'm looking at all my friends speeding through the cosmos with me, and then the tingling stops. I open my eyes and look out the window. Cotton candy clouds hover over the state, miles in every direction.

After sixteen years, the plan is finally set into motion. I pull the notebook out of the pocket and use the table tray. The pages are crumpled and filled with drawings and notes about places, people, and all the things we encountered as naive pre-teens.

Terrene. Fleming Space Ring. Arid. Zaltana. Verglas. The five nations of Ethra—the dreamworld we created together. If I'm honest with myself, half the time Ethra was a terrifying nightmare, but even to this day, I feel a twinge of loss when the birds outside my office don't whisper back.

What the hell am I doing? Am I really going to risk everything?

I look down at the book, and it's open to an entry on Verglas, Jhoana's nation. I'm so fucked up. This is my cousin, the one who stands up for me against my parents, the one who loves me so very much. I don't even know if she's still in there. But I'm sure as hell going to make the others believe she is. I have to get back, even if it means lying my way in, and there's no way I'm going in alone. I cannot end up like Jhoana.

I flip the page. A cut-out portrait drawing of Sólel that Jadis drew is wedged between the pages. I forgot I had this. *Oh Sól, how are you? After all these years, do you hate me?* The last I saw him I promised I'd be home for dinner, but for him, it would be thirty-two years since I made that promise. My finger traces the outline of his short locs. *Is this all worth it? No, I can't be thinking this way, it is worth it. Little brother, I'm coming home.*

"Sir, your shots." The flight attendant's cheery, customer service voice hauls me back to the present.

I close the book and accept the three miniature bottles of tequila. "Payment?"

I lift my wrist to her. She taps her bracelet on mine, and the payment goes through. "Thank you!" I say over the road of the plane. I wait until she leaves and dig in my gym bag for the flask. I begin pouring the little bottles in one by one. That should be enough. I spin the flask's cap to close and turn my attention to the grandma, whose eyes look like they're judging the hell out of me. "I'm seeing a friend I haven't seen in ten years," I tell her, unsure why I feel compelled to explain myself.

"You're fine, my dear. I'll be indulging in a couple of rounds myself when I visit my husband's grave. His other wife will be there too. That wall-eyed hag just won't let it go." She pats my arm.

Okay, Grandma is a G.

The taxi ride was horrible. The one time I wanted to really feel New York life, I was met with near-death experiences and a violent, mustachioed driver whose right hand had taken up residence on the horn. Okay, honestly, it was very New York. I change my review of the experience. A+ for the first time. Once I've staggered out of the cab, I'm standing in front of a truly bizarre building. Seeing it in person makes it even more unreal. I read the huge plaque across the main entrance.

"Flemming Corporations." I wonder, not for the first time, if there is any connection to the space ring where Rictor had spent a fragment of his childhood. Not that he remembers. Of course, Rictor would land someplace like this. My hand searches for the flask in the bag and I quickly turn my head, tossing back a shot. "Yeah, still burns," I choke to myself. I throw the flask back in the bag and enter the otherworldly entrance. "Woah."

This is like a scene from a science fiction movie. The holograms, though, are so obnoxious. I wish what I read about this building wasn't true, but from the looks of it, I wouldn't be surprised if they bought out Central Park and demolished it for their gain. The conspiracy people are saying Flemming Corp. is working on "clean" energy, but it's a cover for all the electromagnetic radiation pollution they'll leak if they build a particle accelerator here. I really shouldn't believe everything I read online, but if Rictor is helping these people do just that, I don't know him anymore. I find the information booth and approach the very pretty lady with red hair.

"Hi, I'm looking for someone who works here. He's an old friend of mine."

"Hello, sir, and good afternoon," she says in a high-pitched voice. "Could you give me his name please?"

"Rictor Mason."

"Ah, you just missed him. He went all the way up there." She points to the ceiling.

I tip my head back, and I see what I think is the roof. How is this building safe? "How do I get up there?"

"Through the elevator behind me." She points to her back. "It's the only one that goes up to that floor, but unfortunately, it is off limits unless you have an appointment, or the CEO requests you."

Her pitch suddenly drops.

Ah, so she doesn't sound like that. That's some extreme customer service voice.

"Has Rictor come back down?"

"Not to my knowledge."

"Great." I tap the counter and head for the elevator.

"Excuse me, sir, you are not allowed—"

"I'm not going up. I'll wait by the elevator." I smile at her winningly. "Don't work too hard!"

"Th—Thank you…" she says, taken aback.

11:18 a.m. Okay, waiting game, got it. I stretch, and I catch a glimpse of security looking my way. It's fine, they can't kick me out without a reason, right? I scan the vast space around me. It's so busy. Do these people ever stop just to look around? City life is a bit too much for me. I don't know how Rictor can handle all this coming from Farmington. That thought clunks into place. Shit, I have to see Rictor again. I have to *talk* to him.

How do I even approach him? Do I go for a hug? What if he rejects me? Shit. I'm overthinking this. I need another shot. I peek at the security guards but they've turned their attention elsewhere. Clearly, I don't look like a threat.

Now's my chance.

Discreetly, I unzip my bag and pull out the flask, glancing again to see if the coast is clear. The tequila scalds its way down my throat, till the flask is almost empty. My neck begins to warm, the sensation crawling to my ears. My eyelids feel heavy, and my face is now hot. Perhaps several shots of airplane tequila on an empty stomach wasn't the most brilliant of ideas.

You got this. When he comes out, hug him! Oh, and show the letter, you need the letter. I tug the letter from my pocket, its edges crumpled from too many rereads. Just as I start to read it again, the elevator doors slide open. I look up—and freeze, gaping at the man standing inside. *Is this him? When did he grow a beard?* I raise my hand with the letter, and I call out to him, "Ricky." After ten years, our eyes meet.

Utter fear overtakes his face, "Security!" he shouts.

"Woah! Ricky, it's me, Emierr." I throw my hands in the air. Three guards come rushing in.

Rictor doubles over laughing and coughs, "No, no sorry, I was just messing with him."

"Are you sure?" the biggest guy says, eyeing me.

"Yeah, I'm sure. Sorry, Kent. Seriously, we're all good!"

My hands are still in the air.

Kent scoffs but jerks his head and prowls back to his position.

"Thanks, guys. I'll tell HR you're doing a great job!" Rictor calls, giving them a thumbs up. "You can put your hands down now," he adds, smirking at me.

"They won't come down," I protest. "Did you see the way he looked at me?" Our eyes meet for a few seconds and we both burst out laughing. For a second, it feels like no time has passed.

"What the!" Rictor's fingers grip my upper arms. "Meer, what—How? What are you doing here?" He crushes me in a hug, and I return it, sighing deeply. *Hug him first, got it.*

"I almost shit myself," I say. "Can you never call security on me again?"

We pull away, and I get a good look at him. Rictor changed a lot. Aside from an improved wardrobe, he's pretty bulky compared to when we were in high school. He put in the work. Surprisingly, too, because he was the laziest out of all of us. The beard is something I'm going to need to get used to, but he sure looks a lot like his dad. His observant eyes are still that unique shade of light hazel. At least something of his old self has clung on.

My eyes are drawn to his ear, and I see the gold pen I gave him for his twelfth birthday tucked behind it. I can't believe he kept it all these years... Made stealing it from my dad's office worth it.

"The pen."

"Oh yeah." He takes it and holds it in his palm. "I did some modifications, though; it works like a smart pen, but it's universal. If it can connect, it works. Especially with holograms." His eyes move to the letter. "So, I'm not the only person who got one."

"Are you going to—"

"Not here," he cuts me off. "I'm about to go home, so let's talk there. But first, I need to stop by my office real fast." He begins walking to the elevator on the left tower from the entrance.

I guess I wait.

He turns around. "Yo, you coming?" He jerks his head at the elevator.

"Oh, yeah. Duh." I follow him, and we get inside the elevator. He punches the fourteenth floor, and we ascend.

"Isn't this place cool?" Rictor's face is shining. It's the same look he had whenever we made a major discovery on Ethra—the world I suspect he and the others have forgotten. I still don't know why I'm the only one whose memories seem intact. Maybe I'll find out soon enough.

"It's alright," I say, folding my arms. Of course, it's groundbreaking and breathtaking but I'm not about to admit that.

"Really?" Rictor scoffs.

"*It's alright.*" I roll my eyes.

Just ahead, Rictor pushes on thin air, as if opening a door and holding it open for me.

"Is this the translucent thing?" I reach out tentatively to feel the door. "I've never seen it in person. Farmington's too poor for that." My fingers make contact. It's really there. Holy shit. "How do you guys not run into this?" I step inside. I think. Sprawling just past the ill-conceived entrance, there is a floor of video game nerds, all toiling away in their cubicles. This is where the magic is made, I suppose.

"Trust me, we run into it constantly," Rictor grumbles. "We're transitioning to sliding doors soon."

"Rick!"

I turn to see a curvy woman with short, curly hair waving at us from across the floor.

"Oh god," Rictor mutters.

She breezes through the beehive of game devs and reaches out for a handshake.

"Hi! I'm Bonnie," she says, a sunny smile lighting up her whole face.

"Nice to meet you," I say, a bit startled. "I'm—"

"Emierr, right?" Bonnie interrupts. "Sorry if I butchered your name."

I allow my mouth to hang open for just a moment too long. "No," I respond hastily, "you said it perfectly." *How the hell does she know my name?*

Rictor looks intensely uncomfortable as his two, very separate worlds collide. "Meer, this is Bonnie, my assistant."

"But we go way back, since college," she adds. "It's finally nice to meet you. Rick speaks so highly of his childhood friends."

"Really?" I had expected Rictor to pretend none of us existed in his new life.

Rictor is glaring daggers at Bonnie.

"Well, that's nice to hear," I say lamely.

"So," Rictor redirects. "I have an announcement to make."

Bonnie gives him a mock bow and gestures to the room behind her. Rictor rolls his eyes and steps forward.

"Hey, everyone," Rictor calls. "Can I have your attention for a moment?"

The hum of chatter and keyboards dulls as faces turn his way.

"I'll keep this short and sweet," he says, grinning. "We got our grant!"

There's a ringing silence for just a few moments while everyone stares, slack-jawed at him. Then, the whole floor erupts into cheers. Bonnie joins in, sticking two fingers in her mouth and unleashing an ear-splitting wolf whistle.

"Congratulations, everyone," Rictor yells over the noise. "You all worked so hard. I am the proudest team leader in all of Flemming right now. And with that being said, I will be taking some time off to cool my head because I'm going to kill myself if I don't."

I swallow my laugh as silence falls.

"I'm kidding," Rictor says quickly, hands up.

I decide to be polite and join in on the pity laugh.

"Okay, maybe I'm not kidding," he mutters, cringing a bit. Bonnie pats him empathetically on the back.

"I'm sure your next joke will land," she stage-whispers. Now *that* has the audience crowing. He narrows his eyes at her.

"In the meantime, Bonnie will be in charge." Bonnie's grin becomes, if possible, even wider and Rictor slings his arm across her shoulders. "Please treat her well."

Someone in the crowd whoops.

"Not that well," Rictor shouts, jabbing a finger at the perpetrator. "Okay, let's get back to work; it's not over yet. And pizza is on its way!" The employees begin to disperse, slapping each other's backs and high fiving.

I study Bonnie as she slips an arm around Rictor's waist, congratulating him once again. I've often wondered what kind of friends Rictor would have outside of our Squad. After we stopped hanging out, he seemed lost. I don't remember him making many friends in high school.

But Bonnie? She seems like an amazing person. The way she carries herself... Her confidence is contagious. I can see why he gravitated towards her.

"Let's go," Rictor says, snapping me out of my thoughts.

"Uh, yeah. Nice to meet you, Bonnie."

"You too. I hope to see you around more. Lord knows Rictor needs the company." She smirks at Rictor. *I love her.* Roasting Rictor is one of my favorite pastimes.

"Ha," he says blandly. "Keep me updated." He hugs her then grabs my arm, dragging me to the hallway.

"So, are you guys fucking or what?" I ask as soon as we're out of earshot.

Rictor barks out a laugh. "You're so dumb. Keep walking."

"This is *your* house?" I'm trying to pick my jaw up off the floor.

"Condo. In about four years, it'll be all mine." He casually throws his laptop bag onto the lengthy white couch. A sleek wooden coffee table stands in the center, flanked by another pristine white couch and two matching loveseats on either side. The walls are all glass. I press my nose to the windows, taking in the incredible city view. Utah has its scenery, sure, but this is something else. If I woke up every day to drones whizzing around, self-driving cars cruising the streets, and skyscrapers dripping with holograms, I wouldn't mind city living one bit.

I glance down at my wrist. 12:33 p.m. I need to speed this up. Rictor heads towards the kitchen area beneath the spiral staircase that ascends to the second floor. This place must cost a fortune. *How rich is this guy?*

He hands me a glass of ice water. "Drink. Do you have clothes with you? You smell like cheap tequila."

"Thanks." I toss the whole glass back. "And yes, I packed some." I pat my gym bag.

"Okay, let's cut the bullshit. What the hell are you really doing here?" He frowns at me. "We haven't spoken in years, Meer, and you suddenly show up at my work? Are we good now? Because I didn't know."

Oh, damn, he's still mad. "When are you um—uh—" I gulp, forcing back the sudden wave of anxiety-induced nausea. "...Leaving to go back home?"

He goes deathly still for a moment before letting out a breath. "Sit down. I reheated some of my leftovers." I let myself fall into the soft, plush couch as Rictor disappears back into the kitchen. When he returns, he's holding a steaming plate of food. The smell rapidly overwhelms my nausea and I grab the proffered fork.

The familiar flavor of spam fills my mouth. "Holy shit, you made this?"

"You can't ever go wrong with spam fried rice," he says and sits down beside me. He doesn't make a move to pick up his fork. "I'm not going, Meer."

I stop chewing. "What?" The final remainder of my tequila buzz vanishes. "Didn't you say you were taking a break from work?"

"Yeah, I am. Stay in for a week, watch shows, or even throw a party, I don't know. But I'm not going back home."

"Didn't you read the letter? You said you got one, right?" I whip around to dig through my bag.

"Yeah, I did. But that's Uncle and Auntie's decision. We can't do anything about it." He crosses his arms and leans back on the couch.

"If we go back with the rest, they'll listen, and we can change their minds."

"Do you truly believe Auntie Ina will change her mind about us?"

"Not her, but Uncle Kit, maybe."

"Seriously, I can't fucking go through this again." He leans forward, elbows on his knees and hands on his forehead. "It's not our fault. We just slept; how would we know Jho wouldn't wake up?"

I pause. *He really doesn't remember.* "What do you mean?"

"We had a sleepover, right? And we just went to sleep, and she stayed sleeping."

"That's all you remember?"

He looks at me, confusion crossing his features. A memory flashes through my mind. I'm sprinting down the basement stairs with a bucket of cold water and Rictor is holding Jhoana in his arms. I can see the fear in his eyes. It looks like the fear I see on his face now.

"I—I only remember the constant pounding in my chest, every day, until I left." His head drops back into his hands. "I mean, over the years, it comes in waves, but it's not continuous. If I go back... I don't want to ever feel that again." His voice catches.

"Jho's gonna die," I state flatly. Saying it out loud for the first time twists my stomach.

Rictor's eyes are back on me. They're glistening in the afternoon light.

"It's not about you or me," I press on. "Our best friend is going to die. We did that." My hand grips the notebook concealed in my bag.

"I'm sorry, Meer, I—I can't." Tears trace lines down his cheeks. I didn't see this coming. After years of planning, I didn't account for this one thing; they all might be just as broken as me. The only difference is I know why I'm broken. I can't make him remember everything now. We all have to do it together.

"What—What if I tell you we can bring her back?" My voice shakes. *I'm really doing this.*

He narrows his eyes, a flicker of anger lacing his next words. "What? What the hell have you been drinking?"

"I know a way." I can hear the desperation in my tone but I'm not strong enough to hold it back. I *am* desperate. "But we need the others to do it."

"*How*, Meer?" he snarls.

I flinch. Some part of me had hoped that this whole amnesia thing was just an act. A refusal to talk about what happened to us. But now, I don't think he's pretending.

"You don't remember *anything*?" I whisper. "The Space Ring? The Terrerium? Al?"

Rage transitions smoothly to bewilderment. "What are you talking about? I told you..."

"Help me get everyone back home," I interrupt. "And I'll explain everything."

"No, dude, you sound crazy. This isn't some fantasy or a game. There's nothing to explain. Why would I go back there after everyone we knew turned on us? If they called us killers when we were kids, what do you think they're going to say now?" Rictor's arms fold around his abdomen, like he's trying to hold himself together. "I'm not going back!"

"Then you're just proving to them that you *are* guilty." My jaw tightens. *I don't mean any of this, Ricky.*

Rictor's expression looks as though I've plunged a knife into his gut. "Fuck you!" He stands. "You know what, weren't you the one who told me to get the fuck away from you? Yeah, I remember *that*. That was the greatest advice anyone has ever given me because I did get the fuck away, and I made a life out of it. I got out and changed how people saw me."

"Good for you, Ricky." I genuinely mean it. "I am proud of you, but Jho will never have the pleasure of living a life like you do."

"Jesus, man. That's so un-fucking-fair."

"Is it fair for Jho?" I counter. Each jab I make at one of my closest childhood friends cuts me deeper but I'm in too far to stop now. "Is it fair for her to be stuck to monitors and tubes?" My voice is trembling now. It's all or nothing. "Let's just... Ricky. Let's save our little sister."

Broken isn't the right word to describe him right now. I just shattered him. *I'm sorry, Ricky. I won't lose him, like how I lost Jhoana. I won't lose our world, even if it means I'll break all of my best friends' hearts. Even if it means becoming the villain in this story.*

"We—c—can br—bring her..." He closes his eyes and takes a few measured breaths. "Can we really bring her back?"

"I know we can."

He takes a step back toward me, eyes boring into mine. *Punch me, Ricky, it's okay.* I prepare myself for impact but instead, his head finds my shoulder and tears begin to dampen the fabric of my shirt.

Fuck.

DUSTIN

My stomach seizes as I puke out my protein shake. This hurts. The mixed stench of stomach acid and almond milk fills my nose, churning my insides further. I brace for the third wave, and my stomach contorts. I squeeze my eyes shut, but nothing comes out of my now-empty stomach.

This is the worst kind of vomit: air. The automatic toilet flushes, and I wipe my lips. I stumble out of the stall to scrub my hands and rinse my mouth. My reflection stares back at me from the wide, spotless mirror. I can't believe they're really doing it. My eyes drift back to the letter on the floor. *Jho...*

I take a steadying breath and pick it up, reading it once more in a fruitless effort to make myself understand. Jhoana will never see one of my games. She won't experience having a family or even getting to love. It's not fair. But maybe this is for the best. She's suffered long enough. I already grieved her long ago; it's about time.

"Dustin, halftime is about to end. Coach is calling for you." Cal comes thundering into the locker room. It's a good thing he scored a job in sports because I'm pretty sure he couldn't fit into a cubicle.

"Yeah, one sec." I move to my locker and shove the letter in amongst the mess of sweaty clothes and damp towels.

"Was that a love letter from one of your fans again?" Cal grins at me, oblivious to my pale, sweaty face.

"No, it's from your mom." I put on my helmet.

He barks a short laugh and smacks me on the back. I wince as the sound echoes between the surrounding concrete walls.

"I might just be your daddy soon," I continue as we jog back toward the field.

"Bruh, I need you to never say the word 'daddy' ever again, cool?"

I force out a laugh and give him a shove on the shoulder. The crowd's cheers swell as we step back onto the field, the noise building like a wave. The stadium lights hit me, stinging my eyes for a second, and I hear the fans above shouting my name. I raise a hand and flash a smile, the kind I've mastered over the years. The roar of applause almost hurts my ears.

"Borja!" Coach Guerrero bellows.

I tear my gaze away from the audience and see him agitated and pacing.

"Chambers!" he roars.

We pick up the pace and join the huddle.

"You boys done with your fan service? I'd really like to win." Coach Guerrero's bulging arms are folded over his barrel chest.

"Sorry, Coach," Cal and I mumble.

"Okay, boys," Coach Guerrero says, redirecting his attention to the entire team. "You're all doing real good out there. But it doesn't mean you get cocky and put your guard down. This is our stadium; we take this one home." He jabs a finger at me. "Borja, this is your team. What's your game plan?"

All eyes are on me.

With heroic effort, I push the letter to the back of my mind and settle into game mode.

"Thanks, Coach. You heard him. This is our town!" My team hoots and pounds at their chests. I can feel the energy rising like static in the air. "We're ahead by a landslide, so let's keep it that way. Cal." It only takes a wink from me to convey the plan.

"Ayy, I follow you. I'm ready," he says, grinning back.

"Okay, boys, we're going with the 'fakey.' "

The boys nod, a few fists bumping each other.

"Yeah, shit, let's have some fun," Harrison whoops. "We might as well show them why we're going to the Super Bowl."

"Atta boy, we all in?" I place my hand in the center and the team piles on.

"Lions, what?" I shout.

"Roar!" the team thunders.

Half-time ends, and we take up our positions on the field. I look out into the sea of people. A surge of energy flows through me as I spot Celeste, my little angel, with her nanny, Dahlia, by the stands. Being away from my girls for long periods of time always kills me. I blow her a kiss, and she returns it with dramatic flair.

Emierr and I came up with this play in high school, and it worked every single time. Turns out, the NFL isn't much different. Cal looks at me and nods.

Diaz, our center, takes his position in front of me The other team's quarterback leers at me. I lean down, readying myself to wipe that obnoxious smirk right off his face. Suddenly, a weight crushes my chest. The thought of my daughter, this game, the Squad, and the letter batter at the fragile barrier I've constructed in my mind. I try desperately to force it back and refocus on the field before me. I think I'm going to puke again. An image of Jhoana smiling at me wavers in my mind's eye.

Jho... "Hut!" I yell through the hazy threat of tears, and around me, the play is set in motion.

Diaz spirals the ball to me, and the helmets and shoulder pads of the left and right guards smash into our opponents, shielding me from any offensive measures. Diaz runs straight for an opening, and Harrison takes off to the right. I lunge two steps back and crank my arm back to toss the ball in Harrison's direction. The other team takes the bait, leaving me, and going for Harrison and Diaz. I fake the throw and spin to my left, where Cal should be running at me to take the ball. But it isn't Cal coming for me. My muscles lock into place and a wave of ice washes over me.

My younger self, with murder in his eyes, is sprinting over the grass, teeth bared in twisted snarl.

The game disappears around me as I drop the ball. He's almost on me. My body moves independently of my brain, almost in slow motion. *He* lunges at me. I don't think. I seize him by the waist mid-air and slam him to the ground. Bones crack as he lands, and his scream of pain echo through the stadium. My vision has tunneled, blocking out everyone around me, and fixing on the face of the boy beneath me.

Pain mixes with fury on his young face. Something about him is... wrong. He reaches out with a bloodied right hand. Two fingers are missing. My stomach lurches at the sight of crimson welling from the empty spaces.

"Borja," someone shouts. My head snaps up and I'm back in the stadium. The game has come to a complete halt and everyone in the field is staring at me in horror. I look down, and it's not my mutilated younger self on the ground. It's Cal, holding onto his shoulder. His teeth are gritted tightly against the pain and his arm hangs at an unnatural angle.

"S—Shit!" I stagger back, away from the scene I'd created.

Medics flood onto the field, hiding Cal from my sight. I look to Coach, as if he might have answers. His crossed arms have fallen to his sides and he's staring at me in shock.

What the fuck did I just do?

Automatically, I scan the crowd, searching for Celeste and Dahlia. Did they see? The seats they'd been in just a few minutes ago were now empty. I exhale, wondering how much of a raise I should offer Dahlia.

I watch as the medical team straps Cal to a gurney and lifts him from the ground. "Cal... I'm sorry." I falter as he passes me, "I blanked out and... got confused." The excuse sounds pathetic, even to me. *Am I losing it?*

"There's no way my mom is gonna like you after this," Cal mumbles, lifting his head to grin weakly at me.

I shake my head and manage a thin smile. "*Par*, you're crazy. I'll pay for your hospital treatment, alright? Sorry, brother."

The medics carry him off the field. "Better win, boys!" he shouts, raising his free hand with a shaka. My team and I raise fists with pinky and thumb out in a salute. The crowd roars as Cal is swallowed by the stadium exit. I look back to where Celeste and Dahlia are sitting. Dahlia has my girl in her lap, and I can tell from here that she looks unnerved.

In my periphery, I can see two new figures standing at the stadium entrance. For the second time today, my blood runs cold. For the first time in years, I see the faces of Rictor and Emierr. After what just happened, I'm not even sure if they're real.

"Borja!" Coach Guerrero calls for me.

I break eye contact with my childhood friends and walk toward the coach in a daze.

"Borja," he repeats when I come to a halt in front of him. "You're benched."

I nod, honestly a bit relieved. I have no idea what was happening to me, and I don't want to dislocate anyone else's shoulders. Without a word, I turn to take my place on the bench. In my line of sight, amidst the sea of faces, I can clearly make out five figures in white button-ups. My first instinct is that they're Mormon missionaries, like back home.

They're dressed the part but.... There are five. They're supposed to travel in pairs. They sit still, their eyes fixed on me. As if my attention was a signal, they all rise as one from their seats. They're smiling down at me, a bit too wide. *What the hell?*

"You sent your teammate to the hospital," the referee says from behind me.

"Yeah... I... I know," I manage to say, turning back. "Coach, um—I'm not in a good way. I just found out my childhood friend is going to... die." Just saying it out loud feels surreal. A quick look back at the bleachers tells me the "missionaries" are gone. Something about them set my teeth on edge.

"I'm—sorry, son." Coach Guerrero takes off his cap.

"Can I go? I—um—I—"

"Yeah, take some time off. I'll let the team know, and I'm sorry for your loss. You'll be in my thoughts."

"The game will resume without Mr. Borja." The referee walks

away and blows his whistle.

"Thanks, Coach."

"Aye, look," Coach Guerrero whispers. "The press is going to do their thing, so lay low."

I nod, understanding that the press is about to chew me up and spit me into the gutter. The crowd is giving a mixture of cheers and boos. I don't let it get to me because there are crazier things happening right now than just the destruction of my reputation. Like these two jackasses finally attending one of my games.

"Hey," Rictor says lamely as I run up to them.

"Hey? That's all I get?" I catch him in a crushing bear hug. "Holy shit. Where the hell have you been, loca?"

"Okay Jacob, I'm team Edward," Rictor wheezes. I snort and release him, take a step back. Rictor has really filled out over these past years. And the beard, just like his dad's.

Damn, my chin stubble could never. "Look at you," I laugh. "You've been working out, huh?" I squeeze his corded forearms. "What you benching? Two-fifty?"

He chuckles. "Yeah. Work and gym, that's my routine."

"Nice." I turn my attention to Emierr, who hasn't changed much since I last saw him a few years back.

"Hey, Dust, about the last time..." Emierr scratches his head uncomfortably.

This drunk *ass*. I can't believe the balls on this idiot after the shit he pulled with that piñata. I shake my head and spread my arms wide. "Come here, man, give me a hug."

"You're not mad?" Emierr says, voice now muffled against my chest.

"Mad at you for ruining my daughter's second birthday? Of course not." I pull away from him. "You only fell onto the food table and broke it. Oh, and got in a drunken fistfight with the piñata. Then there was the incident with the cake..."

"Daughter?" Rictor exclaims, mouth hanging open.

"Oh yeah, I forgot to mention, Dusty's a dad now," Emierr says, slapping a hand down onto my shoulder. "Turns out we didn't have to worry after all, even if they're super small, they *do* still work—"

I swat Emierr's hand off me, laughing. "Now you show up to a game after how many years of me inviting you guys?"

"I never got an invitation," Emierr protests.

"Me neither," Rictor says, looking baffled.

"I email you guys all the time."

"Ah... It's probably in my junk folder." Rictor has the decency to look ashamed.

"I don't like opening my emails," Emierr admits.

"Wow, can you guys not be honest?" I chuckle. "At least you know now, right? I always leave three tickets for you guys every game, just in case you come, and you did tonight."

"Every game?" Rictor looks guilty as hell. "I'll attend some games when I can. I promise."

"That's more than enough. You too, Meer." I punch him again.

"Ow!"

"Where's Jads?" I peer behind them, expecting her to emerge from the shadows in her signature way.

"Sorry, Dust, we haven't been able to get through to her." There's something cagey about Rictor's expression.

My heart twinges for a second. "That's okay. You guys showed up."

"Are you okay, though? We saw what happened." Rictor's tone is hesitant.

My smile fades. "Uh—yeah. I got confused and—it was an accident, that's all."

Rictor still looks suspicious but Emierr claps me on the back.

"You did our play! It looks so much better when the real professionals do it." By the look on his smug face, you'd think he had been unilaterally responsible for my entire career. The tension in my muscles loosens.

"It would've worked if I didn't space out—" I shake my head. "Damn, I'm really happy to see you guys." I wrap my arms around them, pulling them in again.

"Well, under the circumstances..." Rictor ducks out from under my arm, pulling an all-too-familiar letter from his pocket.

My stomach churns. "Oh. Right."

"I'm guessing you got one, too." Emierr's mouth thins.

I don't answer. Of course this is about Jhoana. They're not here to watch me play.

"I'm going to change. I'll take you guys to my place when I'm done." I slip between them and disappear into the locker room. The image of little Dustin lunging at me replays in my head. Home is filled with so many nightmares. It took many years to overcome the fear that accompanied every thought of my town and my family. But what was that vision? Why would my younger self be... after me? I duck into the showers and try to rinse the anxiety from my body. I wish it were that easy.

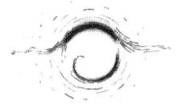

"This is your house?!" Rictor's eyes look like they might fall out of their sockets.

"Now you know how I felt when I saw your condo," Emierr says.

"I have a condo, Meer. Dusty has a mansion."

"Relax, boys, this isn't my main house. I just bought a house in Madrid; I see my family settling there." I smile sardonically, looking at the mansion I bought under peer pressure. That realtor persuaded the hell out of me.

"You regret not going for a football career, huh?" Rictor prods Emierr.

The car doors slam behind us, and my little girl runs to me with arms outstretched. Dahlia strolls in her wake, jerking her chin over Celeste's head. I follow the gesture and spot Sylvia standing with the front door flung open, Holo-phone to her ear, and eyes burning a hole through mine.

"Oh shit," I mutter, and Dahlia takes my gym bag in silent solidarity.

"Come on, I'll show you my house." Celeste releases her vice grip on my leg and yanks Emierr and Ricky through the foyer. Dahlia side-eyes me and joins the impromptu house tour.

"Hi, Mommy," Celeste says without pausing. And with that, my daughter, friends, and nanny have left me to the sharks. Well. Just one shark. I sidle up to my wife, sliding through the doorway.

"I understand that," Sylvia says tightly, "Oh yes, he's paying for all the hospital bills." Her right hand is balled into a fist on her hip. She's kicking my ass after this. "Okay, thank you, Alfonse. I'll make sure he gets an earful. Goodnight." Her hand drops to her side, Holo-phone interface vanishing.

I try to step back, but the front door has swung shut behind me. "Vi, wait!"

She closes the distance between us with two strides of her incredible legs and clamps an arm around my neck, putting me in a headlock. "Again, Dustin Reed?"

"I'm sorry, I blanked out." I try in vain to escape my prison.

She lets go and grabs my face, kissing me. "What's going on?" The irritation in her voice fades to worry. "Is it happening again?"

I nod. I can't tell her yet what's going on back home. She just gave birth to Ana; I don't want to add more to her plate. Sylvia plants a firm peck on my cheek.

"I love you," I say, burying my face in the crook of her neck.

"I love you, too." Her arms close tightly around me as I run my fingers through her silky, black hair.

"Was that... Ricky? With Meer?" she asks, looking in the direction they'd disappeared.

"Yup."

"Oh my god." She steps back and smacks a palm to her forehead. "I ignored them."

"It's okay. Celeste's got them," I say dismissively. "Wait, where's Ana?"

"Asleep. I have the monitor on the counter. She finally went down for her nap." Now, I notice faint purple smudges beneath my wife's eyes and feel a wave of guilt wash over me. Even with Dahlia's help, the past few weeks must have been hard on her. And I haven't been there for half of it. "The food is ready," she says, interrupting my spiral of self-pity. "I'll set up, and you go change."

"Shoot, thank you, baby." I envelope her in my arms, pressing a silent apology into her soft, comforting shape. She kisses my cheek, and a sharp smack follows as her hand lands on my left ass cheek. Wincing slightly, I shoot her a playful glare before we part ways—Sylvia heading to the kitchen while I make my way upstairs to change. As I reach the second floor, I can't help but peek into Celeste and Ana's room. My little one is fast asleep in her crib, her gentle snores, just like her mama's, bringing a smile to my face.

Upon reentering the kitchen in clean clothes, I'm greeted by a spread of Chamorro and Filipino dishes, with trays of barbecue ribs, shrimp patties, pancit, red rice, and lumpia, all neatly arranged.

"Damn." My stomach grumbles, reminding me that I'd lost all my food to the locker room toilet earlier today. I take a shrimp patty and shove it in my mouth, devouring the delicacy. Its flavor is unlike anything I've encountered when traveling. With every bite, a myriad of flavors unfolds; plump shrimp from azure seas, harmonizing with pungent garlic, fiery chili, and fragrant herbs; a testament to Guam's culinary artistry. My eyes roll back in nearly indecent pleasure; this is my favorite Chamorro dish.

"I wanted to welcome you home with all your favorites," Sylvia says, emerging from the apartment-sized pantry. "You haven't been home for a month. It's good that Dahlia told me Meer and Ricky were coming." A lumpia crunches in her mouth. "I said, might as well cook everything. And Auntie Mel helped me with the rest."

"You had your auntie drive? Did she at least bring some food home?"

"Oh, that woman took a party platter with her."

Feeling a surge of overwhelming fondness, I wrap my wife in my arms and press my lips to hers.

"Mommy, Daddy!" Celeste shouts from the kitchen entrance, covering her eyes. "Yuck!"

"What? I can't show I love my wife?" I plaster every inch of Sylvia's face with kisses.

Celeste turns around, ever the polite hostess. "I apologize for my daddy."

My two friends roar with laughter at the seriousness on her round face.

"Don't worry, Celeste, let them be so you can have a little brother or sister," Emierr says, grinning fiendishly.

"I already have one," Celeste says proudly. "My little sister, Ana."

"What?" Rictor's heart might actually give out if we try for that third baby like I want to.

"Two?" Emierr lifts two fingers, as if verbal confirmation isn't enough.

"She's five months old now," my wife corroborates. "Hi, I'm Sylvia. It's so nice to finally meet you, Ricky." She opens her arms for a hug.

"Oh my god, yes, I'll give you a hug." Rictor embraces her. "Congrats on the new baby."

I can't believe my closest friends—my brothers—are here with my wife and daughters. It's almost too much. Heat begins to well in my eyes.

"Hi, Vi," Emierr says apprehensively. "I'm sorry about that party."

"That was a long time ago. Come here." She pulls Emierr into a hug too, squeezing tightly. "You're always welcome here."

Emierr's eyes look glassy over Sylvia's shoulder.

"Hey, no crying here." I point an accusatory finger at him, using my other hand to wipe my eyes. "This is a masculine, manly, NFL home."

The emotional charge that held the room in its grip breaks and everyone laughs.

"Let's eat!" Sylvia claps her hands.

As we dig in, Dahlia announces her departure and is forced to teeter out the front door, carrying enough food to feed a small army.

"Is this Chamorro food?" Rictor asks conversationally over his heaping plate.

"It has to be. There's red rice." Emierr adds two scoops of the rice and five lumpia to his plate.

"Authentic Chamorro food," I boast through the shrimp patty stuffed into my mouth.

"Man, look at you," Rictor says, gazing at me with affection.

"It's reassuring to see that most of us made something of ourselves beyond Farmington."

I don't think he meant it negatively, but we both glance over at Emierr. It gets awkwardly quiet.

"These are really good, Vi," Emierr says quickly, changing the subject. "Dusty wasn't lying when he said it's second best to Auntie Luna's cooking. I had her spaghetti yesterday and—"

"What, you ate my Ma's food?" Rictor interrupts, looking startled.

"Uh—yeah, Ru—I—she packed me some food for the night before I flew out," Emierr mumbles.

"Did you see my dad?" I ask, setting my food back on the plate. A twinge of anxiety sparks in my stomach.

"No, sorry." The answer brings mingled relief and disappointment,

"Who's my mom cooking for?" Rictor insists.

"Our parents, they're helping with the vigil. I guess your mom's the cook. I don't know."

"Vigil? Someone passed away?" Sylvia frowns, a worried crease forming between her eyebrows. My heart drops. She's not supposed to find out this way.

"It's the reason we're here."

Shut up, Ricky. I don't want the high of this long-overdue reunion to end. I don't want to face the reality of our situation. Not yet.

"Someone you know from your hometown is..." Sylvia doesn't finish the sentence.

"My cousin, Jhoana—" Emierr starts to say.

"Auntie Jho!" Celeste interrupts excitedly.

My mouth tightens at the sight of my daughter's shining face.

"Did she wake up already?" Celeste asks. Her big, brown eyes sparkle with delight. "My Daddy says she's like Snow White. Did a prince kiss her?"

I steal a glance at Rictor and Emierr. Their expressions are equal parts soft and sad.

"No, Celeste," Emierr says gently. "Your Auntie Jho's... She isn't going to wake up. She's going to be an angel instead of a princess."

"What?" Celeste's voice trembles, tears beginning to dribble down her face. "Daddy... Don't people have to die to become angels?"

"No..." Sylvia covers her mouth and looks at me.

"Meer!" Rictor hisses. "Let Dustin explain it to her."

Sylvia reaches out to cradle a weeping Celeste in her arms. "You don't look shocked," she says to me. Her eyes have gone icy. "When did you find out?"

"In the middle of the game, I read the letter," I say, trying to keep my voice even, but I can feel my legs trembling.

"When were you going to tell me?"

"After they left." I close my eyes and wait for the rage, disappointment, or whatever it is Emierr and Rictor decided to fling my way.

"So, you're *not* coming." Rictor drops his utensils.

"Really, guys! I just wanted to have dinner." I lean away from the table, pressing my fingers to my eyes. Stars explode behind my lids.

"And you said we would talk," Emierr retorts.

"You shut up, okay—" I say, jabbing a finger at him.

"Is Auntie Jho going to sleep forever?" Celeste's tearful voice breaks as she looks over at Emierr, resting her head on her mother's chest.

"She doesn't have to," Emierr mutters.

"Meer, maybe not here." Rictor says quietly.

Emierr ignores Rictor, leaning forward on the table. "We can bring her back, Dust."

"*What*?" Rage and disbelief collide in my chest. "Now I know you've been drinking again," I say through gritted teeth.

"I swear, Dust, we can bring her back!"

Bring her back? What kind of bullshit is that? It's been nearly two decades, and now he has a solution, right before they plan to put her in the ground.

"How Meer?" I ask flatly. "How do you plan to bring her back?"

"We need Jads first, and then I'll explain everything," he says, looking relieved, as if I've agreed to go along with this insanity.

"No!" I slam my hands on the table and leap to my feet.

Sylvia's arms tighten around the now-wailing Celeste. "Dustin Reed. Don't you dare speak to your brothers that way."

My jaw drops as I stare blankly at my wife's resolute face.

"This is your family, just as much as we are," she says. Poise radiates from her lifted chin and low, even tone. "They have a right to be heard, and they deserve to know the truth." She stands, propping a sniffling Celeste on her hip. "Talk it out. We'll be upstairs." And with that, she sweeps from the room, vanishing up the stairs.

We all look silently at the doorway for a moment before I spin back around to face Emierr and Rictor. "Are you guys fucking happy? You made my baby cry."

"Dust, Jho needs us," Meer plows ahead. "We can save her. She can... She can meet Celeste."

"Don't fucking use my daughter to guilt-trip me, man." Each breath I take feels like a weight in my lungs. "I love Jho, alright? I love her like my own sister. But, after everything... How can you guys be okay? I can't go back there."

"Who said we were okay? I shake every time I even think of that place," Rictor fires back.

"I live there," Emierr points out. "Every day, I'm reminded of what happened."

"What *did* happen? 'cause, I don't remember anything," I snap. "Do you, Ricky?"

Rictor avoids meeting my gaze. "I... don't really remember much," he admits softly.

"See, what the fuck happened? I think you're the only one who remembers, Meer." I squeeze my eyes shut. "And with the shit you're saying, I don't even know if you *do* remember."

"Like I said, when we get Jadis, I'll tell you guys everything," Emierr says doggedly.

"Fuck that, no. I love you guys. I wanted my brothers back but... I have a family of my own now... I can't walk out on them just to relive those nightmares. Not after how hard I've worked to put it behind me."

"Dusty, do you hear me? *We can bring her back!*" Emierr stands up, eyes leveling with mine.

"Meer," Rictor grabs him by the arm, "He said no. Let's respect that." He pulls Emierr back down to his seat.

"There are rooms upstairs," I mutter, avoiding direct eye contact. "Please, stay the night. I'll drop you guys at the airport tomorrow." I catch Emierr shaking his head in my peripheral vision as he gets up and walks wordlessly towards the stairs.

Rictor follows suit, rising from his seat. "I'm sorry, Dusty," he murmurs before walking away.

"I'm sorry, too," I whisper, dropping my head into my hands. My chest tightens, and the hot tears behind my eyes prickle in their desperate bid for freedom. I run my hands over my face and start gathering empty plates. It's a distraction I need. After clearing the table, I head upstairs, briefly glancing at the guest rooms before making my way to Celeste and Ana's room. I peek in and see Celeste sitting up in bed, playing with her doll. Her little eyes still look puffy. I step inside.

"Hi, angel. Where's your little sister?"

"With Mommy, I woke her up when I was crying," she says, eyes fixed on the toy in her hands. I sit down on her bed beside her.

"Angel... I'm sorry Daddy yelled."

"It's okay," she mumbles, still not looking at me.

"Did you have fun showing your uncles around the house?"

She nods. "Daddy?"

"Yes, angel?"

"You have to go back home." She finally lifts her face to look me in the eye.

"What?" *If Emierr told her to say this I swear—*

"You have to save Auntie Jho."

"Baby, I want to stay here with you," I say. My shoulders shudder with the effort of staying calm.

"Daddy…" Her voice trembles. "She's my auntie. And she's your sister. Family, right?" She holds my hands tightly.

"My love," Sylvia calls softly from the doorway, Ana cradled in her arms. "You're going home."

"What?"

"I've packed your clothes. Everything you need is in your luggage."

"Love, I'm not going," I stand up to face her as she crosses the room. "I can't."

"Jhoana needs you," she says simply. "The girls and I will be okay. We have Dahlia and Auntie Mel. You have to do this."

"I'm scared, Vi."

"I know," she says. I pull her into an embrace, Ana pressed between our chests. Celeste stands and grabs my arm, squeezing tightly. For a while, I've only associated family with my girls and Sylvia, but I need to remember I also have a family back home. My Pops, my aunties and uncles, and the Squad.

"Okay," I finally say. "I'll go." I take a deep breath, trying to calm my racing heart. "I promise I'll be home as soon as I've done what I need to do. I'll call you every night." I reach down to pull Celeste up into my arms.

"You're going to be okay," Sylvia says, as if her words can penetrate my fear. "You're not alone. We love you so much." She kisses me as deeply as she can over the heads of two kids.

"I'll go tell the boys," I say. When I've reached the hallway connecting our four guest rooms, I crack open the first door.

"Meer? Ricky?"

There's no response. I close the door and move on to the second room, finding it empty as well. In the third room, I hear the shower running. Spotting Emierr's ratty bag on the bed, I decide to come back later. I tap lightly on the fourth door, and with the first knock, it creaks open. The lights are on, but Rictor isn't in the room.

I notice the balcony doors are ajar. I slip through them, into the cool, early autumn air. There, I find him leaning against the stone railing, lost in thought as he gazes up at the night sky and bathed in the soft glow of the toenail moon.

"It's called a waxing crescent if you were wondering," he says, his gaze still fixed on the sky.

"It still amazes me how you always know what I'm thinking," I remark, standing beside him and looking up. There are fewer stars here in the city than back home in the high desert.

"You're kind of predictable." He chuckles.

I scoff. "A waxing crescent...?"

"I think you used to call it a toenail."

"Hey, I just thought that!"

"Predictable," he repeats with a smirk. "Dust, I gotta say, I'm proud of you." He pauses, pursing his lips. "You know, for creating your own family."

I'm silent for a moment, gaze fixed on the sliver of moon. "Thanks, Ricky..." I finally say. "That means a lot to me. I'm proud of you, too."

We stand quietly under the stars for a while, until I need to break the silence.

"You really did it," I say softly.

"Huh?"

"You became your dad. Aren't you an astrophysicist like him?"

"I was... But he was also an astronaut. I didn't get that far."

"You know you could if you want to." My attention returns to the pinpricks of light above us. This view of the universe feels strangely familiar.

"I'm sorry, Dusty," Rictor says suddenly. It's as if he's been holding his breath. "I'm sorry I didn't check my email."

I look back at him, startled. "It's okay..."

"No, it's not," he says, shaking his head. "Brothers don't *not* speak to each other. I should have called all of you or, like what Uncle Kit said, kept some semblance of a relationship with you."

"Well, don't beat yourself up. I didn't really get in touch with you guys, either. I just invited you to my games. I could have called too, but I didn't." Guilt creeps back into my voice.

"It still doesn't make it right, though," Rictor persists. "I don't know how you and Meer aren't mad at me."

"Because you're not the one who did something wrong." I place my elbows on the railing and gaze blindly into the dimly lit yard. "I know we all pointed fingers at each other, but it took a long time to see that we were also victims. It could have happened to any of us, whatever happened to Jho." I look down. These had been my thoughts for the longest time; it's weird hearing myself voice them.

"You know... I tried to kill myself in senior year," Rictor murmurs.

My eyes shoot back to him, shock lancing my chest. He doesn't look at me. His eyes are fixed determinedly on the twinkling sky.

"Ricky, you don't have to—"

"You deserve to know this because we all went through it." Rictor continues as if I hadn't spoken.

I keep quiet, mind whirring. I wonder if I can cope with what I'm about to hear.

"We were on the brink of graduating. You weren't there with us anymore and I'd stopped talking to Meer and Jads altogether. I felt so guilty that we were moving on while Jho stayed asleep. Jads found me just in time. She came over to talk, but I suppose that kind of gut feeling is what makes us family." Rictor finally steals a glance at me. "She probably knew that I was crying out for help but couldn't find the words. I don't know how long I was hanging, but she saved me. I made her promise to keep it between us."

I can't find my voice. It's being strangled by regret and sorrow for the boy I once called my brother. Leaving Farmington during sophomore year was one of the toughest decisions I ever made. I could have persuaded Pops to stay, but at the time, leaving seemed like the only option. If I had known that Rictor would be all alone during those years, I would have stayed without a second thought.

"Ricky... I'm sorry I wasn't there." I have to force the words through my tightened throat.

Rictor sighs. "Never apologize. We made a life for ourselves. I don't regret leaving. Neither should you. I honestly don't wanna go back—"

"Ricky."

"But we owe it to Jho to try, right?"

I turn to grab both of Rictor's shoulders. He falls silent.

"I'm coming with you guys."

His lips parted in surprise. "Really? That worked?"

"No, my daughter worked. She reminded me of what family means. You guys are family, too. We made a pact. I intend to keep it, to honor Jho."

A voice from the doorway startles us. "You're going?"

Emierr is standing in the open door, wearing nothing but a disturbingly short towel around his waist.

"U—Um..." Rictor's eyes jump to the floor and his face flushes beet red.

"Relax, you act like we didn't shower together in gym class." Emierr snorts. "Dusty, you're really coming?"

"Yeah, I am." I'm unbothered by Emierr's state of undress. I see far worse every time I go to work. I am wondering where he got such a short towel though.

"Yes!" Emierr whoops and captures me in an extremely damp hug.

"I'm not ready to see anyone back home, but I at least have you guys." I smile somewhat apprehensively. "What airline are you guys flying tomorrow?"

"United," Rictor says. He turns to Emierr, cheeks still a bit red. "What are you even doing here without clothes on?"

"I was going to ask to borrow underwear. I didn't pack an extra pair."

"*Borrow*, you're gonna return used underwear?" There is a note of deep disgust in Rictor's voice.

"Fine. Can I *have* a pair?" Emierr amends. "In return, I promise not to give them back."

Rictor heaves a sigh of resignation. "In my luggage."

"Thank you, thank you." He walks back into the room.

"We could use my jet," I offer absently as I open the *United* app on my Holo-phone.

"Jet? Bitch, how rich are you?" Rictor pauses. "Actually, don't answer that. It's rhetorical."

"It's okay, we can ride in style next time. I'll just fly with you guys; can you send me the details?"

"Yeah, here." He pulls out a surprisingly regular phone from his pocket to transfer the flight information.

"I'm going to bump us to business class," I say, and I hear his phone ding.

"Nice!" Emierr shouts from inside.

"Ricky, thanks for telling me all that stuff." I place a hand on his shoulder, squeezing. It hurt like hell to hear it but somehow, it reassured me that I was making the right choice. "You and that idiot in there are my brothers, forever."

Rictor smiles. "You too, Dusty." He leans around me. "Meer, did you get a hold of Jads?" he yells through the open balcony door. Emierr walks out wearing only a pair of Rictor's gray Hanes boxers, and raises his hand to us, the hologram projecting, "*Calling Jadis Salazar*".

A voice crackles to life over the Holo-phone. "Meer?"

"Jads! You answered! I've been calling non-stop. You're on speaker, by the way." Emierr stretches his arm closer to us.

"Sorry, I was on the road. Are you at your house?" Jadis's achingly familiar voice makes my heart leap.

"No, I went to get the boys." Emierr winks at us. "We're flying back home tomorrow, but we can go to you first."

"Don't bother." A deep breath sends static through the speaker. "I'm already home."

JADIS

I drop the call and put my phone in my pocket.

Emierr sounds the same. Not surprised; he never left this hell hole. For as long as I can remember, I've been running away, trying to forget this place, yet here I am, back to where it all began. At least I know that Cam will never find me here. A bruise on my ribs throbs in time with my heartbeat. It has been my steady reminder to keep driving and not look back.

I park my shitty, red Toyota Corolla two houses across the street from my childhood home and climb out. I don't even know if Mom and Dad still live here but the house hasn't changed, with the brick siding still painted in that tacky yellow color. Go figure. Mom and Dad never did get with the times, just like how they constantly compared me to Cadence, their favorite, like it would somehow make me a better daughter.

I don't even know why I ended up back in this neighborhood.

The house's hideous front door swings open, and my heart leaps into my throat. I dive behind my car, seeking cover. Peering through the windows, I catch a glimpse of Mom. She's wearing the coat she bought me in sophomore year. I hated the color. Purple is not me. Dad walks out, still wearing the worn-out brown leather jacket Cadence and I (mostly Cadence) got for his thirty-sixth birthday.

They stand under the porch light, revealing their faces. They've aged so much. It's hard not to notice how time has etched worry deep into their faces. I've never seen them so devastated before. Not even when I left after graduation. Mom clings to Dad's arm, and they move down the driveway, onto the sidewalk. They're going to Jhoana's. Emierr said our parents have been seeing her family. I love that for them, but where were our parents when *we* needed them? I straighten and make for the center of the road. They do not turn back as they continue walking, arm in arm.

This place sets old memories trickling back into my brain. I can only imagine that the onslaught will continue for as long as I'm in this cesspit town.

Jhoana, Dustin, Emierr, Rictor, and I were always inseparable as kids. But within our group, Jhoana and I shared the closest bond; she was the sister I always longed for. As opposed to the sister I actually have. I glance back at Rictor's house, positioned across from mine at the end of the cul-de-sac. The echoes of our collective grief on the day of his dad's and Dustin's mom's passing still linger in my mind.

My phone buzzes, and I read aloud, "I'm here." Shit.

> I'm almost there

I reply with shaking fingers. Dustin's old place is just a house down from Rictor's. He and his dad split during sophomore year and headed off to Michigan. The other guys were pissed at him for a while, but honestly, I was glad he escaped. Reaching my car once again, I swing the door open, and the singular functioning light flickers on, exposing a jumble of my belongings piled in the backseat. It's hard to believe I made it out of the house in time. I hop in and start the engine.

Going through the neighborhood is a big bowl of nostalgia. I drive past Emierr's place, just one house over from mine, and a vivid memory flashes in my mind. It's of Uncle Kit, walking us home after a day of endless play at their house. Our parents were always busy, but Uncle Kit stepped in and took care of us like a second dad. I ease my foot on the brake as I approach Jhoana's house. Several cars are parked around the driveway. Probably her visiting relatives. I spot Auntie Luna, Rictor's mom, on the porch and Uncle Joshua, Dustin's dad, approaching her.

I watch in shock as their lips meet. *What the hell? When did that happen?*

Auntie Luna hasn't changed one bit, still rocking that distinctive white streak in her hair. And Uncle Joshua? He's aging like a fine bottle of wine. His fifties suit him. I steal a quick peek through the open door and spot my parents engaged in conversation with Emierr's folks. It warms my heart to see they still have each other. Regardless of my convoluted feelings for this place, my memories, and these people, I feel content knowing that they will be okay.

Tea's Memory, a cozy café where I worked my first job, is just a four-minute drive from our neighborhood.

Cadence used to give me rides to school until I finally got my license in sophomore year. She stuck around here for college instead of hitting the dorms. Mom said it was to save money, but I bet my sister knew I'd hook her up with free drinks, too. Small towns have their perks, like everything being within arm's reach. I park the car on the sidewalk and sling my backpack over my shoulders. The café's logo has changed, but I hope Mr. and Mrs. Yu are still running the joint.

I glance around for Cadence, spotting a woman who bears a resemblance at the counter. Bells jingle as I step inside.

"Oh, can you substitute the milk with soy?" I hear my sister ask.

"Yeah, for sure." The young barista takes a cup and writes the order on it.

I tap my sister on the shoulder. "Still not a fan of regular milk, huh?"

Cadence spins around, cradling a little bundle in her arms. "Jadis," she breathes, pulling me into a tight hug. A baby is nestled between us.

After ten years, she looks so much older than I remember. There are lines now creasing her forehead and little smile lines at the corners of her eyes. Despite our strained relationship, I can't help but feel pity for her. She looks utterly exhausted.

"Whose baby is that?" I know the answer as soon as I find myself looking into a pair of eyes that so resemble her mother's.

"Say hi to your niece. This is Lyric," Cadence says with a small smile.

"Sorry," the barista interrupts. "Cadence, will this complete your order?"

I'm an aunt? And she named the baby Lyric?

Cadence turns around. "Sorry, Joy, can you just add a matcha latte with extra whipped cream?"

I lean around Cadence, catching the now-familiar barista's attention. "Joy?"

"Jadis? Oh my god, you're back!" She beams, calling over her shoulder, "*Māmā! Bàba!*"

I take a good, long look at her. The last time I saw her, she was in first grade. I always knew she would grow up to be a beauty. And she's still rocking those pigtails. "How old are you now?" I ask.

"Sixteen." She grins with a level of confidence I would have killed for at sixteen. "Omg, your hair is so rad, by the way."

"Thanks," I reach up to touch the strands of deep blue.

Mr. Yu comes out. "What's going on?"

"Joy, you need to start telling customers we're closing soon," Mrs. Yu says, appearing right behind him.

"Ma, there's still an hour left." Joy rolls her eyes at me.

"Hi," I greet my former bosses awkwardly.

Mr. Yu gasps and his wife claps a hand to her mouth.

"Jadis?" Mr. Yu walks around the counter. "Is that really you?"

"Hi, Mr. Yu. Yes, it's me."

Mrs. Yu gives me a once over, taking in the half-shaved head. "*Wǒde tiān nà...* You look like a rockstar." She gives me two thumbs up and a mischievous grin.

"It suits you very well," Mr. Yu agrees.

"Thank you," I chuckle.

"And Cadence! How is your husband doing, ha?" There's an odd note of disapproval in Mr. Yu's voice.

She did end up getting married.

"*Bàba!*" Joy shakes her head.

"Honey," Mrs. Yu says sternly. Clearly there's something I'm missing here.

"He's doing fine, Mr. Yu," Cadence answers, ignoring the barb. "He's coming home tomorrow."

We all fall silent, knowing the reason for his return.

"Okay, I'll bring your drinks to your table," Joy says, busying herself with Cadence's order.

"It was nice seeing you, Mr. and Mrs. Yu," Cadence says, putting a graceful end to an awkward conversation.

"Good to see you too, Cadence. It's nice to see the Salazar sisters finally together." Mrs. Yu says with a reproachful look at her husband.

"We missed you, Jadis." Mr. Yu seems oblivious to his wife's irritation. "Come visit home more often, okay?"

"You can stay longer after closing," Mrs. Yu whispers, and a smile spreads across my face as I trail behind Cadence to a table near the entrance. We take our seats, and Cadence's eyes are fixed on my hair.

"What?" I say, a little defensively.

"Nothing, your hair is really... out there. I like that dark shade of blue." She hesitates. "Mom and Dad are going to freak when they see you." She sits Lyric on her lap, facing me.

My stomach drops. "Did you already tell them I'm back?" Maybe telling her about my visit was a mistake.

"Not yet, why?"

Immediate relief washes over me. "Good. I don't think I can face them right now," I admit, leaning back in the wooden chair.

"Really, Jadis?" Cadence adjusts her posture, Lyric's wide brown eyes watching me unblinkingly. I still can't wrap my head around the idea of Cadence being a mother. Especially since she didn't exactly have a good role model for it. "After ten years of being gone, you still won't see them?"

I scowl at her. "You know how they treated me."

"It's been years, they've changed."

"Did they? Because I'm pretty sure I've been doing everything on my own since I left."

"Well, you didn't make things easier. You're basically a ghost, and no one knows where you are or how to contact you."

"All everyone did in this town was jump to conclusions and accuse me and my friends of doing something horrible."

"I'm sure no one really thought badly of you."

Her words spark fury in my gut. How could she dismiss my trauma with such ease? "Why did I bother coming here?" I mutter.

"Hi, guys." Joy arrives at our table with a drink in each hand. "Honeydew milk tea, substituted with soy milk." She places the drink in front of Cadence. "And matcha latte with extra whipped cream."

"Thanks, Joy," I say, pasting a smile on my face.

"I placed an order for two cakes, too," Cadence tells me, changing the subject as Joy circles back behind the counter. "One for us and one for…" She trails off and looks back down into her drink.

Between her and the Yus, it's clear that everyone in this town knows about Jhoana's fate, and that's why they all stare at me as if I'm broken. Well, maybe I am, but I'm not the one facing a death sentence.

"I'm sorry," I breathe out.

Cadence looks back up at me.

"I know I'm the one who reached out to you. I have no one here… anymore. And you're the only one I sorta trust."

"I'm sorry I disregarded your feelings about what happened in the past," Cadence murmurs. "I don't know how to do this either."

"I didn't think you cared that I left." I sip my drink, my eyes fixed on a chipped piece of the wooden table.

"Of course it affected me. We fought a lot, but we're still sisters. We're supposed to have each other's backs against Mom and Dad." She offers a small smile.

Leaving was no easy decision. After Rictor did it, I'd never felt so alone. The only person I could talk to was Jhoana. I'm happy Cadence can forgive me for running away, even when I can't do that for myself right now.

"But I'm glad you're back," my sister adds.

"It does feel nice being home after all these years." A lie, but one that will make this exchange far less tense.

"I wish it was under better circumstances."

"Yeah… How did everyone find out?" I ask. "Seems like everyone in town knows."

Cadence takes a moment before responding. "Auntie Ina—"

"Say less, I already know." I roll my eyes.

"It's so stupid, why would she—" She inhales deeply and doesn't finish the thought.

"Don't tell me. She invited the whole town like it's a party," I say sarcastically.

Cadence presses her lips together.

"No... You're lying." I put my drink down with a thud.

Cadence mutters, "She went on about how Jho never got to celebrate her birthday for seventeen years, so she invited everyone to celebrate until..."

"I mean, that sounds nice, actually," I confess, letting my indignation cool. Maybe I should cut Auntie Ina some slack.

"Jadis, Jhoana is going to die." My sister recoils as she says it, as if the words might lash out and bite her.

"Yeah, she is." The threat of tears chokes my throat and I close my eyes, shoving them back.

"Wait, how did *you* find out?" Cadence interrupts my internal battle.

"Uncle Kit." The taut muscles of my throat have loosened enough to speak. "He sent me a letter. I think he sent them to the boys, too." I turn to dig through my backpack.

Cadence watches, looking bemused. "That's weird, Uncle Kit doesn't like writing letters."

"That's what I thought but... Wait, I have it, hang on." My hands scour each pocket, fishing out all sorts of detritus but no letter. I drop my bag, thinking hard. A memory of the letter on my bed floats to the front of my mind and realization hits. "I forgot it at my house."

"It's fine, I believe you." She sips her drink.

It's not fine. He could be home now. My palms begin to sweat.

"Where are you staying?" Cadence doesn't pick up on my shift in mood. It's probably for the best.

"I don't know, maybe a hotel."

"Don't be ridiculous; you can stay with me. You don't have to waste money."

"I don't know, Cade, your house sounds full." I look at Lyric pointedly.

She sighs. "Well, I already told Carl you're staying with us, so..."

"I can't believe you married him." I can still recall the look on my parents' faces when Cadence had first brought a white guy home for dinner.

"You don't like Carl?" she asks, sounding a little wounded.

"No, I do. He's not that bad, from what I remember. Mom and Dad hated him, though."

"Now you know why I left home." A humorless laugh escapes her mouth. "You're not the only one who got it bad from them, Jadis. After you left, lashing out at me was their way of coping. I think I finally understood how you must have felt when the whole damn town turned on you."

I never thought anyone would be able to put themselves in my shoes.

"You can stay in Lyric's room; I moved her crib to ours and put an air mattress in there as soon as I got your message."

I smile softly. "Thanks."

"I have to use the restroom; can you hold her?" Cadence gets up and places Lyric on my lap.

"Wait, Cade, I—"

"Just a second, I can't hold it," Cadence says. "Something they fail to mention about giving birth," she adds with a grumble. I hold Lyric awkwardly, and she looks at me with those big brown eyes.

"Hi," I say, and she burbles a laugh. "You're so cute." I pinch her pillowy cheek. "You look like your dad, but you have your mom's eyes." She places a tiny hand on my face, and a warm tingle spreads through me. Even though I just met her I'm absolutely certain that I would take a bullet for this child.

"Are you ready?" Cadence asks, shaking her hands dry.

We say goodbye to the Yus, just in time for closing, and head to our cars. Cadence's house is near the town square, about a fifteen-minute drive. As I follow her car, my mind drifts to the letter. I can't believe I left it. I should have been more careful.

He's going to find it the moment he gets home. Was the address on the letter? Or was it on the envelope? Fuck, he can't find me. Especially not here. I drag my mind away from this prison I'd just escaped from and take in the familiar sights of the town square. It was never like this when I was younger.

So much has changed. Well, at least in this section of the town. This place used to be a snooze-fest, but damn, it's like a whole new world now. The streets are decked out in vibrant lights and trippy holograms. I roll down my window and catch the infectious sound of laughter and chatter filling the air.

Gross. I roll my window right back up. As soon as we leave the tiny town center, the past returns. No holograms, no colorful lights. Just Farmington.

I park my car opposite Cadence's house and grab a handful of clothes to stuff into my backpack. The trash bags in the back seat don't just hold my clothes. My entire life has boiled down to a pile of garbage in the back of a shitty car.

"Are you planning on moving?"

I nearly jump out of my skin at the sound of Cadence's voice.

"It looks like you took all your things with you."

"Yeah, I plan on heading up north after this, maybe Canada."

I follow her up the short walkway toward her front door. "Sounds like a big move."

"Nothing feels too big for me anymore," I admit. I don't know where to even start with my situation. I'll tell her eventually, but there are bigger problems at hand than my drama. "Nice place, feels cozy," I say, jerking my chin at the little house.

Cadence grins and unlocks the deadbolt with a hot pink, Hello Kitty key.

"You know, they have those fancy fingerprint locks now," I point out. "Only authorized fingerprints can unlock the house. No more keys."

"Jadis, this is Farmington. Only the mayor or Auntie Ina can afford that kind of security. You know that woman has power in this town," Cadence scoffs.

Stepping inside, I'm immediately struck by the soft, homey atmosphere that surrounds me. The living room is bathed in warm light and paintings of serene meadows and quirky vases dot the room. The entire space, in all its mismatched glory, really feels like an actual home. This is the world Cadence has built for herself, and it's beautiful. And here I am, feeling like shit for judging her all this time.

"Jadis?"

I turn around to see Cadence with her arms open, tears glistening in her eyes.

Without hesitation, I find myself enveloped in her embrace, and in that moment, we share the weight of all that was lost. I've got my big sister back.

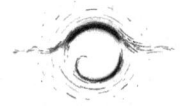

That was the best sleep I've had in a while, maybe even years. Mornings in Farmington are peaceful; even I'm not too bitter to admit that. In big cities, you never get this kind of quiet. After Jhoana's accident, every morning was like this—no one yelling at me, no one bossing me around, just me and my thoughts. At the time, it felt like my parents just stopped caring, but once I left home, I would have killed for this freedom. I pick up my phone from the floor and unplug it. 7:23 a.m. and *twenty* missed calls from Emierr.

"Oh, for the love of white Jesus," I mumble irritably. I'll message them later. I get up, brush my teeth, and hop in the shower. I take a look at myself in the tiny mirror, appraising the trash bag outfit I'd cobbled together. Ripped black jeans, white crop top, and cropped leather jacket. All that was missing were my combat boots downstairs.

"Nice, blending in perfectly," I say dryly. "Why couldn't I have been blessed with no sense of fashion?"

When I enter the kitchen, Cadence is sitting at the dining table, sipping her coffee and reading the morning paper. Like an actual newspaper. 2007 never left this place.

"Good morning. Off to the club?" Cadence asks sweetly, eying my ensemble.

"Shut up, this is my signature style. I'm just gonna drive around and see what's happening around here."

"Sounds good," she says. "Take my keys. I'm not letting my sister drive around with all her worldly possessions in the back seat."

I catch the tossed set of keys and sling my own back at her. "Take mine if you need them."

"I doubt it. Today is my 'me' day. I'm going to binge-watch this series called *The OA* while being a mom."

"I love that for you. Don't wait up." The keys jingle as I wave them at her.

"Make good choices!"

I close the door behind me and breathe in the crisp autumn air. The mountains in front of me rise sharply against the pale sky. It's easy to forget just how big the Wasatch range really is when you're no longer living at the foot of it.

A dark blue 4Runner awaits me in the driveway. This can't be her car; it's probably Carl's. I climb in, panting, and wonder if ropes and hand chalk would be necessary to reach the driver's seat. This car is huge; how does she drive it with a baby?

"Okay, Farmington, let's see how fucked up you got." I put the car in reverse and back out of the driveway. The daylight makes the nostalgia even worse.

This place holds a mix of good memories and a whole lot of trauma. My first stop is Farmington High, my old school. It's so weird driving down these streets. It feels like I'm caught in some freak déjà vu but in reverse. Everything but the town square looks exactly the same as when I dipped out of here—same buildings, same stores, same damn people. It's like time decided to take a nap and forgot to wake up.

It's been ages since I left this place and hit the road to explore the other forty-nine states. As an OG local, it's mind-blowing to see how much technology and progress have turned the world upside down. The places I've traveled had fancy gadgets and mind-boggling gizmos, pushing boundaries I never even dreamed of. Rictor, always ahead of the game, fit right into this tech-savvy world. But stepping back into Farmington is like taking a trip back in time, to a slower, simpler era.

Don't get me wrong, there's something comforting about the familiar. But there's also something unsettling about the fact that nothing much has changed. It's like everyone is stuck in the same routine, day in and day out, with no room for growth or innovation. Just like Jhoana has been. But despite all of that, there's still a sense of home here, a sense of belonging that I can't quite explain.

I park the car at the curb of the high school entrance. Damn, they really revamped this place. It used to resemble a poorly funded prison, but now it looks more like a fancy university campus. The longer I stare, the more blocked memories reveal themselves to me. This was where I spent most of the formative years of my life.

But it isn't just the joyful memories of laughter and innocent friendships that flood my mind. It's also a painful reminder of how we were all treated—Dustin, Emierr, Rictor, and I. The way people acted towards us. The hateful words and accusatory stares come rushing back, reopening old wounds that never fully healed.

They laid the blame on us for Jhoana's coma, like it was all our fault. The police were convinced we'd been doing some kind of drug, despite having no evidence to back it up. And the town had gone right along with it, painting us as a gang of vicious drug addicts, peer-pressuring our sweet, innocent friend. As soon as the police's theory hit the news, we became pariahs. Adults and classmates alike hurled allegations at us like stones, maybe believing that with enough torment, we would break.

But we fought tooth and nail for ourselves and for Jhoana, sticking together through thick and thin, only to face more of the same persecution as we grew older. But as we pushed through and moved on, Jhoana stayed. Unmoving, unchanging, hanging onto life through a machine. Her time was always borrowed and now it's finally run out.

I inhale deeply, then release a long exhale, allowing the memories to settle within me. It's not just the burden of guilt and regret that weighs heavily on my shoulders. It's the fiery anger and deep bitterness I harbor towards Brunner Fischer, that piece of human filth who had the audacity to call himself Jhoana's best friend.

"Expel the killers! We don't want murderers in our school!" Brunner *chanted, his spiteful voice booming through a megaphone.*

I jumped off the school statue where I'd been reading and prowled towards him. A few other students held a big, white cloth spray-painted in red, "MURDERERS IN OUR SCHOOL".

"What's going on?" Rictor appeared beside me.

I turned to face him. He looked like shit. Is he eating? "Brunner's being Brunner."

"What murderers is he talking about?"

Is he serious?

"This school accepts killers; we need them to hear us. Which one of us is next until it's too late?" Brunner's bellow continued.

"There they are!" A student shouted and leveled a finger at us.

Brunner turned our direction and leered, "Murderers! You sentenced Jhoana, a poor innocent girl, to her death!"

"Get out of here!" Another student yelled and the crowd followed.

Rictor grabbed my hand and pulled me behind him as Brunner and his followers surrounded us.

"Go to hell!"

"Kill yourself!"

I shake away the memory. That bastard made our lives a living nightmare. I may have forgotten a lot about this place, but his face, his voice, they're ingrained into my mind. I can still hear his taunts and curses echoing in my head. My teeth clench, and my fists tighten.

There's absolutely no way in hell I'll ever forgive that scumbag. I open the car door and slide into the driver's seat, twisting the ignition and feeling the engine roar to life beneath me. I clench the steering wheel, my hands shaking with rage. The anger surges through me, choking me from the inside out. I rev the engine and zoom out of the road, tires screeching against the asphalt. My grip on the steering wheel tightens and my knuckles turn bone white. A searing heat crawls up my neck to my face.

I drive aimlessly through the town that turned its back on us, that turned its back on me. The weight of the past presses heavily on my chest, suffocating me, and the whispers that once accompanied pointed fingers now echo in my ears.

I remember now why I wanted to leave this place; it's all too painful.

My alarm blares, reminding me to take my birth control. How the hell did it get so late in the afternoon? And how long have I been driving? The gas gauge shows half, but it's better to be safe than sorry. I pull into a gas station to fill the enormous vehicle's proportionately massive tank. Getting through this week is all I have to do. Then I can disappear forever, maybe even change my name.

Being Jadis Salazar is too damn hard.

I place the pump back into its holder and close the fuel tank. Just as I was about to climb back into the car, the gas station caught my attention. It looked oddly familiar. The wheels in my brain spun until—*Oh. Right.* We'd been down this road a million times, riding the school bus. The middle school should be right around the corner. That was the last place we all had Jhoana as a classmate.

I remember Rictor's epic twelfth birthday, where we schemed and plotted to surprise Emierr, making up for missing his special day as we frantically searched for that iPod Nano. Every damn store in Farmington was sold out, but Rictor refused to give up, and thanks to Cadence's role as volunteer chauffeur, we finally scored one from a store outside town. And then there was the playground, our sacred hangout spot, where the five of us would gather at the merry-go-round during breaks and lunchtime. We were just a bunch of kids, but we knew deep down that we were different.

We were the only Filipino and Chamorro kids in our school, standing out like mismatched pieces in a puzzle of faces that weren't ours. When we were little, none of that crap mattered. But once we hit sixth grade, shit got real. Teenagers are mean and Mormons travel in packs.

But even so, I wouldn't trade what I had with them for anything.

Those moments might've been short-lived, but damn, it felt like we had hours of pure bliss. In our own little world, we didn't have to care about fitting in or seeking validation from anyone else. My smile widens as I think about how much I adored those dorky dudes and how deeply I cherished Jhoana. Our bond was unbreakable because we were all we freaking had. Through thick and thin, always having each other's backs no matter what. We were like a family away from home, and that was something damn special.

I make my way towards the school, temporarily captivated by the sky, ablaze with a stunning blend of orange and red hues. I wish I'd brought my sketchbook. I park the car by the sidewalk, not exactly at the school, but close enough.

This spot... My heart weighs heavy in my chest as I approach the park bench; the very same one where Jhoana and I used to plop our butts and swap playground gossip as kids. It's been ages since we last sat here, and yet, nothing seems to have changed. The trees still stand tall, the flowers still bloom, and that crusty old bench, well, it's still here. Waiting for us.

I sit down, feeling memories settle around me. I remember the conversation Jhoana and I had when we were both eleven years old. We had been talking about everything and nothing, laughing in the carefree way only children can do.

"Jho," I said. "*Ricky told me about what Dusty told him, that Dusty sees him as a brother. I feel the same way; you're like a sister to me.*"

Jho smiled, and her eyes crinkled at the corners. "Me too, Jads. You're like family to me."

At once, I'm filled to the brim with pride and relief. "I promise to always be there for you, no matter what. We're in this together, and I'll fight for you as long as I live."

Jho took my hand, her grip strong and firm. "And I promise the same. Sisters forever, no matter what life throws at us."

We'd sat there in a comfortable silence. It was a moment I didn't know I needed, but it meant the world to me. In that moment, our friendship became something even stronger—a bond of best friends and sisters that nothing could break.

But now, I sit here alone. Jhoana is going to die, and there's nothing I can do to stop it. All those promises we made seem hollow now.

I feel the tears trickle down my cheeks as I think about everything we had planned together, all the things we had hoped for. It's not fair that she has to leave this world so soon, not fair that we can't be there for each other like we had promised.

I close my eyes and try to remember Jhoana's smile, her laughter, and her warm embrace. I try to hold onto the good memories, the ones that remind me of why she was so special to me.

But it's hard when the pain feels so raw, so all-consuming. I cry for the loss of my best friend, for the memories we won't be able to create, for the dreams we won't be able to fulfill.

And I'll forever be sorry I walked away from here and didn't come back until it was too late. I get up, get inside the car, and drive away from the old, worn bench whose wood holds all the memories I never want to forget. *I don't know if I can do it, Jho. I don't know if I can say goodbye to you.*

I'm so tired of this place; all it ever does is break my heart.

My pocket buzzes. I pull out my phone and read the message: *"Grab these from the store in the square. Here's the list."* I groan.

I can't complain though; Cadence *is* letting me crash at her place. Thankfully, the roads are pretty empty today. Zipping to the grocery store without any trouble, I park the car and hop out. I'm determined to get in and out as quickly as possible. The last thing I need is to run into a familiar face.

I manage to toss all the items into a basket without incident, save for a jar of carbonara sauce. I scan an aisle for the jar and just as I spot it, my eyes land on a man standing right in front of it. My breath catches in my throat as the realization hits me like a ton of bricks. It's Gordo—Jhoana's little brother. *Holy shit, he's grown up!* I quickly duck behind a shelf of cereal boxes, stealing glances at him. His muscles are peeking through his shirt, and his face is all sharp and defined. And look at him rocking those glasses now, giving off major brainy vibes. How did such an extreme transformation happen? *Wow, he's hot as fuck.*

But there's a bittersweet feeling in seeing him. He was just a kid when Jhoana fell into her coma. I can't help but wonder what she would think of him now. Would she be proud of her little brother?

I can't do this. Not now, not when his sister is about to die. I don't even know how to act around him or what to say.

"Noble Jadis," a voice calls out behind me, and I spin around, seeing no one.

"Hello?"

"Over here," the voice comes again, and I spot someone in my peripheral vision, dressed in white, moving through one of the aisles. It's a woman in a white blouse, her long hair nearly touching the ground. My jaw clenches. Another damn missionary.

"Hey. Excuse me, did you call for me?" I ask. *Why am I even bothering with this? And did she call me "noble"?*

She doesn't respond but turns to glance back at me. Her brown eyes have a weird, coppery ring around the pupil. I'm pretty sure that's indicative of some disease. *What was it? Watson's Disease? Whatever.*

"Okay, I'm not playing this game," I mutter under my breath. I move to walk away from her, but stop abruptly. *I'm... by the meat cooler? How did I get here?* I look around and realize the woman is gone. I shake my head, trying to pull myself together.

"Over here," the woman's voice echoes from inside the freezer unit. I can see her smiling at me between the shelves. A prickle of rage nettles my skin. *I am so not in the mood to be fucked with.* I rip the door open and cool air chills my skin as I step into the meat-filled room. I shouldn't be here, but this Book of Mormon–thumping tampon tunnel is about to learn the hard way that people don't generally appreciate being preached to in the grocery store.

I stop. She's standing with her back to me in the middle of a dead end, chunks of meat littering the floor around her. *What the fuck.*

"Hey, you!" I shout, receiving no response. Slowly, I approach the unmoving figure and reach out to touch her shoulder. She whips around, long hair slashing across my face.

"Save us," she breathes, a tear rolling down her cheek.

"What the hell are you—"

Suddenly, a loud crack shatters the silence looming behind me. I whirl around but never get the chance to identify the source. The woman's arms wrap around me, long dark hair falling over her face. Sister Banshee's arms crush mine to my sides, as unyielding as a bear trap. I yelp, trying desperately to throw her off me. Her wiry arms are alarmingly strong, and I can't seem to break her grip.

"You. Jadis Salazar." Her frigid lips brush my ear in a grotesquely intimate whisper. *How the hell does she know my name?*

"You know the way back. You, who travel between worlds. *Save us.*" The final two words come out a strangled hiss as the back of my head slams into her throat. She staggers back and I hit the concrete floor.

"Ma'am!" A man's voice snaps my gaze to the entrance. "Are you alright?" A perplexed worker is staring between me and the evidently drug-addled woman flinging meat around his freezer. "You're not supposed to be here," he says, offering a hand to help me up. His eyes stay fixed on the woman behind me.

The man escorts us out into the aisle at the back of the store. As he turns back into the fridge, the stringy woman flashes a wild-eyed grin at me.

"Remember us, Noble Jadis. We remember you."

I'm left with my mouth hanging open as she disappears behind a shelf. I've barely regained my composure when—

"*Ate* Jadis?"

Dammit. I turn around and see Gordo looking at me with surprise. "Gordo, hey!" I reply awkwardly, trying to sound pleased and not like I've just been assaulted by Joseph Smith's worst employee.

"Oh my god, I can't believe it's you!" Gordo sets his shopping basket down and gives me a tight hug. "It's been way too long. How have you been?"

I smile weakly. "I've been alright, just taking things one day at a time, you know?"

"Yeah, I totally get it." He nods. "Hey, do you have some time? Let's grab some hot cocoa together."

I hesitate for a moment, not really wanting to go, but also not wanting to disappoint him. I can still feel the woman's desperate hands raking at my skin. "I should probably head home, Gordo."

"Come on, *ate*." He nudges me playfully. "Let's go have some hot cocoa at that new café down the street. It's been years since I've seen any of the Squad."

The Squad... I vaguely remember that term. Maybe talking to Gordo will help me remember more. Or at least, it might distract me from whatever psychotic break I'm experiencing. "Alright, why not? But you don't have to call me *ate*."

We arrive at the café and settle at one of the outdoor tables. He goes inside to order our hot cocoa and returns a few minutes later carrying two steaming cups.

"Be careful. The cup almost burned the fingerprints off my left hand," he warns, placing a cup in front of me.

"Thanks." I blow into it and take a cautious sip. It's creamy and soothing. It feels strange, sitting here sipping hot cocoa with him, like everything's okay.

Gordo hasn't met my gaze. "Where do we even begin?"

I smile and shrug, equally unsure of what to say.

"What are you up to these days?" he asks, clearly choosing the safest route.

"I'm a freelance artist, trying my best to secure a gallery showcase."

"That's amazing, Jadis. I know a guy in New York looking for talented up-and-coming artists. If you're interested, I could link you guys up."

"Gordo, you really don't have to do that."

"Come on, you're my sister's best friend. I'd do anything to support you."

"Thank you." I've always been bad at receiving acts of kindness. And gifts. And compliments. "What about you?"

"I'm in the military, but I came back home for... You know." He can't seem to bring himself to say it. There's a brief moment of silence as I try to find the right words, but they escape me.

"So, what time are you heading to my house?" Gordo asks.

I suddenly feel like a rat backed into a corner. "I... I don't think I'll be able to make it tonight." Shame rolls through me at the dejected look on his face. "I'm sorry."

"You have to be there," he says softly. "It's been so long since you've seen my sister. Just say hi, and then you can go home. I think if she feels one of you there, it might make a difference."

"Gordo... I don't think that's—"

"I know, I know. It's wishful thinking. But it would be good for her, and for you too."

"I don't know, Gordo. I'm just not ready." The admission hangs suspended between us for a few breaths.

"No one is, Jadis," Gordo says finally. "I just got here about an hour ago and I haven't even been home yet. I don't want to see her like that again." Gordo may be a grown man now, but in this moment, he's eight years old again. Those wide brown eyes framed with thick lashes, looking at me like I have the answers.

Fuck... I forgot how soft I used to be. Back when I lived in New York, I didn't bat an eye for anyone, not even those who needed me. Hell, *especially* those who needed me. Then there was my time in California... with *him*. But being back home again, seeing all these familiar faces, I'm starting to remember what caring means. And how much I fucking hate it. I run my hands across my face. "Do you want to go together?"

He looks up, warm surprise spilling over his boyish face. "Can we?"

I sigh and take another sip of my hot cocoa, "Yeah, I just have to drop the groceries off at Cadence's, then I can meet you there."

"Sounds good. I'll swing by my parents' house first." As we get to our feet, Gordo pulls me into a tight hug. "Thank you, Jadis," he says sincerely.

I pat his back uncomfortably. With rising anxiety, I rush back to my sister's place, leaving the groceries on the dining table. Cadence sent a text earlier, apologetically explaining that our parents had taken them on a surprise trip to the zoo. I'm miffed that my sister won't be attending but at least that means my parents will be absent too.

I swap out Cadence's car for my own. As I approach Jhoana's house, I realize I forgot to message the boys. Cadence was right; Auntie Ina knows how to gather a crowd. I manage to find a parking spot dangerously close to a stop sign and quickly send a message to Gordo before stepping out of the car.

As I start typing a message to Emierr, his message pops up:

Meer N.

We're here, in front of their house. We're going in.

I look up and see the trio standing before Jhoana's home. Relief washes over me. There they are, my favorite group of absolute idiots, standing together outside the tomb of our dearest friend.

Home

September 31

"**G**uys, I don't know if I can do this," I say, pacing back and forth.

"Ricky, stand still. You're giving me anxiety." Dustin cracks his knuckles. It's a nervous habit his mother always swore would give him early onset arthritis.

"Come on, guys, you both agreed. Don't back out now." Emierr glances back at us over his shoulder.

"Then you go in first." I chew a nail, feeling apprehension coursing through my bloodstream.

"Hell no."

"Where's Jads? Did you message her?" Dustin is doing nervous stretches as if he's about to run onto the field. He's lucky I'm too freaked to mock him.

"I'm right here," a voice says.

Jadis's presence sends a jolt through my senses. I open my mouth, but the words die in my throat. She isn't looking at me. Ouch. Is that really Jadis? She looks so different. My instinct is to throw my arms around her and apologize for everything, but I restrain myself, unsure of how she'll react. This isn't the appropriate time or place to catch up on a decade of lost time.

Focus.

"Hey..." Dustin smiles at her. "Wassup, rockstar."

"Hi... Guys. Do we have a game plan?" Her voice is the same cool, collected tone it always was.

"We get it over with and uh... Let the whole town know we're back all at once?" Dustin offers.

"Whose bright idea is that?" Her brows knit together.

"Who else?" I narrow my eyes at Emierr.

Jadis's eyes finally lock onto mine but she doesn't speak.

Just say it.
She manages a small smile before turning back to Emierr.
Fuck.

"Hey, it's now or never," Emierr says defensively. "Forget what anyone thinks. We're here for Jho."

"He's right." The words cause a twinge of pain. "This is fucking crazy, it's been ten years, but here we are. Jho brought us back home."

"I feel it, too. Like a tingle," Dustin adds. "I feel like I can take on the world with you guys right now."

"Jads?" I say hesitantly. We all turn to her in apprehension.

"Yeah... I feel the same." The tension that lifts from the group is tangible. "But at least I know my parents aren't in there." She folds her arms tightly across her body. I realize my crossed arms are a mirror of Jadis's. Even after so long, we're using the same body language.

"If we're all being honest, same." Emierr agrees.

"That's the spirit. Okay, let's get in there." I clench my jaw, hoping against all odds that this will go smoothly. As if communicating via telepathy, we stand back and allow Emierr to march toward the door alone.

His hand is on the doorknob before he realizes. "Uh, guys?"

"What, I'm not going first." I shrug, the others nodding emphatically at my sides.

"Really?" Emierr groans. "You gave a speech; you have to go first."

"Meer, Jho's your cousin. We're right behind you," I reassure him. "Well. A few yards behind you."

He takes a deep breath in and exhales. "Shit." He takes a golden flask out of his back pocket and takes a sip. "Anyone else?"

"Me." Jadis charges up the walkway and grabs the flask without hesitation and takes a swig.

"I knew you were drunk when you came to get me." I snorted. "I'll have some." I take a shot. The alcohol burns a flaming path down my throat. I jerk my head from side to side. "What the fuck is that?"

"First-class tequila," Emierr says proudly. How did he fill it up on the plane without me seeing him? "Dust?"

"Absolutely not."

"Okay, that worked." I close my eyes as the alcohol sears down my throat and coils heat into my mostly-empty stomach.

"Bro, you're pink already," Dustin teases me.

"Shut up. People who have red cheeks from consuming alcohol are allergic to it," I retort. An excuse I've repeated so many times it springs to my mouth without thought.

"That is not true." Emierr laughs.

"Google it, bro." I place my hands on my warm face.

"You guys are so dumb." Jadis snorts.

Wow. I haven't heard that in a while.

We all exchange looks, and laughter erupts, shattering the tension in the air.

"Okay, Meer, I'm right behind you. No turning back now," I say after I've managed to contain myself.

Emierr sighs deeply. "If we can fight monsters, we can do this."

I turn to Dustin and Jadis, my eyebrows furrowing in confusion. I mouth the word "What?" to them.

They exchange shrugs, just as puzzled as I am. As we walk into Jhoana's house, the abrupt silence presses against my chest, matching the weight of the situation. The room is filled with a sea of familiar faces—old classmates, teachers, neighbors, and even the mayor is present. All eyes turn our way; their gazes are a mix of curiosity, damnation, and something I can't quite decipher. After two sweeps of the room, I can see that Ma isn't here.

I glance at the others, noticing their gazes sweeping across the room, searching apprehensively for their parents. My gaze pauses on Jadis. She has always struggled with handling emotions like this. She never admits it, but it sends her into a quiet spiral. She grips my shirt, her fear transferring to me. Instinctively, I do the same to Emierr.

It felt like we were intruding on a secret gathering. I try my best to maintain composure, but the scowls and whispers make me viscerally uncomfortable. We quietly make our way towards the living room. As we navigate through the maze of mourners, my eyes scan the faces, searching for a familiar one to anchor myself. And then we see him—Uncle Kit, sitting on a worn-out armchair in the corner.

His letters are what got us here. *He* wants us here. His presence brings a glimmer of comfort.

"Hello, Uncle Kit." Emierr says.

"Emierr?" Uncle Kit slowly rises to his feet, as if he can't believe what he's seeing. "How are—" Then he catches sight of me. "James?" Those eyes are still kind, even under the circumstances.

"Hi, Uncle, it's Rictor." I don't know whether to hug him, shake his hand, or stand at a safe distance.

"You look just like your father," he breathes out. " Dustin and Jadis too?" Uncle Kit steps back, his hand trembling as it covers his mouth, tears welling up in his eyes.

I frown slightly. He seems disproportionately shocked. Did he expect us all to ignore the letters?

Jadis and Dustin shuffle uncomfortably, trying to arrange their features into smiles.

"How are you kids here right now?" Uncle Kit spreads his arms as wide as he can and makes an effort to capture all four of us in a hug. "You're all so grown up." I can feel him trembling. "Jhoanalyn is going to be so happy."

I chuckle. "You asked us to come and here we are." Uncle Kit drops his arms and moves away, brows furrowing.

"What are you talking about?"

We all pause, looking at each other in bewilderment.

"The letters you sent, Uncle Kit," Dustin says with a hint of concern. Have we been gone so long that his memory is going?

"You wrote us to come here." Emierr pulls his letter from his pocket, offering it as evidence. I fish mine out as Dustin adds his own to Uncle Kit's outstretched hand. He stares at them blankly, silence falling over the handful of people listening in.

"Did you write these letters, Uncle?" Dustin finally asks.

Before he can answer, a familiar and unmistakable voice resonates from behind us.

"No, I did."

My heart plummets to my stomach. Auntie Ina emerges from the kitchen, her high heels striking the wooden floor. A glass of rich red wine rests in her hand.

"Hi, Auntie Ina." Emierr's voice is unsteady.

"I wrote the letters," she continues, refusing to acknowledge that Emierr had spoken.

"You did what?" Uncle Kit's voice rises in shock and anger.

All eyes in the room now fix on us.

Instinctively, the four of us draw closer to one another.

Auntie Ina scoffs at Uncle Kit. "I needed to see it for myself." She scans us one by one, a sinister smile spreading across her face. "Look at the four of you. All grown up." Her voice is ice, grating against our resolve. None of us dare look at her.

We never should have come home.

"I want them to see." Her claw like nails lift my chin and force me to look at her. Her gaze pierces into mine. Rage dances like hellfire behind her eyes. Yet the worry lines creasing her forehead and the dark smudges below her eyes tell another version of her story. One of loss, sorrow, and helplessness. I twist my chin out of her hand and drop my gaze to the scuffed wooden floor.

"Ina, enough!"

"Why?" She whips around to snarl at her husband. "They need to see what they did to our baby!"

Jadis is the first to break. She bolts for the door, throwing shoulders at anyone unfortunate enough to be in her way.

"Jadis! Don't go!" A familiar man shouts as she flies past where he stood on the front porch.

Gordo, he's all grown up.

"Don't you dare go after her," Auntie commands Gordo.

Dustin shakes his head and departs, followed by a rattled and crestfallen Emierr. The harsh reality settles into my bones—it was all too good to be true. How dare we hope and think things would be different after all these years?

"I'm sorry," I rasp, my throat tight.

"You should be," Auntie Ina snaps. "You're the one that killed her."

A wave of cold washes through my body. My hands are starting to shake, and my stomach is filled with lead. I want to defend myself. But I can't. Some part of me knows she's right.

I take a few steps back then race for the door.

They don't want us here. The thought sends a bitter taste spearing through my mouth. We're the ones "responsible for condemning a sweet, innocent little girl to an eternal rest." That's what we've been told all our lives. Their vilifying glares drag me back to those excruciating days after the incident, when we went back to school carrying the weight of our guilt.

The conclusion that we'd been taking badly cut drugs was the pervading theory. Cocaine, heroine, LSD—the drug changed depending on who was telling the story. Never mind the fact that all five of us had tested negative for drugs of any kind. There was no other logical explanation, so the story stuck. Everyone who knew Jhoana had considered her a sweet, naive girl who must have been corrupted by her miscreant friends.

In those moments, I felt utterly small and insignificant, like a mere speck in the vastness of the universe. Just when I thought I had let go, it all comes rushing back. As I step outside, greeted by the chill in the air, I feel uneasy. The sky matches my convoluted mood, painted with hues of deep purples and fiery reds. The others are nowhere to be seen.

I rub my hands together, trying to ward off the cold that serves as a constant reminder that I'm on my own and always have been. I guess that was our reunion. Jadis and I didn't have a chance to catch up either.

I pause, trying to think of my next step. I could just pack up and head back to New York.

At least I tried, Jho. I feel a pang of guilt, like I'm running away. I have to do something to honor her memory before I renounce this place for good. With a deep breath, I gather my courage and walk towards the side of Jhoana's house, the silent ghost of my past trailing behind. Just before setting foot in the backyard, I freeze in my tracks then hastily press myself against the side of the house. Jadis stands in the center of the lawn, arms wrapped around her shoulders, and facing the fence that separates Jhoana's house from Brunner's.

"Jads, you, okay?" Dustin steps into view.

"I can't believe Auntie Ina did that." She dashes tears away with the back of her hand.

I shouldn't be eavesdropping. I start to shuffle away.

"Yeah... It's fucked up. Did you see everyone's faces? They still think we did it," Dustin says, his voice laced with resentment.

I halt in my tracks. *Why does everyone think we put Jho in a coma?* When I really stop to think about it, it doesn't make sense, even if they did think we were on drugs. The tests had proven that theory false and yet people persisted in blaming us. We were a bunch of kids, sleeping on a basement floor.

At a slow, measured pace, I slide backward until the cool surface of the wall meets my back once again. I hate eavesdropping, but maybe they remember something I can't.

"Of course, they would. Everyone in this fucking town acts like Jho is already—" Jadis cuts off by a hitch in her breath.

"It's not fair. How do we defend ourselves? Weren't we all sleeping too?"

"I don't know... I don't remember anything from this place," Jadis admits in a whisper. I lean forward subconsciously, straining to hear.

"You too huh?" Dustin sighs. "Ah shit, did I say hi to you already?"

"Yeah, you did." She gives him a watery chuckle.

"What have you been doing the last ten years?"

It seems that I won't be getting the answers I'd hoped for today.

"I got into NYU after high school."

"What! No way! Did you become a dancer? I remember you doing a lot of interpretative dancing when we were kids," Dustin teases.

I can't help but admire him. Despite my reluctance, I'm hanging on every word, listening to Dustin masterfully pull Jadis out from her pain-wrought shell. Even in our childhood, he was our silver-tongued diplomat, always knowing just what to say to keep us out of hot water. If I were the one talking to Jadis, I'd level with her emotions and we'd both just feel like shit, but at least we'd feel like shit together. Slowly, I turn towards them, stealing a cautious glance.

"No," Jadis laughs. "I can't believe you remember that. It's for art; I draw. Well, I used to. I work at Walmart now. School didn't really work out and—" She pauses. My heart aches for Jadis. I wish she had come to me like she used to whenever she needed a shoulder to cry on.

Jadis shifts the topic off herself. "How's being an NFL superstar?"

"It's fun. I might even make it to the Super Bowl. You should watch with the guys sometimes. If they ever come again."

"I'm proud of you, Dusty. And that would be nice."

"I'm also married and have two baby girls." Any negative emotion Dustin was harboring evaporates from his voice.

I smile. Dustin's a wonderful father. I hope that Jadis will have the chance to meet his family too.

"Really, Dusty is a Daddy?" Jadis smiles and shakes her head in awe.

"You're gonna love them. Oh, maybe we can have a big barbecue at my house, the Squad, and our parents. Nothing is more family than a barbecue."

My smile fades and I fall back against the wall. It feels wrong to hear my friends planning a grand reunion when one of us is... gone.

"That sounds fun. But it has to be the 'Guam' barbecue our parents used to throw." Jadis falls quiet for a moment. "Thank you for checking up on me, Dusty."

"Always. We gotta be here for each other, Jads. It's still us four versus everyone."

"Yeah. We should look for Meer and Ricky, then."

Dustin murmurs an agreement and I hear grass-softened footfalls dissipate into the evening air. I realize I've been holding my breath.

This journey has run its course; it's time to go back to my real life, where people respect me and my work. Where I had a friend in Bonnie, who came without dragging painful memories behind her. I glance back at Jhoana's house with its hunter green siding and outdated, pale brick veneer. This house was our headquarters and held many of my memories of the Squad. Now, it harbors most of the pain in our neighborhood, the reminder of the impending end of Jhoana's life. I could almost see her youthful face smiling from the upstairs window, but that smile exists only in memory now.

Across the street, one house down, sits Emierr's childhood home. Bold blue shingles clung to the gambrel roof, standing out against the fading clapboard siding. Echoes of our laughter still seemed to resonate within those walls. A memory is triggered of me and Emierr lying on the floor of his room. We spent endless hours planning imaginary expeditions, just like any other kids our age. At that time, it was harmless, creative fun but these days, his plans seem based in that same imagined reality.

I stop walking and look to my left. Dustin's old house stands solemn with its peeling white paint and rusty red bricks. Grief is what we both shared; losing one parent that young scarred both of us, but it was in this house where I truly got to know him, where he became my brother. *I wonder who lives here now.* I continue walking.

Jadis lived in the house on the right end of the road, its cracked driveway leading to a pale yellow structure adorned with the secret language of our childhood. Every windowpane, every crevice held a memory of the times when life was simpler.

Standing at the left edge of the cul-de-sac, my gaze lands on my home, a maroon fortress drenched in the wine of countless sunsets. I remember wanting it red, fiery, and bright, but Pa painted it maroon, saying it was a softer touch, more dignified.

After all these years, its maroon walls no longer symbolize that soft touch but rather the melancholy that suffocated me and Ma.

In the driveway, Pa's car, an old but cared-for sedan, stands as a silent memorandum to a life cut short. As if clinging to the past, Ma never moved it—instead, she parked her vehicle by the roadside. A sentinel keeping vigil. That's still the case, I guess.

As I scan the second-floor window of my room, another memory sweeps over me.

Jhoana stood where I stand now, her eyes reflecting the pain in mine. I think she felt the agonizing weight in my heart that day, because she became the solace I needed after losing Pa. We spoke in hushed voices in my room, where her empathy blanketed me in a comforting cocoon. I knew then just how deeply she cared for me.

Vaguely, I recall offering her something, maybe a symbol of our bond, yet the memory eludes me like so many others in this place. Even though I don't remember it fully, the exchange stirs a renewed wave of anguish. This house, meant to hold the imprints of a joyful childhood, now bears the remnants of silent suffering.

Why did I walk this way? My eyes find the empty spot where Ma's car usually sits. Nothing. My gaze shifts to the seemingly vacant neighboring houses.

Where the hell is everyone?

Their absence at the wake was weird to me. Ma not showing up today is unlike her.

Questions whirl around in my mind, churning up more unease, more loneliness. I shake off the pointless thoughts and reach for my phone to grab a Lyft—twelve missed calls from Dustin. Great. I ignore the notification and open the app, entering the airport as my destination. Someone accepts it. Now, I wait for them to get me the hell out of here. Bonnie. I dial her number next, hoping her voice can offer some semblance of normalcy.

It rings. "Come on, answer, girl," I mumble. It rings three more times until she finally picks up.

"Rick?"

"Bonnie, thank god, I'm happy you answered." My voice trembles.

"Oh shit… What happened? It's good to hear your voice."

I close my eyes, pressing the phone against my head.

"Rick?"

"God, Bonnie. I—I think it was a mistake coming here."

"What's going on?"

"It was all a lie. The letter wasn't even from Uncle Kit."

"Wait, what? What do you mean?"

"My Auntie Ina wrote them," I say, my voice low.

"Maybe she realized how badly she treated you guys before. You probably wouldn't have given her the time of day. So, she used Uncle Kit's name."

I know she's trying to be helpful. To see the silver lining. "I wish that were the case, Bon. But she explicitly said she wanted us to see what we did to her baby…"

"That fucking bitch!" Bonnie erupts, her rage radiating from the speaker. I instinctively pull away from the phone, but a smile creeps onto my face. "How twisted is she to do that just days before her daughter's death? Are you guys, okay?" The righteous indignation and fierce compassion in her voice fills me with warmth.

"I am now," I reply, the smile lingering on my lips.

"Holy shit, I'm so heated!" I can practically feel her pacing back and forth as she speaks.

"How's everything over there?" I ask, trying to gently pull her back from the edge.

"Rick…" she groans. "If I had known I'd be seeing Oscar in our department this often, I would have started dressing better."

"He's been there?"

"Yeah, like five times a day. Sometimes he stays for hours."

"Wow, that sounds promising." *I hope.*

"I don't know what you said to him, but it worked. He's even ramping up console production."

"What? Already? It's only been two days."

"Last I heard, he's getting an additional five hundred made on top of the three hundred you already have."

"I… I don't know how to feel." And it's true. The jumble of the day's emotions muddles together, creating a hellish soup of excitement, pride, sorrow, and loss.

"Forget about work. I'll take care of things here," Bonnie says dismissively.

"No, I'm coming home, Bon."

"You are?" She sounds equal parts relieved and disapproving.

"Yeah, I don't think I can handle this."

"Hey... When I said I'm with you no matter what, I meant it."

The sound of tires crunching over gravel grabs my attention. "I think my Lyft is here."

"Okay, keep me updated. I can pick you up from the airport."

"Thanks, Bonnie."

"See you soon."

I hang up, shoving the phone in my pocket. I suddenly remember that I came here with luggage and swear under my breath. The car halts abruptly, its position skewed, taking up the center of the road. The glare of headlights floods my vision. I squint, momentarily blinded.

"Hello?" I raise my left hand, blocking the light.

The silhouette approaches me. "Rictor James?"

My heart nearly stops. I've imagined this moment for the last decade, but now that it's here, I feel I might shatter.

"Mama," I whisper. Her face appears within view and her eyes well up with tears. The familiar gray of her irises seems to swallow me. Just around her pupils was a faint starburst of coppery gold; central heterochromia. A trait I'd frequently scolded her for not passing on to me.

She strides towards me, age and worry etched into her face, and the white streak in her hair more prominent than before. Yet, somehow, she still looks youthful. Glowing, even.

As I lay my eyes on my mother after ten years apart, I'm hit with yet another whirlwind of emotions. This affectionate, emotional woman standing before me is the mom I desperately needed when I lost Pa. It's a stark contrast to the absent, cold, and neglectful mother she once was. I don't know how to feel exactly, but deep down, I can't deny the overwhelming sense of longing I've had for her all these years. Despite everything, I've missed her terribly, and I can't lie to myself about that.

Her hands come up to cradle my face, her forehead meeting mine, and it takes every ounce of my strength not to break down.

"Oh, Rictor James," she breathes, her voice a soothing balm to a decade's worth of yearning. "I wish I knew you were coming home... I would've made your favorite food."

Before I can respond, the passenger door opens and out steps Uncle Joshua, Dustin's dad.

"Well, if it isn't the prodigal son," he says, aiming for jovial but striking sappiness instead. He crosses the short distance to pull me into a warm, fatherly hug. It's a comfort I didn't know I needed. Another car pulls into the driveway, and I freeze. Dustin. *Oh, bitch.*

Uncle Joshua is the first to move, crossing the driveway to yank Dustin into a fierce hug. Dustin's lips press into a thin line. He hadn't been looking forward to this moment.

Ma follows, her face glowing with joy and disbelief. Her boys are home, and everything else, at least for this moment, can wait.

I pull my phone out to cancel the Lyft and message Bonnie.

> I guess I'm staying; update you soon.

"Ricky, where did you go? I was trying to reach you," Dustin says over his father's shoulder.

"Um... Well..." I don't want to admit that I tried to make a run for it.

"You saw each other already?" Uncle Joshua pulls back and looks between the two of us.

"We actually came together," I confess. Dustin rolls his eyes. He'd told me that Uncle ditched him right after his high school graduation and never looked back. I guess Uncle Joshua was great at taking care of everyone except his own son.

"I'm glad you two are still in touch," Ma says, a smile on her face.

"Wait a minute." I narrow my eyes at Ma and Uncle Joshua. "Where were you guys? Why weren't you at the wake?" I can't keep a note of accusation out of my voice.

Ma and Uncle Joshua exchange a long look.

"Your Auntie Ina asked us not to come today," Ma finally answers. Her cool, gray eyes flash a hint of guilt.

"Just you two?" I ask, a sense of unease taking root in my stomach.

"No... All of us," Uncle Joshua admits.

Silence hangs heavily in the air. Something doesn't seem right. *This is so fishy.*

"*Anak*, let's get you settled in. I make sure to clean your room every week," Ma says, linking her arm through mine. It's clear they're done discussing whatever happened between them and Auntie Ina but I'm still burning with anxious curiosity.

A car trunk slams, and I turn to see Dustin hauling my suitcase toward me.

"Thanks, Dusty," I say, relieved.

"Check your phone," he whispers. "I'll see you around," he adds to our parents, waving at Ma. "Pop, where you staying?"

Uncle Joshua lets out a sigh. "Your Auntie offered to let me stay at her house."

Tension swarms through the air.

Are they...?

"Dad, I have a hotel. You can stay with me." Dustin may never fully forgive his father, but he can't help playing the filial son.

I glance at Ma, noticing her deliberate avoidance of eye contact with Uncle Joshua.

Dustin's brows knit together, sensing something amiss. Locking eyes with me, he mouths, "What the hell?" and I nod in agreement.

Uncle Joshua looks at Ma, but she continues to avoid his gaze. Finally, he acquiesces. "Okay, son. Luna, thanks for the offer."

"Always, Joshua." Ma's eyes dart up to Uncle Joshua's face. She looks guilty as sin.

"I'll see you around, Uncle," I say slowly.

"It's so good to see you, Ja— I mean, Ricky." Uncle Joshua looks unnerved for a moment before moving toward Dustin's rental car.

"Bye, Auntie. I'll be back for that spaghetti." Dustin waves, sliding into the driver's seat.

She shoots him a big smile. "My spaghetti and I will be waiting."

Once Dustin and his dad drive off, I stand on the street with my luggage, waiting. Ma parks her car by the curb, then together, we walk toward the house.

It's surreal, standing back in front of this doorway again. As I step through the threshold of my childhood home, a flood of memories washes over me, both comforting and bittersweet. I close the door behind me, kicking off my shoes and setting them on the little shelf to my left. It's been a decade since I last set foot in this house, and yet the essence of the place remains unchanged. The air carries the scent of home—a blend of incense, garlic, and the faint aroma of simmering *adobo* that lingers in every *Pinoy* household.

The walls, once vibrant and filled with family photographs, now show signs of age, their paint chipped and faded. The hardwood floors creak beneath my every step, a familiar melody that once signaled Pa's return. I cast my gaze at the tiny living room, with its worn-out coffee table and a threadbare rug. A tapestry of my Filipino heritage.

A haunting echo dances in the air as Ma takes over the kitchen. I close my eyes, and there it is—the sound of laughter. I remember that day, my birthday, when we all sat around this very coffee table, clutching frosty cans of root beer. I take a moment to soak in the memories, embracing the mixture of familiarity and melancholy that swirls around me.

"Ma, I'm going up to my room," I call out, my voice echoing through the house.

From the kitchen, her voice floats back to me, carrying the warmth and love that only a mother's voice can possess. "Alright, *anak*. I'll come get you when dinner's ready."

I make my way up the stairs, the weight of my luggage tugging at my tired arms. As I reach the landing of the second floor, my gaze drifts toward the narrow hallway leading to my parent's room. Or... I suppose it's just Ma's room now. I pay silent tribute to my Pa, to the man who filled this house with warmth and wisdom alongside Ma's unwavering love.

When I reach my room, at the other end of the small hallway, I turn the doorknob and allow the door to swing open with a soft squeak. Nostalgia envelopes me, mingling with the faint aroma of dust.

I take in the sight of my childhood haven. The bed is made up with the solar system sheets I picked out in second grade. And there, nestled amongst the pillows, is my old companion, Carter—the space teddy bear that Pa bought at the NASA gift shop. Or was it Dustin? My memory is still faulty. I reach out, my fingertips brushing against the worn fur. He is a true child's teddy bear with years of stains and smells only familiar to me.

With a quiet sigh, I place my suitcase to the side. I hold Carter to my chest, seeking the protection Pa assured me the bear could offer, before setting him back down.

Surveying the room, I let my eyes dance across the walls plastered with posters of rocket ships and space. A bookshelf and desk stand proudly beside them, bearing witness to my thirst for knowledge. They house my old desktop computer and a collection of books on quantum physics and black holes.

I sink into my bed, cradling Carter in my arms. The day's exhaustion starts to pull at my eyes as I grab my phone out of my pocket and start scrolling through the dozens of messages I'd ignored. Most of the notifications belong to a new group chat, created by Dustin.

Dusticle

Dat was a lot.

Meerina

My bad, I should've brought more airplane tequila.

Jadikins

I feel like I can still hear her yelling.

Dusticle

Meer, y'd u bring us back home?

Meerina

I told you, we talk in person.

Jadikins

I never agreed?

Meerina

Well, you have to now, we're all in this together remember?

Jadikins

F U

Dusticle

No more ghosting each other. 2mrrw, we meet @ da old Twig Bistro resto-bar 4 dindin.

Jadikins

Eww, why do you text like that? Can we go to a new place?

Dusticle

@Jadikins becuz I want 2

Meerina

There's a new joint nearby, they have these huge ass burgers.

Dusticle

@Dicktor, I see u lurking. Speak @sshole.

Lolololololol

Sup bitchessssss

Me down 4 da bistro. Dey also have bar.

Jadikins

Ugh, not you too.

Meerina

@Dicktor <333

Dusticle

@Dicktor dats y ur my fav. Ok, Twigs it is. Settle in evry1. Catch up wid ur fams. See u all soon. I miss u guys.

Meerina

Miss you guys too.

Jadikins

Me too.

Same. Goodnight bitches.

It's only moments after putting my phone down that I succumb to sleep.

"Ricky... Ricky, I'm scared!"

My eyes flash open. Jhoana's voice lingers in my ears. As the sunlight seeps through the cracks in the blinds, I hear the distant sound of a rooster crowing. I reach for my phone, only to find it dead. I'd fallen asleep before plugging it in. Swearing under my breath, I leave it to charge and venture out in search of breakfast. Ma sits at the kitchen table, her coffee untouched and a physical phone in hand. I smile. Maybe that's where I got my resistance to change, although it's possible that Ma just isn't tech-savvy. Either way, it's a comforting thought.

"Morning." I stand in the entryway to the kitchen, waiting to be acknowledged. I don't know the protocol for adult children returning to their parents' house.

"Good morning, *anak*," Ma replies, walking over to me and leaning in to kiss my forehead. "You must be starving; you didn't eat last night."

I take a seat at the table. "Just a little," I concede, my stomach grumbling in agreement.

She chuckles. "Just like your Papa." My gut clenches. "Is it okay if I heat up the food from last night? I don't want it to go to waste."

"Oh, shoot. You cooked for me, Ma, I forgot. I fell asleep." I wince. How have I already blown this reunion?

"I know. You must have had a long day," she reassures, retrieving a serving plate from the closet and placing it on the table. "How was the flight?"

"It was long, but it was business class," I reply, rubbing my eyes. I never imagined I'd be having a conversation with Ma in my childhood home again. It still feels surreal to see how much she has changed. "Oh, and Ma, did you know Dusty's married and has two kids?"

She nods, but her smile bears a hint of sadness. "Have you met them yet?"

"Yeah, he named his oldest one Celeste and their new baby is Ana."

"If Dustin takes after your uncle at all, then I'm sure he's a wonderful father," she says. I frown at that. *Does she really not know that Uncle Joshua went into an alcoholic tailspin?* Ma sets plates and utensils on the table, their clinks harmonizing with the oven's beep. A steaming Tupperware of Filipino lumpia is dumped onto the serving plate in front of me. The aroma makes my mouth water and my stomach grumble in anticipation. Ma sets her beat-up, trusty rice cooker on the table alongside the sweet chili sauce I love. The thing I miss most about Farmington is Ma's cooking.

I scoop some rice onto my plate, carefully selecting a few lumpia and generously drizzling the sauce on top. With the first bite, I'm transported back to my childhood, watching Ma work her culinary magic.

As my weariness slowly dissipates, I look up to Ma and catch her smile, shaded with a touch of sorrow in her eyes. "What?" I ask, my mouth still full.

Ma shakes her head gently, her voice barely a murmur. "Nothing. You just look so much like your Papa." Tears well in her eyes, threatening to spill over.

"You think so, Ma?"

She nods, wiping away her tears. "I wish he could see how much you've grown."

A rush of guilt cascades over me. I had denied her the chance to watch me grow into the man I am today. Pa never had a choice but Ma... That was my fault.

"Ma, I'm so sorry," I say in a small voice. "I'm sorry I left without saying goodbye."

She reaches out, grabbing my hand tightly.

"Oh..." Her tears stream down her cheeks. "No, *anak*, I'm sorry. You needed me. Your Papa was your best friend. I will always be sorry that I left you all alone."

"That doesn't change the fact that I left *you* alone, Ma." Hot tears roll down my face, my regrets threatening to crush my chest. "I held onto my anger for so long. I don't want to be angry anymore."

"Don't be sorry, *anak*," she whispers, rising from her seat to wipe away my tears. "I'm glad you left. You've always had the strength to change how you feel and despite everything that's happened, you've kept pushing forward."

She releases my hands and heads into the living room, returning with a scrapbook. It's filled with newspaper articles and phone screenshots—a collection of my achievements and moments of success. Each page reflects her unwavering support throughout the years. My guilt intensifies, and my eyes begin to ache with fresh tears.

"This is... really cool, Ma."

"I'm so proud of you." Her words fill a void I've had since the day I turned twelve. Overwhelmed with emotion, I bury my head in her chest. It's as if I finally found the missing pieces of a puzzle I've been working on for years. The loneliness I've felt, especially after moving away, amplifies the significance of Ma's unfailing love. I believed for the longest time that becoming someone Pa would be proud of would make me feel whole, but now I understand that Ma's love has the power to do the same.

"Oh, there's something else I have," she exclaims, dashing upstairs, leaving me with the scrapbook. I begin flipping through its pages, wiping my eyes. It's incredible that Ma has gathered all this stuff; ten years' worth of memories—a time capsule preserved for this moment. As I continue turning the pages, I catch sight of articles about the AMOS VR, something I rarely took the time to read myself. But what catches my attention is the extra page at the end of the book.

I eagerly flip to find a picture of the Squad back in sixth grade. Damn, this was the last picture we took together.

In the photo, Dustin and I playfully nudge Emierr's and Jadis's heads together, trying to make it look like they're kissing. But Jadis, always one step ahead, quickly retaliates by pulling Dustin's and my ears. Jhoana's infectious laughter fills the air as she finds herself caught between Dustin and me. The camera captured that joyful moment in a flash.

I carefully extract and tuck the picture into my pocket, treasuring this snapshot of our carefree days.

Ma returns with a mischievous grin, holding the AMOS VR. "I bought one."

"Yeah, you did," I chuckle, standing up from my seat.

"I have a game downloaded. Want to play?"

"What game?"

"Just Dance."

"Oh, Ma, you know you're gonna lose, right?"

"Oh yeah? I've been practicing," she retorts, striking a pose and doing the Stanky Leg.

"Okay, Ma got moves. You're on. Let me grab mine, be right back." I rush upstairs to my room to rummage through my shoulder bag. I unplug my phone from its charger and dash back downstairs. As I return, I find Ma in full Elvis mode. I burst into laughter. This is just like old times with Pa. Their dynamic was the best. Even when Pa had only a day at home, he made sure to be fully present. And now that Ma is here, I appreciate it even more because I know I'm going to need her when I inevitably lose another important person in my life.

I put on my glasses and sync them with Ma's device. "Ready to lose?" I taunt.

"Bring it on!"

Half an hour later, here I am, bent over in fits of uncontrollable laughter, trying my best to imitate Ma's twerk. No matter how hard I try, I can't quite nail the same rhythm and finesse.

When I'm finally able to stand up straight, I pull her into an embrace. "Ma, I love you."

"I love you, *anak*." She hugs me tighter. *Anak...* Pa always called me that.

We spend the rest of the afternoon together. Ma takes me to the old Cold Stone Creamery in town, where I eat my weight in cake batter ice cream. We followed it up with a visit to the train museum in town. I feel like I missed a lot of my childhood.

Why can't I remember things like this?

After that, we stroll through the familiar South Farmington Park. The playground where the Squad used to laugh and play is one of the few places I can clearly recall. A lot of good memories there. But then, Mom leads me to a place I don't recognize. It's not until I see the tombstones that I realize where we are. My heart sinks into an ocean of sorrow and gratitude.

"Ma?"

"I think we both should visit your Papa." Her fingers find mine.

I grip her and sigh deeply. "Okay." My fingers form a stranglehold on hers as she leads me through the rows of tombstones, each one a marker of a life now gone—so many souls are resting here, waiting for a visit from their loved ones.

Thorns needle my veins when I see it—a tombstone painted in a shade of cornflower blue. Pa's grave stands out amongst the dignified stone monuments, a mark of our heritage in a sea of Mormon granite. My legs move numbly across the perfectly cropped cemetery lawn until we are standing before what remains of my Pa.

A white marble rectangle amidst the blue holds the epitaph: *"James Aquino Mason, loving husband, father, uncle, and friend. You can always find me reveling among the stars."* I stand there in silence as the memory takes hold. I remember that night so clearly.

It was the worst night of my life.

A loud, sudden scream echoed from the kitchen. My heart stopped in my chest, and I felt my blood go cold. I had never heard Ma scream like that.

I dropped the Wii remote I'd been holding, and sprinted to the kitchen. I was vaguely aware of my friends right behind me. Uncle Joshua was on his knees, hands pressed against his chest.

"Dad?" Dustin rushed to his father's side. The rest of us stood there, frozen, not knowing what to do. But then, one by one, the parents reached out for their respective children, tears shining on many of their faces. What's happening? My heart had restarted and was pounding against my

ribs. *I spotted Mama by the sink, her head bowed and shoulders shuddering with sobs.*

"Ma?"

She turned around to face me, slowly, painfully. She knelt and took my shoulders in her hands. Her beautiful face was twisted. Something was very wrong. "Baby..." *Her voice shook.* "Something happened while your Papa was at work."

I was silent but felt something squeeze my insides.

"Your Auntie Via... And your Papa..." *She paused, her grip tightening on my shoulders. I winced.* "They're... They're gone, baby. Your Papa's..." *Mama couldn't even finish the sentence before she dissolved into uncontrollable tears.*

Dead?

"My mom?" *Dustin's voice cracked. He was bent over his father's crumpled form, staring at Mama like he couldn't believe what he'd heard.*

Mama was crying too hard to reply. It was answer enough.

"No." *I shook my head, feeling ice spreading through my chest.* "You're lying. They're—he's not dead! You're lying!" *I pushed away from her and ran. My bare feet pounded into the stairs as I tore up to my room.*

"Ricky!" *Jhoana shouted.*

I slammed the door behind me and locked it. The thumping in my chest had become thunder, shattering the ice holding my chest captive. Before I knew it, I had collapsed onto my bed, wailing. I just spoke to Papa; he was just here. *The pillow deadened my scream.* He had been right on the edge of this very bed just hours ago. Papa... you promised...

"Ricky? Please open the door." *Jho's voice was muffled behind the door.*

"Just leave me alone, Jho!" *I cried, my voice catching between words.*

"I love you. I love you, okay? I'll always be here." *Her voice sounded fragile, on the cusp of breaking.*

As always, Jho had come to my rescue. There was no point in shutting her out. I stumbled out of bed, reaching for the doorknob. Inches from the worn metal, my hands halted. Tremors wracked my arms. I don't think you can save me from this one, Jho. *My legs gave out, and I fell to my knees, burying my face in my arms and letting the grief overtake me.*

I didn't know how much time had passed. I was starting to feel weightless; my tears having left me empty. I could feel Jhoana's silent presence from the other side of the door. How long had she been sitting there? Once in a

while, she would whisper to me, telling me I would be okay. That we would all get through it together. She was the only thing keeping me tethered to the surface of the Earth. Maybe if I closed my eyes, I'd wake up and find out none of this was real. It couldn't be real... I was slipping deeper now, my eyelids heavier than ever. Before I completely surrendered to the darkness, I whispered one last word into the empty room.

"*Astralis.*"

The cold stone under my hand brings me back to the present. Heat prickles at my eyes, but I blink away the tears.

Ma's hand touches my shoulder, and I meet her gaze. The warm and cool blend of gray and gold shimmers with tears of her own. I break down, crying like I did the day we saw it in the news. The day I lost my Pa. Ma cries with me, murmuring choked comforts about how proud my Pa would be. But would he really be proud if he knew what I was about to do? If he knew that I was going to abandon Jhoana after sixteen years of her fight to live? And all because I was too weak to bear it all?

I don't know how long we sit by his tombstone, the coolness of the marble base seeping through my jeans. Ma asks about my life and what I've been up to, and I tell her about my job, travels, and dreams. She shares that she became a certified nursing assistant, helping others in their times of need. I ask about her and Uncle Joshua and she hesitates, saying it's complicated, and she feels as if she's betraying Pa's memory. But I give her my blessing and remind her that she's mourned enough. Pa would want her to be happy, not live out her life in sorrow. The afternoon passes with laughter and tears and, as sundown approaches, we make our way home.

Ma pulls the car into her parking space, and we step out onto the pavement.

"Ma, your car keys?" I extend my hand.

"Here." She rummages through her handbag and tosses me a different set of keys.

"Is this...?"

"Your Papa's car keys. It's still running fine. Your Uncle Joshua gave it a tune up two months ago."

I glance over at the aged car. It's a dull blue Ford Sierra; the epitome of a 1980s sedan. I realize that, morbidly, it's a similar color to his headstone. I wonder if that was intentional. "I can really take it?" I ask. It's been years since I last sat in the vehicle's worn, scratchy seats. Ma smiles fondly and tips her head toward the car. "Thanks, Ma." As I climb inside the battered Sierra, I notice the faint scent of Axe still lingers in the upholstery.

"Don't stay out too late, okay?" Ma calls from the front porch. "Love you, *anak*."

"Love you too, Ma."

I take a moment, my hands resting on the steering wheel. It's been a while since Papa passed away, yet I recall why he cherished this rust bucket. Uncle Joshua had given it to him, and, despite its perpetual problems, Uncle Joshua would always come to repair it. Pa used to proudly say that Uncle Joshua simply wanted a reason to hang out with his brother. I can sense both of their presences in this car, their laughter and companionship lingering in the air. It's bittersweet to think about the similarities their friendship had to the one I share with Dustin.

With that, my decision solidifies sharply in my mind. Anticipation thickens in the still air around me. I'm going to do it. Even if Emierr has completely lost his mind, a shred of hope is better than none. I'm going to do what I can to save my best friends. All four of them.

With a turn of the key, the engine splutters to life.

I'm coming, guys. After all these years...

ReUNION

October 1

My left leg won't stop bouncing. The anticipation is driving me crazy. It's 7:15 p.m. Where are they? I can't stand being the only one here, awkwardly sitting at a table for four in a busy restaurant during the dinner rush. I seize the menu and start flipping through it without really looking. Honestly, I'm still craving Ma's cooking.

Suddenly, my phone dings. *Finally!* But it's not them; it's Bonnie.

Bonstance

> Rick, if you see this message, please call me. I need to talk to you ASAP.

Something heavy drops into my stomach. Without hesitation, I tap the call icon. It rings. And rings. And rings.

"Come on, you literally just messaged me," I say, exasperated.

"Rick?" Bonnie's anxious voice comes through the line.

"Hey, what's going on?"

"Have you checked your emails?" She actually sounds on the verge of panic.

"No, I'm totally disconnected out here. Farmington is like a damn time warp."

"So, you don't know yet."

"Know what? Stop being cryptic, Bon."

Bonnie whispers, "Oscar is going a little overboard."

"Define 'a little.'"

"He wants to launch in five days."

"Five days?" My voice rises several pitches and the family sitting at the next table eyes me irritably.

"Yeah, he's pouring in millions and overworking everyone. I take back what I said about you being that kind of boss. This is the worst." I can suddenly hear the exhaustion in her tone.

I swear loudly, earning myself more than one offended gasp from surrounding patrons. "Should I come back home?"

"No, no need for that. I'll talk to Oscar and see if we can delay the launch until you're back. That way, you can have more input. Honestly, big props to you. I don't know how you do all of this."

I force a chuckle. "Well, I have you by my side. That's why."

She groans, "I miss you. I hope you're doing okay."

"I have a lot to update you on, but thanks for taking care of things back there."

"Always, greater together, right?"

"Always."

"Dicktor!" I jump amidst scandalized whispers around me. A few parents have clapped their hands over their precious children's innocent ears. I snort and turn around to see Dustin, Emierr, and Jadis standing near the entrance.

"Who's that?" Bonnie snickers.

"They're here. I'll call you later. Love you." *Well, that wasn't supposed to slip out.*

"Uh—Um, okay. L—Love you too."

I set my phone down, smoothly sidestepping my own humiliation and waving at my friends.

Jadis has a wide grin across her face as she leads the boys to the table. Behind her, Dustin is pointing at Jadis, miming the shape of her hair and swinging his hips lasciviously. I get up from my seat, and Jadis starts sprinting towards me. I meet her halfway, catching her in my arms and twirling her around. She bursts into laughter, and I set her back on the ground.

"I'm sorry I didn't really get to say hi to you yesterday."

"No, I'm sorry," she says, one arm crossing her body to clutch the other. "I wanted to hug you guys, but..."

"Yeah, it was intense." I cringe.

She gently places her hands on my face. "You grew a beard."

"Your hair looks dope; really suits you."

"You look just like your dad," she murmurs.

"Yeah, so I've heard," I reply, feeling a mix of pride and melancholy.

"Hey, lovebirds, don't forget about us! We're here too," Emierr butts in, a mischievous look on his face.

I shoot him a smirk and retort, "Jealous, Meer?"

"Obviously. I miss holding you in my arms, Dicktor." He flutters his lashes at me.

"Look what I found," I say, electing to ignore him. I pull out the picture of us from sixth grade from my pocket.

Jadis snatches the picture out of my hand. "No way. Where did you get that?"

Dustin and Emierr peer over her head at the photo.

"My Ma. She stuck it in a scrapbook with all the random articles I was in." Thinking about that book still fills me with warm fuzzies.

Emierr shakes his head in disbelief. "Was I always that scrawny?"

"Dude, you had a six-pack by seventh grade," Dustin says, stroking his arm and his ego.

"Oh yeah..." Emierr says, mollified.

"I remember this." Jadis's face is glowing, her gaze lingering on our youthful faces.

"Man, I was such a chubby kid. Look at my Justin Bieber hair." I screw up my face, laughing at the memory.

"Were we all aboard the 'Jadeer' ship?" Dustin teases. I'd forgotten the couple name we'd given Jadis and Emierr. The taunting, shockingly, never did lead to a relationship.

"Gross, never in a billion years," Jadis rolls her eyes but chuckles all the same.

"That's not what your mom said," Emierr mutters under his breath. Dustin whacks him in the ribs.

"Check out Jho, she's so happy," Jadis's finger brushes Jho's smiling face.

"My turn," Emierr seizes the picture from Jadis's hands. She makes a grab for it but Emierr is too fast. It's just like old times.

"Dicktor," Dustin calls out to me, motioning to step aside with him.

"Dusticle," I respond.

"About last night..."

"Yeah... Our parents are definitely—"

"Don't even finish that." He shakes his head. "Did you talk to your mom?"

I nod. "She said it's complicated."

"My dad said the same thing," he says, eyes focused over my shoulder. The one thing that hasn't changed about Dustin is his eyes; dark brown with a clinging sadness that serves as a constant reminder of the pain we both carry.

"Hey." I pat his arm. "This is a good thing, you know? I finally get to be your brother for real."

He smiles, the warmth returning to his features. "Yeah, that is a good point."

"We're ordering now," Jadis half-shouts, drawing everyone's attention. I pull out the chair beside Jadis and Dustin takes the seat opposite me. As they browse the menu, I silently observe my old friends. This is so surreal—each of us has built a life over the past ten years, but it feels like we're picking up where we left off. Now that I can finally take it all in, I see just how much they've changed.

Jadis's long, ebony hair is now a midnight-blue pixie cut with half her head buzzed to her scalp. Dustin's childhood pudge has given way to chiseled features and hard-earned muscle. Emierr, once a lean athlete, is now a sentient brick wall. They've all changed physically, but underneath it all, they're still the same people I've always called family.

The waitress arrives with ice waters and takes our orders, Emierr leans into whisper something to her. Probably asking for her number. She smiles but walks off. *Rejected.*

All four of us finally meet each other's eyes and there's only one thing left to do. Catch up.

"How are your parents?" I break the silence.

"My dad's still stubborn. Oh, I bought my old house back," Dustin says, as if that's the most normal thing in the world

"What?!" We're all gaping at him.

"Yeah, he wants to live here again, so I bought it this morning. He loves being around your parents, I guess." He shoots a knowing look at me.

"That makes me happy; your dad is a softy just like you." Jadis overcomes her shock with a weak attempt at a joke. Emierr and I had already gone through the five stages of grief regarding Dustin's obscene amount of wealth, but Jadis was just beginning.

"The first thing my parents asked me after not seeing me for seven years is if they

have grandchildren yet." Emierr shakes his head incredulously.

"Are you dating? Because sorry to her." Jadis closes her eyes in mock sympathy. "My mom says you've been hanging out with one of her employees a lot. A 'Rune,' she said."

"Rune? Like spells? Did she hex you, Meer?" I grin. Classic Utah. It's a statewide hobby to give your kids bizarre names. Rune is far from the worst I've heard.

Emierr rolls his eyes but doesn't answer. "What about you?" he retorts. "You didn't leave with a great parental relationship. Your mom reminds me all the time when she sees me."

"You know, my sister Cadence told me they changed, and I think they did."

"*Ate* Cade..." I smile fondly.

"How is she?" Dustin leans on the table.

"She's a mom now, and I'm an aunt." Jadis seems surprised to hear the words coming out of her mouth.

"Maybe I can exchange notes with her," Dustin says. "Being a parent is hard, guys."

"You should, she's, like, really good with Lyric." *Is Jadis actually complimenting her sister?*

"And your parents?" I prompt.

"Oh yeah, they didn't get on my ass about anything," Jadis says. "They just hugged me and let me know they're sorry. Which is a lot, you know? I always thought they hated me." Jadis's eyes begin to shine with tears.

"That's good. That's really good, Jads." I pat her shoulder.

"Wait, where's your super model boyfriend, Jads?" Emierr props his elbows on the table. "Why you hiding him from us?"

"Oh yeah, Cam Collins, right?" Dustin asks. "He did that one ad for the Olympics. He seems cool."

"Ricky," Jadis looks my way, her face suddenly hard. "How's Auntie Luna?"

Subtle. Maybe they broke up and she didn't want to talk about it. "She's the same, worrying all the time about me," I say, allowing the change in subject. "She's sort of back to how she was before... Well, you guys know how she was after my Pa died. But she's trying and I think..." I pause, locking eyes with Dustin before saying, "I think it's because she's seeing Uncle Joshua."

"Ricky!" Dustin's eyes bulge.

"I'm sorry, but it's gonna get out eventually." I shrug.

"You know, I saw them kiss two nights ago. I wasn't going to say anything, but..." Jadis sips her water, sparing herself from finishing the thought.

"Yeah... Your dad's been back home for months now, and I think he's been staying with Auntie Luna since then," Emierr adds.

"You said you didn't see my dad, when I asked you." Dustin shoots a glare at Emierr.

At least Emierr had the decency to look a little guilty.

"Well, they look happy, and it's cute," Jadis asserts. "I hope it works out for them." We all fall into an uncomfortable silence with my mom and Dustin's dad's sex life dangling between us.

"Woah, something just came back to me," I say, trying to restart the conversation. "Remember when—what's his face—Brunner Fischer? He pulled that stunt, trying to get us all expelled because he sucked. And you tore into him, Jads, like he was a damn toddler. He practically peed his pants."

"No way, she did that?" Dustin looks impressed.

"Yeah, I totally did." She flashes him a wide grin, relishing in the memory.

"I knew you were a badass, but I didn't know you were a

straight-up gangster too." Dustin gives her a fist bump.

"Ugh, that douchebag. I never want to see Brunner's face again. He made living here a damn nightmare," Jadis grumbles.

"Agreed." Dustin raises his glass in solidarity.

"Hey, come on, you don't need to be rude," Emierr cuts in, sounding a bit agitated.

The three of us look at each other, startled by Emierr's defense of our childhood bully.

"Don't tell me you guys are friends or something." Jadis laughs. There's a threatening undercurrent in her words.

"Maybe, Jads, people can change. You all did," Emierr says. He looks genuinely troubled.

"Okay, calm down, I'll be more cordial." She bats her eyes at him, dissolving the tension into laughter.

"Wait, Jads, what have you been up to aside from traveling?" I ask. Jadis is the one I currently know the least about, excluding my ill-gotten intel last night. She exchanges a glance with Dustin, and he subtly tilts his head. "I'm studying at NYU and am about to graduate in liberal arts. I took drawing seriously," she says, stealing another look at Dustin.

"Wow, shit, that's neat! Do you have any of your drawings with you?" Emierr asks.

"Not at the moment, but if you ever find yourself in New York, I'll make sure to invite you to one of my shows," she says, smiling tightly.

She just lied to his face. Why would she lie about that? "NYU? Why haven't you visited me? If I had known you were around the neighborhood—"

"I took this semester off," she interrupts.

"Fair," I say, trying to keep my tone light. "Why did you make it sound like your life was boring? You were always amazing at drawing. Remember that time you drew..." I pause as a faint memory starts to resurface. *Was that a notebook?*

"You okay, Ricky?" Emierr furrows his brows.

"Yeah, just a bit of a headache," I say, pressing my hands against my forehead. "I'm fine." I turn back to Jadis. "Really proud of you, Jads."

She gives me a soft smile in response.

"Oh, here they come." Emierr stands up and intercepts the waitress carrying a tray of shot glasses. "I'll take care of them." He grabs the tray and doles out the glasses.

"Meer, what the hell?" I can feel my eyebrows reaching for my hairline.

"What? We're all grown-ups now, and we've never actually had a drink together," he says, a mischievous glint in his eyes.

"I haven't even eaten yet, but I'm down for it," Jadis says, closing her fingers around a shot glass.

"Yes! See?" Emierr gestures to Jadis as if this is sufficient evidence to do burger joint shots of mystery alcohol in Farmington, Utah.

"You know what, screw it." Dustin grabs a shot as well.

"Damn it, I guess I'll give in to peer pressure. You guys know my mom warned me about hanging out with y'all," I complain. "Just promise not to pressure me into smoking any of that—what do the kids call it—jazz cabbage."

"No can do," Emierr says seriously. "I already put it in my calendar. 'Bully Rictor into smoking jazz cabbage.' "

The howls of laughter from our table are attracting more than a few looks. We are going to have to tip this waitress like crooked politicians.

"The first one is for us, for being back together. Cheers," Emierr calls, raising his glass.

"Cheers!" We all raise our glasses and clink them together before downing the shots. The liquid hits my throat like a peppery punch, making me cough and grimace. I can't even identify what the hell was in that glass.

The waitress reappeared as if on cue with another round.

"The second one is for Jho, our best friend and sister. Cheers," Emierr says, taking a glass.

"Jhoana," I agree, my glass joining Emierr's. The second shot goes down much smoother. That one I like. Still can't figure out what it is but honestly, who cares.

We spend the evening indulging in food that was once deemed too expensive by our parents. Plates continue to pile up: lobster roll dip, salmon tacos, and a sausage and honey pizza—possibly my favorite. Dustin and Emierr opt for burgers, claiming it's bulking season.

The laughter flows freely as we dive into stories from our childhood, reminiscing about the good ol' days. We share inside jokes and tease each other relentlessly. The bond between us, unbreakable and timeless, is evident in every word and every smile. In this moment, surrounded by my best friends, life feels complete. We're back where we belong, and nothing can dampen our spirits.

"Alright, Meer, spill the beans. What's this grand plan you were talking about? And why the hell are we back in Farm-fucking-ton?" Dustin slurs. Raucous laughter breaks out again. Luckily, we'd chased out all the tight-buttoned families several hours ago.

"Yeah, Meer, you said we can save Jho. How the hell do we do that?" I say, only somewhat more eloquently than Dustin.

"He told me we were convincing Uncle and Auntie to put a stop to it," Jadis offers.

Emierr's demeanor shifts, his expression turning wary. "You guys seriously don't remember anything from our childhood, do you?"

"Other than getting bullied by everyone, not really," Jadis replies, sipping her water in an effort to combat the liquor.

"Okay. Um. Damn, how do I do this." Emierr runs his hand through his close-cropped hair. "Look, just don't judge too soon and just hear me out. You need to *remember*." Emierr rummages through his mini-gym bag and pulls out a battered composition notebook. He slides it across the table to us, the cover reading "The Allied Organization Squad".

All three of us stare stupidly at the cover.

"Your evidence," I say slowly, "is an old notebook?"

Emierr groans in frustration and shoves the dilapidated book closer to us. "Just *look*! Really look at it."

Jadis huffs a laugh of disbelief but opens it up to a random page. In our childish scrawl, there are detailed notes on magic spells, fantastical lands, and imaginary beasts. Little pictures dot the pages. Jadis pauses on one depicting a desolate desert scene. I lean closer to the page, squinting at the letters.

"Is that your handwriting, Jads?" I ask her, pulling the book a little closer. I watch her eyes flick over the page before she nods.

"Looks like it."

Dustin cranes his neck over her shoulder. The header of the page read "Arid". We skim through a few more pages, nonplussed. Jadis's entry comes to an end, and the new section is entitled "Terrene". The barely legible writing is undoubtedly Emierr's.

"Hang on," I say, narrowing my eyes at a little drawing of a treehouse. "I do remember this."

"Really?" Emierr unleashes an enormous breath and slumps back against his chair. "Thank God, I was expecting this to be a lot—"

"It's that adventure game we used to play," I laugh. Emierr's face drops. "We used to imagine we were exploring our own little nations, discovering amazing animals, learning stupid magic spells... We turned Jho's backyard into another planet." The memory is fuzzy, like a dream about to slip through my fingers.

"Oh shit, yeah, how did I forget about that?" Dustin says, smiling faintly as he leafed through the pages. "I had no idea we were so detailed about it."

"No," Emierr growls through clenched teeth. "It wasn't—It's not—God, okay." He takes a deep, steadying breath. I raise an eyebrow at him. There's a muscle in his jaw twitching. "Okay," he says finally. "Just let me try one more thing. If this doesn't work, I'll let it go."

"Try what?" Jadis says suspiciously.

"Come on," he pleads. "Go with me on this."

The three of us exchange exasperated glances but nod in agreement.

Emierr hauls himself out of his chair and slaps Dustin's credit card on the table.

"What the hell, how did you even—"

"Come on," Emierr cuts through Dustin's spluttering. "We have to go somewhere else for this."

"The *park*?" Jadis's voice slices through the quiet, evening air. "You dragged us out to the old park?"

"You guys said you would just go with me on this!" Emierr protests. "I swear, if this doesn't go how I think it will, I'll give it up, alright?"

A few grumbles rise up, but no one really pushes back. I was just here with Ma a few hours ago, not knowing I'd be back so soon—this time with the people I made my favorite memories with.

The wide expanse of grass was its main allure back in the day, not the pathetic, one swing-one slide playground. Emierr leads us to the center of the field, his face barely visible in the distant light from the road. He opens his mouth to speak but pauses, staring past us.

"You made it!" he calls out, a broad grin stretched across his face. I twist around, expecting to see a secret girlfriend. Instead, there under the yellow street light stood Brunner Fischer. Our childhood bully.

"Hey, uh. Brunner here... I'm not sure if you guys remember me..." His face is pinched with anxiety. I am at a total loss for words. Awkwardly, Brunner shuffles up beside Emierr, as if readying for a swift exit that would involve using Emierr as a human shield. Anger boils to life inside me. Jadis's face turns red, and Dustin shoots Brunner a disdainful scowl.

"Rune is here to help," Emierr says, his voice imploring.

"Rune... Oh." I put the two together. There was no girl. Emierr had been hanging out with Brunner this whole time.

"What the fuck is he doing here?" Jadis's voice rises with rage.

"What's going on, Meer?" Dustin's teeth are gritted against what I assume is a deluge of foul-mouthed insults.

"We're not the only ones who lost Jho. Rune was her best friend, too."

"You should have fucking told us that you're friends with him," I snap.

"Would any of you have even come if I did?" Emierr shoots back, looking both guilty and defiant.

None of us respond, the silence between us thick with guitar-string tension. There has to always be something... As if we're cursed to never get a happy moment for ourselves. This was meant to be the Squad's actual reunion, but Brunner's sudden appearance, and Emierr's deception—all of it—even this brief joy has been tainted. Yet, for some reason, I don't feel as angry as I ought to be. Seeing Brunner after all these years, I expected to throw a punch to his face, but instead, I find myself pitying him.

"Guys, if I may—" Brunner starts.

"No, you don't get to say a damn thing," Jadis interrupts, her hands balling into fists.

Brunner leans closer to Emierr, whispering, "I told you they wouldn't forgive me. I wouldn't either."

Seizing the moment, I catch hold of Jadis's wrist, hoping to defuse the tension. But as I do, I remember the day Jadis and I were cornered by Brunner's lackeys at school. Time has blurred their faces, but their words still ring clear. They taunted—no—*challenged* us to do the "noble thing" and end our own lives, as if it would make Jho's loss any lesser.

"Guys, let's give him a chance," I hear myself say. I bite my tongue but continue, "Meer is right. Brunner was important to Jho too." Though I'm not sure how much I believe it.

"He put us through hell, Ricky!" Jadis's rage is covering up deep-seated hurt. I can see it mingling with the tears in her eyes.

"I know," I reply, trying to keep my voice steady. But he meant something to her. And that's enough of a reason for me."

"I hate it when you play the mediator," Dustin mutters, shaking his head at me before growling at Brunner, "I'm allowing you to speak. But if you say one wrong thing, I won't hesitate to knock you out."

"Dust," Emierr warns.

"It's okay," Brunner reassures Emierr. His blue eyes fall on the three of us. "I don't even know how to begin apologizing for all the years I tormented you guys."

Jadis flings herself down into the dry grass, slumping low and folding her arms tightly. I lower myself down next to her. The prickly blades needle through my jeans,

"After graduation, I spent five miserable years beating myself up for not being there for Jho. I resented you all, but not because of the coma thing. I knew everything about your adventures, all the crazy stuff you went through. Jho would tell me all about it. She even shared the last thing you guys were planning to do."

"So, what? Just because you had your friendship issues, you made sure everyone in school hated us?" Jadis's voice is terrifyingly icy.

"I'm not proud of it. But I truly am sorry," Brunner says quietly, his gaze dropping to the ground.

"Rune wants to help bring Jho back. Please, guys, he's been proving himself over the past few years," Emierr pleads.

"To you, Meer, not to us," Dustin retorts, lowering himself to the ground with me and Jadis.

Emierr lets out a sigh, looking resigned,

"Brunner, did you receive a letter too?" I ask, sounding calmer than I felt.

"Yeah, I did," Brunner pulls an envelope from his jacket. "It's weird, though. We all got letters when Uncle Kit could have just called us."

We exchange perplexed looks among ourselves.

"What?" Brunner frowns.

"Auntie Ina wrote those letters. She made it seem like Uncle Kit was the one sending them so that we would come back for him. And we did." I clench my teeth.

"It was a damn ambush, and Gordo was in on it too. That's why I was there yesterday," Jadis adds bitterly.

"But if Auntie Ina wrote the letters just to trick you guys, then why did she send me one?" Brunner says, confused

"Maybe because you were close to Jho, and you weren't around during all of it," Emierr suggests.

I glance at Dustin and Jadis, their faces still marked with resentment. I consider allowing them to rip Brunner a shiny, new asshole, but I can imagine Jhoana urging me to put an end to this feud. That fighting won't resolve anything. And as much as I hate to say it, I would agree with her.

"When I got the letter, I felt like the room was closing in on me." Brunner breaks the terse silence.

"I thought I was the only one," I admit, my hands trembling slightly. "I felt like I was choking, like the air was going to be taken away from me. And I kept hearing my younger self's voice, screaming bloody murder."

"Damn, I straight up vomited my protein shake," Dustin says. "The moment I laid eyes on that letter, my stomach couldn't handle it. And then I started having these crazy visions. Out in the field, I saw my younger self chasing after me, and all I could think about was wanting to hurt him."

"So that's what happened." I say, remembering the way Dustin had brought his teammate crashing to the turf.

"Same here," Jadis exhales. "I almost got into a damn car accident on my way here. I saw what looked like a younger version of myself standing in the middle of the road. I wanted to run her over."

The three of us lock eyes. We all hallucinated our younger selves. *What does* that *mean?*

Emierr and Brunner exchange a meaningful look as if confirming something between them.

"What the hell is going on? What do you guys know that we don't?" I demand.

"Okay, remember when you came here and you agreed to go with me on this?" Emierr asks.

"That was before—"

"Please, Ricky, just do this for me." Emierr's voice suddenly sounds so young, so broken. I find myself closing my mouth, arguments dying in my throat. I give him a short nod.

"Jads, Ricky, Dust, I need you to lie down," Emierr instructs, looking relieved. "We're gonna make a circle with our heads in the middle."

I catch Jadis rolling her eyes, but she obeys, settling down on her back. I position myself beside her. Once we're all gazing up at the stars, Emierr begins.

"Take a deep breath. Imagine a wave of relaxation starting at the top of your head and working your way down to your toes."

Stifling my irritation, I try my best to force my body into a state of relaxation. We lie in the dead grass, breathing slowly. Despite everything, I can hear Jadis's breath slowing. In the corner of my eye, the rise of Dustin's chest is nearly imperceptible.

"I'm going to count down from three," Emierr murmurs, "and together, we will say 'Astralis.' "

The jolt of shock in my stomach is muffled by the meditation exercise's effects. How does Emierr know about Astralis?

"Three... two... one..."

"Astralis," we say. Emierr's low voice doesn't join ours.

All at once, my skull is poised to explode, thunderous ringing filling my ears, and something akin to acid boiling my brain. I snap upright and shout a curse, clutching my head, trying desperately to keep the pieces of my skull together. A typhoon of colors, faces, terror, and joy assail my mind. The deluge of memories throbs behind my eyes, roiling, and slowing until I begin to understand. I remember.

"Ethra..." Jadis breathes out. Her chin has collided with her knees and her hands are still pressed to her ears. A steady drip of blood pools below a split in her lip.

"Are you guys okay?" Emierr is on his feet, unsure what to do. Dustin's forehead is pressed into the grass, fingers curled into his short hair. Slowly, he tips his head up to look at us. There's blood streaking his face but I can't tell where it's coming from.

"Uh guys, your noses," Brunner says nervously.

I move my hand down to feel something hot and wet dripping from my nostrils. I look up at the other two. Blood now drips out between Jadis's fingers as she tries to stem the flow. Emierr hurriedly digs into his pockets and hands out pilfered restaurant napkins. I watch scarlet bloom across the restaurant logo.

Jadis is the first to speak. "Arid. The Academy. I remember." A few tears mingle with the blood on her face.

Dustin's whispers, "Zaltana, my tribe."

A fresh pulse of memories overwhelms my mind. An enormous city orbiting the planet. A tangle of impossibly tall trees. Sweeping deserts. Jagged mountains. Frozen tundra. A single tree, its endless limbs reaching for the stars themselves.

Ethra—our shared dreamworld that we created together. Or had it ever just been a dreamworld? We had fought and survived in a world where technology and Magick flowed seamlessly together. Not only had we survived, we had thrived; each of us becoming powerful members of the societies we had chosen to call home. As the whirlwind of memories continues to shatter my brain, my heart begins to hammer against my ribs—the one thing I prayed I would never experience again. The sense of absolute, unadulterated fear Ethra had instilled in me. The reason I had chosen to forget.

Emierr's arms cross tightly over his chest. "So, you guys remember?"

We don't speak. We just sit in stunned silence. The gush of blood is slowly receding. I hold a fresh napkin to my nose, dabbing at the remainder.

Brunner's voice pierces through the shock. "Jho told me. She said that the Squad was breaking up. Meer wanted to grow up, to face the real world rather than hide away in a fantasy. So, you all planned one last adventure, one final mission, to that shadow forest."

Jadis shakes her head in denial. "No. We just fell asleep, that's it." She flings her bloodied napkin to the ground. Her eyes are shuttering closed, trying to push the memories back, not wanting to believe.

Emierr's frustration boils over as he shouts, "You know that's a lie!"

I desperately try to rationalize. "We were just kids. Maybe it was all in our heads. Shared psychosis, you know? That game got too real."

Emierr flings the notebook from his bag to my feet, his voice filled with conviction, "Ricky, you know it's real. You're the one who showed us in the first place. You brought us to Ethra. *You* taught us 'Astralis,' remember?"

The second mention of "Astralis" resurrects the most agonizing memory of all—one I've buried deep within. It was the night of Pa's death; the very same night I first dreamed of Ethra. "We made a pact," I say slowly. "I gave you guys the space rocks from the white hole. The rocks my dad gave me on my twelfth birthday."

"I have mine here." Emierr reaches into his pocket and hands me his shard. It shines like a star dipped in gold; a celestial treasure. It catches the dim streetlight's glow and sparkles like pure magic.

Closing my hand around the glittering fragment and looking up at my friends. "I had mine made into a necklace." I lift the pendant from where it sat against my chest.

Dustin takes off his ring and displays it. "I had mine smelted into my wedding ring."

Jadis rolls up her sleeve, revealing the gold bracelet on her wrist. "I did the same, but as a bracelet." Her eyes are wide with wonder, lanced through with needles of pain.

I sit there, mind racing as I piece together Emierr's plan. Deep down, I already know the answer, but I fear confirming it. With a mix of apprehension and curiosity, I finally muster the courage to ask the question that weighs heavily on my tongue.

"What's your plan, Meer?"

Emierr's response sends a chill down my spine, confirming my worst fears.

"We're going back to Ethra to rescue Jho."

Dustin, Jadis, and I exchange horrified glances.

Unable to contain my fear, I yell, "Are you out of your fucking mind? Why would we risk everything on something *we don't even know was real?*"

Emierr remains resolute, his voice steady. "Think about it. Jho's consciousness is still there. She's probably alive and waiting for us to bring her back."

"You're banking everything on a what-if scenario. What if she isn't even there?" Dustin's tone is heavy with skepticism.

"Yeah, and if everything you say is true, what about us? If we die there, won't we end up like her?" Jadis shudders.

Brunner, seeming agitated by our doubts, looks at Emierr and dismisses us with a scoff. "Forget them. They don't care about Jho. We can go back together and save her."

I retort, "First of all, you'll never be able to fucking Transcend to Ethra, *Brunner*. And Meer, this is a fucking terrible idea."

Jadis abruptly stands up. "You guys can go ahead if you want. I'm not going back there."

Dustin follows suit. "I love you, Meer, but I have my family to think about. I'm not risking everything on a hallucination. I'm out."

I nod fervently and add, "Count me out too."

The three of us begin to trudge back up the low hill to the parking lot. I'm shaking, but not from the cold. How could I have forgotten Ethra so thoroughly? Is this a normal trauma response? If it was, what about the nose bleeds? I jerk my head to the side, as if I can jostle the thoughts from my brain.

Emierr and Brunner remain where we left them. Desperation fills Brunner's voice as he yells after us, "Wait! If it's all fake, then you're also calling Jho a liar. Why did she give me this if I wasn't meant to save her?" Brunner pulls out from his pocket a stone I know very well.

"That's... That was supposed to be for Gordo," I stutter, stunned.

"She gave it to me," Brunner says, his voice the same as always—sharp, accusatory, like everything is still my fault. We stand under the glow of the park street light, casting long shadows on the pavement, but all I can focus on is him, dragging up the past like he always does. His tone reminds me of every time he's pointed the finger at me, never letting me forget I'm to blame.

I walk over to him, grabbing the shard of stone. Suddenly, it emits a radiant glow and pulsates with vibrant light, just like the others before. *Bitch.*

"Look!" Emierr yells, face wild with excitement, "That's proof! You guys have to listen to—"

Without thinking, I rip the shards from his hand, rage heating my blood. Emierr doesn't deserve to touch them. The rocks cut into my palms, but I hold on tight. I can't trust either of them with something so valuable—not after all of Emierr's lies, and the years of Brunner's ruthless witch hunt. "You've genuinely lost it, Meer. I'm taking this back before you go too far. And you." I level a glare at Brunner. "This was never yours to begin with."

Both of their faces are twisted with fury.

"If you guys won't go," Brunner growls, "then you owe it to me and Jhoana to explain everything. From the beginning."

Jadis's hackles rise, and I catch her just before she attains her goal of clawing Brunner's eyes from his skull.

This is not going to end well.

Meeting

October 2

I collapse at the kitchen table, rubbing my bleary eyes while Ma flips pancakes on the stove. I didn't get much shut-eye last night. Everything from my hazy childhood had slowly sharpened into painful focus as the early hours of the morning ticked by. I remember everything now. Ethra... The mystical world we all dreamed up together. All those wild adventures we had, somehow managing to interact with one another in the dream state. How could I have forgotten all of that?

And now Emierr is telling us that Jhoana might still be there? But we saw her... Well. It's not possible. Emierr better have some damn good answers for us.

The mouthwatering aroma of breakfast fills the air, mingling with the sizzle of bacon in the skillet, distracting me from my racing thoughts. These were the mornings I used to have; the ones I missed.

Ma returns with a plate of fluffy pancakes and crispy bacon. It's nice to have someone to talk to in the mornings. Back in my condo, every morning was the same old routine, quiet and solitary. But this, this is what I've been craving. Ma asks if I'm attending the wake tonight, and I tell her not yet. Ma understands that I need some time after the catastrophic events of the first night here.

Between bites, I coax Ma into filling me in on what's been going down at Jhoana's place. I want to pay her a proper visit without Auntie Ina trying to murder me. It turns out that Uncle Kit and Auntie Ina just got back to work last year after fifteen years as Jhoana's caregivers, which explains how she had so much time to stew in her own resentment.

Ma suggests that, if I want to see Jhoana, the best time is around 7 a.m. The nurse starts her shift at 6:30 a.m., when Jhoana's parents both leave for work. She then gives me a sweet smile, rubs my shoulder, and plants a kiss on my forehead before hustling off to the hospital. I scarf down the rest of my breakfast, not wasting a single crumb, and rush to get myself ready.

As I leave the house and stroll along the sidewalk, I think back on my time with the Squad. We used to play our hearts out as kids and have the time of our lives. But it was all taken away when we went on that mission to the shadowy Akeurimja Forest... The mission that landed Jhoana in a coma... The one that I planned. One stupid mistake, and it cost us everything. The echoes of our younger selves' screams resound in my mind, haunting me like a broken record stuck in an eternal loop of torment.

Just ahead, Jadis is standing on the Naputis' porch, facing Gordo with her arms crossed. I can't quite make out what they're saying, but Gordo's emphatic arms and Jadis's stiff shoulders give me some clues. I make my way quietly up the driveway, unnoticed.

"You really didn't know what she was planning?" Jadis's voice is low and guarded.

"You have to believe me," Gordo pleads. "She lied to me too. I just wanted to make everything okay again."

His head drops as I place my foot on the first step.

"Okay, Gordo," Jadis says, gentler now. "I trust you."

I clear my throat and they both turn.

"*Kuya* Ricky!" Gordo exclaims, rushing towards me and enveloping me in a big hug. I can't unsee him as a eight-year-old kid, regardless of the size of the man crushing me in his grip. I squeeze him against my chest.

Releasing me from the chokehold, he grins. "Why don't you and Jadis go see *ate* together?"

I nod at Jadis. "Yeah, I'm in. Can't handle this on my own."

"Fine." Jadis kicks at a rock with her heavy, black boot.

I nudge her. "Love you."

As I step into Jhoana's house for the second time, with no familiar faces around, I feel a sense of relief wash over me. This place, once a safe haven for the Squad, holds a comforting familiarity that I haven't felt in years. Gordo leads us through the dimly lit house, the floorboards creaking beneath our feet. The whole place feels ancient, from the worn-out rug to the peculiar artifacts scattered across the living room. The air is heavy with the scent of incense, mingling with a mysterious aroma I can't quite place.

As we walk, I notice picture frames lining the walls, filled with faces of family members I don't remember. There's the last family portrait they took, frozen in time. Near the basement stairs, I catch sight of a picture of the Squad on the first day of first grade, grinning like fools. I'm surprised Auntie Ina left it up. Maybe Uncle Kit stopped her from ritualistically burning it. One last fragment of the childhood we shared.

We ascend the stairs up to the second floor, passing more picture frames. This time, they hold individual portraits of their family. The house remains the same, yet everything feels washed out, like a faded memory.

Gordo comes to a halt, his gaze fixed on the portraits. "Kinda eerie, huh?" he remarks, indifferent. "None of us smile like that anymore." He resumes walking up the stairs, leaving Jadis and me to exchange a glance. Our eyes then drift towards the wall, where Jhoana's school picture from sixth grade proudly hangs. That smile of hers could light up a room, and those chubby cheeks were always a sight to behold.

Lost in my memories of Jhoana, a warm smile spreads across my face. A smile dances on Jadis's lips, too.

"Hey, you guys ready?" Gordo calls from atop the stairs.

"Yeah," Jadis murmurs. As we continue our ascent, I feel as though we're walking back in time. I'm seven again and Jhoana is showing me her room for the first time. Gordo's room is on the left by the end of the hallway, and Jhoana's on the right.

Gordo introduces us, bringing me back to the present. "*Tita*, this is Jadis and Rictor, two of Jhoana's best friends."

"Hello, *po*," I say, forcing a smile.

"Hi, *po*," Jadis echoes.

A middle-aged Filipina nurse stands before us in her pink scrubs with hair neatly tied back, radiating warmth through her welcoming smile. Her presence immediately puts me at ease, knowing that Jhoana is in good hands.

"Hi, it's nice to finally meet you." She motions us towards Jhoana's bed, which is surrounded by beeping monitors.

We approach with trepidation, my heart sinking as we take in the sight. Jhoana has aged; why was I thinking she wouldn't? Tubes invade her mouth, and her hands are tethered to a multitude of devices. She looks almost lifeless, drowning under wires and straps. My eyes fixate on Jhoana's frail body. Her once-vibrant face now appears gaunt and hollow, devoid of the lively expression I remember. The sight of her emaciated form shocks me, a painful reminder of the toll that time and her coma have taken on her.

This can't be Jho.

"She's been unresponsive for so long, but she's a fighter. I suggest talking about the good times and your memories together. She can still hear you." Ms. Santiago's voice is gentle and compassionate.

"Thank you," I manage to say.

Jadis turns to her, voice cracking, "She hasn't responded to anything at all?"

"No, but who knows, right? Her best friends are here now. Let's stay hopeful," Ms. Santiago replies, pausing for a moment. "I've been in Farmington for a long time, and I know what they say about you and your friends. I don't believe them. Sometimes things happen that we can't explain, and you were all just kids." She places her hands on our shoulders. "Sixteen years is a long time. She wouldn't be fighting this hard if there wasn't hope. I'll leave you to it." She walks out of the room, leaving us alone with Jhoana.

"I'll be in my room. Good luck." Gordo closes the door.

A heavy weight settles in my chest, and I instinctively reach for Jadis's hand. Together, we succumb to our grief, allowing the pain to pour out.

"Hi, sis," Jadis's voice trembles.

"Hey, Jho," I whisper, gripping the bedpost tightly for support.

We release each other's hands and move to opposite sides of Jhoana's bed. Kneeling down, we clasp her hands in ours. Jadis and I share the same broken heart in this moment, our heads resting on Jhoana's bed as we let our anguish consume us. The pain hits me hard, just like that night Pa passed away. The memories I'd spent years tamping down are a bleak reminder that this is my fault. I was the one who brought Jhoana into this mess, and the others followed. *What the hell did I do?*

After a few minutes, our tears subside, but we continue to gaze at Jhoana, her lifeless hands gripped tightly in ours.

"Have you thought about going back?" I ask, looking at Jadis through the twisting medical equipment. She meets my gaze, her expression tense.

"Yeah." She swallows. "We made a promise. We fight for each other, always." Her lip quivers. "I don't want to break that promise, Ricky."

A lump forms in my throat as I fight back a fresh wave of tears. "She... She told me, after my dad died, that she believes we're meant to face all the heartaches together because we're best friends in every life we live." I let out a quavering sigh. "What should we do, Jads?"

"I don't know... I'm terrified to go back. I remember the Academy and..." She trails off, eyes distant. She shakes away the thought and continues, "And the fucking nightmares... I don't know if I can go through that again."

I nod. "It took me years to heal, to find some semblance of normalcy. There's so much pain here. But being in Ethra with you guys was the best thing that has ever happened to me. What if there's a chance she's still alive?"

"But what if she's not?" Jadis's voice breaks, reflecting my own uncertainty.

I close my eyes, feeling defeated. Those lingering "what if" questions haunt me, stirring in the depths of my mind. I wish I was a psychic and knew exactly how things would happen. It would save me from a lot of pain and regret. We spend the next few hours in relative silence. Breaking it only to murmur words of encouragement to Jhoana or to recall a happy memory, just as Ms. Santiago ordered. My legs were beginning to go numb by the time Jadis checked her watch.

"Oh shit, it's 10:15. We're late," Jadis exclaims, interrupting my rapidly spiraling anxiety. Our phones ding, one after the other. "We should go. You know how Dusty is with time."

"Did you just read my mind?" I give her a soft smile.

"We're research buddies, remember?" She smiles back. "The eternal brains of the operation."

We both stand up, reluctantly letting go of Jhoana's hands.

"I'll see you later," I say, kissing her forehead gently.

"Bye, sissy, I'll be back," Jadis kisses her cheeks.

I knock on Gordo's door, and he opens it.

"You guys are leaving?" There was a hint of disappointment in his voice.

We both nod.

"Gordo, just let us know if you need anything, okay?" I say. This poor kid, losing any chance at a normal family so young...

"Yes, *Kuya*," he replies. He offers me a grateful smile.

"You have my number; call anytime," Jadis adds, reaching out to rub his arm.

Gordo looks at us, a mix of relief and uncertainty in his eyes. "You're not mad anymore?"

Jadis shakes her head, "No, we're here for you, Gordo."

Before he can even reply, I wrap him in a tight hug, and Jadis joins in without hesitation. We bid farewell to Ms. Santiago and step out of the house. Brunner's place is conveniently right behind Jhoana's. Before we even take a step, Jadis and I find ourselves locked in a suffocating hug. I messed up big time over the past ten years, losing touch with the Squad. Maybe if we had stayed connected, we could have attempted this earlier, giving ourselves more time. With heavy hearts, we make our way to Brunner's house, and there they are—Dustin and Emierr, standing at the front.

"Yo, you guys seriously need to work on your punctuality," Dustin groans.

"We were at Jho's," Jadis says.

"What? Why didn't you tell us? I wanted to see her too," Dustin's frown deepens. "I don't want to see Auntie alone."

"We didn't plan it, I was just going on my own, but we ended up being there at the same time," I say, looking over at Jadis.

"How is she?" Emierr inquires, sounding unsure about whether or not he wants to hear the answer.

Jadis and I exchange a glance, sharing a heavy sigh.

"On second thought, maybe I'm not ready to see her," Dustin says, his hands slipping into the pockets of his hoodie.

"Where's the asshole?" Jadis asks brusquely, looking around for Brunner.

"Rune is making sure everything's good," Emierr says with his hands tucked into his jacket pockets.

There's a moment of silence, and before I even realize it, my body jerks forward, trying to pull everyone together. "I love you guys," I say, voice somewhat choked.

"I—I love you too, man." Dustin's powerful arms press us together even more tightly.

Emierr pulls back, looking at me strangely. "You okay, Ricky?"

"Just getting emotional from remembering everything," I mutter.

"Just get in the damn hug," Jadis demands.

Emierr finally gives in. "I love you guys too," he says as he wraps his arms around us.

"Me three." Jadis's voice is muffled. We break apart and burst into watery laughter. The door swings open, and there stands Brunner, greeting us with a smile. The tension from yesterday settles in, like fog on a rainy seashore. He motions for us to follow him down to his basement. His home feels so aggressively American compared to ours, which makes sense, considering his dad is a cop. Last I remember, his mom works at a restaurant with Emierr's mom.

"Don't mind the mess," Brunner says, glancing back at us.

"What mess?" I ask, chuckling.

I check out the pictures on the wall, showing Jhoana and Brunner growing up from cute little babies to sixth graders. The rest of the Squad is staring around, too, except for Emierr, who seems familiar with them. It dawns on me how close Jhoana and Brunner were, which I never fully grasped with our Squad always hanging out together. How the hell did Jhoana find time to hang out with Brunner?

Brunner pushes the door to the basement open, and one by one, the rest of us follow him down.

Along one wall is a worn, but plush couch. On the opposite side, boxes are piled up, presumably filled with forgotten treasures. Scattered around them is various golfing equipment, likely belonging to Brunner's dad.

We all gather in the center of the room, our eyes meeting, and an unspoken understanding passes between us.

"Alright, let's just get this over with so I don't have to be around you any longer," Jadis grunts.

"Um, yeah," Brunner says, not rising to Jadis's bait. "My parents won't be off work until six, but they're going to the wake tonight, just like yours are. We've got the whole day and evening."

"That won't be necessary." There's a bite in Jadis's tone.

"Jads, we talked about this," Emierr snaps.

"Meer, seriously, how do you expect us not to be mad?" Dustin shakes his head incredulously.

"No, please. Be mad. I don't expect you guys to be nice or anything; I just want to know what happened. And figure out the fastest way to save her."

"Yeah, I'm not forgiving him that easily," I say, looking at Dustin and Jadis. "But I think we need to talk about it. They're the last memories we have of Jho. It's going to be painful, but maybe we can get closure." I take a deep breath, trying to steady my trembling hands.

Jadis and Dustin sigh but nod in agreement.

"So, who's first?" Brunner scans all of us. We glance at each other. It seems no one wants to begin this group therapy session. "I'll grab some drinks, be right back," Brunner mumbled, disappearing up the stairs.

"How the hell do we even do this?" I scratch my beard, feeling apprehensive about the undoubtedly grueling the task ahead.

"Well, first of all, what do you guys remember?" Emierr sits down on the couch, looking at us expectantly.

"I remember everything, now," Jadis says, her eyes darting around the room. "But it's all a bit hazy."

"I wrote down whatever came to me last night, but it's a mess," Dustin pulls some crumpled papers from his pockets.

I remember every damn detail crystal clear, but I'm not so keen on sharing all of it. Relive the horror I went through in the Space Ring? No thanks, I'd rather keep that locked away.

"Yeah, same here," I lie. "it's kind of fuzzy."

Brunner returns, carrying five bottles that I've only seen in old pictures of our parents back in Guam. They're thick plastic and filled with a light brown liquid. I accept my bottle and take an experimental sip. The lemon tea inside is thick with sugar. It's delicious.

"King Car? Where'd you get these?" Dustin exclaims excitedly, snatching one from Brunner's hands and momentarily forgetting his beef with him.

"My mom gets them from my relatives in Guam," Brunner says, shrugging.

"Right," Jadis scoffs. "Your parents are tight with Jho's. That makes sense."

"Jadis, you knew that. Remember what you said to me during the protest? 'Not even Guam will want you if you ever go back home,'" Brunner reminds her, handing each of us a bottle.

"I said that?" Jadis says, startled.

"Damn, Jads, never mind. You're a bitch," Dustin snickers, a mischievous grin on his face.

"I don't even remember that," I say, furrowing my brows.

"You were saying it with her," Brunner retorts.

"Oh..." I can admit I feel a bit ashamed.

"So, both of you are bitches." Dustin laughs louder, easing some of the friction in the room.

I glance at Jadis, cringing a little. "Research bitches, huh?"

"Well, you deserved that," Jadis tells Brunner, clearly not remorseful in the slightest.

"Yeah, I did," Brunner nods, unbothered. "So, what the hell happened?"

"Since I'm the only one who remembers everything, I'll start," Emierr announces, sipping his King Car and closing the bottle. "Here, you guys can read through the notebook for reference." He hands it to Jadis.

We all settle down on the couch while Emierr positions himself in front of us, standing on the thick, powder blue carpet.

"So, I had this idea to go to Juno, the capital of Zaltana, 'cause they throw the wildest parties," Emierr begins. "But Jads insisted on visiting the Treetop Provinces instead. We flipped a coin, and I lost."

All of us blink at him, completely lost.

"Wait, where are you going with this?" Jadis asks, baffled.

"I'm talking about that time when I got attacked by that fungus-furred flounder ferret in the Treetop Provinces... Jho thought it was cute and wanted me to talk to it, but it got all pissed off 'cause I called it adorable, and it scratched my damn head," Emierr rants.

"That didn't happen." I laugh.

"Yeah, I don't think it went down like that, Meer. You cried because we didn't wanna party. None of us were old enough to drink; we were like twelve." Dustin shakes his head.

"Jho and I were eleven," Jadis corrects. "And you didn't just call it cute, you tried making it your pet."

"No, I swear to god it was rabid," he insists then looks at Dustin. "And we were Nobles, they'd let us drink." Nobles. People who managed to bond with the mysterious beasts that ruled each land. At the time, it had seemed badass that we were all leaders in our realms. But now, looking back, who cares if we managed to tame a Crown Beast, we were children! We had absolutely no business being in charge of anything.

"Wait, Ricky, you weren't even with us when that ferret kicked Emierr's ass," Jadis realizes

"What? I wasn't?"

"No, yeah, he wasn't," Dustin recalls. "You were mostly up in the Space Ring, remember? I think it was only the last two months that you started hanging out with us in Ethra."

"That's right, we had to visit you 'cause those scientists that took care of you were pretty strict," Emierr adds, a knowing smile on his face.

"Dude, this shit is a fucking mess. I can't keep up," Brunner complains. "You all remember things differently, but it's the same damn event. Let's have one person speak, and then the next can tell their version."

"Yeah, that works," Emierr agrees with a shrug.

"Meer, you're *not* going first," Jadis says.

"Then who?" Emierr counters. We all eye each other as if we're in a wild west standoff.

"It's gotta be Rictor." Brunner looks at me. "He created Ethra."

As I feel everyone's eyes settle on me, my stomach grows hollow. But I'll have to relive it sooner or later. "Okay," I nod and stand up, Emierr taking my place on the couch. I try to think of what to say, and it finally comes to me. "We were at, uh, the fields..."

"The Great Eagle Fields," Jadis corrects me, referencing the notebook in her hands.

"Yeah, that's it! We played there most of the time. I remember I could—"

"No, that's too far ahead," Dustin interrupts.

"Oh, um, okay. Well, you guys visited me at the Space Ring, and then I brought you all to the Mecha suits and—"

"You gotta talk about the Terrerium first. That's where we went before that," Emierr interjects.

"What the hell do you guys want me to say?" I fling my hands into the air, exasperated.

Everyone starts talking over each other, and Brunner tries to defuse the situation to no avail.

"*How's* about," Jadis shouts, silencing everyone. "Start from when you first entered Ethra, Ricky, tell us about that."

I pause for a moment, the echoes of everyone's cries resounding in my head. "Okay," I finally say. "It was the day I found out my dad died..."

BOOK TWO:

ALL THOSE YEARS BEFORE

RICKY

I pressed my face against the window and squinted. My breath fogged up the glass, but I didn't care. Beyond the window was a kaleidoscope of glittering stars and swirling galaxies. The whole world was below me; fluffy, white clouds billowing over sprawling land masses and expansive seas. Papa would never believe it. He always said I had an overactive imagination. But this felt *real*.

The clouds below parted, and I could see city lights twinkling along coastlines. I bet Jads would've loved to paint this view. I wished Papa could've seen this with me; then I could float with him among the stars. Thinking of him punched a hole in the balloon of excitement filling my chest, and I tried hard to focus on the wonder unfolding in front of me.

"Hello, there," someone said behind me. I turned to see a woman in a lab coat with ash-brown hair tied up in a bun. Several others in matching white coats were watching me from behind her.

"Hi," I said, eying her with apprehension. *This is some dream.*

"What's your name?" the woman asked.

"I'm Rictor Mason. Nice to meet you." Even if it was a dream, it never hurt to be polite.

"I'm Dr. Hutton, but you can call me Delphini." She reached out to shake my hand. Her fingers were small but warm around mine. My eyes drifted from Miss Delphini's gentle expression to the room around me. This must be the lab where they tested chemicals from the look of all the test tubes. They had a chemical lab at Papa's work, too, but this place looked like a movie set.

"What kind of doctor are you?" I asked her.

"I am a physicist. How old are you, Rictor?"

"I just turned twelve today," I said, puffing out my chest.

"Is that so?" she said with a soft smile. "Then, happy birthday. You seem very bright for your age."

Her words filled me with pride. As I beamed at her, a real-life hologram projected from her bracelet onto her hand. She had a super cool pen that looked all sleek and shiny with glowing lights. Instead of paper, she wrote on a holographic screen. It looked like she scribbled on thin air, but the words magically appeared as if on a notepad.

"Woah!" I leaned in closer to her. "I've only seen holograms in movies."

"Why don't you take a seat first, Rictor? I have some questions for you." Miss Delphini guided a floating, egg-shaped chair towards me.

This place was so advanced. I pushed down on the chair, and it stayed floating. "Science!" I whispered. Miss Delphini and her team chuckled. The egg lowered as if it sensed I was about to sit. Once I was settled, it lifted me off the ground. Miss Delphini drew up her own egg and sat. Automatically, my chair moved to level me with hers, my feet dangling off the ground. I had to resist the urge to swing my legs like a little kid on a Ferris wheel.

"How did you get here?" Miss Delphini asked. Her tone had become more serious. I wondered if I was somehow in trouble.

"I don't remember. It's blurry." My hands started to sweat. *Wait. How did I get here? Why can't I remember?*

"Where are you from?"

"Utah," I said and tried hard to picture my recent journey from Earth. *I guess, if this is a dream, maybe my brain skipped over that part?*

She stopped writing and looked up at me, puzzled. "Utah? Is that in Arid?"

I blinked at her, totally thrown off. "No, the United States. North America." How could an adult, a scientist even, not know where Utah is?

I heard the people behind her start to whisper. I only caught a few words like *"lying"*, *"impossible"*, and oddly, *"string."* I was suddenly acutely aware that I probably shouldn't be there. Miss Delphini's stare lingered for a few more moments. She slowly began to write on her invisible notepad again.

"Could you spell that for me, Rictor? Utah?"

"Uh... Yeah. It's U-T-A-H." The thumping in my chest grew to the point of near-pain. Its thundering was pushing me towards something I couldn't see. I realized I was about to wake up. *Of course it's a dream. I can't remember how I got here because I didn't. I just fell asleep.* The thought put my mind at ease, luring me back from the precipice of waking.

"Do you know where you are?" Miss Delphini continued.

"A space station, I guess? Like the one where my dad used to work."

"Your dad works here?"

I screwed up my face, pondering. "Well. I think so. You're a scientist with NASA too, right?"

She just looked at me blankly. "What's NASA?"

I blinked at her. She had to be pretending... How could a scientist not know NASA? Even if this was a dream, my subconscious knew what NASA was. Maybe it was supposed to be a test to gauge how smart I was.

"It's an acronym for National Aeronautics and Space Administration," I answered, the familiar words lending me confidence. I knew this stuff by heart. "They study space and learn about our universe, but before, they studied our oceans." *Nailed it.*

She turned around to look at her equally baffled colleagues. When none of them offered any explanation, Miss Delphini leaned in a little closer.

"Rictor, what do you call the planet you live on?"

"Earth..." I responded slowly. "Are you sure you're a scientist?"

The whole room went quiet, and everyone's eyes were on me.

"Am I in trouble?" I felt a little ashamed for questioning her intelligence. "I'm sorry, I'm sure you're a great scientist, and I know kids probably aren't supposed to be here." Dream or not, I was embarrassed for interrupting their work by crash landing on their station.

"No, not at all, Rictor. You just surprised us, that's all," Miss Delphini assured me. "You're far from home, aren't you? What is the name of the space station your dad worked on?"

Her question didn't make sense to me. Wasn't there only one space station?

"The International Space Station?" My voice trembled slightly. "Isn't that where we are?"

Miss Delphini shook her head. "No. We're in the Fleming Space Ring. The fifth nation of Ethra."

A thrill of fear thrummed through my limbs.

"Where?" I said hoarsely. I slid out of the hovering chair and dashed back to the window. Earth gleamed below me with its familiar white, green, and blue. Except... the landmass below me was nothing like Earth's.

"Rictor," Miss Delphini said behind me. "I'd like you to meet my husband, Dr. Wolfgang Hutton."

Her husband was a tall, blond man; probably around the same age as Papa. Actually he kind of looked like Papa's German astronaut friend.

"Hello, Rictor. You're making big news on this station." He had an accent, but it didn't sound like the German accents I'd heard. Well, not like Papa's friend, anyway.

"What's going on?" I demanded. I tried to sound strong and bold but all I wanted was to wake up, safe in my bed.

"Don't worry, we're here to help you get back home," Miss Delphini reassured me. She and her colleagues began to circle around me. I tried to move away but the window pressed against my back. *Wake up!*

My eyes flew open, and I sat up, sweating. I held a hand against my chest, feeling my heart punching at my palm under my pajamas. I thought I was having a heart attack. The alarm clock showed it was 3 a.m. I got out of bed and opened the door. The hallway lights were still on.

That had been a very weird dream. Miss Delphini and Dr. Wolfgang's faces were still crystal clear in my mind. Were dreams supposed to be that vivid? Had I been dreaming wrong my whole life? The floorboards creaked as I tiptoed towards Mama's and Papa's room and pushed the door open just a crack. Mama was asleep. I slipped inside, careful not to make a sound. I gave her a gentle shake and scanned the spot next to her. Papa wasn't there.

Her bloodshot eyes fluttered open; she had been crying.

"Ma," I whispered. "I can't sleep."

She sat up, the hallway light casting shadows on her face. "Oh, baby, come here." She made room for me on the bed. I crawled in, and she pulled me close.

I gathered my courage. I didn't want to know the answer to the question I was about to ask. But I needed to know. "Is Papa really dead?"

Mama's lip quivered and nodded, tears streaming down her face. At that moment, I wished that this was the dream instead.

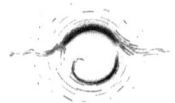

The living room couch wrapped around me like a cocoon. I used to wait here for Papa when he worked late, anxious that he wouldn't come home at all. But now, knowing that was truly the case, I felt numb to everything. It had been a week and five days since Papa and Auntie Via passed away. The burial was just a few hours ago, but I didn't remember being there.

I looked around and understood why the room was so silent—everyone was staring at the kid without a dad. Meer and Jho sat next to me, but even they had been rendered speechless. I didn't blame them. What *could* anyone say? Jads moved around the house and helped Mama with the guests, making sure everyone had been offered food and a drink. She was probably trying to handle her emotions in her own way, staying busy and all. Helping my Mama was just a bonus.

Death was weird. It turned people into someone they weren't. It seemed like no one even noticed that Dusty wasn't there.

The other parents were trying to be strong for both of us, but why did they have to do that? Papa was one of their best friends, too. And it bothered me that Dusty was all by himself. I slipped out of the house. Everyone probably saw me, but I couldn't stay in that suffocating room any longer. I glanced up at Dusty's window next door, wondering if he was hurting as much as I was. Instead of going through the front door, I made my way to the backyard.

There he was, head down, still in his funeral clothes, and sitting on the swing set that we'd all outgrown. I approached him with slow, shuffling steps, buying time as if it would help me figure out what to say. He caught my eye briefly but dropped his gaze back to the dirt under his shoes. We didn't need words right then. I sat beside him on the swing set. I could practically feel the grief radiating off the two of us, sending waves of misery into the air around us. *Oh, Dusty.* Without a thought, I reached for his hand and held it tightly.

After a week and five days of staying strong, on the swing set his mother bought for him, Dusty finally broke down. I cried with him, letting the tears ease some of the pressure in my chest. We stayed together until Uncle Joshua finally came back home. Jads, Meer, and Jho all kept their distance. Maybe they didn't know what to say or how to help. Maybe they were suffering too. After all, we were a family. We had all lost a parent that day.

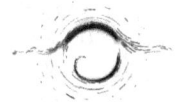

In two days, I had to go back to school. I wasn't ready for the staring, the awkwardness. Not even the adults knew how to talk to a kid who'd just lost a parent. And schoolwork? I was supposed to sit there and learn math equations as if there wasn't a gaping hole in my chest?

As I wandered past my desk, I spotted the space rocks Papa gave me. I picked them up. They were warm in my hand despite the chilly autumn night outside. They reminded me of the dream I had that night, just hours after I'd lost him. I rolled the little shards around between my fingers. *Could I go back to the Space Ring or whatever it was?*

Jads and I had read about lucid dreaming in the library, where you could control and revisit your dreams. We'd both tried for months but never seemed to manage it. I supposed now was as good a time as any to try again. I lay down on my messy bed, focusing on the Space Ring and Miss Delphini. I tried to recall the incredible view out the window and how Miss Delphini had smiled at me from her egg-shaped chair. Slow, deep breaths. In and out. It was working. Just as I was about to fall asleep, I whispered the words Papa had taught me years ago. The final words he'd spoken to me.

"Astralis."

My body tingled and my stomach dropped as a violent force pulled me upwards. My eyes shot open. I was *flying*. I couldn't move my body from its prone position, but my head was still under my control. I looked behind me and saw the cul-de-sac growing smaller and smaller. As I passed through the clouds, I caught a breathtaking view of Farmington from above. *I'm doing it! I'm lucid dreaming!*

The speed picked up and I couldn't prevent a small scream from escaping. I soared through Earth's atmosphere and burst into the deathly silence of space. Behind me, Earth shrank until it was nothing but a glittering marble in the inky blackness. I breezed past the red planet—Mars—and the asteroid belt, where the dino-killing asteroid came from. Before I could blink, Jupiter, the king of the gods with his ginormous swirling eye, was looking right at me. I didn't stop, though, cruising past planets and stars I'd never even heard of. I knew it was a dream, and yet everything was so vivid, so clear. *Jads is gonna be so jealous.*

Leaving the Milky Way behind, I gazed at nebulae in colors I had no name for, stretching across every direction. Everything around me blurred and warped, the light bending into ribbons that twisted and stretched, as if the universe itself was folding in on me. Then, there was nothing but blackness. For a moment, I held my breath in utter silence and darkness. Suddenly, a minute trail of golden dust trickled into view. Its faint, glittering light revealed what was coming—a colossal black hole. I was mesmerized by its vastness, but absolutely terrified of what would happen when I flew inside.

Unable to control my momentum, I approached its warped horizon. Just as I was about to cross the threshold, I let out a tiny whimper. Maybe lucid dreaming wasn't for me. My vision seemed to distort, twisting and turning into a dimension my 3D brain could not comprehend. A planet came into view; the same planet I'd seen from the Space Ring, I was sure of it. Encircling it, a glint of silver caught the nearby stars. It was a massive, metal ring, looped around the entire planet. From a distance, it appeared similar to Neptune's rings, but then I realized what it was. I hurtled towards the Space Ring, somehow gaining speed if that were even possible. I closed my eyes, preparing for impact.

The tingling returned, and my eyes snapped open. I couldn't believe it; I was back in the lab. I quickly checked that all my body parts were still intact. I glanced at the window, and beyond my own excited reflection was the planet. Doubt started creeping in as I watched the clouds migrate through its atmosphere. *Is it really a dream?*

Looking around, I spotted some people in white lab coats at the other end. They didn't even notice my sudden materialization in the lab. I slunk along the back wall and toward the exit. As I stepped into the hallway, my jaw dropped. The glass floors beneath my bare feet and the LED lights on the walls emitted a cool, ethereal glow. I started running down the hall, the soles of my feet slapping against the floor and pure excitement bubbling inside me.

I reached a door, and just as I got closer, it slid open on its own. I stumbled to a halt the moment I crossed the threshold. I'd somehow exited a building—not a space station—and was standing on the curb of a *street*. I was instantly engulfed by a bustling crowd. Conversations melded with the sound of the whizzing of robots and the hum of floating cars. Everyone wore dark blue jumpsuits. They reminded me of Papa's work clothes but, upon closer inspection, I could make out some patterns like stars, flowers, and even shiny, metal skeletons.

Holographic coffee cups, flashing contents and temperature, filled hands. The solid cement street was embedded with LED lights, and showcased holographic warnings and crosswalk signs.

I had never been to New York City, but I imagined it was like this—or at least it would be, five hundred years in the future.

A man's voice made me jump. "Last call for the trolley to the Square Hub." A sleek white cart had come to a halt outside the building behind me. It was an elongated, open-air vehicle with just metallic rails on each side. It reminded me of the tourist carts Papa and Auntie Via had taken me and Dusty around NASA in. The people already on board were not clad in the same, dark blue jumpsuit. Instead, they wore extravagant costumes with materials like feathers and suede. They looked a bit like old photos I'd seen of indigenous people, though their attire glimmered with holograms, chrome zippers, and bits of shiny crystal.

Without hesitation, I flung myself into the floating cart. The people appeared to be tourists, based on the way they were craning their necks over the cart's railing. I spotted an empty seat at the back. The driver's voice filled the air, praising the brilliance of the Fleming Space Ring's Laboratory Sector.

I glanced back and saw the towering, metallic structure of the laboratory. Its walls resembled glass but with a particularly transparent quality. *They don't have any reflections,* I realized. The sign atop the highest building proudly displayed the laboratory's name, "Infinity Research Laboratories".

"Now, we'll take a detour to the Square Hub, also known simply as the Hub," the driver continued, his voice falsely jovial. He was definitely a customer service worker. "There, you'll find everything your heart desires—food, clothes, jewelry, gadgets, and so much more. Don't forget to stop by the Crawdelou sweet meat stall! Traditional Aridian food, cooked the traditional Aridian way."

As he finished, someone beside me snorted. I tore my eyes off the impossible city view, and turned to see a blue creature with big eyes and tiny ears, dressed in a dirt-red robe. I gasped, gripping the railing for support. The thing looked back at me, bemused. Now that I finally was looking at my fellow passengers, I realized that the cart did not only contain humans. Other beings I could have never come up with on my own were interspersed with the human tourists. *What kind of dream is this?*

We sped through the streets, my heart racing—Did they even have hearts like mine? And then, out of the corner of my eye, I caught a glimpse of something I *did* recognize. They looked like a person but as my eyes traveled down, I could see it had the body of a horse—a centaur? *Wait, hold on a sec. Did I really just see that?* A few moments of hard blinking confirmed that I was, in fact, looking at a centaur. He wore an elongated robe which covered his human front, then draped over his equine back. It fell to the middle of his raven-black tail. I pulled my focus back to the alien streets flying by. I couldn't think about the existence of centaurs for any longer or I really would lose it.

All the noises around me echoed strangely, like we were in a giant mall. I tried to crane my neck to check if there was a sky, but the roof of the cart blocked my view. The towering buildings loomed overhead, clustered closely together. I wondered if I had been watching too much of the Sci-Fi channel. Neon signs flashed with all sorts of ads for bizarre things like Holo-phones and some sort of sporting event between people in giant robot suits and... I stared harder at the letters. *Witches?* We'd shot past the hologram before I could even begin to process what that meant.

As the tourist cart continued its wild ride, I was confronted by even more alien faces. Something that looked like a minotaur with enormous horns swinging dangerously over the crowd. A giggling girl held aloft by gossamer wings. People who may have passed as human if it weren't for the lurid colors of their skin. Finally, the cart came to a stop. I stepped out, still a bit shell-shocked by the vivid reality my brain had cooked up.

Maybe I should give up on my goal of working for NASA and write a book instead. The Space Ring was something straight out of my wildest dreams. It had all the things I loved—science, space, mysterious laboratories, and advanced tech. I was a whole lot less sure about the fantasy element of this world. I'd never much been one for fairy tales, but I had to admit, it certainly added another layer of complexity to this dream world.

"Watch out, kid," a gruff voice said behind me. I moved to the side of the walkway automatically, an apology on my lips.

"I'm so—" The words died in my throat. The person eyeing me irritably had appeared human, but then I looked down. The legs of his khaki chinos were bent the wrong way. Poking out from the neatly cuffed legs were two cloven hooves. I backed up, thinking back to the depictions of Satan I'd seen.

Now that I was really looking at him, I could see two small horns protruding from his curly, black hair. But the worst part was his eyes. They were amber, just like a goat and, horrifyingly, with rectangular pupils. He looked like every generic, half-goat demon from old depictions of hell. All that was missing was a baby leg sticking out of his mouth.

I quickly ducked out of his way and moved to the side of the thoroughfare. Something between thrill and adrenaline was flooding my whole body. Admittedly, the goat man hadn't looked that threatening in his sensible office attire. I was pretty sure Satan didn't wear button-down shirts.

I began to walk again, finding myself on a side street filled with little stalls. It reminded me of the farmer's market back home. The stall nearest me sold "ethereal jewelry" which sparkled with gold and resembled tree branches. Another sizzled with grilling meats, though I was hesitant to look closer and figure out exactly what kind of meat it was.

This dream exceeded my expectations, to say the least. Dreams pre–Space Ring were fleeting and fuzzy. I had no idea lucid dreaming was so vivid and realistic, though the mythical creatures puzzled me. Shouldn't my subconscious be focusing on things I was interested in? And why were they here in space?

Suddenly, an eerie clang reverberated behind me, snapping me from my thoughts. It was coming from a narrow alleyway between two slate gray buildings. The air back there seemed darker. Heavier.

It wasn't lit up by the thousands of holograms that engulfed every other street I'd seen so far. I walked cautiously toward the looming tunnel just ahead.

I hesitated. A stench came from the leaking pipelines that dripped from the grimy walls. Rusted sheet metal merged into a sleek metallic walkway, like a maintenance tunnel, with sparse lights that reminded me of the lab's.

These lights were dimmer and curving along the length of the tunnel. Each strike of my bare foot against the cold metal was amplified, leaving me cringing. I was very certain that I shouldn't be here, and also that I should have put shoes on before going to sleep. After a few minutes, the trail came to an abrupt end. I was standing before a massive, metal door. It looked black in the low light, mismatched with the enameled gray surfaces I'd just passed through.

There were strange carvings all around the edges of the door. They reminded me of symbols from a fantasy movie. Curiosity got the better of me and I reached out. As my hands touched its surface, a freezing shiver lanced through me. A low rumble tingled my palms, giving a hint as to just how thick this door was. *Is this some kind of nuclear fallout shelter?*

Just then, a vicious snarl ripped through the metal of the door, sending a shockwave of vibrations through my hands. I leaped away with a yelp.

Nope.

I sprinted out of that tunnel as fast as I could. Within seconds, I was back in the middle of the street, heart hammering and tears of horror welling in my eyes. *Are all lucid dreams like this?*

All the wonder and joy I'd felt evaporated the moment I touched that door. Even though I was mostly sure I couldn't be injured by a dream, I just wanted to go back home. I pinched the skin of my forearm between my nails. That always worked in movies. Other than hurting myself, nothing happened. *How do I wake up?!*

"Rictor?" a familiar voice called out. I almost didn't recognize her. Miss Delphini stood a few feet away from me, not in her lab gear, but wearing regular clothes. I felt immediately more at ease. Here was an adult who could help me. She would know what to do. Miss Delphini lowered her armfuls of shopping bags to the ground and leaned down to place her hands on my shoulders.

"Rictor... Where have you been?"

Before I knew it, I was bawling into her shoulder like a two-year-old. "I want to go home!" I wailed. I was too afraid to even bother feeling embarrassed.

Her arms wrapped tightly around me. "You're safe now. You're alright," she murmured soothingly.

~ ~ ~

"Wait, I thought they were mean?" Brunner raises an eyebrow. "Your Space Ring parents." His voice brings us all crashing back to the present day.

"No," Emierr corrects him. "I said they were strict. They were still nice to him, or Ricky wouldn't have stayed."

"So, they just kind of adopted you?" Brunner asks skeptically.

"It didn't just happen like that," I say. Emierr's description of them as *nice* twisted the mental knife deeper. If only he knew. I suppose he would know soon enough. "That day, she took me all around the Space Ring," I try to keep my voice even as I continue. "And it was way bigger than I expected. We spent hours exploring, and she even got me some of those sick jumpsuits so I could blend in better." Thinking of my Space Ring adventures was a far less painful topic. "But the food. That was the best part. That first day at the market, I ate so much that I barfed on the way home." I laughed at the memory. "I finally learned the name of the planet, too. Ethra."

~ ~ ~

"Miss Delphini, how many different kinds of creatures *are* there in the Space Ring?" I spoke through two cheekfuls of the best lunch I'd ever eaten.

Miss Delphini dabbed her mouth thoughtfully with a napkin. "I believe every species from the terra is represented here. So, around one hundred and thirty-seven, I believe."

"Wow." Space Ring folks referred to Ethra's surface as "the terra" which felt so much cooler to say.

We'd stopped at the Crawdelou sweet meat stand I'd heard about on the tour cart. I had no idea what I was getting myself into, but the tour guide had said to try it, so I found it. Crawdelou sweet meat turned out to be actual meat, grilled on hot bits of broken pottery. Once cooked, the meat was slathered in some kind of sweet sauce and plonked into a sort of bread roll. Honestly, they sort of reminded me of sloppy joes, but way, way tastier.

My stomach growled audibly the whole way to our lunch spot, which Miss Delphini called "the SkyWalk."

"What advanced species do you have on Earth?" she asked.

I laughed. "One, humans. We know about centaurs and fairies and stuff, but they're just in stories. They don't exist."

"Hmmm, it seems like it would be difficult for humans to perform all the necessary jobs of a society by themselves," she said, mostly to herself. "Some of the most populous species on Ethra are humans, centaurs, fae, and giants."

"Cool." I cram the last of my mystery meat sandwich into my mouth, savoring its honey-sweet taste and spicy tang. How could I experience flavors and smells that were beyond anything I knew if this was a dream?

"Rictor, I have another question for you."

"Mmmpf?"

"Do you know how Earth was formed?" she asked, diplomatically ignoring my frantic chewing. We were standing by the railings of the SkyWalk, hundreds of feet in the air.

Normally heights scared me, but I was a spaceman now; gravity could kiss my ass. I swallowed eagerly.

"There's this thing called the Big Bang," I began, feeling important. "It created time and space and everything we know. Earth started as hot molten rock, and over time, asteroids hit it, bringing water. That's when life started to emerge. And now, it's what I know as home today." As I concluded my lesson, I realized there was a glob of sauce on my brand-new jumpsuit. *Dang it.*

"That's interesting," Miss Delphine said thoughtfully. "And this is what NASA studies?"

I nodded. "But what about Ethra? It looks so different from my Earth."

"Ethra is a complex world, but luckily, scientists like me are eager to learn all about it." She smiled. "A long, long time ago, an asteroid hit Ethra and wiped-out seventy-five percent of life."

"That happened on Earth, too! It wiped out the dinosaurs, the original rulers of the planet," I interjected excitedly.

"Dinosaurs? We call the former rulers of our planet 'Ealdorweardian,' which means Old Guardians."

"Um, that's way cooler than dinosaurs," I said, my face reddening.

"But there was another asteroid that hit Ethra and caused similar devastation," she continued.

"Oh, that didn't happen on Earth."

"I thought so," she said. "This second asteroid hit when human civilization was still young and growing. But instead of destroying the land masses, it brought them together."

"Pangea!" I exclaimed. "So that's why Ethra looks like that."

"You know about Pangea?"

"Yeah, before Earth looked like it does now, it was a giant land-mass called Pangea. Over time, it broke apart due to the shifting of tectonic plates," I explained, silently thanking my lucky stars that I was not relying on Utah public education for my scientific knowledge.

"You're a very smart young boy, you know that?" Miss Delphini said with an indulgent smile.

"My dad taught me everything," I replied proudly.

"You should bring him with you someday. I'd love to meet him."

My smile faded a bit, and I looked down.

"Anyway," Miss Delphini's tone became more business-like. "The asteroid had some unique properties. It released a kind of radiation that spread all over the world. The surviving humans were affected by this radiation."

"So, you're..." I trailed off, starting to put the pieces together.

"Yes, every single person in Ethra has this radiation flowing through their veins," she said, nodding.

"Is it... dangerous?" I asked apprehensively.

"No, quite the opposite. In fact, how old would I seem on Earth?"

I may be young, but Mama taught me to never answer this question truthfully.

"Twenty-six?" I suggested politely.

"I'm sixty-three years old. My husband is sixty-five years old."

Mama's lessons immediately vanished from my mind.

"Sixty-three? Where's your saggy arms?" I demanded.

She laughed loudly and ruffled my hair. "I'm not that old! Not by Ethran terms anyway."

"It's just like the fountain of youth," I said, awestruck.

"Fountain of youth... Yeah, you can say that," she agreed. "The surviving humans came together and formed a new tribe called the Tellus. Over the years, the radiation gave birth to creatures humanity had never seen before."

"The aliens," I breathe out.

She laughed a bit too hard. "Not aliens—they're leyfolk. But yes, that's essentially how magick came to be," she concluded.

"Wait, there's actual magic here?" Even after everything I'd seen, done, and been through, I had to draw the line at magic. Sure, I'd seen centaurs, fauns, pixies, and even something I thought was a werewolf. But that was just my brain filling in the gaps. It's not like every alien race would be the little gray men from Roswell. My subconscious had to use *something*.

"There's so much you need to learn, Rictor. I'd be happy to teach you, but there's one thing I want from you in return."

"What is it?" The answer didn't actually matter. I'd give her my left pinky here and now if she asked for it.

"You teach me about your world," she said with a smile.

"That's easy!" I grinned back.

She led me back to the area where we first met, but instead of heading to the lab, Miss Delphini took me to a super cool terrarium. It was like a sci-fi greenhouse filled with floating pods that held plants and flowers I'd never seen. There was no way Earth had anything like this. The dome-shaped enclosure hovered above a bright light that shone up from the ground. I wondered what kind of tech it was. Magnetic maybe?

As we stepped inside, a perfume of soil, greenery, and flowers hit my nose. A man greeted us as the door slid shut behind us.

"Hey Dr. Del, how's it going?"

"I brought a visitor for you," Ms. Delphini said. "Rictor, this is one of our head botanists, Albert. Do you remember him at all?"

I squinted at him. Albert wore a lab coat that was a bit too big for him, making him look younger than he already did. I noted that the nametag on his breast pocket said "Terrerium. Was that a typo? He had a birthmark that covered his left eye which looked pretty badass. Two weathered scars marred his right cheek, adding a few years to his boyish face. *He must have seen some action.*

Albert looked around *Ate* Cadence's age. It was weird because usually scientists were all old and serious, but Albert broke that stereotype. Kind of. He had an energy that I really liked. Plus, his messy hair and glasses just added to his whole nerdy scientist look.

"I don't think so..." I said, frowning. "Did I meet him already?

Albert smiled. "You did. But you hit your head pretty hard when I first got you out of Akeurimja. I'm not surprised you can't remember."

After he got me out of... where? Hit my head?

Miss Delphine was watching me closely. "Do you remember anything before we first met in my laboratory?"

I shook my head, bewildered. "I thought I landed in your lab in the beginning. Did I go somewhere else?"

Albert hummed a little. He looked like he was trying to find a way to say something.

"I was flying over a zone bordering Zaltana called Akeurimja Forest. It's a botanical anomaly so I often travel there to collect samples when I'm not researching in Terrene." He shuddered. "Anyway, when I touched down, I saw you wandering around between the trees. That place is bad news. So, I tried to call you over, but I guess I startled you because you backed up real quick, tripped, and banged your head on a rock."

He grimaced. "Sorry about that. You were passed out so I grabbed you and took you back here. If I'd left you... Actually, I'm not going to tell you."

I had so many questions I didn't know where to start.

"I'm going to leave you with Albert for a while so he can teach you more about Ethra." Miss Delphini patted my shoulder and began to leave the Terrerium. I didn't even watch her leave in the wake of my excitement.

"What's so weird about that forest?" I asked Albert. My voice was quavering with giddiness. *Meer would* love *this.*

"Well, it's something we call a shadow forest—"

All of a sudden, I felt my feet leave the ground. I was ripped upward, through the Terrerium, through the Space Ring, and back into the void of space. My scream was silent in the infinite blackness.

Mama shook me awake. "Rictor... Jhoana's here, she's outside waiting for you. Come on, get up."

Completely disoriented, I jumped out of bed and peered out the window. There she was, standing by the sidewalk with her hands clasped tightly against her chest. I knocked on the window to catch her attention. She looked up and a smile spread across my face.

I couldn't wait to tell her about Ethra.

~ ~ ~

"That was when you first told Jho about it?" Brunner asks, raising the bottle of King Car to his lips.

I nod, lubricating my dry throat with a swig from my own. The burst of sweet lemon tea brings me momentarily back to the sunny beaches of Guam. "Damn that's good. And yeah, we visited Ethra together that same day."

Jadis interjects, "Didn't you tell her about Ethra the day before me?"

I shake my head, casting my mind back. "No, I made her promise not to say anything. I just wasn't ready, you know?"

~ ~ ~

"I can't wait for you to come back to school, Ricky. Everyone misses you," Jho said, her voice soft as ever.

"If they missed me, they'd be here, right?" I sat up on the bed, restless and wondering how to approach the subject of my incredible evening adventures. Would she think I was nuts?

"Give them some time, Ricky. You know how much your dad and Auntie Via meant to all of us," she said, casting her eyes down.

My gaze shifted to the desk, where the white hole debris Papa gave me rested. I stood and reached for them, running my fingers over the sharp, jagged edges, and then glanced back at Jho. I carefully selected one and returned the rest to the desktop. *Is this even going to work?*

"Jho," I started, trying to catch her eye.

She met my gaze. Papa's words echoed in my mind, *"Only those you trust."* I took Jho's hand and placed the fragment of rock in her palm. Just like with Papa, the rock began to pulsate with soft, gold light. Jho's mouth formed a little "o" of wonder.

"What is it?"

"It's the last thing my dad gave me. I was supposed to give all of you one that night. It's a space rock. My dad and I were going to examine them together when he came home, but..."

"Thank you." She used her free hand to squeeze mine.

"There's something else, Jho. I think I created a dream world." I just said it, like ripping off a Band-Aid.

"What? What does that mean?" Her forehead wrinkled in confusion. I could tell the concerns for my sanity were already beginning work their way into her mind.

"Just promise me you won't think I'm crazy, okay?"

"I could never think that," she reassured me, though worry filled her deep brown eyes. I wasn't even sure if this idea would pan out. If it wasn't a dream, could I take people with me? If it was a dream, would I just fall asleep like an idiot, and nothing would happen? I took a deep breath. Jho would never mock me, even if all this ended up being some kind of grief-stricken delusion.

But on the off chance that I might be able to share Ethra with my best friends... It was worth a shot. Some part of me knew it wasn't just a made-up world. Ethra had to exist—I needed it to exist.

"Do you want to come with me?" I asked, feeling my stomach clench with anticipation. "I can show you."

"Ricky, I'll follow you anywhere," she said, smiling gently at me. Even if she thought I was nuts, she would always hear me out. I couldn't help but smile back.

"I love you too, Jho." I threw my arms around her once again. We got to our feet, excitement bubbling inside me. "I think I know where you're going to land. I'm not there right now, but just wait until I come get you. But listen, if you see a dark forest, don't go in there. Promise me." I tried hard to impose the seriousness of my warning through the cheek splitting grin stretching across my face. "And if you see crazy-looking creatures, just ignore them."

Jho nodded, her expression solemn and sincere. She wasn't mocking me at all; she might actually have believed what I was saying. I briefed her on the journey to Ethra and on Albert, who could seriously be our *Kuya*. But the rest, I wanted to be a surprise. *God, I hope this works.*

We both lay on opposite sides of the bed, our heads side by side. I guided her to relax her body and take slow, deep breaths like I did last night. Our breathing synchronized.

In a soft voice, I told Jho that when I counted down, we had to say Astralis.

"Three, two, one... Astralis." Jho's voice joined mine and suddenly, that tingling feeling surged through me again. I opened my eyes, and I was once again speeding up into space. I turned my head and there she was, Jhoana, right next to me. Her eyes were round with shock and fear.

"Holy shit! It worked! Jho! It worked!" I exclaimed, tears brimming in my eyes.

"Ricky, I'm scared! I'm gonna puke!" Jho shouted, excitement tinging the fear in her voice. Laughter escaped me as we zoomed through the vastness of the cosmos.

"Jho, look, clusters of galaxies," I yelled, lifting my head and gesturing. This was really happening—I was exploring the universe with one of my best friends. And I could bring the rest of them too. This meant a lot of things moving forward. There were so many groundbreaking implications, but the most important fact was we'd have our own place to be ourselves. No more pain.

I heard Jho scream as we began to approach the void ahead and it occurred to me that we shouldn't be able to hear each other out here. A puzzle for another day. We saw the golden dust and the supermassive black hole, its gravity pulling us towards it. Everything warped around us and we found ourselves in front of Ethra, growing rapidly as we rocketed toward it.

As I expected, we started separating, going in different directions. I closed my eyes, bracing myself just before slamming into the Fleming Space Ring. I gasped for air, eyes flying open. Miss Delphini and Albert stared at me, alarmed.

"Where did you just go?" Albert asked, jaw hanging open.

"I woke up," I answered distractedly. *I have to tell them about Jho*

"What kind of magick is that?" Miss Delphini murmured to Albert.

Before he could respond, Dr. Wolfgang came running towards us. "I heard he's ret—"

"Hi, Dr. Wolfgang," I said hastily. "Miss Delphini, I brought my best friend with me." Anxiety trickled into my voice. Jho must be scared out there, right by those creepy woods, and who knows what was walking around out there.

"There are more of you?" Miss Delphini's eyebrows shot toward her hairline.

"Yeah, she's really nice and all alone right now. Can I go get her? She should be where Albert found me," I plead. "At least, I think so."

"Akeurimja Forest?" Albert said, worry hitching his voice up an octave.

All three of them exchanged glances.

"Please, I want her to meet you guys." I attempted the puppy-dog eyes routine on them. *Do they even have dogs here?*

"Al, can you?" Miss Delphini muttered. He looked nervous but nodded all the same.

"Thank you!" I exclaimed, giving her a quick hug.

"You're... welcome." Miss Delphini seemed unnerved. Maybe I should have asked them before bringing Jho here.

I turned back and saw Dr. Wolfgang looking after me, and I couldn't help myself—I ran back to give him a surprise hug, too. He sort of reminded me of Papa. Albert loaded me into an automated flying car; a taxi by the looks of it. He poked at a map of the station in the center console and the car was off. Through the perfectly transparent windshield, I could see that we were making a beeline for a fleet of white spaceships. As the taxi landed us neatly on the ground, I stared up at the crafts, my mouth agape. The spaceships were shaped like crescent moons with elegant gold accents.

They look like my white hole rocks. Nearby were massive mecha suits, parked in a docking area.

I peppered Albert with questions, flapping my hands like a complete dork at each new technological marvel. Albert boasted that only specific people like him could fly these awesome spaceships. I agreed; he was the coolest scientist out there. We hopped inside one of the crafts. The walls curved gently, creating a sense of spaciousness. The lighting cast a warm glow throughout the cabin.

The interior was adorned with high-tech displays and controls, each panel glowing gently with information about our destination. The seats were plush and comfortable. And then there were the windows. They stretched from floor to ceiling, offering what must be breathtaking views of the cosmos outside.

After a few moments, we got clearance for takeoff from the troopers on the ground. With a whoosh, the ship glided through a force field and we started our descent towards Ethra.

As we approached, I couldn't believe my eyes. It was like a whole new version of Earth if humans hadn't wrecked it. Amidst a fortress of enormous trees, the most colossal of them all stood tall and proud. It emanated the same golden dust as I always saw just before the black hole. I wondered if it was the same radiation that Miss Delphini told me about. The mountain ranges stretched as far as the eye could see, towering over deserts, valleys, and forests. The glaciers at the northernmost point of the planet were even bigger than those in Antarctica, and they glistened with an otherworldly glow.

We slowed to a hover and Albert pointed out where he'd first spotted me. I peered out the massive windows and saw the shadow forest he'd mentioned. The leaves were a deep maroon color and gave me the heebie-jeebies. We slowly sank toward the terra, sticking to the edge of those eerie maroon trees. I noticed that their bark looked black, as if it had been burned. My heart skipped a beat as I spotted Jho peeking out from behind a tree on the normal side of the forest. I waved excitedly, unable to contain my joy.

With a gentle bump, the spaceship touched down on Ethra's surface. As I stepped out of the spaceship, Jho rushed into my arms. She was in shock, trying to explain that she saw some strange animal but couldn't quite figure out what it was. Albert joined us, greeting Jho with a warm smile. I told her that we were going up there, pointing to the sky where the Fleming Space Ring hovered, and she stared up at it with wide-eyed wonder.

We ascended the ramp and re-entered the spaceship. Jho and I peered out of the window, taking in the breathtaking views of this newfound world. Albert was clearly taking us on the scenic route.

Impossible trees surrounded us, stretching into the clouds above. Advanced cities glittered in the distance, gleaming structures blending beautifully into the surrounding landscape. They were nothing like Earth's cities; built on deforestation and mass habitat loss. Albert told us that the colossal tree was named The Ethereal Tree. Seeing it this close was incredible. I didn't even know how to describe what I was feeling. We caught glimpses of the "alien" creatures that I now knew were called leyfolk.

They looked to be going about their day in a sprawling village built into the roots of The Ethereal Tree itself. I caught sight of several more centaurs and Jho jammed her finger in the excitement of trying to point out a unicorn.

As we soared through the skies of Ethra and back up to space, I was wrestling with a series of complicated emotions. I was thrilled by the discovery of this world. What kid wouldn't be? Yet I felt guilty for leaving my real life behind. Like I was leaving Papa behind. But finally, I had found a place where we could leave the hurt behind and experience joy again, like we did before. I was just so tired of hurting.

I reached for Jho's hand and we watched together as our ship re-entered the Fleming Space Ring.

Ricky's Confession

I struggle to hold back tears as my voice chokes up.

"Ricky, what's wrong?" Jadis offers me her drink. My hand accepts it automatically.

I take a shaky breath before finally managing to speak. "That memory of Jho... It's just... really great. I can't believe they're pulling the plug on her."

No one speaks. There's nothing much to say.

Brunner is the first one to break the silence. "Ricky... What happens next...?"

He just called me by my nickname. "I went back to school. For a few weeks, it was just Jho and me during break and lunch time. The others stopped hanging out with us. But you know, we were having too much fun to even notice." I shifted guiltily and fixed my gaze on the wood paneling behind the sofa. "We started mapping out the Fleming Space Ring with the notebook she got me for my birthday. Whatever we remembered, we wrote it down. Eventually, after being in Ethra for a while, my par— Miss Delphini and Dr. Wolfgang asked me if there were more of us. That's when Jho suggested I finally tell you guys."

"Did you ever think they were just trying to get information about Earth from you?" Emierr asks.

"Well... Obviously. They made it clear from the beginning that they wanted me to teach them about Earth. About our science, our cultures, about you guys. But I didn't care if they were using me because genuinely, I think they did start to care. My Ma—" I pause. It's hard to think back on those days, when Ma was little more than a husk. "My Ma started working at the diner with your mom around that time, Meer. She wasn't around much but that gave me more time to spend on the Space Ring. At least in Ethra, I had parents. Or... Something like parents."

The Hutton's faces swim to the forefront of my mind. I can clearly recall the delicate laugh lines that framed Miss Delphini's hazel eyes. Dr. Wolfgang was always perfectly clean-shaven, and his blond hair neatly styled. Those faces were once a source of immense comfort to me. All the research we did together, the dad jokes Miss Delphini and I suffered at the hands of Dr. Wolfgang, or those times when she challenged her husband to the all-you-can-eat Crawdelou, and she would always beat him. I desperately wish that I could say these are happy memories, but they aren't. Not after what they did to me.

"Rictor?" Brunner tugs me back to the present. "You mentioned Jadis was the next one you brought in?"

Jadis shifts uncomfortably in her seat. "Yeah, I was next," she grumbles.

"Yeah, yeah, yeah, she believed you right away," Dustin cuts in, his tone dismissive. Jadis aims a shove at him but she might as well have slapped a brick wall. "How did Meer react?"

"I think Ricky's not the only one with memory problems," Jadis huffs. "You really think I heard all that bullshit and just went along with it?"

"What is it you guys always say?" Dustin feigns thoughtful pondering. "Science before hoes? Research besties forever? RBF; research bitch face—" Jadis's smack lands this time.

I chuckle. "No, man, that was the first time she was skeptical about anything I had to tell her."

~ ~ ~

"Jads, I've been there. Ricky isn't lying," Jho said, sliding her lunch tray to the side and propping her elbows on the table. The little cafeteria was buzzing with middle school drama. A massive cluster of boys were huddled around a table in the corner. They were all muttering and shooting glares at a group of snickering girls on the opposite side. I was so out of the loop these days, I wondered who had dumped who. The resulting din of the lover's spat was great cover for our conversation, though.

"No way," Jads sat up straight, her eyes blazing. "Do you guys hear yourselves? You guys sound crazy."

"Jho, never mind, it's okay." I looked down at my food. Meatloaf again. The turd-colored mash oozed into the other compartments of my metal jailhouse tray. I used my spoon to rescue the steamed peas.

"Ricky..." Jads paused. She didn't seem to know what to say.

I looked up. Behind her head, the gaggle of girls had begun flicking wadded up paper balls at the boys. The kid in the middle—Mark Anderson—flattened out one of the balls and read the note inside. His face turned beet red with fury. Over on the girls' side, Anamari Smith was screeching with laughter. I guess I knew who did the dumping.

"I'm sorry. I don't know how to—" Jads fell silent again. Her shoulders were tense, and she didn't even seem to hear what was going on around us.

"I know." I meant it. If the teachers didn't know how to talk to me, how could I expect a kid to? "It's okay. I miss them both a lot, too."

Jho grabbed both our hands, blanketing them in warmth.

Jads sighed. "It's not just your dad and Auntie Via. I've been missing you guys, too..." Jads stared hard at the crusty, white tabletop between us. "Okay, I'm not saying I believe it, but this dream world... How do we get in? And if we're meeting after school, I'm not ready to be at your house, Ricky, sorry."

I understood. Even *I* wasn't ready to be at my house. I watched a beautifully crafted paper plane soar the length of the cafeteria before striking Anamari directly in the forehead.

"We can use my house. If that makes you more comfortable?" Jho suggested. She gave Jads's hand a squeeze.

"That's okay with me," Jads agreed. Her shoulders had relaxed and she seemed the tiniest bit excited, despite herself. "If it doesn't work, I'm not trying again."

Jho brushed her elbow against mine and nodded. I dug a pale, glinting stone out of my pocket and slid it to Jads. She looked at it and, for a moment, seemed to she recognize it.

"Is that a meteorite?" She reached out and brushed the golden markings with her fingertips. She looked up just in time and missed the golden pulse that emanated from the rock.

"Yeah, it is," I said, surprised. "How did you know?"

"My dad has a similar picture of one. I think it was from when Uncle James went on his space expedition."

My Papa's first and last voyage into space. He'd gone many years before I was born but I still sometimes wondered if I was the reason he never went back up.

"He told me to give it to only those I trust," I murmured.

"Thanks, Ricky, I'll keep it safe." She took the stone in her hand and nearly dropped it when the glow sparked between her fingers. Her jaw dropped and she looked wordlessly at me for answers. I just grinned.

"Now we all have one." Jho pulled hers out and stretched her palm. I added mine to the circle. Just then, I saw Mark sprinting at Anamari with an actual armload of banana peels and made the executive decision to cut our meeting short.

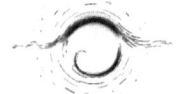

Fear pumped through my veins and my heart felt like a freight train. Each slam of my foot against the forest floor sent agony wrenching through my muscles. I risked a look over my shoulder. It was still chasing me. The beast was the size of an elk with needle-like teeth and unnaturally long front legs. Arms? Its head was covered in thin white fur, but its body and neck were a scabby, mottled brown. Its claws send clods of mud and decaying leaves flying in its wake.

"Jadis!" I screamed.

My feet betrayed me, and I stumbled hard, crashing onto the ground. Pain shot through my shoulder as I scrambled back to my feet on pure adrenaline. The creature reared tall on its hind legs, snarling and salivating. But just as it lunged towards me, Jho's voice echoed from the right, her words like a battle cry.

"Over here, ugly!" she shouted. The monstrous creature whipped its head in her direction, lips pulled back from the long, thin teeth. I realized that the protrusions I'd thought were ears were actually ivory-colored horns. Splinters and cracks ran up to their broken tips, ending in deadly shards.

Something whizzed, plunging into its side. The sound that came from it was unlike anything I'd heard. A horrible screech of rending metal, coupled with a cougar scream. I staggered backward, away from the nightmare fuel before me.

To my left, Jads clapped her hands together. A deep light, the color of pomegranates, began to spread across her palms. She began moving her fingers through the air, as if drawing on an imaginary canvas. She pushed her arms open, conjuring three massive, bladed stars from thin air. The shimmering, blood-red weapons soared across the space between her and the beast, striking the creature's leg and narrowly missing its head. With a final, spine-chilling scream, it dropped down to its grotesquely long arms and loped away. I watched, shaking, as it vanished between jet trunks and purplish leaves.

"Bitch," I exhaled, letting myself collapse to the mossy forest floor. Jho rushed to my side, clapping her hands together. Her hands glowed in a soft, light blue. She began to twist her hands like Jads had moments before. It was called weaving; a form of magick. Or at least, that's what the witch in the Square Hub had told us. I was still convinced that this "magick" was just some kind of misunderstood science.

Jho's swift hands followed the patterns of the healing spell she learned in the Square Hub a few days back. She placed her palms gently over my shoulders, middle three fingers intertwined. The glow intensified, transferring healing energy to me. I felt a comforting warmth spreading through my injured shoulder, and the pain began to fade away.

"Thanks, Jho. So glad you befriended the clairvoyant." I smiled and rolled my shoulder experimentally.

"Don't thank me. Jads did all the work." She looked at Jads, who was picking her way through the twisted roots to get to us. "I knew you could do magick," she added, throwing Jads a huge smile. I was beyond grateful that Jho had insisted upon teaching Jads how to weave an offensive spell before we taught her how to Transcend.

"It helps that I watched *Naruto*, I practiced weaving the Jutsu hand signs," Jads admitted with a shaky laugh.

"That explains the shurikens." I grunted as the girls hauled me to my feet.

"I still can't do conjuration magick," Jho complained. "And you did it on your first try."

"Wait," Jads stopped dead. "You taught me a spell that *you didn't even know if I would be able to do?*"

"Well," Jho said with a shrug. "I was pretty sure."

Jads rubbed her temples and sighed. "I guess I can help you figure it out."

Jho smiled at her and Jads winked back. *Am I missing something?*

Jads tilted her head to look at me. "What happened? Why wasn't I in front of the ship like you said I would be?"

"I don't know, but you were near it at least." I winced apologetically.

"I'm just happy we didn't end up monster food." Jho reached down to brush a clump of moss off her knee.

"Okay, we don't tell Al about any of this." I turned to Jho, bracing her shoulders in my hands. "As far as he knows, we went to look for Jads nearby and got a little turned around. That's it. If he tells Miss Delphini and Dr. Wolfgang I almost became demon shit, I will get in so much trouble."

We all stared at each other and broke into a fit of laughter.

"Ethra," Jads said, once the laughter had subsided. She turned on her heel to walk backwards, taking in her surroundings.

The trees around us waved in the brisk evening air, their yellow-green leaves drifting lazily along the air currents. They looked almost like Earth trees until you got close. The leaves were soft and fragile. The stems they sprouted from were delicate in a spider-like way, and the smallest change in the wind set them moving. The way they bobbed in the air was also unlike the trees I knew. They were in perpetual slow motion. I'd even tested it by giving a limb a good, strong whack.

After scolding me soundly for "mistreating the flora," Al said it was because they were connected to the Ethereal Tree. If we visited forests further out, their trees would obey the laws of physics.

Jads, Jho, and I made it back to the spaceship and let Al give Jads the flyover tour he'd treated Jho to. Once we were back in the Space Ring, life amongst the stars was second nature for Jads. She soaked in Ethra's lore and history faster than Jho and me combined. Al started hosting trivia nights to supplement his history lessons and Jads would destroy us every time. When we were out exploring the Space Ring, she'd talk to the locals, interrogating them without shame about their magick, home nations, and family structure. And to think she called us crazy in the beginning.

But even more impressive than her wealth of history and lore knowledge was her magick. Before Jads, I'd been impressed by people who knew two or three schools of magick. Jads? She picked up all five as the weeks went by. She was always sneaking out to have long conversations with the witch at the Hub and coming back with eight new spells every time, like it was nothing.

I knew it was her calling the day I watched her copy the weave signs of a spell she saw on a hologram, perfectly mimicking each movement without even knowing what the spell did. Jho and I were then hit by a giggle spell and spent the next *hour* laughing. Jho and I compared our abs afterwards, convinced we'd developed six packs.

Back at home, Mama was barely around. Even when she was home, she was just in bed, and she hadn't spoken to me in a while. But that was why Ethra was the perfect place. I didn't have to be miserable here.

After I was sure that Jads had settled in, I told the Huttons about Meer. He was easy to convince. Well, Jads helped a lot by threatening him, but the main selling point was Terrene; a nation that reminded me of Earth's Amazon rainforest. I'd never visited myself, but I knew there were more plant species in Terrene than in any other nation on the planet. The crawling vines, floating flowers, and vibrating saplings in the Space Ring's Terrerium were just a drop in the ocean.

I still didn't fully understand how Ethra worked. Was I creating it? Was it possible for people to lucid dream together? When Jads and Jho showed up, the world seemed to become richer and more complex. My working theory was that each of us was contributing to this imagined reality. No way did my brain have the bandwidth to populate an entire planet with flora, fauna, cultures, technology, and whatever else I had yet to discover. I was pretty sure Meer was just the guy I needed to flesh out Terrene.

When I gave him his space rock, out of all the things I told him, he didn't believe that the rock was from outer space. He was convinced that it was battery-powered because it glowed and was touch-sensitive. In the World of Meer™, my Pa could just "make stuff" as a scientist. I mean, he wasn't totally wrong but still pretty close to it.

When the four of us finally gathered at Jho's house to bring Meer into the fold, we had to spend a little extra time Tetris-ing ourselves on Jho's floor. We were running out of real estate. I tried leading us through my usual relaxation routine, but Emierr kept bursting into giggles. It wasn't until Jads got involved that we were successful. She took it upon herself to twist his ear each time he laughed. His ear was scarlet by the time he managed to drift off. As we had risen into the star-studded void of space, I'd looked over at Meer, grinning, before realizing I'd forgotten something.

Meer's fear of heights rivaled my own. I was wracked with guilt the entire trip, watching the mask of horror that had taken over his face.

He got used to it after a few tries and found his own niche in the Space Ring, just like Jho and Jads. Meer was the one who discovered that time didn't tick the same in Ethra. An hour in real-time was two hours in Ethra. We came up with a neat schedule that let us hang out in the dream world and still do our usual stuff back on Earth. We were the definition of living a double life, secret second family and everything. It was pretty easy for me since Mama was never home and when she was, she didn't seem to notice whether I was there or not.

The more we explored the Space Ring, the more Dusty infiltrated my mind. He should've been the first one I spoke to about Ethra. He was the one who had lost just as much as me. I guess I was worried that he would accuse me of trying to replace or forget our parents. It's not that I wanted to, I just didn't want to hurt anymore. I wanted the same for Dusty too. My life had been weird without him.

The others said they had tried talking to him, but he was never up for chilling with anyone. I had to make the move before it was too late to reach him. I finally made the decision to do it after we'd spent an afternoon just outside the Hub. We discovered an obstacle course called Fleming Ghelcarii Warrior where anyone who could complete it would win a giant katana filled with encased *lightning*.

As soon as I laid eyes on the crackling blade, I knew this was the final straw. I couldn't deny Dusty a lightning katana just because I was a wuss. *I'm coming, Dusty.*

The familiar, chipped front door opened, and Dusty's eyes met mine.

"Dusticle."

"Dicktor." He managed a wan smile. "Come in."

I walked in and placed my shoes to the side. It was quiet, just like my house. Just like a tomb.

"Where's Uncle Joshua?"

"He's out. There's pizza if you want."

We sat on the living room rug, pressing our backs against the couch. *SpongeBob* was on and that yellow bastard still hadn't gotten his driver's license. Three episodes ticked by, punctuated only by the chewing of cold pizza. I sighed, trying to find a way to start.

"Just say it, Ricky," Dusty said, his eyes still on the screen.

"Where have you been? You don't hang out with us anymore."

He looked at me and shrugged.

"We all missed you on your birthday, Christmas, and New Year's." I was working very hard to keep my voice light. "I don't think you should be alone, Dust."

"Ricky." He turned to fully face me. "How are you?"

"I'm a lot better now," I said hesitantly. It felt wrong saying it when we both were going through the same thing.

"That's good, I'm happy for you." He looked back at the TV. "My dad's a drunk."

I didn't say anything. That caught me off guard. Mama becoming a workaholic was bad, but not alcoholic bad.

"He said maybe if he had shown more attention to my mom than me, he could've convinced her to quit her job sooner."

"Dusty..."

"I got her killed, right?" His voice cracked.

"Bro, you can't think like that!" I shoved myself away from the couch to face him. Hearing the words come out of his mouth had sent a jolt through my whole body. I was wrong. Dusty wasn't just bad. He was worse than I could have imagined.

"It's true. My dad was helping me a lot with school and now my mom's dead," Dusty's voice gave out and he began crying in earnest.

"That morning, I tried convincing my dad to stay," I yelled, stunning him into silence. "I begged him not to go! He told me he was quitting after one last trip, so I let him go. I replay it in my head over and over again, as if I just tried harder, I could have changed things. But it's not gonna change anything. It's not our fault."

Dusty whimpered.

"It's not our fault, Dust." Tears spilled down my face as I pulled him into a hug. He sobbed into my chest. I had been so lost in my own grief that I didn't realize Dusty was going through it worse than I was. I was so scared he would push me away, but this whole time, he was crying out for help. My fear had pushed me away from him. My fingers scrabbled in my pocket for the jagged rock inside. I jammed it into his quaking hands, and it lit up, filling the dim stillness around us with golden glow.

Dusty gasped. He wiped at his nose with his sleeve. "That's... My mom told me about these. How did you get one?"

"My Pa, he gave it to me that morning. This one is yours." I gave him a shaky smile.

"My mom and your dad studied these until the very end. Thanks, Ricky." He gripped it as if it were a lifeline and hugged me. "You're a good brother."

Brother? That choked me up. "You too, Dusty." The words barely managed to leave my throat. Yes, that's what I felt about him, too. Dusty was the brother I always wanted and now the one I'd always have. "Wanna get out of here?"

We broke our embrace. "Where?" he asked, brushing away the last of the dampness on his cheeks.

"Somewhere to take away all this sad shit." I got up and stuck my hand out to him. "The others are waiting. You just gotta trust me on this one."

"Yeah, I'm done with the sad stuff." He grabbed my hand, pulling himself up, and we walked arm in arm to Jho's place. Uncle Kit gave us a warm welcome, crushing Dustin in an embrace, and waved us to the backyard. I'd been right; Jho's room was officially too small now that Dusty was here.

Everyone leaped up from the browning grass and tackled Dusty to the ground. There was laughing, crying, yelling, and a little bit of punching (Jads). Seeing us all back together hit me right in the feelings. These four right here were everything to me. And now, together, we were all heading to this world that was a gift just for us. No more hurting; just being kids, living out a life of excitement and exploration. Meer started "explaining" things to Dusty in his own unique way which ended with me questioning if I even knew what

Ethra was.

Jho stepped in, literally stood in front of Meer to block him from view, and broke it down. Hearing her and Jads talk about Ethra send swirls of pride and joy through my veins. They knew our world so well that I didn't even need to be a part of the conversation.

Dusty was all in, no questions asked. I couldn't believe I had wasted so much time worrying about his reaction. Once I'd briefed Dusty on the entry and landing procedures, we all decided to set our meteor pieces next to each other, in the middle of our circle. The tingles were extra intense now that we were all here. The shards seemed to know they had been reunited. We stretched out on the grass with our heads forming a ring around the stones and legs creating a five-pointed star. We linked hands, our arms drawing a secondary line in the center of our star. I started leading them through the guided breathing. Dusty, thankfully, was not prone to the giggles. We all eased into the dreamlike state just before sleep.

"Three... two... one... astralis."

~ ~ ~

"I know I remember everything, but having it all laid out again is wild," Emierr says. "Like I'm reliving it."

"Or... You don't have any memory at all, and you're just pretending like you know the whole story," Jadis grumbles.

Emierr rolls his eyes and turns an imaginary crank, raising his middle finger at her.

Brunner ignores them. "Okay, then, what came after that?"

"We all traveled to Ethra," I say, thinking hard. "Since there were five of us and five nations, we decided to split up. Miss Delphini and Dr. Wolfgang suggested we each pick a nation to explore more in depth. Sort of like an anthropological expedition." *Of course, now I know that was never their intention.* "Jho picked Verglas, the ice nation, and Jads chose Arid, the hidden desert nation."

"Arid is also the magick capital. It's where all the witches and wizards come from," Jadis adds, her eyes skimming the notebook in her lap. "Wow, my handwriting was terrible."

"Dusty chose Zaltana, the mountain nation in the skies, and Meer chose Terrene," I finished. "I stayed in the Fleming Space Ring. We took turns writing everything in the notebook."

"So, you all split and started living your own lives?" Brunner asks, brows creased.

"Before the Jho incident, we didn't see each other in Ethra for almost three months," Jadis says, nodding. "We figured that we could learn more about Ethra a whole lot faster with each of us covering one nation. And we still had our regular lives to hang out."

"Yeah…" My voice is joined by Emierr's and Dustin's, each of us hanging our own heavy weight on the word.

"Why did you guys say it like that?" Brunner might have an inkling of what we went through but it was clear that Emierr had skimped on a lot of the details.

"Because Rune, the nightmares." Meer shakes his head and gets up from the couch. His feet wear a trail in the plushy, blue carpet as he paces.

"Splitting up wasn't… It wasn't the best idea," I mutter. "Shit went down."

"I went through hell in those weeks before Jho—before we left for good," Jadis confesses. "I barely slept in real time because I didn't want to go back. And I'd lost control of the Transcending. It happened whenever I fell asleep."

"So, we all just acted like shit wasn't going on? I'm seeing a pattern here." Dustin's joke is half-hearted at best.

I shift from one foot to the other, heart sending adrenaline racing through my veins. I don't want to relive these memories. What happened to me in the Space Ring was something I'd planned to take to my grave. I never even told Jho. But Dustin's wife, Sylvia's words echo through the fear. *They deserve to know everything.*

"I have to tell you guys something," I say. My hands are shaking, so I stuff them into my hoodie pocket. "I never told you what really happened to me in the Space Ring. And I think you deserve to know."

Everyone turns my way, stunned.

"The week you guys left for the other nations was tough for me. All of you became Keepers and got cool powers, and I didn't. I was feeling left out in my own world. Then you guys all became Nobles after a month."

"What are Keepers and Nobles?" Brunner interjects, his eyebrow reaching for his hairline.

"Keepers are people who, um…" I trail off. "Shit, I don't know how to explain it without launching into an hour long lecture"

"They're people who jump in Ethereal Waters." Jadis comes to my rescue. "Ethereal Waters are bodies of water imbued with some form of energy directly from the Tree itself. The chosen few permitted to enter usually come away with powers." She snorts. "Magick exists and people want tree powers instead." She rolls her eyes.

"But aren't powers themselves magick already?" Brunner argues.

Emierr sighs and formulates a thought. It looks painful.

"From what was explained to me, magick is the source that anyone can tap into, but innate powers are abilities that are transferred via the Ethereal Waters. They're different because magick has limitations, but people who have powers, the Keepers, basically can do whatever they want with their ability."

"Oh, that's cool. Keepers, because they're keepers of powers."

"Nobles are people who bond with Crown Beasts," Emierr continues. I'm surprised his train of thought ran this long. "Only one person at a time can bond with them. The Crown Beasts are like guardians of each nation, so if you bond with one, you're like a sort of human guardian."

"Okay, you guys keep saying these words like I understand them. Crown Beast? Guardian? And why the name Noble?" Brunner mouth tightens, suppressing a laugh. I get it. Imagining grown ass adults calling a gaggle of eleven and twelve-year-olds "Nobles" is pretty ridiculous looking back.

I just shrug. "I guess we thought it was so cool we didn't question it."

"Crown Beasts are supposedly shadows who take on the image of the first animal they encounter outside Akeurimja Forest," Dustin offers. "At least that's what I remember from the Brae's history lessons."

At Brunner's blank look, Emierr jumps in, "Shadows are basically an unknown species from the shadow forest between Zaltana and Terrene. I still can't say the name right."

"Akeurimja Forest," Dustin repeats.

"Yeah that. The most we know is that they're black and formless. People who go into the forest don't usually come out. Even Al never went more than a few meters in for his botanical research."

"Before you ask any more questions, Brunner," Jadis cuts in. "There's not much else to know about shadows. All they are, is dangerous. That's what every person said when we tried asking around." The pages of the battered notebook rustle in her hands.

"Okay... Very insightful." Brunner says sarcastically. "Ricky, you can talk again."

"Uh yeah. Where was I?" My mind was a whirlpool of shadows, stars, and Ethran creatures. I haven't accessed this part of my memory in over a decade. I'm starting to think it might have a cobweb or two. "Oh! The Huttons. They were disappointed you guys became Nobles because it meant all of you had duties to your nations. You couldn't keep assisting them with their research anymore, so they only had me, with no powers and not a Noble."

"That's so dumb, you literally gave them so much information about space and geology. I swear, adults are so ungrateful when kids help them out." Jadis scoffs. "You never needed to prove anything, Ricky."

"Yeah..." I cringe. "And yet..."

"What?" Jadis frowns, closing the notebook.

"Well... I had a theory. I wanted to impress the Huttons so I figured I had to do something drastic. Remember that creepy door I found on my second trip to Ethra?"

Scattered murmurs of affirmation fill the basement.

"I knew it had to be hiding something big. And I also knew that, somewhere on the Space Ring, the Fleming Crown Beast was locked up." I wince, sneaking a peek at Jadis. Her forehead is creased and I can see her putting the pieces together. There's a reason I've never told them the full story. I swallow hard and continue. "I went and snapped a picture of the door and sent it to Jads, asking for her help to decipher it. She ended up figuring out it was an incantation. By then, I was almost certain that the Fleming Crown Beast was behind the door."

"If I had known what it was," Jadis growls. "I wouldn't have done it for you." Her eyes pierce right through me.

"Yeah, I know. That's why I lied and said Al thought there was a lost Terrerium in there."

"That's sneaky, Ricky," Dustin says, chuckling. That does nothing to assuage the pang of guilt I feel as I chance another look at Jadis.

"So... I unbound the spell on the entrance. I thought he'd pounce on me the moment I went through but he was locked in a cage." A memory, unbidden, rises to the surface. Penetrating yellow eyes, coarse black hair on a body too large to be any natural animal. Snarls rending its throat through predatory teeth. I shiver at the thought. Younger me was reckless, braver maybe, but I couldn't lie—I was terrified out of my mind. Still, that stupid, stubborn preteen sense of invincibility had pushed me forward. "I had no clue where the key might be," I went on. "He'd been locked in there for almost a hundred years. But what I did have was a stolen kit of maintenance tools."

Emierr laughs. "You picked the lock on a hundred-year-old cage with a rabid monster growling at you inside?"

"I didn't think you had that in you," Brunner says, impressed.

"Yeah, well, anyway." My face is hot. *Am I blushing?* "The Crown Beast's name was Aigerim. He took on a wolf form but..." I hesitate. "You know how none of the Crown Beasts seemed to get the shape quite right?"

"Yeah man," Dustin agrees. "I thought Ade' was an actual tiger 'til I looked him in the eye. Snake eyes. Like his pupils were vertical."

"Maral wasn't even trying to look like a normal elk," Emierr mutters.

"Tana gets a pass," I concede to Jadis. "Who the hell knows what a normal phoenix looks like."

"They probably have less than eight toes on each foot," Jadis says nonchalantly. All four of us gape at her.

"Tana had *eight*—" Dustin starts, thunderstruck.

"Can we let Ricky get back to the topic at hand?" Brunner snaps. His patience must be wearing thin.

"Right, yeah," I try to regain my train of thought. "To make a long story short, I managed to bond with him. I was the first in almost a hundred years, so I figured the Huttons would be impressed."

~ ~ ~

It worked. Now I'm important, too. Aigerim may have been absolutely terrifying and definitely almost ate me, but I understood how he felt about being trapped. I had been, too, since I arrived.

Three weeks had passed since I became the Noble of the Fleming Space Ring. My new status freed me to explore the terra and visit my friends after weeks apart. But before I did any of that, the Huttons asked me if I could help them with something. I felt so proud and even a bit relieved that they needed me again. The Squad could wait just a little longer.

Miss Delphini and Dr. Wolfgang took me to a cold, white room with a plain, steel table and chairs.

They wanted to decode how the Crown Beast bonds worked, and I was the perfect guinea pig. At first, the tests were harmless, just checking my senses and reactions. But as the days went by, they became more intense. And, on some days, outright painful. I told them that shock therapy never worked on Earth. But Dad said maybe they could control how the bond worked through my survival instincts. I agreed, in the name of science. *They won't hurt me, right?*

I hated it. I hated that anger, fear, and pain were my new default settings. But my parents saw the trials as a success and kept pushing the experiments. Day after day, I sat in that chair and allowed them to stick electrodes to my skin. I clenched my jaw and fought the screams as the people I saw as parents sent lightning coursing through my body. How was my pain a success? Wasn't the sound of my suffering enough to make them want to stop? I hadn't seen my friends in a month and they had no idea I was up here being tortured. *Why does nobody care?*

When I was awake, I tried my hardest not to fall asleep. I wanted to tell someone, anyone, what was happening to me. But I also knew that this world was still the escape my friends needed. I couldn't ruin that for them; I had promised fun and happiness for all of us. And it was useless to stop Transcending. That's what Jads started calling it when we went into Ethra. She told us it was a spell that, according to her books, was basically committing suicide. You sent your consciousness to a different plane and never returned.

That's not exactly what we did since we could go between the two worlds, but it was the closest explanation we'd been able to find. These days, when I slept, I just went straight to Ethra. I had stopped saying "Astralis" long ago, not wanting to taint my final memory of my father. And yet, each night, I was back in that lab, strapped to that chair, and unable to do anything about it.

Two months into their twisted experiments on me, Dr. Wolfgang thought they needed to kick things up a notch, even though Miss Delphini warned that the voltage could kill me. He didn't listen. He shocked me harder than ever and through the crackling agony, I kept thinking to myself that death was better than this. *Mama, please wake me up.*

The electricity surged through my veins, the straps digging into my skin as my body convulsed against them. The warmth of their smiles—the comfort they once gave me—was gone, replaced by cold, detached stares.

"No... please..." I gasped, biting down as the pain intensified, every nerve in my body set ablaze.

How could they do this to me?

"Higher—he can take it."

I didn't scream anymore. My body was past that, locked in a desperate fight to endure. I thought I could have parents here. I thought this was an escape from the pain of my decimated family back on Earth. How stupid I must have been.

"Wolfgang, that's too much!" Miss Delphini's voice cut through the haze.

"He can take it!"

It felt as though a million needles were stabbing into me at once. And then, something inside me snapped. "Mama, please!"

A surge of power emanated from my chest, and I let out a scream that shook the room. The machine generating the current shattered.

I could feel Aigerim's power in my chest, fueling my rage and lending me the strength I needed to save myself from this nightmare. The steel table beside me smashed into the glass where the Huttons stood, cowering. I hadn't even touched it. I gathered all my strength and blasted through the door, flinging every person in a white lab coat out of my way. I made a run for it, drums pounding in my chest as I tore in the direction of the docking area.

I knew what I had to do. I managed to skid to a stop outside an escape pod and threw myself inside. My hands shook with terror and adrenaline as I locked in the coordinates for Terrene.

Meer's tribe would protect me, I was sure of it.

After several seconds of an agonizingly slow countdown, the pod dropped into the unknown, hurtling towards the planet below. I would never be able to return to the Space Ring.

I thought they loved me.

JADS

Rictor's confession shatters us. The room falls into silence, with every gaze fixed on him.

What can we possibly say to him? For so long, he kept up this charade, always wearing a smile, as if Ethra were the paradise we all sought. Yet, all the while, he endured the worst of it. He lost his dad, his mom distanced herself from him, and in Ethra, his stand-in parents tormented him like a lab rat. Despite it all, he laughed and smiled alongside us until the bitter end.

How can we ask him to return to Ethra now?

Rictor squeezes his eyes shut, suppressing a surge of tears.

"Why didn't you tell us?" Dustin approaches him the way one might approach an injured rabbit. "You didn't have to go through that on your own."

"It's like Brunner said. I'm the one who brought you all into this. I didn't want to destroy everyone's escape just because I was having a hard time."

"Fuck that," I sit bolt upright. "That's bullshit and deep down, you know it."

"Jadis... He doesn't need that right now," Brunner says, holding an arm out to trap me against the sofa.

"No!" I shove his arm off me and leap to my feet. "Ricky, you're the one who said our pain is your pain, too. It goes both ways and... and you..." My voice hitches. "You lost your dad. He meant everything to you. We're supposed to be the ones who make you feel better, but all this time, you were only thinking about us." I shake my head, angry and ashamed. "We were supposed to be your best friends and we didn't even notice."

"I don't know what to say. I'm sorry," Brunner's voice is filled with genuine remorse. "I'm, uh, I'm just gonna get more drinks." He steps back and disappears up the stairs.

Emierr is the first to reach out and tug Rictor down onto the couch. The four of us are a tangle of arms, tears, and guilt. I press my cheek to Rictor's shoulder, staring unseeingly at the opposite wall. I don't know how long we stayed like that.

"Jads, can you check on Rune?" Emierr asks, his voice spearing the quiet. His arm is curled protectively around Rictor's waist.

"What? You do it. He's *your* best friend," I throw at him.

"Please?"

I shake my head, tugging my arms free. "Dusty, you talk to him."

But when Dustin looks up at me, his eyes are hollow. Just like the night he lost his mom. I didn't pause to think about how triggering this must be for him too. We all have trauma to unpack, but Rictor is the only one of us who's still pretending he's okay.

"Ugh, fine," I say, throwing my hands in the air. "I'll go check up on him, but if I'm not back in five minutes, it's because I'm hiding a body."

"Thanks, Jads." Dustin manages a chuckle.

As I head for the stairs, my phone vibrates in my hand. There are numerous missed calls from an unknown number and a flood of messages. Dread hits my stomach like ice, and morbid curiosity guides me to opening the messages. They contain fragments of a nightmare wholly different from the one I was about to relive downstairs.

It hadn't always been this bad. I'd stupidly found Cam's jealousy endearing and confused his possessiveness with caring. I was like the frog in the metaphorical boiling pot until one day, he snapped my phone in half after reading the name "Alex" in my messages. He didn't even apologize after I told him, sobbing, that Alex was a woman. He screamed that I was an "insolent bitch" and caught a fistful of my hair when I mentioned the Squad, accusing me of wanting to cheat on him with my oldest friends.

The final message stops me cold: "I'm coming for you. When I find you, I'm going to kill you." My heart slams against my chest as memories of that night surge back—the night I realized he had drugged me, the crushing betrayal of discovering I was pregnant, and the desperate decision to leave after the abortion. I can't seem to catch my breath. My lungs are frozen, and I remember exactly how his hands feel on my throat. I block the number and delete the messages. The others don't need to know. I'm too ashamed.

I close my eyes for a moment and will myself to take a deep breath. When I open them, I can feel Rictor's eyes on me. I don't want to meet his penetrating gaze. I continue up the stairs, my mind racing. I find Brunner in the kitchen, leaning against the sink. I approach him cautiously. I haven't decided whether to punch him, slap him, or let him go unscathed.

"Hey... You alright?" The words sound so wrong coming from my lips.

He glances back. "Shit... How the hell are you guys okay?"

"Who said we were?" I scoff. *As if any of us could be okay.*

"I fuckin'... All those years... I made your lives hell when you already..." He lets out a shaky breath. "Ricky really felt it? The pain?"

I nod. *Am I actually feeling sorry for this guy?* "I don't even know how to explain it. The dreams, Ethra... It felt as real as Earth. It's not like we were playing VR." I look at my right hand, remembering the corded burn scars that once wrapped around it. "Even if it wasn't real, the pain was."

"Did you go through that too?" he asks me.

"No, nothing like Ricky."

"I don't think I want to hear any more," he murmurs.

"Well, too bad. I'm next. And I think you'll want to know how badly Ethra messed me up." I smile at him, trying to lighten the mood. God, *me* trying to make *Brunner Fisher* feel better?

He chuckles and presses his fingers onto his eyes, like he can push the tears back. "No. I never wanted that for any of you. I just—Thanks for checking up on me."

"I was forced to."

"I know."

I return to the basement with Brunner, carrying chilled bottles of water for everyone. We're going to need to stay hydrated if the waterworks keep going at this rate. I take up the position in front of the couch, signaling that it was my turn to share. I take a deep breath and begin.

"I should've said no."

~ ~ ~

I rushed home after school, dropping my backpack and books in my room before heading to Jho's house. I hadn't found anything in the school library or on the internet about dreams making you crazy. They didn't have the symptoms and signs for it, at least. I did feel crazy searching up, "What does it mean when you can visit your friend in a dream?"

Mom walked into the room and greeted me. "How was school today?"

"Fine," I replied absently, my mind occupied with thoughts of the world Ricky and Jho had revealed. I was caught between anxiety, excitement, and suspicion. It sounded too incredible to be true and I didn't want to get my hopes up but... What if they were telling the truth?

"Did anything interesting happen?" Apparently, my mom was still here.

"No," I responded. Another one-word reply.

"So, where are you heading now?"

"I'm going to Jho's house to hang out with her and Ricky," I said, hoping to wriggle free from this conversation.

Mom nodded and smiled. "That's good, *anak*. Be there for Rictor." She hovered around momentarily as if she wanted to say something more, but then she simply touched my shoulder and walked away.

She'd been weird lately. Usually, she bombarded me with questions and advice. But this time, she seemed to hold back. I didn't even know she was capable. I half wondered what it was she wanted to say but not enough to dwell on it.

I said goodbye to Mom and headed out.

Half of me was hoping that nothing would happen. That their insane story would end up being just that; a story. I just wanted all of us to go back to being normal kids again. Of course, the other half of me desperately wanted it to be real.

I glanced across the street at Dusty's house, worry creeping up in my chest. *I hope he's okay.* I passed by Meer's house next. He probably wasn't home, since he joined the football team. I wondered how he was holding up. Crossing the street, I approached Jho's house. I spotted Uncle Kit outside, sitting on the porch patio, gently swaying back and forth in the wooden rocking chair Uncle Joshua made him. He looked lost in his thoughts. *Maybe I should say hello and check on him.*

"Hi, Uncle Kit," I said as I stepped up onto the porch. His vacant expression sharpened into pleasant surprise.

"Hey there, Jadis, it's been a while, hasn't it?"

"You alright, Uncle?" I asked.

He laughed dismissively, brushing off my concern. "I'm fine. You know your uncle, always in his head. Oh, can you tell your dad to stop by here sometime this week?"

I nodded then pressed, "Why are you home so early? Shouldn't you still be at work?"

He sighed softly, and a hint of sorrow tugged at his familiar features. "Well, I won't be going to work for a while. I want to spend more time at home with Jhoana and Gordo."

I thought I knew where this was coming from. "I hope that makes you happy, Uncle."

With a warm smile, he said, "Thank you, Jadis. Now go, they're for you in the back."

Waving goodbye, I went around the house and found my two dreamers lying on the grass, busy doing some weird hand signs.

Curiosity sparked within me as I approached. Or was it nerves?

"Hey," I said.

"Jads, you came!" Jho pushed herself to her feet.

"What were you guys doing?" I asked awkwardly. It felt ridiculous to treat this as a serious matter, but it would be insulting to treat it as fantasy.

Ricky gave me a little smile, and I returned it.

"I was just showing Ricky the spells I learned from the witch," Jho said, grabbing my hand and leading me to the center of the yard.

"Magic, huh?" I tried my hardest to walk that line of polite skepticism.

Jho placed her hand on her chest, explaining, "The witch told me that magick—"

Ricky cut her off, "That's magic with a k."

Jho fought back a smile and continued, "Magick comes from within you. You have to believe in it for it to work."

"Yeah, like the fairies in *Pixie Hollow*," I joked.

Ricky snorted and nodded. "Exactly what I thought."

"Ricky, come next to me and do it with us," Jho instructed. He stood between us, grinning at me.

Jho clapped her hands together, and we mimicked her. "This is the 'astral weapon' spell."

"Weapon? Why were we learning fighting magic?" I furrowed my brows. *Am I taking this seriously?*

"Um, because, well..." Ricky faltered, looking sheepish. "When you first get there, it's like a spawn point. And—"

"I think I saw Bigfoot," Jho interrupted.

"What?" My lips quivered as I tried not to laugh.

"Just to be safe, I think it's a good idea to learn some defensive magick," Ricky concluded, clearly not noticing my stifled giggles. "The landing point is near a dangerous place."

"Are you guys at the landing point?" I asked, deciding to play along with their game.

"Yeah, Al said he would wait for us. The ship should be in front of you when you get there," Ricky said. "So you shouldn't worry too much about something happening."

"Al's really nice," Jho added.

"Okay, teach me the spell," I said. It looked fun, like those *jutsu* motions from *Naruto*, even if I really didn't buy the whole magic thing.

Jho clapped her palms together and interlocked her fingers. She then flexed her fingers into claws and linked her fingertips horizontally before pushing her arms outwards. "You have to think of the weapon you want to conjure. The witch said the more tangible it is in your head, the stronger the spell is. I don't know what 'tangible' means."

"It's something you can touch," Ricky supplied.

"I guess we have to imagine the weapon in detail?" I asked.

"Yes. I'm thinking of a bow and arrow," Jho said with a smile.

"That's cool," I said. I was excited to give it a try, imaginary or not. We practiced the motions several more times. Once she was satisfied with our technique, Jho taught us a healing spell. This game was so advanced—I couldn't believe they came up with all of this. The urge to rush to the library and do some research on dreamworld psychosis tugged at me, but I pushed it aside. I didn't care if it was all made up; I was going to let myself get lost in this magical world with my friends. So, when they sat me down and gave me a crash course on Ethra, I listened.

It seemed simple enough, if I suspended my belief. Magick was real, mythical creatures existed, and the world was shaped like Pangea. Some of it sounded like Ricky's invention but the magick and mythical creatures?

I didn't think he even believed in anything besides science, but it was nice to see him enjoying himself again. We lay down on the grass, our heads forming a triangle, and held hands. Ricky guided us, instructing us how to breathe and calm our minds. I sank deeper into the moment, my breaths slow and steady. I faintly heard Ricky's voice, "In three... two... one..."

"Astralis," we said in unison.

My body dropped. My veins felt like static as an unseen force pulled me upward. It was exactly how I imagined being abducted by aliens would feel. When I opened my eyes, I was passing through a layer of puffy clouds.

Ricky shrieked with excitement, and I turned to see him soaring upward, looking utterly free. Jho glided beside him, her arms outstretched like wings.

"I can't move!" I shouted, panic rising in my chest. *Holy fuck this is really happening.*

"Don't worry, you'll learn how to move around. For now, enjoy the ride!" Ricky called to me, pirouetting in the air. I'd either had a total mental break or... *Could this be real?* Our speed picked up, and Earth became smaller and smaller behind us. My eyes grew wide as we passed right by Jupiter's storm tossed atmosphere. Uncle James and Auntie Via would have never believed this.

"Look!" Ricky pointed in the distance, where there were clusters of galaxies in every color I could imagine, and some in colors I had no name for. The light around us began to stretch. I felt Ricky and Jho grip my upper arms. Before I could ask what was going on, everything was black.

"Guys?" My breath quickened in the darkness.

"We're here," Ricky said. I couldn't see or feel them, but it was comforting to know they were with me. A flicker of golden stars began to twinkle, and the light slowly revealed Jho and Ricky, both in awe of the dust clouds around us. They should have been used to this by now, but I understood—I'd never get over this view either.

"What is it?" I asked, straining my eyes to look sidelong at Ricky.

"I think it's coming from the black hole."

"What?" I looked ahead again and there it was—a supermassive black hole that hadn't been there just seconds before.

"Ricky thinks that the dust comes from Ethra. It's the same stuff that sheds off the Ethereal Tree," Jho said.

Above the maw of the void in front of us, I spotted other black holes drifting across each other. Their flame-hued edges bent and warped around each other's gravity. It was terrifying. I began to feel thin. Like I was becoming less substantial. "I think I'm going to wake up!" I yelled.

"No, fight it!" I saw Ricky grip my hand, but I couldn't feel it. "We're with you." He smiled and wrapped his arm around my waist while Jho placed her arm across my shoulders. Their free hands held mine.

"It's happening!" Jho shouted into my ear. Everything around me began to distend. I screamed, trying hard not to let myself return to the body I'd left in Jho's backyard. And then, we were sucked in. What looked like the moon blinked into existence. We were propelled right over it, heading for a planet just behind it. It had to be Ethra. Its scudding white clouds and blue oceans felt familiar. However, the massive metal structure encircling it was less so. The Space Ring made Ethra look like a crude recreation of Saturn.

"We'll see you soon!" Ricky said as they let go of me. Jho soared beside him, and they braced themselves in a sitting position. The force that had pulled me through time and space became a crushing pressure as I entered the atmosphere. *This is it—I'm going to die!* I screeched and squeezed my eyes shut. But the impact never came. Instead, a tingling sensation ran through my body and I heard the sound of wind rustling through trees. I opened my eyes and gasped. I was alive. I was here, on Ethra.

I gawked at my surroundings as I pushed myself upright. I was in a forest all right, but we didn't have trees like this on Earth. The leaves were all maroon and seemed to give off a faint, plum-red glow. The grass beneath my feet was different, too—softer, like cotton. With every step I took, a neat print was left behind. A group of butterflies migrated around the trees, their wings changing colors as they fluttered by. The world my best friends had created was truly magickal, with a K.

A voice echoed in the distance, *"Jads!"* The ship was supposed to be in front of me, but maybe I'd landed a little off center. I started walking in the direction of the voice. "Ricky? Jho?" There was no response. A jolt of panic shot through my chest as I heard Ricky scream. The sound of pounding feet bounced between the coal black tree trunks. Then, I heard a menacing growl slink between the shadows. My heart dropped. *What the fuck is that?*

"Jho! Ricky!" I shouted again, a sob catching in my throat. All I heard were the snarls echoing in every direction.

Ricky's scream was unmistakable now. I took off in his direction, weaving between charred limbs and velvety leaves. There, up ahead, was Ricky. He was on the ground, clutching his shoulder, his face distorted with pain. But that wasn't what concerned me. Looming over him was a beast out of the deepest, darkest pit of hell.

It held unnaturally long arms out and away from its mottled brown body. The head was disconcertingly white and furry. I could see its thin teeth from here, like an anglerfish. The guttural sounds that echoed around me must have been coming from its twisted throat, and yet the noise continued to bounce from tree to tree.

"Over here, ugly!" Jho bellowed from Ricky's other side. Her arm cocked back, and she hurled a stick at it, as if *that* was going to do anything against this living nightmare. I clapped my hands together, as if on instinct, and they began glowing with a deep red aura. *Woah.* My fingers sprinted through the motions I'd drilled just minutes ago in the safety of Jho's yard.

I thrust my palms out, focusing with all my might on the mental image of a razor-sharp dagger. Out of absolutely nowhere, a dagger seemingly made of pure, pulsing red energy shot out from the space between my hands. It pierced the beast's side, and the horrific, shrill screech of rending metal filled the air. I'd done something, but it clearly wasn't enough. *Is it even bleeding?*

I clapped my hands again. This time, I thought of an enormous shuriken, and I weaved the spell. Three huge shurikens appeared before me. I took a deep breath and launched them towards the beast. The spinning blades danced through the air, one landing deep in its leg while the other two narrowly missed its hairy head. The beast let out one last shriek, the sound of rusted metal scraping rock, before bolting away. I got the sense that it was more annoyed than pained. *Shit, that was close.*

I looked back at Jho, and her hands were on Ricky's shoulder, glowing light blue. *Why's her color different from mine?* I had to keep reminding myself that none of this was real because it sure as hell felt real. We helped Ricky up, and he made us promise not to mention the near-death detour as we headed for the spaceship.

A man who looked like he was a few years older than *Ate* Cadence stood at the ramp of the ship. "I was beginning to worry," he said as we approached.

"Sorry, Al." Ricky smiled apologetically.

"We saw butterflies that changed colors, and got a little turned around following them," I volunteered.

"Ah, the Laelynn butterflies. They're pretty, aren't they?" He had an interesting birthmark over one side of his face and looked every bit the dorky scientist I expected Ricky to grow into.

"You must be Jadis," the man said. His voice was warm and welcoming.

"And you must be Al." I stuck out my hand.

"It's a pleasure." We shook hands. "Alright, let's get out of here. There are Calithoceres around these areas." He scanned the surrounding forest and motioned for us to get in. "They're usually nocturnal but I'd rather not risk it."

Is that what tried to eat us?

"Al, do you have those butterflies at the Terrerium?" Jho asked eagerly. Of course she would want to see them.

"No, but we can get some for you kids," he said, flashing a big smile. He felt more like a cool older brother than a scientist.

"Yes, please." Jho's grin creased her eyes into little lines.

"Alright everyone, buckle up." Al tapped one of the many incomprehensible buttons on the dashboard. A seat belt wrapped itself around my chest. It felt secure but surprisingly unrestrictive. *Damn. Science.*

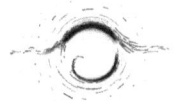

"Kids, time to wake up," Uncle Kit shook me gently.

My eyes blinked open. All at once, the three of us let out a gasp. We had been on our way to the Quantum Plaza's cyberboxing arena, excited to see a mecha suit pilot battle a wizard. Magick versus science—that would've been so awesome.

"Daddy, why did you wake us?" Jho rubbed her eyes, and we all sat up.

"Jadis, your dad's here to pick you up."

"What time is it?" I asked as I got to my feet. I felt a little disoriented, but I guessed rapidly shifting realities could do that to a person.

"Almost eight," Uncle Kit said. "*Anak*, dinner's ready. Your brother won't eat until you do. His stomach's growling so loud the neighbors are gonna call animal control." He chuckled but Jho looked a bit guilty.

"Eight? We slept for four hours?" I turned to Jho and Ricky, alarmed. They just shrugged.

"Come on, Jadis, your mom's going crazy. Say goodbye before your dad gets in trouble." Uncle Kit started to walk back to the house.

"Is my mom here?" Ricky frowned, helping Jho up.

Uncle Kit stopped in his tracks, looking back at Ricky. "You're eating here tonight, okay? I'll drop you home after." He reached back to tousle Ricky's hair and strolled back inside the house.

I saw Ricky's eyes fill with hurt. He knew the truth. I forgot for a moment; pain still lingered here.

"It's okay, Ricky. Eating always makes me feel better," Jho said, putting a comforting arm around him.

I walked up and gave them both a hug. "Thanks, guys. That was... incredible. I'll see you when we sleep?" I added in a whisper before releasing them.

"Yeah," Ricky nodded. "At nine."

"See ya then." I waved goodbye as they entered the house through the sliding back door. When it snicked shut, I made my way through the side yard. Dad stood on the porch, talking to Uncle Kit.

"This is for the best. James and Via told me to watch over the kids, so I'm going to do it," Uncle Kit's voice cracked.

I stopped walking and took a few steps back. Watch over us?

"I don't think they meant quit your job, Kit," Dad said in a hushed voice. "How does Ina feel about it?"

"She's on my side," Uncle Kit retorted.

"We are, too," Dad said grimly.

This is bad. Sounds like they might argue. I should step in.

"It doesn't feel like it, Manny." He paused. "I'm the only one who got letters from them. Why didn't any of you?" Uncle Kit said, his voice turning to a plea.

"Dad?" I interrupted Uncle Kit.

"*Anak*," Dad said, turning his back on Uncle Kit, as if nothing had happened. "You ready to go home?"

"Yeah, I just said goodbye to Ricky and Jho. Sorry again, Uncle, for staying out late on a school night," I tried to play it cool, pretending I hadn't overheard their conversation.

"Don't be sorry, and you're always welcome here any time. It's your mom I'm scared of." Uncle Kit laughed, clearly pretending the same thing.

"*Sige, pare,*" Dad said to Uncle Kit, in Filipino.

"*Sige, pre. Ingat nalang,*" Uncle Kit replied.

"Ready, Dad?"

"Yeah." He nodded and gave Uncle Kit a one-armed hug. As we turned to walk away, Dad placed a hand on my shoulder, pulling me in closer. "Your uncle said you guys were sleeping on the grass?"

"We got tired." I wrapped my right arm around his waist. "Dad, are you okay?"

"Why wouldn't I be?"

"Ricky's not okay. Dusty, too, he doesn't wanna talk to any of us."

"Well, it's hard, *anak*, you know, they just lost a parent. I'm sure Dusty is very sad, but you should always be there for him."

"Do you miss them?" I looked up at him and saw the question took him by surprise.

"I'm always going to miss them." His voice sounded strained. I tightened my hug. "Remember the wish you made on your birthday when you were seven?"

I shook my head.

"You wished out loud, 'I wish my best friends stay my best friends forever.'" He chuckled.

I cringed. Hearing someone else say it sounded so much worse.

"That's how I feel about your aunties and uncles, too." He wiped his eyes. Mom and Dad hadn't said much since the funeral. It was like everyone was walking on eggshells. I didn't like any of this. Why couldn't it go back to the way it was? In Ethra, we were happy. But here? It sucked so bad. Tears welled up as I remembered Ricky's and Dusty's devastated expressions that day, and how everyone's faces stayed broken ever since we said goodbye to Uncle James and Auntie Via.

"Then what can I do, Dad? How can we make everyone happy again?" Dad stopped walking and knelt down, his hands cupping my face.

"Nothing. You do nothing, okay baby girl?" he said, looking into my eyes. Dad used to smile a lot. Now, he looked as though he'd aged a decade in a matter of months. "All you need to be doing is keep being a kid. Play with your best friends like you did today. Be there for each other. As long as all of you are okay, we will be too." He pulled me into his arms and held me tightly.

"Will you really be okay, Dad?"

He wiped the tears off my cheeks. "I'm going to try." He kissed my forehead then said, "Come on." He turned around, offering me his back. "I think I can still do this."

I jumped on his back and giggled. "Dad, you're old already!"

He wrapped his arms around my legs, and I clung to his shoulders. "Let's go home." We crossed the street and saw Mom standing by the window with her arms crossed, shaking her head. "I found her digging the trash cans," Dad joked once we got close enough.

"Dad!" I laughed.

Mom chuckled, shaking her head. "Manuel, you're going to turn our daughter into an animal."

"Mom!"

"*Sabi ko nga*, she got that from you." Dad winked at her.

"You guys are losers." I hopped off Dad's back.

"Did you have fun?" Mom smiled, placing a hand on my cheek.

"I did. A lot. I missed them."

"That's good, *anak*. Let's have dinner." Mom kissed my forehead.

~ ~ ~

"I just remembered that," I exhale. "They always seemed so cold to me." I turn away from the boys, wiping the dampness from my cheeks.

"That's what Rune said," Emierr says. I look back to them, confused. Emierr gestures to Brunner.

"Yeah, I was reading up a lot on mental health stuff at the bookstore. Trauma does a lot to a person, and from what the town, your parents, and..." he hesitates. "What *I* put all of you through, I feel like you all might have developed survivor's guilt. And that comes in many forms."

"Like PTSD," Rictor says, arms crossed, leaning back on the couch. "Which explains the faulty memories. I mean, I think I've always known that."

"Survivor's guilt?" Dustin's eyes dart from Brunner to Rictor.

"Did y'all ever wish it was you instead of Jho?" Brunner asks.

We don't say a thing; everyone's eyes are trained on the ground.

"That's survivor's guilt," Brunner says to Dustin. "And me too," he adds. "If only it had been me, the world would have kept spinning. Nobody would fight for me anyways." Sad, but true in my opinion. I know I wouldn't fight for him, even if Brunner's been fighting for Jhoana for most of his life. It's actually a bit strange to me just how hard he's been fighting. And then it dawns on me.

Oh shit... Brunner was in love with Jho. Or maybe he still is. It all makes sense. I glance at the others, wondering if they've drawn the same connection.

"Rune," Emierr shakes his head. "That's not true."

Of course, he would fight for Brunner.

"Don't ever say that again," Dustin admonishes. "Brunner, you're a dick, but I'd never wish anything like that on you."

Way to make me feel like an uber bitch, guys.

Brunner turns his head away from us. That comment probably meant a lot to him.

Rictor speaks up. "Let's stop blaming each other. It doesn't do Jho any good." There's a beat of silence.

"Keep going, Jads," Emierr finally says.

~ ~ ~

"I knew you were giving me harder stuff!" I smirked. "It's cool, I liked the challenge."

"You've already learned four kinds of magick. Do you know how amazing that is? You Earth kids are intriguing." Madam Evanora reclined back in her velvet chair, one hand twirling an unlit bone pipe. The scarlet silks overhear blocked out the artificial sunlight streaming over her fortune-telling stall.

"Jho said there are five. I wanted to learn them all." I was positively oozing confidence. Possibly a bit of egotism as well.

"Do you want to be a witch?" she asked. Her emerald eyes shone from under her hood in the surrounding candlelight.

"Yes," I said, without a second thought.

"Why?" It was more of a demand than a question.

"I want to protect my friends," I replied. The answer felt as if it had been pulled from my lips.

"Pretty noble of you," she said, reaching out to trace lazy circles on the crystal ball that sat between us.

"Hey!" I shook my head, trying to clear the disorienting sensation. "Did you just use a truth spell on me?"

"You catch on fast, don't you?" She smiled without a hint of apology in her face. "I'm a Diviner. Divination magick is my specialty."

"But how did you cast it? I didn't see you do any weaving." I was more impressed than angry.

"You've got a lot to learn, little duck." She pushed her robe's hood back and let it fall to her shoulders, revealing long, beautifully braided, dark blue hair. Little white flowers were woven in. The black robe changed colors right in front of me, becoming dark purple with gold lines that ended in spirals. "I am a High Priestess." She clapped her hands together and they began to glow in a shade of blue that perfectly matched her hair. I wondered which came first; the hair or the magick. Around each of her intertwined fingers were glittering, astral rings of gold.

My mouth hung open in total amazement. I'd been drinking tea and learning spells from a High Priestess?

"Mastering a kind of magick lets you cast some spells without weaving them." She extended her right hand. "Did you want me to show you?"

What was she going to do? I hoped this wouldn't suddenly wake me. I put my hand on her palm, and her fingers closed lightly around mine. She took a deep breath and her emerald eyes slowly started fading, like the color was being sucked out. I tensed, waiting for something to happen. Madam Evanora gasped, ripping her hands away from mine.

"You!" she snarled. "Little usurper. Stay the hell away from the Academy. You understand, duck? It's *mine*."

I stepped back, shocked and confused.

"You might not even know it yet, but you will soon enough. Let me give you a warning." She leaned in, an unfamiliar sneer on the face I'd seen day in and day out. "I promise that you will not leave the Academy alive."

I felt like she'd punched me in the gut. *What did I do wrong?* Madam Evanora clapped her hands together, weaving a spell I had never seen before. The red silks that framed the roof rippled in the breeze. The sealed portal at the edge of the Hub opened, revealing an empty void, not unlike the black hole we passed through each day. The witch cast one last look of loathing over her shoulder and stepped through. The seal snapped shut behind her and the runes around its edge resumed their glow. *What just happened?*

"Jads!" Meer called me, waving me over. As I moved toward him, I felt the eyes of the whole damn Hub on my back. Embarrassment and hurt roiled in my stomach. Madam Evanora was the only witch who hung around the Space Ring, not because she cared about technology, but just to shake off boredom. She spent her time at the Quantum Plaza, sharing her magick as the resident clairvoyant, mixing a bit of mystique with the tech to keep herself and the crowd entertained. Her skill as a fortune teller was the reason many people came to the Space Ring. *Did I mess things up for everyone?*

"Is it starting?" I asked, trying to act like nothing happened.

"Just about. Where were you?" Meer held two big buckets of popcorn, one in each arm.

I took one bucket from him and tossed a piece of popcorn in my mouth. "I was chatting with the fortune teller," I answered. It tasted like peaches.

He glanced at Madam Evanora's empty booth and returned to his popcorn. "You scared her off, huh?"

"Shut up," I retorted and selected another piece. *Whoa, now it's pineapple.*

"The flavors change with each bite. So cool, right?" Meer's eyes crinkled into a grin.

"Is Dusty here?" I looked around the endless crowd.

"No," he shook his head. "He said he and Uncle Joshua are in the city for his birthday." His eyes darted away for a moment, and I could feel disappointment emanating from him.

"He doesn't want to see us, right?" I stuffed another handful into my mouth, looking for a distraction. Now it was orange-flavored.

"Can't do much about it," he muttered. "C'mon. The match is starting. Ricky's convinced the mecha suit will win this time." Meer smiled, but his eyes still looked sad. Together, we went to find our seats.

I looked up and saw Ethra in the sky. *As above, so below.* "Happy Birthday, Dusty," I mumbled as I grabbed another piece of pop-corn—gross, now it was lemon.

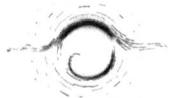

Al led us to where Jho kept her bug specimens. Inside dome casings, those color-changing butterflies co-existed alongside all kinds of strange Ethra insects, each in its mini-biome. The room was filled with countless hovering domes, each one a perfect circle removed from its resident's home ecosystem. Meer and Ricky were totally into the plant life domes. I vaguely overheard Meer rambling about the plant species endemic to Terrene while Ricky ooh-ed and ahh-ed appropriately. I'd bet my whole piggy bank that he wasn't retaining a word of it.

I gave Jho a nudge, pulling her attention from the Laelynn butter-flies. I clapped my hands and weaved a delicate, little spell. Perfect little clones of the captive butterflies appeared before us, fluttering their iridescent wings. Her eyes lit up and she reached out to touch one. Her fingers passed through it, and it dissolved into silvery mist.

"Wow," she whispered. Al ran off for some urgent meeting and left us wandering the space age Eden.

"When can we go back down to Ethra? I wanna see Terrene already," Meer moaned.

"There's a lot of Terrene plants in here," Jho said, gesturing to a cluster of flora-filled pods.

"Yeah... But it's not the same as *really* being out there, you know?"

"I agree," I say suddenly, surprising everyone, including myself, by agreeing with Meer. "We've practically been everywhere we can go here and already mapped out the Space Ring in the book. I want to see Ethra too... Even if we almost died the first time I was there." Meer laughed at that. Easy for him, he hadn't been there. *Maybe I can project a Calithoceres into his bathroom...*

"I know, I'm sorry guys. The Huttons are just a little... You know." Ricky sighed and dropped his gaze to the floor, where a violently blue slug was sliming over the toe of his boot.

"I wish Dusty were here," Jho murmured. A quick look around our little group confirmed that we all felt the same way.

"He really doesn't want to hang out?" Ricky asked, leaning down to deposit the slug back into its habitat pod.

"I tried yesterday after practice, but he said he just wants to go home," Meer said. He jammed his hands into his jumpsuit's pockets.

"I saw him taking some kind of medicine in the nurse's office earlier," I offered, suddenly recalling the brief encounter.

"Is he okay?" Jho asked, worried.

"He might've just had a headache, guys," I pointed out. "But I offered to come over, and he said he has practice today."

"No, we don't," Meer contradicted. "We only have it four days a week."

"I know." I sighed. "He's lying to us now. Things are probably really bad for him."

"Poor Dusty," Jho said softly.

"Could it still be about—"

"It probably is." I interrupted Ricky, shooting him a warning glare.

"It's been three months, hasn't he—" Ricky started but trailed off. Patchy splotches of shame colored his cheeks.

"Ricky, have *you* moved on?" Meer asked pointedly.

"No... But I'm not as sad anymore." Ricky gave us a faint smile. "I'm here with you guys.

An awkward silence followed. We're all together, but not with Dusty... *We're such bad friends.*

"Bitch..." Ricky sighed as if he'd been thinking the same. "He's been all alone. I'm the worst. I should have talked to him already."

"Don't say that," Jho reassured, hugging his arm. "You're a great friend."

"Thanks, Jho," Ricky smiled, resting his head on hers for a moment. There was a flicker of something in Jho's expression, but it was gone before I could place it.

"Why haven't you talked to him anyway?" Meer asked. He folded his arms over his chest.

The question seemed to bother Ricky. He fidgeted with his fingers; a sign he was trying not to bite his nails.

Ricky blew out a breath. "I might sound like a dick, but Dusty just brings me down. Whenever I'm around him, I think about my Pa and it... it hurts."

Ricky's admission surprised me. He was usually an open book when it came to emotions, but I got the sense that he'd been holding things back these days.

"It's alright to feel that way," I said after a moment. "You've been through hell these past few months. But Dusty is our friend. We have to be there for each other." I paused then admitted, "We haven't been doing a good job, though."

"I know," Ricky muttered, rubbing his face. "I'm going to talk to him. Is it too late?"

"Well, we've been here for two hours, which means around an hour has passed on Earth. It's about three o'clock right now," Meer calculated. He noticed all of us gaping at him. "What?"

"When did you figure *that* out, cousin?" Jho asked, impressed. We'd never bothered to actually sit down and work out the whole-time exchange thing. Honestly, I'd kind of assumed it was random.

"I had to use the bathroom last night, so I woke up," he said with a shrug. "It'd been an hour since we arrived here, and I checked the time before we slept—only thirty minutes had passed. I tested it again, and I got the same result. We were here for six hours, but only three passed. So, it's half of the time we spend here."

"I cannot believe none of us figured that out." Ricky fist-bumped him. "Alright, I'll catch you guys later. I'm going to bring our friend back." He smiled, and his body began to shatter then crumbled into fragments. Metallic golden lines raced along his figure, outlining the shape of his body before he disappeared completely. Watching the others Transcend back to Earth would never stop amazing me.

"Later guys, I'm hungry. I'll head home to eat first and then come back." Meer threw up a peace sign and vanished in another cascade of golden splinters.

Jho and I exchanged glances before sharing a giggle.

"I guess it's a girls' day today." I linked an arm through hers. When Al returned, we relayed the message that we needed a ride to the landing point in about an hour. Our final friend was arriving today. Al's face lit up. He happily agreed then shooed us out of the Terrerium. He had a report on his recent expedition to Zaltana to write. Jho and I headed for the SkyWalk to give ourselves something to do while we waited for the boys. Ricky said it was his favorite place to go when he needed to think. It had been a while since Jho and I had time alone like this. The moon shone brightly in the distance, and below, the artificial nation buzzed with activity. Car horns battled in the levitating roads and the pedestrians swarmed along the walkways.

"I was thinking," Jho said, "that when we become masters together, we should have a coven. Just the two of us."

"A two-person coven?" I grinned. "We'd need a catchy name if we're going to stand out."

"I thought of that, too. How about Sororitas Coven?" Her eyes were shining up at me. "It means sisterhood."

All of a sudden, I felt my throat constrict. *Chill out!* I berated myself. "Sororitas Coven sounds perfect, Jho," I finally manage to get out.

Jho's head found its way onto my shoulder. She did this often with Ricky, but never with me. There was something comforting about it, a closeness I'd never experienced with her. I stole a glance at her. The way she looked at Ricky and how she always stood up for him... I knew there was something more between her and Ricky.

"Jho?"

"Yeah?"

"You like Ricky, don't you?"

Her cheeks turned pink. "Yeah."

"I knew it!" I crowed, spinning to face her. Now she was beet-red.

"Jads, please don't tell anyone."

"Our secret. Promise."

JADS'S TRIALS

My eyes open. Somehow, I'm surprised to see myself still standing in Brunner's basement. My face feels like a canvas, painted with streaks of tears. *Sororitas...* This is so messed up. How is it that my only memories of Jhoana are from when we were kids?

"Wait," Rictor leans forward, sitting up straight. "She didn't like me!" And just like that, Ricky is twelve again.

"Seriously, Ricky? Are you that clueless?" Emierr raises his eyebrows.

"She had the fattest crush on you, man." Dustin nudges him.

"You alright, Jadis?" Brunner gets up, ignoring the schoolyard gossip and handing me a packet of tissues from his pocket.

I hesitate for a moment, then take it. "Thanks," I say, genuinely grateful.

I take a few moments to compose myself then redirect my attention to Rictor. "Ricky, you're book smart, but you couldn't even tell that Brook Daniels was obsessed with you throughout middle school."

"Oh yeah, Brook Daniels. I remember her... um, attributes." Dustin pressed his lips together, stifling a laugh.

Emierr snickers, shooting Dustin a wink.

"Brook wasn't into me," Ricky argued "And besides, she wasn't the brightest, guys."

We stare at him, perplexed.

"Seriously!" he protested, clocking out expressions. "She always needed help with science. She kept getting the same answers wrong each time." He shakes his head. I'm almost impressed by his total lack of awareness.

"See? Oblivious." Emierr chuckles.

"Ricky..." I say, placing a hand on each of his shoulders. "She was our valedictorian in high school. She pretended to be clueless so she could hang out with you."

Realization, fourteen years too late, dawns in his eyes. "But Jho's like my sister," he protests, glossing over the revelation.

"Think about it, Ricky," Emierr says, in a tone one might use to explain basic math to a child. "Jho didn't treat any of us the way she treated you."

Brunner settles back onto the couch, looking up at the outdated popcorn ceiling. His jaw is set. Clearly something about this conversation was upsetting him.

"That doesn't mean squat." Rictor wrinkles his nose.

"Rune?" Emierr asks, grinning.

"What?"

"Did Jho ever tell you she had a crush on Ricky?" Dustin asks, elbowing Rictor in the ribs.

"No," Brunner snaps. "We didn't talk about that kind of thing."

"Ouch, seems like you guys weren't as tight as you thought." Dustin reaches over to prod him in the side.

Brunner scoffs. I can see a muscle in his jaw twitching.

"Brunner," I say carefully. He peers up at me, a touch of resentment in his eyes. "You're *still* thinking about Jho that way, aren't you?"

"W—What? No!"

I can see the others connecting the dots.

"*That's* why you treated us like crap." I jam a victorious finger in his direction. "Sure, your best friend fell into a coma, but you also lost the person you were in love with. If we're going to be real with you, you should start being real with us."

"And so what if I am?" Brunner throws back, face going red.

The room's silence is deafening.

"How could I not fall for her?" Brunner's tone has shifted to pleading. "When my grandma passed away, she spent the week with me, and lied to you guys about going to the city with her dad. She was here, making sure I was okay." His voice cracks. "Then Ricky's dad and Dustin's mom passed two weeks later, so she had to divide her time. Every week, she gave me a book to read, something to distract me from my grieving. And it worked."

Well, I'll be damned. I didn't think I'd feel sorry for him a second time.

"You just called me Ricky again." Rictor gives him a faint smile.

"That's why you read so much and work at the bookstore," Emierr says in realization.

Rictor extends his hand to Brunner, who stares at it for a moment. Rictor gives him a reassuring nod, saying, "That's the kind of love we need to fight for Jho. Don't give up." He gives Brunner's hand a squeeze then reclines back on the couch. "What's next, Jads?"

I cross my arms taking a slow breath. "We split up."

~ ~ ~

Ricky took forever, seriously, almost half an hour after the time he told us to meet.

"Ricky James, are you okay?" Jho asked him as we walked to the docking area.

"Yeah, why wouldn't I be?"

Something's up. Jho wouldn't ask that for no reason.

"Dude, you avoided me at school today," Dusty said, shoving Ricky's shoulder. I still couldn't believe Dusty was here, even though it had been nearly a week since he first landed.

"Yeah, did we mess up or something? You ignored me too." Meer raised his brows.

"Sorry, guys. I was just making sure my surprise for today worked." Ricky heaved a dramatic sigh.

"Surprise?" Meer's face lit up but Jho's concern didn't abate.

"I had to do some serious talking, but I pulled it off." Ricky beamed at us.

"Pulled what off?" I asked suspiciously.

Ricky fished out a bunch of thin, clear, rectangular blocks from his pocket and handed one to each of us. I inspected mine, but it was nothing I'd ever seen before.

"What's this?" Meer tossed his up into the air and caught it.

"Double tap on it," Ricky instructed. I narrowed my eyes at him but did as I was told. A hologram depicting a landmass shot out in front of me. I studied it for a moment then looked up at Ricky. "Arid?" Each of us seemed to be holding a different nation of Ethra. *Does this mean...*

Ricky nodded, smile growing wider. "Dust, you're heading to Zaltana. Meer, Terrene's all yours."

Meer closed his eyes and tilted his head back. "Finally!"

"I get to go to Arid?" I interrupted. Excitement thrummed through my veins. The home of Ambrosia Academy.

Ricky glanced at me. "Didn't you wanna master all magick?"

I was rendered speechless. Ricky would have to accept a thumbs up.

"Jho, you're off to Verglas," he continued. "You always talked about wanting to visit Iceland someday, so this is my way of getting you close."

Jho didn't answer at first. "But what about you?"

Ricky's smile faded and he blinked at her a few times, clearly thinking fast.

"Rictor James," Jho said seriously.

Everyone fell silent, looking nervously between Jho and Ricky. Ricky sighed heavily and finally met her gaze.

"You're not coming with us." Jho didn't need to ask.

"Aren't we supposed to do this together?" Meer's ecstatic grin melted away into a frown.

"I'm sort of coming... I'm going to drop you off with Al."

All at once, the others began to protest

"That's not what we—"

"How are we supposed to just *go*—"

"You *promised* that we—"

"Guys," I raised my voice over the yammering. "Let him talk, geez."

Ricky shuffled from side to side, not meeting our eyes. "I told you; this is the best solution I could come up with. The Huttons agreed—"

"Who cares about their rules?" Dusty interrupted angrily. "This is our dream, our creation."

"Yeah, you're right," Ricky agreed. "We're the ones who built this world, but... I want to stay here. There's a lot for me to do, and I can actually make a difference. I'm good with not seeing Ethra right now. I'll visit, of course, and we can go on adventures... But until then, I'm staying here. Where I'm needed." Ricky's tone was final.

I glanced at Jho and saw that she wasn't buying it either.

"Come on, guys..." Ricky pleaded. "You get to see Ethra! This is a cool thing! We'll stay in touch, don't worry." He dug another clear device from his pocket. "These are cell phones, so we can all call each other anytime."

The four of us exchanged looks.

"Ricky, I don't think this is a good plan." I shook my head.

"Just for a week, okay? If you want to come back, I'll come pick you up," Ricky coaxed.

"Will it make you happy, Ricky?" Jho asked, reaching for his hand.

"Yeah." His face was so genuine, I almost believed him.

I took his other hand and gave it a squeeze. Jho twined her free fingers with Dusty's, and I offered my left hand to Meer.

"Are we really doing the hand-holding thing?" Meer said incredulously.

"Just hold on, dummy," I said, rolling my eyes.

"Fine, sheesh." Meer grabbed my hand and then Dusty's.

"Listen, we still have school, so we'll keep each other posted when we're awake," Ricky reassured us. "When we're here, we're gonna explore every corner of our world.

"I wish you could come with us," Jho murmured.

"Yeah, this feels off," Dusty grumbled.

"Don't worry about me." Ricky dropped my hand and pulled us into a group hug. Even Meer returned the embrace. I could tell it wouldn't just be a week apart.

"Oh, you kids."

We jump apart, turning to look at the doorway. Al had his hands on his hips and a warm smile on his face. "Ricky, did you give them the phones?"

Ricky nodded. I thought I saw the barest hint of sadness cross his face.

"Alright, squad. I guess that wraps up the briefing." Al clapped his hand together. "The Dr. Huttons have spoken with all the nation's leaders, and they know you're coming. They're going to host you and look after you while you're there."

"Thanks, Al. For everything." Jho flung her arms around him. The rest of us joined in, one by one, trying to squeeze our gratitude into him.

Al's voice sounded a little weepy. "I'm just a call away, alright? If you need me or Ricky, we're there." He let go and covertly dabbed at his eyes.

"Okay," he sniffed. "Time to get you settled in your new homes."

We glanced at each other. It felt wrong to be separated after reuniting so recently. One by one, with sad smiles on our faces, we turned away from Ricky. Our footfalls carried us in Al's wake, closer to Ethra and further from the Space Ring.

"Jads," Ricky called suddenly.

"Yeah?" I glanced over my shoulder at him.

"You've got the book, right? Write everything down, then pass it on to the next person."

"Got it." I nodded. He gave me a soft smile and began to trail behind us. *Just tell us, Ricky, we won't go if you say it.*

~ ~ ~

"Do we really think Ricky came up with the idea for you guys to survey the nations?" Brunner asks. His voice is skeptical.

"I already told you; it wasn't me. The Huttons convinced me to get you all on board," Rictor reiterates, his head now resting on Dustin's shoulder.

"What was their hidden agenda, then?" Brunner persists.

"Their motive was purely scientific." Rictor straightens up to stretch. "All I remember is that nobody in Ethra dared to touch the Ethereal Tree. Even the scientists were too nervous to study it." He eyes Emierr accusingly.

"True," Emierr agrees. "It's the one rule everyone on the whole planet obeys."

"Yeah, and you broke it," Rictor jabs at Emierr with his finger.

"No, I didn't," Emierr protests, swatting him away.

"So... This is their fault. The Huttons."

Rictor blinks at Brunner, startled. "How do you figure that?"

Brunner leans forward, eyes blazing. "They sent Jho on that journey to survey Verglas. They separated all of you and it landed you guys in the shadow forest. Maybe they didn't intend for their precious *research* to have casualties but—"

"We're getting there," I interject. "You wanted the full story from the beginning. There's no point in throwing blame without seeing all the sides. That's what drove us all apart last time."

"I should have put my foot down against you guys going," Rictor says quietly. "Maybe that would have changed the course of things."

"Yo, what did Jads *just* say," Dustin chides. "You can't blame yourself. We became Nobles out of nowhere. No one could have predicted that and we sure as hell weren't equipped to be diplomats in the sixth grade."

"How long were you guys apart, anyway?" Brunner asks, looking between us.

"According to Meer's calculations," Rictor says slowly, thinking back. "We got Dusty to join us in January and they all set off to the nations about a week later. That was the end of January. Then Jho's accident occurred in March."

"So about a month and a half here, three months in Ethra," Emierr clarifies.

"Three months living apart?" Brunner gapes. I guess Emierr skipped over that detail in the pre-meeting brief. "No wonder you guys were so attached to your host families. Wasn't it hard, not seeing each other?"

"We did, during school at least," I say. "But it was only once or twice a month in Ethra," I pause for a moment, delving into a part of my memory I hadn't seen in over a decade. "Jho was the first to become a Noble. She became a Keeper around the same time and gained her powers, too."

"What about you?" Brunner leans in, looking at me more intensely than I would like.

"I went to Ambrosia Academy."

"The magick school, right?"

I nod. "I wish it had been anything like Hogwarts. I should've listened to Evanora's and stayed away but I couldn't resist. And..." I close my eyes against the onset of hot tears. "Magick was our thing, mine and Jho's. We vowed to master it together. I loved being a witch, but the experience was... trash." It isn't entirely true. I have some fond memories of the school that gave me my magick and sense of purpose. But most of it makes me wish I'd spent those months slowly removing my left eye with a melon baller.

"I remember," Emierr says somberly. "They treated you like shit."

"You used to say you enjoyed it there." Rictor looks even more miserable now. All that time, he'd held onto the idea that he was helping us when the reality was far bleaker.

"I did, in a way. I loved learning the spells and inventing new ways of utilizing magick. But when the rest of the world has magick, the race to be the best gets ruthless." I clench my hands into fists. Reliving what I went through at the Academy is not my idea of a good time. But Rictor bared his soul, so I owe him this much.

The words begin to tumble from my lips. "I've only ever shared this with Jho. But if we're uncovering secrets..." I squeeze my eyes shut one last time, steeling myself for what needs to be done. "The first few weeks weren't terrible. Before starting classes, I had to take a placement test to determine which magick school suited me. I was an anomaly, they said, 'cause I was a fit for all the schools."

"What are the schools?" Brunner interrupts.

"So many questions," I say irritably. "They're in the notebook, Brunner, it's a shame you never learned to read." I see his mouth open to defend himself but don't give him the chance. "The schools are Abjuration—focused on protection; Conjuration—summoning; Evocation—dealing with elemental magick; Divination—mind reading, illusions, and enchantments; and the fifth and last is Mending—centered on healing."

"It says here that Conjuration and Evocation are like sister schools," Brunner points out, gazing into the notebook. I give him a slow clap and he shoots me a withering look.

"I know about this," Rictor chimes in. "Each type of magick has its own chemicals—I mean Mana, and our bodies can usually handle only one type at a time. Like chemical reactions, your cells are trying to figure out which Mana it reacts to the best. Of course," he adds, "There are some exceptions."

I jump back in. This is *my* specialty. "Evocation magick used to be a part of Conjuration before becoming its own school of magick. That's why so many people choose Conjuration; it's a way to branch into mastering two types of magick." I'm actually pretty impressed by my own recollection.

"But you managed to master all of them?" Brunner sounds awestruck and I hate to admit that I'm flattered.

"I was the youngest ever first-year student promoted to fifth year without taking the Test of Hearts." I pretend to dust my right shoulder off, covering my very real pride with humor. Can't let things get too serious. "I attended every class from each school, learned and mastered as much as possible. I even made a friend my own age; Elyssa Cabot." I smile fondly at the memory. "She reminded me a lot of Jho. But we got separated when I moved up, and I never got the chance to talk with her after that."

"They wouldn't let you speak to her anymore?" Brunner asks, perplexed.

"It's not that; it's just that I wouldn't run into her anymore, different classes and that kind of stuff. There was also this massive bitch, Ronan Delvaux. She was fifteen and hated me on sight. Classic mean girl." I can still see her pinched little weasel face in my mind's eye. I shook the memory off and continued. "Rumors started spreading that the Council had me in line as the next Supreme. Last one died without an heir, so it was about time someone took the job."

"*Supreme?* Like *Doctor Strange?*" Dustin asks, laughing.

"Actually, that's a good comparison," Rictor says seriously.

"I thought they called her supreme because it was short for 'super powerful.'" Dustin says, confused.

"Brawn, but no brain." Emierr chortles.

"How did you stop her from bullying you?" Brunner asks me, ignoring the boys. His tone shifts into something uncomfortable, as if the topic of bullying triggered him. *Good.*

"Well, the rumors were true in the end. The Council summoned me, and it was between me and another witch. Madam Evanora."

Emierr gapes at me. "That day at the Space Ring, when she held your hand, she saw you become the Supreme."

"Maybe," I agree. "But I declined the offer. I just wanted to be a master so Jho and I could go on adventures. Oh, and because I was fuckin' eleven years old." I snort. I still can't believe an entire school of witches decided that a literal child should be in charge of anything more complicated than a toaster. "Though, even after I refused, they didn't name Evanora the Supreme. The real nightmare began when the annual Tests of Hearts started. I had to compete if I wanted to get to sixth year." I heave a sigh. "The Test was super exclusive; the only way to participate was by getting a rec-ommendation from a professor. A special case would be if a student showcases—"

Brunner cuts me off, his eyes glued to the notebook. "Showcases potential in exceptional magickal qualities, they may volunteer on their own accord."

"Glad to know you're literate after all," I smirk at him. "But that's not complete. They'll match you with a student of similar magickal ability, and you duel to determine whether you'd continue as a regular student or be placed in a higher year to further your training."

"That sounds like a great bargain to me," Brunner says with a shrug.

"For the winner, sure," I say, "But if you lose, you're expelled and stripped of your magick."

Brunner stares wordlessly at me. "That's... harsh," he finally says.

"I remember now," Dustin says, "You asked us not to come. You got paired with—"

I finish his sentence. "Yeah, with the devil's spawn herself. I didn't want you guys to see what I was turning into. I knew, afterwards, that I didn't want to stay at the Academy."

~ ~ ~

I scanned the benches around the arena. Predictably, most of the students were chanting for Ronan. Amidst the sea of pinch-faced weasel supports, was Elyssa, casting an illusion of a flapping banner with my face emblazoned on the front. The intangible fabric glittered above her fingers and I could see her eyes shining with pride. At least I had one person at my back, even if we hadn't spoken for nearly two months. I'd wanted to call the others but I was too ashamed to show them the truth of my time spent in Arid. I didn't want Ricky to know that I was being whittled away into a vengeful spirit of my former self. It would mean his sacrifice was for nothing.

For now, Elyssa was my only ally. *Just get through this and if you survive, call them after. They'll come and save you.*

Ronan strolled into the arena; her hair tied so tightly that it seemed to be lifting her eyebrows skyward. I felt a stab of pity for her hairline, but, with a flush of heat racing along my cheeks, I scraped my own lank hair into a ponytail. Could I look any less prepared? This was probably the most crucial test of my lifetime and here I was, scraggly hair and shit posture. The crowd shrieked and leaped to their feet as Ronan swept into a dramatic bow in their direction. I caught Elyssa's voice coming from somewhere behind me, a lone beacon of support.

In my periphery, I see Madam Evanora with the much smaller audience of adults, including the teachers and the Council. She grins maliciously at me. The wise fortune teller I had once known was long gone. A cold, ominous feeling crawled up my spine. This crazy old lady did something. Then, without warning, a bell clanged.

It's starting already?! Before I had time to even think, Ronan cocked her arm back and hurled a blazing fireball straight at me. I didn't waste any time. Slamming my hands together, I weaved a shield spell, forming a protective bubble around myself. The fireball exploded in a burst of scalding embers which disappeared on impact.

I shot a look at the Council, and they were just... vacant. Their faces were blank, expressionless. Spells that had the potential to permanently maim or kill weren't allowed, regardless of how cutthroat the competition. This was a school, not a colosseum. But Ronan was not holding back in the slightest. She was going for the kill. Ronan thrust another spell at me. Sharp rocks burst from the ground, twisting in midair and careening straight for me. They slammed into my shield, leaving behind a spider web of cracks. *She's really going to kill me.*

I had to start thinking offensively. I knew the spells to inflict injury. But, hurting another human, another student... I didn't know if I could do it. I supposed there wasn't any other choice.

My hands and fingers whipped through the motions I'd practiced a thousand times. I sucked as much air into my lungs as I could, then held my breath. I brought my arms, quivering, above my head. Ronan let out a gasp as the invisible force seized her, lifting her into the air. She struggled for a moment before she was launched bodily across the arena. She hit the opposite wall with a sickening thud, her head cracking against the concrete. I unleashed my breath and gulped down fresh air. Ronan fell to the floor, landing in a crumpled heap. The force field around me disappeared, and I saw Ronan's arms buckle as she failed to push herself back up.

"You little...!" she cried through gasping breaths.

As she finally staggered upright, I frantically shuffled through my repertoire of spells. Settling on one, I swept my hands out, finger splayed. I took in another lungful of air and shouted, "Puls-enlin!" A powerful wind rushed out from my palms, obeying each motion of my hands. Using it the way an artist wields paint; I formed a spinning circle around my opponent. Into the whirling spiral, I screamed, "Flamorphus!" A fiery stream laced into the wind from my palms, riding the current and transforming into a ring of flames. The burning strands wove a lethal basket around my opponent. The crowd's voices were muddled by the wind and flame. I couldn't hear whether they were thrilled or terrified. Frankly, I didn't give a singular fuck.

From within the flaming tornado, I caught a glimpse of Ronan with her hands raised. Her thin voice barely pierced the roar of my magick. "Aguarenin!"

Torrential rain cascaded down onto me and my flames. I watched them extinguish. The sight didn't make me feel hopeless or afraid. It made me *angry*. Moving my fingers in a complicated series of motions, I weaved illusions of myself all over the arena with a mirage spell. My clones dashed off, working to confuse Ronan as I crouched behind a boulder.

"What did I ever do to you?" I yell. My voice is amplified as my illusions mirror my words.

"Who do you think you are, just waltzing in here and taking all our glory?" she snarled, "The rest of us have worked hard since day one in this academy. You think you can just swoop in and reap the rewards when you're not even one of us!" She drove a second fireball my way and I felt heat soar by, narrowly missing its target. I clapped my hands together, my fingers weaving the shape of the astral projection spell. As I rose out of my body, I scoured the arena, searching for the other witch.

There she was, standing at the corner of the arena. She was

peering over a boulder, clearly looking for me but not intelligent enough to use magick to do it. Her freckled face was twisted with rage. "Only cowards hide," she grumbled under her breath, as if she wasn't hiding herself.

I had to do something she couldn't expect. For all my talent as a witch, I was still a kid and Ronan was years ahead of me. But there was one thing I knew she couldn't do. Something I'd only ever theorized, hunched over the notebook with Jho at my side. I turned back toward my body and urged my astral self to re-enter the physical plane. This was insane. I had no time to regain my bearings as I landed back in my body. I directed my focus on the stone behind Ronan. This terra spell should work.

I lifted my right hand and whispered, "Orcoré-ibaraz." Behind her, the rock pulled itself shakily from the ground, coming to a halt in midair. Taking the bait, Ronan spun around, her arm jutting toward the newly levitating boulder and firing a series of ice shards into it. The ice shattered pathetically against the rock's pitted surface. That was my signal. I weaved the astral projection spell again to create two extra, astral arms, and then clapped all four of my palms together. My physical pair of hands curled and shifted, weaving a telekinesis spell, while my astral hands simultaneously thrust outward to project the astral weapon spell.

I held my breath, clinging to hope that this would work. My real arms snapped out, shoving Ronan telekinetically and making her stumble, but not topple over. She laughed loudly and began weaving a spell I only recognized from reading an ancient tome of outlawed magick. *Surely, she can't be...* I took a quick glance at Madam Evanora. A cruel smile twisted the features I'd once found graceful and elegant. Neither the teachers nor the Council budged. I'd suspected they wanted me gone after I refused to be their Supreme, but I never imagined they'd go as far as letting a teenager murder me to do it.

I caught my breath, steeling myself to retaliate against what I thought was coming, when suddenly, the entire arena went silent. For a moment, I wondered if it was an aspect of the spell. Then I saw innumerable pairs of shocked eyes gazing out at me from the crowd. Ronan's own eyes widened in terror as a ring of astral spears whirled delicately around her. I'd done it. I'd cast two spells at the same time.

Ronan was frozen with fear, her fingers still claw like from her weaving. It was at that moment that I stopped seeing an opponent. In her place stood a scared girl, like me, caught up in a grudge that belonged to neither one of us. I exhaled and released the spell. I refused to play the puppet in the Council's messed up vendetta. Elyssa broke the crowd's silence with a cheer. At her cry, the audience rallied behind me. I supposed they cared less about the winner and more about a good show. But I wasn't looking at them. I was watching Ronan. Fresh rage roiled in her eyes. She stretched her hands, left over right, picking up the complex spell where she had left off.

Before I could react, she screamed a battle cry, sending out the forbidden spell I'd seen in that crumbling old book. Dragon's breath. Huge, emerald flames rushed straight at me. The blistering heat sent panic surging through my entire body. My hands scrambled to weave the shield spell, but they couldn't work fast enough.

The lashing tongues of green fire reached me. I instinctively flung my bare hands over my face. The deadly flames kissed my right hand, singeing my skin. I screamed as the scalding pain shot through my body. Then, just as soon as it had happened, it stopped. A force field had appeared, cloaking me in a veil of protection.

"Enough!" The High Councilor had stepped in, strangling Ronan's spell with a casual wave of his hand.

The crumbling force field resembled molten glass after its encounter with the dragon fire. I collapsed to my knees, clutching my scorched hand. Through tears of pain, I looked out at the crowd around me.

I think I just lost.

Meer

"Jads…" Rictor rises, moving toward her as one might approach a rabid animal.

Jadis remains unmoving, tears streaming down her cheeks. My leg twitches, but I control myself, balling my fists around the fabric of my jeans. Saying the wrong thing is not an option. Seeing Jadis and Rictor in this state, it's making me think. I can't react like this when it's my turn to share. If they realize… they'll figure it out, especially Rictor. He's always irritatingly perceptive of emotional shifts. He'll know I'm lying.

"I gotta pee, be right back," Brunner announces a bit too loudly before disappearing upstairs.

"Jads?" Dustin gets up, reaching for her tentatively. Rictor places his hands on her shoulders. Jadis jerks back, her eyes wild. I'm suddenly transported to that day. I remember Jadis screaming at Jho to wake up, her face a mask of panic much like it is now. I feel my insides writhe.

"I really thought I was going to die that day," Jadis whispers. "But the pain… I'd take death over dragon fire."

Rictor takes her into his arms. "You're alright. It's okay," he murmurs, guiding her to the couch and sitting beside me. Dustin retrieves her water and perches on the arm of the couch.

Is this my punishment? How am I supposed to handle this? My face falls into my hands.

Brunner shuffles awkwardly back into the room, holding a mug. "My mom makes tea whenever I'm upset," he mumbles, handing Jadis the steaming cup.

I glance at Dustin and Rictor, and they exchange looks before turning their gazes to me, nodding in unspoken approval. Brunner is doing it. He's being the kind person he truly is, the one I have been privileged to know throughout these past years.

"The gloves!" Dustin exclaims suddenly, making all of us jump.

Jadis winced. "I always wondered why you started wearing gloves."

"You never healed yourself?" I ask, trying to imagine the knotted burn scar that forever marred her hand. A twinge of shame rolls through me.

"I didn't want to forget what they did to me," she says, staring down at her unharmed hand.

"So... you lost?" Brunner asks, taking up a seat on the floor. "But you didn't lose your magick?"

"Yeah. I vividly remember what happened after the test. They had to take Ronan away because she completely broke down. Then, without my consent, they declared me the Supreme. They announced it right there in front of everyone. People who had been calling me names just a few months ago suddenly wanted to be my friend. The Council said that I lost to technicality, but as the Supreme, I could challenge the ruling."

"They made you choose." Dustin realizes. "Keep your magick and become Supreme or lose magick forever."

"Yeah... They were fucking desperate. They didn't want Evanora to become the Supreme." Jadis's eyes are unfocused, lost in memory.

"I bet Ronan was pissed," Brunner says.

Jadis sighs deeply. "That night, I was at the courtyard trying to video call with Jho when Ronan's worker bees ambushed me. They charmed me and dragged me to the creepiest part of the Academy. There were rumors that they had a Crown Beast stashed deep within the school. They threw me into a room where they supposedly kept it, but Evanora found us. I thought she might at least put a stop to it but instead, she asked them, 'Did anyone else see you?'"

I can see everyone's faces drop as Jadis goes on.

"They slammed the door shut on me and locked it from the outside. They left me for dead."

"How were there not dozens of deaths at that school each year?" Brunner scoffs. "Those kids were vicious."

Jadis shrugged. "Maybe there were. But anyway, I thought of Jho and how she managed to become a Noble. So, I decided to go on a Crown Beast hunt."

"You're a real badass, Jads," Dustin says in admiration.

"Don't get me wrong, I was scared shitless and stuck there for hours. The room led into a cave system. I was wandering the tunnels for ages, and I started to think the legend might just be a myth. But then the temperature started rising, and I saw it—a massive phoenix." I'd seen her phoenix only a handful of times, but I knew I would have needed a new pair of pants were I in Jadis's situation.

Jadis stares unseeingly at the wall, as if she's back in that cave, staring down her death. "But I stood my ground, showing I wasn't going out without a fight. Then its eyes—like mirrors—started to shine with tears, and I let myself cry too, like really crying for the first time. I couldn't believe it when it brushed its head against my shoulder. I had this instinct to throw my arms around her neck, so I did. After that, I felt a surge, like when we Transcend. I knew right then I'd formed a bond with Tana."

"I felt something like that too," Rictor affirms. "Just as I reached out to touch Aigerim, it was like he mirrored my emotions. He placed his head under my hand and that was it—we bonded."

"Same here." Dustin agrees.

"My bonding with Maral was a different experience altogether," I say with a shrug. Flashes of the preternatural elk come to mind, none of them pleasant.

"Wait, what happened to Ronan?" Brunner asks.

Jadis lets out a huge sigh. "I thought that, after Auntie Via and Uncle James, I wouldn't experience death so soon but..."

Rictor gasps. "Bitch... She passed away?"

Jadis's lips tremble. Ronan may have been an enemy, but a death is a death. "After taking on the Noble role," she says, "I committed to being Supreme, too. I wanted a better future for all the wizards and witches. I sent Evanora away to a remote place where she couldn't mess with any of us, and I pardoned Ronan's worker bees. I just wanted a safe haven for me and Jho to learn magick." Her voice cracks.

"You don't have to talk about it anymore, Jads." Rictor places a hand on her lap.

"No, I need to get it out of my system." A muscle in her jaw twitches but she continues, "When I finally had some time alone, I asked about Ronan to see if we could bury the fucking hatchet. But they told me that after solitary, she was called back home—her father was dying from an illness that no magick could heal. I learned that she came to the Academy to find a cure, but she couldn't..." Jadis shakes her head. "She couldn't do any of the higher-level Mending magick. They said as soon as her father took his last breath, she didn't hesitate—she cast the healing spell we all knew, and it worked..."

"Oh no," I whisper.

"The Law..." Dustin sighs.

"Wait, I remember reading about that in the book." Brunner flips through the pages. "The Law of Equivalent Exchange. When something is taken, something of equal value must be given."

"When she brought back her dad..." Rictor's voice trails off.

"She used up her own life force in exchange. She understood that. We all did." Jadis's eyes are glassy, but she doesn't allow the tears to flow.

"I'm not sure I get it," Brunner says slowly, closing the battered notebook.

"The Law," Rictor repeats. "Ronan attempted to resurrect her dad by healing him back to life. The Law demands balance."

"Oh..." Understanding dawns on Brunner's face. "There wasn't enough life force available, so the spell—"

"Took hers instead," I finish Brunner's sentence.

"And it was all for nothing, too. She brought back her dad, but he was still sick. He passed away again a few days later," Jadis says, her voice now muffled from behind a tissue. "Dead at fifteen for nothing."

Just fifteen... Jhoana was barely twelve. Dustin was twelve. Rictor was twelve. I was twelve. And Sólel was nine. We were all just kids, too. How is it possible that we can find it within ourselves to sympathize with Ronan, when our hometown can't do the same for us; even after sixteen years have passed.

"Alright, let's take a break." I exhale. "I skipped breakfast, and I'm a bit hungover. What the hell was in those shots?"

"You ordered them!" Rictor laughed.

"I can call Francisco's for delivery," Brunner suggests, sparing me from answering. "How do you all feel about Mexican food?"

"Mexican sounds good to me," Rictor says.

"I love Francisco's," I agree.

"Jadis, you okay to eat?" Brunner asks.

"Yeah."

I get up and stretch. My muscles protest after such a prolonged period of tension.

Brunner expands his Holo-phone's interface. "I'll just get a bit of everything, sound good?"

There's mumbled agreement alongside my enthusiastic, "Hell yeah."

"Hey, Dylan, it's Rune. Could I make some delivery orders?" Brunner meanders up the stairs and out of sight. I follow him. He's got to be reeling from the overload of information. He's turning aimless circles in the kitchen when I make it to the top.

"I said what I said, Dylan, yes five burritos. Yes, on top of the rest of it. *No*, it's not all for me!"

I walk over to the walls with the picture frames of Jhoana and Brunner. There are photos spanning first to sixth grade. She'd be forty-four in Ethra by now. I've done the math more times than I care to admit. If she's still there, would she even want to come back? I know I wouldn't. Behind me, I hear Brunner hang up. His footsteps move closer to the frames.

"That was a lot, huh?" he says, casting a look over the photos.

"Ten years..." I sigh. "And way more in Ethra."

"You good?"

"*Me?* How are you? Jadis ate you alive," I chuckle.

"She's still scary, man." He shakes his head. "I thought I'd still be a little mad seeing them, but... it's fucking sad, dude."

"Yeah... I saw a little bit of Ricky's and Dusty's life out there and they're exactly who I thought they'd turn out to be. But having them back here, it's like we're picking right back up when we were twelve. We're the same kids but just older, sadder, and more fucked up." My right hand touches the sixth-grade photo. "I don't know if I can do it," I confess.

"Do what?"

I froze for a second. "Share my story," I lie. *Keep your mouth shut, moron.*

"It's gonna work, man. We save Jho and maybe after this, we can all be friends." He glances at me and smiles. I squeeze his arm, trying to be reassuring but ending up more robotic than anything.

Am I really going through with this? Betraying all my friends... Jho, you'd understand, right?

"How's about you bring some drinks down to them," Brunner suggests, easily reading the distraught look on my face. "Dylan should be here any minute. That kid thinks he can outdrive death."

I give him an appreciative nod, accepting the excuse to slip out of the room. The air in the stairway feels lighter. Less throttled with memories. I go to the fridge and make a valiant effort to stack all five water bottles in my arms. I only dropped them once. Maybe twice. I meet Rictor on the stairs on my way back down.

"I needa pee, move bitch." He shoves me to the side with a grin and scrambles up the rest of the stairs.

Dustin and Jadis are still on the couch. Her face looks less puffy than before. I check the stairs one last time before whispering, "Are we gonna tell Ricky about—"

"Do we need to?" Dustin asks, something like a plea in his voice.

"It could help him understand why..." Jadis doesn't finish her thoughts. "Then again... fuck."

"Maybe it's best he doesn't know," Dustin sighs. The sound of footsteps on the stairs cuts our conversation short.

"Food smells amazing," Rictor says, with Brunner trailing him down the steps.

"Let's eat." I throw myself to the floor, stomach practically howling.

"Sorry, let me get chairs," Brunner says.

"Nah, it's cool." I wave him off. "I'm okay on the floor."

"Okay." Brunner says, shrugging. He and Rictor sit on either side of me.

As I inhale my bean burrito, I survey the loose circle of my friends. They look happier with food in their hands. It reminds me of our summer break sleepovers where we traveled from house to house, seemingly on an infinite rotation. I'd taken it for granted then. Pushing my half-eaten burrito aside, I rise from my seat, a decision made.

"Okay, while you guys eat, I'll spill my version, the honest truth of what went down."

"C'mon, Meer, let's just enjoy the food," Rictor mumbles around a mouthful of beef and cheese.

"I wanna hear this," Dustin says, whacking Rictor's arm with the back of his hand.

"Here we go," Jadis mutters.

Cracking my knuckles and exhaling, I say, "Honestly, I thought you guys were on drugs."

~ ~ ~

"Jads, this is the boys' locker room. Get out!" I yelled, standing in my boxers and using my hands to cover myself. I could feel the heat radiating from my cheeks.

"You're hanging out with us after school, and that's a threat," Jads said, jabbing her finger at me.

"I—I can't. I have practice," I said, desperately trying to wriggle out of it. I couldn't handle it. The grief, the emotions... It was too much for me.

She crossed her arms and glared at me. "I talked to the coach. Practice is canceled. He wants you guys to take a break after losing two games in a row."

"He said that? Damn." I winced. "Fine, wait by the bleachers, I'll change."

No point in fighting it any longer I supposed. I couldn't avoid my friends forever and Jads pouncing on me at my most vulnerable sure made it convincing. Jads gave me a sly look, pointing two fingers at her eyes and then at me before heading out of the locker room. I shook my head. Did she have no shame? I hosed myself off in the showers, got dressed, and walked over to where Jads was sitting on the bleachers. I sighed and sat down next to her.

"What are we even doing?" I asked.

She gazed intensely at me, catching me off guard. "How are you?" she asked, a curve in her lips.

"I—I'm cool," I said, playing it off but feeling my heart rate accelerate. "You?"

"I'd be lying if I said I'm good. But I'm good," Jads said with a smirk, and we both chuckled.

"What've you been up to?" I asked, fidgeting with my fingers. It felt wrong to be so awkward with someone who was one of my best friends. I hated how things had become.

Jads stared across the gym, lost in thought, before turning back to me. "Are you over it?"

"Over... what?" I asked, perplexed.

"Uncle James and Auntie Via."

I stared at her, momentarily lost for words. "What do you mean? Of course not." *How could she even ask that?*

"Since you joined the football team, you don't have time for us anymore. It's like you don't want to be friends."

"Dusty joined, too," I protested. "Why aren't you mad at him?"

"That's different and you know it," Jads scoffed.

"How's that different? They were my auntie and uncle, too. I'm grieving like the rest of you."

"Meer, Dusty lost his mom. You still have two parents. You can't actually think it's the same." Jads scowled at me, but the stern look rapidly faded as she continued to gaze at me. "Why *did* you join?"

"Because... Uncle James and Auntie Via were doing what they loved when they died. Maybe I want to figure out what I love, you know?" It wasn't until the words had left my mouth that I had even considered why I had done any of this. Grief didn't have time for why.

"And football is what you love?" Jads tilted her head. Her curiosity seemed genuine, but I couldn't honestly fault her if she was being sarcastic. Even I would have never predicted this.

"Maybe?" I shrugged. "Who knows? That's why I'm doing it. And you didn't answer me. What are you up to?"

"I've been hanging out with Jho and Ricky. He wants you to come after school."

"Why can't he ask me himself?"

"Because he doesn't know how, dummy. You know Ricky. He's an overthinker. He won't admit it and when he's overwhelmed," Jads said. Her eyes flashed with a moment of frustration before she sighed, slumping down to put her elbows in her lap.

"Fine, what about Dusty? Did you ask him?"

Jads's eyes drifted down for a second before returning to mine. "Yeah. He doesn't want to come. It's okay."

"Yeah... He hasn't really spoken to me either. He's in and out of practice, but that's understandable."

"I just hope he snaps out of it soon," she said softly. As if realizing she'd gone a step too close toward "feelings territory," she jumped to her feet. "Okay, I'll see you later then. Jho's house."

"I didn't agree," I called after her.

She huffed a laugh but said nothing. Rather, she pointed her two fingers at her eyes again, then again at me, before walking away. If I ever went missing, I hoped the police would talk to her first.

"I believe it; I think you guys are onto something," I said, struggling to keep my expression serious. The corner of my mouth twitched.

"Meer, just give it a chance," Ricky said softly.

My grin faded and I pursed my lips. He looked so tired. I still didn't know what to say to him; even during the funeral, I'd been at a loss. I'd wanted to give him a hug, but I couldn't. I just watched him walk out of the house. Now that I was seeing him after a month, I felt like shit. No one told us how this works. I was just scared I'd say something stupid.

"Okay," I said finally. The least I could do was hear him out.

He pulled something from his pocket and reached for my hand. My breath caught. Was this going to be some kind of revenge prank? I tensed as Ricky put his fist in mine and deposited a... rock?

As soon as it touched my palm, a golden light began to shimmer around its edges. "What is it?" I whispered. "I've never seen a rock like this." I held it up close to my face. It was small and jagged, made of some sort of white mineral with gold veins tracing oddly circular patterns through it.

"It's a meteorite," Ricky said. His smile looked just a bit stronger.

"We all got one." Jads took hers out of her pocket as proof. Jho and Ricky added theirs to the circle of glowing, outstretched palms. Each shard was similar, like they'd broken from the same source.

"You guys are lying," I laughed. "This can't be from outer space." I might not be as space smart as Ricky, but I was pretty sure meteors were black or gray. Also, the idea that I was holding something extraterrestrial in my hand was a bit too much for me right now.

"My dad gave them to me on my birthday." Ricky's fingers closed around the rock in his hand, knuckles going white.

"Okay, yeah, but he probably bought these online or something," I said dismissively. It had to be a joke or a prank. Maybe some silly make-believe game. But no way was I holding a legit space rock in my hand.

"You do know his dad worked at NASA, right?" Jads said, her voice thick with sarcasm.

"Well, he actually stole these." Ricky admitted with a chuckle.

"*That* I can believe." I snorted. Uncle James may have been some bigwig at NASA, but he sure didn't act it. He used to bring home all sorts of equipment from work to help us with our idiot kid "science experiments." Once, he'd brought home an air velocity meter in order to officially settle who was the superior burper. Of course, he'd also supplied us with an enormous bottle of Fanta each. Fighting back a laugh at the memory, I suspended my disbelief and said, "So... Ethra?"

"Cousin, you can hold my hand the whole time going there," Jho said, patting my arm.

"What? Why would I need to hold your hand?" I raised an eyebrow at her.

"I can't wait to see this," Jads said. I didn't like the look in her eyes. She was far too happy.

"We have to teach you some battle magick first."

"Sorry, you have to teach me some *what*?"

Grinning like a maniac, Jho grabbed my hand and led me to the center of the yard. The other two formed a circle with us and Jho stuck her arms straight out. She clapped her palms together, a crack of sound shooting through the air. Ricky and Jads mimicked the action and looked at me expectantly. I couldn't believe this. I'd spent weeks sidestepping these three because I didn't know how to act around them. Now, here I was, back in Jho's yard, surrounded by my friends, without even a hint of grief in the air. Despite the ridiculousness of the situation, I clapped my hands together.

After a bizarre crash course in *Naruto* magic, we went up to Jho's room. It was a tight fit with all four of us lying down, heads together. Ricky led us in a sort of meditation, and it took all of my willpower not to make fun of him as we did it. I couldn't entirely restrain the giggling, but Jads got me to shut up real fast with a few well-placed tweaks to my ear. Finally, I managed to drift near unconsciousness, just like Ricky described.

"Astralis," I said, my voice joining the other three.

As if on an amusement park ride, I felt gravity press me hard to the ground, right before a force yanked me up, causing sharp prickles to lance through my body. My eyes shot open as I passed through a foggy layer of cloud. I burst through the top, and the sprawl of dreamy cotton below took my breath away. Not for long though. I screamed as I rose higher and higher into the air. When I tried to move, I found I had no control. All my limbs were locked; I couldn't even bend my spine.

In my periphery, I could see Jads. Flying. *What the hell is going on? Wait, I can move my head.* I snapped my head to the left and saw Jho, her arms outstretched like a featherless bird.

"Do you believe us now?" I heard Ricky shout.

"Why can't I move?" I yelled, ignoring his smug expression. I was way too panicked to deal with "I told you so." I turned to look back and, with growing horror, I realized. It was fucking Earth. I was high enough to see the entirety of Earth.

"It's a first-time thing," Jads called. I could hear the smirk in her voice and refused to look.

"You'll get used to it, cousin." Jho soared near enough to reassure me without raising her voice.

I barely heard her as I squeezed my eyes shut, bracing to hit the rapidly approaching moon. When the impact never came, I peeked through my eyelashes, terrified of what I'd see next. Holy shit. I was in space. I was seeing the planets. The asteroid belt Ricky said he liked passing by. It was all here, just like they said it would be.

"Meer, you, okay?" Ricky asked. I didn't get how he could look so casual. We were flying through space, but it felt like endless falling. My stomach churned and I felt acid rising in my throat.

My stomach hardened and I felt this afternoon's cafeteria food depart on a journey of its own. I turned my head just in time to save my friends.

"Space barf!" Ricky shouted. Somewhere behind me, I hear Jads hollering a string of curses, some of which I'd never heard. Her voice got nearer as she planted both hands on my shoulders and hissed into my ear, "You are so lucky that missed me."

Ricky seized one of my arms while Jho braced the other. We were rapidly picking up speed. The lights stretched, exactly like in *Star Wars*, when the Millennium Falcon jumped to light speed. Just when I thought I couldn't produce any more adrenaline, I saw it.

"What the fuck is that!" I screeched. A massive void yawned just ahead, fiery orange light illuminating the edges. Gold dust was rolling out from within the abyss.

"Hold on!" Ricky barked. Six hands tightened across my upper body. I couldn't even make myself shut my eyes this time. The blackness that consumed my vision was more than dark. It was a total absence of all light. Like someone had simply removed a piece of reality.

"I hate you guys!" I cried. Everything around us warped as we slipped through the black hole. There was complete and total silence. For just a moment, I thought I knew what death was like. Then, as soon as we had entered, we fell out the other side. *Really* fell, plummeting toward the surface of a planet that was and wasn't Earth.

Oh shit, this is it. I'm going to splat all over the ground. I closed my eyes one last time and the tingling returned. Ringing exploded in my ears, and I gasped, eyes snapping back open. I didn't know where I was. The buzzing in my veins was not letting up. *Fuck, I can't do this, my heart's going to pop out of my chest!*

"Argh!" I wrenched my body upright.

I was back in Jho's bedroom.

~ ~ ~

"Oh yeah..." Rictor chortles. "You woke up the moment you Transcended in Ethra."

"I can't believe you vomited in space," Brunner says, abandoning his burrito with a look of disgust.

Everyone snickers.

I shake my head, trying not to laugh with them.

"I knew Meer was afraid of heights, but I didn't think he was *that* scared," Dustin says thickly, through a mouthful of rice and beans.

"Oh, I'm still the worst one when it comes to heights. But it was pretty funny seeing the vomit swirl past Jads's face." Rictor snorts.

"Eww, I'm still eating, Ricky!" Jadis smacks Rictor's arm.

"Wait... Didn't you tell me when you first Transcended, you were moving around already?" Dustin arches a brow at me.

"I'm still telling my story, guys," I protest. "Where was I?"

~ ~ ~

I heaved in a lungful of unfamiliar air. I'd managed to get myself back into the headspace to return to Ethra. My chest was still pounding. I could feel I was on the cusp of waking up once again, but Jho's lessons flooded into mind. The silly tai chi we'd done in the backyard was feeling a whole lot less ridiculous. I took a deep, controlled breath and let it hiss back out through my trembling lips. Determination steeled my wobbling legs. I whispered to myself, "I'll show them."

My eyes roved up the trunks of surrounding trees, and there it was—the Space Ring, Ricky's home. A distant slash of silver through the sky, turning ever so slowly beyond the horizon. I watched its placid progress for a few open-mouthed moments before returning my gaze to Ethra's surface—the plants, the flowers, and the insects.

The colors of the flora forcefully reminded me that I was on an alien planet. Fallen leaves in hues of deep purple and warm green fluttered with every step, as if they were not entirely affected by gravity. The trees around me were a gradual blend of sunlit green and maroon. In one direction was an expanse of amber bark and thin, velvet green foliage. Even the grass was soft and swaying under golden rays. In the other direction, a sea of blackened trunks and purple leaves led to a desolate void. It reminded me far too much of my very recent trip through the black hole.

Tendrils of shadow seemed to be slipping between the trees. I shuddered and jogged a few meters to put myself solidly in the green zone. Excitement reclaimed me as I leaned down to inspect the plant life around me. There was a kind of silky grass that swirled beneath my fingers as if underwater. A bush beside it boasted glossy pink leaves and lemon-yellow clusters of berries. I touched every plant I passed, completely failing to consider that any one of these alien plants could be toxic.

As I wandered farther, I stumbled upon something more alarming than over-bright foliage. There was some kind of creature rolling around in a patch of deep orange moss—a creature I had never seen. It crawled over on strangely long, mottled legs, its wide, leaf green eyes fixed on mine. It had a long snout, a bit like a canine, but narrower, with a patch of white fur on its head.

It started licking my hands with a scarlet, forked tongue. Though some part of me, common sense most likely, screamed at me not to, I reached out to pat the thing's soft, fluffy head. It made a strange keening sound and leaned in for more. Two little nubs within the fur looked like the beginnings of horns. *Maybe it's a baby?*

Suddenly, I jumped a foot in the air as twigs snapped behind me. The little beast in front of me warbled a howl. I spun around to find a fully grown monstrosity snarling at me through long, needle-like teeth. It had white fur coating the narrow skull and mottled, brown skin stretching over horrifyingly long legs. I was almost certain that I had just met my new friend's mother.

I was locked into place. What were you supposed to do when confronted by a living hellhound? My frantic mind replayed a clip from a YouTube video on bears, saying to stay calm and not show fear. I had no idea if that advice was applicable here, but what else could I do? I took a deep breath, slowly raised my hand, and extended my palm. I forced myself to look directly into its slitted, green eyes.

The brute came closer, the rumbling in its chest low. I was just beginning to consider if dying here would kill me in real life or just wake me up when, suddenly, it started to rub its enormous, furry head against my hand. The little one joined in, bumping its head against my legs. I was terrified to take a breath. This thing could turn on me in the blink of an eye. It was then that I noticed the presumed mother was limping. Still holding my breath, I slowly leaned down to check her grotesquely long, spindly legs.

There was a gash through one of her hind legs, crusted with ochre blood. I frowned, forgetting my fear and crouching down to look closer. I realized this might be the same beast that attacked Jads when she first got here. This mother didn't look as scary as they said it was. She certainly wasn't attacking me. Good thing I learned the healing spell. I clapped my hand, and they lit up, glowing like a cartoon's rendition of radioactivity. The beast twitched a little at the sharp sound, but didn't move.

I admired my shimmering palms for a moment. *Badass.* I started weaving the spell, stumbling a bit over the complex motions. The spring-green glow centered in my palms, and I held them to the creature's leg. The wound began to knit together, flesh and muscle reaching out to mend the gash. Within a few seconds, all that was left was a tiny scar. The beast stared down at the little mark and gave it an experimental lick, her snakelike tongue slithering between the thin teeth that lined her narrow jaws.

She looked back at me and I prayed that she was intelligent enough to realize I had helped her. She snorted gently through little, horizontal nostrils. Her nose reminded me of a goat's. After a few more anxiety-inducing seconds, the beast turned away from me, grunting at her offspring. I sagged with relief as I watched them amble a little way off, then nestle down for a nap in a pile of velvet-soft, gravity-defying leaves.

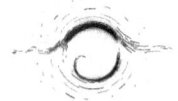

I was perusing through the moonflower biomes in the Terrerium, fascinated by the idea of flowers popping up only in moonlight. How did they photosynthesize? It messed with everything I knew about plants, showing how life could adapt in any circumstances. Just when I was gearing up to stick my finger in it, Al showed up. I whipped my hand back, grinning to hide the guilt. Al was like the big brother I always wanted. He was tall, chill, and quickly became one of my favorite people in Ethra. He took one look at me and said, "You snuck away from them again, huh?"

I heaved a sigh and nodded, eyes on the floor. Al didn't say anything else, just came to look into the moonflower pod next to me. After a few minutes, he said, "They have that sticky pool of sap inside because they get their nutrition from moths."

Completely side-tracked, I gaped at him. "They're carnivorous?!"

Al grinned and unhooked a little container from the nearby wall. "Want to feed it?"

I spent a good five minutes happily sticking the unfortunate moths into the bluish pool of digestive sap at the heart of the moonflower. Once the flower was satiated, Al returned the moth container to the wall and asked me, "Have you seen the Solaris flowers? They're one of my favorites." His eyes sparked as he led me to the floating biome. He gestured at the red ones with pointed petals, explaining, "Those are the Solaris. They only grow around the village of Solaris, hence the name."

"Whoa," I gasped, staring in awe at the flower. It was like fire trapped in petals, glowing with golden veins. Tiny sparks twinkled inside, miniature stars in a cosmic dance.

"They're one of a kind. They store energy within them, and having one can extend your life tenfold, as it carries the energy of life within it."

"Because the sun creates life?" I asked, and Al nodded. I was quiet for a moment, thinking hard. Then, I asked, "What does the Ethereal Tree have to do with magick?"

He gave knowing smile. "You finally asked. Come with me." He headed for the window, and I tagged along behind. There, down below, on Ethra's surface, was the Ethereal Tree. From this angle in space, you could clearly see the gold dust drifting across the entire planet.

"The tree sprouted from an asteroid buried deep in the surface. When it hit the planet, it nearly wiped out civilization," Al began.

"Like the one that wiped out the dinosaurs?" I kept my gaze at the tree, watching the shimmering motes swirl lazily through the atmosphere.

"Yes, the dinosaurs. Ricky told me about them," Al said. It was odd, hearing an adult admit that his entire store of knowledge regarding dinosaurs had come from a twelve-year-old. "But this one happened again several million years later," he went on. "Instead of causing destruction, it brought all of the landmasses together and bestowed upon the world the gift of magick; a power we still don't fully understand."

"So, the tree is the source of all magick?" I asked, a thrill traveled up my stomach. "Do you think if the tree dies, it will destroy magick all together?"

"That's a good theory, but we may never know. The Ethereal Tree's sanctity stands as the most sacred law of the world and tampering with it is strictly forbidden."

"No one's ever tried to get samples?" I found it somewhat ridiculous that the source for all magick was above scientific research. If this was on Earth, people would have died, wars would have been waged over this tree. Ethra was a much better world for sure.

"Many have attempted before," Al answered. "But the Tellus Tribe, the human clan of Terrene, are the guardians of the Tree and they're ready to stop anyone who tries to get their hands on it. Regardless of the cost." He said this as if he had firsthand knowledge of what it was like to be on the receiving end of that protection. Maybe that was where he got the scar on his face. I wasn't about to ask.

The fact that it was forbidden only made me more desperate to know. I could be the one to unlock the secrets of the Ethereal Tree. *Maybe if I befriended the Tellus Tribe then snuck up to the tree in the dead of night—*

Jho came crashing into the room, derailing my thoughts entirely. Her eyes burned with excitement. "Cousin, the match is about to start," she half-shouted at me.

I pumped my arms into the air with whoop, all thoughts of magick and science swept right out of my mind. I started to dash out after Jho but remembered to spin around and call, "Thanks, Al! I'll come back!" Jho and I sprinted for the Quantum Plaza. It was my first time seeing a match between someone in a mecha suit and a witch or wizard wielding magick—an upgraded version of WWE.

As we navigated the lively streets, I asked, "How did you find me, cuz?"

"I knew I'd find you at the Terrerium when we couldn't find you. You would stay there forever if you could." She smiled. Her words held no tone of accusation or hurt, just understanding.

"Don't tell them," I pleaded. The last thing I needed was for my friends to accuse me of liking plants more than them.

"Our secret." She crossed her heart. "I'll say you got hungry, and I found you by the food stalls."

We laughed and, hand in hand, we dove headlong into the crowd, pushing our way through to the arena.

~ ~ ~

"Meer?" Brunner pulls me back.

A single tear drops on my cheek, and I quickly wipe it away. "Sorry... I know I remember everything but it's a different feeling when I'm reliving them. I miss my cousin." My voice breaks.

"Wanna take a breather?" Brunner offers, standing up.

"No, I can do it. It's going to be like this for all of us, right?" I attempt to joke. "I gotta suck it up and see it through." I'm trying to cling to the sweet memory of Jhoana's smile and laughter to avoid breaking down. "Uh—where was I?" I pause, mentally flipping through chapters of my story.

"You were going to the arena with Jho," Brunner reminds me.

"Right, thanks." I glance at him but avoid locking eyes with the other three. "Okay, we talked about the Space Ring already, which leads to Dusty joining us. But we already covered that. We flew around space; that was fun." I start cracking my knuckles mindlessly and pacing from side to side. "Then we got phones and decided to go our separate ways and learn about the nations. The first to go was Jads, and then me, then Jho, and then Dusty. Terrene's where I met my Ethra parents and Sól—" I stop myself. Saying the name out loud feels like a punch to the gut.

"Meer, slow down." Dustin's looking at me with slight concern.

"Sólel... Oh my god!" Rictor's face split into a smile. "I forgot about him. Mini Meer... That's what we used to call him. He followed you everywhere. He was like the Ethra Gordo. He followed Jho everywhere, too."

Oh shit. Why did I bring him up, fuck! My heart is hammering in my chest. *They can't know.*

Meer's Dilemma

A soft poke woke me up. Pop's face filled my blurry vision. "Hey, come on, your mom cooked breakfast. Let's go eat," he said.

I groaned, "It's Saturday, Pops. Can I just sleep in?" I buried my face under the pillow.

"Your mom got a night shift; get up and show her you love her." He grabbed my legs, dragged me out of bed, and carried me into the bathroom. I was laughing by the time he placed me in front of the sink. "Wash your face and head downstairs."

I took my sweet time, letting the cool water wake me. In Ethra, I was all set to visit the village of Moore View, where half-human leyfolk were said to reside. I wanted to ride a centaur so badly but something told me they wouldn't take kindly to the request. Downstairs, Ma and Pops sat at the dining table. As I took my seat, Ma insisted on a hug and a kiss on the cheek first.

"How's working at that 50s diner, Ma?" I asked as I loaded my plate with Longanisa, scrambled eggs, and garlic fried rice. Ricky and I would always switch lunch boxes; he loved his breakfast food. Auntie Luna always cooked him the kind of fancy food I loved for school. It was a symbiotic relationship.

"It's hectic. Who knew a diner is what Farmington needed. I'm just happy they gave me the night shift so I can see your naughty face." She winked.

"What about football, Emierr?" Pops sipped his coffee. "You're still in football, right? There's a game coming up, and you still haven't asked us to come."

"I was going to tell you guys about it," I mumbled.

"A game? Is it anytime soon? You know, I have to request time off early, Emierr," Ma scolds.

"He's been hanging out at your brother's, Rose. He plays with the kids. Cut him some slack."

"Two weeks from now. Friday," I said, not looking at her. I continued to mechanically shovel food into my mouth.

The house phone rings.

"Christopher, can you get that, please?" Ma said absently. I could feel her eyes on me, like an x-ray machine.

Pops' voice floated in from the hallway, "Yes, I will make sure he gets there on time today. Thank you, Coach Danny."

My hands went cold as my dad strode back into the kitchen.

"Our cat's funeral, huh? You should have invited us."

I cringed, casting around, looking for some kind of excuse or explanation that would save me. I was coming up blank.

"And some trouble keeping track of time? Do we need to buy you a watch? Coach tells me you're late a lot these days.

"*Emierr Naputi.*" Ma's eyes blazed.

"Is there anything else you want to tell us?" Pop asked. His tired eyes held no anger, but the knot in my stomach tightened.

I didn't answer.

"*Ai adai*, son," Pops said in Chamorro. "I'll drop him. I need to go buy something at the hardware store anyway."

"I'm sorry," I say quietly. "I just miss my friends,"

They glanced at each other, irritation evaporating from their expressions.

"Come here." Pops said.

I got up, eyes trained on the floor.

"Hey." He placed a hand on my face. "If you don't want to play football anymore, it's okay."

"No, I do. It was just—I'm having so much fun with them. I promise I'll talk more and go to practice on time... Just please don't ground me."

Ma shocked me by shaking her head and laughing, "You're such a naughty boy. But you're doing your best." She hugged me and Pops put his broad arms around both of us.

"We love you, son."

~ ~ ~

"Fuck." I breathe out. "I—I don't know why I brought that up. I've never focused on so many memories before I—"

"It's okay, Meer," Jadis says. "It's nice hearing about Auntie Rose and Uncle Chris."

"You don't understand. The last thing I said to them seven years ago... I said I wished it was them who died instead."

Everyone's jaws drop. Stunned and horrified silence rapidly fills the room. Brunner stares at me like he no longer recognizes who I am.

"I told them about Ethra and how we can save Jho." The words gushed from my mouth, squeezed from my throat by the constriction of tears. "They just dismissed me like everyone in this fucking town, looking at me like I'm just—they don't care about Jho. No one fucking does except for the people in this room... and Gordo." The hot tears break loose, spilling over my face.

"But—" Dustin starts.

"You told them about Ethra?" Rictor interrupts, his eyes locking on mine. For once, I couldn't read them.

"Yeah," I nod. "I couldn't anymore. I couldn't wait for any of you to come home. I just wanted my cousin back..." I bow my head, shame coursing through me. It was only half of the truth. *I do want her back... But I also want to be with my little brother.*

"What did they do when you told them?" Rictor asks. His voice is too calm.

"Nothing," I spit. "That's when I fucking lost it. The one time I wanted them to be parents, they just stood there like they didn't hear me. After I said what I said, I immediately regretted it, but their faces... Ma looked so hurt." Pain crushes my chest and I stand still for a moment, unable to breathe.

"Maybe Dusty can take his turn," Jadis suggests gently.

"Yeah, bro. I'm okay to speak," Dustin says emphatically. "We'll go back to yours after, if you're still feeling up to it."

"No," I shake my head, forcing my lungs to expand. "I'm good. I haven't even talked about how I got my powers. Let me do this, guys, for Jhoana." *Just tell them about the powers, and then you're done.* I take a few more calming breaths and steel myself. "I became the chosen one."

~ ~ ~

It had been a month since we split up but, somehow, the events of an entire year had taken place. Jho had leveled up big time—she wasn't just a warrior, but a Noble, bonded with a water Wyrm named Eyre. Oh, and she fell into a cave pool and became a Keeper. It happens to the best of us sometimes. Once she had climbed, spluttering, out of the water, she realized she could make force fields without the use of magick.

Jads went even higher on the leaderboard and became the Supreme, the big boss of all witches and wizards, which we all thought was insane considering she hadn't even hit her twelfth birthday. She bonded with the phoenix Crown Beast named Tana, making her a Noble, too.

Dusty got a Keeper upgrade that allowed him to use his own body as a human duffle bag. Whatever he wanted to carry around, he just had to press it to his skin and an outline of the item appeared as a tattoo... The Brae called people like him "Inkweavers" which I thought sounded super cool. Although there was something innately wrong with a heavily tattooed sixth grader. Yesterday, he went Noble and teamed up with a white tiger Crown Beast named Ade' with Jho's help.

Today was my turn to join Team Keeper, and Sólel's too. It was the day of our baptism in the Ethereal Lake, where Maral, the great elk Crown Beast, could be found lurking among the trees, waiting to grant us her blessing. As the minutes ticked by, I was starting to become slightly hysterical as nerves and excitement continued to build pressure inside of me. It was becoming a real possibility that I might be able to shit diamonds at this point. I had spent weeks imagining what kind of incredible powers the sacred water would give us.

I'd met Elara, a Keeper in my village with healing powers. All she had to do was touch an injury and weeks of healing would flash before your eyes. Then, there was Nolan, the tracker. When he'd successfully become a keeper, he was given something called selective perception. He explained it to me as being able to choose a sense and pour all your energy into it. The other four senses weakened as their energy was rerouted but that made it all the easier to focus on the fifth. He could track down anyone or anything. Coincidentally, there had been a marked decrease in petty crimes since he'd been baptized.

The baptism was a colossal event in Terrene where all the tribes came together. There was Tellus—the human tribe, Commisceo—the half-human tribe, Sperclen—the fae tribe, Giga—the giant tribe, and the Bundac Tribe. They were harder to categorize as they sort of collected any leyfolk who didn't belong anywhere else. The miscellaneous tribe, if you will. Each year, all five gathered to witness the baptism and place bets on who would be chosen as the new Keepers of innate power. Sólel told me that, way back, anyone could dive into the waters which obviously led to a whole lot of people with superhuman abilities. But then, some wizard had placed an unbreakable curse on the lake after the Great War.

Now, if you wanted a shot at an innate power, you must be pure of heart. That was the deal with the "Keeper" title.

Since I was essentially adopted by the Terrene's High Chief Berkarys and Chieftess Nalani, I was permitted to try my hand at gaining an innate power with their real son—my little brother, Sólel. The festival was incredible. I felt like my Filipino and Chamorro heritage was somehow being showcased here in the blending of different cultures, all celebrating the baptism. There was a mix of dances, colors, and traditions from each tribe. But most importantly, there was a colossal spread of each tribe's food.

All my best friends were rolling in to show support—Jho, Jads, Dusty, and even Ricky was flying down from the Space Ring. We had school to see each other when we were awake, but I'd been missing them like crazy here in Ethra. Ricky was the only one I hadn't laid eyes on since our last visit. I often wondered what kind of cosmic adventures he'd been having out there in space.

My little phone chimed, showing me a photo of my friends by the lake. I sent one back, a shot of my cheeks jammed with some sort of breaded fish wrap. The thrum of excitement was building up within the endless sea of attendees; the parade was about to kick off. Once we got there, Father would open the ceremony, marking our significant rite of passage. A single peal from the massive, lakeside bell rang out, followed by a cacophony of drums. The baptism was beginning.

"You ready, Sól?" I glanced at him, decked out in his traditional ceremony attire. The younger boy had light brown skin and his hair had been carefully twisted into little baby locs. He stood at the level of my chest.

"I'm ready, *Kuya*," he said, his young voice high with enthusiasm. I'd taught him that word. It felt good to hear a bit of home while I was living out my second life.

"Me too." I grabbed his hand, and we began marching. Leading the procession was a series of musicians and dancers. The musicians played flutes whittled from bone, beat drums of stretched scalehide, and blew hollowed Calithoceres horns. The dancers wore heavy racks of shed elk antlers as they moved, honoring the Crown Beast of Terrene.

Before I knew it, we were standing by the lapping waters of the Ethereal Lake, and I spotted four familiar faces waving frantically at me. I broke away from the procession and dove into my friends' waiting arms.

"Thanks for coming, guys" I said, pulling away to look at them properly.

"We wouldn't miss it, cousin," Jho said proudly.

"It's so good to see you." Ricky's voice didn't quite match his smiling face. I hadn't checked up on him in a while. Maybe we should take a day to visit him up there again. That always made him feel better.

"I really missed you guys, even if we saw each other in class today," Dusty said sheepishly.

"I didn't think I'd be doing so much reading as the Supreme. I just want to go out and explore with you guys," Jads said, a plea in her tone.

"Okay, so..." Ricky paused, and we all looked at him. He looked embarrassed. "We don't have cool power-infused waters in the Space Ring."

"Spit it out, Ricky," I said, nonplussed.

"About our conversation... Can you ask Chief Berkarys if I can also be baptized?" His big, light brown eyes shone in the sunlight. He looked like a sad dog at the dinner table.

"Oh." I thought fast. It *had* been my idea, but I wasn't even sure Father would allow it. When I'd jokingly suggested Ricky become a Keeper with me weeks ago, I didn't think he'd take it seriously. Sólel and I had done a lot of studying and endured a number of long discussions before Mom and Father approved us. I opened my mouth to explain just that, but the words died on my lips at the look on Ricky's face. *Shit.*

"Okay, I'll ask him. Hang on. Sólel!" I called out. "Come say hi!" Sólel was standing with his best friend, Evera, talking excitedly in fluent Comminsceoan. I liked the little faun girl, but it was embarrassing that Sólel had to translate for us.

He waved goodbye to Evera and ran down the gravelly embankment before skidding to a stop in front of us. "Hello, *kuyas* and *ates*," he said, winded.

"Oh my goodness, he reminds me of Gordo." Jho walked over to him and gave him a hug. Sólel, being the little extrovert he was, threw his arms around her without hesitation.

"Okay, I'll be right back," I said, glancing over at Father. "You guys talk to Sól."

Leaving my brother and friends, I walked over to where Father was standing with the Tribe Council, an imposing collection of humans, leyfolk, and those in between.

Father was easily the largest man in our village. He was built like a tank with bulging muscles akin to boulders. It was the physique of a man who had not only dedicated his life to physical power, but also to protecting his people, his land, and his most sacred charge, the Ethereal Tree.

He wore a chief's tribal clothes, dark green with shining gold accents. The sparse strips of fabric left him almost shirtless, likely for the purpose of showing off those epic muscles. Everyone swore that when he walked, the ground shook. His call could rival a thunderclap, commanding respect from everyone within a mile radius. Okay, maybe some of that was slight exaggeration but the best legends always had a basis in fact.

Coming to stand beside him, I felt downright puny. "Father, I'm going to ask you something, but I hope you don't get mad."

He looked down at me and I wondered, not for the first time, if he could even make out my face from that high up.

"Out with it, Emierr." His voice rumbled right through my chest. It was the voice of a man who was said to win battles with a single war cry. It was the voice of an absolute badass.

"Ricky... My best friend... Um, from Earth... Well, he's from the Space Ring and you know they don't have any Ethereal waters so he was hoping, well, *I* was hoping... Can he get baptized, too?" The words sounded stupid as soon as they tumbled out of my mouth.

Father blinked then let out a booming laugh. "I thought you were going to back out of the ceremony. Of course, son. He is an honored guest; he has brought you home to us. If you vouch for him, I trust your judgment. He may go first, before you and your brother." Still chuckling, he turned back to the Tribe Council.

"Thanks!" A wild grin spread across my face, and I dashed back to the group. "Ricky, you're going first!" I yelled, grabbing his shoulders and shaking him.

A deafening cheer rose from our little group for Ricky, who looked dumbstruck.

A wide smile appeared on Sólel's face, and he threw his arms around Ricky, catching all of us by surprise. "I hope you get the best power, *kuya*, so you can come down here and play with us too."

Sólel's comment brought everyone to a grinding halt. I peeked at the others' faces. They all looked almost relieved, though it was marred with apprehension. Someone finally said it. We all wanted Ricky to join us down on the surface but none of us had known how or when to bring it up.

"Did your *kuya* tell you I'm sad up there?" Ricky said, tousling his hair.

Sólel nodded, his lower lip poking out. "My *kuya* is also sad down here. He misses all of you." Before anyone can answer, a booming voice fills the air.

"Welcome, everyone!" Father's voice sounded electronically amplified but I knew there wasn't a single microphone up there. His Keeper powers let him copy any voice he'd heard, at any volume he desired. He was the voice of Terrene.

I reached down to grip Sólel's hand, telling Ricky, "Wait here," before dragging my brother to where Mom was waiting. She was wearing her tribal gown; billowing, gauzy green with gold bits glinting in the sunshine.

"My esteemed kin of Terrene," Father rumbled, "honored guests from distant tribes, and cherished friends who have journeyed from diverse lands. I stand before you with a heart full of gratitude."

The centaur Tribal Council member translated for the leyfolk through earpieces. Eona was a glossy chestnut mare with legs easily confused for tree trunks. Matching hair cascaded down her front like a lion's mane. She wore a cloak woven from autumn leaves and feathers. It draped across her human torso, and lay like a blanket across her equine back.

"Your presence at the sacred Ethereal Lake is a testament to our unity on this momentous Baptism Day for my beloved sons, Emierr and Sólel," Father said. "As the Chief of Terrene, let me express the profound significance of becoming Keepers. It is a solemn pledge to uphold our sacred vows, to harness our newfound abilities with pure hearts, and to be stewards of the balance in Ethra. Today, I announce a special addition to this ceremony. In acknowledgment of the warmth and camaraderie the new Nobles have shown Ethra, we are honored to have a distinguished guest join the baptism. I call upon Rictor, an emissary from the Space Ring, to stand alongside Emierr and Sólel." Father welcomed Ricky with a massive, outstretched hand.

The crowd swelled with cheers, whoops, and inhuman calls as Dusty pushed Ricky a step forward. Looking a bit pale, he took his place next to me.

"Before we proceed, let us seek the blessing of Maral, the great elk, guardian of the Lake. Together, we shall sing the Lullaby of Maral, calling upon her to grace us with her presence, and bestow her blessing upon this sacred ceremony. May the harmony of our voices reach the heart of Maral, and may her spirit guide these three young boys in their journey as Keepers."

The tribes' song surrounded us—the soft murmur of a bedtime story whispered by firelight. The song told the legend of how Maral had transformed herself from aimless shadow to forest deity. A gust stirred, the melody peaked, and I looked up to see Maral, descending from the treeline as a daunting silhouette against the brilliant sky.

These Crown Beasts were massive, far larger than any land animal I had ever seen. Maral's antlers grew like ancient, gnarled tree limbs from her skull. Her antlers were said to have been stolen in a battle against a mighty bull who thought her a prize to be won. Dazzling white fur made for a stark contrast against the dark, aged bone.

The singing cut out, the breeze whispered low, and everyone, even Jads, Dusty, and Jho, bowed their heads. Maral's enormous hooves carried her regally toward the silent crowd. She came close enough for Ricky and Sólel to feel the huff of her breath. Sólel bowed his head, setting an example for Ricky, who followed suit. Sólel then glanced up at Maral, who lowered her own head in acknowledgment. With that cue, Sólel and Ricky straighten up. I admit, I was shitting myself as the unnaturally large animal's breath rolled over my skin.

Her deep brown eyes locked onto me. Her nostrils flared as she took in my scent. I felt as though I was being x-rayed. I bowed, even though my heart was threatening to leap out of my throat. Getting rejected would be so embarrassing. "Meer," Ricky whispered, prompting me to look up.

Maral's eyes listed over us once more before she took a step back and dipped her head, antlers falling within an inch of my nose. Gold dust, just like the substance emitted from the Ethereal Tree, began to glimmer around her antlers. It swirled around the three of us, dancing in the wind for a few beautiful seconds before dissipating into the air.

"There we have it," Father called triumphantly, "The blessing has been granted." The crowd went wild—Maral just gave us the sacred thumbs up.

Maral turned away, seeming to have immediately lost interest. She was probably tired of doing this for however long she'd been doing it. I didn't blame her. She strode past the wide-eyed crowd to settle further down on the lake's shore. As she dropped heavily to her knees, Father called for the crowd's attention and declared it was Ricky's time to experience the baptism. He reached down to take Ricky's hand, guiding him toward the lake.

Before they went further, Mom knelt to Ricky, their foreheads touching. My stomach jolted. Auntie Luna used to do the same thing. Ricky's eyes squeezed shut and Mom gently brushed a thumb under his eyes. Then, she stood and allowed them to pass.

Father and Ricky walked, hand in hand, into the cool, green waters of the lake. The gold dust that hovered just above the surface did a little river dance as they pushed on. Father continued to guide Ricky deeper into the lake until the waters lapped at the lobes of his ears. Spectators whooped as Ricky took a deep breath and Father used his massive hand to plunge Ricky below the surface. The gold dust kicked up into a luminous glow, swirling over the ripples where Ricky's head was moments before.

After five, seemingly endless beats, Father hoisted Ricky up. He gasped for air, possibly not expecting to be held under that long. Father's solemn expression turned to one of concern. The onlookers weren't cheering anymore. A low buzz of worried voices hummed from the throng. Something was up.

Sólel leaned in, whispering, "I think *Kuya* Ricky didn't get a power."

~ ~ ~

We wince, averting our eyes from Rictor.

"Does that mean... Ricky wasn't pure of heart?" Brunner lifts an eyebrow.

"I think at the time, Ricky wanted so badly to have something for himself. The waters didn't deem him worthy because of it," Jadis says. We'd discussed a multitude of theories as to what happened that day. When Rictor wasn't around, of course.

"No, yeah, I agree," Rictor says. He's showing no sign of pain at the memory. " That's partly why calling it 'magick' never sat right with me. It's all about chemical reactions and the chemicals my body was producing at that time didn't react to the magick. I'll admit I was disappointed that I didn't get anything, but I understand now that I was being selfish going there. I just wanted to fit in. I got telekinesis anyway, so I'm not as bummed out about it." Rictor shrugs.

"A win is a win, am I right?" Dustin slaps Rictor's back.

"A silver lining, I guess," Rictor agrees. "Anyway, keep going, Meer."

~ ~ ~

The crowd rippled with whispers as Mom and Father led Ricky out of the lake. I watched as Mom worked her magick, steam rising from Ricky's wet clothes until they were dry. The gang surrounded him, trying to offer comfort through their confusion, but a weird heat stirred inside me. I couldn't help but curl my lip at Maral. *Why would that monster turn Ricky down?* He deserved this more than anyone. I gazed at the beastly creature, and, for a split second, she looked just as confused as everyone else.

"Uh—Please everyone, let's calm ourselves. It is Sólel's time to enter the waters." The crowd's voices fell to uneasy whispers at Father's voice, but they clearly weren't about to gloss over the failure of the baptism. Sólel gave me a tight hug before walking up to Father, whose eyes now held a hint of worry. I wasn't sure when someone had last been rejected, but it was evident that Father now feared his son might face the same fate. Anticipation filled the air. Everyone's gaze was fixed on my little brother. Father gave him a tense smile, attempting to conceal the doubts I just had glimpsed moments ago.

Mom knelt beside Sólel and whispered something to him before pressing her forehead against his. Then, Father guided him into the lake and the process was repeated. Sólel sank into the waters, gold dust spiraling over the surface. But this time, it intensified, flooding the entire lake with brilliance. Sólel was bathed in golden light, as if flames had engulfed the waters, and a hush fell over the onlookers.

Sólel's head broke through the water's surface. He straightened up, with eyes closed and arms raised. Strings of sunlight seemed to pour into him. The radiant energy surrounded him, and his hair lashed around his head, encased in tongues of fire. The flaming aura whirled around his entire body, filling his eyes with white heat.

Sólel rose into the sky, a little sun radiating warmth. He was a spectacle. The crowd all reached for him with their hands, hooves, and other limbs I had no name for. His soothing glow could be felt all around us. I became aware my jaw was hanging open when a gnat hit my uvula.

I glanced over at the gang, where most of them stood frozen with awe. Not Ricky. He lingered at the back, tears streaming down his face. Jho noticed and gave him a comforting hug. My mind flashed back to the conversation Ricky and I had a few weeks ago. The one that triggered his failed scheme in the first place.

"Meer, do you think your power will be flying or something?" Ricky asked, fiddling with his computer's camera.

"Why the sudden interest in the Ethereal Lake? I thought you didn't believe in that," I replied. I was lying down in my treehouse room, sprawled comfortably over a mattress of furs and leaves.

"I'm just curious," he said, his eyes glued to his table.

"I don't know. I wish we could choose our powers. Maybe I should just practice magick like Jads said. We could both give it a try."

"I did try. It doesn't activate for me. I mean, I see it, I believe it's real, but I guess the fundamentals of magick don't click with me. But the powers, though. That's something I could get behind." He stopped suddenly, as if self-conscious of his rambling. He reminded me so much of Uncle James. We hadn't spoken about him in a while. I wondered how Ricky was really doing.

"Hey, maybe you can cannonball in after me on Baptism Day." I grinned at him. I wasn't emotionally equipped to have a real talk with him. Not yet.

Ricky's face brightened. "Yeah! If I had an innate power, I could keep up with you guys and not be a damsel in distress." His laughter echoed through my speakers.

"Thank the Tree." Father murmured, bringing me back to the present moment.

Oh, Ricky.

Sólel descended gracefully and, as his feet touched the ground, the radiant aura surrounding him dissipated, sending the crowd into a frenzy. Father scooped Sólel up, spinning him around. The fearsome sun god vanished as Sólel giggled in his father's arms, just like any eight-year-old boy. I was torn right down the middle with joy and sorrow. I was about to join Sólel as a Keeper, but in the process, I had to leave Ricky behind. Should I back out and just practice magick with him instead?

"Up next is my son, Emierr, the most recent addition to our family." Father's thunderous voice interrupted my thoughts, and Sólel dashed over to throw his arms around me in a stranglehold. The tips of his hair were still smoldering.

"Come on, son," Mom said, smiling as she reached her hand out to me. My head spun as I took her hand. The walk to the lake's edge felt like the longest distance I'd crossed in my life. Father reassured me that I would be safe. Mom put her forehead on mine before I waded out into the lake. Chilly water formed little whirlpools in my wake. Before being submerged, I glanced at my best friends. Locking eyes with Ricky, I silently asked for his blessing.

He gave me a thumbs up.

Suddenly, Father's iron grip forced me down in the waters. My eyes slammed shut against the onslaught of water, glittering dust, and probably fish crap. After a few heartbeats of darkness, my curiosity got the better of me. I squinted through my lashes, looking into the greenish depths. In the lake's deeper center, I noticed little trails of gold dust meandering out from a central point. *Where does that go?* A tingling sensation spread through my entire body, and I closed my eyes once again.

I shot up, gasping for air, and felt a very physical shift. *Did it work?* I blinked the lake water from my eyes and caught Father looking down at me with pride.

"Come on, son." Father's hand extended to me, and I took it. "I'm so proud of you." His smile was a reassurance. It worked—I've gained a power. But... what power? The crowd erupted into cheers and I shared a triumphant smile with my friends, especially with Ricky, who was still giving me that thumbs up. Had it truly been just a few seconds I'd been underwater?

"You did so well." Mom beamed at me.

"Thanks, Mom." I shivered, looking around, and realized that all eyes were trained on me, human and nonhuman alike. Some hung from branches while others lurked in the shadows, the giants were at a distance, but most of the faces seemed to be looming over me. Their chattering filled the air and, weirdly enough, I was pretty sure I could understand what they were saying. Mom weaved an evocation spell, drying me off. Gusts of warm air blew through me and so did her pride.

"Did it work?" someone to my right said. It was a satyr, elbowing his friend. "I wonder what power he got."

"I'm wondering the same thing," I said to him nervously. The satyr's jaw dropped.

"You can understand me?" he asked, astonished.

I nodded, confused. He had been speaking plain English... Hadn't he? Despite my weeks down here on Ethra, I had not picked up a single word of leymara. Nor any other tribe's language for that matter.

Another creature with overly large eyes, maybe from the Bundac Tribe, jeered, "The filthy alien got the ability to talk to satyrs, what a useful skill."

His friend, some kind of goblin, cackled shrilly. *Filthy alien?* I was enraged. Something that wasn't even human had the audacity to insult *me* for being an alien?

"Apologize!" I snapped at him. But the voice that left me wasn't my own. Not entirely. It had taken on a strange, threatening quality. The creature shuddered and bowed his apology. *What did I just do?* Silence fell over the onlookers.

Leaning down, Father looked at me intently. "Son, your eyes. They mimic his." He pointed at the quivering thing I'd reprimanded. My gaze shifted upward to the towering trees, away from the now-fearful faces that watched me. I stared right back, just as worried as they were. From a nearby limb, Evera was cheering my name. I could see her big, floppy ears poking up through wavy, golden hair, even at this distance. Her mood was a stark contrast to the serious faces on the ground.

"Can you understand me now, Meer?" she hooted. I grinned and started to call back when the branch beneath her cloven hooves broke. The crowd exploded in horrified screams as Evera plummeted to the ground. Instinctively, I lunged for her despite knowing rationally that she was too far for me to save. Vines that had been wrapped around the trunk of Evera's tree ripped themselves from their host, obeying the motions of my fingers.

They caught the tumbling faun, ensnaring her in a sort of net. Slowly, I settled her down on the ground. She pushed herself up on her sandy brown legs, shaking. Gasps echoed across the lake's placid surface and Sólel dashed to Evera with panic in his eyes. The Tribe Council gaped at me. The confusion in their eyes spoke louder than Father's powers ever could.

The Tribal Seer, a truly decrepit old man who was over two hundred years old, stepped forward. All eyes were trained on him as his frail voice called, "Behold! The Fatebringr! We have all waited a millennium for you. Finally, you are here, Chosen One." He knelt on both knees and bowed all the way to the gritty lake shore.

Confused, I stuttered, "The what now?" As soon as the words escaped my lips, a horde of people and leyfolk swarmed me, each expressing their worries and requesting my assistance, as if I were some medieval king tending to his peasants. Mom and Father positioned themselves in front of me, creating a barrier between me and the teeming crowd. *What did I just become?*

~ ~ ~

"Damn." Dustin exhales. "I know we were there but damn."

"I remember that. It was so intense." Jadis shakes her head. "Everyone wanted you to solve everything for them. That old guy really stirred shit up with the "Fatebringr" title."

"So, what, you got two powers instead of one?" Brunner asks.

"Yeah, it had never happened before." I reply. "The prophecy stated 'the one who wields the power of two, will decide the fate of Ethra: Destruction or salvation.' Like that isn't a lot of pressure for a kid."

"What happened after all of that?" Brunner asks, his focus intense. I appreciate his dedication to learning every detail in his efforts to rescue Jhoana, but homeboy needs to chill out a bit.

"Well," I say, humoring his seriousness, "I dove straight into my lessons. Being the Chosen One wasn't exactly on my bingo card. Since I ended up as the translator for everyone, I spent a ton of time with that. Eventually, we decided Ethra needed one global language, and it just happened to be English. The Space Ring made that easier—English is mandatory up there. Ethra calls it the 'tongue of the first,' which, honestly, sounds way cooler."

~ ~ ~

It had been a month since they dubbed me the Chosen One and avoiding my parents had become a professional sport. Some ancient prophecy supposedly pegged me for this fate. Someone who possessed two innate powers would decide Ethra's destiny. Now they were cramming lessons down my throat, trying to turn me into the world's best Fatebringr. Yay.

Tired of the endless lectures, I snatched my bag and bailed from my treehouse room. I snuck a glance into Sólel's room and found him all packed. I motioned for him to join my great escape.

Just as we were about to ninja our way out, someone pulled a classic throat-clearing move. And, of course, it was Mom. Sólel froze, caught in the act of joining my rebellion. She leveled a look at both of us, one eyebrow raised.

"Where are you two going?" she asked, tone light but stern.

"Mom..." I swallowed. "Sólel and I are gonna get some training in, like you wanted. I mean, it's good to start young and you're only young once—" I was rambling. Mom was the kindest person I had ever met, but she was still the Chieftess.

Her mouth thinned and she looked at Sólel, who would absolutely break under the mom stare. *You got this, little bro, don't cave!*

"Yeah, Mom. It's time we learned how to hone our abilities," he said, not even breaking a sweat. *Good man.*

Mom's lips stayed pressed, but she relented. "Okay." She clicked her tongue. "But remember, Emierr, you have a meeting with the Council later tonight. Do not be late again, or else." She leaned down to place her forehead on mine and I nodded.

"You be careful too, my brave little one." She turned to touch her forehead to Sólel's.

"See you in a little bit," I said and took Sólel's hand.

"Love you, Mom," Sólel said with a jaunty wave. I was pretty damn impressed with my little brother. He was learning my ways well.

"Love you, boys. Remember, tonight!" Mom called after us.

Sólel and I burst out of the village. The villagers who spotted us bowed respectfully, always reminding me of my new, celebrity status. The whole Squad, busy with their own duties, was actively shaping the world. Jads as Supreme and Noble of Arid, Dusty as an Inkweaver and Noble of Zaltana, Jho as a Keeper and Noble of Verglas... Then there was Ricky.

Ricky's news about becoming the Noble of the Fleming Space Ring had thrilled everyone. Maybe he hadn't become a Keeper, but being a Noble was even more impressive. I wasn't a Noble but Keeper and Chosen One were enough for me.

I seized Sólel and tossed him onto my back. In a fit of giggles, he linked his arms around my neck. I sprinted to the edge of the village with his little body bouncing on my back, the wind stealing our laughter. I called a vine to my outstretched hand and we swung through the forest. The sun-warmed air roared in my ears, drowning out several whoops of admiration from below.

I landed high on a tree branch in one of Terrene's massive, buttery trees. The yellow of the leaves turned sunlight to gold as it filtered down to the forest floor.

"I have an idea," I said as Sólel clambered off my back and dug his fingertips into the tree's grooved bark. Scanning the sky, I spotted what I was searching for. A small flock of enormous birds, coasting high above the treeline. Argentavis, as they were called here, were similar to the now-extinct condors on Earth, other than the fact that they had wings so big they could cover half a football field. Oh, and they were roughly twelve times the size of said condor.

With a burst of power, I summoned them, my call woven with the lake's gift. They wheeled along the currents of air to descend gracefully into our tree. A striking black and white Argentavis landed first, his two companions close behind.

"Can you take me and my baby brother for a flight?" I asked. It suddenly occurred to me that it might be rude to ask a dinosaur-sized, sentient eagle to give me a piggyback ride.

"It is an honor," the bird responded, dipping his finely feathered head. Sólel, fearless as always, scaled the proffered wing and settled into midnight plumage.

"What's your name... sir?" I asked as I climbed aboard. I barely knew Earth manners, what were you supposed to call a talking apex predator?

"North Star," he replied. He waved a semi-truck–sized wing at the other two. "Beak and Snow."

I stared at the first one, a golden brown and tawny creature. *Did he just say Beak?* Surely, I was imagining things.

"Ready?" North Star twisted his head back to look at me. His eye was a brilliant, fiery shade of amber.

"We're ready," I said, curling my fingers around thick feathers. But as we launched off the branch, headed skyward, my fear of heights kicked in, and I let out an involuntary yelp. The clouds were puffs of cotton candy against the cerulean sky. The Tree Top Provinces were far below us, a village nestled atop colossal trees. Bridges were crafted from huge, twisted vines which connected the lofty structures.

I watched our host's powerful wings rustle under rivulets of cold air. His snowy flight feathers glistened against the blue-black expanse of wing. Below us, Terrene slipped away as the nation of Verglas came into view. I knew that, somewhere, Jho resided among the towering glaciers. The icy mountain tops gleamed in the sunlight, and faceted glacial ice cast rainbows on valleys of shadowy snow. Above us, the Fleming Space Ring had reached its peak and blotted out the sun. We were plunged into darkness.

It was something I had grown accustomed to but it still made me uneasy every time.

The soft glow that always radiated from Sólel these days turned him into our makeshift lamp. The forest below transformed into an illusion of a city blanketed in twilight. The bioluminescence that had first drawn me here twinkled like stars from this altitude. I remembered the first night I spent in Terrene, where I'd spend an hour collecting an armload of glittering leaves from the Amadas Lux trees, hoping to use their brilliant white light as room decor. I learned the following night that plucked leaves didn't glow for long.

I turned to look at Sólel, who had the biggest smile plastered across his face. I never knew what I was missing as an only child. My free arm wrapped around him, and he gazed up at me. "Happy Birthday, Sól," I said, giving him a squeeze.

"Thanks, *Kuya*." He leaned into my embrace.

We could have been flying for minutes or hours, I wouldn't have been able to tell.

Eventually, North Star mentioned that he and his flock were getting hungry and suggested landing near the Sperclen Tribe's Lavender Sky Island for some fish. My stomach grumbled and I dug into my backpack, fishing out a birthday cupcake, a sneaky souvenir from my tedious "Fatebringr" lessons. I gave it to Sólel. His eyes sparkled with glee and without hesitation, he broke it in half, handing a piece to me.

Just then, the Space Ring did its rotation thing, and the sun returned. In the distance, Lavender Sky Island unfolded—a burst of color with vibrant plants, flowers, and of course, the lavender trees. That was probably my favorite thing about Ethra. Nothing here was just green.

After depositing us on the shoreline, North Star and his comrades veered off to their favorite fishing spot a few miles away. We watched Beak and Snow dive into the water, snatching up impossibly large fish with their lethal talons. Dolphins swam around the carnage, hoping to score a lost catch from the Argentavis. On a whim, I shouted to them, asking if we could catch a swim. They agreed in a flurry of whistles and clicks.

I couldn't swim, but something told me that, here in Ethra, I could. That was what Ethra was about wasn't it? If you believed it, you could do it. We waded out into the crystalline water and grabbed onto the dolphins' flippers. Taking a deep breath, we plunged below the surface. The underwater world was jarringly silent, yet stunning—corals, seaweed, and a vibrant neon city of bioluminescent fish surrounded us. My panicked lungs urged me to return to the surface and the dolphin obeyed the unspoken plea.

I kinda hated that whole commanding thing that came with talking to animals. After a few deep breaths, I opened my mouth to ask the dolphin to take me back down when suddenly, it whipped its flippers free from my grasp and vanished into the depths.

"Emierr!" North Star cried. I saw him swoop down and pluck Sólel from the water. He looked so small in the cage of ebony talons.

I felt the water ripple below me. Heart beginning to race, I glanced down and saw the horrifying glint of something immense and scaly cruising towards me. I struck out for land, my body following some muscle memory I had never taught it. At that moment, the colossal creature leaped from the water, hoisting me into the air with its momentum. I was weightless for a moment, but not in the freeing sense I'd felt from the back of the Argentavis. It was the kind of weightlessness I imagined one felt moments before death. I barely had time to catch my breath before I was hurled back into the water.

I frantically scanned my surroundings. It was there, where the water turned murky blue. It looked like it could be the cousin of the Loch Ness monster. Its small head was set with jagged teeth and perched atop a long, sinewy neck. From what I'd seen of the Loch Ness monster, it had seemed pretty peaceful.

This thing, on the other hand, seemed absolutely feral, and out to turn my guts into spaghetti. My limbs flailed, trying desperately to push me shoreward.

"North! Beak!" I screamed. I could see them, high above, turning their bodies into a coordinated dive for me. Sólel had been placed safely on Beak's back. Thank goodness.

Ahead, the monster's massive fins rose. Panic rose in my chest. Panic and something stronger. I screeched, "Stop!" The monster froze. I could see every gruesome detail of this horror's body. It was slick, black, and spiny. It looked like photos I'd seen of deep-sea creatures. "I am not an enemy; I am a friend. We are your friends," I said through the tremors that wracked my body. The monster lifted its head, snarling through sharp teeth, and its reptilian eyes locked on me. "Friends," I repeated, trying to put the full force of my power into the word.

To my shock, it replied, "No friends."

"Well *I* am," I said, slowly reaching out and placing my hand on its hideous snout.

"And birds?" it asked, slitted eyes flicking skyward.

"Yes, friends. They're just looking for food," I explained. I couldn't believe I was having this conversation with a several ton death machine. The beast's eyes returned to me. A third eyelid slid across the reddened iris.

"I help catch food," it rumbled. I was completely frozen with shock as I watched it submerge. Just as I was starting to feel my limbs again, I felt the creature under me, lifting me out of the water. I cried out in alarm. My legs dangled on either side of its head. North Star dipped down next to us and I made a clumsy jump to his back. Ethran Nessie plunged back into the depths, momentarily leaving behind a crater in the sea.

I felt North Star jerk slightly beneath me. Sólel had leaped off Beak to land behind me, his hands grasping the ebony feathers. He scrambled forward and caught me in a hug, crying. "I thought you were monster food," he sobbed.

"I'm okay, little brother," I reassured him, though my heart rate was far from returning to a regular rhythm. A powerful spray of water hit us from below. The three Argentavis squawked in alarm. The sea dragon below had breached the surface again, blasting an entire school of fish into the air from its mouth. The three Argentavis acted instinctively, catching them in their mouths and talons. We were smacked soundly by more than one wriggling body. Sólel and I stared at each other before dissolving into laughter, the relief and adrenaline creating the perfect storm of giddiness.

Sólel and I were still soaking wet. He slid his arms back around me, and I could feel his Innate warmth emanating from him. As he clung to me, concentrating on his inner sun, my clothes began to dry. I shook my head to speed up the hair-drying process. I had been moments away from becoming monster shit. I should have been scared out of my mind, but I couldn't feel more alive.

I leaned over North Star's side and called to the dragon, "What is your name?"

Its crude little skull swiveled skyward. "I am Mirul."

"It is an aequoyong," North Star supplied. "They usually live in family groups. It is strange to see one alone." My heart broke for the misshapen beast below us.

"Thank you, Mirul! We will come back to visit you!" I yelled back, this time a little choked up. It gave a warbling keen, then plunged back into the depths.

The flight back home was serene, the clouds catching the hues of the sunset—purples, reds, yellows—all blending together. As we were approaching our village at last, my eyes drifted to the Ethereal Lake. The day of our baptism swam to the forefront of my mind.

Rictor not getting a power was stupid. I wanted answers, not just for him, but for me. My successful evasion of death had me feeling bold. I called down to North Star, asking him to drop us on the lake shore. After our feet were finally back on solid ground, we thanked the Argentavis.

North Star invited us to call on them if we were ever around Zaltana. I knew that I would have to make my way there if I ever wanted to get to the bottom of Beak's name.

I watched them force their massive bodies back into the sky, inconceivably powerful wings sending gusts of wind over the water.

After they were too high to see clearly, I walked toward the lake. Now that the sound of wingbeats was gone, I realized our surroundings were eerily quiet.

"*Kuya*, we should head back. We're not supposed to be here," Sólel whispered, tugging my arm.

"I'll explain to Mom and Father if we get in trouble. Don't worry, I just need to get some answers." I covered his hand with mine and gave him a comforting squeeze.

"Hey!" I called, my voice ricocheting between the trees. "Maral, I know you can hear me. The animals have told me they always see you lurking around here. Come on out. I need to ask you something." I felt untouchable. If I could control a demonic Ethran plesiosaur, I could handle Maral.

"*Kuya*, don't do that. Crown Beasts are not kind to unkind people," Sólel said in a low, urgent voice.

I scoffed, ignoring his fear. "I didn't know you'd be scared of a twelve-year-old!" I taunted into the trees. Their limbs waved in the breeze as if they, too, were trying to warn me.

Twigs snapped, echoing impossibly from every angle around us.

"Please, let's go," Sólel pleaded. He looked absolutely terrified.

The righteous anger in my chest dimmed as I looked down into his wide, golden eyes. Even when filled with fear, little flames danced in them.

I relented. "Okay," I said, "I'll come back on my own to deal with this." I took his hand and his whole body slumped with relief.

Just as we started walking towards the trail home, a clear woman's voice rang out, "You dare call me then walk away, Emierr of Earth?"

I froze, Sólel looking up at me. All the bravado that had filled me minutes before drained right out. Slowly, we both turned, our feet crunching in the gravel. It was her—Maral.

"Have you a question? I may have the answer," she said in a mocking tone. She shook her enormous head and gold dust spun off her antlers. I had forgotten the sheer size of the elk, like something out of the Ice Age on Earth. She was standing on the lake's glassy surface; a Cervidae Jesus.

"Get behind me," I said, pulling Sólel to my back. I tried to scrape together the last shards of the swagger I'd landed here with. "Why didn't you give Ricky a power when you blessed him that day?"

"Child, I do not grant powers," Maral says, her voice tinged with pity, but not kindness. "That is not within my ability. I am merely a watcher. These Waters belong to those pure of heart, and I protect them, but the final word is not mine." She pauses, her gaze narrowing. "It is the power you carry now that allows us to speak." Hellish laughter escapes her velvet lips, a sound straight from a nightmare.

I shuddered, trying to shake off the sound. "Then why didn't Ricky gain one?" I demanded, though my voice had lost any remaining bravado.

"I am as surprised as you," she acknowledged. "He had all the intentions of being pure. I smelled it off him. But *you?* Two powers? Now, how did that happen?" Maral made no effort to hide her disdain.

"What does that mean?" I furrowed my eyebrows.

"*Kuya*, what is she saying?" Sólel murmured from behind me. He was no longer a sun god, but rather a scared little boy.

"You didn't deserve either of them." Her voice rang out across the water. "The heart that I smelled off you wasn't pure. You don't even know what you want and who you are." She stepped closer, head lowered in a challenge. I realized her eyes were wrong. They didn't hold the horizontal pupil of an elk, but a round, disconcertingly human pupil. She took another step toward me, the water rippling below her. She was in the body of an herbivore, but at that moment, she was a predator. And I was her prey.

"Stop!" I yelled, the panic cracking in my voice.

"You can't command me; I am not an animal." Maral no longer sounded like a woman. Her voice was inhuman. Perhaps it was her true voice. "You answer to me." Another hoof struck the lake's surface. Her hooves were wrong too. Three toes, not two. "Why?" she crooned. "Why are you afraid?"

"Because I'm scared to die!" My admission echoed over the water. The snowy elk paused,

"*Kuya?*" Sólel's small hand touched my back.

"After my uncle and auntie passed away, I didn't really understand what death was." I was shocked to hear my own voice. These words were being pulled from some deep, dark part of my brain. Was Maral pulling them out of me? "I didn't understand how Ricky and Dusty were feeling. I hated that everything and everyone had changed, and I just wanted them to come back. But they're gone. And all I think about now is how can I not let that happen again?" Tears fell to the shallows of the lake, shattering my reflection.

"Your heart is wise, Emierr." Maral suddenly sounded gentle, as if my weakness brought her back to herself. "But you are still a child. You must understand that you do not play any part in who death takes because, eventually, everyone dies."

"But... I don't wanna hurt anymore," I whimpered. "I don't want anyone to hurt at all. I wanna protect my family, my aunties and uncles, my best friends... and my little brother." Tears began to flow in earnest now. All the pain I had been shouldering over these months was flooding out, joining the waters of the lake.

Sólel looked up at me, his eyes gleaming with tears and confusion.

"And who will protect you?" Maral was only a few feet away from us. I didn't bother trying to look up to meet her eyes.

"I don't care about me as long as everyone is safe," I said quietly.

"Then you are worthy, Fatebringr." Startled, I looked up. Maral closed her eyes and leaned her head down to me. Her antlers cage me in age-darkened ivory, gold dust flaking off them. I wiped my tears and placed a hand on her head, right where the white fur parted to meet bone.

I just became a Noble.

Dusty

Emierr's usually a ball of energy. Full of laughs, always cracking jokes. Seeing him broken like this rewinds the clock to when we were twelve years old and clueless.

I can't shake the memories. It's like a punch in the gut every time he wears that guilt on his face. I remember the day Jhoana didn't wake up. The weight of it, the shock, and that damn look that's plastered on his face. We didn't have a chance to save Jhoana. Everything just spiraled out of control too damn fast.

"That's so much responsibility for a kid..." Jadis reaches for Emierr's hand. "You can stop here."

Emierr takes a deep breath in and exhales. "I didn't know how to be there for any of you. I just stayed away, hoping everything would come back to normal."

"That's what I hoped, too." Brunner admits. "Even before Jho's coma. I was hoping everyone would just be normal. I knew exactly how you all felt. My grandma passed away a couple of weeks before everything went down with your parents. I didn't like seeing my grief on you guys."

"So, we all were just protecting each other from the hurt? Now I know we're really best friends," I say with a little laugh.

"Sólel..." Rictor looks at Emierr. "Do you think he's still there?"

Emierr doesn't meet Rictor's eyes.

"Do you guys remember the song Jho would always sing when we're feeling sad?" Emierr asks.

Rictor's eyes narrow at Emierr's blatant sidestep. It's a weird topic to avoid. He used to love talking about his little brother.

"It was a lullaby she made up, right? I still remember the tune." Jadis smiles.

"Jho sang to you guys, too?" Rictor looks slightly put out.

I can feel a smile tugging at the corners of my mouth. I remember. I remember it so well. She would sing that song to calm us.

"She named it, "Hush Now, Little One," I supply. She sang it when I was fighting with Ade'. She even sang it before we left for the Akeurimja Forest.

"That's right... How could I forget?" Rictor 's eyes are distant now, trying to recall a melody he'd nearly lost to time.

Jadis starts singing. *"Hush now, little one. Don't you fear, I'm here..."*

Without warning, Brunner buries his face in his hands. His shoulders shake with silent tears.

"Rune..." Emierr looks at him, seeming alarmed.

Rictor, unsure of what to do, places a hand on his shoulder. Jadis and I glance at each other.

"Geez, I didn't think I was that bad," Jadis jokes.

Brunner sniffles and shakes his head. "No. It's not that. My—When my grandma passed away, Jho would sing that song to calm me down. It was the one thing that really held me together. It gives me comfort knowing she did it for you guys, too. She was a rock for so many people experiencing death for the first time and she was so young." He wipes his arm across his eyes.

"Do you guys know why she always sang it?" Jadis the room at large.

None of us answer, eyes darting around the circle.

"Gordo cried a lot," Jadis says. "He wanted to play with us, but Auntie Ina told him he was too young, and nobody would watch him." Jadis purses her lips. "She came up with the lullaby to soothe him, and then she eventually sang it for us too."

Silence presses down on us. I can see it in their faces; they each remember a time Jho sang to them. A memory I thought I lost comes creeping back in... I shake my head and get up. "Sit down, Meer. It's my turn."

He's all too happy to step aside and collapse into the couch beside Jadis.

"I can't believe this is it. You're the last one." Brunner sighs. "I've learned so much about what happened, yet I feel like I've only tapped the surface." He looks up at me. "What heartbreak are you gonna share, Dusty?"

I crack my knuckles and, after a steadying breath, I say, "My mom died."

~ ~ ~

"She's not dead!" I shouted, like saying it out loud will make it true. Behind us, the kitchen TV blared.

"Breaking news from NASA headquarters, coming to us live from our reporter on the scene," the anchor said. "It appears that the cause of the explosion within NASA's particle accelerator is currently unknown. As of right now, there are two casualties, both NASA astrophysicists."

My heart raced. *Please be anybody else but them.*

"We don't have any confirmation yet on the identities of the victims, but we have more details with Casey who is now with one of the employees who narrowly escaped the facility."

The camera switched to the lady who normally did the weather reports. "Thank you, Dennis. I am here with Dr. Oscar Wilder. Dr. Wilder, can you please tell us what happened?"

"I—I... I tried to get out as many as I could." He paused and looked straight into the camera, eyes fixed in a strange, dead stare. "I'm so sorry, Luna, Josh. I tried." He broke down, turning his face away from the reporter.

The room felt airless.

"Mommy..." I choked, my fingers refusing to let go of Dad. Everything was falling apart around us. And I was falling apart with it.

~ ~ ~

"Oscar Wilder? As in the CEO of Flemming Corp?" Brunner crosses his legs.

"And my boss," Rictor adds. "He told me before I left with Meer that he and my Pa were 'like brothers.' "

"He didn't attend the funeral or the wake. I would know. I helped your mom with the guest list." Jadis crosses her arms. "Some brother."

"I don't know. He looked pretty hurt to me when he was talking on the news. Maybe he couldn't stomach attending." I shrug. I sure as hell couldn't.

"I mean, he did say I can talk to him outside of work. Maybe we can get some answers," Rictor says thoughtfully, tugging on his beard.

"Dusty..." Emierr breathes out. "I'm sorry." Everyone looks at him. His eyes are glued to the floor. "I'm sorry I wasn't there for you as much as I was for Ricky."

"Yo, don't do that. You made me love football. I owe my success to you."

"No, Meer is right. I didn't realize it, but I focused on Ricky more. I'm sorry too, Dusty," Jadis says softly.

"You guys were there for me." I pause, remembering the isolation and misery I'd faced in the months before finally joining them in Ethra. "More than you guys know."

~ ~ ~

The empty caskets were lowered into the ground. Why wasn't I crying? Jads would probably have said I was numb, but that wasn't it. I was feeling everything, every damn thing. Ricky was falling to pieces at my side. Maybe it was because I wasn't focused on the phony burial. My mind was scrabbling against this entire situation. It didn't make any sense, how could they just bury an empty casket? I was tired of hearing the same, vague excuse.

We just can't bury her, okay sweetie?

What, was I five? I had a right to know, even if it meant hearing that my mom was blown into pieces so small they couldn't even sweep her up. Why wouldn't someone just fucking tell me?

At some point, I noticed the burial was over. I was alone in the cemetery. Dad had forgotten me. I stood by the dirt-laden casket that should've held Mom. Since it had happened, I felt like I was trapped in Ricky's kitchen, reliving the sounds of grief-stricken sobs and the businesslike tone of the newscaster.

The sound of an engine revving filled my ears, and I turned to see Dad pulling up. He finally realized I wasn't with him. I wondered how long I'd been standing there. His truck came skidding to a stop next to me and Dad flung himself out of the driver's seat.

"Dustin, I'm so sorry, I thought—"

"It's okay, Dad," I cut him off and climbed into the truck.

Dad inhaled deeply through his nose and rubbed his face. I watched him through the windshield, struggling to compose himself. Finally, he hauled himself back behind the wheel. The drive home was quiet, but it didn't take long for Dad to start shaking with tears. I just stared out the window, watching the sun shine bright. It was a good day to be out. A fucking good day.

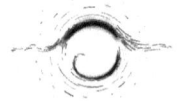

The door slammed downstairs, and I snuck a peek out the window. Dad had taken off for Ricky's place. They were doing the wake there because our house was smaller, and Auntie Luna had thought it'd be better to mash them together. My computer buzzed with call notifications from Guam—family I didn't even know I had. Mom was gone, and now they were adding me. It turned out that Dad had lost touch with them when he, the uncles, and the aunties all moved to America. We never really talked about relatives, so I didn't know which of these people were the real deal.

I was still dressed in my funeral clothes when I walked downstairs. Dad was supposed to take me to the wake. I took a step toward the front door but paused. I didn't want to be there, surrounded by grief and pity. And all those people... No. I slipped out the back door instead.

I picked my way through the grass, toward the swing set I'd gotten for my seventh birthday. It was a bit tighter than I remembered. Mom used to push me so high I thought I could touch the sky. Closing my eyes, I waited for her to give me that push. It never came. Footsteps crunched and I lifted my head.

Ricky? How long was I sitting here? I looked at him but dropped my gaze back down. I don't know what to say, especially to him. How could I comfort him when I was just as broken as he was?

He sat down on the swing beside me, not saying a word. I wished I knew what was going on in his head. Suddenly, he grabbed my hand, holding it tight. It caught me off guard. Ricky started crying, his fingers shaking in my hand. I could feel his pain traveling through his body and into mine. I wasn't numb. I was feeling it all, just deep inside. But with Ricky silently sharing my grief, everything bubbled to the surface. My eyes welled up, and together, we succumbed to the tears.

My stomach growled as I dragged myself downstairs. The house reeked. Dad had been hitting the bottle hard this past week, way more than usual. Before, he drank with the uncles, but lately, it was just him alone every night. Beer cans were scattered all over the dining table. I sighed and got to cleaning.

After an hour, the dishes were done, the trash was out, and my dirty laundry was ready for a wash. I headed for the basement but paused in front of the stairs. Mom's lab was down there, and I hadn't been able to face it yet. I stayed for a heartbeat longer, then decided Dad could deal with the laundry. I left my basket by the basement door. My stomach grumbled again, but this time, it was accompanied by a sharp pain. I pulled the fridge door open to reveal a single carton of eggs. My mouth thinned.

I grabbed the carton, slapped it on the table, and climbed up on a chair to check the cabinets. Spam. Nice. As the spam and eggs sizzled, I found a bit of bread left over and some cheese. I built two sandwiches and was just sitting down to eat when the doorbell rang.

Seriously?

I swung the door open. "Jho."

A wobbly smile crossed her face. "Dusty... How are you feeling?" she asked tentatively.

I didn't answer right away. *Do I be honest or brutally honest?* "I'm okay, Jho. Don't worry about me. How about you?"

"I could be better," she said, her eyes scanning me like she wanted to ask about my eating habits. She always cared about things like that, but this time, she didn't bring it up. "I'm checking up on Ricky too. Why don't you come with me?" Her voice was gentle, like she was coaxing a nervous cat out of hiding.

"I don't think I can," I said, shaking my head. "I'll talk to everyone when I'm ready. Thank you for seeing me."

She swiped a hand over her eyes, voice cracking. "We love you, Dusty. I love you, okay?"

"I love you too, Jho," I said, reminding her as much as myself.

"Please don't go too far away from us."

"I won't," I agreed, crossing my fingers behind my back. *I don't know if I can stay, Jho.*

Farmington Middle School's football field had seen better days. I was standing on the sidelines, watching the seventh graders jog laps around the ring of dry grass. I wasn't sure exactly what possessed me to suddenly join the team. My family had never been big on football. Yet even so, here I was, robotically thanking Coach Danny for letting me join so late.

"Don't even worry about it. Just make sure to come to practice after school, okay?" Coach said. There was an interesting mix of discomfort and sympathy on his face. "And um... I'm sorry about your mom; she was a really nice person. At least to me." He cleared his throat. "Anyway, we start at 3 p.m. sharp."

"Thanks." I turned my back on the field, one step falling automatically in front of the other. Dad used to say Coach Danny had a crush on Mom. Apparently, he'd tried to join our parents' little clique but was too awkward for them to tolerate. He must've really liked Mom.

Everyone did.

My feet carried me to the cafeteria. Dad hadn't made breakfast for the last few weeks, and only getting to eat at school had been something I couldn't get used to.

Today's menu was iceberg salad, cold fries, and cheese pizza; a pancake-sized cheese pizza. I tapped my meal card and shuffled along the lunch line, collecting my steel tray from an ill-tempered lunch lady. As I scanned for a spot to sit, I saw my friends, all laughing at a table in the far corner. Meer was showing them some weird hand signs. Ricky laughed and joined in, somehow mimicking the motions perfectly. What game were they playing? I started walking towards them on instinct but stopped. Each step closer made the dull roar of grief ever so slightly louder. I wasn't ready yet. *I'm sorry, guys.*

I turned away, moving for the door. I slid my pizza into one hand and ditched the tray in the trash, ignoring the tray return table on the far side of the room. I wandered to the old merry-go-round, where we used to play when we were younger. I didn't spend long there. The ghosts of our happier selves haunted the chipped metal. I could almost hear the conversations long since passed. At least the limp cafeteria pizza had quieted my grumbling stomach.

I floated aimlessly through the rest of the day. Somehow, it was already eighth period; the last class. Science was only fun because Ricky loved this class. We'd been classmates in science since elementary school. We even joined the science fair together last year. He left me alone to use the restroom for like two minutes, and I had no idea how to explain our project—a model of jet boots inspired by a show called *Xiolin Showdown*. Uncle James helped turn them into a working model.

Ricky came back to find me trying on the shoes and, well, let's just say the fire part worked. Something like a laugh rose in my throat, but I wasn't sure I remembered how to release it. A folded bit of paper slipped across my and Ricky's shared table. I turned my head just enough to see Ricky smiling at me. I opened the paper—it was a crude drawing of me smacking an alien on the head. A smile formed on my face, but it faded away as soon as it came. I slid back the paper to him, unable to bring myself to do something as carefree as doodling.

A shadow of guilt echoed through my chest. *Just say something, Ricky. I'll talk if you do.* But he took the paper back and said nothing further.

It was 2:45 p.m. I was sitting in the locker room, waiting for Coach to roll in with the team. Honestly, I didn't even want to do this, but going home was worse. Dad... He hadn't been Dad for a while now.

And I was starting to hate him for it.

The team strolled in, shooting me furtive looks.

"Borja, your uniform," Coach called, "A large, right? You're a big boy." He opened one of the lockers and tossed me the uniform. Number 7. Ricky's favorite number. Great.

I didn't know much about football. Maybe it hadn't been a good idea to join mid-season. Everyone else knew what they were doing, and I didn't even know the rules. We ran some drills, but I was lost for every single one we did. Coach stopped yelling, and I looked back at him. It was Meer. *He's on the football team?*

"This is the third time you've been late, Naputi. Do you see how much everyone wants to be here? If you're late again, you're benched next game," Coach threatened, jabbing a finger at him.

"Yes, Coach, sorry." Meer hung his head.

"Well, since you've graced us with your presence, you might as well make yourself useful. Go show Borja how to do the drills." Meer spun on his heel, eyes wide, and began jogging my way. I smiled at him. At least, I think I did. It'd been a while since I saw this doofus. He leaped into a hug, embracing me tightly.

"Dusty, what the fuck? When did you join?" We both shucked our helmets to get a better look at each other. He had already changed so much. How long had it been?

"Just today," I admitted ruefully.

He put his hands on my face, shaking me with something akin to affectionate rage, and then crushed me in his arms. "I fucking missed you."

I paused for a second and slowly returned the hug. "I missed you too, bro." I meant it. I missed all of them.

He let go and punched my shoulder. "That's for not talking to me." He looked back at Coach. "Let's catch up after. Coach is gonna have an aneurysm if I don't get you in shape for the game. I have so much to tell you." He motioned for me to follow with a smirk. "You have no idea how football works, do you?"

"I've seen it on TV."

He chuckled and patted my shoulder. "You trust me, right?"

It was the dumbest question I had ever heard. "Always."

I was feeling slightly more confident by the time practice ended. Everyone rushed to the showers. I didn't bring any extra clothes or a towel. Shower at home it was. As I stepped out of the school entrance, I was relieved to see the sun was still up—thank god for daylight savings. I didn't tell Dad about joining football, but would he even notice I was gone? He was probably drunk by now anyway. I'd walked home with the Squad before; it wasn't that bad. I could do this.

Parents parked their cars along the curb, waiting for their kids to finish their after-school activities.

"Dusty, where's your dad?" Meer had clearly showered in record time. Maybe he'd skipped the soap part.

"He's on his way," I lied. The last thing I needed was for people to realize what things were like at home. I didn't feel like being suffocated with pity.

"Want me to wait with you? I can tell my Pops." He looked down the road and waved. I looked over my shoulder to see Uncle Chris pulling in.

"I'm good, Meer. Thanks." I said. I kept my voice even, hoping it would be enough to quell his suspicions.

"Dustin?" Uncle Chris lowered the passenger seat window. "I thought you were home. When did you start playing?"

"Just today, Pops. Coach had me train him," Meer said proudly.

"Come on, I'll drop you home." Uncle Chris motioned for me to get in.

"My dad's coming, Uncle," I said, almost believing it myself now, but Meer frowned at me. I could feel him studying my face.

"Does your dad even know you're in football?" Meer asked quietly, readjusting the strap of his gym bag.

My face heated. My mind was flitting around, trying to think of a way to get myself out of this car ride. I didn't have the energy to talk about Mom or even acknowledge anything dealing with grief. I just wanted to be distracted, but now it was backfiring. Before I could think of something to say, Uncle Chris grimaced at me.

"I knew it," he growled. "Get in, both of you. Now." Meer dragged me to the car by my arm. I gave in without a further thought; I'd never heard Uncle Chris raise his voice like that. Now, his eyes were boring into me through the rearview mirror. Even Meer was quiet, for once. I didn't know he was capable. "Were you going to walk home, Dustin?" he asked. His tone told me he was in no mood for nonsense.

"Yes," I said in a low voice, looking out the window. I could feel Meer staring at me, but I didn't want to look at either of them right now. The air in this car was too thin. I couldn't breathe.

"That's dangerous, Dustin. What if you got hit crossing the highway or taken by somebody? If anything happens to you kids..." He paused and took a deep breath before muttering, "I can't believe Joshua would be stupid enough to even—"

"He's trying," I snapped, finally looking up into the rearview mirror. I could feel my chest tighten as the words left my mouth. I desperately wanted to believe in them.

Meer's fingers wrapped around mine; there was no need to tell me he had my back. I saw it in his face. My grip tightened on his hand, and I wiped my eyes before tears started flowing.

Uncle Chris's eyes lingered on me. After a few moments, he said, "I know, okay. I know he's trying. We all are."

It got quiet. All I heard were the tires rolling and my sniffles. Meer keeps his hold on my hand despite the sweat leaking from our palms; I didn't want to let go either.

"Dustin, I'm sorry... But I'm going to beat your dad up." I saw Uncle's eyes crinkling into a smile and I chuckled at the thought. Maybe Dad did need a good beating, at least to get some sense into him. Uncle parked the car in front of my house. Meer and I let go of each other, and he gave me a fist bump.

"I'll see you at practice," I said, opening my door.

"See you, Dusty." His smile was softer than usual.

Uncle Chris climbed out after me, slinging an arm around my shoulders. "Let's go," he said, and together, we walked to the front door. Uncle Chris pounded on the door. It took a few moments for Dad to get the door open. Once he managed it, he stood there with unfocused confusion on his face.

"Dustin? Weren't you in your room?" he said. His words were slightly slurred, like he was harboring a cotton ball under his tongue.

"Hi, Dad." I went to walk right past him but paused to turn and throw my arms around Uncle Chris, trying to pour the thanks I couldn't express into the gesture.

He squeezed me tightly and said, "Go shower, you stink." I passed by Dad, catching the whiff of beer that seemed to constantly ooze from his pores these days.

"Son!" Dad shouted.

I froze with one foot on the stairs that led to my room.

"*Lanya*, Joshua," Uncle Chris reprimanded. I slunk halfway up the stairs and sat down on the steps. Uncle Chris scared me when he was serious, but not too much to stop me from being nosy.

"What?" Dad sounded really out of it. But then again, what was new?

"Did you notice where your son was?" Uncle Chris sounded like a parent talking to a poorly-behaved toddler.

"He was in his room, wasn't he?"

"Joshua," Uncle said with exasperation. "He was at school. For football practice. Did you know he was about to walk home all by himself? If I had come a little later, he would still be walking by now. *In the dark.*" Anger was starting to bleed through his voice.

"It's a good thing you did, right?" Dad chuckled. Maybe Uncle Chris really would beat him up.

"You're drunk again. You're about to lose your job and your son..."

Uncle Chris fell silent.

"What?" Dad slurred. "Say it, Christopher."

It was quiet for a moment as Uncle Chris struggled to find the words. "You... You need to get your shit together," he said finally. "If not for you, for your kid. That boy is going to grow up resenting you. He needs his dad, Josh."

"You know what I need? A fucking beer," Dad laughed harshly. His indifference was like a punch to the gut.

"You read the letter they gave Kit. Via and James said to protect our kids, we ne—"

"Why the fuck did he get a letter, ha?" Dad cut him off. "He and Via were probably sleeping together, huh? That fucking guy."

"What the fuck, Josh. How the hell could you even think that!"

I clutched onto the stair's wooden railings, heart thundering, hands shaking. *Please, Uncle Chris, don't hurt my dad.*

"What? It's true isn't it?" Dad was almost shouting now.

"*Lanya.* Put it together, *par.* Kit was the one who got us out of Guam, remember? Even when he lost his dad, he kept going to make sure we would leave without a doubt. He got us our homes, and found us jobs until we could stand on our own feet. He's always been the most reliable. We'd all be falling apart right now if it wasn't for him keeping his promise to Via and James." Uncle began choking on his words. I wanted to run down to stop the entire conversation, but I was finally learning something. "He quit his job to watch over his kids. He quit, Joshua. *Kit...* The one who loves working for this goddamn town."

"What?" Dad's voice suddenly sounded fragile. I risked a peek and saw Dad leaning on the doorway. Everything really was falling apart. Uncle Kit loved his job. He loved helping Farmington with Auntie Ina. Jho said he was going to run for mayor. Did that mean he was stepping down because Uncle James and Auntie Via said to protect us? What did that even mean?

"Why is this happening, Chris?" Dad whispered, sounding choked. "James is dead... and Via... How can they just not exist anymore, Chris?"

I couldn't help myself anymore. I slid down a few steps to peer at my dad. The last thing we needed was for Uncle Kit to send him down an even deeper spiral than he already was. Seeing them now locked in an embrace was not at all the scene I expected. Dad broke away and, unbelievably, he started laughing. They'd seen me. Uncle Chris played it off, too, chuckling with him, his eyes flickering to mine.

"*Asta i despues.*" Uncle Chris said in Chamorro. I regretted that I still couldn't understand it. Meer, Jho, and I hadn't learned any

Chamorro, bar a few words here and there. Our parents promised to teach us Tagalog too, with Jads and Ricky. But after everything, we'd probably be speaking English for a while longer. I did know when they started speaking a different language, they were hiding something from us.

Uncle James never would have kept things from us. He would have explained it and made sure I knew what was happening. He'd be disappointed if he could see his friends now.

Dad waved me over and took hold of my arm, guiding me to the kitchen. Uncle Chris waved goodbye and closed the door.

"Pineapple pizza, just like you like, right?" Dad's alcoholic reek was worse than usual.

"Yeah," I said with a small nod.

Dad wobbled a bit and sat heavily in one of the chairs, still smiling and staring at me. "Football, huh? You should've called me to pick you up."

"No phone, Dad," I said with my mouth full.

"Then let's get you one." He yanked my hand and stole a bite of my pizza.

"Hey!" I laughed, pulling my slice away. It was nice to see a glimmer of who Dad used to be, even if it was under the influence of 3.5% Utah piss water.

He got up, washing his face in the sink. "You want to go to the movies tonight?"

"On a school night?" I said, shocked. "Yeah!" Five minutes ago, I was seriously about to jump between Dad and Uncle Chris before they started throwing fists, but maybe Uncle Chris got through to him.

Maybe he was going to be okay after all.

Dusty's Decision

"**M**y dad wasn't okay, guys." I snort.

No one says a thing.

"It just got worse after that." I sigh, placing my hands in my jacket pockets and looking at the floor. "It felt like I was healing for both of us. I was eleven. Whenever he got really drunk, he got mean. It started with making me feel stupid. I'd ask for help with school, but he'd belittle me for not knowing math or science like my mom. Then it became about blaming. He'd blame me for how shit his life turned out and how it was my fault his wife died. He didn't seem to consider that I lost my mom, too."

I look up at all of them, noticing their glassy eyes. My first instinct is to break up the tension and say something stupid, but I don't. There's so much I want to say, so much I want to go over, but this isn't about me. This is about Jhoana. And all this time, deep down, I'd already decided; I'm going to save her. I have to save her. I release the air I've been holding hostage in my lungs.

"After Jho... When she didn't wake up... that was like the last straw for my dad. We left a few years later. Being in our house, this town... It was too much for him. He thought a fresh start might help us leave my mom's ghost behind. It didn't, of course. As I got older, I worked really hard to not turn into him. But I am my father's son. It didn't take long for me to turn to the bottle, just like him."

"But you're also your mother's son." Brunner says, blinking against the pooling in his eyes. I'm surprised, despite knowing I shouldn't be. This man who'd spent the better part of a day immersing himself in our nightmares... He isn't the cruel, damaged kid I'd known. He was Jhoana's best friend too, even if we never really let him in. I'm made up of pieces of the people I surround myself with and Brunner is a piece of Jhoana.

"Don't sell yourself short, Dust," Brunner finishes.

"You have Auntie Via's kindness," Jadis says with a sad smile.

"You have her compassion," Rictor adds.

"Her smile is yours, too." Emierr's face looks hollow, mismatching the warm words that came out. "I remember feeling so loved by her smile. And how much your smile made me feel the same way. When she died, I couldn't help but think how lucky you were to have someone who loved you more than the universe itself."

That one hit home. I close my eyes against the wave of prickling heat. After all these years, I still feel everything.

~ ~ ~

DCEMBER 12, 2007

Happy Birthday Bro!

I miss you. Football is over, but I had the best time with you! Next year again?

Love, Meer.

December 12, 2007

Happy Birthday, Dusty

Please come back, Meer got more annoying since you hung out with us. I can't handle it anymore. I miss you, Dusty. We're always here.

Love, Jads.

December 12, 2007

Happy Birthday, Dusty!

You promised you wouldn't go far away :(But
I hope you enjoy the spam sandwich I made for
you. I love you.

Love, Jho.

December 12, 2007

Happy Birthday, Dusticle

    I hope your 12th birthday is galactic! I miss you.
Please come play with us, we have a new game.

                          Love, Ricky.

P.S. I'm getting tired of Meer, so come hang out!

I read their birthday letters over and over again. Uncle Chris dropped them off before he went to work.

This year, I didn't want to throw a party; I didn't want to celebrate my life. This year, I just wanted to sleep. Dad took the day off to stay and celebrate with me, just us boys he said. But I was already tired of expecting anything from him.

I was tired of expecting anything from anyone. But I couldn't lie; I wanted my best friends here more than ever. I wanted to play whatever game they had invented that seemed to fill their lives up again. I wanted to laugh right next to them. *But...* I sighed. *Why does there always have to be a but.*

I headed downstairs to see what Dad was doing. Music was coming from the kitchen, and water was running from the sink. Dad wasn't here. I turned the water off and spotted his phone on the table, with a huge mixing bowl full of confetti cake batter. The easy-bake cake box was on the floor next to the trash can; he probably threw it like a basketball and missed. I felt a warm smile forming on my face. Dad was making me a cake even though he couldn't cook for shit.

At least I knew he was trying. Today anyway. *Where is he?* I heard some clanging echoing from the basement. I felt my heart sink. For a split second, I thought it was Mom. What the hell was he doing down there? He'd been doing all our laundry at a laundromat to avoid going to the basement. I grabbed the doorknob, hesitantly opening the door. A little crack of light broke through the space between the wall and door. With one steadying breath, I swung the door open.

The clanging and banging were louder now, and I could hear Dad mumbling something. The Chamorro music playing from his phone started to fade into the background as I walked down the stairs. Wordless vitriol needled my mind, cursing my dad for making me face my dead mother's lab. It would probably look how she'd left it. Like she had just stepped out for an errand. I didn't want to be here.

Air froze in my lungs when I reached the bottom stair. There was broken glass scattered across the floor and Mom's research papers were strewn everywhere. A dull thud filled me with primordial fight or flight. My eyes trailed along a splatter of stark red, rapidly soaking into the coarse, concrete floor.

Thud.

It didn't sound anything like the movies. The tendons of my dad's arm clenched as he forced his fist into the battered wall. The white paint was splintered with hairline fractures, emanating from a scarlet central point. I watched with mounting horror as my dad's bleeding knuckles collided with the wall. Blood slipped down to the floor; faster than the colored corn syrup I'd seen on TV.

"Dad!" The scream that rended my throat barely sounded human. I bolted across the sheafs of paper that held Mom's life's work. Shards of shattered glass lodged into my bare feet, but I barely felt them. I caught Dad's arm, slick with blood, and pulled it from the wall.

"Move!" he roared, shoving me with all his strength. I crashed to the ground. The pain of the bruise now forming on my hip and the burn of glass in my soles hit me all at once. Hot tears coursed across my face. They were still warm when they landed on my arm.

"Wouldn't it be better if I just go too?" he slurred, to me or himself, I couldn't tell. "No one cares that Via is dead. Everyone wants to forget her." He glared down at me, "Even you. You want me dead, don't you? Don't you wish she was the one alive?" He whirled and struck the wall again. The thud was so quiet, like it shouldn't have caused any damage at all. When he drew his hand back, a fresh rivulet of blood was rolling toward the floor. His knuckles were shredded and raw.

I was sobbing now, "Dad, stop, stop, stop…"

"I'm better off dead!" he bellowed at the ceiling, straight through to the heavens.

"Dad!" The panic made my voice unrecognizable. The sound startled him. He turned back to me, dazed. He seemed to wake up, looking around him, taking in the shattered glass and gore. Finally, he raised his hands to look at the mutilated knuckles. Horror bloomed in his expression.

"Dustin?" His voice was higher now; thin, fragile. He reached for me, but I flinched and scuttled backwards on the concrete, raising my shaking hands like two pathetic shields. My breath came in shallow gasps. A vice-like embrace enveloped me. *Mom?* It was hard to see through my tears, but I could smell the beer; it was Dad. He held me tightly, choking on his sobs in a way I'd never seen a grown man cry. Somehow, I felt it. I felt Mom wrapping her arms around us. I clung to Dad, fearing that if I let go, we might both break.

"I'm so sorry, son." Dad's frail voice began to echo. "I love you so much, please forgive me."

~ ~ ~

Dusty!" Rictor hollers. My eyes snap open. I'm in Brunner's carpeted basement and no blood slithers down the walls. "You're okay, bro." He grips my shoulders, holding me firmly to the earth.

My face is damp with drying tears. It was just a memory. Dad, to his credit, got better in the end—for him and me.

"Let's sit down," Rictor says, leading me to the couch. I allow him to guide me, and the others make room for me in the middle.

"Guys..." I start. "I'm sorry for not messaging or calling. I keep saying I'm here for you guys, but I never reached out. I think that would have changed a lot, at least for me." I start cracking my knuckles, a habit Sylvia pointed out when I get anxious. Clenching my fingers shut, I try my best to steady myself. I can hardly feel Emierr's hand as it lands gently on top of mine. One by one, they all reach out to hold onto me, even Brunner. At this moment, Jhoana's smile flashes in my mind.

I'm so tired of being the way that I am. *It's time to share the burden. I can't keep carrying it alone.*

~ ~ ~

The new year started how I figured it would: shitty. Dad didn't lose his job, but he was starting to talk about leaving Farmington. NASCAR trainer, he said. It was cool he had a distraction now, but... I sighed. I'd made up my mind. I'm going to be with them. Whatever time I had left, it was theirs.

A knock on the door interrupted my thoughts. I hastily turned the TV on and SpongeBob's obnoxious voice filled the air, covering the sound of paper crunching as I jammed it under the couch. Whoever it was pounded again. My money was on Dad forgetting his keys. Again. Resigned, I got up to open the front door. But it wasn't Dad. It wasn't even a creepy pair of teenage missionaries.

"Dusticle," Ricky said.

"Dicktor." I grinned, feeling oddly light at the sight of his face. "Come in."

I'd once read a theory that every person has their own mundane superpower, like always making the perfect pancakes, or never stepping on Legos. Ricky's power was showing up at the right time and saying the right things. Him appearing today, just at the moment he did... It just made my decision feel even more right.

"Where's Uncle?" Ricky asks, scanning the house.

"He's out. There's pizza if you want."

We sat on the floor, leaning back against the couch, watching SpongeBob and eating pizza in silence. He sighed quietly yet audibly, and I hid my grin; that was his way of hinting that I should speak first. But I wasn't going to be the one to start this conversation.

"Just say it, Ricky," I said.

"Where have you been? You don't hang out with us anymore."

I met his gaze and shrugged. I knew this was coming, yet the truth felt too deeply buried for me to dig it out.

"We all missed you on your birthday, Christmas, and New Year's." His voice was soft, maybe a little hurt. "I don't think you should be alone, Dust."

"Ricky." I stopped myself. *Start small.* "How are you?"

"I'm a lot better now." He tried to smile.

"That's good, I'm happy for you," I said. I was unable to force much feeling into that response. *I wish I was happy.* "My Dad's a drunk." I said, catching even myself off guard.

Silence.

SpongeBob did his goofy laugh, and I snuck a look at Ricky. His face said everything. The thoughts I'd been keeping locked up were all boiling up to the surface. I pressed on, "He said, maybe if he had shown more attention to my mom than me, he could've convinced her to quit her job sooner."

"Dusty…"

"I got her killed, right?" My voice cracked, tears welling in my eyes. I didn't really need any external validation. I knew it was true. It was my fault. But a part of me still wanted someone to tell me a comforting lie; that I was not the reason my mom died.

"Bro, you can't think like that." He sounded genuinely shocked. Couldn't he see the truth of what I'd done? "Don't ever think that!" he repeated, reaching for my hand.

"It's true," I choked out. "My dad was helping me a lot with school because I'm stupid, rather than taking care of my mom and now she's dead." There it was; the thought that had been festering in my mind ever since that empty coffin went into the ground.

Ricky didn't argue. Instead, he talked about how he tried to stop Uncle James that morning. He'd been replaying that day over and over again, just like me. I wanted to tell him that there was nothing he could've done, but I knew I couldn't say it without excusing myself. His grip on my hand tightened, just like that day at the swing set. But this time, it was me sharing my pain with him. I let the tears fall, unable to hold them back any longer. I should've reached out to him. He was the only one who could understand me.

"It's not our fault, Dust," he said, his own eyes damp. He pulled me gently into a hug.

His chest was warm, maybe from my crying, but it felt safe. I thought I'd built up my walls enough to numb the pain of Mom's loss, but it turned out I'd constructed those walls with paper. Everything crashed back into me all at once, my defenses flapping pointlessly in their wake. Ricky fidgets with something in his pockets and pulls out a weird-looking rock. Startled, I pulled away and wiped my eyes. I knew what this was. Mom had pictures of these space rocks in her lab.

"That's... My mom told me about these. How did you get one?" I asked, catching my breath. The distraction helped settle the howling storm in my chest.

"My Pa, he gave it to me that morning. This one is yours." He smiled shakily and handed it to me. As it touched the skin of my palm, it began to glow.

Despite myself, I was completely sidetracked. *What kind of mineral can glow like that?* "My mom and your dad studied these until the very end... Thanks, Ricky." I curled my fingers around it and reached for one last hug. "You're a good brother." The words left my mouth before I could even comprehend what I said, but it was true. Ricky always felt like more than just my best friend; he felt like the brother I always wanted. I glanced up at him, suddenly self-conscious. Would he laugh at me?

"You too, Dusty." His voice hitched as he said it. "Wanna get out of here?"

"Yeah." I nodded.

Ricky led me to Jho's house, where he told me the others were waiting. As we walked through the door, Jho, Jads, and Meer rushed forward. We were a tangle of arms, legs, tears, and smiles. Meer tried to explain everything in a flood of excited babble, but he lost me practically as soon as he started speaking. So, Jho jumped in and broke it all down; the world they had discovered, the adventures they'd been on, and the friends they'd made.

I tried to listen seriously, doing my best to keep an open mind, even though it sounded like some kind of babyish make-believe. I took mental notes on Ethra, the magickal world with creatures and magick spelled with a "k." I had to admit it was pretty in-depth for an imaginary game. They must have put a lot of time into this. Ricky grinned a lot as we listened to the girls rave about Ethra. It suddenly felt as though time had hardly passed at all. I was back where I belonged; doing something ridiculous with my best friends.

At last, we lay down on the grass, heads all in a circle and holding hands. Ricky's voice guided us, telling us to close our eyes and breathe in slowly. I started feeling light and my heart began to race. Was there even a possibility that this was all real?

As Ricky counted down, together, we all said, "Astralis."

My body sank briefly into the ground before a second force yanked me up into the sky. My eyes snapped open, and I was passing through clouds.

"Holy shit!" I yelped, trying to twist my body in the air, but my limbs didn't obey.

"Don't worry, Dust, you'll get use—" Ricky started to say.

Panic filled my muscles with adrenaline, contracting them against whatever force gripped me. I could feel the veins in my neck and my teeth clenching so hard I feared they might break. My heart pounded once, twice. Just as a burn began to overtake my muscles, I felt the bind shatter, and just like that, I was flailing in total freefall. Ricky caught my hands, steadying my trajectory.

"How did you do that?" Ricky's eyes were round with awe.

"I—I don't know," I said, confused. Couldn't everyone move around their first time? "How is this real?" I yelled over the roar of cosmic wind.

"It's real for us," Ricky's eyes were filled with wild joy and starlight.

"You trust us, right?" Meer's smiling face was cast in greens and blues from a passing nebula.

Who gives a shit whether or not this is real? "Always," I said. We flew hand-in-hand through the universe, and we were infinite.

~ ~ ~

Brunner chuckles, interrupting our reminiscing. "After hearing this the fourth time, I remembered something." He gets up and stretches, fingers brushing the old-fashioned popcorn ceiling. "When Jho first told me about Ethra, I laughed it off. I thought it was just her way of dealing with Ricky's grief. But then she mentioned Jads went with both of them to Ethra, and then Meer joined. She constantly updated me with everything you guys did. At the time I really didn't think much of it. But one day, she went on about how Ricky was going to bring Dusty back to the fold." He fidgets with his fingers. "I saw all of you that evening from behind the picket fence. And for the first time, I saw how much you all loved each other." He pauses.

"Rune..." Emierr murmurs. "You don't have to explain."

"No, let him." Jadis jerks her chin at Brunner.

"I got jealous. For the first time..." He sounded ashamed. "I wished I could be with you guys. I wanted it so badly, to be with my best friend's best friends. But I don't know why you guys didn't want me to be." Brunner's eyes would have fit perfectly on a humane society ad.

No one has anything to say, not even Emierr, who probably should have a response by now.

"So... instead, I let myself be angry." He sighs deeply. "What I'm trying to say is I'm really sorry. I should've believed Jho all those times and just asked to tag along... but I let my anger get in the way."

"No one would have expected you to believe Jho," Emierr says reasonably. "If they'd told me what they were doing, but never actually took me to Ethra, I would have thought they'd completely lost touch with reality."

"You made our lives a living hell, Rune," Jadis says, her voice low and eyes unfathomable. "And I don't know if I can ever fully forgive you for how you treated us. But, remembering the past, hearing how much you cared for Jho... I wish you could've been part of our group." We all stare in total disbelief at her. Brunner's mouth is hanging open. No one could have predicted those words exiting Jadis's mouth.

Did Jads hit her head? "Yeah, Rune. What you did was fucked up," I add, pouncing on the chance to make peace while everyone was busy gaping at Jadis. "I'm still angry about it, but when I think of Jho, I see all of us together, including you. If they can forgive you, then I can too. Holding onto grudges is pointless anyway."

Brunner seems to be at a total loss for words. Shock, gratitude, guilt, and warmth roll over his face in shallow waves. I decide to rescue him, partly because I want to get this over with.

"Anyway," I say loudly. "Where was I?"

~ ~ ~

"Yeah!" I whooped as the mecha suit guy got blown clean through the wall of the arena.

"Yes!" Meer cheered, popcorn flying from between his fingers and bouncing off a nearby nymph's emerald hair. She shot him a leaf green glare over her shoulder.

"No!" Ricky wailed, hands grabbing fistfuls of his own hair.

"I'm telling you, these wizards come here to just kick ass." Meer laughed, replenishing his handful of popcorn, much to the nymph's dismay.

"Next one, Ricky. He'll get him for sure," I said with a bracing pat on the back.

"You got this, Alabaster!" Ricky shouted, leaping to his feet. His lone voice echoed through the entire stadium. A ripple of laughter moved through the crowd and more than one face turned our way. "Kick his ass!" He threw his arms up and threw two huge thumbs up at the mecha pilot hauling himself out of the Alabaster-shaped hole in the wall. He brushed his chrome knees off before turning around and giving Ricky an appreciative wave.

"Sit down, you're embarrassing us," Meer hissed, yanking Ricky back into his seat. Ricky huffed and folded his arms, his back hitting the seat with a little too much force. "Who do you think can beat Mr.

Wizard over there?" He leaned around Ricky, eyes sparkling with violence. "He's won every match three times in a row."

"Jads told me he's part of the Council in Arid. No wonder why he's so good," Ricky scoffed.

"Isn't that cheating? Can professionals join amateur things like this?" I asked, surprised.

Both their heads slowly rotate to face me.

"Don't ever say that again," Meer growled.

"Yeah, bro. This *is* professional," Ricky snapped.

I rolled my eyes. They always took these things way too seriously. "Then I think they need to make the mecha suits magick resistant. Can't you tell Al or the Huttons that, Ricky?" I helped myself to some of the popcorn, and a dozen different flavors danced in my mouth.

"It's not that easy, Dust. Magick—"

"Oh, here we go, you got him going now," Meer groaned.

"As I was saying before I was so rudely interrupted, it's not that easy," Ricky said, shooting a glare at Meer. "It's hard to get any samples of the source of magick, even though we all have it in our bodies. Extracting it from our cells won't work because the moment it touches the air, it disappears."

"Woah." I was no science whizz like Ricky, but even I knew that was some impressive trivia. I always forgot how long they'd been here. How much did they learn or make up? I still had no idea how they even created this place, but I tried not to think too hard about it. Don't look a gift horse in the mouth and all that.

"No, yeah, it's a lot to catch up on. But you'll learn it all, trust me." Meer fell back against his seat, waiting for the next match to start.

"The source is... the asteroid, right?" I asked Ricky. "Why haven't they just gone down there and gotten samples?"

Meer answered for him. "It's forbidden. Also *dragons* exist here, Dust. What other scary shit might be creeping around their life source?" Meer cut off his musings with a screech as the new mecha suit dude deflected his wizard opponent's rain of softball-sized hail.

"They're not just scared, it's more that the Ethereal Tree is untouchable," Ricky amended, eyes glued to the match once again. So many rules here; how did they have the time or foresight to create such a detailed reality? I knew it must have been something to do with the white hole stones, but that was where my theories ended.

"Dusty." Meer's voice made me jump. "You should see the mecha suits they have parked by the docking area. Those are huge."

Ricky gasped, startling me again.

"Can you guys *stop*—"

Meer bolted upright. "Oh shoot, time to go." He leaped to his feet, dragging me away with Ricky close behind me.

"Where are we going?"

Neither one answered me. Ricky clamped his hands on my shoulders to push me while Meer continued to drag me along. We came to a stop in front of the Terrerium, the two of them grinning and giggling like the little dumbasses they were. These two had something planned; they were going to prank me; I could feel it.

"Cover his eyes," Ricky ordered Meer.

"Hey, if you guys put anything crawling on me, you're dead," I warned them.

They both snickered and pushed me inside the Terrerium. I heard the doors slide open. Meer's hands fell away from my eyes.

"Surprise!" Jads, Jho, and Al chorused, blowing into noisemakers.

"Happy birthday, Dusty!" Meer and Ricky pounced on me in a crushing hug and the girls piled on. A nice holographic sign shone with the words "Happy Birthday, Dusty" and pictures of me with different expressions floated all around. I didn't know how to react; my birthday was two months ago.

"We're sorry we missed your birthday." Ricky punched my shoulder affectionately.

"We planned this with Al for months," Meer added.

My chest swelled, and my eyes felt hot. I couldn't help it; I was so fucking happy.

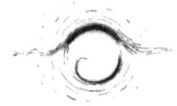

The icy air was slicing right through me—through my pointless Space Ring jumpsuit, through my skin, through my muscles, and into my bones. Jho's warm arms slipped around my shoulders for a tight squeeze before I hightailed it back inside the safety of Al's ship. A large man, roughly the same size as the Chief of Terrene, and dressed in Inuit-style clothes, approached Jho and wrapped her in a thick, furry blanket. Al shook the man's hand and they exchanged nods. Al then knelt down to a sniffling Jho. I couldn't make out what she was saying but it looked like a familiar scene.

After several more rounds of crying, hugs, and farewells, we were all back on board, waving at Jho from the window. She looked so small against the frozen expanse of Verglas.

Ricky pushed away from the window and went to sit, not in the passenger's seat, but where Jho had been minutes before. I joined him and the seat belts pulled snugly around us. Safety first. We were now on our way to Zaltana, the nation in the sky. I liked the thought of a whole bunch of people living up high in the mountains. I wanted to visit when I heard about it, but I never thought I'd get separated from my best friends so soon after reuniting.

Al was quiet. Saying goodbye to three kids he basically took care of on his own must have been tough for him. Goodbyes were always hard. I looked at Ricky again and reached his hand. He returned my gaze, trying to regain control of his breathing.

"Why are you sending us away, Ricky?" I asked quietly.

"I don't want to, Dust. But... this is the only way we can all be happy."

"But we're happy *together*. Isn't that why we made this place?" I looked down; his hand was so warm. "I don't want to go." My throat constricted. I just got them back; I didn't want to be far away from them again. "Can I just stay with you?"

Al looked back at us. "You guys all right?"

"Trust me. Please." Ricky's voice cracked. Meer's words echoed from my first day at football practice.

"Always," I whispered under my breath.

"We're okay, Al." Ricky rubbed his eyes. We stayed like that until we arrived in Zaltana. It was the last time my hand felt warm.

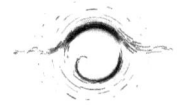

The sun felt nice on my skin as I took in the chilly mountain air. It had been almost a month since we all went our separate ways. Jho called us yesterday with some big news—she was now the Noble of Verglas, and had acquired some kind of force field capabilities. I didn't even think that was possible, but now it was. I hoped we would all get cool powers and could go on epic adventures, just like the video games we played.

I thought exploration and escapism was the reason Ethra even existed, but these days, it seemed more like drudgery.

Man, these routines were killing me. Same old stuff every day; heading with the tribe to Lumina's Reach to learn Brae ways. Every time I visited, I couldn't help but stare at Zaltana's Ethereal Lake. It was a magickal pool of stardust, mirroring the sky's vibrant hue and bioluminescent flowers lit up around it. It felt like a secret spot where the mountains had conversations with the stars, and the water listened in. They said the lake granted mystical abilities to those chosen to swim in it.

I'd put in the effort, and I hoped it would pay off. I also met a few kids during training, but I never stuck around long enough to get buddy-buddy. They were all about traditions, which I didn't think would be a thing, especially in the technologically advanced capital city, Juno. The Brae had a really cool history. There were five human chief councils of the Tellus Tribe and all of them decided to part ways. The Brae Chief wanted cosmic knowledge, so he and his followers settled in the mountains and studied the stars, like Mom.

And now, it was one of the most progressive nations in Ethra. The blend of culture, tradition, and progress fascinated me. Ricky would totally fit in here.

Zaltana was the sister nation to the Fleming Space Ring. Engineers in Juno initially built the Space Ring, and now it had become its own nation. We were all connected by life's threads.

I missed my friends. I wanted to explore Ethra together, not be scattered around, plodding through our solo expeditions. But, Ricky said we'd be back together after surveying the land and I was taking his word for it.

The best part of my day, especially after cramming so much knowledge into my skull, was coming up to this mountain top and looking out over all of Ethra—over all my friends, regardless of how far away they were.

"So, this is where you go after your training."

I spun to my left and saw Chief Arun, sitting like me, soaking in the sun.

"I'm sorry for interrupting you, Grandpa." I bowed my head. *How did I not see him?*

"Never be sorry for enjoying such a magnificent view." He smiled reassuringly. Chief Arun was extremely zen. He was everybody's cool grandpa, always in some fancy traditional attire; loose gray pants tight to the ankle, a long, layered tunic stitched with indigo thread, and thick, woolen overcoat on top. A woven scarf was also looped several times around his neck. While each Brae overcoat was completely unique in its intricate designs, Chief Arun's stood out the most. The entire thing was snow white and covered with jagged black stripes, representing Ade', the Crown Beast of Zaltana. It was inspirational. Maybe my job could be sitting on a mountain in tiger print one day.

"Why doesn't this place have a name?" I asked after a moment. "Every other settlement in Zaltana has one."

"Because we are not just one place; we are all of Zaltana combined. Our spirits will return here, the place all our ancestors have called home."

"Sweet." The word sounded stupid as it tumbled out of my mouth.

"You know, my daughter used to come here, too. You remind me of her." His expression was distant.

"Really? I heard she and her sister are... no longer here. What happened to them?" I knew I shouldn't ask, but I was tired of marinating in my own pain. Talking about someone else's might be refreshing in a morbid sort of way.

Chief Arun sighed, still gazing out at the world beyond.

"Sorry, Grandpa." I really shouldn't have said anything.

"No." He shook his head, seeming to pull himself back. "I love talking about my daughters. They were incredible—spitting images of my dear Calista, whom we lost during her second birth. Her heart could not handle the journey, but she gave pieces of it to both of them. The youngest, my Little One, was to take my place as chief. Like her mother, she practiced witchcraft, and she was a breathtaking sorceress. Do you know much about the magick here?"

"Yes. Everyone has it in their blood; we all can use it, but some people practice it more, and they can do better spells," I rattled off, desperate to prove myself not a fool.

Chief Arun chuckled and nodded his head. "That is a very simplified take on it, but essentially yes. But there is also old magick. Have you ever heard of that?"

I shook my head.

"Old magick existed long before the great asteroid blessed us. And some people, like my beautiful Calista and Little One, could tap into it. My youngest was destined to help forge a new Ethra but she was taken too soon." Chief Arun heaved another sigh, laced with longing. It was so long ago, but his hurt sounded like it was just yesterday.

"What about your eldest?" I asked tentatively.

"My firstborn, she was more like me." He laughed affectionately. "She was a problem child, always getting scolded by her mother. And I would get scolded after."

I snorted a laugh, picturing the scene.

"Ful was an explorer of knowledge; she loved learning about the world and the stars. She was through and through a Zaltanian. But she also carried her mother's heart, her kindness, and her willingness to protect her own. I see those qualities in you, Dustin." He smiled at me.

"I don't know about the knowledge-seeking part, Grandpa," I said. "But your daughters sound awesome."

"What about your mom?" he asked, catching me off guard. "What was she like?"

I gaped at him, puzzled. "How did you know?"

"You arrived here with sadness in your heart, my boy. A kind only one who has lost a mother would know. My firstborn carried it very much with her, but she never let it break her spirit."

"My mom was... She was everything. She was actually a lot like... Ful?" I waited for a nod to confirm my pronunciation. When it didn't come, I continued. "My mom loved learning about space and the world. My friend Ricky, his dad, and my mom became best friends. They said they hated each other at first, but I can't imagine it. Sometimes, I think their friendship was stronger than my dad's and Uncle James's." I smiled at the memories. "She was my best friend, too." My voice suddenly broke.

Chief Arun untied the thick, red scarf at his waist and wrapped it around my shoulders. "She is a part of you. Carry her memory, and let it be all the great things."

I pressed closer to him, gripping the woolen scarf. He smelled like something Uncle James would've worn... Axe body spray. *Do they even have that here?*

"Thanks, Grandpa."

He smiled down at me. "It was Ful's. It once kept her warm in this very place. Now it shall do the same for you."

I leaned my head against him, and we stared out at the view in quiet remembrance of those we'd loved and lost.

After a few moments, Chief Arun let go of me and asked, "Are you ready for the ceremony?"

"I am now." I pushed myself up and helped him to his feet.

~ ~ ~

"It's crazy how there are only two bodies of Ethereal Waters in all of Ethra," Brunner comments.

"Well, two that the world knows of," Rictor points out.

"There're three, remember?" Emierr corrects them. "Jho found the secret one that her Crown Beast, Eyre, was living in."

"She made us all promise not to tell anyone, right?" Jadis looks pointedly at Brunner.

"It's in the notebook, Jads." Emierr rolls his eyes.

Jadis flicks him off.

"Okay, explain to me again why Zaltana's Ethereal Waters only give out one power but the one in Terrene is random?" Brunner flips through the pages of the notebook. He looks like an overenthusiastic college kid. Or maybe a massive Dungeons and Dragons nerd.

"It's like what Chief Arun said about old magick." Rictor really sounds like his dad. "Though there is so much science present about how magick works, there are still plenty of things the science can't prove. We know the origins, but we don't know why they function the way they do."

"So, it's still a mystery?" Brunner closes the book, looking slightly crestfallen.

"Who knows, it's been years since we've been there, maybe they figured it out?" Rictor almost sounds excited by the prospect.

"But it's all a dream, right? You guys can just make it up and that's it." Brunner raises an eyebrow. He's on a roll, asking all the right questions I never thought of asking, and I'm starting to wonder too.

"The longer we were there, it started to feel more real than if it were a dream," Jadis says slowly, contemplatively. She looks to Rictor for help. "How *did* you create Ethra?"

All of our eyes are trained on him now. As kids, we always thought Rictor just came up with this game out of nowhere, but it was so detailed and vivid. We started to think that maybe he was hypnotizing us and "Astralis" was the trigger word. When we were young, we didn't question much. Then, after Jho... Well, we stopped thinking about it entirely. Now that we're all here, sharing memories, things aren't adding up.

It's not possible for Ethra to just be a dream.

"I didn't really *create* Ethra," Rictor answers slowly. "It was a dream I was in, and I kept going back every time I slept. I just assumed it was a form of lucid dreaming. Jads and I read some books about it in the library, so I thought I'd just managed to do it." He meets Jadis's gaze. "It was all just dreams."

"But how did we share the same dream? Isn't that impossible?" I argue.

Emierr and Brunner glance at each other like they know something.

"I think because you guys always said "Astralis" before you slept, maybe that's like a spell? I don't know." Brunner seems to realize that the suggestion of Earth witchcraft is somewhat ridiculous and shuts his mouth again.

"What does "Astralis" mean again, Ricky? And what language is it?" Jadis asks.

"I don't know the language, but my Pa taught me it. It was like our goodbye. He said it meant 'to be revealed by the stars', I don't know why I had us say it every single time, I think it was just a way to comfort myself," he confesses. "But it did feel real."

"If it was real, all of it, then that means Jho—"

"Do you guys know string theory?" Emierr cuts Brunner off.

"What now?" I am most certainly out of my depth with anything that ends in "theory."

Rictor is staring, mouth ajar, at Emierr. I can practically see the cogs whirling. Of course he knows what that is.

"Yes, but what does that have to do with anything?" Jadis crosses her arms.

"What's string theory?" I ask again but, again, I'm ignored.

"Think about it guys—"

"Wait, we're getting off topic here. Dusty still hasn't finished his story." Rictor interrupts Emierr.

"Right, let's get through everything first and then we can talk about theories," Brunner agrees. Just as he said that, Jadis's phone dings, drawing my attention for a brief moment. The screen lights her face, just enough to highlight the look of horror that spreads across her face. I watch her shaking fingers fumble for a second before she drops the phone facedown, as if it's a venomous snake. She catches my eye and subtly shakes her head.

What the hell was that?

"Shit." I rub my forehead, tracing my mind's eye along the memories. *What's next...*

"I became a Noble..."

~ ~ ~

"Thanks again for coming with me, Jho." I peered at her. She'd changed a lot. In Ethra, she lost weight, but in the real world, she was still her chubby self. Today, she looked like a true Ghelcarii warrior—what she had been training for. Her armor had metal plates on the arms and legs, but the rest was made from a tough leather. Something told me I didn't want to know which creature's skin Jho now wore. There was fur on her wrists, ankles, and neck for warmth. Her hair was braided in the traditional Verglasian style, with beads and feathers woven in. She looked like a total badass.

"Of course. I'll always be there for you guys." Jho's warm smile was at odds with her attire. We were on the outskirts of Glaedhaven, one of Zaltana's villages, where Verglas's glacial currents met Zaltana's high cliffs. The trees, coated in eternal frost, towered above. Inkweavers, the Keepers of Zaltana who lived around this area, liked to sport flame tattoos for warmth. I was glad I'd taken some a few days ago.

"How are you doing in Verglas, Jho?" I asked. My breath billowed in the frigid air.

"Now that I'm a Noble, I get to leave when I want. It's nice getting out of Verglas. All they care about is becoming warriors." She wrinkled her nose. Jho's gentle nature would have never fit in with a nation of frozen Spartans. "I'm thinking of moving to Islaug instead."

"Islaug? Your nation's capital? Isn't that at the south pole of this place?" I traced the flame tattoos on my forearms onto my palms, letting out a flicker of green light.

"That's so cool!" Jho leaned in, placing her hands over the tiny flames.

"Feeling warmer?"

"A bit. Wait, I have an idea." She raises her hands, takes a deep breath, and exhales, pushing out her arms to create a light blue force field of translucent dragon scales around us. "There, so we can get warm faster."

I nodded appreciatively, letting the flames grow a bit, a soft heartbeat in my hands. "If you're thirsty, I packed some drinks on my left leg." I chuckled. Becoming an Inkweaver had its benefits. I could take something, anything really, and turn it into a tattoo on my skin. It was like having a secret storage space right on me. When I needed that thing again, I just summoned it back. I was sure most Inkweavers didn't use it for food or ice-cold drinks, but it was pretty handy.

I continued, "But why Islaug? It's so far away."

"There's so much more I can do there. I'm not a fighter, Dusty," Jho said. That was an understatement, despite her current appearance.

"Islaug sounds great, Jho. I mean, I'm not really into fighting either," I said as we emerged from the forest onto a mountain road. "But I kinda wish I picked Verglas instead."

"But Zaltana feels more like you. And you've always wanted to learn more about our Chamorro side, right?" Jho suddenly slapped a hand to my arm. "Remember Boyko, the big guy who greeted me when you and Ricky dropped me off?" she asked.

"Yeah, the one who looks like Meer's father from Terrene."

"Well, Boyko and his wife Valda took me in. They're nice people, and Valda is my favorite. She reminds me of my mom without the craziness." Jho snorts and I can't help but laugh too. "They tell me stories about Zaltana and its culture. From what I've heard, Zaltana is a lot like Guam. When our parents on Earth spoke about their home, community and family were important values in their way of life. If that's what being Chamorro means, you belong in Zaltana." Jho's eyes gleamed as she gazed ahead, not seeing the road.

"Wow, now that you say it that way, I guess I'm glad I ended up in Zaltana." I appreciated the way Jho could always make something seem fated. "You really like it here, huh?"

"I like being with my adoptive parents in Verglas, but being with you guys is the best. What about you?"

"I still can't believe this is a dream world. It all feels so real; sometimes, I forget it's just a dream."

"But *how are you*, Dusty?" Jho's eyes burned into mine.

"Can you keep a secret, Jho?" I asked, and she nodded.

"I'm happy, but I don't know where I fit in all of this. It looks like you guys found your purpose here," I admitted. It was something that had been weighing on me since I arrived here, late to the party. They all had their superpowers, their high status as Nobles, and a task. I may have gotten the powers but as for the other things. . .

"Is that why you want to face Ade'?" Jho furrowed her brows.

I jerked one shoulder up in a half shrug. "Maybe becoming a Noble will make me feel needed." It sounded strange to hear my thoughts aloud.

"You don't need to be a Noble to be needed. We always need you, Dusty." Jho dropped the force field around us, and the wind blew out the fire in my palms. Jho took both of my freshly extinguished hands. "We rule Ethra. This world is ours. Come on, I know where a Gate is; we can go through it and pick up the others. Let's go on an adventure." Jho's hands were warm, like Ricky's.

"The portal? We don't know the spell to open it."

"I do." She grinned devilishly.

"Okay then," I said, impressed. I scanned the area up ahead. "Oh, shit. It's a dead end." We stood a few feet away from where the road came to an abrupt halt. A cascade of fallen boulders had eliminated the trail.

"Dusty!" Jho shouted. I spun around, fists clenching on impulse.

A preternaturally large tiger was hunched over the middle of the trail, barricading us into the dead-end road. I couldn't so much *hear* the growl as I could *feel* it. The sound reverberated in my chest, sending adrenaline coursing through my veins.

Ade's pale yellow eyes fixed on mine, and I took an involuntary step back.

"Holy fuck."

"Come on, Dusty!" Jho sweeps her arms skyward to form transparent steps rising up and over Ade'. Without checking to see if I was wise enough to obey, she took off up the little floating platforms.

Ade's piercing stare did not leave me, seeming to glow against the snow white fur. I pelted after Jho onto the force fields and, though it felt wholly wrong to be running on something so seemingly intangible, it was stable under my footfalls. The force fields dropped behind us as she cast her arms ahead, calling more stepping stones. If I hesitated even a second, the steps I was bolting across would disappear. This was probably the worst trust exercise I've ever endured. Below, the massive tiger's predatory gaze followed us through the glasslike shields. I could still feel his low snarls in my chest cavity.

Jho slid to a halt, floating on one of her shields.

"Dusty, go," she panted. With a flick of her wrist, a trail of shields arranged itself into a set of stairs leading back down to the ground.

"What about you?" I asked frantically.

"I can protect myself; just go! I'll be right behind you." Jho turned to face Ade', her arms rising to meet his impending attack.

I didn't doubt her for a second. I thundered down to the ground and made for the road leading back to the forest. Just as I was nearing the tree line, Ade' slammed to the ground in front of me. I went skidding in the loose dust and hit the terra, hard. My body was now refusing to obey my commands.

MOVE, COME ON, MOVE!

Ade' towered over me, lips drawn back to expose his teeth. He had two sets of canines in his top jaw.

I was frozen, fused to the hard-packed dirt beneath me. Ade' was now so close, I could see saliva glinting on yellowed fangs. Each silent step of his enormous paws was a slow, torturous walk to my end.

"Dusty! Fight back!" Jho shrieked. Two glowing blue arrows struck the ground in front of me, narrowly missing my boots. Ade' leaped back and unleashed a blood-curdling roar in her direction. As if electrocuted, my body jerked back into motion. I rolled from my back, lifting off my shirt, and slammed one knee on the ground, pushing myself upright. I yanked my arms across my body, reaching for the inked outlines of firearms on either side of my ribs.

A blinding green light swelled at my sides as I pulled two laser guns from my skin. I had acquired them in Juno. I may or may not have stolen them to show off to Ricky. A scream ripped through my throat as I wrenched the triggers back.

With shocking agility, the tiger twisted and whipped its body between each blast. When the light dissipated, the beast was gone. For now. Jho darted behind me to haul me to my feet. We readied our stances, backs pressed together. I felt her arms rise as she conjured two force field shields the size of tractor tires on her hands. I slapped the guns back to my ribs where they melted back into tattoos.

I then prized the battle knives out from where they were etched into my forearms. They were traditional gifts for anyone who successfully became Keepers in Zaltana. I slid back into position, clicked the buttons on the handles, and felt the blades begin to heat. The razor-sharp steel began to burn red.

Where the fuck are you?

"Dusty," Jho whispered. I spun around to follow her gaze. He was there, in the trees, his pale, striped pelt blending into a copse of aspens. I watched, body taut with fear, as he took a soundless step toward us. Then another.

I made the foolish mistake of blinking and, in that moment, he charged. His muscles bunched under the rippling fur, propelling him over the forest floor faster than I thought possible. I expanded my lungs, taking in as much oxygen as I could get. *Bring it on!* But just then, Jho dropped her shields.

"Jho?" Did something happen? Did her power fail?

She shut her eyes and clutched her chest. Her shaking voice echoed as she began to sing. *"Hush now, little one. Don't you fear, I'm here."* To my utter disbelief, the tiger stopped dead in his tracks. *"In the wind, heartbeats under your chin..."*

It was... working? Jho was calming the Crown Beast down. Gripping the knives tighter, I seized the opportunity and dashed toward the tiger. He snapped out of his trance, locking eyes with me. I screeched a battle cry and dove at the tiger. That was when the pain surged. I fell short of the beast, collapsing to my knees.

My chest felt as though my heart had grown spines and, with each beat, a little more of me was sliced apart. Blinding tears splashed to the ground. Though I had just put myself in the most vulnerable position imaginable, I no longer felt fear. Ade' lowered his enormous head, the soft fur touching my forehead. My knives lay abandoned on the ground, and I pressed my face against his.

"I'm sorry," I whispered. "I didn't want to hurt you. I was just afraid." A tingling feeling wrapped around me, filling me with thousands of little novae. Just like that, I'd bonded with Ade'.

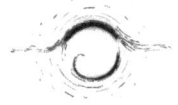

I made a decision when Ricky brought me back to the Squad. It had taken me a while, but I was ready now. It was two in the morning, and each step down the dark staircase felt like a warning cry. Dad should be asleep by now; he'd been getting better too. I flicked on the living room lights and reached under the sofa. I found the crumpled piece of paper, slowly smoothing out its creases.

I carried the paper to the basement, turning on the lights as I descended. I hadn't been down here since my birthday, and it was just as Dad and I left it. Leaving the crinkled paper on Mom's desk, I got a wet rag from the laboratory sink and began wiping the dried-up blood from the wall. Scrubbing it away was easy—the memory, not so much. I swept the loose papers into a pile, trying halfheartedly to restore some order to the chaos. Dropping the haphazard stack onto the desk, I fell into Mom's rolling chair and grabbed the picture of her and me from the NASA space camp with Ricky and his dad. Mom's hair had turned white faster than all the other parents.

I closed my eyes and let the memory play out.

"Dustin Reed."

I took a bite of my pizza and raised my brows. "Yeah, Mom?" *I said through the mouthful.*

"What did I say about talking with your mouth full?" she said, momentarily sidetracked by my manners.

"Sorry." I took a swig of root beer.

A soft smile formed on her face, and she shook her head indulgently. Her eyes were gray, almost silver in the light, though with an odd copper burst around the pupil. "Are you having fun, Piggy?" The nickname I'd earned by talking with my mouth full.

Her question confused me. "Of course, Mom. I'm just glad Ricky's here with me, he really loves it here."

"You sure? You're not just saying that because I work at NASA? You know you can be honest with me, I promise not to be hurt if you think your mom's job isn't cool." She put on a mock sad face.

"Mommy." I chuckled. "I think you're really cool. Cooler than Dad anyway."

"Now I know you're joking with me." She leaned back in her chair, smiling all the same.

"I swear! I don't understand much about the science stuff, but I have

Ricky to explain it to me." I turned around to see Ricky and Uncle James still at the gift shop, holding onto a black t-shirt that had the NASA logo on it. I saw a teddy bear in there earlier, Ricky might like it.

"Dustin." Mom recaptured my attention. "Do you remember what I said to you? About if I were to go on an expedition that could take months or years?"

"Yeah?" Mom was acting really weird. "You said that I have to be there for Dad as much as he will be there for me. I must have a strong heart."

"Good. Always have a strong heart, okay Piggy?" She pinched my cheek.

"I know, Mom." I pulled away. "Can we buy something in the gift shop? I wanna get the teddy bear for Ricky, I think he'll like it." I smiled wide, relying on the last bits of baby fat in my cheeks to get me what I wanted.

"You want to get Ricky a toy?"

"I just know he'll like it, Mom," I wheedled.

"Okay, fine. Finish your food first."

"Thanks!" I balled the remainder of the pizza slice and shoved it into my mouth "Les' noh say I go' it o'ay?" I mumbled around bread and cheese.

"Dustin Reed." Mom scolded me again.

I took a moment to swallow. "Tell Uncle James to say he bought it for him. I don't wanna make it weird."

"All right, Piggy, whatever you say," she agreed, tousling my hair affectionately.

"I'm so sorry, Mommy," I whispered to the picture frame. "I'm sorry I didn't have a strong heart."

I unfolded the crumpled paper. I'd decided to not go through with it; the Squad had convinced me of that, but I needed to read it just one last time.

HEY RICKY, MEER, JADS, AND JHO,

WHEN MOM LEFT, IT FELT LIKE SHE TOOK A PIECE OF ME WITH HER. DAD'S TRYING. HE'S REALLY TRYING TO KEEP GOING FOR ME... BUT I CAN SEE HIM FADING, JUST LIKE EVERYTHING ELSE AROUND ME. AUNTIE LUNA, MOM'S GARDEN, EVEN MY OWN REFLECTION... IT'S LIKE IT'S ALL SLIPPING AWAY.

BUT THEN I LOOK AT YOU RICKY, AND YOU'RE DIFFERENT. YOUR DAD WAS YOUR BEST FRIEND, JUST LIKE MOM WAS MINE. SO WHY DON'T YOU LOOK AS LOST AS I FEEL?

WHEN I SEE YOU, IT'S LIKE THERE'S STILL LIFE IN YOU. YOU'RE HOLDING ON, KEEPING EVERYTHING BRIGHT, KEEPING EVERYONE GROUNDED. AND THEN THERE'S ME, STANDING HERE, FEELING LIKE THE GRASS BENEATH ME HAS TURNED GRAY, LIKE I'M SINKING INTO IT. I DON'T KNOW HOW TO PULL MYSELF OUT. I'M WILTING, AND I DON'T THINK ANYONE CAN MAKE ME GREEN AGAIN.

BUT I NEED YOU TO KNOW, I LOVE YOU ALL. YOU'RE MORE THAN FRIENDS, YOU'RE MY BROTHERS AND SISTERS. AND PLEASE, PLEASE TAKE CARE OF DAD FOR ME.

LOVE, YOUR BROTHER DUSTY

I crumpled the paper one last time and threw it in the trash.

THE DAY IT HAPPENED

My arms wrap instinctively around Dustin, my head resting on his shoulder as the weight of his pain spills out in silent tears. In the toughest chapter of our lives, love enveloped me from all sides, but for Dustin, pain embraced him more.

I wish Dustin could have felt the love that surrounded me back then. Instead, he was haunted by thoughts of ending it all, and the guilt eats at me for not being the brother he needed. As Dustin breaks down, we press in from all sides, trying our best to drown the pain.

"Fuck. I'm sorry, I'm sorry," Dustin manages between jagged breaths.

"Dusty, *I'm* sorry," I murmur. "We agreed to be brothers. I should have been there for you. You've always been there for me."

"No, Ricky. You gave me Ethra. It was everything to all of us. It meant everything to Jho... to me. Thank you, guys, for pulling me off the edge." Dustin is so strong, yet so fragile, and witnessing his breakdown makes it even harder to deny how fucking depressing our past is.

There are no words; all we do is hold one another.

We take a moment to regroup, pulling ourselves together after the emotional storm. It's been a few hours now, and we're approaching the most critical part of the story—the one that unveils the mystery of how Jhoana slipped into her coma. Even Brunner, who's taken every tale in his stride, remains unusually subdued.

"Obviously, we can't stop now." I break the uneasy silence. "I thought about it, and I'll be the one who tells the story. None of us wants to remember how Jho... but I brought you guys into this mess, so let me be the one to talk about the day we left Ethra for good." My chest tightens, and I make a conscious effort to slow down my breathing, listening to the faint echo of Bonnie's voice, *"Slowly, steadily."*

At that moment, something catches my eye. Two men in white shirts and black slacks are staring down into the window well, feet planted on the browning grass above us. We stare right back. What is it Emierr calls them? Mormon 2.0? One of them opens his mouth to speak, just as the plastic blinds drop down to cover the window.

"Every time, I swear," Brunner mutters, releasing the cord. "Alright, Ricky." He lowers the shades on the remaining three windows and falls back into the sofa. "How... How did Jho die?" The words hang in the air, heavy with the weight of the past and the anticipation of an answer none of us are truly prepared for.

~ ~ ~

Tomorrow would be Jho's birthday, and maybe our last Squad hangout. Meer thought we should put Ethra away for good and start living in the real world, but that was just dumb. Why couldn't we grow up with Ethra? Tonight, I'd show them why we needed it. I'd give them the best adventure yet. If they wanted excitement, I'd bring it to them.

I closed my eyes and let myself drift to Ethra. I woke up in the room I had shared with Meer ever since I started living in Terrene. He wasn't here yet. He'd better come. The sun was high in the sky; the Space Ring had just finished its shadow cycle on Terrene. I checked on Sólel, peeking through his window. He was packing his backpack when he spotted me and ran outside, with a big grin across his face.

"*Kuya* Ricky! Did you speak with my *kuya*?" he asked, slinging the backpack over his shoulder.

"Hi Sól. Your brother is coming, I promise," I reassured him, giving him a one-armed squeeze.

"Why hasn't he been coming? You know Mom and Father miss him," he said, his voice lower. He actually looked a bit taller. Time dilation was weird here. I'd known Sólel for nearly three months, but in real time, it had only been a month and a half. He was growing right before my eyes.

"Your *kuya* is becoming a teenager, that's why. But he'll come around," I told him with a smile.

Sólel nodded solemnly. "Oh, and *kuya*, my parents are asking if the Squad can have dinner here with us tonight. I'll ask the rest, but I just wanted to bring it up with you."

"It's your *Ate* Jho's birthday tomorrow. I think she'll like that," I replied, heart warming at the thought of a Terrene birthday celebration. Although I hoped to avoid the decapede egg salad this time around.

He brightened. "I'll be right back. Mom said she prepared food for all of us. I'll just let them know." He rushed off to the main part of the treehouse. I gazed around at the smooth wooden walls, adorned with all manner of furs, bones, and art. How could Meer want to forget all of this? I checked my phone. No messages. It was so weird; they never missed meeting time. *Where are they?*

A door slammed shut. "Loser."

I turned around to see Meer coming out from our room.

"Finally," I chastised him with a grin, "I was beginning to think you were going to flake on us again."

"I'm here, aren't I?" He lifted his eyebrows, and his lips curve, trying not to smile. We both laughed and reached for a hug.

"We miss you, man." I pulled back.

He sighed, "Ever since I started baseball, it's been eating up all my time. I get too tired to do anything."

"Then come here when you sleep; this place is supposed to make us feel better, that's what it was made for." I punched his shoulder.

"Yeah," Meer agreed with disinterest. "I'll try next time." An awkward pause filled the air. Meer was not the same anymore. He wasn't the guy who wanted to explore the world as a burgeoning botanist. Maybe he'd outgrown us.

"*Kuya!*"

We turn around to see a wide-eyed, smiling Sólel bounding towards us with a vine-woven picnic basket. He placed the basket on the ground and leaped into Meer's arms for an embrace.

"Sól, look at you, you grew!" Meer hugged him tightly. "When did your locs get this long?" Meer and Sólel's relationship had become one of my favorite things about Ethra. Meer had changed a lot when he became an older brother. Maybe that could explain why he thought he needed to grow up; maybe he wanted to be better for Sólel? It was no use trying to decipher any of it right now. I had to convince him to want to stay because if he left, I just knew the rest would start feeling the same way.

"Mom and Father have been dying to see you; let's go see—"

"Later, we have a mission to get to," Meer said, cutting him off.

"Oh, okay." Sólel's smile faded, and he picked up the picnic basket.

I tilted my head. "What mission?"

"The others are meeting us by the meadow."

"What? I thought we were all meeting here?"

"No, we said meet at the meadow." He eyed me. I could see a flicker of authority there.

"When did we say that?"

"I talked to them and—" Meer sighed.

"You guys had a meeting without me?" A mix of confusion and

hurt welled up inside me. *When did we start keeping secrets from each other?* Maybe I was the odd one out, stuck in my little fantasy world while my friends inched toward adulthood.

"No, Ricky. Um, we—" Meer looked at his feet. "I saw them outside before coming here and they don't want us to wait long. They'll meet us halfway. Come on, they might be there already." He grabbed Sólel's arm. "Can you take the basket?" he asked me.

I frowned, slowly reaching for the basket. Maybe I was just over-thinking it. It was nice of them, wasn't it? To make it easier for us to reach them?

Meer knelt down looking at Sólel, "Just like the old times?" Sólel's smile returned, and he hopped on Meer's back. "Hold on tight."

Meer tugged a vine down, wielding it to swing them up in the air. I let go of the basket and made it levitate next to me. Since I'd been in Terrene, I practiced a lot with my telekinesis. The ability to not carry things and just make them hover next to me was my favorite thing. I could already hear Jads's voice telling me I was lazy. She was not wrong. I raised my left hand to a vine and pulled it down to me. I took a deep breath in.

I clamped my fingers around the thick tendril and leaped forward, gaining momentum before I gave myself a telekinetic push to swing up in the sky. And just like that, I was in the air. It took a while for me to learn how to smoothly swing with the vines. Fearing heights didn't help, but Meer was a great teacher. Swinging up here with him and seeing Sólel happy again made me more determined not to let this go.

We reached the meadow they always talked about. Lush greenery stretched as far as the eye could see and, in the distance, Zaltana's majestic mountain ranges brushed the sky. Big, puffy clouds hung in every direction, almost like we were in one of Jads's drawings of white against the vivid blue. The Space Ring hovered above, casting its shadow on other parts of the world; a reminder of the magic that brought us together.

We rarely got to see each other, busy with our roles as Nobles of the nations. Being scared to go out and having the Huttons find me made everything so hard to do. I hadn't told the Squad about what happened in the Space Ring, and I didn't think I could. I had to confide in Chief Berkarys and Chieftess Nalani. Thanks to them, I'd been kept hidden, even when Dr. Wolfgang and Miss Delphini came down to the village. The Chief and Chieftess lied, saying they hadn't seen me in months. It was something they would never usually do. But they did it for me.

I owed a lot to them, but today, I was putting aside all of my worries. I wanted to have fun with my best friends.

There, not far along, Dusty, Jads, and Jho stood in the grassy field. I stopped walking. *Ethra stays with us, no matter how far we go. Even if this is the last day we see this place, we're never truly gone. We are Ethra.* Next to me, Meer gave me a nudge.

"Last one is a rotten egg," he said and booked it.

"Hey!" I shouted; anxiety shoved to the wayside. I dashed behind him and Sólel, the basket chasing us all.

The others spotted us and waved in our direction. Sólel found himself wrapped in Jho's tight hug; his prize for winning the impromptu race.

"Hi, Ricky," Jho said, letting go of Sólel and sidling up next to me.

"Hey, Jho, is Gordo feeling better?"

"He still has a cough, but he'll be better before we know it," she answered brightly. I still wasn't used to seeing this version of Jho. She had slimmed down; her face was all sharp with no more chubby cheeks. Her hair was longer and intricately braided. But what really got me was how strong she looked. Her movements were those of a warrior; confident and powerful. She hadn't changed much when we were awake. She was still chubby and shy back home, but here, she seemed ready to take on anything.

"My mom made lots of food for us," Sólel announced proudly, turning to look for the basket. I raised my right hand and urged the basket to him.

"Should we take a break?" Meer asked me. We were both still panting from our mad dash. My stomach grumbled.

"That's a yes," Jads laughed.

"Where we gonna sit? The grass is tall as fuck," Dusty frowned, hands out, brushing the velvety blades.

"I got this." Meer cracked his fingers. He lifted his hands in the air and lowered them. As he did, the grass around us began to retreat into the ground, making what was unmistakably a crop circle.

"Nice." Dusty fist bumped Meer. "Are you the one behind all the ones on YouTube too?"

"Yeah man, I have a little cardboard UFO and everything."

Sólel opened the picnic basket, and the sweet aroma of honey wafted through the air.

"That smells really good, Sól," I said.

"My mom made us sub sandwiches. She took inspiration from your Earth recipe, the Subway footlong? I know it's your most sought-after delicacy."

"Now, who told you that?" Jads asked, crossing her arms and fighting back a laugh.

"*Kuya* did," Sólel said, looking pleased with his high level of Earth knowledge.

"What, it's true. Subway is the best," Meer said, reaching for the basket.

"Can I show you guys what I've been practicing?" Sólel asked once everyone had settled in for the meal.

He was met with scattered nods and encouragement.

"Yes!" He jumped up and wheeled around to stand in front of us. "I wanted to make sure I could keep up with you guys. I'm no Noble, but I am a Keeper." He grinned.

"We believe in you, little bro," Dusty said, cheeks packed with an enormous mouthful of sandwich.

"He sounds a lot like you, Meer. What are you turning him into?" I teased.

"Please don't turn sweet little Sól into a mini you," Jads pleaded, a sly grin cutting through her act.

"Guys, stop bullying my cousin," Jho complained.

Sólel scoffed. "I'm better than him already!"

"Okay then, show us what you've been practicing," Meer said, gesturing to the center of the circle. "Thanks, cuz," he added to Jho.

Sólel took a deep breath in and spread both his hands out. Suddenly, strings of sunlight like solar flares, pierced through his deep brown skin, as if leeching the light from the actual sun. After a few seconds, he tightened his body, and he transformed into something we hadn't seen before.

His locs turned sun-bright yellow, and his eyes glowed with golden fire. An aura of light surrounded him, almost like light refracting off a diamond. The grass around him began to grow again, slowly undoing Meer's handiwork. He rose up into the air, his ascent gentle and controlled. In a flash, he was jetting across the clearing, shooting in circles around the tree line.

"Dude!" Dusty stood up, the rest of us close behind. "Sól, that's *sick!*"

Sólel soared back down to us and doused his blinding light to reveal the regular nine-year-old beneath.

"Okay, my turn," Dusty declared, moving to the front.

Apparently, it's talent show time.

"Alright." Dusty cracked his neck and shook out his fingers. "Behold!" he shouted, swinging his right hand in front of him like a shield. The tattoo of a spear on his forearm glowed green then appeared in front of his arm with the same emerald aura. Instead of falling, it levitated for a few seconds before dropping on the ground.

"Dusty! How did you do that?" Jho asked, surprised. I watched her approach the spear and crouch down to inspect it closely. "Was it magick?"

"I think innate powers aren't as magick-centered as people think they are," Meer said.

"Then how did you do that, Dusty?" Jads pressed, intrigued. My interest was also piqued, seeing as magick and I didn't get along so well.

"I was thinking like you guys, honestly," Dusty admitted. "I was observing the other Inkweavers and—"

"Woah," I said, shocked, raising my hands in the air. "That's a big word, Dust."

"I hang out with you nerds too much, shut up" he retorted, laughing. "But yeah, every time I take things out of me—"

"Eww." Meer's disgust interrupted Dusty again.

We all snickered, ever the peanut gallery.

"Every time I *summon* things from my skin," Dusty amended irritably, "I can feel the tattoo like it's still a part of my body. When the thing becomes tangible again, the connection or something gets cut off, and I don't feel it anymore."

"So, you found a way to let it continue when it becomes solid. Like tethering it for a few seconds." My inner scientist was kicking in.

"Yeah, what you said. I keep the tether until I can't hold it anymore." Dusty bent down and pressed the spear back into his forearm, returning it into its shrunken, tattooed form. "I think I could do it for longer if I practiced."

"Okay, my turn." Jads tapped Dusty out and he surrendered the grassy stage. Jads clapped her hands together and a red glow emanated from inside the gloves she'd been wearing for months now. Except this time, little golden rings materialized on all ten fingers. She raised her hands and slowly wheeled her arms into a wide circle. As she did, eight astral arms appear in sequence, like a long-dead Hindu goddess.

She weaved a new spell, and her extra hands mirrored the motions. She pushed all ten of her arms out and a giant projection appeared of the Squad on the day of my birthday. We were all chugging root beer and burping with abandon. It was from Jads's point of view, but regardless, it made me emotional. Everyone looked at me, but I was too immersed in the memory. I was powerless against the grin that split my face; that was one of my favorite moments with them. Uncle Kit walked into the living room, and the projection disappeared.

"That was cool, Jads," I said, feeling my words fall flat.

"I learned that the astral arms could weave spells the same time you cast one. I've been experimenting with how far I can go, and I think you can cast the same one to give it more juice or you can cast different spells at the same time."

"And that's why you're the Supreme." Dusty said appreciatively.

"What about you, Jho, is it still just the shields?"

"Oh, I learned something new too." Jho took Jads's place at the front. "Stand back." We shuffled a few feet back, unwilling to fully rise to our feet. We watched Jho create a glowing, blue shield with her right hand. She thrust her hand forward, and the shield exploded, firing a quick, sharp gust of wind toward us. I had to catch myself on my elbow as the force shoved me backward.

"What was that?" Dusty demanded.

"Sonic boom?" I guessed.

"Close! I can charge my force fields to explode with energy or collapse the energy inside the force field." Jho did it again, this time aiming at the sky.

"What about you, cousin?" Jho asked, casting her gaze back down amidst our applause.

Meer, who was attempting to eat his sub the way an anaconda might consume a wild hog, shrugged. "You guys already saw me de-grow the grass." It was impressive that he could speak so clearly around so much... blockage.

"When did you become so lame?" Dusty taunted.

"My turn." I directed an evil smile at Meer. He gulped, probably in an effort to avoid choking on my next move. I raised my right hand, extending my inner force at him, and he began to float.

"Ricky! Put me down!" Meer yelled frantically. His limbs were spinning in wild circles. It reminded me of what happens when you hold a puppy over water.

In response, I raised my left hand, lifting everyone off the ground.

"*Ate!*" Sólel started giggling uncontrollably and tried to reach for Jho.

"Not too high!" Meer pleaded, and I laughed; all five of them looked like they were swimming or, in Meer's case, drowning. I took pity on him and set them gently back in the grass.

"Sorry, Meer. Didn't mean to scare you," I said, grinning.

"I wasn't scared!" he protested. "I was full; I didn't want to puke or something."

For the rest of the next hour, we continued the supernatural talent show. Even Meer joined in, drawing a knot of roots from the ground and deftly crafting them into the shape of a middle finger.

~ ~ ~

"After that, it would be the last time she sang her lullaby for us, right?" Jadis looks at me intently.

I nod, trying to keep my emotions balanced.

"Was it because we were going to the shadow forest? I know I was really anxious about it." Dustin begins trying to crack his knuckles again, despite there being nothing left to crack.

"No." Emierr corrects. "It was because I wouldn't let Sól come with us. Akeu—the shadow forest is the most dangerous place in Ethra. If anything happened to him, I don't know how I could have lived with myself."

"So, he just went home?" Brunner sounds surprised.

"No. Of course he wouldn't just go home." I smirk.

"So Jho sang the song to calm him down, just like she did with Gordo," Brunner says, smiling. "Seems about right, Jho's singing could do that. She was probably singing for all of you."

I'll never forget that song, that day in the meadow; it was the last time I ever felt calm.

"After we said our goodbyes, Sól flew home by himself. And I promised I'd come back." Emierr's lips press tightly together, like he's holding back tears.

"And we went the other way, out to Akeurimja Forest," I finish.

~ ~ ~

Meer waved to Sólel, who was flying home all teary. Dusty patted Meer's back and whispered something. Meer nodded, forcing a smile that looked more like a grimace.

"You'll see him soon, Meer," I said reassuringly. I used to be able to read him clearly before, but now it was more like a guessing game. I didn't feel like I knew my friend anymore.

"Before we do anything," Jho began. "Can we just be together?"

"We *are* together," Dusty said, looking confused. Like a caveman asked to perform trigonometry.

"No, like the backyard," Jho clarified, fiddling with her fingers.

"You want us all in the same place? On Earth?" Jads asked, sounding similarly perplexed.

"Whenever we're next to each other, it feels more real than when we weren't. I like waking up with you guys around." Jho's unfamiliar, thin cheeks glowed faintly red.

"Are we sneaking out again?" Meer's eyes lit up.

"Just like old times?" Dusty grinned.

I felt a smile spread across my face, thinking of the old days.

"Last time we did that, we were grounded for a week." Jads rolled her eyes.

"But the view was awesome, remember?" Meer reminded her.

"How'd you even find that hill, Ricky?" Dusty asked.

I'd dragged them all up a massive foothill at the base of the mountains in the dead of night. Our parents had not been impressed by my adventurous spirit.

"My Papa said there's a shortcut through the neighborhood," I said, shrugging. "He drove that way one night, and the streetlights looked like stars. Wanted to show you guys."

"It did look like stars on Earth," Jho agreed. "But it had nothing on Ethra."

"Biking up that hill was the worst," Jads groaned.

"We even left our bikes in front of our houses when we got home. That probably gave us away." I laughed. Rookie error. Our parents had gotten up for work the next morning and the evidence of our crime was laid out neatly on the lawns.

"But if they find us together again, they won't get mad. They all want us to hang out," Meer said without hesitation. "And we're not driving halfway up a mountain. I'm in. Where are we meeting?"

"Let's use my basement. I sneak down there to watch *Adult Swim* sometimes." Jho said slyly.

"That works for me." I said, chuckling at the idea of Jho sneaking downstairs to watch *Robot Chicken*.

"I've got root beer; I'll bring it," Meer said, as if he was the twenty-one-year-old bringing beer to an underage party.

"My dad bought a ton of chips," Dusty pitched in. "I'll grab some."

"I have nothing to offer, but I'll be there." Jads said. "Someone's gotta keep you boys from getting Jho in trouble." She smiled at Jho.

"Yeah, inviting you over is like having a pack of hyenas in the basement," Jho teased.

"That's Meer." Dusty pushed him.

"No, that's *you*." They seized each other and tumbled to the ground.

The two girls started giggling.

I had to remember this moment; this might be the last time we were here, together, like this. I tried to hide my sadness and smile, like I'd been doing all this time.

"Okay, see you guys in a few."

I awoke in my bed. I glanced out my window as I stood and stretched. I could see Jads turning on her lamp and Meer switching on his lights. I looked at my reading desk for just a moment, wondering if I should grab my stone, but I shook my head. The last thing I needed was to lose it in the dark on my walk over there.

The four of us made quiet exits from our respective homes and met in the middle of the cul-de-sac. Meer had root beer cans wrapped in his arms and Dusty strolled over with a bunch of chips. We tried our best to be stealthy as we moved through the pools of streetlight, giggles echoing through the sleeping neighborhood. Jho waved from the backyard, signaling us to go that way instead. We slid past the door and tiptoed through the house, the wooden floor creaking beneath us.

We gathered in the middle of the basement, on an outdated red and white rug, flanked by a couch and Dusty's old TV at either end. It had been a while since we'd all been down here. We formed a circle, all in our very on-brand PJs. Meer's had a pine tree pattern, Dusty's had palm trees, Jho's had butterflies, Jads had a flowering cactus on the chest, and mine had a honeycomb, circuit board pattern. We were probably too old for these, but no one said it out loud.

"I can't believe we're doing this again," Jads said, shaking her head but smiling all the same.

"I'm scared, but excited," Jho said, accepting a can of root beer from Meer.

"Are you guys ready for Akeurimja Forest?" I asked. I could feel my heart rate gaining speed. The excitement I expected to flood through the basement never came. The other four looked sidelong at each other. "Come on, are you seriously scared?" I asked incredulously.

"Ricky, I'm always down with whatever you say, but this might be dangerous," Dusty said, avoiding eye contact.

"Yeah, we can go on an adventure, but the shadow creatures? No one knows what they even are," Jads said. "Remember how scared Al was of them? And he went to Akeurimja like every other month."

"We're Nobles. We rule Ethra. Remember?" I felt like a politician. "As long as we're together, we'll never lose."

"I'll protect you guys," Jho said confidently. "My force fields are strong."

"I guess my laser guns and battle knives will come in handy," Dusty relented. "Do you guys think I can store a shadow creature in me?"

"That would be stupid," Jads laughed. "But I'd like to see you try. I know a lot of defensive magick, I can finally use them on real targets instead of practice dummies."

"Meer?" I asked tentatively.

It took him a few seconds, but he finally met my gaze. "Look... Um..." His eyes moved to Jho and then back to me, "Okay." He let out a sigh. "I've been meaning to try a vine whip, like Bulbasaur." He lifted his hand and pretended to snap a whip.

We all laughed, and it started feeling warm. Just like it did before...

Are we really giving up Ethra? I popped open the root beer and raised my can to them. "Happy Birthday, Jho." I took one good, long look at her. The girl with the softest eyes in the world and a smile that came with them.

"Happy Birthday, Jho," everyone chorused in hushed cheers.

"I love you guys," Jho said before taking a deep drink.

Jads surprisingly burped first. "Oh shit. Sorry." She covered her mouth.

The one that came from Jho a minute later could have rattled the windows. We all covered our mouths, trying not to laugh out loud. As I was trying to relish this remaining piece of childhood, I couldn't help but think about how we were all growing up. I knew it was unavoidable, and probably for the best. But it still hurt, regardless. We put the chips and cans to the side and lay in a circle like we always did in Jho's backyard. The rug was soft enough and should put us to sleep easily. Our hands interlocked, our breaths synchronized, and in unison, we say, "Astralis."

~ ~ ~

"That was the last time you guys Transcended." Brunner says it as more of a statement than a question.

I nod slightly.

"And that's when you guys decided to stop visiting Ethra, right?" Brunner asks, glancing at all of us.

We all nod again, the rest looking at the ground.

"Why? Ethra was everything."

"Ask Meer," I say, perhaps a bit too sharply.

"It wasn't just me." Emierr furrows his brows. "We all talked about it."

Jadis and Dustin glare up at him.

"So, you guys did meet without me. Was Jho a part of it?" My voice is calm, my breathing steady. It's too late to be angry, too late to be sad; all I can do now is accept the facts.

"Yeah," Dustin admits quietly. He sounds ashamed.

His reaction strikes a nerve within me. So much for accepting the facts. "*All* of you agreed to stop going?" I feel like I'm twelve again. Waiting for Mama to get up and hold me, waiting for Papa to come home and tuck me into bed, and trying my hardest to walk alongside my best friends. But even in those moments of happiness, I'm pulled away, back to walking right behind them. Something always has to happen, and I end up always waiting.

"It's more complicated than that, Ricky." Jadis sighs.

"It doesn't sound complicated; you all decided on it. I mean, I knew that was probably the case, but I thought one last adventure could make you guys stay." It's not Rictor who's speaking anymore; it's twelve-year-old Ricky who wants to hear his best friends justify that leaving Ethra was the best choice.

"Ricky, it was—You didn't think to ask if we wanted to stay?" Emierr finally asks, meeting my eyes.

"No man, if you didn't, then you would have said so."

"I told you I didn't want to," Emierr says, raising his voice.

"You said you wanted to grow up, but you never said you didn't want to stay." My breathing is coming faster now.

"I wanted to stay." Dustin says, startling me. "I never wanted to leave."

"Then why did you choose to?" I shoot at him.

Dustin sighs deeply and looks away.

"Because—Ethra was an escape, Ricky," Jadis answers for him.

"Yeah? For us to be happy." Flaming tongues of hurt and rage flick against my heart.

"No." Meer shakes his head.

"What do you mean no?"

"It was to escape reality, Ricky. Your dad. Dusty's mom. None of us could have handled it if we didn't have Ethra." Jadis suddenly chokes up.

"I would've stayed with you, Ricky. You know that, right? Brothers," Dustin says pleadingly. "But I didn't want our parents' deaths to be the only thing holding us together. That's why I agreed to make you believe—" He stops talking and clenches his jaw at the sight of Emierr and Jadis's sharp looks.

"Make me believe what?" I demand.

"Guys, maybe we should take a breather," Brunner suggests.

"No. What did you agree to make me believe, Dust?" I'm not angry, not at them, but if this reason is why things ended up the way they did, I might not forgive them.

All three of them look at each other.

"Just fucking tell him." Emierr says, throwing his hands up in defeat. "He's going to find out sooner or later."

Dustin takes a look at me and purses his lips. "Jho made the plan. It was all her idea."

"What? You guys are fucking sick. How are you going to blame her?" I'm starting to see red, despite my efforts to remain calm.

"No..." Jadis says. "Jho knew. She knew we were going to leave. Meer is just an idiot and told you he wanted out before even talking to any of us, but Jho called for a meeting without you. She knew how much it was going to hurt you... with us leaving."

"So, she asked us to just go with her plan," Dustin continues. "To make you believe you were throwing the last, best adventure you can think of."

"Make me beli—" Realization sets in. "She did tell me we should try going to the shadow forest. She planted the idea... I didn't notice."

"She said, 'Let's make him believe he tried his best.' She convinced us to just go with it, as her birthday gift. To make you happy." Emierr rests his chin in his hands, elbows propped up on his legs.

"That's why we were late coming that night; she had another meeting to make sure we pulled through with the plan," Dustin says in a low voice.

"No..." I shake my head. "Jho wouldn't do something so risky."

"For fuck's sake Ricky, she loved you," Jadis cuts in. "She did it because she couldn't stand seeing you hurt. She wanted you to see it on your own, how change is good too."

"She wanted to grow old with you," Dustin murmurs. My eyes move instinctively to Brunner whose eyes are filled with pain.

"Then what the fuck happened to her, guys?" Brunner growls, catching all of us off guard. "What the fuck happened to my best friend?"

~ ~ ~

My eyes popped open, and Dusty helped me to my feet. The sun was getting low in the sky. We stood in our crop circle in the meadow, staring out into our secret kingdom. This place was ours. But it might be time to say goodbye. I glanced at my best friends who were lost in the view. They were all I'd ever known, so maybe they were right. Maybe it was time to step up, keep pace with them. I wanted to be side by side, not lagging behind.

"Last one's a rotten egg!" I hollered and took off into the trees.

"Hey!" Jads shouted, and they all scrambled after me. Jho used her force fields as stepping stones and skipped further ahead.

"That's cheating!" I laughed and focused on my feet, propelling myself up with each step. Each step struck midair. I snuck a peek at the others and watched Dusty tap into Ade's bond. His eyes went an unnerving, pale yellow and boom, he was right behind me. Jads eyes were dancing with the flames of her phoenix. Rather than bolting ahead like Dusty, fire coated her arms like feathers. They caught the wind, carrying her up and over us all. Meer stopped running altogether.

"Loser!" Dusty shouted at him.

Without moving a single step, Meer rocketed forward, carried on the tiny stems of a million helpful blades of grass.

"How're you doing that?" Jads called from the air.

"Just letting the grass push me," he said casually, then he stuck his tongue out and glided ahead, turning to flip us off.

I smirked and extended my right hand, mentally shoving him. He tumbled over, his fall softened by obedient, green tendrils.

"Asshole!" He clambered back up, but it was too late for him to reclaim first place.

The race to the forest was a close one, but Jho beat us to the trail after using a force field like a catapult. The road that used to be there was covered in a tangle of weeds, roots, and vines, leading straight into the forest.

As we walked down the nearly invisible trail, dead leaves crunched under our feet. The ones that escaped us drifted in gentle clusters around our legs. I was in the lead with the others hot on my heels.

"Aren't you guys gonna miss this?" I turned around, walking backward.

"Miss what?" Meer's hands were stuffed in his pockets.

"The floating leaves." I grinned, reaching out with my left hand to disturb their delicate dance. They swirled around the other four, despite the lack of wind.

"Ricky?" Jho's voice came from the back, and Dusty moved so we could see each other. "This isn't the spawn area, right?"

"Nope, that's at the other end of the forest. This is the scenic route, if anything."

I gazed up at the sky, blending pink and purple hues between gnarled branches.

"What if we see one of them?" Meer asked, staring at the ground.

"Then we fight." Dusty nudged him.

"It's still so crazy to me how nobody knows anything about these shadows," Jho said. Her eyes were darting between the spaces in the trees.

"Yeah, 'cause anyone who tried to know died," Jads retorted.

"Can't they send robots or drones to get information?" Meer asked me, finally glancing up from his evidently fascinating boots.

"You think they didn't try?" Jads argued, before I could open my mouth to answer. "It all came back corrupted, right Ricky?"

"Yeah, I watched all the archives, and right before they go into the forest, the file goes all jagged then black."

"We sent the best field witches and wizards, and they all just come back saying the same thing, 'Those things are evil.' "

"The only thing we know is that they're the same species as the Crown Beasts," I said, thinking back to the pathetically small file I'd read on them.

"Why are there only five Crown Beasts out there?" Dusty asked, forehead wrinkling.

"Maybe... we could ask our Crown Beasts about their history?" Jho suggested. "None of the past Nobles in Verglas ever tried that, not that I remember reading anyways."

Jads stopped dead in her tracks. "Why did I not think of that?" she half-shouted, smacking a hand to her forehead. Dusty frantically shushed her, staring around at the forest like any one of the waving limbs might reach out and throttle him.

Now that I heard it out loud, it seemed stupid that I hadn't tried. Aigerim had proven himself to be quite the conversationalist once our telepathic connection had kicked in. I didn't know why I'd expected him to have the intelligence of a regular animal.

"Guys," Meer called out, his voice a pitch higher than usual. Everyone stopped in their tracks.

I turned back to face the front, impressed I hadn't hit anything while walking in reverse, to see the blackened branches of Akeurim-ja Forest looming over us. This was the entrance. The comfortingly brown bark had steadily grown darker as we moved between the trees. Now, a wall of coal black and maroon leaves choked out the green.

"Are you guys ready?" I looked over my shoulder at them.

"Wait." Jho wriggled past Dustin. "Shouldn't we put a sign or something..."

Everyone blinked at her, bemused.

"I mean... We're Nobles but what if other kids hear about this and decide to come exploring too?" She looked troubled. "Shouldn't we leave some kind of warning?"

Always worrying about others. "Okay," I agreed. Something fluttered in my chest.

"What sign are we gonna use?" Dusty asked, casting a look around us as if expecting to see a disused sign shop.

"Stand back, peasants." Meer strode to the front and faced the side where the trail met the wine-hued grass of the forest. He stretched both his hands to the ground then twisted them, palms up. The ground shivered for a moment, then roots began climbing from the soil below. They braided themselves together, forming the vague shape of a sign. He closed his fingers slowly, and the roots started to harden. When his fingers slammed shut into a fist, the roots had compressed themselves into a flat, smooth rectangle.

"Woah, when did you learn to do that?" Jads looked awestruck.

Meer pretended to blow on his nails. Jads scoffed.

"That was sick." I said, reaching up for a high five.

"Here." Jho had slipped away while Meer was doing his thing and came back with five huge leaves and a bag full of berries. I didn't even notice her leaving. "Take these berries. Then grab a stick and smush them on the leaf." She demonstrated. "Ink!" We obeyed and, before long, we had more than enough berry paint for our marker. Jho used her finger to carefully spell out "DO NOT ENTER." Her finger came away deep purple.

"My turn!" Meer bent down to the sign.

"Or else?" Jads huffed a laugh.

Meer grinned.

"Move." Dusty hip checked Meer, knocking him to the forest floor. With a berry-stained finger, he wrote, "Who let the dogs out?"

We all stared at the sign. Then Dusty. Then each other. We waited for further elaboration. None came.

"What?" I finally said.

Dusty barked. We burst into howls of laughter.

I really don't want this to end.

"Let's sign it!" Jho suggested, once she was able to form words again.

One by one, we took turns signing, marking our warning. This was one way to immortalize us.

"There. Happy, Jho?" Meer slung an arm around her shoulders.

"I love it." Her smile was dazzling. Together, we placed the sign against the trunk of an ancient tree and Meer bound it tightly with creeping vines.

"Alright, let's go," I said. The temporary spark of joy from our project dimmed. *I hope this convinces them.*

"After you." Dusty shoved me forward, and I took the first steps in. The air in here felt thicker. Damper.

Black branches clung to dangling, maroon leaves. Meer had once told us about the current theory of the shadow trees. They only grew in this part of the world—something about heavy magickal properties buried deep within the soil. It caused everything to grow like that here, like shadows. Of course, the theory was untestable.

The grass was strangely feathery and waved with each footfall. It was quiet here, but it felt safe, somehow. For now. I glanced behind me and saw the Squad still at the entrance.

"C'mon, scaredy cats," I teased. With some grumbling, they followed me in.

"Do you know where to go?" Jads asked, falling into step beside me.

"We just go. C'mon." The forest was calming. Sure, the black trees were creepy with their maroon leaves like drops of blood, but the cool darkness was weirdly relaxing. I spotted a few bugs and animals that looked like squirrels, but were definitely not. Normally, I would have asked Meer to talk to them, but he was already looking jumpy.

"How much longer are we going to keep walking?" Dusty complained.

"Yeah, Ricky, there's nothing out here. Maybe there aren't any more shadows." Meer said hopefully.

"We have to see one, or else this would've been all for nothing," I argued.

"It's okay, Ricky. We at least get to say we entered the shadow forest," Jads pointed out.

I sighed in frustration, looking at the endless soot-colored trunks around us. Even the dusky light was gone, leaving little relief from the press of blackness.

"It's really okay, Ricky. Thanks for getting us in here." Jho placed a hand on my wrist.

"Wait. I have an idea." I pulled away from her and turned to a nearby tree. Its jet bark and rotted whorls gave the impression that it was once struck by lightning. I took a few running steps then propelled myself into the branches. The telekinetic weightlessness made scaling the tree a breeze.

"Ricky, be careful," Jads shouted. I could hear Dusty hissing profanities at her.

"I got him," Jho said, casting a force field safety net around the base of the tree.

I reached the top and poked my head out through the leaves. There, looming in the center of the purplish canopy, was... something. *A mountain?* No. That couldn't be a mountain, could it? It looked artificial, with unnatural obsidian planes and neat, linear edges.

"Ricky?" Dusty whisper-yelled from far below.

"Oh, so it's okay when *you* do it?"

"Shut up, Jads!"

I ducked back below the mottled leaves and crawled out to the end of my limb. After a quick look down, I flung myself into the open air, catching myself with a mental parachute. I hit Jho's force field lightly, and she dropped it. I fell the last few inches to the ground. Bruised leaves whispered around my ankles.

"There's something in that direction. It's kinda huge." I said, panting a bit.

"Like shadow creatures huge?" Meer asked, his voice even higher.

"Like, mountain huge," I said, trying to think of how to describe what I'd seen. "It sort of looked like one anyway. But also not. Something about it was not natural. It was too smooth and perfect."

"A mountain? In the shadow forest? That is weird." Jho frowned. "None of the maps have it marked."

"I'm good to go back." Jads said slowly. "But... I also love a good mystery."

I was inclined to agree. "It's going to kill me not knowing what the hell is it."

"I don't know guys, that's a red flag in horror movies," Meer said, unconvinced. A twig snapped off in the distance and he jumped.

"You need to stop watching so many movies, man." Dusty scoffed.

"These movies are going to save our lives, trust me," Meer retorted.

"Come on, this way," I pointed in the direction of the structure I'd seen. "Let's just check out this "mountain" and then we can head back to Terrene. The chiefs want us for dinner anyway."

"You didn't tell me that," Meer complained.

"I'm telling you now." I patted his back and began walking.

"One last mission," Jads said, heaving a sigh that seemed equal parts intrigue and burnout.

I didn't look back. *One last mission...* They really were done with Ethra. Maybe I never had a chance at all. We walked in silence for the next few minutes. Jads's words roiled around inside me. I thought I had a shot to change their minds, but I was pretty sure they'd made up their minds a long time ago. I felt like I was on autopilot, staring down at my feet, mindlessly walking into an abyss. Maybe I should just stop now and end it for everyone. This was a bad idea; why did I let Jho talk me into this?

"Ricky." Meer said. His voice ricocheted off something in front of me.

I looked up from my brooding and was met with an unfathomable wall encompassing my entire field of vision. My eyes widened, and my jaw dropped. It wasn't a mountain. It was a temple. "Holy shit."

"That's... really... big," Jads managed.

We all gaped stupidly at the building; it was nothing like anything we'd seen in the nations. I didn't think it resembled any of the cultural buildings I read about in the Squad notebook. It was like a pyramid but layered strangely. An illusion of some kind tricked the eye into believing that each progressive layer floated just a few inches above the other. Or... was it an illusion? The peak was unmistakably shaped like a mountain's top, or was it perhaps a mountain before it became... this?

Bizarre symbols were scattered across the forest floor, singed into the ground around the temple. They looked like runes, but they weren't. At least, Jads didn't seem to recognize them.

"Did any of your people ever report this?" I asked Jads, glancing at her.

"No." Jads shook her head. "I don't think they ever got this far."

So how did we?

"Well, someone did. But they didn't make it back," Jho whispered. Her face was lined with revulsion, eyes fixed on something just behind a twisted, violet bush. We moved nervously to follow her gaze, then collectively leaned back, aghast.

"The shadow creatures probably got him," she said quietly. The bones of an unnamed person lay scattered around the bush. The bones were cracked and ghostly white. They had been here a long, long time.

"How many more do you think are here?" Meer whispered, taking a horror-struck step toward the remains. "The clothes, they're Terrenean."

"Are we staying to find out?" Dusty asked, panic filling his voice.

"Yeah, maybe we sh—" Jho halted mid-sentence and jerked her body behind the cover of the nearest tree, hauling Jads with her. Dusty and Meer did not hesitate as they threw themselves out of sight. I dropped to the ground, crouching in the midst of the former Terrenean. None of us had seen what Jho had. But I could sure as hell make an educated guess.

Jho and Jads's hands were clamped over their mouths, eyes filled with terror. Dusty had Meer wrapped up tight in his arms, acting as a human shield. Meer's hands were clapped over his ears, his eyes were squeezed shut. I chanced a look above me and there, tangled in the branches of the ebony trees, was something that God never intended to be witnessed. It was made up of black strings, all intertwining with each other continuously. It looked like videos I had seen of an octopus rolling its tentacles together, but if that octopus had been painted by H.P. Lovecraft. I held my breath, staring at the coiling mass of tendrils as it passed over me, through the canopy.

It had no eyes that I could see, and it didn't appear to notice us as it made its way to the temple, each motion slick and grotesque. As I let my breath out, I lifted my head slowly from the cover of the bush. I saw the others moving to peer from behind their trees. There were more now, a horde of demonic jellyfish surrounding the temple.

"Let's get the fuck out of here," I hissed.

"I think I'm going to throw up," Meer whispered back.

"I'll lead the way." Jho's voice was barely audible as she took Jads's hand. Dusty pressed his hands to Meer's back, urging him forward, step by step. All of us had our heads on a swivel, expecting another living nightmare to come oozing from between the clawing limbs around us. I crawled a bit away from the bush before standing up. As I straightened, Dusty's eyes widened in alarm. He leveled a shaking finger just over my shoulder. My heart dropped. I waited for shadowy strands to take hold of me when, instead, I felt something crawling on my shoulder.

Slowly, I looked down. Perched on my shoulder was the biggest, nastiest spider I had ever seen. I emitted an ear-splitting shriek. I telekinetically whipped the spider off me, splattering it against the tree. The relief was short-lived when I realized what I had done. Behind me, the knotted webs of mangled shadow turned to face me.

"Run!" I shouted, and we bolted. There was a sickening hiss in the fallen leaves strewn along the forest floor. I risked looking back to see dozens, possibly even hundreds of shadows streaking after us. Their stringy limbs dragged in the leaf litter below, the only sound coming from the hovering horrors. I mentally propelled myself again, launching my body through the air, legs still pumping. Dusty ripped his laser guns from his skin and fired over his shoulder at the gnashing throng of ragged darkness behind us. Just as the lasers were about to find their marks, the shadows' bodies gaped open, forming round holes big enough to let the fiery beams pass through.

"Just keep running," I half sobbed. Nothing but the sound of my friends' pounding feet answered me. I shut my eyes and felt my muscles tightened as I tried to channel Aigerim. I hadn't used the bond before. A primal rush surged within me. All of my senses sharpened to a point of near-pain. I could hear, see, and smell *everything*.

I noticed a slight wind pelting the left side of my body, rattling my focus on the bond. I whipped his head around to see a shadow careening toward me, its oscillating tendrils reaching for my face. A burst of energy exploded, shredding whatever matter formed the creature's body, and it collapsed. I slid to a screeching halt, staring back at the shadow. The crumpled pile of oily matter did not move. Was it dead? Unconscious? Could it even be either of those things? Jho's force fields were glowing around her hands; she had saved me.

"Let's go!" she called, hurling more of her shimmering grenades at the onslaught of shadows. The blasts took a few more out, leaving them like Morticia Addams's moth-eaten curtains on the ground. Meer took up a position at the center and raised his hands in the air. Black roots plunged out of the ground around us, stretching up high into the sky and twisting together into a fortress.

"That should stop them," Meer said shakily. Orange light blazed up against the newly formed wall. Jads's phoenix wings enveloped her arms, and she flung herself into the sky. As she attempted to clear the trees, a shadow lurking on a tree branch sprang at her, bringing her down.

"Jads!" I screamed. Everyone was tearing toward her as she and the shadow tumbled across the ground. Jads kicked it off her, and she used the momentum to land firmly on her feet.

"Don't touch me, bitch!" she spat, and swiped her wings at the shadow. Crescents of flame slashed through the air and caught as they made contact, lighting like a spark to a scrap of paper. She heaved two more at it and an agonizing, grating screech rended the air. Its tentacles curled up as they burned, and it fled into the darkness. "I hate this fucking forest!" Jads yelled.

At that moment, I felt the wind again. Reacting on instinct, I spun to face my attacker. I reached out and seized the shadow with my mind. Nausea swelled in my stomach as the slick, oily tendrils clung to my skin. Its body was too soft, too pliable to crush.

"Ricky!" Meer roared. "They're climbing over the wall!"

In my periphery, I saw two shadows fall gracelessly to the other side of the mangled root wall. The top of the wall was coated with pitch fingers, waving like Satan's ivy in the still forest air. I curled my fingers and did the only thing I could think of: ripping the shadow apart. The sound that came from it was nothing that could be replicated on Earth.

"Ricky!" Jho's warning jolts me from the overwhelming sound surrounding me. The pulverized shadow disintegrates, fading into nothingness. More shadows had cleared the root barricade, and they began to swarm us, blocking any semblance of moonlight that had managed to touch the ground. I backed away; mouth open in a silent scream. My back hit Dusty's steadying arms. Just as the nearest tendrils began to stretch toward us, Jho sent a force field crashing down around us. Denied their prey, the shadows' sickening limbs writhed against the shield, searching for an opening.

"What do we do?" Dusty gasped. We formed a circle, back-to-back.

"Stop!" Meer attempted to command them, but the shadows continued to pile their flaccid bodies onto the force field. "Figures," he panted. "Not animals."

"I can detonate the force field; that should knock them out," Jho said, arms trembling with the effort of holding the shield in place.

"It might not be strong enough. There're hundreds of them." Jads said. She had gone cold, and matter-of-fact. Her defense mechanism was working overtime to keep her safe from the nightmare I had walked them into.

"Why did I agree to this?" Meer wailed, covering his ears.

My heart was pounding out of my chest. *How do we get out of this?*

"Ricky!" Jho's strained voice brought me back. "What's the plan?"

I stared wordlessly up at her. Fear had paralyzed my vocal cords.

"Let's just wake up!" Meer yelled, now curled into a ball on the ground.

"If we do that, we might not make it back," Jads snapped.

"Oh shit!" Any shock we might have felt at Jho swearing was overshadowed by the sight of her force field starting to crack.

No, this doesn't end here. "Jho, blow it up," I yelled, banking on my gut feeling. We would not die here. Not because of me. Jho's eyes searched mine for a moment. Then she nodded once, tensing her muscles.

"What if it's not enough?" Jads snarled, the flaming feathers along her arms blazing with fear and rage.

"Then we'll make it enough!" I shot back. "When she detonates the force field, I'll push as hard as I can in every direction."

"Can you even do that?" Dusty ground out.

"I don't know, but I have to try." I forced myself to meet his gaze. "Trust me."

"I do." Dusty said, returning his attention to the splintering shield. The entire dome was plastered with slippery, void-black strands, all sweeping along the surface, prodding for a weakness.

"I can make a huge gust of wind." Jads slammed her palms together. "Let's blow these motherfuckers into smithereens."

"What do I do?" Meer asked, his voice guttering.

"When we push them away, call a vine, swing like we do at home." I told him. He was useless like this, I just needed to get him out.

"Fuck, okay." Meer breathed out, uncurling and raising his arms.

I whipped my head to the other side. "Fly out of here, Jads."

"Jho, your stairs," Dusty added, jerking his chin at her.

"Got it!" Jho closed her fingers into fists and crossed her arms in an X over her chest.

"In three... two... one... Now!" I bellowed. Jho flung out her arms, and the force field exploded. At the same time, I felt a tingle in my stomach. I clenched my abdominal muscles as tightly as I could, pushing my arms out and releasing a burst of telekinetic energy. Jads screamed an incantation, and a sharp gust of wind roared out in every direction. The wind melded with the explosions, blending seamlessly into a concussive wave.

The shadows were blasted away, some catching on tree limbs and other pelting the trunks. Their bodies hit like something congealed and rancid. Sharp cracks rang out like gunfire as trees took the hit. Meer yanked vines from the branches and pulled himself up, swinging away from the devastation. Jads's wings cloaked her arms in fire once again and she soared up into the air. Jho's force field steps shimmered into existence, and she fled, disappearing up above the trees.

"Ricky, let's go." Dusty urged, he hounded after Jho, up the translucent steps. I propelled myself up to the third step and landed right behind them. After what felt like an eternity of running, we stopped to catch our breath somewhere deeper in the forest, far from those fucking shadows.

"Holy shit, that was close." I wheezed. Fear was etched in each one of my friends' faces.

"Fuck you," Meer let out, breathing heavily.

"We made it out, didn't we?" I snapped. "It could have been worse." I knew the anger was a thin cover for overwhelming shame. We damn near hadn't made it out and not one of us knew what would happen if we died here. I was honestly about to shit my pants.

"Could have been worse? That was the worst thing that could have happened, Ricky. Sometimes I think you don't care about us." Meer's hurled accusation hit me like a punch to the face. "All you care about is your *adventures*."

"Woah. Back off Meer." Dusty stepped between us.

"No, Meer is right. That was so fucking bad. We could have been ripped to shreds like that guy we found." Jads planted herself on Meer's side. "I wasn't planning to test our Ethran immortality today."

"If you got something to say, Meer, spit it out," I growled, ignoring Jads. I knew he was right. I had brought us here. But it wasn't like any of them had tried to stop me.

"Ricky, just forget about it." Dusty turned his back on Jads and Meer and placed a hand on my shoulder.

I glanced over at Jho, who hadn't yet spoken up. She had both hands on her chest, as if she was struggling to say something.

"You never asked us," Meer finally said.

Dusty turned his head to look at Meer.

"You never asked us how we felt, or how we were doing. I get it, it was your dad who passed, and Dusty's mom, but they were our family too. And you never asked..." Meer's voice cracked.

Jads twisted around to stare at him. "That's different, Meer. You know that."

"That's not fair." I meant to sound harsh, but the words came out in a whimper. "It's not fucking fair for you to say I don't care." Meer's words felt as though they had driven a nail through my chest. "How do I ask you how you're feeling about *my* dad dying?" Tears peppered my cheeks, and an iron vice clamped itself around my aching ribs. I couldn't breathe.

Dusty's hand tightened on my shoulder, eyes on mine.

"I don't even know how to talk about it without breaking apart. But I *do* know how bad it is for you guys too." I drew the back of my hand across my face. "If I didn't care, then why the fuck am I trying my best to keep all of us together?"

"Guys!" Jho cried out. "Please stop fighting! It's my birthday." Her last words were said in such a small, young voice.

We all looked at her. My anger immediately began to fade. Dusty squeezed my shoulder and half smiled. Meer glanced at me, and I caught his stare. I knew he was sorry, and I was too. I nodded at him, offering an unspoken apology. I read one in his face too.

A branch snapped behind me.

"What the fuck?" Meer said as we took instinctive steps closer together. What we were looking at was not possible.

"Is this an illusion?" I asked, reaching for Jads's arm, unwilling to break eye contact with what had just arrived in the forest.

"I don't think so." Her voice trembled.

"What the fuck is this?" Dusty hissed.

Five kids, exact copies of us, stood across the narrow clearing we'd landed in. They—*We* were all uniformed in something I had never seen in any nation, not even in the Space Ring. Black jumpsuits blended into the trees behind them, with a sort of polyhedral body armor reflecting meager moonlight off their chests.

Everyone locked eyes with their doppelgangers.

"We should get out of here," I whispered, staring into my own eyes. Were mine filled with just as much rage?

"Astralis!" Meer shouted, startling all of us. His whole body dissipated into golden outlines of the nervous system. He was always faster at Transcending back than we were.

"Ass," Dusty swore and pulled out his blasters, aiming them at the other us. Before he could even fire, the blasters were ripped out of his hands. The other me had his arms raised, guiding the blasters away from their owner.

Fuck. They have our powers too. My doppelganger crushed the blasters into a ball of metal and let them drop to the ground. I snarled and pushed out with both hands. My clone staggered backward, his spine striking a tree. Jads's doppelganger had vanished. I whipped around and, from the branches, I saw it dropping behind the others.

Before I could yell a warning, it uttered something and sent Jads tumbling, catching herself on one knee. Fiery wings blasted out the side of her arms, and she slashed the crescents of flame at her twin. A force field appeared around the doppelganger, blazing tongues outlining the field. Right behind Jho stood the other her. With no hesitation, Jho spun around and wrenched a force field towards her clone, where it exploded on impact, knocking it—*her* back. I looked back at Dusty and let out a cry of shock. Meer's doppelganger had his arm wrapped around his neck.

"Get off him!" I shrieked. I reached my hand out to mentally grab hold of Meer's twin but before I could, I felt my body constrict.

I turned my head to the right, fighting the resistance, and saw my twin holding me from afar. Jads was fighting herself, exchanging spell after spell while Jho and her clone competed in force field explosions. Dusty raised his right hand and swung his knife down toward my twin, but of course, it stopped in midair. My clone dropped its hold on me, and I tapped back into my bond. Everything slowed and I started to see ripples.

Is this air? How can I see air? No, these are waves; they're sound waves, and they're coming from the knife that's flying straight at my face.

I was reacting faster than I thought possible; my hands lifted to catch the knife before it could lodge itself in my skull. Suddenly, I felt a force push me off balance. I watched the blade slip through my fingers in slow motion. *I'm going to die.* At the last minute, just as the tip entered my right eye, I telekinetically redirected the knife upwards. It flicked up through my cornea, splitting my cheek, slicing up through my eyebrow. I fell to the ground and felt a sharp sting heat my face.

"Ricky!" Jho screamed. Dusty was on his knees, still wrapped in a headlock. His twin walked over to him, eerily calm. It reached down to take his hand, looked him dead in the eye, and brought his teeth down on two of his fingers, severing them as if they were no more than carrots. Dusty's agonized scream echoed through the forest as I lay among the fluttering leaves. My stomach rolled with nausea, and Aigerim's eyesight honed in on the bleeding stumps that remained on Dusty's hand. Jads hurled a giant shuriken at Meer's twin. One of the blades hit its target, striking the clone in the head and rendering him unconscious. Dusty's twin spat Dusty's ring and pinky fingers onto the ground with a grin. There was blood between his teeth.

"Dust!" I screeched, trying to see though my own blood, flooding my eye. As I struggled to push myself up on shock-numbed legs, Jho's force fields erupted on the Dusty and Ricky doppelgangers, thrusting them away. Dusty fell to the ground and began to drag himself across the dampened dirt. Jho and Jads came roaring to Dusty's defense. My vision was blurry, but I could see enough to know they were putting up one hell of a fight. Not even my twin could manage to grab them. I looked at Dusty, who was sobbing, holding onto his bloodied hands.

"Guys! Wake up!" I screamed. It wasn't worth it, none of this was worth it.

I managed to haul myself upright, the word "Astralis" on my tongue, but Jads's twin seized a fistful of her hair. My voice died in my throat. The other Ricky raised his hand toward Dusty, and, like a grotesque puppet, Dusty's hand mirrored the clone's. He screamed in horror and pain as the tattooed spear from his hand tore free of his skin and flew into my twin's waiting grasp. It was all happening so fast; I couldn't keep up. "Wake up!" I sobbed, lifting my hand to try to free Dusty and Jads.

I heard Jho gasp. My heart dropped. Everything went silent. The handle of the spear was protruding from Jho's gut. My twin stared at me, smirking as he picked Jho up, the spear lodged in her body, like some kind of hunting trophy.

"Jho!" Jads shrieked. I dropped my hand from my savaged eye and reached out for Jho. Suddenly, a force ripped me up into the sky, and I saw Ethra fading away, my body spinning out of control.

My eyes cracked open.

I jolted up and I found myself shivering violently. I was drenched in cold water. It felt like I was just slammed into my body. Everything hurt.

"That worked; you guys weren't waking up," Meer said. There was a bucket in his hands.

Dusty and Jads both stared at me, their expressions shocked and eyes filled with tears. They were both soaked, too.

My right eye is still blurry. How can that be? "Jho," I gasped. She was still sleeping.

"Why isn't she awake?" Dusty whimpered.

"I saw her—" Jads cried.

"I'll get more water." Meer bolted out the basement.

"Jho, come on! Wake up!" I shook her. Her head rolled lifelessly under my hands.

"Did she die?" Dusty choked.

I shook my head, more denial than answer. I crawled around to sit beside her, scooping her into my arms. "Jho..." I shook her again, harder this time.

Dusty and Jads were watching us, trembling with terror. This was the real world. There was no waking up from this.

Meer came back down with the bucket of water and froze at the sight that met him. "What's going on?"

I looked up at him hopelessly. "What did you do?" My voice trembled.

"I—I woke you guys up. Why... Why isn't Jho awake?" The bucket in Meer's hands shuddered.

"What do we fucking do?" Dusty reached for Jho's face, touching her cheek.

"Jho... Wake up!" Jads wept, clutching Jho's wrist.

"We have to call an ambulance," I whispered.

Meer dropped the bucket on the ground and ran upstairs.

We just got our best friend killed.

Meer's Plans

October 3

"**W**ake up, Jho!"

　　　"Please wake up..."
How did it end up like this?
"Wake up, Ricky!"

My eyes snap open, and beads of sweat trickle down my forehead. That nightmare—it happened. That's how we lost our sister. I take deep breaths, my palms damp with sweat. I roll over in my childhood bed, and the springs squeak in protest.

"Fuck!" My younger self stands beside my bed, a bleeding gash over his right eye. I subconsciously slap my hand over my own eye, and little Ricky vanishes, replaced by a sudden flood of sunlight into my room. My hand comes away clean, my eye undamaged.

Am I still dreaming?

I sit up and cringe as I peel off the sodden sheets. I wipe my forehead with a shaky hand, then let my face fall into my palms. After recalling Jhoana's fate, we'd had to stop. The emotional toll was too great. But we had at least agreed on one thing: We're going back to save our sister.

I grab my phone; it's 2 p.m. The Squad chat is buzzing; everyone's already at Brunner's. I shoot them a message, saying I just woke up, and drag myself out of bed. Staring at the full-length mirror beside the door, I try to visualize my younger self once again. Why had I seen him? Trauma, perhaps, but it felt too real. I retrieve my shirt from the rolling chair and head downstairs to the kitchen.

There's a covered meal on the table, and a note from Ma. I read it aloud. "I'll see you tonight; tell Emierr happy birthday for me. " With a jolt, I check my phone; it's October 3rd.

"Oh, shit." I sit down in front of my breakfast. I dial Bonnie's number and place my phone on the table, activating the hologram. I've just taken an enormous bite of sausage when Bonnie's face pops up.

"Rick!" She grins brightly. Clad in a vibrant yellow floral blouse, she screams professional, but fun." Her hair is different, curls straightened to beachy waves. Red glasses add a nice touch.

"Bon," I say, swallowing. "You're looking great." I smile for the first time in what feels like forever, leaning into the hologram.

"Always am."

"True. I wanted to call and check if you did what I asked. It's Meer—Emierr's birthday today."

"Oh yeah." She opens her hands, and a hologram pops up for my inspection. "It should have arrived in your mailbox this morning."

"Thanks, Bonnie. Damn, I miss you. It's good to see your face." I now sense something different about her; something I can't quite pinpoint, but I like it.

"How was..." She trails off. "Um..."

"It was a lot. But...." I look down, unsure if I should delve into it. *Will she believe me?*

"Rick... Ricky," she says. It's the first time she's called me by my childhood nickname. "I'm still holding up our promise."

As the words left her lips, I'm transported back to our final day of our economics class at CUNY.

We were the last ones left in that lecture hall, sitting there in silence for a few minutes. That was the only class we were both going to have together, different courses and all. Then she broke the silence.

"Promise me then, Rick. If we ever need each other, for anything, we'll always be there. No matter what it is. No limit on help, even if we both lose our minds along the way, let's lose them together. To the moon and back."

"Can you talk?" I say, decision made. "I need to tell you something."

"Funny, I cancelled my meetings this morning to talk to you," she says. Her voice is light and airy, but not enough to hide the undercurrent of concern.

"Bon..." I sigh deeply.

"I'm right here." She leans in closer.

"We're... We're going to try and save Jho." I wait for her to call me insane or have me committed. Her expression remains unchanged, free of judgment.

"How?"

"There's a lot more I didn't tell you about my childhood. I only just started to even remember myself." I exhale.

She stays silent.

"We created this world as kids." My eyes focus on my food. "It was the best thing we had ever done, and we could only visit it through our dreams. And..." I chance a look at her; she's smiling.

"Okay," she says, encouraging me to keep going. She's just like Jhoana—a safety net. I detail exactly what happened to Jho, and how everything went to complete and utter shit. Bonnie, respectful and understanding, asks necessary questions, carefully navigating through the stickier subjects. I appreciate it. Throughout my explanations, I sense she believes me.

"But is it safe? After everything you just told me, what if you get hurt there and you don't come back?" Bonnie's voice is serious. She isn't patronizing me. She really is worried.

"We know the risks. But there's a chance. We owe it to her to fight."

"I know. I'm not stopping you." She sighs. "If there's a chance that this is all not real, I'd like to believe in that instead. I don't want you to—" She looks away. "But I know you're telling the truth. You don't have it in you to lie about something like this."

"Bonnie. I promise I'm coming back. We have a game to release, remember?" I force a smile, trying to reassure her as much as I need to reassure myself.

"I'll man the ship until you return. Please, Ricky, come back home to me—I mean... Come back home." Her voice is strong, but her eyes tell a different story.

"I will. I promise." I don't know if it's even something I *can* promise, but I'm sure as hell going to try. "How's Oscar, by the way?"

"He hasn't spoken to me since you got there. I swear, he better have gotten all my messages about waiting for your return. He's seriously going to make me lose it." She rolls her eyes.

"You're doing really great. Thank you for everything, Bon. I owe you." The words aren't strong enough to convey my sincerity. I don't know what's going to happen in the next few days, but I want her to know how much I care about her, if something were to happen.

"Ricky, don't say it like that. You're not saying goodbye."

"Okay, okay." I chuckle. "I'll see you later."

"You better come home, jackass." She flips me off and smiles.

I shoot one right back and grin. "I love you, Bon."

"I love you too, Ricky. Update me."

I wave goodbye and end the call. I push the chair backwards to go retrieve Bonnie's package from Ma's mailbox. The cold floor beneath my feet seems to momentarily tether me to this Earth, preventing me from spinning out of control. The journey to the mailbox becomes a tangible connection to normalcy.

Opening the front door bathes me in warm sunlight but is instantly countered by chilly morning wind pelting my skin. The mailbox, a simple metal container, waits patiently at the end of the drive. I flip it open, revealing Bonnie's package among the envelopes and flyers. When I return to the kitchen, I tear the package open to reveal Emierr's birthday surprise—a gold necklace with a rectangular pendant, perfect for his meteorite shard. Another necklace with a square pendant is meant for Brunner.

When I ripped the shards away from Emierr and Brunner at the park two nights ago, I was sure they'd never hold them again. But after yesterday's revelations, things look different now. It feels right to let them carry a piece of this hope, too.

Finishing breakfast, I retrieve the space rocks from my old desk. The basement, untouched since my time with Pa, holds the tools I need to craft these delicate pieces of art. Flipping the light switch on, the room looks as I last saw it, and the creaking floorboards are reminiscent of memories with Pa.

I'm transported back to the hours I would spend here, doing homework while he worked on his projects. It feels like it was yesterday. Sunlight illuminates his table, revealing research papers and a disorganized mess of tools.

"Okay, let's get to work." I crack my knuckles and approach the desk, letting Papa's worn-out rolling chair envelope me. Wobbling wheels accompany my search for the electric Dremel I know is here somewhere.

I recall him using it to craft Ma's earrings; trimming rubies, and joking that he bought them from a store when, in reality, he obtained the rubies from his excavator friends in Florida. Among the papers, I discover his notes from his master's dissertation, titled "The Existence of White Holes and How to Find Them." The parallels between our research are striking—without consciously knowing it, we'd both delved into the mysteries of white holes and black holes, each from our unique perspectives.

"Ah, there it is." Beneath the mess, I find the Dremel. Placing the research paper to the side, I take the shards from my pocket.

Starting with Emierr's pendant, I outline where to cut on its widest facet. "I hope this still works," I mutter to myself. Precision guides my movements, and it feels as smooth as cutting through butter.

I'm bringing this back to New York with me.

I meticulously carve the shard into a perfect shape and size, slipping it into the pendant casing. Pressing down, I feel the stone click snugly in place.

A clean cut removes the protruding part of the shard, and I test its security by shaking and tapping the pendant against the table. It doesn't budge. I give myself a triumphant high-five, then replicate the process for Brunner's. Holding both necklaces up, I marvel at my creations. My phone buzzes, and the hologram activates.

Emierr's message appears

Meerina

> Are you coming or what? We need to talk about the plan.

Hanging with them these past few days is influencing me; I'm beginning to think I should get the Holo-phone. I shove the necklaces in my pocket and pick up my phone.

> Coming, be there in a few.

I bring my golden pen with me this time. I didn't take a jacket on this trip, which was pretty idiotic in hindsight, so I borrow Pa's leather one, a gift from Uncle Joshua. It's a perfect fit and somehow still smells like him. Then again, I'm pretty sure AXE has a half-life of three hundred years.

The walk is nice, with the warm sun buffeted by fall winds. It just feels like home. I knock on the door three times and place my hands in the jacket pockets. The door opens, and to my surprise, I'm met with Brunner's father.

He's a cop for sure. His cul-de-sac of thinning hair is counteracted by a spectacular mustache. His ruddy cheeks are rough; the face of a man who thinks skincare is for women. I think Brunner said he's the chief of the Farmington Police Department now, but he certainly seemed to be finding time to hit the weights. My eyes are drawn to the tattoos on his left arm. I don't know what they are, but they make him look like a badass.

"Uh, hello Mr. Fischer." I smile, trying not to look how I felt; like a kid caught misbehaving. *Those bitches didn't mention his parents were home.*

"Rictor. It's been so long, son. Please come in." His voice is so deep, just like those blue eyes.

"Thanks." I take my shoes off in the entryway and place them on the side.

"Rictor James."

It's Mrs. Fischer, wearing an apron with her curly hair tied in a bun. She's the one who gave Brunner his smooth, brown complexion. She exudes island life, something I envy. If I make it through this suicide mission, I'm moving back Guam, like Dustin did.

"Mrs. Fischer, hi." *She hasn't aged at all has she?*

"Oh. Look at you." She places her hands on my cheeks. "You look so much like your father."

"Thank you." I can feel my cheeks lifting in her hands.

"Nei ponira," Mr. Fischer said warningly. "Let's not bring up something he might not want to discuss."

"I'm so sorry, I'm sorry." Mrs. Fischer pulls her hands away from my face. I can hear her accent now. Papa shared stories about the Chuukese community in Guam, renowned for their deep cultural roots. Through festivals, dances, and traditional practices, they ensure that their heritage thrives, passing it on to each generation. He also said they were some of the most loyal and kindest people he had ever met. And I see that in Mrs. Fischer.

"It's okay; I love talking about my dad. Did you guys know him well?"

"We weren't close to him like the others were. But I had several conversations with him and a few rounds of beers." Mr. Fischer smiles fondly.

"He was very kind to us. When Jayson was still in the academy and I couldn't drive yet, your father would take me to work on his way, and drop my little Brunner off at school."

"That sounds like my dad. It's good to know that other people remember him the way I do."

"Would you like a beer?" Mr. Fischer offers.

"Fokun?" Mrs. Fischer throws a sharp look at him.

I chuckle, "Not right now, Mr. Fischer. I'll take you up your offer some other time, though."

"Mr. Fischer is my father, call me Jayson."

I nod. "Okay, Uncle Jay."

"You can call me Zuwena."

"Auntie Z," I say with a grin.

"I like that." She winks at me.

"Is Brunner here? I'm supposed to meet him." I feel like a kid, asking the neighbor if his son can play.

"He's in the basement with your friends. What are you guys up to? Gambling, drinking, illegal weapons?"

The blood leaves my face. "Uh... we're just..."

"I'm just messing with you, son. Just don't do drugs in my basement. That's what the shed out back is for." He laughs when his wife smacks him on the arm.

Fuck me. "Noted." I force a laugh.

"Brunner!" Auntie Z calls.

"Yeah!" His voice echoes up the staircase.

"Come up here!"

Footsteps thud up the stairs, and Brunner walks in with a smile on his face. "Ricky! Why didn't you say you were here; I would've come up." He reaches out with a fist.

I bump it with my own. "I was just talking to Uncle Jay and Auntie Z."

"Ugh, did they say something uncool?" Brunner rolls his eyes dramatically.

"Uncool? The only uncool one here is you." Uncle Jay fires back good-naturedly, rubbing his fist into his son's hair.

"Okay! Okay!" Brunner yelps. He ducks out of his father's reach and motions to the stairs behind him. "Let's go?"

"Yeah." I nod. "It was nice talking with you, Uncle and Auntie."

"I'm happy you can be here." Auntie Z says.

"Mom," Brunner glances at the basement and back at Auntie Z, cupping a hand around his mouth and whispers, "Did you start cooking yet for the surprise party?"

Auntie Z raises two thumbs up.

"Okay, thanks." Brunner grins at his mom and drags me to the basement door.

"Talk to you later." I say, stumbling under Brunner's grip "By the way, I have Meer's gift," I say to him as I follow him down. "Came in this morning."

"Nice."

"Wait."

He stops walking to look at me.

I dig through my pants pocket and pull out his pendant. "This is for you." I hand it to him.

His eyes widen and he takes it from me.

"I put your meteorite in there, so you have one like all of us." I hope that this conveys what I'm trying to tell him.

"Ricky... You didn't have to." Brunner touches the stone tentatively, as if afraid to break it.

"I just thought maybe it would be nice to not have it rolling around in your pocket." I chuckle.

"Bro, thanks. I appreciate it."

"That's all I get? Dude." I open my arms. "Gimme a hug."

Brunner leans in for an awkward hug. I crush him against my torso and feel him relax.

"Don't mention it," I say as we pull apart. "No really, don't mention it to Meer. Wear it after I give him his."

"Yeah, of course." He shakes his head and drops his necklace into his pocket. We both glance up and realize his parents can still see us.

"What?" Brunner furrows his brows at them.

"Nothing. Go." Auntie Z shakes her head, grinning, and shoos us away. I don't get it; why didn't the other parents get close to them? They seem like great people. We shuffle down the remaining stairs and into the basement. The others are on the couch, studying the notebook like they haven't read it cover to cover a hundred times since we got here.

"Ricky, finally." Emierr stands up. "Did you eat a heavy meal or something? Hibernation is two months away."

"Ha ha," I say sarcastically. "Were none of you guys tired? Yesterday emotionally wrung me out." I slide into Emierr's spot on the couch.

"I couldn't really sleep," Jadis muttered. She looks cranky, with deep purple rings below her eyes.

I wisely decide not to provoke her. "Hey, Dusticle. How was sleep?" He was sitting at the opposite end of the battered sofa.

"Dicktor," he drawls, still leafing through the notebook. "I had a long talk with Vi; she wants me to come home."

"Understandable." I frown, thinking back on my conversation with Bonnie. Had she wanted to ask me to come home?

Brunner drags a chair from the side of the room and sits down. I guess he brought some down after yesterday. Thank God, the floor did a number on my ass.

"At least none of you got an earful; she called to scold me." Emierr grabs a second chair and parks next to Brunner, wincing.

"You deserve it, always." I smirk at him.

"Yeah, yeah, yeah, whatever." He waves a dismissive hand at me.

"I had to tell her everything. She thought we all were exploring the use of magic mushrooms as a trauma treatment." Dustin chuckles.

"It sounds like it, really. I was trying to tell Cadence and Carl last night, but they probably think we're all on something too." Jadis folds her arms in sync with mine. We catch each other's eye and laugh. "But I don't care what anyone thinks," she adds. "We're saving Jho."

"Period." I nudge her. "I told my... Um..." *What is Bonnie? A best friend? My assistant? Colleague?*

"Bonnie?" Meer supplies.

"Who's Bonnie?" Dustin leans back and looks at me with interest.

"Yeah, who's the mystery girl, Ricky?" Jadis asks with a mischievous grin.

"She's my best friend outside of you guys. Well, she's also my assistant, but we met in college. We had a class together and we just clicked." I sound defensive.

"She sounds important if you told her about the drugs," Brunner jokes.

Jadis shoots at him with a withering look.

"She is important. And if anything happens, I want her to know how much she means to me." I say, surprising myself a little. I'm not sure when I decided to admit that out loud. Silence fills the air. I'm sure we're all thinking the same thing: What will this outcome be? Of course, the one we're aiming for is to get Jhoana back, but there's a fifty-fifty chance we could end up like her. Maybe those odds are generous.

"What's your plan, Meer?" I ask, dispelling the uncomfortable atmosphere I'd single-handedly created. Emierr had, after all, lured us all here with his grand scheme and now it was finally time for the big reveal.

"The plan." Emierr sighs.

All eyes turn to him, awaiting some form of elaboration, but he remains silent.

"Bitch," I mutter under my breath.

"Well..." Emierr winces.

"The plan was to get you all home," Brunner interjects.

"And now that you all are here, the plan worked," Emierr tries to give us a winning smile but is met with ice.

"So, the plan is there is no plan?" I raise an eyebrow at Emierr, my skepticism probably painted across my face.

"Meer," Jadis groans, letting her head drop into her hands.

"I thought you said you've been planning this for months!" Dustin nearly shouts the accusation.

"We were planning the planning, but we didn't think it would start this soon," Emierr protests.

"Yeah... Auntie Ina changed her mind out of nowhere. We thought it was happening next summer," Brunner says, coming to Emierr's defense.

"So, what are we going to do? I'm putting my family on the line, Meer. This has to be foolproof," Dustin's voice is harsh. He has the most to lose. I have to make it a priority to ensure he gets out unscathed.

Glancing at Jadis, who seems to be attempting to formulate a response, but is coming up blank. I guess it's time for me to step back up as leader.

"Then how are we going to start this?"

Emierr gets up, producing a tablet from his backpack. "I digitally recreated the map of Ethra, and..." He clicks on a folder, revealing a hologram above the tablet. "We'll spawn back at where we last were, the shadow forest." He zooms in on the forest.

"This is impressive, Meer." Despite myself, I have to admire his work. I take the tablet from him, studying the details of our desti-nation. I can't believe we're going back. And not just back. We're going to Akeurimja.

"Wait, Rune never Transcended before, won't he spawn some-where else?" Dustin points out.

"Yeah, but remember when we all Transcended with you the first time, and in the last second, you separated from us?" Emierr asks.

"Yeah?"

"What I'm thinking is, we don't let go of Rune. Maybe he'll land with us."

"Hmm." Dustin nods slowly. "That might actually work."

"But that's suggesting we can move freely like we did before," I argue.

"Yeah, it's been years; I would think it works out like muscles; you know? We need to be actively practicing it, or else our bodies won't be used to it anymore," Dustin agrees.

Well, damn, I guess all those footballs to the head didn't do as much damage as we thought.

The boys exchange glances with each other before turning their gaze towards me.

"Then we hold hands," I propose. "If none of us can move around like before, we make sure we're tethered to each other."

"There we go; now we're planning." Emierr nods, a satisfied smile on his face.

"Guys," Jadis interjects, her gaze fixed on the floor. "It's been sixteen years since Jho was in her coma."

"Yeah, we're aware," I say.

"That means, she's been in there for thirty-two years, "she says, finally looking up. Her eyes are walls, damming up any emotion behind them.

We're silent. Of course we'd all done the math, but none of us wanted to consider the implications. The thought of Jho, well into her forties, having been trapped for thirty-two years... It was too much for my battered mental state to handle.

"Imagine Sól," I say, altering the conversation to something I can deal with. "He was the youngest, but he'll be older than any of us now." It's horrifying and doesn't need to be said, but it's better than talking about Jhoana. I suppose misery loves company. "Meer, you think he'd still be in Terrene?"

Emierr avoids making eye contact with me. "Let's talk about where we're going first."

I frown at him. He's avoided every mention of Sólel outside of last night, when he recounted his memories of Terrene. Does he still feel guilty for abandoning his little brother?

"Wait, that's just her consciousness, right?" Brunner's still stuck on Jhoana. "Her mental age would be older, but she's still twenty-eight. I mean, her body is." I can see him chewing at the inside of his lip.

"Honestly, we don't know. There's still a chance she might not even be there," I say bluntly. "She could have died that day." Saying the words lodges a knife in my chest.

Jadis's entire body has gone rigid. "But if she's not in there, then we leave right away," she says tightly, as if each word has to fight a battle to leave her throat. "None of us risk anything if she isn't there." As much as she must want to find Jhoana, she knows we need to return safely. There is no honor in dying for a ghost.

Another silence cuts the air. I can tell from the others' faces that we're all thinking the same thing: Jhoana has to be there. Dustin breaks through our rumination by rising from the couch.

"Okay." He stretches, fingers brushing the low ceiling, then flops down onto the floor. He lies back on the carpet, placing his hands behind his head.

Jadis peers down at him. "What are you doing?"

"If we're going to plan this out, we might as well get comfortable," Dustin replies with a smile. If he's trying to break up the tension, it's working.

"Shoot." I stand up to join him. "My back is killing me and I think I *might* have outgrown my rocket ship bed by a few years." I lie with the top of my head touching Dustin's. The outdated, powder blue carpet is still thick and plush.

"I'm in." Emierr moves his chair away and lies down beside me.

"It's a good thing I cleaned the carpet." Brunner positions himself between Dustin and Emierr.

Jadis, still perched on the couch, grimaces down at us. I pat the spot next to me and force a smile.

"You all are literal idiots," she says, rolling her eyes. Regardless, she gives in and joins the circle between me and Dustin. We're kids again, lying in the grass before Transcending to our dreamworld. Warmth from the memory is marred by a needling against my heart. The last time we lay like this, Jhoana died.

"Now *this* is like old times," Dustin says. I wonder if he feels the same stab of pain I do. If he does, his voice doesn't betray it.

"Alright, let's head to Terrene first," Emierr says, businesslike.

"But wasn't Verglas her nation?" Brunner asks.

"She didn't even like Verglas," Emierr counters.

"But she did love Valda and Boyko," Dustin argues. "They treated her like a daughter from day one."

"Yeah, she genuinely loved them as if they were a second set of parents," Jadis agrees.

"Maybe we should reach out to them. I'm sure Jho would turn to them if she was in trouble." I can still recall their faces from photos Jhoana had sent me, though time has blurred their features.

"If you survived an attack from your evil twin, would you return to your nation, where they'd expect you to go or head to Terrene where it's easier to stay hidden?" Emierr presses doggedly.

I pause, thinking. "That's a valid point," I finally agree.

"Jho has those secret Ethereal Waters" Dustin argues. "She was pretty sure she was the only one who knew about them. She could be hiding out there."

"Oh, right. That's a good theory too," I say before leaning towards Jadis and whispering, "You're enjoying this, huh?"

"Five bucks they're gonna get into it," she whispers back.

"Bet," I nudge her.

"She's my cousin, bro; I know her," Emierr throws at Dustin.

"Do you? You barely hung out with her in Ethra or in real life," Dustin retorts.

"Bro, shut the fuck up. You don't know anything."

"Yeah, like you know what the fuck you're doing."

"Hey! Dumbasses, knock it off." Jadis sits up, jabbing a finger at both offenders. I stifle a laugh. "Are you guys twelve? We're here to save Jho, not see whose dick is bigger. Tone the attitude down, both of you."

"Sorry, Mom," Emierr says snidely, but falls silent all the same. Satisfied, Jadis lies back down.

"I told you," she whispers, the grin on her face devilish.

I chuckle softly, "I'll PayPal you; I don't carry paper money."

She scoffs. "Forget it. The prize was scolding them."

"Do you guys argue like this all the time?" Brunner asks.

"What do you expect? They're brothers." I chuckle. "You should've seen what they considered a 'friendly spar' in Ethra. There were superpowers involved with that one."

"The whiplash I get with you guys," Brunner says, though he sounds amused.

"But we really *should* head to Terrene," I say, steering the conversation back. "Meer is right; it's the best place to hide. And the Chiefs would keep Jho safe if she went to them. They did that for me."

"Arid is too guarded," Jadis agrees. "If Jho brought trouble there, all hell would break loose." She pauses, contemplating, her arms folding absently across her chest. "And anyway, she wouldn't risk leading our sadistic doppelgangers into a settlement. They would probably cut down anyone in their way to get to her."

"So, Arid and Verglas are a no-go," Brunner concludes. "She definitely wouldn't bring any danger into Verglas."

"And the Fleming Space Ring," I add, suppressing a shudder at the thought of returning to the orbiting city. "Tickets are expensive, and the Gates are challenging to access unless you're a high-level magick user. Jho may not have known the specifics of what happened to me up there, but regardless, I can't imagine she'd willfully trap herself in a closed environment like that, full of innocent bystanders." I cross my arms. "Not with the anti-Squad after her."

"What about Zaltana?" Dustin asks.

"What about it?" Emierr retorts. "I don't think she would go there."

"You *really* didn't know your cousin when she was in Ethra. She visited Zaltana a lot. Her ties with the Brae were strong," Dustin says. I can almost hear his eyes rolling. "She had a significant connection with them. She led expeditions to reclaim a parcel of land taken over by bandits. Because of her, the people of Glaedhaven have their homes back. She was well-respected there." Dustin presses his fingers into his temples. "Holy shit. My head's fucking throbbing. I just remembered that."

"That's really her—always helping wherever she can," Emierr says softly.

"Okay, so, Terrene first, then Zaltana." I unfold a finger for each destination.

"That sounds good to me. The sooner we get back out of Ethra, the better," Jadis says, voice drawn like a bowstring.

Emierr and Dustin murmur their agreements.

"But if she's not in Zaltana either?" Brunner voices the concern none of us want to think about.

"Then we come home and say goodbye to our best friend." As the words leave my mouth, an instant wave of sadness overtakes me.

Brunner doesn't respond.

"I'm sorry, Rune," I say, propping myself up on my elbows. "I'm sorry, everyone. But this is another reality we have to face. Just be prepared for that possibility." My throat constricts.

"Okay, well." Dustin sits up. "If the plan's set, let's take a break, and meet back here in an hour? I wanna talk to my wife and kids."

As the others stand and stretch, I glance at Dustin. He's trying to be subtle about wiping his glassy eyes.

Silence fills the room once again. I'm sure all of our minds are running a mile a minute. This has to work. If it doesn't, I don't think I can bear to witness the death of someone I love a second time.

Allied Organization Squad

I let out a leaden sigh. "Fuck."

This isn't any easier than it was sixteen years ago. The weight of the day settles on my shoulders like a cosmic force I can't escape. Celebrating the day Emierr was born is supposed to be a moment of joy, but the looming thoughts of Jhoana's possible demise casts a heavy shadow. Everything around me feels distant as I stare at Pa's car from the porch of my childhood home.

But amidst the swirl of contemplation, my thoughts drift to Oscar. My boss, who was somehow at the place where our lives were destroyed. Sure, Dustin was convinced by his seemingly genuine pain in that newsclip. Yet Oscar's reaction when I asked him about Pa, like someone with skeletons in his closet, left me uneasy.

What does he know, and why the hell hasn't he been talking to Bonnie?

I retrieve the AMOS VR from my pocket and put it on, its familiar weight settling against my temples. Scrolling through my contacts, I find Oscar's number and dial. The rings echo through the speakers and real-world sunlight streams through the augmented lenses.

"Rictor, good to hear from you," Oscar's voice sounded through my speakers. "How's your vacation going?"

"Hi— Hello, sir. Vacation is going well—Uh—Actually, it's not a vacation. My—"

"I heard. I'm sorry you're going through that. If you need anything, please let me know."

"Thank you... for that, sir. I'm actually calling to find out why you haven't been connecting with Bonnie."

"Relax, I'm about to go see her right now." His voice is a strange mix of politeness and aloofness.

"Oh. Okay, that's good," is all I can mutter.

"The game is exceeding all my expectations, Rictor. What you made here changes everything."

"I'm glad to hear about your involvement, sir. I'm hoping you can wait for me to get back before the launch. I'd love to be there when it all happens." Despite the tremor in my voice, I muster every ounce of effort to exude confidence. I feel like I'm still peering down at Central Park from his office, and my fear of heights is clinging to every word.

"Of course. You have to witness the fruits of your labor. Finish whatever you need to do there, and we can start when you arrive."

This is good, this is really good. Time to strike.

"I wanted to talk about my dad," I say in a rush. "There are a lot of questions I have and you're the closest thing I have to answers from that day. If you have the time, it would really—"

Oscar interrupted, "Not here. We can't talk on the phone about any of this. But there is something I need you to see. Something I don't understand. I'll send it two minutes after ending this call. Make sure your phone is encrypted. Whatever you do, Rictor, make sure you come back home. We will talk about it then. There's a lot you need to know, and I can't do it through here. I have to go now. Remember, encrypt your phone." He hangs up without a goodbye.

"Oscar—" *What the fuck?*

There is something looming beneath Pa's death, and Oscar holds the key, or at least a piece of the puzzle. I released a shuddering breath before going to my phone settings and switching on the encryption. A message from Oscar appears a few seconds later. It's a video attachment. As the video begins, my arm hairs bristle. Security footage from Pa's lab the day I lost him begins to play.

In the heart of the scene, a colossal device dominates the center, encased in gleaming glass that overshadows most of the video feed. Alarms start flashing and, despite the lack of audio, I feel like I can hear them piercing the air. Pa, clad in a lab coat, races towards the apparatus. It's striking to see Pa again—I do look like him. He has his hands pressed against the glass casing. I can't hear what he's saying but he looks frantic, and I can't tell if his words are directed at someone out of frame or at the machine in sheer desperation.

Auntie Via steps into view. I almost don't recognize her. Her fingers are flying across a tablet but the footage is too grainy to see the screen. Auntie Via drops the tablet and darts out of frame. Pa's panicked gaze follows her, then returns to the mysterious device at the heart of the chaos. Suddenly, it hits me. I recognize the machine. *What's Pa doing with a particle accelerator?*

Pa's words echo in my mind. *"I promise, when I come back, I'll quit."*

He places his head on the casing, a poignant moment frozen in time. Then, as if orchestrated by some form of divine intervention, the particle accelerator ignites, casting an eerie glow through the lab before everything erupts. The footage abruptly statics and I jolt. I flip the phone's screen away from my face, trying to control my breathing.

A movement in my periphery catches my attention. Twisting my head, I see him. A younger version of myself stares down at me from an upstairs window in the abandoned house next door. After a heartbeat, the apparition vanishes. That's the second time today.

I continue to watch the abandoned house, its weather-beaten façade casting a foreboding shadow over the neglected lawn. The windows are shattered, like eyes hollowed out by time's cruel hand. The porch sags, and paint peels away in curling strips, exposing the decaying wood beneath. Weeds choke the path leading to the door, and a sense of unease settles in the pit of my stomach. Ma mentioned it's been vacant for nearly two decades. So much time has passed, I struggle to remember who lived there, and why it was abandoned.

As I stare into the house's empty husk, a memory unlocks—Mr. Dawson. A drop of blood falls from my nose, splattering onto Ma's concrete porch. It was hidden away, just like my memories of Ethra. But why would I have blocked out Mr. Dawson? He watched over us before Uncle Kit left his job. It can't be a coincidence that I saw my younger self in his old house. Something had to have happened there, but what exactly? I delve deeply into my strained memory, searching for the scattered answers.

As the pieces fall into place, my mind begins to race. *What was it about hallucinations that my therapists said? Fuck. Do I follow the ghost of my past?* I shake my head, attempting to clear the fog of uncertainty. On instinct, I open the Squad chat and type, "SOS, meet at my house now." Adding Mr. Dawson and the abandoned house to my list of unanswered questions makes my skin crawl.

Just as I send the message, I notice a man wearing a tucked-in, white button-up shirt approaching from my right. A wide, unsettling smile stretched across his face.

"Bitch." I mutter, shouldering my way back inside the house. *Seriously? I've got bigger problems than this right now.* I can't be bothered with another psycho missionary, not today.

I glance at the clock—3:56 p.m. The secret surprise birthday party kicks off at 5. Time's ticking, and if we're aiming for answers, we need to move. A knock on the door interrupts my thoughts, and I swing it open. The missionary has vanished.

"Say hi, angel." Dustin angles his hand my way, flipping the hologram.

"Hi, Uncle Ricky!" Celeste greets me with a beaming smile. "I miss you. Can you and Daddy come back home now?" Her pouting lower lip pulls at my heartstrings.

"Hey, best friend," I say, waving at her, and the radiant smile returns. "I miss you too! Once we're done here, I'll swing by, alright?"

"Yay!" Celeste bounces, little arms raised in triumph.

Dustin redirects the hologram. "Okay, angel. Daddy's gotta go. Kiss your little sister and mom for me, okay? Love you."

"Okay, Daddy. I love you!" Celeste blows a kiss, and the hologram fades.

"Best friend? When did that happen?" Dustin strolls inside without invitation.

"She showed me her boat. Said I could keep it." I grin, shoving down the tangle of anxiety in my gut. No point in dwelling on it until everyone's here.

"Excuse me, no one's taking my yacht."

"Hey, no take-backsies. I don't make the rules." I close the door behind him, taking one last deep breath to steady myself. "Did you see a missionary outside?"

Dustin scans the living room. "Holy shit. It's like stepping into—"

"A time machine," I finish his sentence. "The nostalgia doesn't fade; it's like living in a memory." I head to the living room, sinking into the embrace of the old couch, a reminder of the day of Papa's wake.

Dustin joins me. "Did you say missionary? One of Meer's Mormon 2.0s? Didn't see anyone."

Must have been. Real missionaries aren't allowed to be alone, are they? "I don't know if I'm seeing shit or losing my mind at this point."

Dustin shrugged. "Got beer? I think I need it."

"I think your dad's stash is still here." I head to the fridge. "Where are the others?"

"They went to grab boba from Jads's old job, remember that place?"

"Real? Man, I was craving boba." I open the fridge, retrieving two San Mig Light bottles.

"That's your fault. You bolted out of Rune's place before they could even ask you. And SOS? What's going on?"

"I'll explain when everyone gets here." I pop open his bottle cap with mine and hand him the bottle.

"Damn," he says.

"College was a different time for me." I grin, using my teeth to open my own.

"Cheers." Dustin raises his bottle.

"Cheers." I tap his beer with mine and we both take a swig. "Meer really forgot his own birthday, huh?" I say.

"That boy's memory is Swiss cheese." He takes another big gulp before placing it down on the coffee table.

A knock interrupts us.

"*Dust-in* time," he says with a chuckle that lasts far too long for the quality of the joke.

"You're such a dad." I get up to answer the door. The trio of traitors. "Well, well, well, if it isn't my..." I raise both hands to sign air quotes dramatically. *"Friends."*

"Hey." Brunner sounds nervous, like he's in trouble.

"I brought you a matcha frappe with whipped cream." Jadis hands me the drink and casually steps in, slipping off her shoes and placing them to the side. She still remembers my favorite.

"With soy milk?"

"Righto, Captain Lactose Intolerance."

My attention shifts to Brunner, still standing on the porch and shifting anxiously.

"You coming in?"

"Uh, yeah." He dusts off his shoes before entering. "This is my first time here."

"Runey, over here." Dustin pats the seat next to him on the couch.

"Make yourself at home," I chuckle. My gaze lands on Emierr, seated in front of the coffee table, engrossed in his tablet. "Meer, don't sit on the rug. I can get you a chair." I set my frappe on the table.

"Nah, it's okay. Makes it feel like old times." He doesn't look up.

"Okay, whatever. If you need one, help yourself." I fetch myself a chair from the kitchen, settling between the couch and Emierr. The cold, sweet matcha is a welcome distraction.

"You good?" Jadis furrows her brows at me.

"I guess I'll forgive you for not inviting me." I say, wiggling my drink at her.

"You know what I mean, asshole. You sent us an SOS."

"Guys, can we talk about theories now?" Emierr interrupts, clearly having not listened. "Over the years, I did my research about Ethra. I felt so stupid searching on Google, 'My friends and I created a dream world, is this possible?' and the internet made me feel even more stupid." Emierr runs a hand through his short hair.

"You've got your own kind of smart, Meer," Dustin says with mock sympathy.

"Please raise your hand if you're going to say something, Mr. Borja," Emierr retorts in his teacher voice. "Okay, seriously. In high school, I did an intensive search on the net and I found a post on Reddit, and... Well." He fidgets with his tablet, and a hologram pops up.

Everyone leans in to read the post. There's a long pause as eyes flit across words.

Finally, Dustin announces, "I don't understand any of this."

"It's about string theory again," Jadis murmurs, eyes still scanning. "The post was made by someone called StarSeed89."

That sounds familiar. Oscar and the abandoned house next door slip from my mind as I squint at the tiny print.

Dreams are a conscious state of mind where the soul wanders the never-ending possibilities of realities. What if I told you dreams are a gateway to worlds beyond your knowledge and wildest dreams? What if there is a way to transcend yourself to another version of you, another universe.

"Transcend?" I say, startled.

"What?" Dustin leans in closer.

Jadis and I share the same wide-eyed look.

"Why didn't you show me any of this?" Brunner asks Emierr, accusation in his voice.

"Because... just keep reading."

I read aloud. "What if there is a way to transcend yourself to another version of you, another universe? I have proof that string theory exists, and it will break the fundamentals of science. If there are any of you who want to free yourself from this existence, now is your chance to learn. Who will you be in this vast multiverse? Astralis." The word doesn't register in my mind before it leaves my mouth. But a simultaneous gasp comes from the rest.

"What the fuck?" Dustin grabs the tablet and scrolls through the post.

"What?" Brunner was equally dumbfounded.

"How is that possible?" I breathe out. Ethra. Transcending. Astralis. All of that was between the Squad. We *created* it. If it weren't Brunner's pale face, I would have thought he and Emierr had written it to fuck with us.

"Exactly what I said," Emierr says. "I read all of StarSeed's entries, and basically, it's a guide on how to Transcend. Except no space rocks."

"You didn't make this to mess with us, right?" Jadis shoots at Emierr. She's clearly more suspicious than I am, even if we're riding the same train of thought.

"Why would I do that?" Emierr looks genuinely wounded.

"No, yeah. Look." Dustin places the tablet on the table. "The thread was posted on January 17, 2008. It was two months before Jho went into the coma. Reddit was created in 2005. The website was still pretty new, and sixth-grade Emierr wouldn't have been able to spell half of these words."

Emierr looks outraged, but Brunner interrupts him. "The only ones who really knew how to use the internet were Jads, Ricky, and Jho. But as smart as all three of you are, I don't think any of us would understand a concept like this at that age. And definitely not write using this vocabulary."

"I mean, I had a vague knowledge because of my dad," I say. "In, like, a really dumbed-down version of it. The thing about space is that it's so vast, we still don't know how big it is. Even with all the technology we have, there's no way to pinpoint it. But my Pa talked about it to me sometimes, and how NASA is..." I pause.

"Is what?" Jadis looks intently at me.

"I—I don't remember." *That's weird; why is there a block on that memory?* "But yeah, even though I kind of understood at the time, I wouldn't have been able to use that kind of language to explain it. I didn't even know about Reddit until high school."

"Then who the fuck is StarSeed89?" Dustin says, and we all look back at the hologram, like a final inspection would reveal answers.

"You guys seriously don't see the connection?" Emierr gets to his feet. "This... *person* knows about Ethra. They had to."

"Are you suggesting that Ethra—" Jadis starts.

"Yes!" Emierr cuts her off. "Ethra is a version of Earth where magick exists."

Emierr's words ring in my ears, as clear as the memories of my childhood.

I didn't create Ethra; it was always just there.

"I mean, if you really think about it, Ethra is literally an anagram for Earth," Brunner says, his deep, blue eyes wide.

"Yeah," Emierr's hands start talking with him. "Wasn't the lore of Ethra *super* specific? It mirrored our history until another asteroid struck it. StarSeed89 suggests that dreams are gateways to the realities you inhabit..." He stares around at all of us, expecting someone to complete his sentence, but we're all at a loss. "We don't exist in Ethra."

Jadis fishes for some kind of plausible denial. "Are we really going to trust someone who posted something crazy online sixteen years ago?"

"I mean, it closely aligns with our experiences, and it's too much of a coincidence not to be related to Ethra or us," I argue. "How else could they know the word 'Astralis?' "

"My head hurts." Dustin reaches for my frappe and takes a sip.

I don't bother slapping his hand away.

"So, Ethra could be from another reality?" Brunner asks, examining the tablet.

"That's the theory," Jadis leans in, peering over his shoulder.

"String theory is about different realities, right?" Dustin looks at me for confirmation.

"Well—" I begin.

"Yes!" Emierr interrupts, grinning triumphantly. "Let me take this one, Ricky."

"Sure, go ahead." I recline in my chair, amused. "I'm curious to hear your version."

Emierr directs his attention to Dustin with a grin. "Alright, picture yourself at McDonald's."

This is already off to a stellar start.

"Yep," Dustin nods.

"You've got to decide between a cheeseburger and a McChicken."

"McChicken," Dustin interrupts.

"I didn't mean—Whatever, fine, you choose the McChicken." Emierr rolls his eyes. "That choice creates a split. In one reality, you picked the McChicken, but in another, you went with the cheeseburger. Both choices exist simultaneously, in different branches of reality."

Dustin frowns.

"Now, think of the universe like a forest," Emierr continues. "Each tree in the forest is a possible reality, a different version of events. But the trees don't grow randomly—they're all connected by tiny, vibrating strings. Those strings form the particles that make up the trees—or, in this case, realities."

Dustin hesitates. "Particles..."

Emierr raises an eyebrow. "You do know what particles are, right, Dust?"

"I'm not some dumb fucking jock, okay? Of course I do! They're like... dust... particles."

Jadis, Brunner, and I exchange quiet snickers.

"Close enough, but think more like atoms," Emierr corrects. "Each string vibrates, and the way those strings move determines how the particles behave. That's what shapes the reality—like roots growing a tree. And when those vibrations change, they create new possibilities, new branches on the tree."

"So, string theory is about proving that these branches, these possibilities, are what form different realities?" Brunner traces invisible branches in the air.

"Exactly," I confirm. "Every decision, every event, could create a new universe—like new trees sprouting in a cosmic forest."

Dustin looks both confused and intrigued. "So... the multiverse is like a giant forest with different versions of reality?"

"Right," Emierr says. "Each tree—each reality—is connected by those vibrating strings. And just like in a forest, what happens in one part can affect another, though it's not always clear how. The cosmic wilderness is full of countless possible worlds, all existing side by side."

"Hence, the multiverse." I nod and fist-bump Emierr. "Well done, Mr. Physicist."

"I learned most of it from you."

"So, there's a universe where I didn't become a football player." Dustin looks disquieted by the idea.

"There's one where I hung out with you guys when we were kids." Brunner smiles faintly.

"One where Jho woke up with us." Jadis sighs.

"One where my Papa didn't die," I say and all eyes turn to me.

"And one where my mom is still around." Dustin's gaze locks with mine. Perhaps there is beauty in the fact that some other version of us is living those realities.

"But look at Ethra—it's so different," Emierr presses "What if other universes exist, hidden alongside ours?"

"Like a superstring," I reply. *How much did he research? If this is all true, then it would change everything we know about science.*

"Exactly! Thank god you know about superstring; I had a hard time understanding it and was so not looking forward to explaining it," Emierr admits.

"There's more?" Dustin sounds like he's worried there might be a test at the end.

All eyes turn to me.

"Right. So, like Meer explained, string theory suggests that the universe isn't just one single thing—it's made up of multiple, possibly infinite, realities stacked within a larger structure. Think back to the McDonald's analogy, where you have to choose between two burgers. That choice splits reality, creating two branches—one where you picked the McChicken, and one where you picked the cheeseburger. Each branch continues on its own path, and that splitting can happen infinitely." I pause, glancing around to see if they're still following. Heads nod slightly, so I take that as a good sign and continue.

"Now, superstring theory adds another layer. It's not just about splitting realities—it's about the tiny strings that make up every-thing in the universe. These strings vibrate in different ways, which creates the different particles, forces, and even realities we experi-ence. Our universe, with all its branching realities, is just one part of a much bigger system. Imagine each universe is like a forest with its own unique trees, leaves, and seedlings. But there are countless other forests—completely independent, with their own rules, trees, and ecosystems. They might follow entirely different laws of physics or have elements we can't even understand. These 'forests' don't interact directly with each other, but they all exist side by side in this bigger multiverse." I'm trying my best to simplify it, but no matter how I explain it, it's still a complete mindfuck.

"And Meer thinks Ethra is in a superstring universe?" Jadis clarifies.

"I'm sorry, guys, this isn't my area of expertise in theoretical physics," I confess. "I studied black holes and white holes; I haven't really read up on the multiverse and I might not be explaining it correctly."

"Bruh, I'm still processing yesterday's meeting. But this... It changes everything, right?" Brunner looks to us, seeking some form of reassurance.

"Well, we can't be entirely sure this theory is the real deal." Jadis has her arms tightly folded around herself. "Like yeah, the evidence is fucking compelling, but there's still no solid proof to back it up, and if it *is* true..." She pauses, her face deep in thought. I'm a step ahead of her.

"If it's real, then Jho could have really died in Ethra," I finish.

The weight of that realization settles on everyone's faces and I can see them grappling with the potential consequences of this theory. I stand up to pace, unable to sit still any longer.

"If I'm being honest, I never knew how or why we could visit Ethra in the first place. It's not normal to visit each other in our dreams... I'm still on board with the idea of shared psychosis. But, if Ethra is another, *real* universe, this truly does change everything." I don't need to look at my friends' faces. I pull my phone out to check the time—4:22 p.m. "We should head back to Brunner's."

He blinks at me, startled. "Wait, didn't you call for an SOS?"

"Oh, shit, yeah." All this string theory talk had driven my reason for calling this meeting right out of my mind. I sigh. I really do not want to watch this footage again, but I don't have a choice. "I spoke with Oscar. He was really cryptic, but he sent me a video." I pull the video up on the hologram, placing the phone on the table. "Dust, this might be tough to watch,"

He nods.

I take the gold pen from my pocket and click the button. The silent video unfolds. I stand next to Jadis, watching their faces as the events in the lab play out. For so long, we wondered what happened, and now, after seventeen years, the answer unravels before them. Their eyes fixate on Pa and Auntie Via in the video. Gasps fill the room when the explosion hits. Jadis covers her mouth, and Dustin turns away.

"Oh my god," Jadis breathes.

"So, it was a malfunction," Dustin says, his voice hoarse.

"Yeah, it looks like it," I say.

"Can you go back to before the explosion, like seconds before?" Brunner asks. His brows are knitted together and he's staring hard at the pixelated footage.

I rewind the video, and we all lean in to watch.

"Right there," Brunner points and takes control, rewinding it himself. "Before the explosion, look at, uh, Uncle James." He stumbles over my Pa's name, likely unsure whether he has the right to refer to him that way.

I move closer, staring hard at the hologram. Pa places his hands on the glass casing and then looks up just before the explosion.

"He looks up?" I say, perplexed. "So what?"

"It's like he's being forced. Look at how his head jerks back," Brunner rewinds the video again. Pa seems to resign himself to his fate, but then suddenly, something yanks his head back. The more I watch, the more unnatural it seems.

"That's strange," Dustin mutters.

"Yeah, something doesn't feel right. I'm starting to feel queasy," Jadis says, sitting up straight and tightening her arms around herself.

"Oscar said to watch it carefully... Maybe he was referring to that. But what does it mean?" A crease forms between my eyebrows.

Brunner sighs. "Looks like you'll have to get that answer from Oscar himself."

I take a deep breath in and exhale, remembering what I saw right after I watched the video. "I saw myself again. My younger self, with the bleeding eye and all."

"It's still happening for you?" Emierr's face contorts with concern.

"Yeah, saw him when I woke up, then again and at the house next to mine."

"The abandoned one, right? Not my parents'?" Jadis asks nervously.

"Yeah, the abandoned one. It was right after I watched the video..." I pause, glancing at them. "Do you guys remember Mr. Dawson?"

Silence fills the room. I can see all four of them straining their battered memories.

"Three... two... one," I cajole. Just as I expected, they all gasp when the mental barrier breaks.

"Yes! He was the one who watched over us, right?" Jadis claps her hand to her forehead.

"Yeah," I say, trying to wade through the swamp of faded memories in my own mind.

"I just remembered him too," Brunner says, puzzled. "I used to watch you guys play in his backyard, and he always let me watch but I was never allowed over. What happened to him?"

"Wait, why didn't I remember him at all?" Emierr's brows knit together. "I'm supposed to be the one with my memory intact."

"Mr. Dawson... He was around our parents' age, right?" Dustin rubs his stubbly chin.

"Yeah, but are we going to ignore that Meer didn't remember him?" I ask, jerking my head at him. I'd expected Jadis and Dustin, but not Emierr or Brunner.

Everyone's attention shifts to Emierr as he scrolls through files on his tablet.

"I don't have any notes on him, or any mention of him. That's so strange." Bewilderment is written across Emierr's face.

Jadis lets out a deep sigh and stands. "Okay, let's go."

"Go where?" Emierr asks, startled.

"We're getting some answers." She extends her hand to Emierr, and he allows her to haul him to his feet.

"If we're doing this, let's do it now. It's *4:30*," I say, casting a meaningful look at Dustin, Jadis, and Brunner.

"Damn, right." Dustin jumps up.

"Yeah, let's get this done." Brunner strides toward the door.

"Why the rush, guys? Wait, we're *breaking into* the house?" Emierr scrambles after us. "Brunner's dad is a *cop*. And anyway, it's boarded up, someone's going to notice us tearing it down."

"We could sneak in through the back door. There's no house behind it, and a fence blocks the view," Brunner suggests, ignoring Emierr's first question.

"Perfect. I've got a pry bar in the basement," I announce, dashing downstairs to find it amidst Pa's tools. When I return, I toss the disused tool to Dustin.

"Why can't we just do this tomorrow?" Emierr asks, adjusting his gym bag strap.

"Dumbass." Dustin shakes his head.

"What?" Emierr asks, bemused.

"We're Transcending tomorrow," I remind him, finding a plausible reason for our haste.

"Oh, shit, right."

"We'll get answers and then head to Rune's place for more planning." Jadis's tone is authoritative as she leads the way out the front door.

The rest of us follow obediently. We quietly make our way to the back of Mr. Dawson's house. All the windows are boarded shut, as is the door. Dustin starts prizing off the plywood with disconcerting ease.

"See, he's the muscles," Emierr says, leaning comfortably on the wall while Dustin works.

"Um, guys, how are we going to get in if the door is locked?" Jadis asks, eyeing the doorknob.

"Easy. We have a Rune," Emierr says with a wink.

"Don't ask me why I have this," Brunner mutters, pulling out a silver case from his back pocket and extracting some miniscule tools from it. He begins to fiddle with the doorknob as Dustin sets the final board aside.

"Is that... a lockpicking toolkit?" Dustin stands up, dusting off his jeans.

"Why do you have it?" I'm watching the practiced motions of Brunner's fingers with equal parts interest and concern. "And do you just always keep it in your pocket?"

"I told you not to ask me," Brunner says. The door clicks. He pushes the door open. Its rusty hinges emit a painful shriek. The wind stirs the contents of the entryway, filling our noses with the smell of dust and abandonment. "Ready to meddle, Mystery Inc.?" Brunner grins.

"It's darker than I expected," Jadis remarks, failing to hide her nerves.

"Phones out," Brunner instructs, activating the flashlight on his Holo-phone. Jadis and I turn on the lights from our physical phones, two lone rebels against the Holo-phone takeover. I'm struck by how familiar this feels. It makes me think of the early days of Ethra, when we spent our time exploring the darkest parts of the Space Ring.

"This place has definitely been abandoned for years. There are still Kidz Bop CDs here," Brunner scoffs as I step into the house.

"That's a throwback; I haven't seen one of those for years." Dustin scans the living room, eyes alert and cautious.

"Don't go through the kitchen area; there's mold in there," Emierr warns, retreating from a dank doorway.

"I don't like it here," Jadis mutters, eyeing the forgotten family photos on the walls.

"Does any of this look familiar to you guys?" I grab a Kid's National Geographic magazine from a nearby shelf and check the date: November 2007.

"I've never been in here, so I couldn't tell you," Brunner says unhelpfully.

"No." Dustin shakes his head. "I mean, remember a little, but nothing here seems familiar."

"This feels wrong." Jadis moves to stand closer to me.

"What does?" I ask.

"We don't remember this... It's like—"

"Dude! Guys!" Emierr's excited, somewhat panicked call interrupts Jadis. He comes jogging back to us, clutching a piece of paper. "We were here, look." He holds the paper out to us, and we all huddle around it. It's a drawing of us playing on a lawn. "It's Jho's. She drew this. See, Rune is even in it." He points at the darker-shaded kid in the drawing.

"Yeah, that has to be me," Brunner snorts.

"She drew me and her holding hands." Jadis smiles, brushing her fingertips over her own portrait.

"Are there any more drawings?" Dustin asks Emierr.

"No, that was the only one on the table." Emierr takes the drawing back from Brunner, folds it, and puts it in his bag.

"Why can't I remember?" I shake my head. It feels like I'm throwing my weight against a pane of frosted plexiglass. With a secondary wall of concrete behind it. The memories have to be there, but I can't get to them.

"Maybe we don't need to solve everything right away. Let's just concentrate on gathering more information," Jadis suggests, resting a hand on my shoulder, and giving it a significant squeeze.

Right, the party. "Yeah, fine, let's split up. One group looks around down here, and the other goes upstairs. I saw myself up there, so I'll go check it out. Who's coming with me?"

"Not it." Dustin quickly places a finger on his nose.

"Not it." Jadis's finger shoots to her nose tip.

"Not it." Emierr hand flies up to his face.

"Scaredy cats. I'll go with you, Ricky," Brunner volunteers.

"Call out if you find something," I tell the others, exasperated. "Let's go, Rune."

Brunner and I move cautiously up the stairs. I am not a fan of the groaning sounds coming from under my feet. I step into the hallway at the top and glance to my right. I could see my bedroom window through a grimy pane of cracked glass.

Brunner positions himself to my left. "Do we start with the least scary side first?" he asks, peering down the hallway. Its walls seemed to be papered with floral patterns. Sunlight stumbled through the filth on the windows.

"I saw my younger self in one of the rooms on this side."

"Thank God," he says. "Ricky..."

"Hmm?"

"I wanted to ask a few things. I don't know if the others would even answer, but I thought maybe you would." He hesitates.

"Shoot," I say, opening the door on the right and shining my light inside. It's not the right room.

"Why didn't you guys go back to check if Jho was alive?" he asks. The room smelled peculiar, neither moldy nor pleasant. I scan the area. There's no bed, just a desk covered in a colony of dust.

"Rick?"

I glance back at him; he's still lingering outside the door. I sigh. "We were kids. We were scared. We didn't know what happened, and going back meant... We were kids, Rune." I don't know what else I can say. We weren't right to just give up on her, but we were also kids way out of our depth. We had already shouldered far too much responsibility in Ethra, more than anyone should have asked of us. And when we lost Jho...

"This isn't the one," I say, brushing past Brunner.

I understand why he hesitated to ask the others; Jadis would've reacted differently. But I don't blame him for asking either; it's a valid question. I just can't tell him outright that none of us wanted to end up like Jho. I look into the next room and feel my stomach drop.

"This is the one for sure," I say, shining the light on the door at the end of the hall.

"Sorry," Brunner mutters. "That was a loaded question. Of course, you guys would go back if you knew what was going on. It was stupid to ask."

"There are no stupid questions, Rune. Everything we know about the world started out as a question," I nudge him. "So, keep them coming."

"Okay." He smiles tentatively at me. "Thanks."

"You ready?" I ask, gripping the doorknob.

Brunner nods, and I swing the door open. It's a master bedroom, poorly decorated by a man who lived alone. Brunner rummages through the closet, while I inspect a table cluttered with jewelry and perfumes.

"Was Mr. Dawson a drag queen in his spare time?" Brunner calls. "There are a lot of dresses in here."

"Or maybe he was *married*." I snort. Nothing stands out to me. By the bed, a lamp table sits, and a picture frame faces the bed. It's a portrait of a couple. *Is this him?*

"There's nothing here. Just clothes and shoes, none in my size," Brunner reports with clear disappointment. A short laugh escapes me.

"I don't remember what he looked like," I comment, holding the portrait closer. "I don't even recognize him here." The woman might have been his wife. As I continue to pound at the unyielding wall in my brain, nothing is coming up about this man.

Brunner takes a look at the frame. "Okay, here's my next question," he says. "If Mr. Dawson watched over you guys before Uncle Kit quit his job, were you guys visiting Ethra when you were with him? The timeline isn't making sense to me."

"I think so?"

"What the hell happened in this house that made you guys forget?" He glances up at me nervously. I'm worried we're thinking the same thing.

"That's a great question, but I don't have the answer for this one. My guess is we focused so much on what happened to Jho, we got mixed up with the details? Mr. Dawson was irrelevant, I guess." It's not what I really believe, but I don't want to contemplate the idea that something bad happened to us as we spent time in this grown man's house. The last thing we need is some more real-world trauma to add to our Ethra trauma.

"Honestly, I remember talking to someone," Brunner says slowly. "But not the face. Is that weird?" He sets the frame back on the table.

"Meer didn't either, so it's safe to say something is going on here, more than just our memories being lost," I sigh. *God, I hope it's not what I'm thinking.*

"Follow-up question. Why didn't you want me to be a part of the Squad? Jho said you were the most uncomfortable with me hanging out with you guys."

My gaze meets his, and I feel shame rise in my cheeks. *Jho told him that?* "I don't know, Rune. It was... so long ago. I guess I—" My phone rings, cutting me off.

"Nothing down here, but we're headed to the basement. Meet us there," Emierr says on the other end.

"On our way. Nothing up here either." I hang up and gesture to Brunner. "Let's go."

"Hey, you owe me an answer," Brunner insists.

I don't want to admit it to him. That I was jealous of their friendship. I don't think I romantically felt that way for Jhoana, but I did feel something more than mere friendship. My therapist said it sounded like she was my soulmate. I didn't understand that concept when it was first introduced to me, but with all this multiverse talk, maybe in every universe, I do have a version of Jhoana with me.

"Hurry up, loser," I say with forced levity. The layout of the houses in the cul-de-sac is so uniform that it always feels like I'm descending into my own basement. The wooden stairs creak under our weight.

"Ricky, I don't think there's anything in this house." Jadis flashes her light at us as we come down.

"There are boxes here, maybe they have something," Emierr says, already elbow-deep, rummaging through the stack in the right corner of the room.

"Nothing so far on this side," Dustin says from the left.

"Guys, do you remember what Mr. Dawson looks like?" I ask the room at large.

There is a pause in the sound of paper and cardboard rustling.

"I don't think I do," Jadis admits. "It's like a blank face if I try to think about him."

"I remember someone watching over us, but I can't picture their face," Dustin agrees.

"I should be able to, but I'm drawing a blank," Emierr says.

Jadis cocks her head at me. "Why do you ask?"

"Just curious," I reply, exchanging a glance with Brunner. "I'm drawing a blank as well."

"So am I," Brunner chimes in. "I've got a question for all of you."

All eyes turn to him, shining in the light from our phones.

"Why'd you guys settle on 'Allied Organization Squad' for the group name, and who came up with it? It's like something straight out of a superhero comic."

"I'll take this one," Dustin volunteers, raising his hand. "The idea behind it is that, in the past, the Nobles focused only on their own nations. But we wanted to break that mold and unite to support each other. Plus, it gave us an excuse to spend more time together." He chuckles.

"It brought a lot of good things for the nations," Jadis adds. "I remember in my meetings with the leaders of Arid, they always talked about how great it was that the Nobles were tying stronger bonds, and maybe they shouldn't just be for one nation."

"But why that name and who came up with it?" Brunner asks. His questions pull me back to a seemingly mundane time in Ethra; the day we came up with our group's official name.

"I'm thinking 'Allied Organization Squad.' " Meer struck a superhero pose and I snickered.

"Dude, I like that, the Squad." Dusty fist-bumped Meer.

"That sounds fitting," Jads agreed begrudgingly.

"It has a nice ring to it. Good idea, cousin." Jho smiled at him.

"Thanks, thanks." Meer gave us a bow. He was loving this. "How about you, Ricky?"

"It fits all of you, as Nobles." I forced a grin.

"What, no. This isn't about being Nobles, Ricky. It's about having a name for us. People will know our story. With or without powers, they'll talk about the Allied Organization Squad, and that includes you." His hand landed on my shoulder.

"Shit." I chuckled, feeling my throat constrict. Not getting an ability was *really hard. But I had to remember why this place existed in the first place. It was for all of us. I managed a true half smile. "Thanks."*

"I forgot it was Meer who came up with it. I could've sworn it was you." Jadis looks at me and then turns back to Emierr. "It's a few years overdue but, thanks, Meer, for doing that for Ricky. That was sweet."

"Uh, yeah, let's get back to searching." Emierr returns to his box, flustered. I approach a wall plastered with pages from magazine articles. I turn off the flashlight on my phone and retrieve the AMOS VR, putting it on and clicking the low light button. The room illuminates in green, just like those cheesy ghost shows. It's a good thing I designed this thing to function at night. Maybe I can spot something using the infrared lights. I inspect the room from top to bottom. There's nothing more than the remnants of a life long gone. After a while, Jadis suggests we head back. It's already 4:57.

"Yeah, sorry guys. I thought there was something here." I turn back around to look at the wall papered with magazine cutouts one last time.

"The boxes are just junk." Emierr says, sitting back on his heels.

"It looks like Mr. Dawson was about to move out." Brunner throws a handful of silverware back into its box.

I press the record button on the glasses. I could go over the footage more closely later. As I pan over the wall, I notice something strange. I take off my glasses, and it all looks normal. But once they're back on, there's a bump hidden under the posters. Removing my glasses again, the bump vanishes, buried under magazine pages. Typical—I always find the quirks. Mr. Dawson's idea to use pages from the old Zoobooks wasn't exactly genius; he should've picked something less obvious, like the political sections of newspapers.

"Guys," I interrupt their conversation. "I think I found something." Pressing on the bump, a clicking sound resonates, and the wall cracks.

"Holy shit," Dustin exclaims, jumping away from the box he'd been rifling through.

I cautiously push on the wall. It swings open, revealing a secret door.

"This is why my younger self was here," I say excitedly. "Let's find out what the fuck happened here."

Dustin squeezes right up next to me with Emierr hot on his heels.

I lead the way into the dark passageway. In here, the low light makes me feel like I'm in a found footage horror movie. I pull out my phone and turn on its flashlight.

"Can you see where it ends?" Emierr asks.

"I see a door." I stride forward, leaving a trail of dust in my wake.

Jadis sneezes. The door at the end is enameled steel, oddly white against the years of dirt in the hallway. I reach for its dull silver handle, excitement twinging alongside anxiety. I press down and hear a resolute click. Locked.

"Allow me," Brunner says, maneuvering to the front. A few seconds of scraping ,and we all hear a clunk.

"Boom." He grins at us, then steps inside. "Holy shit. You guys have to see this."

We exchange glances before following him into the room. It looks like an entire second basement, nearly identical to the one we just left.

Jadis shines her flashlight in to reveal walls covered with pictures and notes, reminiscent of Pa's research area.

What is this?

No one can think of anything to do besides stare.

"Look, our parents were friends with Mr. Dawson. I think that's him," Jadis whispers, gazing at a framed photo on the wall.

"My parents are in that group picture too. I thought they weren't close at all." Brunner's expression is completely perplexed.

"Dude, is that us?" Dustin asks, peering at a snapshot of five kids lying down on the ground, their heads in a circle.

"That's not creepy at all," I mutter. "Yeah, that is us."

"Um." Emierr waves a piece of paper at us. "Check this out. Entry logs." He begins to read aloud. "Rictor is the first to broach the subject of an alternate realm. Over the past three months, he's spoken frequently about a world he visits in his dreams. However, he hasn't divulged the method or means by which he accesses this dreamworld."

I stare at Emierr, dumbfounded. "He was... taking research notes on me?"

"Wait, this was dated June 7th, 2007. Three months before Ricky's birthday," Emierr says, frowning at the piece of paper.

"What? How is that possible?" I snatch the paper away and squint down at it. "I first entered Ethra *after* my birthday."

Emierr picks up another sheet of paper and reads, "The tragedy of James's and Via's passing weighs heavily on us all. With the parents destroyed by grief, their attention understandably strays from their children. Rictor introduced Jhoana to the concept of the dreamworld, hinting that he may soon involve his other close friends. Perhaps he'll disclose his method of entry if he plans to include them. This presents an opportunity for me. I must exercise caution; the situation has become precarious. My next journal entry will be from the new bunker I've been constructing for the past month. I've been vigilant about avoiding attention, yet it seems someone is observing me. I must maintain a low profile." Emierr finishes reading and lifts his gaze to meet mine.

"I swear guys, I don't have memories of that. I think I would have known if I had started dreaming about Ethra before my birthday," I say defensively. "And why the fuck is the neighbor guy taking notes on me like I'm his lab rat? And talking about being watched? He was obviously paranoid." The hidden room feels too small, like not enough air is making its way below the earth.

"It's like what you said earlier, this is more than just memory loss." Brunner looks at me, worry creasing his forehead. "And if our parents trusted him... Was he trying some sort of experimental therapy?"

"Why would he be giving Ricky therapy three months *before* we lost our parents?" Dustin shakes his head. "Ricky, no one suspects you of lying or anything, but if you did enter Ethra before your birthday, we need to figure out why you can't remember it." He presses a hand to his head and closes his eyes. "Is it this house? Something did feel off when we got in."

Jadis stays quiet, but her arms snake up to hug her midriff.

"Oh, fuck," Emierr exhales sharply, now clutching a yellow legal pad. "I know why Mr. Dawson was paranoid." He turns the pad toward us. "He's StarSeed89."

It's Not Fair

"**B**itch!" I half-shout.

Dustin's face is twisted with rage. "That fucking dick, he used us."

"Nobody believed him, though," Emierr reminds us.

"*Someone* took notice if they were watching him," Jadis says grimly. "Posting about the multiverse and how to transcend this plane of existence on a 2008 forum? That definitely got him on the FBI's or someone's radar for sure."

"So, all this time, Mr. Dawson was experimenting on you guys?" Brunner is probably feeling grateful he was never allowed over, now.

"That perv probably did something to us when we were sleeping," Dustin growls.

I wince, feeling my stomach clench. I guess I wasn't the only one to think that. "If that's the fucking case, I'm just glad we don't remember anything."

"I don't want to be here anymore." Jadis says, her dark eyes darting around the cluttered room.

Dustin reaches for Jadis's arm, but she flinches, pulling away instinctively.

"I'm sorry, I just wanted to make sure you're alright," Dustin says, his hand now hovering in midair.

"No... Shit, I'm sorry. I just... I wasn't expecting to be touched. I'm okay, Dusty." She tries to shrug it off, but I've noticed over the past few days that she's jumpy, like she's afraid every touch will hurt. What isn't she telling us?

"Okay, fuck this. Is there room in your gym bag, Meer?" I start scooping papers off the table.

"Yeah?"

"Then let's grab whatever the fuck we can and get out of here." Everyone starts filling their arms with the papers scattered across the table and the pictures hanging on the wall. The bag quickly fills up, yet there remains a pile of additional evidence stacked against the other side of the room.

"That's all we can get." Emierr says, forcing more papers in.

"We'll come back after we get Jho," Dustin mutters. "Let's just get out of here."

"I really don't want to be here, Ricky," Jadis says anxiously, standing in front of the exit.

"We're leaving, Jads, one sec." I walk over to the wall and click the record button. "Just in case we can't get back in." I scan the wall with my visor and flip through the yellow legal pad.

"Ricky, let's go," Brunner whispers.

"We'll come back later." Jadis's voice is higher than usual.

"Okay. That's good enough." I toss the pad back on the table.

Within a minute, we're out of the house. The neighborhood is quiet. No one seems to have noticed our little break-in. I take off the glasses and retrieve my pen from my pocket, positioning it over the AMOS VR to transfer the data.

"That was so fucked up." Dustin mumbles, jamming his hands into his pockets.

"I had a thought," Jadis says suddenly. "We started remembering what happened here the moment we came back. But there's a mental block at the mention of Mr. Dawson and his house. It's like... There are memory spells in Ethra. They weren't used much when we were there, but during the Great War, when they would capture enemies, they'd tamper with their memories and send them back, making them believe their former nations were their enemies."

"Are you saying that Mr. Dawson put a spell on us?" Emierr scoffs.

"How is that possible?" Brunner asks. "Magick doesn't exist here."

"Who knows, right?" Jadis shrugs. "If it's a superstring universe, we don't know the implications."

"So, you *do* believe it." Emierr grins

"No, I don't... fully. I think it's still a flawed theory." Jadis side-eyes him. A small smile spreads across my face; their constant bickering never fails to amuse.

I halt in my tracks. "Or it could be something *like* magick." The others blink at me. "The closest thing we have to a memory spell here is hypnosis. I've been seeing a therapist for years for the anxiety and night terrors. Biting my nails is one of my trauma responses."

None of them look surprised. I guess the habit isn't as subtle as I thought.

"It took a long time, but I eventually got to live with it. I couldn't stop hearing Jho's screams. They haunted me for years. Then they started blending in with my own screaming. It woke me up every night." I shiver. "I asked my therapist if there was any way they could get rid of the memory and they suggested hypnotherapy. There's so much research on it now—Dr. Liem is like the founding father of—anyways," I catch my rambling before it can sweep me away. "I was desperate, guys. And it worked; I forgot. It can't erase memories, but it can bury them. Coming home was the trigger that made me remember everything. Well, not everything evidently." I sigh deeply.

"Can you give me your therapist's number?" Dustin chuckles darkly. "I think I'm going to need it after all of this."

"Can you just bring us as a group, Ricky?" Emierr grins, but it looks artificial. "I can't afford it."

Brunner nudges him, "What's the point of getting insurance if you're not gonna use it?"

"What? We can use it for that?" Emierr's startled face elicits a genuine peal of laughter from everyone.

"Yeah, let's all go together and explain that our best friend is in a coma because she died in the dreamworld we invented. My therapist is gonna lose her shit." I snicker. "Let's talk about this inside, we're almost at Rune's."

"Do you all think that's what Mr. Dawson did to us? Hypnotized us into forgetting?" Dustin presses me as we walk.

"Magick, hypnosis... They smell the same." I cast a glance at Dustin as we all gather in front of Brunner's front yard.

"You..." A woman in a white blouse and a dark green coat appears across the street, catching us off guard.

"Shit, not you guys again," Emierr mutters. "Mormon 2.0."

Just our luck. She steps off the sidewalk, and we instinctively shuffle backwards.

Jadis remains just ahead, crossing her arms like a human shield. "Oh great, just what we needed—another self-righteous prophet. Looks like you've lost your buddy; better go find Sister Smith before you earn a spot in outer darkness."

"They were at my game that day too," Dustin whispers to us.

"I saw them all the time in New York. Have they been following us?" I murmur, glancing around before returning my gaze to the woman. Her eyes widen as she looks at us, as if she's witnessing a miracle take place before her very eyes.

"I can't believe it... It's really all of you." That's when I notice—her eyes look like Ma's. But instead of gray, hers are a vivid green with that same coppery burst around the pupils.

How does she know who we are? Was she around when we lost Jho?

Emierr sniffs the air and then shakes his head. "You guys deal with her. I'm going for whatever Auntie Zu is cooking." He heads for the door without another word. We realize too late what's happening.

I whip back to the street—the woman's gone.

"Wait!" Brunner lunges at Emierr, but he's already swinging the door wide open.

We're all caught off guard when we find our parents clustered together, grinning ear to ear. They burst into a rousing rendition of "Happy Birthday," all eyes on Emierr, who's looking slightly shell-shocked and red-faced. As we pile in behind Emierr, Uncle Chris and Auntie Rose make their way through the crowd toward their son. In their hands are two cupcakes, each bearing a flickering number candles: two and nine. The soft glow of the tiny flames lights up Emierr's face, and I can't help but smile at the look of joy that has quickly overtaken his features.

"Happy Birthday, Meerina." I wave an inviting hand toward the cupcakes. He closes his eyes, blowing out the candles as everyone applauds. I let go of Emierr and lean over to Dustin, "What the fuck is going on?" I whisper.

"Beats me, man," he mutters back, hands still clapping robotically. "I thought they'd be at the wake."

"Here, this is from me and your dad." Auntie Rose hands Emierr a tiny box wrapped in metallic green paper. All eyes are on him as he peels through it like a child. He opens the box and reveals a key with a potted plant keychain.

"A key for what?" Emierr looks at his parents.

"A key to the house," Uncle Chris answers. "We want you to come back home, son." His voice cracks.

"Or you can come visit us if you don't want to move back. Just come home, anak." Tears spill down Auntie Rose's face.

"Pops... Ma. Thank you," Emierr says, diving into an embrace with his parents.

After a few moments, he steps back, takes his mother's hand and brings it to his forehead. He repeats the gesture for his father. It's called Mano Po, a sign of respect and reverence in Filipino culture.

Dustin explained once that, in Chamorro culture, they have a similar custom called Manngingi."

As the rest of the parents close in, it's a sea of hands to foreheads as we follow Emierr's lead. After hearing everyone's stories over the past two days, a newfound sense of understanding colors moments like these. They take on a deeper significance. It's not just a house key; it's Emierr's forgiveness. I hope it brings him the closure he's been seeking.

The whirl of faces and joyful tears pushes Mr. Dawson out of my mind. The same comment comes from everyone; that I resemble Pa. I can see in their faces that, in their eyes, Pa is back with them. Dustin is experiencing something similar. He may not be the spitting image of Auntie Via, but his presence brings her back to life in a way.

Jadis receives compliments on her hair from everyone, including Auntie Dana, her mom, who loudly announces her plans to replicate it. It's endearing to see how much time has softened our parents. I suppose the saying "absence makes the heart grow fonder" holds true.

"Ma," I say, giving her a tight hug. "You got off work early."

"I wouldn't miss it. Zuwena called me this morning about the surprise party, and I told the charge nurse that my baby is home and I need to spend all the time I can with him." She kisses my forehead.

"Really?"

"I may have to work the whole day tomorrow, and I know it's your birthday, but I'll figure it out. I just needed to be here for you." She hugs me tighter.

"Oh, don't worry about tomorrow, Ma. Me and the Squad, we're um..." I pull away from the hug. "We're going to take... uh... a trip and be back on the last day. So, we'll celebrate here." I smile, trying to cover my pathetically ill-planned lie.

"A trip?" She eyes me suspiciously.

"Hi, everyone," Auntie Z calls, catching everyone's attention. "First off, I want to apologize to the kids. When my little Brunner told me he wanted to throw Emierr a surprise birthday party, I knew I wanted all of the parents to be here." She casts a fond smile at Emierr. "Emierr has been a great friend to my son and if it wasn't for him, Brunner would still be unemployed and running up our electricity bill."

Everyone chuckles, poking at a red-faced Brunner who attempts to conceal himself behind Emierr.

"I would also like to say something." Uncle Jay interjects, draping one arm around his wife.

Brunner winces, shuffling further behind Emierr.

"It's great to see everyone here. My wife and I have been part of your lives since you all moved into the neighborhood. Kit and Ina couldn't be here tonight due to the wake, but on their behalf..." Uncle Jay lifts his beer, and the other uncles follow suit. "Having fellow islanders as neighbors really made it feel like a little slice of Guam was just around the corner. Though Zuwena and I weren't as close to everyone as we were to Kit and Ina, helping you all settle in was the best decision we've ever made. It created a community where our kids could thrive." He pauses, scanning the familiar faces. "It started with James and Via, both of whom are greatly missed, and now with poor Jhoana. But seeing my boy with the people he admired the most makes me happy to have this moment. Let's raise a glass to James, Via, and Jhoana."

"Cheers!" Uncle Joshua wipes away his eyes and raises his bottle. There's a beat of silence as everyone drinks. The front door bangs open, startling the room at large.

"Sorry we're late!" Cadence walks in with a white box, breathing heavily. "Oh, man, did we miss it?"

"I told you to pick up the cake sooner." A man holding a baby walks in behind her, shaking his head.

"*Ate* Cade!" I shout. Even if we all die tomorrow, at least we had one more evening truly together, just like old times.

"Well, if it isn't the Allied Organization Squad. It's been a minute."

Dustin and Emierr join me in crushing Cadence into a hug.

"Guys, the cake!" she wheezes. The man uses his free hand to snag the box from her. Is this Carl? He looks so different from the last time I saw him; the military bulked him up.

"Look at you boys," Cadence says, taking a step back, massaging her ribs. "I used to be able to hold all of you in my arms."

"I missed you, *Ate* Cade," I say. She has not aged at all.

"*Ate*? No one calls me that anymore. Jadis stopped calling me that when she got to high school."

Cadence lingers her gaze on me, and I already know what she's going to say. "You—"

"I know," I say before she can finish. "I look like my dad."

"No." She shakes her head. "You did it," she says, her smile broadening.

"Did what?"

"You became an astrophysicist. That's all you ever talked about when you were a kid. Your dad would be proud." She places a hand on my cheek before turning to Dustin. "As I live and breathe, we have a celebrity in town. There's someone I'd like for you to meet." She turns back to Carl, who is no longer the calm and collected man he was mere seconds ago. She takes the cake box back from him.

"Mr. Borja, I'm such a huge fan," Carl stutters, shifting his daughter to the other arm in order to vigorously shake Dustin's hand.

"It's a pleasure," Dustin replies, flushing slightly.

I keep forgetting that Dustin is famous, especially when nobody in town recognizes him as an NFL player. Here, he's just Dustin. I think he appreciates that, even though the constant recognition has mostly been replaced with cold stares.

"Who's this little princess?" Dustin crouches down to the baby and gently brushes his fingertips along her plump cheeks.

"This is Lyric. Say hi to your uncles," Carl says, picking up a chubby arm and assisting her in waving at us.

Lyric? Seriously?

Lyric giggles and gives me a gummy smile.

Cadence brazenly asks if Dustin can secure game tickets for Carl. Overhearing this, the dads instantly scheme a guys' trip to one of his matches. Not to be outdone, the moms insist on joining to cheer for their nephew. Amidst the excited planning, Jadis cradles Lyric in her arms and playfully chides her sister for igniting the frenzy. I chuckle as I watch our parents all talking, laughing, and teasing each other like they're young again. It's moments like this that make me almost regret leaving.

Dustin mumbles, "No one's come to watch my games in years besides Vi and Celeste."

The words drop a stone into my chest as I remember the unused tickets Dustin kept reserved for all this time, never giving up hope that one of us might appear. I place a hand on his shoulder. For so long, we've been focused on survival. But tonight, we're simply a family. Looking over at Brunner, I realize that I might be gaining a new brother as well.

The party is in full swing, and I can't help but think it's just what we need. Things have been so heavy lately, but tonight, it's nice to see a bit of happiness around us. Jhoana would have loved to be part of this. I decide to let myself just live in the moment, just for a while.

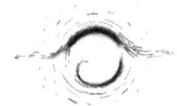

"I'm so full. That cake from Tea Memory... The Yus know how to do it right." Emierr rubs his distended stomach. "I can't believe you guys threw me a surprise party."

"I can't believe you forgot your birthday." Jadis shoots a look of disbelief out of the corner of her eye.

Emierr sticks out his tongue at Jadis. "Ricky, it's your birthday tomorrow. We can postpone... it... to the next day if you want."

"No." I shake my head. "I don't celebrate my birthday anymore. If anything, we're celebrating it together, right now." I force a smile as they all exchange dubious glances with each other. Brunner enters, saving me from further interrogation. A bag and a Nintendo Switch are nestled in his arms.

"We're playing video games?" The smile is real this time.

"Meer said you guys used to play *Mario Party*? I only have *Super*

Smash Bros."

Dustin and Jadis groan.

I laugh. "I'm game. Do you have enough controllers?"

As the game kicks off, we're no longer adults pushing thirty. We're kids, sprawled on the living room floor while the adults laugh and drink. We sit forward in our seats, staring intently at the screen. After a few well-timed button smashes, it's down to me and Dustin.

"I'll avenge all of you." Dustin is locked in, fully standing up out of his chair. I glance at him, and it feels like I'm staring at twelve-year-old Dusty, before all the heartbreak. Returning my attention to the screen, I realize his character is in range. My finger is about to go in for the kill, but I hesitate, and he powers up a punch instead, knocking my poor Pikachu out of the game.

"I won!" he yells. "Yes!"

"Finally."

"Wait." He stops jumping. "You *let* me win, dick!"

"Who, me?" I say innocently. "No, I would never do that. I'm simply no match for your natural joystick skill."

"There's never a true victory with you," Dustin sighs and sits back down.

"Fine, let's take a break. I got you something, Meer," I announce as I rise from my seat.

"What?"

"I'm not going to take credit for this party because it was Rune's idea, and Dusty and Jads helped make it happen. But I'm taking full credit for your gift." I reach into my left pocket and pull out the pendant. "It was a little last minute, but..."

"Woah, is that..." He takes it from me. "I thought you wanted it back?"

"I did, but I was wrong. It's yours."

"Thanks Ricky..." The gold glitters in the artificial light of the Fischer's living room, complimenting the luminescence of the pale meteor within. Emierr fastens it around his neck.

"Happy Birthday," I say, eyes on the stone.

"Ricky got me one too." Brunner fishes for the pendant in his pocket and slips it over his head.

"Now we all have our memento." I grin, feeling it stretch my cheeks to their limit.

"Oh shit." Jadis mutters, eyes on her phone.

A knock sounds at the door and Jadis stands up. Auntie Z opens it, and we watch shock spread across her face. Before she can even speak, Auntie Ina strides in.

Bitch.

Uncle Kit walks in behind her, followed by Gordo.

"Ina," Ma says in surprise. Auntie Ina is greeted warmly by the other parents, and handed a glass of wine.

"Gordo," I call out. "Hey buddy, glad you can make it."

"Hey *kuyas*, and A—Jadis." He'd trying to sound bright, but his face tells a different story. "My mom cancelled the wake tonight. She said we should attend the party. I know you guys don't want us here—"

Our vehement denials jumble together as we reassure Gordo that his presence is welcome.

"Shut up," Jadis tells him succinctly.

"Where's the birthday boy?" Auntie Ina says in an oddly cheerful tone. "Ah." She walks over to us, heels clicking, and hands Emierr a green gift bag. "It's last minute." Her gritted teeth are probably meant to be a smile.

Emierr digs through the bag and pulls out his gift. "It's my old *iPod Nano...*"

Auntie Ina, still baring her teeth, rejoins the parents in the kitchen, without another word.

Emierr stares after her. "In junior year, she took it from me, saying it belonged to Jho because Jho used part of her allowance to buy it."

"Who the hell does that to a kid," Jadis hisses, glaring at Auntie Ina's back.

"Sorry, *kuya*." Gordo cringes.

"Everyone, please come to the living room." Auntie Ina's voice clangs through any remaining conversation. "I have something to say."

The uncles move to stand nearby while the aunties settle onto the couch, leaving the Squad and me standing in the center. Uncle Kit, standing behind Auntie Ina, catches my eye, and gives me a good-natured wink. Some of the violent butterflies inhabiting my stomach dissipate.

Auntie Ina starts, "First off, I want to thank you, Zuwena, for having us tonight. Sorry we're late; we had to let everyone know the wake was canceled and then call Angie to watch Jhoanalyn at the last minute." She tries for a chuckle, but the room remains silent. "She would've loved to be here. And I need to... *apologize* to the kids. I said some harsh things a few nights ago."

I glance at Jadis, whose breaths are deep and measured.

"You, okay?" I whisper.

She nods, clenching her jaw.

"What I wrote in those letters is true. I meant every word," Auntie Ina continues. If that was the case, why did she sound like she was being forced to swallow sandpaper?

"Letters?" Mama says, raising an eyebrow.

"I'm the reason your kids are home," Auntie Ina's voice is soft now, and so are her eyes. It's almost scarier than her yelling. I can't dare to believe she might be telling the truth.

"That's half of it," Brunner whispers.

"I'm sorry. I haven't been kind to all of you. I know..." She pauses "I—"

"Come on, Ina," Uncle Kit says encouragingly, reaching out to rub her shoulder.

"I know you... I know you all didn't have anything to do with... with it." Her voice trails off, and suddenly, her face twists.

"No," she snarls.

"Dammit." Uncle Kit heaves a sigh.

"It's not fair!" she shrieks. "You all get to grow up, but not my baby girl! It's all your fault!" She jabs a finger in my direction.

"Ina, all you had to do was say you're sorry," Uncle Kit says, exasperated.

"Ma..." Gordo pleads.

"Sorry? Sorry that my baby is dying because of these kids?" Her voice booms.

"You know what?" Jadis snaps back. "It's not fair that you're blaming us! We were kids; we didn't know what was happening."

She actually did it. She talked back to Auntie Ina.

"You drugged her, all of you are drug addicts!"

Adrenaline overtakes me and I straighten up, though my knees keep trembling. These insane accusations are stopping now, even if I'm sixteen years late. "You really think a bunch of twelve-year-olds would be on drugs?" I say with a humorless laugh.

"You little... And you!" Auntie's finger stabs out at Brunner. "You called her your best friend, and you let this happen. You killed her."

Brunner looks to his parents, who don't say a thing. "Dad?" But Uncle Jay doesn't look at him.

Brunner looks back at Auntie Ina, horrorstruck. "I..." He drops his head, letting the words fade away.

"You don't get to blame us anymore." I curl my hands into fists. I can feel my heart hammering blood through my veins. "After all these years, you've been nothing but a sour, old harpy. You didn't bother looking around you and seeing all the love and support you got from your best friends. You could've focused all of that energy on your child that's still around, but instead, you want to stay a bitter, cold, fucking bitch!"

"Hey! That's enough!" Uncle Joshua finally steps in, except he's not looking at Ina. He's looking at me. "You don't talk to your Auntie that way. Any of you, got it?"

"Control your kids," Auntie Ina hisses.

Jadis scoffs, glaring right back at Ina with defiant eyes.

"You should leave, Ina," Uncle Manny says, stepping in front of us.

Auntie Ina shakes her head before storming from the house, followed by Uncle Kit who half-smiles in apology as he leaves.

"I'm sorry," Gordo mumbles before trailing after them.

"You all need to learn some respect," Uncle Manny admonishes us.

"Respect, Dad?" Jadis raises her voice, prowling around to stare him down, like a leopard on the hunt. "Did you see how she screamed at us? What she accused us of?"

Dustin stands alongside her, fixing his gaze on the parents. "Why the hell did you all stay quiet?"

Emierr, Brunner and I linger behind, our eyes fixed on the scene unfolding before us. How could they remain silent while one of their closest friends accused their children of murder?

"Hello?" Dustin's voice rings out, demanding a response.

"Mind your tone, boy," Uncle Joshua snaps at him.

"Mind my tone? I can't believe this." Dustin throws his hands into the air, anger throttling his voice.

"Do you guys even know?" Emierr demanded. "Auntie Ina is the reason Rictor and Jadis left. She constantly blamed us for what happened to Jhoana, and we all started to believe it. She kept reminding us that it should've been us instead." His voice shakes but his eyes are bright. "So, when you talk about respect, make sure you earn it first."

"That's our sister you're talking about," Auntie Rose interjects. "You better choose your words wisely, son."

"I can't believe it. Nothing's changed. Your kids are telling you what happened to them, and you still won't listen." I'm in disbelief. The bubble of warm, fond childhood memories has burst and left behind the bleak reality of the past. We suffered, and our parents did not save us.

"*Anak*, your Auntie—" Ma starts.

"We were kids!" I roar. "We were just kids. And none of you believed us. The whole town called us killers and murderers, and none of you protected us. *You* let them hurt us. *You* made us leave." I dash tears from my eyes. The Squad is standing in a loose formation now, protecting each other's flanks.

The parents at least have the decency to look ashamed.

Uncle Chris exhales heavily. "Kids, we understand."

Auntie Dana dabs at her tears with a handkerchief. "We know what the town thinks about all of you."

"For the past sixteen years, I've been labeled as the father of a murderer," Uncle Chris says ruefully.

"That sounds better than being known as 'Death Sentencer's' dad," Uncle Manny quips, his laughter dark.

"We don't say anything to people because we don't believe them. We believe you," Mama says gently. Her words are soothing, though not healing.

"And we know it's not right, letting your Auntie say those things to you guys," Uncle Joshua adds in agreement, voice softer.

"I've wanted to slap some sense into her so many times," Auntie Rose admits. "She's family, but..." She shakes her head.

"Hoy." Uncle Chris chuckles.

"Then why *did* you let her say those things?" Brunner asks, eyes still full of resentment.

"Because son." Uncle Jay looks at him. "Losing a child is one of the worst things a parent can go through. It's supposed to be us first before any of you."

Auntie Z comes to her husband's defense. "Ina... Her whole life she wanted to start a family. She was very jealous of Dana and Manuel when they had Cadence. She wanted to be next. But we all know how she is with her work. She ended up being the last to have a child... Oh, that poor girl. Jhoana is everything to her, that's why she's fighting so hard."

"If it were any of you in Jhoana's place, I'd be the same," Uncle Joshua says.

"We are all so proud of you for sticking up for each other, but never do that to your Auntie again," Uncle Manny says. His tone is firm but understanding.

I'm unsure how to process this. While their intentions seem genuine, their approach to protecting us feels misguided. Pa once explained how they were raised to suppress their emotions and endure silently. It's evident here; they want to support us, but their instinct is to remain passive.

I shift my focus back to the Squad. "We need to tell them."

"What?" Dustin nearly broke his neck whipping his head around to gape at me. "You don't mean—"

"All of it."

"Ricky, I don't know," Jadis murmurs, folding her arms across her body protectively.

"I think it's worth a shot," Brunner says, glancing at his parents. "What if they know something? "

"The worst they can do is call us crazy," Emierr says.

"Tell us what?" Ma demands, worry lining her face.

If *we* end up in a coma, they'll blame themselves. We can't let them carry that guilt like Auntie Ina and Uncle Kit have. Even if they think we're insane, we have to warn them. They'll know we were telling the truth one way or another after tomorrow.

"We can't have another Jho," I whisper. One by one, I see my friends' faces blanche.

"Okay." Jadis sighs. Her arms don't drop.

"Yeah, let's just do it. Just in case," Dustin mutters.

Brunner and Emierr nod once. I pivot back to face the parents. They're all gazing at us, mouths drawn, and brows crinkled.

There's really no good way to say it so, in one breath, I blurt out, "We can save Jhoana."

"What?" Ma gasps, and a chorus of voices begins talking over one another. I can hear words of confusion, disbelief, and even outrage.

"We don't even know where to start, but there's a way we might be able to wake her up before they pull the plug," I plow on, ignoring the admonishments and incredulous outbursts. "Auntie Ina won't listen to us, but you have to trust us, like you guys say you do."

"What on Earth are you talking about?" Auntie Rose's face has shifted from concern to anger.

"Kids," Uncle Chris says, clearly trying to bring some rationality to the conversation. "Jhoana is gone."

"We know that saying goodbye is hard." Auntie Dana's expression is soft. Pitying.

"No," I snap, taking her aback. "Just listen."

Ma opens her mouth to chastise me for my rudeness, but I manage to silence her with a pleading look.

"Jho's in Ethra," I begin, causing everyone to fall silent. I can feel the Squad holding their breath as their parents stare blankly.

"It's the imaginary world we... created," I stumble on the word, knowing now that it isn't true. "It's the reason we spent so much time sleeping." I need to get it all out before they think I've completely lost it. "In Ethra, we have powers, responsibilities, and other families that took us in. That's where she died, but Emierr believes she's still alive. Tomorrow, we're going there to bring her back."

The air is thick with tension. Will they listen? Hell, would *I* listen if someone started spewing this lunacy? As our parents blink at us, clearly at a loss for words, I see something in their expressions change. Their faces make a smooth transition from bemused to completely blank. I get the feeling that they're no longer seeing us anymore, but rather through us. My heart skips a few beats. They look like they've been hypnotized.

"Um, hello?" I say, cold tendrils of fear pooling in my gut.

Emierr is staring, slack-jawed, at the zombie-like faces before us. "Ma? Pops?"

"What's wrong with them?" Jadis moves hesitantly toward her

mom and waves a hand in front of her face. Auntie Dana doesn't even blink.

All of a sudden, the room is back in motion. I jerk backwards, alarmed.

"What were you saying, *anak?*" Mama says, looking at me with a politely puzzled expression.

I stammer, "W—What's the last thing you heard?"

"Uh..." Mama pauses, considering.

"We're going to Dustin's next game!" Uncle Joshua says with a grin, clapping Uncle Manny on the back.

I glance back at the Squad, bewildered.

"Well, it's getting late," Auntie Dana says as she rises from her seat. "I have work in the morning."

There's a hum of agreement and they start tidying up, as if I'd never started speaking at all.

"What just happened?" Dustin is standing close behind me, his voice in my ear.

"I don't know, but I'm starting to believe Jads about it being a spell," I mutter back. "Which is completely impossible."

"Guys," Jadis pulls us in and shows us a message on her phone.

"I heard everything. I want to help bring my ate *back. We can use my house's basement when my parents are at work. Please let me help save my sister."*

"Gordo," Emierr exhales softly. "Looks like whatever happened to them," he jerks his head toward the bustling parents, "didn't happen to him."

I clench my jaw. "I guess that's it then. We've exhausted all our options. We've done everything we can."

"What the fuck is going on?" Brunner whispers.

Transcendence

October 4

"*I* *t's not fair! You all get to grow up but not my baby girl!"*

My eyes flash open.

That was real. I inhale deeply and exhale. Auntie Ina's hateful words echo in my mind, spoken so openly in front of our parents. Yet I can't help but feel sympathy for her. Her daughter has been in a coma, stuck at eleven years old, while all her best friends got to watch their children grow and move out into the world. How does someone cope with that? A streak of light from the hallway cuts through the darkness of my room. My hand fumbles around for my T-shirt, but it's nowhere to be found.

I must have tossed it onto the computer chair. Rolling onto my side, I find Carter, my childhood teddy bear, lying next to me. I lift him up with both hands. His space suit had once been white, a long time ago. It was decidedly gray now, but his little NASA logo still gleamed bright blue. This worn little bear had been my guardian against monsters and aliens since I was a child.

I remember now. Dustin had said Carter was a gift from my dad but I'd known it was bullshit from day one. I think it's really sweet of him, trying to hide the fact. It didn't make me feel any less fond of the ratty little bear before me. If anything, having a physical token of my brother's love made me feel tethered.

"Hey, Carter." I hold him tightly to my chest. "I'm going to need your protection again."

My phone buzzes, pulling me out of my memories. I wriggle to the other side of the bed, reaching for it and glancing at the screen. It's 10:15 p.m. and messages are flooding into our group chat. The Squad is still reeling from Auntie Ina's outburst. Jadis is relaying that she met in secret with Gordo to discuss everything and outline the plan. Emierr says he attempted to broach the subject of Ethra with his parents again, but they seem to have forgotten once more. It's like anything related to Ethra is erased from their memory as soon as it's mentioned.

Meerina

> This is so fucked up.

Dusticle

> Does dis mean u could tell dem a deep, dark secret den follow it up wid Ethra and dey'd forget?

Jadikins

> Try telling them you've joined a polygamist cult and have a child bride then just yell ETHRA and see what happens.

Runey

> Okay THAT is fucked up.

Dusticle

> Wat bout dat Mormon 2.0 lady? Wat was dat bout?

Runey

> At least she wasn't damning us to Hell, amirite?

Jadikins

> Outer darkness*

I snort, scrolling through the conversation. Dustin suggests a sleepover, but I kind of want to be alone right now. My thumbs hesitate over the screen, unsure whether to respond. Ultimately, I set the phone aside, choosing to be alone with my thoughts.

Once I'd gotten home, I'd spent an hour scanning all the papers and pictures we collected from Mr. Dawson's house. I'd taken the time to save all the data on my pen then fell asleep immediately afterward.

I release a sigh, my fingers gently kneading my temples in an attempt to alleviate the sudden headache. A cool breeze slips through the open window, causing a shiver to run down my spine. Switching on my desk lamp, I locate my shirt. As I rummage through the jumble of clothes scattered near the closet, I come to the disappointing realization that I've only packed jeans. Maybe some of my old high school clothes are still tucked away in the drawers, if Ma hasn't donated any of them yet. I think the third drawer used to hold my shorts. I tug at the handle, sending a flurry of dust particles dancing around me.

A smile plays on my lips as I discover my old basketball shorts neatly tucked away— surprisingly, they still fit. Despite the chill, I pull them on.

A delightful aroma wafts through the hallway, leading me downstairs and into the welcoming embrace of the living room. My stomach rumbles in anticipation as I follow the scent and make my way towards the kitchen.

"Ma," I say softly, trying not to alarm her. My stomach emits an inhuman sound.

She pivots towards me, shutting off the faucet with a twist and then drying her hands on her apron. "Oh *anak*, you're awake. Sit, sit."

She gently guides me to a chair, where I settle down obediently. She's wearing the apron I crafted for her back in eighth grade sewing class. We'd gone to the local quilt store together to pick out the fabric. It was a deep blue cotton with the black outlines of waves flowing across it. Despite having eaten only a few hours ago, my mouth waters at the sight of the feast before me.

"I know tomorrow is your birthday, but we're celebrating tonight."

"Mama..."

"The stores were closed so I didn't get you a cake. Sorry *anak*."

"Ma, it's okay. This is a lot." I can't even see the table through the sheer volume of food spread across its outdated, floral tablecloth.

"Here, I'll make your plate."

"Ma, I can do it myself." I chuckle, but let her do it all the same.

My gaze drifts to the plate on my left—it must be Pa's. I select two lumpias and a chicken leg, placing them in the center of the empty plate. Ma purses her lips, a smile tugging at the corners of her mouth. My heart aches at the realization that she still sets aside food for him.

She moves around the table, pressing a kiss to my forehead before taking her seat across from me. One hand reaches for mine while the other rests beside Pa's plate. I mimic her gesture, feeling a pang of longing. We both bow our heads in silence.

Ma begins to bless the food. Thoughts of Pa flood my mind, and suddenly, a hand touches mine from where he used to sit. Startled, my eyes fly open, but there's no one there. I glance up at Ma, who's still deep in prayer. I lower my head once more, patiently waiting for her to finish. *I really am losing it.*

"Amen," she murmurs, lifting her gaze.

"Amen," I echo quietly. In that moment, a second realization hits me—this might be my final supper with Ma. I study her intently, taking in her petite frame, with streaks of white hair that always reminded me of Rogue from *X-Men*, her gray eyes with their strange copper ring around the pupil. I once asked Pa about the other half of my ethnicity, but he admitted that he didn't know either. It always seemed odd that Ma never talked about it, but it's never really bothered me. There must be a reason she doesn't want to talk about it. At this point, I don't care much about it. She's more Filipino than I am anyway, with the way she cooks.

Sometimes, I catch traces of an accent in her speech, a trait I blame Pa for. Time has certainly taken its toll—I can see the faint lines etched into her skin, marking the years she waited for me to come back home. It's unbelievable how swiftly time has flown. I've only had four precious days with her. How do I bring myself to say goodbye again?

"You're not eating, *anak?*" she asks, her hands coming to rest on the table. "What's the matter?"

A tear slips from my eye, and I voice the thoughts that have been weighing heavily on my mind since I arrived here.

"I'm scared, Ma," I admit. "I've been trying to hold it together, but I'm so scared."

She reaches out for my hand, and I instinctively grasp hers, holding on tightly. "You don't need to do anything," she reassures me gently.

"I know," I reply, my voice barely more than a whisper. Silence descends upon us. "But we can bring her back," I say, trying fruitlessly to bypass whatever magick, hypnosis, or mind-warping she's being touched by.

"That is insane, Rictor James!" she says sharply, hand withdrawing from mine. "You cannot bring Jhoana back." She closes her eyes and collects herself. "I know you wish you could. It's never easy to feel so powerless."

"Please just trust me, Ma. I can't tell more now, but please, just trust me," I implore, my hands trembling. "When we accomplish the task, she'll... she'll wake up from the coma and continue living, just like the rest of us." I recapture her hands and squeeze, trying to convey my unwavering confidence in my—*our* ability to see this through."

She's quiet for a moment, searching my face. "Can you tell me what it is you're going to do?"

"I can't, Ma. Not yet."

"Are you going to end up..." she swallows hard. "Is there a possibility you will end up like Jhoana?"

I pause. Some part of her must know. Some piece of her memory is still in there, even if she's unable to bring it to the surface.

"It won't happen again. Not like Jho. We're older now, not children anymore. I'll be okay." I know I'm convincing myself as much as I am her.

"You're only telling me so that I'll know what happened if something goes wrong, aren't you?"

"No," I lie hastily, mustering a façade of assurance. "To reassure everyone that we're bringing our best friend back."

"But—"

"They would do the same for me if I were in Jho's place. You would do the same for me," I murmur, unable to meet her gaze. My heart is heavy with the fear of losing my mother forever. But deep down, I know she would want me to pursue this, if she could just remember.

"If you had the opportunity to bring Papa back, you'd take it, wouldn't you?" I finally look up at her, grappling with self-disgust for manipulating her like this. I feel like Emierr when he was convincing me to come back home.

"Absolutely. I'd do anything it takes. But that's not possible anymore; your Papa is gone for good, and now there's only you. I can't bear the thought of losing my baby." Tears well in her eyes.

"Ma..." My shirt catches the droplets that fall from my cheeks.

"But you're so much like your Papa. So hardheaded." She pats my hand, offering a watery smile. "You'll always do the right thing. And if you really have this chance with Jhoana. Who am I to stop you from trying?"

"I promise, when I return, I'll share everything with you, no more secrets," I vow, releasing her hand. As she stands up, she envelops me in a tight embrace.

"Ma, I promise. I swear," I repeat. I wish I could tell her everything. I wish she could feel the outpouring of love I had for her. I never want to let go, and I was a fool to turn my back on it in the first place. For a few heartbeats, all the years of longing for her dissolve into the warmth of her arms.

Then, in a spectacular showcasing of poor timing, my stomach grumbles once more. A blush creeps up my cheeks.

She chuckles, sitting back in her chair. "Just like your Papa. Let's dig in."

I twirl spaghetti around my fork, pausing to savor the moment. Mom's cooking is the epitome of home for me. I take a bite, the sweet flavors exploding in my mouth, sending me into a state of total bliss. It's like tasting happiness itself. Next, I grab a piece of crispy chicken, cooked just the way I like it, and sink my teeth into its juicy goodness. The satisfying crunch fills my ears like music.

But as I indulge in these familiar tastes, weight settles back in my chest, and tears begin to flow. Sniffling, I avoid Ma's eyes.

"Happy Birthday, *anak*." She strokes my arm, allowing me to shed tears as I savor her cooking. With each mouthful, I find comfort in the childhood flavors that evoke memories of home. Taking a lumpia, I dip it into the sweet chili sauce reserved exclusively for such treats, relishing the harmonious blend of flavors in my mouth. As I indulge in mouthful after mouthful, the twinge of sadness continues to tug at my heart—a stark reminder of the time lost over the past decade.

Though I was once skeptical, I now understand the healing power of food made with love. As the evening unfolds, a tranquil atmosphere settles around us, a rarity in my recent years. We share stories, laughter, and tears, weaving new bonds and memories together. Silently, I make a wish for time to stand still, yearning to prolong this moment indefinitely, treasuring every precious second spent with Ma.

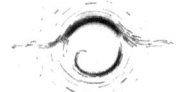

Stepping out of the shower, I reach for my towel hanging on the rail and briskly dry my body. The bathroom fills with steam, clouding the mirror's surface. Wrapping the towel around my waist, I glance at my reflection.

Staring back at me is the younger version of myself. I recoil, taking a step back, but the reflection remains, silently observing me. A steady drip of blood falls from his ruined eye.

Summoning my courage, I take a step closer to the mirror. To my surprise, the younger reflection mimics my movements. I raise my right hand and watch his hand lift in unison. My breath quickens as I tentatively place my palm against the glass, feeling my hand tremble alongside the reflection's. We lock eyes.

In one swift motion, I swipe my hand across the mirror. As the mist dissipates, my own anxious, bearded face stares back at me. This encounter marks the third time since my return—what message is my younger self trying to tell me?

Pushing my unsettled thoughts aside, I dress in a pair of high school basketball shorts and my favorite shirt—a souvenir from space camp. It was the last black NASA T-shirt available that day, and although it was far too large for me then, it fits now—slightly baggy, but suitable, nonetheless.

Ma left for the hospital at 3 a.m., sacrificing her rest to celebrate my birthday. My alarm chimes at 6:30 a.m., reminding me that Auntie Ina and Uncle Kit should be departing for work right now. An hour ago, I requested a mail bot to collect my pen and deliver it to Bonnie. In case of an emergency, she'd be informed of everything and hopefully come to save my ass. The bot should be here soon.

My trusty black fanny pack, a favorite from my collection, rests atop the bookshelf. Retrieving it from retirement, I secure it around my chest and slip the letter I penned last night into its back pocket. As my phone dings to signal the bot's arrival, I realize I have ten minutes to reach Jhoana's house. We'd all agreed—it just feels right to do this with her close by.

Staring at my reflection in the full-length mirror, I realize that this might be the final moment I see myself in this way. My hair is short, faded on the side, and casually styled. I brush my hands on my neatly trimmed beard and mustache, my light hazel eyes betraying a hint of fear. My body is in the best state it has ever been in, though the shirt I'm wearing conceals it. I'll never admit it to Dustin, but he's been my inspiration for maintaining my physique. If he finds out, he'll never let me hear the end of it.

The neighborhood remains ensconced in slumber, the morning air crisp and refreshing. With a jingle, I tuck my keys into my bag and steal one last glance at my home before setting off. The mail bot hovers near the mailbox, and I tenderly kiss my gold pen farewell before placing it inside the bot. I then look around to double check that none of the neighbors witnessed my moment of objectophilia.

"Thank you," I whisper to the little bot. It beeps cheerfully and departs. *I better see that pen again.*

As dawn begins to break, the morning light paints the sky in hues of pale blue and pink. The streetlights still illuminate the sidewalk, resembling stars guiding my path. I tread along the familiar route that passes by Jadis's and Emierr's houses. With each step, brown-orange leaves cascade from the trees like delicate feathers. I recall the night I returned to Farmington, exiting Jhoana's home while enduring the cruel eyes of the entire town. I was ready to head back to New York right then, to Bonnie, and leave that fear behind forever. Yet, I chose to stay, enduring it all.

Now, as I take these final steps back to Jhoana's house, the same fear that has shadowed me throughout my life seizes me once again.

My gaze catches Dustin emerging from his house on the opposite side of the street. I envision a fragment of time long past—little Dusty hauling ass across the street with an infectious grin plastered across his face. But as I snap back to the present, he stands before me, devoid of that familiar smile.

"Morning." I break the silence.

"Yeah, morning." His breath forms mist in the chilly air.

"How was your first night back in your house?" I ask, releasing a puff of warm air from my body.

"It's still a little dusty but it feels like home." He offers a tired half-smile, his eyes heavy with purple smudges.

He didn't get much sleep either.

"Emierr and Jadis just got there. I think Rune should—oh there he is." He jerks his chin to my left.

Brunner strides over to us, hands tucked into his pockets.

"Morning," he says with a shiver. I wonder if it's cold or nerves.

"You guys got any sleep?" Dustin raises a brow.

"No." Brunner shakes his head.

"Same." Dustin sighs, his nose crinkling slightly. "We'll be getting plenty of sleep in the next few days, though."

Neither of us laughs.

"Too soon?" He chuckles. Brunner and I opt to ignore him.

"You didn't have to pick us up, Rune." I slip my hands into my pockets.

"Meer took the book back from me and honestly, I needed the fresh air."

We stand in silence for a few minutes, all trying to wrap our exhausted minds around the gravity of what we are about to do.

"Let's go," I say finally. I take the lead, walking ahead with the others just behind. As we proceed, the streetlights blink off with the sunrise. As the sky is gradually dyed pink, we find ourselves standing across the street from Jhoana's house. Brunner is the one who finds enough courage to knock. Within a few moments, Gordo is swinging the door open and ushering us inside.

"Ms. Santiago just got here; we should be okay," he reassures us. We move through the house, our own happy faces watching us from picture frames along the walls. Brunner opens the basement door in the hallway, and we file down the carpeted stairs. Jadis is seated on the familiar green couch, where we used to share stories and drink too much root beer. Emierr is on the rug—the same one with the red, gray, and white circle patterns—nervously flipping through the Squad notebook. I'm surprised Auntie Ina and Uncle Kit kept the old rug. It's the place their daughter died. The mini fridge that Uncle Kit bought for us in fourth grade sits beside the couch, and the old TV we "borrowed" from Dustin's house stands across from Jadis.

The basement remains unchanged, just as I remember it.

"Finally," Jadis exclaims, sitting up.

Emierr raises his head to look at us.

"I'll be right back," Gordo murmurs, heading upstairs.

I sit down heavily on the couch, unable to staunch the flow of recollections this couch holds. *We're almost back to you, Jho.*

Dustin settles beside me, letting out a deep breath. "I'm ready to sleep."

I huff a quiet laugh.

"Meer," I say. "Sit with me for a second. Jads, scoot in, and Rune, get over here."

Dustin and I press together, trying to make space, but like every couch we've recently shared in someone's basement, it's just too small for us now.

"Do you think Jho will recognize us?" Brunner asks, voice quavering a bit.

"The real question is, will we recognize her?" Dustin says. The dark rings below his eyes look even worse down here, under the fluorescent bulbs.

"She changed a lot in just the five months she was in there, and she's way older than any of us now, but I think we'll know when we see her," I say, timid hope lacing my words. Silence falls over us again. I wonder what's running through their minds. I'm scared shitless. This is finally becoming a reality.

"Did you seriously cram us all onto this couch to have a conversation we could have had without moving?" Jadis asks irritably. Dustin shoulders her and she slides down to the floor with a grunt.

A notification lights up my phone.

"Oh, bitch," I mutter, clicking on the link Bonnie sent me. It's an article from CNN about Dustin's incident at his game, and it's making headlines. Everyone peers at my phone.

"I thought you said it'd blow over," Emierr says, grimacing.

"It will, don't worry," Dustin replies dismissively.

"They're looking for you, bro. It's a good thing Farmington is a ghost town," I remark, putting my phone away.

Footsteps echo down the stairs and Gordo returns with a crooked smile on his face.

"You guys ready?"

A wary mutter of agreement rises amongst our ranks.

"Okay, let's go," he replies, turning back toward the stairs.

"Wait, where are we going?" I ask, startled.

"My *ate* wants to see you guys," he says with a smile. "Come on."

We exchange apprehensive glances, but I rise to my feet all the same.

"Let's go see our sister," I say with a shrug. I guess Gordo considers Ms. Santiago trustworthy.

Brunner remains seated. "I'll be honest, I haven't visited Jho in years," he admits, not meeting our eyes. "I'm not sure if I want to see her like that."

"I haven't seen her in five years," Emierr says. "Let's do this together." He extends his hand, hauling Brunner to his feet.

"It's a good thing you have us," Jadis says, prodding him with her elbow.

"Dusty, it's been a while for you too, right?" Brunner asks. He's looking a bit pale.

Dustin nods, lips pursed. He looks miserable. Did he sleep at all? Maybe I should have stayed over at his house. As we ascend the stairs, Gordo awaits us by the door.

"Ms. Santiago won't say a word," Gordo assures us. "Let's go." He leads us through the house and up the stairs. I reach for Dustin's hand, gripping it tightly, and he reciprocates. With his other hand, he grasps Jadis, setting off a chain reaction of intertwined fingers. A morbid game of Red Rover. We follow Gordo into Jhoana's room. The walls are a serene, light blue; something I hadn't noticed the last time I came here with Jadis. It's calming, almost like walking into a gentle breeze. The furniture, all wooden, is painted a crisp white, giving the room an airy and bright feel.

Scattered across the walls are posters from teen magazines, featuring the boy bands and pop icons from 2007 that she loved. What truly captures my attention, though, is the large, framed drawing prominently displayed above her bed on the main wall.

How did I forget that?

It's a depiction of Dustin, Emierr, Jadis, Jhoana, and myself—all lying on a grassy field, laughing under the sun. The joy and the unbridled laughter we shared are so vividly captured in this drawing. It's more than just a piece of art; it's a portal to a cherished memory, making me feel as though that carefree, sunlit day is still within reach, even if everything else feels like the calm before the storm.

As they step into the room behind me, I hear a few gasps. Aside from Jadis, the Squad clearly had not anticipated what Jhoana would look like, all tangled in wires and wasting away beneath a loose gown.

A familiar, kind-faced woman steps between us and the shapeless, spiritless form of our sister.

"Hello, I'm Angie, Jhoana's nurse, but I like to think of us as friends," the woman says with a warm smile. "Nice to see you again, Rictor and Jadis."

Returning her smile, I glance back at the Squad. Dustin, Emierr, and Brunner are clearly struggling with the sight before them.

"This might be a little tough for all of you. I understand how much you care about Jhoana," Ms. Santiago continues, her voice filled with empathy. "She's been fighting so hard all these years to get a moment like this. She's listening; let her know you want her back home. Guide her back to us."

Ms. Santiago smiles one last time before excusing herself from the room, leaving us to our visit with Jhoana.

"I'll be in the basement," Gordo announces, shuffling awkwardly from the room.

We gather around Jhoana, and I'm struck by how thin she looks, despite having seen her just a few days ago. Dustin is the first to break down, his tears flowing freely, followed by Emierr.

"Stop holding it in, Rune. Let it out," Jadis whispers. Her eyes are bloodshot but tearless, as if she's run out of sorrow. Instead, it's been replaced by a grieving emptiness.

Brunner walks over to Jhoana and collapses beside her, clutching one of her hands tightly as he too begins to sob uncontrollably.

"Jho." Dustin kneels beside her on one side of the bed. I watch a tear splatter onto the woven blanket covering Jhoana.

"Cousin," Emierr chokes next to Dustin, gripping her other limp hand like it's the last thing holding him to Earth's surface.

Jadis and I are barely holding it together. I walk over to Brunner and wrap my arms around him, allowing myself to feel the ache of loss. Jadis drapes herself over the other two, blanketing them in solidarity and comfort. For the first time in sixteen years, the Allied Organization Squad is complete again.

As a moment passes and the sobs begin to subside, leaving only a few lingering sniffles.

"Is this it?" Dustin mutters, his voice thick. "Is pain the only thing that's connecting us to each other anymore?"

His words catch me off guard. Pain has indeed been a powerful force binding us together—as well as guilt—preventing us from fully escaping Farmington. But it can't be the only thing holding us together. There has to be more.

"No..." Brunner looks at him, his voice trembling. "Pain can't be the only thing that connects us. I refuse to accept it." His voice wavers but holds out. "I have to believe that love connects us too. It was love that brought you guys back home." His lips quiver. "How it brought me closer to all of you. Our love for our friend is stronger than the pain it gave us."

I squeeze him tighter, wiping away my tears as we linger a bit longer, surrounding Jhoana with our love.

"Cam is abusive," Jadis blurts out suddenly, catching all of us off guard.

"What?" My mouth falls open. Jadis is one of the toughest people I know. For her to be the one to fall victim to a violent partner... But then again, men like Cam never show their true colors until it's too late. Shame colors my cheeks as I think back to all the signs I missed. Her flinching away from touch, the way she keeps her arms folded defensively across her body, the look on her face whenever she checks her phone... I should have realized.

"The reason I was already here when you guys called... I ran away from him. He's been hurting me for years." She hesitates, her gaze falling on Jhoana's face. "I didn't know how to tell any of you."

"That fucking bastard," Dustin hisses, fists clenched.

"I'm sorry I didn't say anything. I don't want pain to be the only thing holding us together, either. But... he's been threatening to kill me if he finds me, and I'm scared—terrified, actually—that this time, he means it." Tears spill down her face and her body shudders convulsively.

Brunner's voice is a low growl. "I'd like to see him try."

"When I get my hands on him..." Dustin can barely contain his fury. The trailing tears have dried from his cheeks, and the pain in his eyes has been overtaken by fire.

I close my fingers tightly around hers. "We're here for you, Jads. We won't let anything happen to you."

"We'll figure this out together," Emierr says, his eyes glowing with rage. "I promise."

"I never finished school," she confesses, shaking her head. She's laying it all out, exposing every insecurity. She's braver than she gives herself credit for. "I'm so embarrassed. You all finished, and here I am, acting like I have the right to judge anyone."

"None of that matters," I say immediately. A degree is the last thing on anyone's mind.

Jadis nods quietly, accepting our bracing hands on hers.

"It's time," I say after a few more moments of silence. I rise to my feet, wiping my face with my shirt. One by one, the others each give Jhoana a soft kiss on her cheeks—silent promises to return soon. I lean down to her, placing my forehead against hers and closing my eyes.

Can you feel this all the way from there? "I'll see you soon, soulmate," I whisper.

When we return to the basement, we find Gordo standing in the center of the room, his back turned to us. It looks a bit like a horror film, honestly.

"Gordo?" I furrow my brows and reach out for his shoulder. Gingerly, he begins to rotate to face us.

"Happy birthday to you," he begins singing, holding a green cake, possibly matcha, with a lit number twenty-nine birthday candle on top. I'm at a loss for words. I can't even blame Emierr anymore; I've forgotten my own birthday too.

The rest join in, "Happy birthday dear, Ricky. Happy birthday to you."

"Make a wish," Gordo says. His smile is warm but there's something sad just under the surface.

My throat tightens. "Guys, this isn't important right now."

"Your birthday *is* important," Dustin rebukes, patting my back.

"Make a wish, dumbass." Jadis clicks her tongue at me.

I pull Emierr closer to me, feeling overwhelmed by the moment.

"We already celebrated my birthday yesterday," he protests.

"Traditions," I retort, putting my arm around his neck.

"Make a wish, Libra babies," Brunner croons, raising his bracelet to snap a picture.

"Wait." I block Brunner's waiting Holo-phone with my palm. "All of you, come blow the candle with me."

"I'll take the photo," Gordo offers, handing me the cake and opening the camera interface on his own Holo-phone.

"One... two... three!"

The candle dies under the gust of our combined breath.

"As annoying as you both are, happy fucking birthday," Jadis says, hugging Emierr and me tightly.

"Come here," Dustin says, grabbing my face and planting a kiss on my cheek.

"Dusty!" I laugh, feeling a warmth spread through me.

"You too," Dustin says, seizing Emierr and planting a kiss on his face.

Brunner opts for the less invasive gesture of patting my back. "Happy birthday, Ricky."

"Thanks, guys, this means a lot. We'll eat this when we wake up." I put the cake back in the mini fridge as if the promise of dessert will be enough to bring us back. Glancing at the time, I realize it's already 7:15 a.m. We're running late.

"Okay, let's set the room up." Emierr starts clearing the floor, shoving the furniture to the edges of the room. Jadis positions the five pillows that Gordo provided us in a circle, arranging them so our heads would be close together. Dustin and Brunner retrieve the notebook and thumb through it one last time. I stand there, simply watching, feeling a mix of anticipation and nervousness paralyzing my muscles. This could be the last time I see my own world. This could be the last morning I spend awake.

"*Kuya?*" Gordo takes a step toward me, his voice filled with concern. "You're gonna be okay." He takes my hand and pulls me to the rug. "Guys." He raises his voice to address the group. "Thank you. I can't even begin to describe..." He trails off, his words seeming to fail him. Finally, he simply says, "Please bring my *ate* home."

"We will, Gordo," I vow, curling my hand into a fist to stop the trembling. "And we're coming back home together."

All the faces around me are solemn as Gordo seems to wrestle with his emotions. Hope, sorrow, fear, worry, excitement.

"I'll be back every thirty minutes to check up on you guys," he manages after composing himself. "By the time you come back, the wake should be starting. I'm going to the hardware store to buy something to soundproof the door. Your alarms are gonna go off and I don't want my parents catching us. Oh, and here, I got some crackers for you guys. I know none of you ate breakfast. That's all I have for now." He sounds apologetic but, at this moment, I truly feel that there has never been a greater delicacy than these crackers.

He takes one last, long look at all of us before disappearing up the stairs.

I stride over to the fridge and grab five cold water bottles, distributing one to each of us. "Drink up, we need to stay hydrated." The water is icy as it trickles into my hollow stomach. I can already hear the crackers protesting.

"Brunner," I begin, "This is your first time. It's going to feel really weird, but remember to fight waking up. You can't break the connection."

"Remind me again what would happen if I do?" Brunner's tone wavers with nerves.

"I don't know, none of us has ever done it. Even Meer made it to Ethra's surface before he woke up that first time. But in theory, if you have no destination, you could be stuck in limbo." I purse my lips. It was a worry I really didn't want to add to our growing list.

"So... I won't wake up?"

"Maybe? But let's not find out today," I respond, turning my attention to the others. "Guide him; we all know where we spawn the first time, but let's make sure he Transcends with us. Assuming we're right about this anyway."

Jadis, Dustin, and Emierr accept my orders with weary agreement, the sleepless night evident on their faces, but determination shining in their eyes.

"Um, and what if I get yanked away from you guys?" Brunner fidgets. "I did not like the stories about the spawn point."

I've thought about this already. "Just wake up. If you get pulled away, it's not worth it."

"And to do that, I just have to say 'Astralis?'"

"Right. Try to do it somewhere hidden just in case you're a slow Transcender."

Brunner swallows hard but, to his credit, he doesn't back out. I return my attention to the others.

"We're all out of practice, so try your best to see if you can open your eyes or move. If you can't, just focus on where we last were." I squeeze my right hand to steady myself. I'm giving orders like I'm some kind of expert but I'm acutely aware that I could be getting each and every one of us killed. I close my eyes briefly, shutting that thought out. I don't have time to think about that now.

"Please, don't lose me," Brunner implores, interlocking his fingers over and over again in a nervous tic.

"Don't worry, you're with professionals." I attempt a lighthearted, jaunty tone but I'm not sure I've managed it.

"Yeah, all we have to worry about is saving our little sister," Dustin says resolutely.

"Then let's sleep." I feel as if I've hit a point of acceptance. It's really happening.

We each select a pillow and settle down, setting our alarms for 7 p.m. We tether ourselves together with clenched fingers, and form a circle with our extended arms.

"Okay, close your eyes and focus on my voice." I dive deep into my memory, searching for the old, guided meditation I had always used to lead us to Transcendence. "Slow your heart rate and breathe in sync with me. Inhale... Exhale... Inhale..." Gradually, everyone's breathing falls into rhythm.

"Now, feel yourself becoming lighter; allow yourself to sink deeper." I notice Brunner's grip loosening on my hand, along with Dustin's. "Experience that weightlessness." My mouth is on autopilot. Below me, the carpet covering the hard concrete floor has melted into water. I float alongside the others.

"Counting down from three," I whisper, my voice barely audible, "Three... two... one."

"Astralis," we say in unison.

My body tingles, shifting into numbness. Suddenly, a force hauls me upwards, leaving my body behind. The jolt of panic and fear exacerbates the sensation of falling. Some part of me had believed that this wouldn't work; that it really had all been an insane fever dream. But as we hurtle off the face of the Earth, I'm forced to accept that it was real. That it had been real all this time.

Our essences travel through space, the vibrations pressing in like water when you dive a little too deep. I try to open my eyes, but my eyelids are heavy. I feel like I'm trying to pry my eyes open far too early in the morning. I manage to crack them open after a few more seconds of straining against the paralysis.

The stars blur into fine lines, and far off in the distance, I see clusters of galaxies swirling. I look to my sides, above, and below. My friends are holding the positions in which they fell asleep as we soar. As expected, Brunner's transcendent form begins to glitch, trying to escape from our grasp. Our breakneck journey slows until we're suspended in space.

My eyes open fully, and I'm greeted with the sight of a binary star, one orange-red and the other blue-white. It's an incredible sight, almost too vivid to be real. This is something NASA needs to learn about, but they'll never believe me. My head breaks free from the pressure, and I can freely swivel my neck. Everyone's eyes are still shut, and we're stuck in the same lying position. "Guys! Open your eyes!" I call out, my voice echoing as if in a grand hall. But they don't budge.

A small, red planet collides with another, the explosion silent, sending debris hurtling in all directions. We're not dangerously close, but the fragments are heading our way. Brunner starts glitching erratically, his body flickering this way and that as Transcendence tries to rip him from our ring. My limbs are still frozen. Bitch, we weren't ready for this. My heart pounds heavily as a chunk of planet spins violently towards us, but then, in the blink of an eye, we're transported to another part of the universe.

Brunner's spasmodic movements threaten to pull us off course. If this continues, we could *all* drift away. I want to urge the others to guide him, but I'm still unable to move myself. Space dust swirls around us and my heart rate begins to slow.

Suddenly, I feel a tight grip on my left hand. It's Brunner, pulling me back from the brink of losing myself. If I'm the only one conscious, then it's all up to me now. I've never tried this before. *Please don't fuck this up.* I need to anchor myself to them. I concentrate hard on Ethra, like a moth to a flame, and gently pull their essences along with me. It feels a little like using my telekinesis.

The momentum propels us forward, and we're back on track. The pull of the super massive black hole is mesmerizing, its beauty overwhelming. A tear escapes my eye, drifting away like a crystal in the void. The knowledge that I was truly seeing something real makes the incomprehensible vastness so much more powerful. I am here.

This place is not a creation of my grief-stricken mind. It exists.

My muscle memory guides us through the black hole. I squeeze my eyes shut and brace myself as we slip through the event horizon. A familiar sensation of pressure and buzzing in my veins engulfs us. Just a little further, we're almost there.

The numbness dissipates, the nerves in my face tingle frantically, trying to regain their bearings as sensation returns. With a gasp, I sit up, surrounded by swirling, maroon leaves defying gravity's pull. *Am I really back?* Despite what my senses tell me, I remain suspended by disbelief. Flexing my limbs, I take stock of my body. Everything seems to be in working order. Toes all good, fingers working perfectly. As I move, feeling the solid reality of the world around me, I lose grip on that last sliver of hope that none of this is real.

I have returned to Ethra.

The grass is a sickly, moldy black, drained of life. The sky above is clearly visible through the few remaining leaves that cling to cracked twigs. This is wrong. The forest should be lush and dim, with a thick canopy blocking out the sunlight. *What happened to the forest?*

A glow from around me announces the materialization of my friends. I push myself up and out of the leaf pile we'd landed in, just as the others began to gasp to life. They're blanketed in fallen leaves, as if they'd lain there for a very long time. I'm jolted by Brunner's sudden, wordless cry. He's frantically patting himself down, as if to ensure all of his body parts had survived the journey.

None of us speak. The memories of this world are solidifying into reality, and I feel certain the others are undergoing the same, unnerving experience. What I remembered before was fragmented, like broken shards of glass, but now it's as if the pieces have fused seamlessly together.

We're all here, clad in the clothes we fell asleep in. Thank god I'd remembered to have everyone put their shoes on just in case. I wasn't about to forget my first, barefoot journey to Ethra anytime soon.

I turn and take in the sight of my friends' Ethran bodies, noting the changes. Emierr sports a deep scar on his left eyebrow, a memento from the encounter with that adorable yet lethal fungus-furred flounder ferret. Jadis, on the other hand, has her long hair back. I watch her expression turn to horror as she runs her fingers through it. I remember the same expression on her face the last time we were here, as her clone's fist closed around the silky strands.

Meanwhile, Dustin is staring down at his three-fingered hand, nausea rolling across his features. The bitten stumps look long healed and are knotted with thick, purple scar tissue. I have to look away as my own stomach clenches at the sight.

"Ricky. Your eye," Emierr whispers, his gaze fixed on me.

I touch the scar running from my eyebrow down to my cheek.

"I can... see?" I thought for sure that eye was a goner. "My eye is healed?"

"No..." Dustin looks up from his mangled hand.

"Oh my god!" Brunner's eyes widen in shock. "That isn't a human eye." He scrambles to his feet, chest heaving. "I wanna go back! I'm gonna have a heart attack!" He's nearly hyperventilating yet unable to pull his gaze from my damaged eye.

"Ricky, your eye is..." Emierr hesitates. "It looks like a wolf's eye. It's all yellow with no white."

I blink at him, processing. *I'm still bonded with Aigerim. It sounds like his eye.* That means the others must still be bonded too. I raise a hand to my eye. It doesn't feel much different other than the rope of scarring. At least seeing won't be a problem.

"Aigerim," I mutter, unable to elaborate further.

Brunner drops his head down between his knees, still breathing hard.

"Relax, Rune. You're fine, you have all your body parts," Dustin says. "Ricky's eye is fine too, his Noble bond is doing its job. You're gonna have to chill out, my guy."

Brunner glances up at Dustin's outstretched hand and groans at the sight of the missing fingers there. His head falls back between his knees as Dustin hastily drops his arm to his side.

"He's gonna wake up if he keeps reacting like this," Jadis mumbled, pushing herself to her feet.

The rotted grass squelches as I stand.

"Jads, can you calm him down, please?" As the person with the fewest visible injuries, I think she has the best chance. She heaves a sigh and pats Brunner on the back.

Emierr grips a withered tree, its trunk split down the middle. He leans in, inspecting it closely. "Everything is dying," he murmurs, locking eyes with me. "What the hell is happening here?"

"I don't know," I admit, reaching out to touch the tree.

"We're near Zaltana!" Dustin's voice cracks, gazing out towards his home in the mountains. "It'll be faster to go there."

"That's not the plan," Emierr says sharply, dropping his hand from the papery bark of the dead tree.

"But it—"

"I'm fine!" Brunner says loudly, slicing through the burgeoning argument. "I'm good, I'm good." He wobbles as he waves Jadis away. "I don't even know how to ask about how you guys aren't dead. Those injuries look really bad." His face is looking a little green but at least he's upright.

"I guess our bodies here reflect the ones back on Earth," I say, glancing around. "Since we aged, I think our injuries healed over time, and since we weren't physically here, we didn't lose blood."

Brunner stares stupidly at me, the gears in his head almost audible.

"How am I going to use this hand?" Dustin grumbles, touching the space where his pinky and ring finger used to be. "Oh shit, my ring is here," he adds in surprise, raising his right hand. The ring containing his white hole fragments glinted on his finger.

"Huh?" I reach for my necklace. Metal and stone meet my fingers.

"My bracelet made it too," Jadis says, raising her wrist.

"We both have our necklaces," Brunner adds, jabbing a thumb at Emierr.

"We never actually had the stones with us whenever we Transcended," I say slowly. "And now that I'm thinking about it, why are we wearing the clothes we fell asleep in? Shouldn't we be stuffed into our twelve-year-old Ethra clothes?"

"We did sometimes Transcend with the stones," Jadis recalls, ignoring the clothing mystery altogether. "But we always had them in a pocket or something, so I guess we never thought about it. I can't believe we didn't lose one... But I think the stones are imbued with magick. These *are* space rocks, right?" She directs the question at me.

"Yeah, from the—Well. My Pa gave them to me." Even after all this, I had never actually been fully honest about the rocks' origin. I promised Pa that I could keep the secret about the white holes. Up until now, I had kept my promise. The idea of breaking it sends a twinge through my gut, but I'm starting to think I probably should.

"Actually," I begin hesitantly, "there's a little more to the story."

Jadis folds her arms and shifts her weight to one leg. "Spit it out."

I close my eyes for a moment. "Before my Pa ever gave me those rocks, he told me a secret. He made me promise not to tell anyone, even you guys." I open my eyes and am met with stony silence. "Way before we were born, NASA discovered something. It was a phenomenon that was heavily mocked in the world of astrophysics. The white holes."

Dustin's brows are lowered in concentration. "So... It was a black hole but like... lit up?"

A laugh escaped my lips despite the tension building in my muscles. "No, Dusty, but A for effort. It's basically the opposite of a black hole. Nothing can go in, but it can spit things out. Anyway, somewhere down the line, the theory of white holes started getting attention. One opened up right next to our moon."

Jadis's mouth falls open. "You're just telling me about this *now*?"

I shrug apologetically, not meeting her gaze. "So... Yeah, my Pa told me about it, and he said that these pieces," I hold up my necklace, "came out of the white hole."

Jadis's eyes harden. "Ricky, this changes everything. If you had told me this before, we could have worked things out so much sooner. We would have realized it wasn't imagination and magic, it was science."

"I didn't think that far ahead when I was a kid, Jads," I mumble, "I was just thinking that I made a promise to my Pa."

Dustin shakes his head slowly, still trying to make the connection Jadis had seen instantly. Emierr and Brunner eye her cautiously. I can tell they don't want to stick around if she starts yelling.

"This is proving the superstring theory more and more," Jadis says under her breath. "Rune might be right then, maybe 'astralis' is an incantation, and us coming into contact with the stones was the ingredient needed for the spell to work. Remember how they glowed that first time? It's kind of like the real Transcendence spell, but with a loophole."

"Uh, why didn't you just evaporate?" Brunner asks.

She shoots him a withering look. "Intent to leave is half the process. You don't just disintegrate if you accidentally say 'astralis.'"

We fall silent. Hearing Jadis say all of this makes me think of the Superposition; my life's work waiting to launch back at Flemming Corp. Something about all of this feels like it's connected to the game. After all, I had used flakes of the rocks to create the device. At the time, it felt like having a bit of Pa with me and it didn't hurt that they seemed to work like quartz. *If the rocks are imbued with magick and I smelted the rocks onto the device's chip, then that means...* I gasp.

"Fuck!" I slam both hands on my head. "Fuck, fuck, fuck." I pace back and forth, my mind racing. "I messed up, guys, really bad. I need to wake up and call Bonnie. The game can't launch."

"Take it easy, Ricky," Jadis says, looking alarmed. "What are you talking about?"

"I borrowed VR tech from NASA to integrate into the new game device I created," I pant. My heart is going to burst from my chest. What have I done? "I also took a chunk of the space rock samples they brought back, years ago. The white hole facilities were basically abandoned so I thought it was fair game. The properties of the rock... They're indescribable. It made the device work, but it wasn't supposed to."

"What does that mean?" Brunner asks, baffled.

"We don't have the technology advanced enough to make a device that can transport your consciousness into a game. But the space rock made it possible. Once I ran out of those stones, I couldn't just go back to NASA and get more so I did research. The rocks' energies are similar to a charged particle accelerator. I got some scientists to work on how we could get those energies onto more chips. We did it, and the impossible was possible."

"Is it releasing soon?" Emierr's voice is throttled with forced calm.

"Yes, but Bonnie's trying to postpone it."

"Then when we wake up, we'll make sure it doesn't happen," Jadis asserts, reaching out to stroke my hand soothingly.

"Guys, I made the chip with the *space rocks*," I emphasize. "The game is literally Ethra." At this, their faces blanch. "When I made the concept, the world just felt familiar, but I didn't connect the dots until now. I even let players say 'Astralis' during the touch ID process." With my memory barricaded all these years, I hadn't been capable of realizing what I was doing, what would happen to the players. "They're going to activate the stones," I whisper. "People are coming here... They're all going to end up like Jho." *And it will all be my fault.*

"How many did you make?" Brunner demands.

"Three hundred with the space rock chips," I breathe.

"Three hundred..." Jadis exhales sharply.

"Shit..." Brunner mutters.

"I'm waking up," I say through gritted teeth. I have to fix this before it's too late. No one tries to stop me.

"Astralis." I close my eyes and wait for my body to evaporate. Nothing happens. "What?" My eyes blink open. The other four are staring at me, confusion on their faces. "Astralis," I repeat, but still nothing. "What the fuck?"

"Astralis," Jadis shouts. Her body remains solid, bare feet planted on the oil-slick forest floor. Everyone else tries too, but there's no reaction.

"What's going on?" Brunner's voice is pitched high with fear.

Bitch. "Maybe we're too tired. None of us had a full sleep, right?" I hope to god I'm right because the alternative is not something I want to think about. "Someone has to wake us up..."

"Our phone alarms will do the job, right?" I can hear Brunner's breathing pick up speed.

"Yo!" Dustin snaps, startling us from our hysteria. "Jho might be here, guys. We have to stay focused on the plan." He then directs his gaze to me. "Ricky, it's gonna be fine. Bonnie has you. She'll keep it from launching."

I pinch the bridge of my nose and take a deep breath. He's right. The game won't launch today. I can deal with Flemming Corp when I wake up.

"We got this," he says forcefully.

Emierr stays silent. I look to find his gaze fixed on the ground.

"Okay, fine," I relent.

Brunner breathes out, taking in his surroundings. "So this is Ethra." He changes the subject gracelessly, watching as charred, purplish fronds float for a few seconds before drifting to the forest floor. "Woah."

"Woah, indeed," I murmur to myself. Taking a deep breath, I let the essence of this place envelope me. Never in a million years did I think I'd be back in Akeurimja Forest, where everything ended for us. The scent of this place is indescribable, but the air feels denser, heavier; maybe because we're not native to this realm. My brain is muddled by a turbulent mix of sadness, fear, longing, and fucking everything. I shake my head, trying to clear my mind.

"How do we get out of here?" Jadis directs at me.

"Let's head to Zaltana, it's right there," Dustin repeats, gazing out at the vast mountains. They resemble the Alps but are larger and harbor an entire civilization atop them.

"Like I said, Dust, we're going to Terrene," Emierr finally speaks, his tone harsh.

What's going on with him?

"Agreed, let's stick to the plan and find our way out of here. The sooner, the better," Brunner agrees.

As I turn to look at Brunner, a feeling of fear that doesn't seem to be my own engulfs me. I stare at him. The feeling is radiating off of him in little rivulets of terror.

Am I... sensing his emotions? I've read about empaths before, because Emierr always suggested I could be one, but it seemed beyond the realm of possibility. On Earth, anyway.

"I think I know a way out," Jadis declares, cracking her knuckles, revealing burn marks. "I'm a little rusty, so no judging." She slaps her hands together. They emit a bright red glow, with golden, spectral rings appearing on every finger. She weaves signs expertly, muscle memory taking over. The rings' light pulsates. Suddenly, a projection of our hand drawn map of Ethra from the notebook appears.

Brunner stares in awe—his first magickal experience. We form a circle around the map.

"If we can see Zaltana, that means we're here," Jadis explains, pointing at the edge of Akeurimja Forest.

"We're not running with the shadow creatures again. We go around the edges," Emierr plots, tracing the lines where Jadis's finger is pointing. "Here," he adds, indicating Terrene on the map.

I glance at Dustin, noticing his demeanor shifting. There's a weird fire in his warm, brown eyes. Even Emierr seems more serious than usual. If I don't intervene, these two are bound to clash.

"Alright," I say. Jadis drops the spell. "We don't have time to make detours, so I'm sorry, Dusty, we can't go to Zaltana right now. Heading to Terrene is already a half-day's journey. Let's focus on getting Jho, and then we're out."

"Okay, yeah. I understand. Next time." The angry light fades from his eyes. Now I'm sure that I can sense the mixed emotions around me. Brunner wants to explore, Dustin longs for home, Emierr is eager to return to Terrene, and Jadis remains the most level-headed among us.

How can I feel these things? I never had this ability before, not even as a Noble. Unless being here is already making my imagination run wild.

"Holy shit," Brunner says, head tipped back and gaping at the withered canopy above us. My eyes widen as I gaze between dried leaves clinging weakly to shriveled branches. Above us orbits the Fleming Space Ring, the fifth Nation of Ethra, my home. Even my memory hadn't captured its grandeur accurately. I can't believe this place truly exists. If it was incredible back when I thought it was a dream, now I no longer have the words to describe it. Thoughts of Miss Delphini and Dr. Wolfgang flood my mind—how thirty-two years have already passed in this world? I don't even know what to feel about them. Are they even still alive?

"Do you think you'll ever go back there?" Dustin asks, eyes on the Space Ring.

"Nah, I don't care about that place. Besides, can you imagine the ticket price after thirty-two years of inflation?" A smile plays on my lips. Regardless of any negative emotions I have about this place, I can't deny the underlying current of homecoming.

"I can't believe you all liv—" Whatever Brunner had been about to say is cut off by a scream.

I whip around to see razor-sharp talons sink into Brunner's shoulder before ripping him from the ground, sending the floating leaves spinning off into the trees. In less than a second, Brunner's echoing wails are all that remain of him.

A deafening shriek emanates from the sky. A giant bird I'd never seen before, with a rainbow of feathers glowing in the half-light, flashes overhead. Then, just like that, they're both gone.

"Bitch." I breathe.

BOOK THREE:

ETHRA

ETHRA

VERGLAS

ZALTANA

ARID

TERRIENE

FLEMING SPACE RING

Luminous Reach

Ethereal Lake

Kingdom of the Forefront

Juno

Bayun

Ambrosia Academy

Desert of Sabarra

Glasthaven

Arcourette's Forest

Isle of Vereilles

VEREILLES

Treetop Province

Ethereal Tree

Solaris

Ethereal Lake

Great Eagle Fields

Lavender Sky Manor

Moore View

Illusia

TERRENE

"What do we do?" Dustin shouts. His eight remaining fingers have become claws, gripping his head hopelessly.

Shit! Shit! Shit!

"Meer, command it to stop!" Jadis snaps.

"I—I can't! It's too far, it won't hear me." Emierr's eyes are wide with horror.

"Brunner!" Dustin's useless cry echoes through the abandoned woods.

Jadis slams her palms together, summoning an astral bow and arrow. Her feet slide into their stance, and she takes aim at the bird. It's nothing more than a glittering speck in the distance.

"I can't risk it. I might hit him," she says, her breath quickening.

My body moves on instinct, and before I know it, I'm sprinting along the bird's flight path.

"Ricky!" Dustin's voice rings out from behind me. I ignore him as my feet pound the dead ground beneath them.

"Faster!" I hiss, feeling the muscles in my legs tighten. Suddenly, I recall the race we had at the meadow; our final day in Ethra until now.

Propel. Like gliding on air.

Concentrating on my steps, I pick up speed. Ahead, I spot some rock formations that might serve as a launch pad. Brunner's shrieks continue to echo, though they're growing alarmingly distant. I let out a cry, leaping onto the rocks and propelling myself skyward, extending my arms towards the bird.

A tingling sensation courses through my fingers as an invisible surge of energy emanates from my hands, extending toward the bird like taut strings, until I make contact. *There, I feel it!* My fingers curl as if grasping onto the creature, and suddenly I'm lifted briefly into the air. Just as I rise, I begin to fall, dragging the bird with me.

"Shit!" I yelp, bracing myself for impact with the ground. With a quick adjustment, I push down with my feet. An invisible force cushions the landing as I touch down on the grass. The bird screeches above, held in my grip. Its fiery eyes burn above me as its wings work the air. The powerful flight muscles drag me a few feet across the grass.

"Ricky!" Brunner dangles helplessly from the raptor's claws, blood already soaking the shoulder of his t-shirt.

"Guys!" I call out desperately, glancing to see the three of them running toward me. The bird unleashes another ear-splitting cry. I attempt to pull it down toward me, but it's like trying to lift hundred-pound dumbbells after years away from the gym. It's futile. I switch tactics, backing away and using every ounce of the strength in my legs to drag the creature down through the treetops. With each step, I groan, feeling every muscle in my body burning. Somehow, I manage to hold it long enough for the others to come to my aid.

The bird's call is like a blade through my ears. Its wings beat harder and wilder, jolting me into the air as I lose my grip on it and collapse back to the ground. Gasping, I watch Brunner reach down, stretching fruitlessly to reach me. Multicolored feathers cascade down like rain. Free of my telekinetic grasp, the monstrous creature soars back into the sky, leaving behind a trail of Brunner's pleas.

"Fuck!" I curse, slamming my hand onto the ground. I'm struggling to keep myself from falling apart.

Dustin swears loudly.

"Rune..." Jadis's gaze is fixed on the sky where Brunner disappeared.

I rub my face, attempting to gather my thoughts and regain focus. *Come on, Rictor, keep it together!* Glancing at Emierr, I notice he remains still. It's oddly calming me, though a shadow creeps over his face. The plan has already blown up in our faces.

"Okay..." I get back on my feet. "Here's the new plan. The original plan is out the window until we rescue Rune." I meet Emierr's gaze, but his unwavering expression unnerves me. *Why isn't he freaking out like the rest of us?*

"I think what took him was an Argentavis," Dustin states, his gaze shifting towards the mountains. "Huge ass birds that flock together. They're usually by the ranges in Zaltana, though."

"Then why the hell was that one all the way out here?" Jadis asks, her tone incredulous.

"Your guess is as good as mine," Dustin responds with a shrug.

"So, its nest would be out by Zaltana?"

"Yeah, it should be."

The three of us turn towards Zaltana, the nation in the skies. That

Argent—whatever its name is—it's taking Brunner there. Now the only question is, which of those mountains is it taking him to?

I exhale heavily. "All right, we head to Zaltana and hope to god he's still alive."

A haunted expression settles on their faces.

"No," Emierr says. We all pivot to face him, stunned. "We go to Terrene, continue as planned." His face is pale, the mask of calm cracking.

"What?" Jadis furrows her eyebrows in confusion.

"Dude, if we don't go after him, Rune's gonna be breakfast," Dustin says, raising an eyebrow at him.

"Meer, he could die here if we don't move now," I say, shocked it even needed to be said aloud.

"We all understood the risks," Emierr responds, his gaze dropping. There's a palpable shift in the air. The emotions coming off Dustin and Jadis flood through me. Fearful apprehension morphs into seething anger. I struggle to disentangle my own feelings from theirs, but they all blend together.

"Are you out of your mind?" Jadis snarls.

"Are all of you?" Emierr's glare intensifies. "Risking us all dying for him?"

"Bullshit!" Dustin shouts back.

"Stop pretending like you care about saving Rune. You just wanna go to Zaltana first because your tribe's there," Emierr retorts.

"If you think that's more important than saving Rune, I oughta kick your ass right now!" Dustin steps forward, fists clenched tightly, ready to throw a punch.

"Enough!" Jadis interposes herself between both of them.

"Forget it! I've waited sixteen years to return to Ethra. None of you are going to stop me. Go on your own, I'm going to Terrene with or without you." He turns his back on us and strides away. Emierr is emitting a wave of emotions too, but instead of anger or fear, I sense sadness. My throat tightens, and tears well up in my eyes, almost overwhelming me.

This... isn't just about Jho.

"Gonna leave us again? Just like you did last time?" Dustin taunts.

Emierr halts in his tracks, taking a deep breath before turning back to face us. Something in my newfound senses pushes me forward.

"Meer, what the hell are we doing here?"

"What? What do you mean?" he snaps.

I halt my approach. "What's in Terrene?"

"Sól—" Emierr growls before clamping his mouth shut. The anger is still ebbing off of him, but now, eddies of shock, dismay, and shame coil with it.

"Fucking *ay*." Dustin shakes his head in disbelief.

"Bitch..." A heavy feeling settles in my stomach and I retreat a few paces back. "Is that why you kept avoiding questions about Sólel? Do you... care about Jho at all?" My hands clench into fists. "It was never about saving her, was it?" My breathing comes in sharp gusts, and a flush of heat races across my face.

"It's all about his fake little family." Dustin scoffs.

"Is that true, Meer?" Jadis's voice catches. "Because if it is, that's really fucked up."

"You guys don't understand." Emierr's lips quiver, and his eyes start to well up. "Sól... he's my little brother."

"He's not your real brother! This place isn't real!" The frustration in Dustin's voice swells, bouncing off nearby trees.

"Look around you, asshole! Everything here is real! He's as real as all of you!" Emierr roars.

"Jho is real. She's your *actual* cousin," Jadis shouts at him. Her face is twisted with hurt and rage.

"I have my own family, you dipshit. You made us risk *everything* because you missed your imaginary brother?" Dustin makes a threatening lunge at Emierr but Jadis grabs hold of his arm just in time. "Do you even care about Jhoana?"

Everything, every damn thing, was a lie. Meer sent us on a fucking suicide mission. "What the fuck, Meer... How could yo—Jhoana! Our best friend! How messed up are you?" My voice trembles, devoid of anger, and hollow with realization. *He's going to get us killed.*

"*Me?*" His incredulous voice feels like an arrow through my gut. "I did everything! When all of you left... I stayed, damn it." Emierr's voice is shaking now. Anger? Sorrow? Regret? I couldn't differentiate any of the emotions lapping at the edges of my mind. What a stellar time for this newfound ability to manifest. Emierr took an unsteady step forward. "You all blamed me for... for being scared! But I blamed myself more than any of you..."

"Bullsh—"

"What bullshit?" Emierr interrupts Dustin. "You all got ten years! Ten goddamn years of forgetting everything. You." Emierr's finger stabs toward Dustin, "You got your family and your career as a football player. Ricky became a scientist and makes video games." He glances in my direction. "You're literally the smartest guy I've ever known."

"Meer," I exhale softly. The weight in my chest is nearly unbearable now.

"Jads, damn it, you're out there traveling and creating art. I couldn't do what you guys did, just leave and forget. I tried to make something of it, okay. We screwed up with Rune, he just wanted to be friends with us, but we treated him like shit, and look what we turned him into. We weren't the only ones who lost Jho. He was her best friend outside of us," Emierr covers his mouth, hands shaking. I think he just realized what is happening to Rune.

"Enough, Meer," Jadis cries out, her voice breaking.

"All my life, I've only ever had one fucking thing... and it's this... All of us. It's always been enough for me. My life ended when all of you left me alone to fend for myself. I thought we were all supposed to be together forever." He halts, his voice choked with emotion. "And Sól... He was the closest thing I had to any of you." He shuts his eyes and lowers his head. "I was never going to leave, Ricky. We were falling deeper into Ethra everyday and I got scared. Because I wanted this to be real. To me, our real life is our dreamworld. I belonged here. How could we leave all this behind? But our parents, they lost two of their best friends. How would they handle losing all of us too? So I made the decision. My cousin..." He wipes his tears away, his breaths coming in sharp gasps.

I approach him slowly and extend my hand. He flinches and steps back, more caged animal than man. *What have we done to you, Meer?*

"I'm sorry, Ricky. I'm so sorry." His younger voice blends with his own as I envelop him in a hug. I can feel his body shuddering against mine.

"Thank you for staying back and enduring when the rest of us couldn't." I clench my teeth, fighting a losing battle against the sharp waves of tears. Jadis stands beside me with rivulets cascading down her face and holding hands with a glassy-eyed Dustin. I take hold of Jadis's hand and we form a ragged circle. I can feel their emotions, their guilt weighing heavy. Emierr weeps into my shoulder. Everything he says is true; we unknowingly crucified him for it, trapping him in Farmington, while we had ten years away from the trauma. He bore all the town's hate, yet he still found space to smile, even if it was forced.

It doesn't excuse what he has done to us today, but pain can drive people to do desperate things. And desperation is all we'll have if we continue to let pain be the only thing bonding us together.

"We don't have much time, Meer. We need to rescue Rune first, all right?" I say gently, releasing him. "Can you hold on just a little longer?" If reuniting him with Sólel would get him on the path to healing, then that's what we would do. But it doesn't change the fact that we now have two friends in dire need of help.

Emierr nods, retreating half a step back. "Dust, I'm sorry, man," he says, his voice still shaky.

"You were going to sacrifice Rune," Dustin holds his breath, but remains composed. I can feel the warring shame, pity, and anger radiating off of him.

"I—I didn't plan it," Emierr shakes his head. "I didn't expect Rune to be taken like that, I just knew I had to get home. To Terrene." He doesn't look up to meet Dustin's even gaze.

"We're good." Dustin grabs the back of Emierr's head, resting his forehead against Emierr's. "No more lies, and you owe Rune the apology."

Emierr unleashes a shaky sigh. "I will."

Jadis punches Emierr on the arm.

"Ow!"

"That's for lying to us," she says, then leaps into a hug. "And that's for being our hero."

"What hero?" Emierr hugs her back, though his shoulders still tremble.

"For taking the town on for us, and watching over Jho."

"Okay." I rub my eyes one last time. "Now that the dramatics are over, let's make our way to those big ass mountains."

Emierr pulls away slightly, glancing at the others. His voice falters as he speaks. "But... what if our clones show up again? What do we do then?"

Dustin steps forward, crunching leaves beneath his boots. "Then we fight them," he says with unwavering resolve. "We're ready this time."

I nod, clenching my fists. "Dusty's right. We've come too far to back down now. We can handle whatever they throw at us." I don't know if I can really face our demonic doppelgangers again, but I can't let my friends see that. If it comes down to it, I'll have to push through—do whatever it takes to keep them safe.

"I'm with you," Jadis says, voice low. "No more running."

An hour has passed since we arrived in Ethra, yet only thirty minutes have elapsed back on Earth. Emierr's reminder about the Gate near the entrance of Akeurimja Forest sparks a new plan. Instead of enduring a day's journey to Zaltana, we opt for a shortcut through Zaltana's Gate. Might not be the safest plan but the quicker we find Brunner, the better.

As we traverse Akeurimja, the once-mystical mauve trees now

stand gray and lifeless, their branches reaching out like skeletal fingers. The absence of leaves intensifies the desolation, casting an eerie webs of shadow over our path; a world stripped bare by some unseen calamity. It's as if nature itself mourns the passing of time.

But that doesn't mean all danger is gone. Shadow creatures must still live in these woods—a threat everyone seems to have forgotten the moment that Argentavis sank its claws into Brunner. I don't feel any immediate danger, only a pervasive sense of dread and uncertainty radiating off of everyone.

"Meer," I say, jogging a few steps to catch up to him. "What do you think is happening with the forest?"

"I don't know, but I tried to create more trees, and it wouldn't work. It's like the soil itself is dead," he responds, eyes still distant. "My father should have answers. We'll find out when we reach Terrene."

Dustin groans. "This is taking forever. Remind me why we can't use a teleportation spell?"

"I told you already; it's going to take all of us to cast the spell, and Mr. Science over there doesn't *believe* in magick," Jadis grumbles. "But if you're okay ditching him then..."

Dustin smacks her arm and Emierr fake coughs, smirking.

I scoff. "How many times do I have to tell you guys that 'magick' is just another form of radiation here? Space is filled with radiation, and an asteroid from space, that glows mind you, is just another form of radiation we don't know about."

"Oh, here we go," Jadis mutters under her breath.

"I'm betting there's another way to activate the radiation chemicals in our bodies without *believing* in magick," I assert firmly, refusing to yield.

"Then let's see," Jadis halts and pivots to face me. "Prove it to me right now," she challenges, crossing her arms and grinning.

"What? I need to conduct plenty of testing before I can provide evidence," I stammer.

"See, what did I tell you guys?" She looks at the other boys, and they chuckle.

"Fine. I'll prove it." I'm not about to let this cohort of magicians win over science.

"It's on. You know how it works, clap your hands," she prompts.

I hesitate.

"Do you need a demonstration? Boys, let's help him."

Dustin claps his hands, and they emit a white light. Forest green shines from Emierr's and a vivid red encircles Jadis's.

"Your turn," she says.

You got this, Rick. Show her the undeniable proof of your theory! I inhale deeply and clap my hands together.

"Ha!" I shout, as if performing a taekwondo maneuver. Nothing happens. Another clap rings out as I try again but still, nothing. Humiliating.

"I guess you can't use your *pixie dust*, after all," Jadis teases, shaking her unnervingly long hair out. All three of them laugh and strut off, leaving me staring irritably at my palms.

"Come on, activate!" I clap my hands repeatedly, feeling like a seal in an aquarium. With a sigh of defeat, I break into a jog and regroup, head hanging. "Experiment fail," I mutter.

"It's okay to be wrong sometimes, Dicktor."

"We can agree to disagree, how about that?" Jadis shoves me, and I manage a half-smile. "Although it doesn't exactly help the teleportation issue."

"Apology accepted," I say, patting her shoulder.

"Get down!" Emierr hisses. Without question, we all drop down into sickly, overgrown grass. A man in a uniform—one I haven't seen worn by any of the nations—stands several feet from us, speaking into his wrist. His attire resembles the jumpsuits from the Space Ring, but upgraded into a sort of body armor. He appears to be around our age, and built like a warrior—perhaps from Verglas? But if he's here, maybe from Terrene or Zaltana? Either way, he looks dangerous, especially with that gun-like thing strapped to his waist.

His gaze sweeps the undergrowth and catches on the four obvious indents within the blades. I curse silently. Four grown adults, Nobles of nations, Keepers of the Ethereal Waters, hiding in the grass like a bunch of idiot toddlers.

"On your feet," the man orders calmly, weapon moving from his belt to his hands. "Move slowly and nobody gets hurt."

Wincing, we rise, palms up in surrender.

"Relax, bro, we're just lost," Dustin says, offering a smile. I can't help but appreciate how personable Dustin is, despite staring down the barrel of a gun.

"Getting lost in Akeurimja Forest seems pretty intentional; nobody wanders here," the man remarks, his finger resting on the trigger.

"You're here," Dustin points out, eyebrow quirked.

"See this badge?" He gestures to his chest. "That means I'm allowed to be."

"We don't have time for this," I snap. My left hand casts intangible threads of power and tugs the weapon out of the man's hands and into mine. He lets out a startled yelp. We drop our hands, and I examine the gun. The metallic barrel gleams in the weak forest light. Compact and lightweight, it fits snugly in the palm of my hand.

Bright LED indicators and touch-sensitive controls dot the gun's surface.

"You are not authorized to handle that weapon!" The man claps shaky hands together, coating them with a dark maroon aura.

"I wouldn't, if I were you." The deep scarlet emanating from Jadis's own hands accentuates the warning.

"It's okay, we don't mean any harm," Emierr assures the now-pallid man.

"Dude, that looks like one of my laser guns," Dustin says, snagging the gun from my hands. "I wouldn't mind an upgrade." He winks at me.

"H—How... How did you do that? You didn't even weave the spell." The man looks at me bewildered and possibly afraid. *Definitely afraid*, I determine, feeling the man's ebbing fear lap at me.

"I don't use spells," I reply, glancing at Jadis.

"Ricky, now's not the time!" She shakes her head, stifling her laughter.

Realization dawns on the man's face. "Wait." He drops his hands, and the glow disappears. "Telekinesis... Holy shit! It can't be." His eyes widen as if he's seen the dead return to life, an ironically impossible event here. "You're the Noble from Fleming, Rictor Mason. It's um—It's an honor, sir." He bows his head.

"I guess my reputation precedes me," I say, taking the gun from Dustin and handing it back to the man.

"Thank you, my Noble" he says, placing it back in its holster.

"Just Rictor is fine," I snort.

He inhales deeply. "No one's going to believe this. You're all back. The legend herself, Lady Supreme, Jadis Salazar, and Noble of Arid," he continues, looking at Jadis with an expression of reverence. Jadis relaxes her guard. He then scans the others. "Dustin Borja, Noble of Zaltana, and Emierr Naputi, Fatebringr and Noble of Terrene." His eyes move beyond us. "Aren't there five of you? It was assumed you died; it's been so long since you've been seen."

"Yeah..." The word leaves our lips in unison. I wonder if the others catch what his words imply. None of us have been seen. That means no one in Ethra has seen Jhoana either. Fear trickles into my veins.

"But we're here now," Dustin says, his tone not inviting further questions.

"And who are you exactly?" Jadis folds her arms in time with me.

"My apologies," he says, clasping his left hand on his right hand. He bows low. "My name is Jae Navarrosen. I'm an Allied Force soldier from the Kingdom of the Forefront."

The fuck is the Kingdom of the Forefront? Jae appears much younger and more inexperienced now that he isn't pointing his gun at us. I glance at Jadis, and she's examining Jae from head to toe. *This bitch, she's checking him out.* I try to suppress my smirk. I wonder if Jae knows how fortunate he is at this very moment. I admit he's not a bad-looking dude. Close-cropped black hair, deep brown almond eyes, high cheekbones, and full lips. *Okay now* I'm *checking him out.*

"Allied Force?" Jadis probes.

"It seems you truly have been gone all these years. It was inspired by you, Nobles," Jae answers. "The Allied Organization Squad changed a lot of things for Ethra; it brought the nations together, creating a much stronger united front. When you all disappeared, a few of the world leaders came together to uphold what you guys stood for. The Kingdom of the Forefront was created, and so was the Allied Force, extending their hand to every nation. That is your legacy."

"Wow," Emierr breathes out. His excitement prickles my skin, like I've been whacked with an electric fly swatter.

"Enough of the formalities, man," Dustin says, lifting Jae's shoulder to straighten him up from yet another bow. "We need your help."

"Anything."

"We kinda lost our friend, he got scooped up by an Argentavis."

"Is it Noble Jhoana?" I flinch at the sound of her name. "Damn birds, they've been making a mess out of things the past few months," Jae growls. "There's a plague hitting Ethra. Something is poisoning the magick. It started here, in the forest—trees dying, chasing away the creatures that lived here."

A plague? So the shadow forest isn't the only place dying off. I try not to imagine what the other nations must look like.

"No, she's... not with us at the moment." Dustin's eyes are the only part of his expression that betray his composure. "The friend we lost is a man with blue eyes, brown skin, and dark, curly hair. His name is Brunner Fischer."

Jae nods with military precision. "Which species of Argentavis got him?"

Dustin pauses. "I think it must have been a Scarlet Lorik from the colors but I've never actually seen one before."

Jae's eyebrows only raise a few millimeters before raising his wrist and repeating the descriptions into whatever communication device he has strapped there. "The man taken by presumed Scarlet Lorik has dark skin and hair, blue eyes."

"Is the Ethereal Tree in trouble?" Emierr blurts out. The prickles of excitement are replaced with cool blades of worry. I wonder for a moment why Emierr is so much easier to feel than the others. Jae lowers his wrist.

"No, the Source is guarded well. The chief has kept his duty strong all this time."

"When did this happen?" Jadis asks, stealing a glance at the gray, lifeless landscape around us.

"Years ago. I was in training when it happened. Shadow creatures started leaving the forest. They've been contained over the years, but the forest will die soon... and that means its residents are being forced out." Jae's suddenly haunted expression tells me that we are not the only people to come face to face with shadows.

"That's... not good," I say lamely.

"That's really not good." Jadis sighs. "What has the Council done about this?"

"I'm not supposed to talk about such matters," Jae says, but quickly reconsiders from the look on Jadis's face. "The word is, since the death of the Supreme after you, the Council is on the brink of disbanding." Jae shifts nervously from one foot to the other. I like this guy; he knows the tea.

"Is that bad?" Dustin questions. We all stare at him. Jadis rolls her eyes so deeply that I lose track of her irises.

"If there's no one overseeing magick—" she says slowly, with the air of explaining basic addition to a particularly dense first grader.

"Then it's anarchy," I finish, rubbing my temples. "No laws. Just chaos." *How bad have things been here?* When we were kids, it never seemed that serious, but then again, we thought it was all a dream and we were *children*. Who the hell decided it was a good idea to let five twelve-year-olds be in charge of anything more dangerous than a temperamental copy machine?

"Who was the next Supreme?" Jadis asks.

"Madam Evanora, the Overseer."

The name elicits a reaction from all of us. I remember the witch who had turned so instantly on Jadis. How she watched in the audience while Jadis had nearly been killed.

"She was the next one in line to Ascend, so..." Jadis trails off, nodding. "What happened to her?"

Jae exhales, hesitating. "Where did you all go?" His eyes flit between us. It seems that Jae needed some reciprocation before he allows us to continue our interrogation. "My father had told me the stories, how you all would come in and save hundreds of people, like it was a game to you. But with all that hope, after you left, there was no one to protect the peace and... a few humans and leyfolk began using blood magick."

"*Blood* magick? I've never heard of it." Jadis looks vaguely nauseated at the implications.

"It defies everything we know. Over the years, they grew into something they now call the Vermillion Sages—blood magick users created by The O'rians. It was a group that once promised change, but quickly became a force of corruption in Ethra. They've taken out cities within days and..." He shakes his head. "My father would be happy, seeing his heroes return."

The Squad remains silent, exchanging glances. How could people remember a band of children as their saviors and heroes? In our absence, our legend has clearly outgrown the reality of what we were: traumatized kids way in over their heads. The overwhelming uncertainty that everyone is feeling seeps into me, and I feel like I'm going to vomit.

What did we come back to?

"Listen... Our friend is new here. He could be in serious danger. We really need your help to find him," I say, clamping down on the acid roiling in my stomach.

Jae turns his head to his right, as if listening to something. He raises his left hand and speaks into his wrist. "Copy. Surveillance ends. Tell the chief that I didn't find any more birds, but I found something better. He's not going to believe this." He grins at us.

"My father?" Emierr says longingly.

"Or my grandpa," Dustin points out.

"We got your friend. They rescued him from a nest in the Zaltanian Mountains. It's a good thing I called it in. Saw him screaming for his life," Jae chuckles. "This is what I'm saying, the balance is tipping. Feeding grounds for those birds are gone. Whatever's poisoning the magick, it's creeping into other parts of the land and seas, spreading further each day and chasing away their inhabitants. Argentavis mostly fed on fish, but now they're eating animals and people. They were starving and now they're... well." He looks down. "Anyways, come on, this way."

"To where?" I furrow my brows.

"To my hovercraft. I'm taking you to Terrene. Once they make sure your friend is good, they'll drop him there."

"Are you... going to tell people that we're back?" Emierr asks hesitantly.

Jae glances back. "Are you kidding?" he scoffs, shaking his head. "Look, I personally don't have any grudges against any of you, but a lot of people do. They're upset at the state you left the world in."

"We were kids." *Even here people blame us...*

"Yeah." He nods. "That's what I always tell people, but you're also Nobles. You had duties, those were your roles." He sighs. "But right now, the world doesn't need to know you're back just yet. Come on, let's beat your friend to Terrene. I'm sure almost being bird food wasn't his first idea of a fun time." Jae turns and walks off, a signal for us to follow.

"You got what you wanted," Dustin nudges Emierr. "You ready to see Sól?"

Are we ready to find out what happened to Jho?

We reach the hovercraft, parked in an open area, not far off. It's exactly what I expected it to be, resembling an SUV in size but far higher tech than any SUV on Earth. Its sleek, metallic, maroon paint gleams under the sunlight.

As I settle into the passenger seat, the others take their places in the back. Jae activates the vehicle with a simple button press. Instantly, the seat belts wrap snugly around us, securing us in place as the hovercraft lifts smoothly off the ground. It's a seamless transition from stationary to airborne. As we ascend, the majestic Ethereal Tree looms, its massive branches stretching towards the heavens in defiance of Ethran constraints.

The Space Ring casts its shadow over the landscape, with the tree serving as a colossal beacon, illuminating the surrounding area like a giant nightlight. It's a mesmerizing sight, drawing our gaze like moths to a flame.

Beyond the tree, the Zaltanian mountains are jagged teeth against the sky. As we speed through the air towards our destination, the world below us glows with twinkling lights from the villages of Terrene. Stars tethered to Ethra's surface. I can feel a swell of joy pressing from the back seats. Despite themselves and despite our situations, there is a piece of all of us that is happy to be back.

As the familiar view sets in, my heart sinks. *Chief Berkarys, Chieftess Nalani, and Sólel, it's been so long. If they don't know where Jho is...* I stop that train of thought dead in its tracks. I refuse to let myself consider the alternatives. Holograms below pull me back into the moment. Terrene appears more urban than before, but I can still see pieces of the home I once knew. The citizens below dress in a modern fashion, less cultural than I remember. Yet, it's unmistakably Terrene, with men sporting flashy tank tops and women clad in flowy dresses. Even the leyfolk are dressed similarly. It's like walking in on fashion week in New York, category: "bougie forest."

"They beat us here, damn it," Jae grumbles. A metallic emerald hovercraft is parked in something that could be a parking lot, though there aren't any other vehicles present. Hovercrafts weren't a thing when Emierr and I lived here. A light green ogre with decoratively carved tusks, and dressed in the same uniform as Jae steps out of the driver's seat, shaking his head as we descend a few feet away from him.

"That guy is kind of a dick. I haven't told him who you guys are, so I apologize for his... comments," Jae mutters.

"I wonder how Rune reacted seeing an ogre." Meer chuckles.

Jadis laughs. "That boy is going to need those therapy sessions after all of this."

"All right, just follow my lead. You're all from Fleming, okay?" Jae appraises us, clad in our comfortable Earth clothes. "Yup, Fleming people are odd. You all fit the description." He turns the car off and the seat belts unbuckle. He exits the car before I can voice my indignation, and we scramble out after him.

"Do you see Rune?" Dustin's head is on a swivel.

"I think he's still in the car," I reply, feeling my palms begin to sweat. What state is Brunner going to be in?

"Borge," Jae calls out to the ogre. "No traffic in the skies? I'm surprised you didn't hit an Argentavis on the way here."

"Didn't I tell you? If you're not at the location before me, there's a 50 drin fee." Borge extends his right hand. I'd forgotten the name of Ethran currency until now.

"We're supposed to be on the same team, Borge." Jae shakes his head but reaches out, tapping his wrist on the ogre's.

"The law demands it, I just follow." Borge snickers.

"What law? The one you made?" Jae sighs. He's probably used to this by now, but I can still feel his annoyance and the urge to punch this guy in the face. Not that punching a tusked face is the most brilliant idea.

"Are these the Fleming citizens?" Borge looks at us.

"Uh... S'up." I raise a hand, cringing internally at myself. When the others make their own awkward attempts at a greeting, I quickly realize that Jae's cover for our behavior was upsettingly accurate.

"The guy's pretty shaken up. Took a while for him to stop quivering." Borge leans towards Jae. "These Fleming folks treat everything like a sightseeing attraction, *ay*?" He snorts.

"Please, we were worried sick," Jadis says, her voice high and eyes doe-like. I can feel the irritation bubbling off her. She should have been an actress.

"It's a good thing I got him before he was dropped into their nests; they've ripped good people to shreds before," Borge comments casually. "Hey, come on out, your friends are here."

The door opens. My broad smile instantly slips from my face and a pulse of shock strikes me from the others.

Emierr lets out a quick, sharp gasp. "That's not Brunner."

BRUNNER

T he thunderous flapping of the colossal bird's wings deafens me, completely drowning out my screams. I watch in horror as Rictor plummets to the ground, and a desperate cry of his name escapes my lips. As my hand stretches toward him and he reaches back, the distance between us becomes painfully clear. A tingling sensation nibbles at my fingertips, only to vanish as the bird carries me farther from Rictor's grasp. I wince as its claws constrict around me. Its keening pierces the air.

To my right, a silver-winged bird carries another wailing man. Our eyes lock briefly before we're torn apart. Dizziness overwhelms me, and I lose consciousness. It feels like I'm in the Transcendent phase: pitch black, calm, and drifting. A distant voice echoes through the darkness. "Wake… run… up!"

Freefall jerks me awake. I land face-first, but I'm too dazed to feel the pain. Disoriented, I scramble to my feet, adrenaline surging through me. As the bird circles the mountain, I seize the opportunity to escape. With trembling hands, I scale the nest's walls, gripping any protrusion I can find. My stomach churns as I look down at the dizzying height. Trees blur far below me, a hundred feet or more down.

My gaze shifts behind me, to the nest's contents—three eggs as tall as me are nestled ominously nearby. At least they aren't hungry chicks. I heave myself up to the edge of the nest, belly pressing into the massive tree limbs it's built from. It's a straight drop below. The nest is set into the face of a cliff. There's no way out.

"Astralis," I mutter desperately. I close my eyes and wait for the tingles to take me, but nothing happens. "Wake up! Astralis!" I screech into the roaring wind, but still nothing.

This isn't supposed to happen. Why did I think nothing could go wrong? Jho died here and I thought I could just waltz into her world?

Fear claws at my chest as I wrack my brain for a solution. Then, cracks pierce the air. I whip around, thinking the nest is starting to crumble from the cliff. But it's worse. Cracks are spreading rapidly along the eggs' ivory surfaces. Terrified, I recoil as a yellow beak pokes its way through a hole at the top. I don't know how long I stay there, clinging to the nest wall as talon-tipped feet crunch through the shell. Then thin, wet wings. I curl into a ball, hoping their senses will be dulled at first. One by one, the silvery chicks collapse from their eggs, lying in piles of white shards.

It doesn't take them long to find their feet. I'm frozen, terrified to even breathe as they wobble upright. To my horror, their bright, onyx eyes fix directly on me. I scramble to higher ground, narrowly avoiding their snapping beaks. But my reprieve is short-lived.

The mother bird's calls echo through the air, signaling her return. My knees tremble as I look below. I either fall to my death or get ripped apart by Ethran dinosaurs. What kind of choices are those? A gust of wind knocks me off balance and, with a loud shriek, I fall from the nest's edge. *This is it; I'm dead.*

Air rushes out of my lungs as I plummet hundreds of feet, the icy winds howling my eulogy. I crash into the trees below, their branches gashing my frozen skin, and limbs battering my body like a cruel game of pong. Miraculously, my hand snags onto a tree branch, halting my painful descent. That must've been a few hundred feet. It doesn't matter; I'm still high up this mountain. The trees that cradle me sprout straight from the rocky side of the cliff. I strain to pull myself up, but exhaustion has sapped my strength. Peering below, I spy more trees, all huddled in a circle.

This is a good sign, maybe it's a cluster of trees connected to the ground. If I'm lucky enough to catch another branch, perhaps I'll survive. At least, I'm more likely to survive than if I just let myself rot up here.

"Okay..." I breathe out and mentally count down. *One... two... three!* My body refuses to obey. I let out a weak cry as my arms begin to falter. Jhoana's face flashes in my mind—her smile, her soft eyes, her laughter. I have to survive for her.

"Fuck!" I groan in pain. Taking a deep breath, I release my grip, trusting whatever chance I have at survival.

Plummeting toward the treetops, I brace myself for impact, aiming to grab hold of a branch. Instead, I crash straight through the branches as if they were mere illusions, unveiling a cavern below. Trees surround the gaping hole, their branches stretching toward the light—a deceptive facade of my only chance for survival.

Silence fills my ears.

As I hit the water's surface, pain shoots through me, cracking something deep within. I sink further, gazing up at the distant shimmering light. *Why can't I move? Is my spine damaged?*

Shimmering gold lights emanate from below, and for a fleeting moment, I feel like I'm adrift in space. Glittering stars dance around me, offering a surreal spectacle in my final moments. *Is this what dying looks like?* But then, the stars converge, enveloping the water in a brilliant glow before dissipating into darkness. My body convulses involuntarily, desperate for air. In that moment, a tingling sensation grips my chest.

As desperation consumes me, a distortion ripples through the air, fragmenting the images around me. Though I stay motionless, everything lurches forward, the light above growing nearer. In a blink of an eye, I find myself on the surface of the cave pool, bringing a cascade of water with me. Gasping and retching, I gulp in a lungful of air, the agony of the fall washing over me in full force.

How did I do that?

I begin to crawl from the pool, but I'm met with searing pain coursing through my entire body. I've taken more damage than I thought. Not even a few minutes here, and I'm already out of commission. Summoning every ounce of strength, I wrench myself onto my back, tears mingling with laughter as relief floods over me—I could've been impaled by tree branches or splattered on a boulder. My mind whirls with thoughts of the Squad, likely mourning my presumed death.

How the fuck am I going to find them? There's now way I'm surviving this alone.

The healing spell comes to mind—the most important spell to remember. Though the others didn't teach me, I practiced it last night. I guess it's time to put my magick ability to the test.

"I'm coming, guys," I whisper, determination fueling my weary limbs. With the last reserves of my strength, I clap my hands together and a soft orange glow blossoms from my palms. *It works!* Seeing it in person is definitely better than picturing it in my head. I breathe a sigh of relief as I weave the spell over myself, hands resting on my chest.

My eyes close and a soothing energy washes over me, the pain gradually fading as whatever had cracked inside me knits back together. The glow dissipates, leaving only the echo of pain.

My eyes snap open, and I sit up, patting down the areas that hurt.

"I'm a fucking wizard."

A laugh of disbelief echoes through the cave as I rise to my feet. The shimmering water catches my attention. A cavern hiding a small pool of Ethereal Water... *Did I just become a Keeper?* It matched Jhoana's description of her secret cave, but I couldn't be in Verglas, could I?

As questions race through my mind, I shout, "Astralis!" My voice reverberates through the cavern, glowing with mystical light of shimmering crystals whispering secrets in the air. It was worth a try. Dustin said these mountains are Zaltana, so if I'm here, that means the Brae, or other citizens must be around. But will the Squad come looking for me here in Zaltana, or head straight to Terrene? The thought of them choosing Terrene stings, but my priority is finding Jhoana, no matter what. I can't fault them if it's their priority too.

Casting one last glance at the cave of wonders, I mentally note my discovery before turning toward the bright lights ahead—the way out. Peering out from the cave entrance, I'm greeted by a wall of furry vines, their white tendrils intertwining like delicate lace. Slowly, I push through them, emerging onto a dirt road.

I glance cautiously in both directions, spotting dark gray grass leading to an expanse of forest across the road. Great, more forest. Looking back at the vines, I realize their enormity, covering most of the mountainside. From this angle, the mountain looks even more colossal and jagged, looming ominously over me.

I take stock of my surroundings. *Which way would civilization be?* A soft growl to my right interrupts my thoughts. Turning, I come face to face with what I think is a plain old grizzly bear, standing tall on its hind legs.

"Oh shit," I mutter, taking a slow step back. *The astral weapon spell!* I clap my hands together, summoning the orange glow. The bear drops to all fours, growling menacingly. As I attempt to cast the spell, I realize I've forgotten the signs. Panic surges through me as I fumble, but before I can react, the bear charges.

"Fuck!" I bolt in the opposite direction.

My heart pounds like a drum as I sprint along the path, the hungry growls of the bear drawing closer. Approaching a fork in the road, I veer left at random. The path narrows, and my legs threaten to give out. Ahead, I see the end of the road—a wall several feet high blocks the path. Glancing behind me, I can see ropey saliva splattering from the bear's jaws, its eyes pitch black, as if possessed.

My chest feels like a nest of hornets as I focus on the top of the wall. My surroundings begin to fragment like rippling mirrors, but at the last second, my gaze shifts to the base of the wall. It's as if I can see beyond it—the continuation of the path. With renewed hope, I thunder forward. Panic grips me as I watch the ripples close. I try to focus on keeping the path open, but it's like trying to flex a muscle I didn't know I had. With one last flicker of the path, It vanishes, leaving me to collide with a very real stone surface. My back hits the dirt hard. I groan, the wind knocked out of me.

As my vision clears, I spot a figure atop the wall, black strings intertwining endlessly and its eyeless gaze fixed on me. My heart stops. A shadow. All of Rictor's storytelling could have never prepared me for this. It jerks its head behind me. I lift myself onto my elbows and look over my blood-crusted shoulder. The bear is fleeing, leaving a trail of dust in its wake. When I turn back to the shadow atop the wall, I realize it's gone. In its place stands another bear, unlike any bear that could exist on Earth. This one is larger than anything I've ever seen, towering from its perch on the wall.

The beast stands tall and majestic on his hind legs, its fur a mesmerizing blend of gold and silver, radiant in the sunlight. Its sharp, intelligent eyes bore into me, sending goosebumps rippling across my skin. The shadow transformed into a Crown Beast.

You have got to be kidding me.

I edge backward on trembling arms, fixated on the creature above me. As the bear descends from the wall, its massive paws move with a regal grace. It advances with a menacing snarl. It's over. I've failed to keep my promise. With a heavy heart, I close my eyes, resigned to my fate for the third time today.

"I just wanted to see her again," I whimper, tears streaming down my cheeks. "I wanted her to know it was always her from the beginning. I'm sorry, Jho." I whisper my final words, bracing myself for the impending attack. The Crown Beast's hot breath washes over me, its growls deafening my senses, drowning out my thoughts. Just as terror consumes me, a slobbery, wet tongue oozes across my face.

I spit out the beast's saliva with deep disgust and wipe my face clean. The terrifying monster that had approached me is gone. Instead, an enormous pile of silky fur and shiny, amber eyes lies before me. Maybe luck's not done with me yet. Remembering how the others bonded with their Crown Beasts, I wonder if this is that moment. I really don't want to end up like Dustin with missing fingers or, worse, a limb.

With a mix of nerves and curiosity, I tentatively raise my right hand. The beast closes its eyes, likely sensing my uncertainty. Taking a deep breath, I gently place my hand on its head.

A surge of energy courses through me and images flood my mind, vivid and unexpected. The first scene unfurls within Akeurimja Forest, where I'm encircled by a horde of shadow creatures, their forms shifting and twisting in the dim light. Abruptly, the vision shifts to a meteorite, much larger than the shard I carry, hurtling down from space.

A realization hits me hard—these are the Crown Beast's memories.

The montage continues, snapping back to just moments ago. I see the rainbow-feathered bird that abducted me, its powerful wings beating the air as it carries me away. The scene changes again, and now the shadow trails behind us. It watches as I'm dropped into the nest. Determination fills its essence as it climbs the mountain's rugged face, peering over to see me plummeting.

Without hesitation, the Crown Beast leaps down the mountain, its movements a blur of speed and agility as it races toward the ground. It reaches a path and pauses, its heightened senses tuning into distant screams—my screams. Following the sound, it scales a rock wall and comes upon the bear menacing me. In that instant, the Shadow morphs, taking the form of the bear, its presence enough to send the real bear scampering away in fear. Our eyes lock, and I feel an intense connection snap into place between us. The bonding is complete.

Pulling back slightly, I try to process the rush of emotions and newfound connection. Then, the beast addresses me, not through audible sounds, but directly into my mind.

"*Can you understand me now?*" Its deep, grizzly voice resonates inside my head. It sounds distinctly male.

"Yes," I whisper aloud. *This cannot be happening.* All at once, I feel all my fear leave my body.

"*I did not think I would need to become a beast, yet here I stand,*" he snorts.

"T—Thank you. For saving me."

"*I didn't do much, child. You survived that fall all on your own.*"

"But still. Thank you." I get up. I shouldn't be shocked anymore—I've already been abducted by a dinosaur-sized parrot, nearly been eaten by its offspring, fallen from a mountain, landed in possibly-magic cave water, and healed myself with glowing hands. But the sight of this otherworldly bear still had my jaw hanging open.

His eyes scan me, and without warning, he unleashes a blood-curdling roar that hits me like a strong wind.

"*If you are to ride me, I do not wish to be wet.*"

I think I peed myself a little. I gulp, patting down my instantly dried clothes. *I'm seriously going to die here, aren't I?*

"Ride... you?" I say without thinking. "I mean, where to?" I quickly add, hoping not to offend the gigantic bear who could easily devour me in one gulp.

"*To the sixth nation. They're guarding something that holds immense power.*" The bear kneels, waiting for me to hop on his impossibly broad back. I can see silver guard hairs overlaying a golden undercoat. *The* sixth *nation?* I open my mouth to ask but shake my head. I have more important things to deal with right now.

"My friends," I say instead. "I lost them, I need to head to Zaltana."

"*The Nobles? I sensed their bond with the other Crowns. You'll see them again, I promise you.*"

It's a good thing I know what these words mean. "I can just walk, it's no trouble." I laugh nervously.

"*There's not enough time,*" he growls. "*Something malevolent is happening here. We must warn the people, so hop on.*"

"Okay." I give in, not wanting to piss off the giga bear. I grab onto his fur, unsure how to mount an animal the size of a school bus. But then, he stands, scooping me into the air with his left paw. With a startled yell, I land squarely on his back. I have to seize two fistfuls of fur to keep myself upright as he takes off into the trees. I lean into the wind, bending low over the massive head in front of me. I'm riding a damn bear.

The landscape blurs past, vibrant with magickal flora and shimmering streams. Enchanted creatures flit through the air, their wings leaving trails of sparkling light. I can hardly believe it—I'm finally in the world Jhoana always spoke about. Everything feels surreal, yet so incredibly alive. The colors, the sounds, the energy—it's overwhelming. The Squad's stories don't even come close to capturing this wonder. This is beyond anything I ever imagined.

"Um, excuse me..." I yell over the rushing wind. "Uh... What do I call you?"

His large, golden eye rolled back to look at me. Something like amusement sparkled there. He seemed to ponder for a moment before replying.

"You may call me Oberon."

"Oberon? Like the fairy king?" I ask, nonplussed. Then, louder, I say, "I'm Brunner."

Oberon chuffs a laugh. *"I know."*

"How does this bond thing work?" I ask, leaning closer to his ear.

"We believe it to be a curse." The deep voice in my mind sounds eerily clear, unaffected by the roar of wind.

"The shadows. Can you communicate with each other?"

"Of course we can. Did you think we were just mindless creatures, roaming that forest for eternity?"

Is this thing being sarcastic? "Yeah, actually," I say honestly.

"The answer is yes. We speak to each other the way I communicate with you. Most shadows are quite dramatic. You would be, too, if you could only speak to the same beings for a millennia. But it may startle you to know that we don't like violence."

"Then why do you kill? Countless people have died entering the forest." My tone is not of judgment, but genuine curiosity. That's all I've heard about the shadows. Dangerous.

"We are provoked. We cannot understand you creatures more than you can understand us. But time and time again, they come to attack and to rob us of our home. What else are we meant to do?."

"Couldn't you leave?"

"You think we haven't tried?" Oberon snorts. *"We can't. The forest binds us."*

This new information sparks my urge to excitedly add lore to the notebook. Cursed to stay in the forest... But here he is, roaming until he found me. Something isn't adding up.

"Were you always a shadow? What even *are* you?" As the words leave my mouth, I realize I'm getting too comfortable.

"I believe we were something else entirely before we were "shadows." But none remember. Hold on tightly."

I have just a second to twist my fingers deeper into his fur before he leaps into the air, sailing over an obscenely large, felled tree. From this vantage point, I can see the Ethereal Tree glimmering in the distance. How did I miss that when I was up on the mountain? I begin to rise up off Oberon's back as gravity reclaims him. I clamp my legs around his sides and tighten my grip on his fur. The world around us blurs momentarily before coming back into sharp focus as we touch down.

We emerge from the forest into a vast meadow, where the tall grass waves like an emerald sea under the gentle breeze. Everything looks almost oversaturated, the colors more vibrant than anything I've ever seen. In the distance, a horde of massive animals—some with long necks, others with armored plates and spiked tails—thunder across the meadow. *Those look like... dinosaurs.* The ground trembles beneath their weight, and I can feel the vibrations through the bear's powerful frame.

The heavy beat of enormous wings echoes above me. My eyes shoot to the sky, terrified yet another bird has come to finish the job. But it's definitely not a bird.

"Holy shit," I whisper.

Above us, a dragon with iridescent scales glides gracefully through the sky. Its wings span so wide, they cast a shadow over us. The dragon's eyes, gleaming like molten gold, lock onto mine for a heartbeat. If I wasn't sitting on a yacht-sized, magic bear, I would have been horrified. Then, as if deeming us unworthy of further attention, it continues its flight, disappearing into the horizon.

I'm seriously going to die here.

The meadow stretches out endlessly, a vibrant expanse of life and color. As Oberon carries me forward, I feel a surge of determination. This place, with all its marvels and mysteries, holds the key to finding her. And I won't stop until I do. I need to learn as much as I can.

"Hey, the bond, you said it was a curse?" I ask, leaning down near his left ear.

"You're not going to keep quiet, are you?"

"No." I grin despite myself.

He chuffs again. *"Yes, a curse. Allowing yourself to accept the form of a Crown, you condemn yourself to one physical form for all of eternity. To be trapped is a feeling many of my kind abhor. As a shadow, we are bound by nothing, to only exist. Our minds are not like those of physical creatures. We do not experience emotions in the way that you understand them. But to be a beast, bonded to one of your kind—"*

"Means to burden yourself with emotions," I finish aloud. Even here, people are a problem.

"Yes. Becoming a Crown means we lose our connection with the shadows. Once a Crown bonds with another, they inherit a piece of them. For something as free and shapeless as a shadow, to forever join oneself to a

*being built on a foundation of problems... Well. Of course we consider it
to be a curse."*

"So... Why do you do it?"

A sigh gusted from Oberon's muzzle. *"The first beast to abandon the
shadows fell in love with worldly beings. She chose a life of endless form
and became a guardian of the Ethereal."*

"Was it Maral?" The first nation was Terrene and she is the one
who claimed guardianship over the Ethereal Lake. She also sounded
less animal than the others when I heard Emierr's description. A
female elk with antlers, ghostly white fur, and human eyes. I think
Emierr even said she had three toes instead of two. As if the first
transformation from shadow to beast had been a test run gone
slightly wrong.

"Yes," Oberon answered. *"She is the mother of beasts. Four others
followed her, and it's been many years since another has turned. Well, not
until me."*

"But if you guys were trapped in the forest, how did the Crown
Beasts escape?"

"They turned into beasts," he said simply. *"A forest of shadow cannot
hold that which is not shadow."* The sound of his paws striking the dirt
slowed. *"It has been five hundred years since I last spoke to another being.
It feels very strange to talk so much."*

"Five hundred? Hasn't it only been two hundred years since your
species arrived here?" All the information I studied in the notebook and learned from the Squad is locked tightly in my brain's
core memory box. Jadis said it was two hundred years when they
appeared out of nowhere, I'm sure of it.

"We have existed for far longer." He sounds amused again and his
breakneck pace resumes. *"But as I told you, we have no memory of the
time before the forest. We do not know what brought us to those woods,
nor what trapped us there. But our existence far exceeds that of humanity.
Of that, I am certain."*

This talking bear is a treasure trove of information and I have
absolutely nothing to write it down with. I sigh, mentally storing
this conversation in my head.

"We're here." His paws lumber to a stop.

I snap upright and look around. I'd been so immersed in shadow
revelations that I didn't even notice the trees change. We've left behind the looming, craggy trees of Zaltana. Now, I'm surrounded by
shorter trees, their smooth, white bark marred by black markings.
Their leaves are an array of autumn colors: red, gold, orange, and
vivid yellow. They tremble in the chilly breeze, giving an illusion of
shimmer. The pale expanse of autumn majesty is harshly broken by
a massive swathe of pitch black.

A gate stands before us, made of obsidian-like material that gleams in the sunlight. Intricate carvings of ancient runes and symbols weave across its surface, pulsating with a faint, ethereal glow. The gate is set into a pristine, colossal white wall, stretching as far as the eye can see in both directions. It blends smoothly into the chalky bark of the trees. The wall is decorated with elegant frescoes, depicting legendary battles where children appear as heroes, intertwined with swirling patterns of silver and gold.

So this is the sixth nation. The Squad only mentioned five, but I guess a lot can happen in thirty-two years. Regardless, there should be actual people here. Maybe they can help me find Jhoana or at least put me on the right track to regroup with the Squad. The air hums with magick, and I feel a surge of hope.

"*Before we go in, remember, you are a Noble now,*" Oberon rumbles. "*This nation's people worship the Nobles in a more... Ah... unique way than other nations.*"

My heart gutters to a stop at this. I knew in theory that I was probably a Noble now, but I was holding out hope that Oberon was just a very polite shadow. Not even two hours in, and this place has slung power on my shoulders that I'm not equipped to deal with.

"So... they're like a cult?" I finally say. *Wonder if this is the Mormon 2.0 origin story.*

"*Devout followers,*" he corrects me. "*They will not permit me entrance as a shadow. We're going to need each other for this. You translate what I have to say, and you can find your fellow Nobles.*"

"Okay, wait." I shake my head. "You and I both know that I'm not sticking around to be a Noble. I'm here to save my friend and get home. You need to tell me what it is you're up to so I play my part in whatever scheme this is." I cross my arms, an eyebrow raised at him.

He growls and I take a step back, bravado quashed.

"*You speak strong words for a creature made of meat.*"

My blood runs cold and I prepare to run for my life. Then he grins. A bear just grinned at me. It was horrifying.

"*You saw my memory of the night the sky turned to blood.*"

I cast my mind back, sifting through the jumbled mess of our combined memories.

"Yes. A meteorite fell, right?"

"*Meteorite,*" he says slowly, as if rolling the word on his tongue. "*That... meteorite... is of that which birthed magick. When it fell, it landed here, and a society was built around it.*"

"So," I say, frowning, "You want me to go in there and, what, steal it?"

Oberon blinks his amber eyes at me and a strange snuffling overtakes his body. *Is he... laughing at me?* "

"*No*," he responds when the sound subsides. "*It's too powerful; it's safer here.*"

I stare at him, perplexed. "Then what do you want from me?"

His enormous head sways irritably. "*These people and what they protect are in danger. I cannot warn them alone. I must speak through you.*"

I suppose that's better than robbery. I feel like I just unlocked a side quest.

"All right," I agree. "I'll be their new Noble." Saying it out loud almost makes me cringe, but the title undeniably has power. I feel way more important than the Barnes and Noble manager I am in reality.

"*You are looking for a girl.*" The bear's observation catches me off guard. Of course it works both ways. "*She appears often in your memories.*"

"She's one of the Nobles," is all I can say. I don't know why I can't just admit that I love Jhoana. Maybe because I know how it looks from the outside. An adult man pining after a girl who died at twelve. The Squad saw right through me, but even then, I never said it out loud. Oberon's eyes linger on my face. I just shake my head and begin walking toward the obsidian gate. The ground behind me shakes slightly under the tread of gargantuan paws.

As we approach, an unseen sensor activates, bathing me in a soft blue light which scans me from head to toe. I must have passed the test because a low grinding sound vibrates through the soil as the gate parts, its massive halves shuddering apart. Beyond them, a vibrant, magickal city lies, bathed in soft, golden light.

People and leyfolk fill the streets, dressed in flowing white garments laced with intricate patterns, similar to the ones along the outer wall. They look nothing like what I imagined. Each person and being seems to float along the curving pathways, their clothes billowing in the autumn breeze. Even the buildings are washed with limestone. A seaside town in the middle of the woods.

Amidst the crowd, I notice elegant leyfolk with long, pointed ears and luminescent skin—they're from the Sperclen Tribe, the Fae. Their clothes shimmer with silver embroidery. Tiny, winged figures flit about, leaving trails of sparkling dust. Their dresses are patterned like butterfly wings—they're pixies, I think. More members of the Sperclen Tribe.

Larger, horse-like beings with human upper bodies stride confidently through the crowded roads—centaurs. Their upper bodies are draped in spangled robes, while their lower halves are concealed in the robe's overlong train. Aquatic figures with iridescent tails swim in water channels alongside the streets—mermaids? Or merfolk? Their clothes are adorned with seashells and pearls. They belong to the Commisceo Tribe, half-humans.

I spot another type of creature, resembling majestic lions with eagle wings, walking among the crowd—I can't believe I'm staring at actual griffins. Their white and gold feathers are dazzling. Each wears a colorful halter and pulls a cart laden with fruits, vegetables, or cloth behind them. In the notebook, it said they are impossible to tame, but here they are, domesticated in this hidden city.

I take a deep breath, excitement swelling within me. I want to dash through the crowd, peppering each resident with questions about their species, this city, their tribe, everything. But I can't do that. This is my chance to seek help, find answers, and maybe, just maybe, discover Jhoana's whereabouts.

The moment I step in, everyone on the street stops and turns to stare at me. Gasps of shock ripple through the crowd, and someone shouts, "A Crown Beast!" Instantly, people surround me, bombarding me with questions I can't fully make out. I try to step back but the throng of excited beings continues to close in.

"I told you, they're devout followers."

Panicking now, I look back through the gate and yelp, "Help me!" The bear, towering as tall as the gate itself, hunches down to enter. His lips raise off those steak knife teeth as he growls a warning at the stampede.

I, however, am distracted by what I see in Oberon's mouth. *Do bears usually have that many teeth?* I lean in just a bit closer. *Is that a third nostril?*

Griffins flap their wings and take to the air as the onlookers cautiously step back, their faces masks of fear and respect. The bear's presence beside me is both intimidating and comforting. I chuckle nervously and say, "Thanks."

"This is the second time I've saved you," he says, blowing hot air from his three nostrils. The closest people scuttled further away. Is this what Emierr meant when his Crown Beast was mean to him?

"Thank the Tree." A man in a white suit stands before us, his wild, colorless hair framing eyes that gleam with manic intensity. The suit, pristine in color yet oddly rumpled, accentuates his eccentricity. He looks like a madman dancing on the edge of genius and insanity. "Could it be... a new Noble?"

"Yes." I swallow. Here I go. "Uh. I will be your nation's Noble." My imposter syndrome is positively howling.

"Good. Tell them I am taking Vereilles under my guardianship," Oberon says. *"Or something to that effect."*

The crowd creeps around once again, fear leaving their faces to be replaced by admiration.

"Is it true?" a human mother asks. Her chubby-cheeked baby is swaddled in endless folds of cottony cloth. Just behind her, I see one of the merfolk leap into the air, its scales glittering in the sun. Wait. Not just from the sun. In a rush of magickal dust, the tail splits and twists into legs, though they retain the grayish, scaly color.

"Have the Nobles returned?" he asks. Several more merfolk join him on land. One woman with strings of pearls in her hair makes eye contact with me. I realize she's wearing nothing below those streaming green locks. She winks at me. Heat rushes into my face and my eyes leap to the ground, staring hard at a little piece of quartz by my toes.

"Well?" The man in the white suit is watching me expectantly. My mouth opens and closes like a beached fish. *What the hell do I say?*

"Tell them Oberon has chosen me to deliver a message to all of you," the bear says, not breaking his stare with the people.

"Oberon, the Crown Beast, has chosen me to be his... champion... to deliver a message to all of you."

"I feel that you are attempting to sound impressive and falling sorely short."

I purse my lips, side-eyeing the beast. *Do I look like I know what the fuck I'm doing?*

"Just repeat what I say," Oberon instructs. *"Word for word."*

His voice echoes in my head and I repeat, "Listen to me, people of Vereilles. I speak through my Noble now, so that you may hear me. I am the sixth Crown Beast of Ethra."

Silent awe blankets the crowd.

"Yes, you are right," I continue, channeling the rumble that vibrates my skull into speech. "The Nobles have returned. They journey in secret now, but soon they will be among us once again. The man you see before you is the first Noble of Vereilles: Brunner Fischer."

A cheer erupts, my name a chant on the lips of every person and leyfolk before me. *This is so culty.*

"But there is grave news befalling—"

The man in the white suit cuts me off. "Thank you, *Noble.*" He nods slightly at me and turns to the crowd. "Brothers and sisters, we must rejoice, for the gods have answered our prayers, our beloved Nobles have returned. The Day of Awakening is upon us!"

The crowd roars and wild-eyed joy blazes across the sea of faces throttling the city entrance.

I don't know about asking for help anymore. They really give me Mormon 2.0 vibes.

"What does this mean? Mormon 2.0?" Oberon echoes in my mind.

"Wait. You can hear my thoughts?"

"From the moment we bonded, yes."

"Why are you only telling me now? This could've been a lot smoother without me shouting in your ear the whole way here."

"Perhaps I enjoy watching you fumble." His low laugh resounds in my head.

Great. I had to be bonded to the insufferable one.

"I heard that."

"Good." I try to suppress the grin forming on my face.

"Let us prepare for the festival!" the man I assume is the leader continues. "Our saviors will arrive and bless us with their presence. Until then, we must keep our fires lit, our food hot, and our drinks flowing!" The man sweeps his arms out, as if dispelling a puff of smoke. The crowd disperses at once, filling the streets with a thrum of excitement.

The leader's tone shifts to serious as he turns to us. "I do not appreciate you spreading bad news unannounced."

I stare at him blankly. Do these people not get bad news? Or does all bad news just go through *him*?

"You need to let him know we do not come to disrupt their way of living but to warn them." Oberon's voice booms in my ears.

I clear my throat. "Sir, um—"

"Amos."

"Amos, we don't mean to bring down your spirits with bad news." I choose my words delicately. If I screw this up, it's all over. I may never find the others, and I won't be able to find Jhoana.

"Tell him not all is bad news. Yet it is crucial that we convey it as Vereilles's new Noble and Crown Beast."

And just like that, I'm subjugated to responsibility. Exactly like the Squad was as kids. But these are all just words, and I have to fake it till I make it, for Jhoana.

"But, Oberon, he brings not just bad news. Your nation has no Guardian and no Noble. We are here to offer protection. Delegate for your seat at the table with the other nations."

"Boy, what are you doing?" Oberon snarls.

"Trust me, I've read the Art of War. *We let them hear what they want."*

"Do you forget where you are? They'll fish out the truth from you."

I ignore him. Even if they can read my thoughts, they still have to cast the spell first, so I'm safe for now.

"From what exactly? We are not blind to the world outside. All of us have suffered from the instability of these difficult times, but we found this place and made it our sanctuary. No one has ever discovered our walls; not until you." Amos looks me in the eye, almost piercing my façade.

Oberon's voice echoes in my head, and I deliver his message. "They're after the meteor shard you protect."

Amos's face becomes grim. "H-how did you kn—"

"Oberon witnessed it fall from the skies. He saw your people discover the shard and watched you build your fortress around it. He believes in what you stand for. The only ones who can save us all are the Nobles from Earth." The name of my home planet triggers thoughts about superstrings. They are aware of Earth, but do these people know about the multiverse?

"Wait." Amos raises a hand. "That is enough for me to let go of my hesitance. I would like to speak to Oberon directly."

"Only Nobles can speak to their Crown Beast," I say, confused.

"I know. That is why I will be in your head. The bond is a connection through the mind. A simple mind reading spell would theoretically allow me to hear Oberon's voice and, as I project my thoughts to you, he would hear mine."

"Can that work?" I ask Oberon.

"I'm not sure. Technically, I am only a few hours old."

"Ha ha." I sigh through my nose.

"The spell, of course, will only work if you allow me into your mind. I swear to you that I will not read anything else." This is so strange; I'm really having a conversation about using my brain as a telephone.

"Why don't you just do it? Wouldn't it be easier to steal all the information you need? Skip all the formalities," I say without thinking. I'm getting too comfortable again.

"I'm not a savage," Amos says with disgust. "We uphold our values in Vereilles, and nothing is more valuable than honesty. You have my word." He claps his hands together, and they glow a bright lavender. I'm surprised it isn't white. He weaves the spell, his fingers and hands moving in fluid, intricate patterns, like a dancer performing tutting. As he completes the spell, he extends his glowing hand to me. "The spell breaks once you deny me."

"Do we trust it?"

"You heard him, you can break the spell anytime you like," Oberon rumbles.

My hand lifts above Amos's, hesitant, but willing to show we're on his side. His fingers close around mine, and then the glow disappears as we both let go.

"Did it work?"

"I can hear you." Amos pierces through my head. It's getting too crowded here. *"Oberon?"*

"Amos," Oberon replies.

"It worked," Amos says. *"Let's walk."* He turns and begins to lead us

down the expansive main thoroughfare.

"The... meteorite, *you're keeping it here, right?*" Oberon lumbers along to my left.

"*It is safe with high-level magickal security. Only I know the disenchantment spell.*"

This feels like I'm schizophrenic.

We make a turn, edging between neatly tended gardens and dome-like homes. Walking through the narrow, cobblestone streets, I marvel at the seamless blend of ancient charm and futuristic design. The ground beneath my feet glows faintly with enchanted flagstones guiding our way, each step illuminating a path forward. The buildings look like earthen mounds, coated in protective layers of limestone. Creeping vines hold each home in a protective embrace and feature windows with digital displays showing weather updates and news. Terracotta roofs are interspersed with solar panels, harnessing the sun's energy.

Amos leads us past an aged well that hums with an otherworldly energy, its water infused with a soft, blue luminescence. I don't think I will ever stop being awed by all of this. I saw a dragon earlier; I'm never getting over that.

I hope I can find someone who knows anything about Jho.

"*Are you not listening to us?*" Oberon brings me back to my thoughts.

"*Jho? You mean the Noble of Verglas? Has something gone wrong?*" Worry laces Amos's thoughts.

"*Sorry. Ethra is so much more magical than I had imagined.*" I admit, my head still on a constant swivel. I need like twelve more eyes.

"*I'm sure Earth is just as magickal,*" Amos says courteously.

"*Yeah... no. You wouldn't survive one day in my world.*" I snort, imagining Amos attempting to file his taxes.

"*If you want to find your friend, he's the best person to ask,*" Oberon cuts in through my idiotic fantasy.

"*Yes, we will do anything for the Nobles,*" Amos agrees immediately. "*Vereilles was founded by my father, who was saved by the Allied Organization Squad. He believed the Nobles would return one day, and here you are. We will do everything in our power to aid you.*"

Amos's words seem genuine. His eccentric behavior is questionable, but his loyalty feels real. I believe him, though this could just be an effect from the spell.

"*I need to be honest,*" I say after a few minutes of quiet walking. "*The Nobles didn't abandon you or Ethra; they just didn't realize the stakes. They were a bunch of kids who thought this was all a game. They returned to Ethra today, not to resume their duties, but to rescue our friend, Jhoana. She's been trapped here since the Nobles disappeared. We don't even know if she's still alive, but her time on Earth is running out. She's been asleep for so long, and...*" I close my eyes against a sudden wave of tears.

"*This changes everything.*" Amos stops walking and looks at both of us.

"*Then you understand now what this all means.*" Oberon growls. "*I need to speak with the other Crown Beasts.*"

I, on the other hand, am totally lost. "*What does this all mean?*"

"*This really is your first time here, isn't it?*" Amos shakes his head.

"*I have so many questions.*" I grin.

"The looming threat of the O'rians means that balance will be tipped in the coming days," Amos says, switching from mind to actual speech. "If they are looking for the shard we protect, that means they need the power of the Source for their plans. In their hands, it could break everything we know."

He says all of these things very quickly, as if I understand what any of it means. "The... O'rians?"

"*Blood magick users,*" Oberon offers vaguely. I trip over a jutting flagstone. *Blood* magick? That definitely wasn't in the notebook. What is happening to Ethra?

"*I must warn the nations,*" Amos says, but his eyes wander.

"*What is it?*" Oberon breathes.

"*If they're looking for Vereilles, then there's a probability they're intercepting frequencies. I will not put my people in danger. I have to send a messenger through the Gates.*" Amos presses on his left ear and murmurs something I don't catch. A human woman wearing a flawless white blouse appears from a side street as though summoned by magick. Maybe she *was* summoned by magick.

"*Then I must be on my way as well.*" Oberon turns his enormous head to me.

"*What, no, you can't leave me,*" I say, panic spiking in my chest.

"*You will be safe here until your friends find you.*"

"*Oberon is right.*" Amos's thoughts spear right through the verbal conversation he's having with the woman. He's a hell of a *multitasker.* "*Vereilles has Diviners using illusionary magick. As far as anyone can see, this area is just a forest. And no one passes our border wall.*"

"*Where will you go then?*" I ask Oberon, trying to steady my breathing.

"*The Crowns are long overdue for a family meeting. If all six Crown Beasts come together, the world will listen. Everything from this moment changes.*"

I purse my lips and manage a nod. Since I've been here, Oberon has been my only safety net. I don't know if it's our bond, but he pushes away all my worries. If he's not here to protect me, then I'm as good as dead. Okay, that's probably a touch dramatic.

"*Brunner, do not be afraid. Remember, you survived the Argentavis all on your own, you're braver than you think.*" He presses his head against my body, knocking me off balance.

"I don't know what I'm doing," I admit. I'm not supposed to feel this way, I promised I'd do whatever it takes. But... my hands, they won't stop shaking. "Please... I—"

"*I'm never far. Our connection is forever. Your thoughts will be with me, and when you truly need me, I will come back for you.*"

That worked. Oberon's words cut through me like butter, and I let out a sigh of relief, placing a hand on the soft fur between his rounded ears. Were those... a second pair of ears?

"*I thought you didn't like me,*" he snorts.

"You saved my life twice," I lean closer to inspect the top of his head. "*Why do you have four ears?*"

"Noble Brunner, you have our protection, I guarantee it," Amos says. The woman beside him flashes a soft smile.

Oh man, she's beautiful.

Amos clears his throat. My cheeks flush red.

"Denied," I blurt out, severing his connection to my brain. I'm never letting anyone in my head again.

"*I must be on my way,*" Oberon's voice echoes. "*My brother, Ade' is the closest. He was always the easiest to talk to.*"

"He sounds a lot like the one he's bonded to," I say fondly. "*Tell Ade' his Noble is a father now. He'd be proud of what he's become.*"

Oberon nods.

"He's going to Zaltana first," I tell Amos.

"Then we must do our part as well. Please follow my understudy, Noble, she will take you to your quarters." Amos gestures to the pretty brunette at his side.

"*Thank you again, Oberon.*" I give him one last farewell pat.

"*I didn't just choose you on a whim. You've always been worthy.*"

"*You peeked at my memories, not fair.*"

"*Until we meet again.*"

"He's leaving," I tell Amos. Oberon stands on his hind legs, a silent promise in his eyes, before dropping back to all fours, and padding off to find the other Crown Beasts.

"*I'll be borrowing this,*" he rumbles in my head. Suddenly, he blinks out of sight. *Did he just... Does that mean I can... Okay, they can use our Keeper abilities.* More mental notes as well as a reminder to figure out how the hell I can tap into that power too.

The citizens rise, and all eyes are glued to me again. I stare back down at the dirt uncomfortably. Amos and the woman rise from the road with their fellow cult members. They are the Mormon 2.0. Emierr will agree when he sees them.

"Much to do," Amos says, businesslike. "I'll be right behind you." He raises a hand and waves everyone back to whatever they were doing.

"My Noble, I am Livia," the woman says. Her eyes are a warm brown, matching the deep cinnamon shade of her hair. A smile curves the corners of her full lips. "I am pleased to meet you. We've waited for quite some time for the Nobles from Earth to return. It is an honor." She bows her head.

"Um... No need for that. Just Brunner is fine." I chuckle nervously. "Lead the way." My body spasms between a bow and a gesture to go ahead. *What the fuck was* that? She gives me a soft laugh and begins walking back down the little alley she came from. I cringe and shuffle along behind her.

"Please forgive my father; he is a gentle soul, I promise you," she says, glancing back at me.

"*Father?*" I choke. "He looks like he's just a couple of years older than I am."

"Ah, of course. I forget how different aging is on Earth. Father was eighteen when he last saw the Nobles. He is now fifty."

"Right," I say, trying to remember Rictor's explanation about Ethra's fountain of youth–radiation. . "Your dad seems like he really loves this place. No need to apologize for that."

She nods, a true smile cracking on her face.

"Um. How old are *you*?" I regret the question the moment it exits my mouth.

Livia laughs aloud at this but does not answer.

As she guides me through the narrow, winding streets, each uneven cobblestone beneath my feet feels like a step back in time. The houses in this part of the city are taller, two or three storeys, but coated in the same snowy layer of limestone. Their walls are shared, creating a wall of residences and shops, unbroken by side alleys. The ivy is thicker, forming a shaggy coat across the building façades. Vibrant flowers spill from window boxes, adding bursts of color.

If the city is beautiful, it has nothing on Livia. Her presence feels almost surreal, like a vision from a dream. Her long, flowing hair catches the sunlight just so, and her deep, expressive eyes seem to hold their own magick. I can't believe Amos is her father. *Gross, he heard me checking out his daughter.* A chill of embarrassment runs down my spine.

"Have you ever met the Nobles?" I break the silence.

"No, I wasn't born yet." *Okay, under age thirty-two, noted.* "But it feels like I have a sort of connection with them. I grew up hearing about their stories. They saved a lot of my people. Vereilles is a melting pot of people and leyfolk of each nation. Well, almost every nation." She glances up at the streak of silver in the sky. "The nations did their best to help those whose towns were raided by bandits, but there are some of us who weren't so lucky. The Nobles saw us and advocated to help. Noble Rictor, even from up there in the Space Ring, did his best to make sure we weren't forgotten. With the combined efforts of the Nobles, they gave us a voice, and we got to live another day."

This changes a lot for me. The five of them, completely going through one of the hardest times of their lives, still thought of helping others. They came here with the idea of forgetting their pain from losing Uncle James and Auntie Via, they could have been selfish and done as they pleased, but still, they helped. They saved so many lives, and they never knew the great changes they made. Yet, I tortured them for it without knowing the full story.

"Noble Jhoana... What were her stories like?" I ask, eyes fixed on the path ahead.

"I admire her the most. She saved my father's life."

Surprised, I turn my gaze to her.

"After the Nobles disappeared, the nations' relationships with one another grew stronger, and from the Nobles' absence came the treaty of the Allied Nations. Change was ushering a new era of peace, but the O'rians came and disrupted that peace."

"Blood magick..." I say, remembering the fragmented conversation in my head.

"Yes. It's what took my grandfather from us, and so many others. My father would've been one of them, but Noble Jhoana, she came in just in time and protected him for a second time. Since that day, he vowed to make Vereilles a safe haven for anyone, even getting us to be recognized as the sixth nation, despite our secrecy. In honor of the Nobles from Earth."

I'm so proud to call Jho my best friend. "She was exactly like that for us too, always coming to save us." My eyes well up.

Livia shares a smile with me. "We're here."

The building before me is utterly astonishing. Its white marble shimmers in the sunlight and gothic windows, framed by intricate carvings, reflect the deep blue sky. Arches and spires stretch upward, their details almost too perfect to be real. A meticulously crafted stone pathway, bordered by vibrant greenery, leads to the grand entrance.

"*This* is where I'm staying?" I know I'm gaping like a complete half-wit but I seem to have lost motor control in my jaw.

Livia's eyes linger on my face for a moment before she nods. I can't read the expression that crosses her face. She stretches her arms, crossing them both. Her pinkies drop and the next fingers follow suit, before she closes them into fists. She then spreads her arms, and the doors creak open.

As I step inside, pulsating lights within the walls greet me. A large mirror stands at the center, capturing the magic of the intricate ceiling. Each section of the roof celebrates a member of the Squad, their images immortalized in exquisite detail. Stained glass windows bathe the floor in a kaleidoscope of colors, the patterns shifting with every step. This doesn't look like a living space. As I gaze up at Jhoana's image, something clunks into place.

Livia said Jhoana saved her father twice, the second time being when the O'rians began to rise. *She was here after the Nobles disappeared. That means Jho didn't—*

"There's no doubt about who you say you are," Amos's voice appears behind me. "But I have to make sure you're not a danger to my people."

I whip around to look at him. "What are you talking about?"

"Normally, this process takes months, but we don't have that kind of time."

I feel my blood freeze over. I really do not like the sound of that.

Amos continues, "The mirror will show you who you truly are, and if the doors open, that means we can trust you, but if it doesn't... Well."

"You... You lied!" I turn on my heel, striding for the open entrance. My hands curl into fists as my feet pound the stone floor, but as I reach the doorway, my body slams into an unseen wall, and I fall to the ground.

"I believe in you, Noble," Amos says calmly. "But I need to be sure. Once you get out, we can talk about Noble Jhoana." The doors begin to close. I catch one last glimpse of Livia. She turns away from me, something like remorse lining her face.

"Hey! Please no!" I crawl towards the invisible wall, banging on it as the light from the outside world disappears. *Oberon, I need you. They locked me up.*

Silence.

I don't think he can hear me from here. Distance or magickal communication blockers, I'm not sure. The shimmering walls begin to show markings; they look like runes. I turn back to the hall; the mirror stands regally in the center, its frame a masterpiece of silver vines intertwined with delicate, golden leaves. The glass itself is impossibly clear, reflecting not just the room but amplifying the colors and lights around it. It looks almost fluid, as if it would ripple under my touch. As I gaze into it, the mirror seems to draw me in, reflecting not just my image, but the essence of the world around me.

A quiet corner of my mind, one that has watched too many horror movies, expects a hand to lash out and drag me inside.

Just to the left of me, a silhouette of a person appears in the reflection. "Jho..." I breathe out. Jhoana's dark hair cascades around her shoulders, framing her gentle face. She clutches a book in her hands, her eyes soft and reflective, carrying an air of mystery and quiet strength that has always captivated me.

"Where the hell have you been?" I demand. "Since the Squad got back in town, I stopped seeing you."

"I never left. I kept an eye on you. Those birds, they almost got you, didn't they?" Worry laces her voice and her hands tighten on the book I lent her—back when I saw her alive for the last time.

"That was you." Tears begin filling my eyes. "You're still saving me."

This is how she would have looked if she never went into a coma. Or at least what I thought she would look like. When Rictor, Jadis, and Dustin said they started seeing their younger selves, I wanted to tell them I've been seeing Jhoana for years. She's the one that told me to call Emierr. She's the one that prepped me to ask all the questions to them. Her spirit, or my manifestation of her memory, whatever it is, has kept me going.

"This mirror... It's going to show you things you don't want to see. This might be one of the hardest things you have to do yet. But I'm always right here with you."

Her smile soothes my nerves. *It's always been for her.* Then, like everything else in my life, darkness consumes the mirror, and the reflection of Jhoana disappears. It's just me now. Except... I lean in closer, horror rising in my veins. My teenage self gives me a malicious grin.

He sneers, "You seriously just gonna stand there with that stupid face of yours? Man, I grew up to be a pathetic loser, huh?"

"You're not real," I say through gritted teeth.

"Of course I'm real, I'm you. Don't act like you don't remember me. How angry you were at those freaks. What they did to Jho, and what you were going to do to them." He chuckles, reaching for his waistband. My eyes follow his hand. I'm frozen, unable to speak as I watch him pull out the pistol he'd hidden at his back. He waves it at me tauntingly.

"No... That's not true!" I step back. I can't pull enough air into my lungs.

"Let me recount the plan you made."

"No, stop."

"You were going to fake an apology—"

"No!" I cover my ears.

"Bring them to the woods—"

"Stop! Stop! Stop!" My screams overpower his voice, but before I can turn away, he raises the gun at me.

"I'm sorry," I said, my voice admirably shaky. I almost believed myself, despite knowing what would come next. I imagined those losers standing in front of me, their eyes watching, judging, waiting for me to admit my wrongdoings. I could see it in their faces—their disbelief, their anger—but I pushed through, pretending like they might accept my explanation.

"I was hurt... I didn't mean to do it," I continued, the words sounding emptier the longer I spoke. Maybe if I practiced it enough, I'd sound sincere. But behind me, my hand gripped the pistol tighter with every word that came out of my mouth. The apology was falling apart in my head, the lie becoming unbearable.

Anger started bubbling up, heating my chest, rising through my throat. My teeth clenched as I spoke, pretending I was sorry, pretending I could make amends for everything I'd done to them. But I couldn't.

Before I realized it, my arm jerked, the gun already raised, pointed right where Rictor would be standing. I didn't even think, just saw his terrified face at the end of the barrel. My finger pulled the trigger, and the blast ricocheted off the foothills. Recoil shot through my hand, the noise ringing in my ears drowning out any echoes still shattering the forest.

I wasn't ready for how the gun would feel—the power of it, the weight of the shot. It hit me hard, harder than I ever expected. My heart raced, panic swelling inside me. I dropped the gun, and the metal thudded against the dirt. I stared at it, rage gone in an instant, replaced by something darker.

What had I tried to do? How could I have even thought *of doing this?*

Jhoana would hate me. My parents would never forgive me. And right then, I started hating myself too. I couldn't stand to look at the gun. Without another thought, I turned and ran, as far and as fast as I could, away from the gun, away from everything. I couldn't face it—I had come so close, too close.

I didn't stop running. I couldn't.

I cry, falling to my knees, feeling the air leave my lungs. "I.... I didn't want them dead. I was... I was..." The words are getting trapped in my throat. What was there left to say? The mirror just showed me what I really am. "I don't want to be a monster."

"You're not." Jhoana's voice comes from my left, but no one is there. I glance at the mirror and there she is, on her knees, holding my reflection. She looks at me in the mirror and gets up. "You are the furthest thing from a monster." She's in my room now. I remember this; it was after I visited Emierr, when we got the letters. I reach out to touch the mirror's liquid surface and feel myself fall into the memory

"It's finally happening, Jho." I paced back and forth. "I'm going to save

you."

She walked over to my bed and sat down. *"I never thought it would come."* She doesn't smile.

"What's wrong?"

"Rune... It's time now you start accepting that there might not be a me to find. The easier you accept this, the less heartbreak you'll have if things go wrong."

I scoffed. *"We talked about this, I don't care if you don't like me back, it's all about getting you home, that's the only reason I'm holding onto."*

"No," She shook her head. *"I could be really dead."* All the time she'd been around, she'd been her usual self, but now, it was as if she was preparing me for her funeral.

That was a reality I had to accept; we may fail to get her back home. The scenario that was more likely to be real was one where I had to say goodbye to my best friend forever.

"Don't be sad," Jho murmured.

"How can I not be? You're not here. You haven't really been here for a very long time, Jho." My throat ached. *"This version of you that I made up in my head, I don't even know if it would be you now."*

"Maybe not." She stood up. *"But I'm still here. Real or not real."* She took my hands; I wish I could feel her touch. *"To the moon and back, remember?"*

To the moon and back... The promise we'd made to each other since we were seven. It meant so much more now; to Ethra and back.

"You've always loved me, Rune. In another life, I know I would return your feelings. Don't give up on me." Her hand perched on my cheek. *"Find me. I gave you the stone for a reason."*

A bright light overtakes my bedroom, blinding me and whisking Jhoana away.

I'm back in the marble building, staring at my own tear-soaked face.

"You did it." Amos's footsteps halt right behind me. I hear him sigh with relief. "That guilt you were carrying, it's what's holding you back. Whatever power you have, you won't be able to control it with all that burden."

"You read my mind. You promised you wouldn't." My voice is barely a whisper.

"I know and I'm sorry, but we've run out of time. We just have to trust each other now." He walks over and places a hand on my shoulder. "Now, let's talk about Jhoana. I think I know where she is."

EMIERR

"This can't be happening," Dustin mutters, pacing back and forth. "Astralis!" he shouts, but the incantation does nothing, just like the last eighty times.

"Dusty, relax, you're driving me crazy," Rictor pleads, his voice tense and strained.

"*Relax?* Rune could be dead right now—we didn't even teach him the healing spell or how to summon an astral weapon," Dustin argues, panic rising in his voice.

"Oh my god," Jadis sighs, her voice thick with disbelief. "We didn't teach him *shit*. We brought him here completely blind."

"Guys, this isn't helping," I cut in, feeling the tension rise around us. "We can't fall apart now. I know Rune seems clueless, but he's actually a quick learner; his never ending questions always worked in his favor. And the dude played baseball in high school, he's got a mean swing. Just like how we survived as kids, he'll adapt here too." I pause, trying to calm my own racing heart as much as theirs. "If he doesn't make it, I'll never forgive myself. But I believe in him; he's going to pull through." I sigh, glancing at the others and then towards the man Borge rescued. "Let's just wait for Jae and his partner to bring us more info."

The man Borge had assumed was Brunner has glasses that barely hang onto his nose, and his blonde hair looks like it's been through a storm. He's decked out in a rugged jumpsuit equipped with high-visibility strips, mesh vents, and reinforced knees—totally something a field researcher from Earth would wear. He looks absolutely nothing like Brunner. What was he digging up in Akeurimja Forest, though? There's a tired relief in his eyes as he explains his story to Jae and Borge. I'm hanging on every word, hoping he drops some clues about Brunner too.

"Okay." Dustin begins stretching. I glance at Jadis, who's staring at the ground, deep in thought. Rictor is biting his fingernails;

something is up with him. He's been a little extra reactive since we got here.

"There's a Gate near here," Jadis says, looking up. "We'll go straight to Zaltana once we know more."

"I'm sorry I'm no help. Something is happening to me," Rictor says, rubbing his chest.

"What's up?" Dustin walks over, placing a hand on his shoulder.

"Since we got here, I—It's hard to explain. But I think I'm... reading everyone's emotions." Rictor's face twists in discomfort. He's usually the guy with all the answers, but now? Seeing him this lost... I'm not sure what to make of it.

"Maybe a divination spell, did you weave one?" Jadis suggests, her eyes narrowing in thought.

"I think it's clear I'm unable to use magick," Rictor replies with a hint of sarcasm.

"Remember what you said about your injuries," I say slowly, sliding puzzle pieces together. "Because you aged, they healed, but you weren't here physically to bleed to death. What if it's like that with our powers?"

"We were kids back then, so our powers weren't fully developed." Dustin nods thoughtfully. "But isn't Ricky's telekinesis *not* magick related? The Waters imbued us with powers, but they're still magick. At least, that's what my grandpa—Chief Arun—told me during my ceremony."

"Exactly. It's all Ricky's brain," Jadis chimes in, nodding. "His brain wasn't fully developed at twelve. But now that he's back here, his brain is catching up with his age."

"I told you, you're an empath." I grin at Rictor, vindicated. "Even on Earth, you always read people to a T."

"Well, here it's like I'm absorbing nausea instead. The more I feel everyone's emotions, the more it makes me want to vomit," Rictor mutters, swallowing hard.

"I wonder what else you'll develop. Mind reading?" Jadis muses, eyeing Rictor like a lab rat she's ready to experiment on. How is she so much scarier when she's excited?

"Rictor Cullen *does* have a nice ring to it." Dustin snickers.

"If he starts sparkling, I'm jumping off a cliff," Jadis says, shaking her head.

I hiss at all of them, and we break into laughter. But then I spot Jae walking over to us, cutting through the brief semblance of normalcy.

"I'm sorry," Jae interrupts, his expression serious. "The other Argentavis victim did see your friend; they flew right by each other."

"Does he know what direction or mountain they went to?" I ask, fists clenching with hope and anxiety.

"Look, I'm from Zaltana and know those ranges like the back of my hand," Jae began, clearly attempting to be gentle, "but when we can't find someone taken by an Argentavis, it usually means—"

"No," Dustin interrupts, refusing to hear it. "Meer has Argentavis friends; they'd know us."

"Yes, *you*, but didn't you say this is your friend's first time here?" Jae just blew right by the phrase "Argentavis friends." I'm impressed.

"Then we're heading to Zaltana." Jadis squares her shoulders, our decision obviously made.

A part of me wants to say I'm staying, but Rictor's right. I can wait a little longer. "Let's get Rune," I agree. Neither Dustin nor Rictor voice opposition.

"I'll accompany you," Jae offers. "I know that Nob—Dustin is from Zaltana too, but I can speed up the search and rescue process."

"Hold up," Borge interrupts, striding over with the other man. "We need them to file an incident report before they go anywhere."

I frown at the ogre. *He's nothing like Shrek—at least Shrek was funny. This guy is just... He's like Coach Danny. Ugh.*

"I'll take care of it after I escort—" Jae protests.

"Escort? You do know if you do this, you'll be responsible for them. And if any of them die, you'll be sanctioned," Borge says harshly. Is that concern I hear?.

"I understand, Borge. But I have to help," Jae replies, determined.

"Sanctioned?" Jadis asks.

"Stripped of my magick," Jae replies, avoiding her gaze.

"And you're willing to sacrifice everything you've worked for, for a bunch of strangers?" Borge steps closer to Jae, grabbing his shirt. "After what Salamance and Frey did for you, you're gonna throw it all away?"

We all take a step back, tension rising.

"Let him go," Dustin commands.

"Or what?" Borge challenges.

Jadis claps her hands threateningly, while Dustin tightens his fists and cracks his neck, clearly ready to throw a thoroughly non-magickal punch.

I dart in front of Dustin, stopping him. We don't need this turning into a brawl. We're the *Allied* Organization Squad for Christ's sake.

"We're Nobles," Rictor blurts out, catching us all off guard.

"What?" Borge drops Jae at once, then bursts into laughter, his tusks on full display. "The Nobles? They've been gone for decades! The Nobles are dead."

We all flinch at his words.

"And even if they weren't, they'd be in their forties by now, but you... you look like you just grew out of your teens. No way you're the same kids who left Ethra!"

Rictor glances around. Borge's laughter is still bouncing through the trees. I don't like the look in his eye.

"Right here, Ricky?" I whisper, my heart racing.

He nods, closes his eyes, and takes a deep breath. When he opens them, they glow a bright yellow. I side-eye the others. They nod, no words needing to pass between us. I fill my lungs and let my eyes drift shut. I search the dusty, disused corners of my mind for the bond. A tingling sensation starts in my brain, spreading throughout my body.

There you are, Maral. It's been so long. My eyes snap open, my vision sharpens, and my surroundings seem dilated; every sense is heightened. Jadis's eyes reflect the fiery essence of Tana, the phoenix, while Dustin's eyes mirror the fierce spirit of Ade', the white tiger. Together, we all turn our frankly horrifying gazes toward Borge.

He and Not-Brunner gasp, stepping back. Shame and shock wash over Borge's spring-green face.

"My Nobles, I apologize." He bows so deeply, I worry he'll bang a tusk on his knees.

I scan the area and notice we're attracting the attention of passersby. I blink away Maral's sight. Jadis and Dustin, too, return their irises to their usual, far less threatening brown. Rictor, of course, can't quite manage to do the same—his left eye stays lit as a backup for his ruined vision.

"Okay, no need for that," I say, gesturing for Borge and Not-Brunner to stand upright.

"Please forgive me, my Noble," Borge says, his voice softening as he looks down, visibly embarrassed. "You saved my parents from a forest fire years ago, and with your kindness, everything the fire took was restored. You're the reason I joined the Allied Force." He glances up, meeting my eyes briefly. I remember that day. Sól and I had made a bet to see who could put out the forest fire the fastest. It was just a game to me, but for people like Borge, their lives changed drastically that day.

"Don't thank me. Sólel did all the work," I say, tapping his shoulder.

"Borge—" Jae mumbles.

Suddenly, Borge bows his head, cutting Jae off. "I apologize for my behavior. As your commanding officer, I should set a better example."

I glance at the others, and they all shrug, just as confused as I am.

Standing upright, Borge adds, "Whatever I can do to assist you and aid the Nobles, I am happy to help."

The sudden change in attitude is impressive. I wish Coach Danny had that kind of adaptability. And significantly less interest in Thai sex workers.

"For starters, no one knows we're back besides Jae," Rictor says. "Well, including the two of you, so that's three, but anyway, we'd like to keep it that way for now. No calling us Nobles."

"Yes. Understood, no Nobles here," Borge says with a wink.

"Excuse me," the man in the jumpsuit says, peering out from behind Borge. "Do any of you have a phone? I'd like to call my people to let them know I'm safe. The last thing I said before leaving all my equipment in Akeurimja Forest was... Well, actually it was just me screaming, so... I'm Joven, by the way. It's a pleasure to meet you all."

His accent sounds like a Brit. Is there an Ethran equivalent to England? I glance at Rictor, catching the amusement on his face. He loves British accents; he once spoke like that for a week straight in sixth grade. I chuckle and shake my head. Dustin and Jadis start snickering too, turning Rictor's face red with embarrassment.

"I'm so sorry, did I say something wrong?" Joven asks.

Borge claps a massive hand on Joven's shoulder. "Don't worry, they know you probably clean up great!"

"For the Tree's sake, here." Jae opens a pocket on his chest and pulls out a transparent block, handing it to Joven. "Make it quick."

"Thank you." Joven takes the phone and walks a few paces out.

"Are we ready?" Dustin asks.

"You weren't going to say hello?" a deep, resonant voice calls from our left. We all turn, and something deep inside me starts to stir.

Ever since we arrived, everything has felt like a dream, but this moment—this feels achingly real. "Father," I manage to say, my voice trembling.

Disbelief spreads across his face, tears welling up in his eyes. "Son... It's really you." Father opens his arms wide, and just like that, all those years melt away. There he stands—not just the Chief of Terrene, but my dad—older, yes, and his once broad shoulders are not as imposing. The tattoos that sweep across his skin still tell our tribe's tales—of battles fought, of peace won, each line a story inked deep.

His wild, thick hair now has streaks of white and it frames a face etched with sharp wisdom, lines carved by time and duty.

It's been sixteen long years for me and twice as long for him, but here he is, arms spread wide, waiting to pull me back into the fold. And it hits me just how much my whole being missed this—missed him.

Without hesitation, I sprint to him and leap into his arms. This is real. Every moment we spent here was real.

"I thought I'd never see you again, son." Father's embrace tightens, and I squeeze him even tighter in return.

"I've missed you, Father. I'm sorry it took this long to come back."

We pull away, and he places both hands on my shoulders.

"You're back, that's all that matters." He presses his forehead to mine. I never thought something as simple as our foreheads touching could unleash all the emotions that have been numbed over the years. I'm home. I'm finally home

"Is that the Squad?" Father asks, looking behind me. I turn to see them, eyes all filled with tears—even Joven, weirdly enough.

"Hi, Chief," Rictor smiles.

"Astro?" Father's face goes pale. He walks over to Rictor, placing both hands on his cheeks. "Could it be you?"

"Chief, it's me, Ricky."

Father looks unnerved. "You look just like someone I knew years ago..." He shakes his head and gives Rictor a dazzling smile. "Ricky, you've grown into such a fine man." He places his forehead against Rictor's. "Dusty and Jads too?" When everyone has received a bone-crushing hug and a forehead press. Father takes a step back to drink us in. "My children are all home." His brows furrow. "Well, almost all of them. Where's Jho? She didn't come with you?"

We glance at each other, sharing the same worried expression. We just got our answer: Jhoana never came to Terrene.

"That's why we're here," Jadis finally says, her voice heavy with the weight of the truth we can't bear to tell him.

"I see," Father nods, understanding more than we say. "Thank you, Jae, for bringing them here."

"Of course, Chief. The situation at Solaris has been maintained, but I'm afraid we couldn't retrieve the stolen Solaris flowers."

"That's unfortunate. Regardless, you're doing a great job."

"The O'rians breached Solaris?" Borge exclaims, his eyes wide with disbelief.

"Al showed me those flowers back at the Terrarium. He said one flower can extend someone's lifeforce tenfold," I tell the Squad. "These O'rians are planning something big if they're breaking sacred laws."

"Chief," Dustin says hesitantly. "Um, there's another problem we have. We brought a friend with us from Earth, and he was taken by an Argentavis to the ranges."

"This gentleman here was taken as well around the same time," Borge adds, crossing his arms. "Jae called it in, and I was in the area. I found Joven and assumed he was the victim in question. I saw no others around the nests."

"Thank you, Borge. I'll be sure to send Captain Kaelor briefings of your work and findings." Father turns to us and lets out a huge sigh. "Oh kids. The balance in Ethra has been tipped since you were last here. This plague... It has destroyed the natural order of things. The Argentavis were great companions for Zaltana and Terrene for many generations, but they've become savage with hunger. But hear my words, your friend is going to be okay. If he's anything like any of you, you'll see him again."

Father's words calm me. I can see it having the same effect on the Squad. *Rune, you better fucking survive.*

"Let's take this discussion indoors. Nalani has been yearning for all of you every day," Father says with a warm smile. "And so has Sólel."

Rictor places a hand on my shoulder and gives it a soft squeeze. *Sól... We're home.*

"What can I do to help?" Borge asks, turning to Jae hopefully. I feel bad for the ogre. He started out as this cocky son of a bitch, but now he just wants to be part of the team.

"Alert Zaltana officials about another Argentavis taking. Let them know that someone of importance from the Tellus has been abducted. That should get them on their feet," Father instructs Borge.

"Yes, Chief." Borge salutes and hurries to his car.

"Joven, stay with me until your people come to get you," Jae instructs the quivering researcher.

Joven does not object in the slightest.

"Do you boys remember your way back home?" Father asks, placing a hand on Rictor's and my shoulders as we begin walking.

I take my first steps back into the heart of where I grew up. Massive trees, their trunks as wide as houses, stretch up toward the sky, their branches supporting sprawling treehouses. These aren't just the simple wooden huts I remember; they're complex structures, their surfaces embedded with soft-glowing lights and energy streams that pulse with a life of their own. Pathways, illuminated by a gentle, bioluminescent glow, weave through the leaves, creating a network of light that dances with the wind.

As we walk, the street below us is alive with a mix of human faces and leyfolk—all nodding their heads in a quiet salute as their chief passes by. The air is thick with magick from the Ethereal Tree nearby. Every corner of this place, enriched with the touch of advanced tech, feels deeply familiar yet astonishingly new, pulling me back into memories I thought I'd left far behind.

"Meer," Rictor murmurs, his voice awestruck.

"I know." *Me too, Ricky, holy shit.* The world I remembered couldn't capture the depth of what I feel now. I recall Uncle Jay's dream of building a community where we could thrive, where his son was beside us, and I realize that what the Squad has built in Ethra is exactly what he wanted for us.

"Are you an Inkweaver like me?" Dustin asks. I glance back to see him talking to Jae.

"No, I never reached that level."

"But you got the blasters!" Dustin exclaims, eyes lighting up. "Those are made in Juno, right? I recognized them!"

"Dusty, you *stole* your blasters from Juno, remember? Aren't blades the weapon given to Inkweavers?" Jadis teases.

Dustin's face reddens as he sighs, "Oh, shit, yeah."

"Don't worry, Dustin, I didn't hear a thing," Jae reassures with a grin.

I let out a small chuckle, turning my head back on the path, and shaking my head.

"Son?" Father turns to me, his tone shifting.

"Yes, Father?"

"How are you holding up?"

"I'm doing good," I say, though I'm sure Rictor can sense the lie. Despite finally seeing Father after all these years, the weight of Jhoana's absence and the mess I've caused with Brunner presses heavily on me.

"It's okay, you're not alone anymore," he says, pulling me in for a tight embrace that seems to steady the storm inside me.

He definitely knows.

"Terrene has changed so much," Jadis observes, looking around.

"Yes, it's more 'with the times,' as Sólel would say," Father agrees. "Thanks to your people, Ethra is powered by solar energy. After you left, Arid developed a system that absorbs and distributes solar energy throughout the nations."

"Like a giant solar panel for the world," Rictor says, impressed.

"I'm not sure how it works, but Sólel spent years helping them incorporate it. Now we have all this. The world is always changing, but we must learn to preserve our roots while adapting to 'the times.'"

"Is Chief Arun... still with us?" Dustin asks hesitantly.

"Yes, we recently celebrated his 162nd birthday," Father says, as if that's a common occurrence. Although, I suppose it is here. "That old man is still going strong. You're planning to visit him after this, aren't you? He talks about you all the time."

"Oh... That's really great to hear." Dustin's voice trembles slightly. Chief Arun was like a grandfather to him during his time here, probably the one person he missed the most from Ethra. I'm relieved he'll get to see him again.

"I must say, Terrene is such a beautiful place," Joven comments.

"My family and I vacationed in the Treetop Provinces a few years ago, and I've been wanting to return ever since."

"Where are you from again?" Jae asks, furrowing his brows.

Joven opens his mouth to respond but Rictor gasps, interrupting him. "Whoa, the treehouse looks exactly how I remembered it."

I turn to our house, and déjà vu hits me instantly. It's like stepping back into my memories, reliving the day Father brought me home. Our treehouse isn't anything grand—it was just like anyone else's home at the time. The sprawling limbs are big enough to support a living room, kitchen, and our parents' room. Simple, really. Sólel's and my rooms were in a separate tree just behind the main house. I wonder if he'd taken over both rooms when I disappeared.

I once offered to grow the tree bigger, thinking royalty should live large, but Father insisted that, to understand the people, we had to live like them. And now, standing here, I see it—everything Father stands for is right here in this house, this home.

"We left it the same, hoping that when you returned, you'd recognize your home," Father says, looking back at us. "Ready to see everyone?"

"We're right behind you," Rictor says with a smile.

"We'll be out here," Jae calls, pausing a few feet away from the entrance. Joven has stopped even further back, but he gives me an encouraging nod all the same.

Father opens the door and steps inside. "My queen, I've brought company," he announces, shooting us a wink.

"Berkarys, I told you to give me at least two hours' notice so I can prepare something." Mom's scolding voice reaches us from the depths of the home.

I take a deep breath and let it out before stepping to the door. This feels like the day we arrived in town after receiving Auntie Ina's letters—walking into Jhoana's house, fear engulfing us under judging eyes. But this is completely different—I'm excited.

A warm heaviness fills my chest as I see the woman who has always shown me kindness and love. Her dark red, fiery hair, now streaked with silver, frames her light skin, which still radiates the warmth I remember. She's wiping down the table, her powerful build an indicator of her years of leadership and resilience.

"Hello," is all I can manage to say.

"Please come in. It's a pleasure to hav—" Her eyes meet mine.

"Hi, Mom."

Her eyes widen in shock. Then, with a rush of emotion, she stumbles toward me, tears welling up. She cups my face in her hands, her touch warm and familiar, and I feel the years between us vanish.

"Could it be?"

"Yes, it's our boy," Father says, his voice choking with emotion.

"By the Tree!" A voice comes from behind Mom. "Emierr?"

As I lean around Mom's shoulders, a jolt of recognition runs through me. This has to be Evera, Sól's childhood best friend. I remember the day I rescued the little faun from falling to her death on the day of my baptism. My eyes drift to her belly, swollen with life. *Did Sólel and she end up together? Is he going to be a father?* Her wavy, light brown hair, decorated with delicate leaves, highlights her expression of utter shock. She wears a flowing maternity gown that gracefully reveals her distinct, hooved legs.

She presses a much more human hand to her mouth, tears flowing as she runs to join me and Mom. The gentle clopping of her hooves on the wooden floor stirs a blend of nostalgia and sadness within me. How much have I missed? She joins our embrace, completing the circle of reunion. Almost.

"The Squad is here too?" Evera asks, switching to English, and smiling warmly at the rest of the group.

Mom peers over my shoulder, but falls silent as she stares at Rictor.

"Astro?" she breathes out, glancing at Father. I look back up at her, frowning. *Mom too? Who is Astro?*

"It's me, Auntie. It's Ricky," Rictor says, his voice cracking. Mom took an instant liking to him when he started living with us. I could see in her face, and in Father's, too, how much they loved him after everything he went through. I'm glad he gets to see them again.

"Yes. Of course," she said, shaking her head. "You remind me of an old friend—you look just like him." Mom places a hand on his cheek. "What a gift it is to see you again." She pulls him into her arms. Rictor hugs her back just as tightly.

"Where's Sól?" I ask, trying to contain my excitement and nerves.

"We were just talking about you." Evera wipes her tears. "He wanted to show me a box of memories from all your adventures. He's in the room you and Ricky shared."

"Go, see your little brother," Father says, wrapping an arm around his wife.

"Good luck, Meer." Dustin gives me an encouraging nod.

As I navigate the familiar twists of our old home, my legs move instinctively, guiding me to the treehouse's back door. This isn't just any path—it's the bridge back to Sólel, the brother I left behind. Each creak of the worn wooden steps echoes with whispers of the past—every laugh, every painful goodbye, every promise made and broken. My heart pounds with dread and anticipation as I reach to knock, but the door swings open before I touch it.

Sólel stands before me, no longer the shadow of a boy who once trailed my every step, but a man as tall as me, his locs falling past his shoulders, and his deep skin marked with tattoos like our father's. I pause, struck by the sight of him—a stranger with familiar eyes. Those eyes, still the lightest shade of green, hold the same purity I remember, yet now reflect a tapestry of pain.

His presence mirrors my betrayals—the lies I told, the trust I broke, the family bonds strained by my absence. As our eyes lock, a torrent of emotions swells between us, and rivulets of tears roll down Sólel's cheeks, his sobs echoing those of a nine-year-old boy who thought he'd lost me to the sea monster all those years ago. The heaviness in my heart spills over as I pull him into an embrace, crushing him to me with the urgency of lost time and regret.

"I'm sorry," I whisper, the words escaping repeatedly as if to mend every broken moment between us. Holding him tighter, each apology feels like a stitch mending our torn past.

In this embrace, under the canopy of our childhood refuge, two brothers reunite—not just as siblings, but as spirits reconciled through forgiveness and love. This is the moment I've been waiting for, the healing I've wanted after all I've been through. As I hold Sólel, the world's burdens fade away, and for the first time in years, I am truly home.

"Emierr," a voice calls from behind us.

Sólel peers over my shoulder. "Evera, what is it?"

I pull myself away from the weight of our bittersweet reunion and turn around.

"A friend of yours is here. He wants to see you."

"A friend?" I frown.

"Someone named Albert?"

Sólel and I exchange a glance, both startled.

How did he find us so quickly?

Jho's Survival

32 YEARS AGO

"**I** told you, didn't I? It was too soon," a woman's voice said, waking me.

I struggled to pry my eyes open. *Where am I?* I had no strength left in me. *What is happening?* I shivered as the cold sting of the metal bed seeped through my clothes. I tried moving, but restraints held me tightly by my wrists and ankles. The last thing I remembered was...

"Jho!" Ricky's screams echoed in my head. I peered down at my stomach and saw the tear in my shirt, where the spear had protruded. I was healed.

"They were all there alone. It was the perfect time to attack," a man said, annoyed.

"And look what happened. You didn't get any of them. I specifically said Jadis Salazar, and you brought me the wrong one."

I turned my head toward the voices, and to my complete and utter shock, Madam Evanora stood just inches from my manacled hand. I'd recognize her cloak and stupid blue hair anywhere. Of course she's the mastermind behind all of this. I scanned my surroundings. I was in a lab—a really old one. If Ricky were here, he'd joke about the equipment turning to dust if we picked it up. *Where are they? Did they get captured too?*

"The kids weren't ready, I'll admit that," the man said, sounding defeated.

Madam Evanora moved out of the way, and I got a clearer view of him. He looked about my daddy's age and sat leaning against a metal table, his lab coat hanging awkwardly from his shoulders, as if weighed down by his troubles. I watched his eyes shift with a haunted intensity as he spoke to Madam Evanora, his voice tinged with hesitation.

"But the only ones who can take on those Earth kids are them-selves," he said, looking up at her.

"This is *why* we plan. You think making those things *now* was the best idea?" Madam Evanora snapped. "They're going to be stuck as children. We could have waited until they were adults. At least then, the Earth kids' powers would have been developed."

The doppelgangers... Those copies that attacked us were made? *How? There's no magick that can do that.*

"Do you know why that's a bad idea?" The man stood up abruptly, finally looking the witch directly in the eye.

"No, but you're going to tell me anyway," Madam Evanora grum-bled.

"Those Earth kids will be the end of everything. They are a catalyst for a lot of suffering." He paused and slumped back down. "They'll end up betraying us as adults."

"You're talking about those *things* you made? How could you know they'd betray us?"

"I just know," he whispered.

"Abbadon, if you don't start being honest with me, I can just take the information myself." She raised her hand, which emitted a dark blue glow.

Abbadon...

"Try me, witch. Remember, I can easily send you back into exile," Abbadon threatened.

What are they talking about? I tried again to move, this time using my force fields. I opened my hands and wiggled my cuffs, but noth-ing happened. *What? Where are my powers?* The clanking of the metal cuffs caught their attention, and they turned toward me.

"She's awake already?" Abbadon said, standing up and reaching for something on the table.

"I told you these kids are not to be underestimated," Madam Evanora said as she hovered over me. "You poor thing, you were even my favorite." She placed a hand on my forehead.

"Why are you doing this?" I cried, still writhing against the re-straints.

"You're an abomination. You're not supposed to exist," she said indifferently. "Knock her out." She waved a hand and turned away.

"No! Astralis!" I wailed as Abbadon strode over, jamming a needle into my arm. I gasped as the sting traveled all over my body. A faint whisper escaped my lips before darkness took over.

"Ricky..."

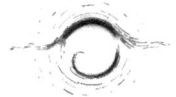

The four walls of the tiny room felt like they were going to swallow me alive. I sat on the hard bed with my back against the wall, my arms wrapped tightly around my legs. I had no idea how much time had passed, and all I could think about was what was happening back home. How was my family? Why hadn't my best friends come back for me? Were they too scared? These questions spun endlessly in my mind, distracting me even when Abbadon and his evil scientists performed those strange experiments on me.

They'd been injecting me with some sort of liquid that Abbadon had created by drawing energy from pieces of the Ethereal Tree. I didn't even know how he got his hands on it; Meer's people would have never let it happen. Unless someone from Terrene helped him. Which was also bad in itself. He said it had something to do with making my body adapt to the natural source of pure magick. But so far, it hadn't affected me at all. Each session, Abbadon lost his patience with me.

With the experiments becoming less frequent, I was left alone with my thoughts in this dingy room, wondering if anyone was coming to save me.

The door beeped open, and there stood my guard, the only face I saw each and every day. I'd tried asking his name once but he'd just jabbed me with his electrified baton. So, I'd taken to calling him Brickface in honor of his rough, chapped face and unfortunately square head.

"You know the drill—against the wall," Brickface said as the baton buzzed to life.

I obeyed, placing my hands against the cool surface and spreading my legs. They had me wear dark gray clothes that made me look like a patient in a mental hospital. After everything they put me through, I wouldn't be surprised if I was. A metallic band had been wrapped around my right hand since I came to, and it was only ever taken off when I was experimented on. A Stasis Band was what Abbadon called it. It had strange runes carved around it that glimmered a little, almost like they were alive. I had never seen them before; they could be new rune symbols for all I knew. Despite how heavy the band looked and its cold touch, it felt as light as a hair tie.

Nothing like this had ever existed before—something that could block the use of Innate Powers or magick—but here it was, wrapped around my wrist.

Brickface grabbed my arms and placed magnetic cuffs around my wrists, activating them so they stuck together. "It's your lucky day; you're allowed to eat with the other kids," he said, nudging me to start walking. I knew there were other people they captured, but other kids? Not for the first time, I allowed myself to wonder if they had gotten the others too. The thought of my friends, trapped alone in bleak cells like mine, set my heart racing.

What is Abbadon doing here?

For however long I'd been in this rundown facility, I'd only ever been to three places: my room, the toilet, and the experiment room. Walking the halls on a different route than usual was a little exciting. I knew it was bad to feel this way, but I was relieved that I wasn't alone. The corridor leading to the experiment room loomed ahead, a place where they made me hone my fighting skills and the use of my force fields. They pushed me harder than any of my training in Verglas. If I disobeyed, they'd electrocute me. It got so bad once that I went into a brief coma. At least, that's what they told me.

I never wanted to feel that pain again.

As we walked to the cafeteria, I noticed the stark gray walls were lined with flickering fluorescent lights. Gray was the only color in this dreary place. The thud of Brickface's footsteps echoed against the metallic floors, amplifying my sense of isolation. The hallways were lined with doors that seemed to lead nowhere, each one a reminder of the confinement that felt more like a prison than anything else. Pipes and wires snaked along the ceilings and walls, humming with a strange energy that seemed to seep into the air, filling it with a sense of dread. Each step felt heavier than the last, and for the first time, I felt like hope was slipping away. Maybe I was finally losing myself.

"Noble has reached the cafeteria, permission to enter, over," Brickface said behind me. The doors were massive; everything always seemed massive to me. "Copy," he said, leaning toward a sensor near the door and lifting his face mask. The sensor scanned his face, now ingrained in my head. "All right, you best behave, or it's solitary confinement again for you," he threatened, releasing the magnetic cuffs. The sensor turned green, and the door slid open. "Play nice." He shoved me into the room, and the door shut behind me.

It was a pretty standard cafeteria; smaller, but still spacious. Two guards stood in a corner, and the glass walls revealed the bright greenery outside, which had never looked so pretty. The winds were dancing with the trees, something I'd only ever seen in the forests of the first nation. *I'm somewhere in Terrene.* In the far right of the room, a group of kids my age sat across from some teenagers, all wearing the same gray suits as me.

Aching relief mingled with selfish disappointment as I frantically scanned the tables for the Squad. They weren't here. I tried to convince myself that it was good they weren't here, even as the yawning hole of loneliness grew larger in my chest.

To my left was the food station, if I could even call it that, where a masked woman stood behind a table with a huge pot of the slimy gray gunk I'd been eating—the stuff that was supposed to have every nutrient my body needed.

What I would do to have Valda's geluer stew.... She always made the best. I'd had the version the Academy made, and it never tasted as good as hers. Boyko and Valda must be worried sick. I promised them I was going to be okay.

The sludge plops on my tray.

"I'll have another plate please," a girl my age said, standing beside me.

The lunch lady scooped up another ladle full and slapped it on her tray.

"Thanks." The girl turned my way. "You must be—wait, Jhoana?"

Did I hear that right? "You know me?"

"Of course." She bowed. "You're the Noble of Verglas."

"Please, you don't have to do that." I grab onto her shoulder with my free hand.

"I'm sorry, it's just custom for us to show respect to the Nobles." A smile forms on her face. "I lived down the hill from you. *Tante'* Valda and *Tante'* Boyko are great friends of my mothers'." Her tone was proud. Hearing my adoptive parents' names spoken out loud was like a balm on that hole in my chest. Tante' was the Verglasian word used as a sign of respect for any older family member or elder, regardless of gender. It was a word I barely took notice of at home, but hearing it here, of all places, feels like a piece of home was with me.

I smiled. I didn't know what to say. When was the last time I'd even had a conversation?

"I'm Faye," she said, her voice clear and bright. Her piercing blue eyes showed a keen intelligence, and her silver hair flowed over her shoulders like a waterfall of frost. Even in the same dark gray clothes as me, Faye had a spirited, adventurous look.

"Come on, meet the others." She strode ahead to the table which sat the cluster of kids. I saw her lean in and say something I couldn't make out. All eyes turned to me.

I stood there for a few seconds. I didn't think I was getting out of here any time soon, so I supposed I might as well make some friends.

Faye sat down and the other kids slowly rose out of their seats. As I approached, they all bowed their heads.

"I *just* told you guys she doesn't like that." Faye looked at me and mouthed, "Sorry".

"No," the oldest boy said, shaking his head. "It's custom for us to show respect to a Noble. Who we are is the one thing they can't take from us." He smiled at me. "It's an honor to eat alongside you."

I guess that was another little piece of normal I could hold onto.

"Please sit," the boy next to him added.

Faye made space, and let me sit between her and a younger boy.

"I'm Aurelian," the oldest boy said. His eyes were a bright amber, and his messy auburn hair fell around his face. "Terrene is my home."

"I'm Sylas," said the boy with curly black hair next to him. His crooked smile and relaxed posture set me at ease. "I'm from Arid."

"I'm Lyra." The girl next to Sylas had dark, wavy hair with hints of deep blue, which was at odds with her freckled complexion. "Lumina's Reach is my home."

"Harmon." The boy on the edge nodded at me. His stormy gray eyes were sharp and watchful. His square jaw gave him a serious look, and there was an intensity about him, like he was always ready for anything.

"Harmon's from Flemming Space Ring," Faye added for him. "And to your left is Aris," Faye pointed to the boy next to me. He had sandy hair and quiet hazel eyes.

I turned to Aris, who gave me a soft smile. Something about him made it easier to address the group. "I was, um—When I heard there were more kids here, I expected a bigger group," I admitted.

"We're the only human kids here. They separate us from the leyfolk kids," Sylas said, taking the last bite of his sludge.

"How long have all of you been here?" I asked, suddenly feeling hungry enough to start my mystery meal.

"Aris has been here for three months," Harmon answered. "Lyra and I got here on the same day. Five months for us. And Faye was the first human girl here eight months ago."

"Nine months as of today," Faye said, sounding a bit tired.

"I've been here for eleven months," Sylas said. "But Aurelian's been here the longest—three years." He grabbed Aurelian's hand and looked at him fondly.

They're in love. A soft smile spread across my face.

"Three great years, for the cause," Aurelian said with a bittersweet smile, his eyes a little distant. "At least I got to meet all of you."

"Why do you say it like that?" I asked, frowning.

"He's turning eighteen this year, so he's moving to the adult unit,"

Sylas said, his voice catching slightly.

Aurelian gave a soft smile and placed a reassuring hand on Sylas's cheek. Then he turned to me. "What made you join the cause?" he asked gently.

"Cause?" I repeated.

"The Convergence," Aris spoke up. I didn't expect such a deep voice from him.

"What's that?" I asked.

"It's because of you and the other Earth Nobles," he said, his eyes wide with excitement. "We were chosen for a higher purpose. The O'rians are going to unite all the nations."

I kept looking at him, not really sure what to say. "But why us?" I asked. "Why does it have to be kids?"

"They say we're the future," he explained, sounding proud. "The O'rians think that if they train us to be like the Nobles from Earth, we can make peace everywhere."

Faye nodded. "They think we can learn from each other and share what we know. It's about making a better world together."

I wanted to believe them, but I knew it was all a lie. The O'rians were led by Abbadon and Madam Evanora, and they didn't care about unity; they had their own twisted plans. Everyone at the table seemed so sure, so brainwashed, and I wasn't sure if I should tell them the truth. Would it help, or would it just ruin everything? I stayed quiet, wondering if there would ever be a good time to speak up.

"How old is everyone?" I asked, putting my utensils down on the tray.

"Thirteen," Faye said. "Aris is fourteen."

"I'm fifteen," Lyra said.

"Me too," Harmon nodded.

"Sixteen," Sylas said quietly.

"I recently turned twelve," I said, pursing my lips together.

"Twelve..." Faye sighed.

"You're so young," Lyra said, her empathetic eyes meeting mine. Was I showing emotions? I was usually pretty good at hiding them these days.

"Are the other Nobles joining us too?" Aurelian asked, smiling.

Instinctively, my hands rose to my chest, squeezing together tightly. I looked around at their hopeful faces. But there were bigger things happening here—it wasn't just me. It was all these kids they were rounding up, injecting with whatever Abbadon was messing around with from the Ethereal Tree.

"It's a lie," I said quietly. "I don't know what they promised you, but there is no unity. They ambushed me and my friends, attacking us and..." The memory flashed in my mind—Dusty's bleeding hand, Ricky's eye, and the spear in my stomach. "I barely made it, but my friends got away. After all of that, I woke up in a lab and was tied down. I heard everything."

Stunned silence fell over the group. Hopelessness, denial, anger, fear... Each pair of eyes told a different story.

"See!" Faye exclaimed in a hushed tone. "I told you guys something weird was going on. Besides us looking like prisoners, their training feels more like punishment. The Ghelcarii Academy in Verglas is tough, but not like this, right, Jhoana?"

I nodded.

"That can't be true," Aris mumbled, looking down at his tray.

"You're lying," Aurelian said flatly. How could I expect him to understand? He'd been here the longest.

"Do you think a Noble would lie about this?" Lyra leaned on the table, frowning at him.

"We left our homes; our parents think we're doing something good." Harmon put both his hands on his head. "We willingly got ourselves kidnapped. It can't all be for a lie"

"Maybe you're mistaken, Noble." Aurelian had pushed back the rage flickering in his eyes and forced his tone into one of politeness.

"Then explain to me why we're all wearing these bracelets." I put my hand on the table. "If they wanted to train you as Guardians, then why block your powers?" My words seemed to hit Aurelian hard. He had to know deep down that what I was saying was true.

"Or give us powers..." Faye said.

"Give?" I turned to her. Just then, the speakers blared, announcing the end of lunch.

In one fell swoop, I'd caused my new friends' worlds to crash down around them.

"Okay... This is a lot to take in. Everyone, pull yourselves together for now," Sylas whispered. "We'll go over it at dinner tonight. Just act normal—they're always watching us."

The cafeteria doors slid open, and one by one, guards strolled in, ready to escort us back to our rooms.

"You play nice, missy?" Brickface smirked at me.

"Yes, sir," I said, meeting his eyes for the first time. It felt good to finally speak, even if it was just one little act of defiance.

"Hush now, little one," I sang softly, my voice barely a whisper in the quiet room. I hummed the rest, letting everything else fade into the background. More than a couple of months had passed since I ended up here. My little brother probably isn't okay. My parents are definitely blaming my friends for me not waking up. The Squad isn't coming for me. These thoughts used to swirl in my mind as questions, but now they felt like facts.

I sat upright on my bed, repeating the names of my new friends to keep them in my mind. "Faye. Aris. Lyra. Harmon. Sylas. Aurelian." If I ever escaped, I wanted to remember the people who helped me and who I'd try to save if it came to that. I'd learned a lot about them in my time here.

When Faye mentioned their powers were given to them, she meant exactly that. Abbadon had managed to get enough Ethereal Lake water to baptize those who didn't have Innate Powers. By law, breaking the sacred rule would get you sent to another plane of existence, permanently imprisoned in the void, never to return. At least, that's what Jads told us when she discovered the transcendence spell. She theorized that what we were doing was a version of that spell, but with the ability to return to Earth. So, whoever's helping him is willing to risk everything.

The water still granted powers, but with the same conditions: only if you were worthy. If someone didn't receive powers, they were sent back home—or so they said. But I didn't believe that; they were probably dead. *Kids my age...*

Luckily, they were all worthy. Faye's ability let her freeze time in a small area around her for approximately fifteen seconds. Time spells were super hard to cast, and only a few people could do them, so having it as an Innate Power was awesome. Aris could project illusions, and he told me he'd been training to make his illusions cover big areas. Lyra could feel emotions and change them. Even though her powers were blocked, she had a natural way of talking to people and understanding them so easily. She definitely kept me sane through all this.

Harmon could control vibrations, which I was dying to see. How would that even work? Sylas was a Transmutare—he called it his "shapeshift power"—where he could reshape inorganic materials, changing their form and composition. Aurelian, on the other hand, could change the size of any plant life, which reminded me of my cousin. I bet they would get along. Once we got these bracelets off our wrists, we'd be able to use our powers to escape and put a stop to the O'rians.

My eyes snapped open, and I let out a big sigh. Our plan had to work, but I knew from experience that things might not go the way we hoped, just like with the Squad. Everything depended on us getting these Stasis Bands off.

The night we all talked at dinner, Sylas brought up the plan to escape before Aurelian's eighteenth birthday, which was four months away from then. We knew that once he turned eighteen, he'd be moved to the adult unit, and our chances would be even slimmer. The idea was to gather as much information as we could about what the O'rians were up to so that when we got out, we could tell the world.

Faye learned a lot from her guard, who loved to chat and complain about being stuck at the children's unit when he thought he'd be more useful in the adult unit. Through his whining, we found out that the children were the key to a successful "Convergence," whatever the Convergence truly was.

Sylas told us how he had been part of the group Abbadon was bringing together from Terrene and Arid every Wednesday. They were being asked all sorts of questions about certain plants, especially the poisonous ones, and any knowledge they had about a mysterious figure of legend.

Most people had heard of Elke, the clandestine witch of the Slough. She lived about five hundred years ago, though actual records of her birth and death could not be found. Her knowledge of all plants and herbs brought her to near-legend status. Her guidebook could be in almost every home in Ethra, filled with tips on how to use plants for healing and cooking. But the people from Terrene knew about her dark secret—how she used magick in herbology to create poisons far deadlier than any natural toxin. She was a figure of respect, yet a Terrenean boogeyman whose name kept small children from popping unknown foliage into their mouths. It seemed that her darker aspect was what drew Abbadon.

Harmon overheard a bunch of the scientists talking a few weeks ago, about "focusing on the Ethereal Tree". They had already taken a piece, were they wanting to get the rest of it? It made me wonder, why were they researching poison and the Ethereal Tree? One theory we'd thrown around was that they were planning to poison magick itself. The idea of magick being damaged was terrifying. If magick stopped working, how could I go back home?

I hopped off the bed and started pacing, my mind racing. There wasn't time to overthink things; in the next hour, the plan would be set in motion, and I needed to be in the right mindset if we were going to pull this off.

For the last few months, we had grappled with the knowledge that we couldn't do this on our own. There had to be someone on our side with access to the building. It felt like a big gamble, and if we chose the wrong person, the whole plan could fall apart. It took us about two and a half months to decide on the lunch lady, Miss Ethel. She was from the same village in Terrene as Sylas—Solaris. He said they knew each other, and their families were close. She used to walk him to school when he was little. She even came with him the day they brought him here. Sylas was really sure we could trust her, and I hoped his intuition was right.

It didn't take long for Miss Ethel to agree to help. In fact, she already knew something was off about the way the training was going and how much information was hidden from the support staff. She snuck us some paper and pencils so we could explain everything to her. She was shocked by the harsh conditions and the experiments they were running on us. That was what convinced her to help us escape. She said she was getting close to one of the guards, and when she got the chance, she'd steal his Syncros—the device that could unlock our Stasis Bands. Everything was coming together, and I could hardly wait to feel the wind in my hair.

Soon, I'd finally get to go home. *Go over the plan again.*

"Okay, Miss Ethel will unlock our Stasis Bands," I mouth to myself. I didn't know if the room was bugged but I wasn't about to test it now. "Faye will freeze time but not us. I'll blow away the glass walls in the cafeteria to get us out of here. Aris will create an illusion to make us invisible so we can lose them. In the forest, Aurelian will turn the plants into giant barricades. And then I'll finally go home to Mom and Dad in Verglas."

I repeated the plan silently, over and over, until it felt like the words were burned into my mind. Just as I was getting into a rhythm, I heard the familiar beep of the doors sliding open. This was it.

"You know the drill."

"Against the wall." I finished Brickface's sentence and faced the wall next to the bed. He placed the magnetic cuffs on me and led me down the hallway toward the cafeteria. Each step felt like a drumbeat in my chest. I was just a few steps away from escaping. Everything I'd learned at the Academy in Verglas had led up to this moment. My heart was racing, but I tried to keep a calm face, just like they taught us.

As I walked, a memory flashed in my mind. I was back in our little house after my first day at the Academy. Mom was sitting on the edge of my bed, gently tending to my wounds. They didn't let us use Mending magick for injuries unless they were really bad, so I had to deal with the pain. I could still feel the sting in my swollen eye and the ache in my bruised lip. I had sparred with the best fighter that day, and she hadn't gone easy on me. They were never supposed to go easy.

"I hate this," I remember crying, my voice small and shaky. "Please don't make me go back in there."

Mom's face was soft and sad as she dabbed ointment onto my eye. "Oh, my little one," she said gently, "I know it's hard. We all had to go through the training—it's brutal, I remember. I got bruised and beaten up too, just like you. But if you stop now, they'll send you far away, and we won't be able to be there for you. We just want to keep you safe. We don't want to lose you." Her words hung in the air, heavy and real.

"Please... please." The sting in my eye hurt even more as I begged, my voice trembling.

"Listen to me," Mom said softly, but firmly. "People with the biggest hearts often have to handle the biggest pain. And you, Jho-analyn, you have the biggest heart I know. The way you love your friends, the way you care for everyone you meet, it shows me just how strong you are. That's why I know you'll get through this." She hugged me tightly, her warmth making me feel a little braver. "Pain is temporary, I promise you that."

"Okay..." I whispered, trying to stop my tears. I didn't want to go back to the Academy, but the thought of being sent away, away from Mom and Dad, was even worse.

"Strong heart, little one. Remember that," she said. I nodded, holding on to the strength she believed I had.

I blinked the memory away as we reached the cafeteria doors. Mom's words echoed in my head. The memory was a reminder of why I had to be strong—why I had to get out of here and make it back to them. This was the only chance I would get. I had to focus.

Brickface took the cuffs off me and the doors slid open. Before they closed behind me, he said, "Good luck." I twisted my head to look back at him, but was met with cold metal.

Why did he say that? I saw the other kids at the same corner, all looking away from the entrance. It was just like any other day. I got a tray of the gray gunk, and Miss Ethel gave me a secretive nod. I was always the last one to come in for lunch. She then walked away from her post and went through a door only she had access to. Making my way to the benches, I sat in between Aris and Faye.

"Happy Birthday, Aurelian." I smiled at him.

The faces around me were grim, but determined.

"My only wish for today is to celebrate outside with the wind." He gripped Sylas's hand so tightly his knuckles were turning white. One by one, we formed a ring of linked hands, Aris and Faye taking mine.

"We go home today," Sylas says in a low voice.

"No matter what happens, I'm happy to have met all of you." Lyra whispered, tears in her eyes.

The Squad's faces flashed in my head. *I'm coming, guys, wait for me.*

"Where's Miss Ethel?" Harmon looked back at the door she'd left through.

"Do you think she got caught?" Faye let go, breaking our circle.

"No, if that was the case the alarms would be going off by now," Aurelian pointed out. His voice is steady and calm, but something didn't feel right. It was starting to feel like the Akeurimja Forest incident, somehow.

The main entrance slammed open and there was Miss Ethel, her chest heaving. "I have it!" She raised the Syncros towards us triumphantly.

We leaped up from our seats and bolted for the center of the room.

"Give it to me, please," Sylas said, taking a step and extending his arm.

Miss Ethel stretched out an arm, letting the Syncros hover just above his palm, but pulled away at the last moment.

"Before I let you kids out of here," she whispered, "there's something you need to know."

My gaze flickered around our group. Were they thinking what I was thinking?

"We don't have time, *Hara*," Sylas hissed, using the Terrenean word for *Tante*'. I'd never used it for her though. She'd agreed too easily to our plan, and something didn't sit right with me about it. And at that very moment, my hunch would either be proven right, or wrong.

Miss Ethel glanced behind her again, then back at us. Her worried expression had melted away under the light of a disconcerting grin. She always looked so innocent, the way she spoke, the fragility of her advanced age, but all of that was gone as she raised the Syncros. She wiggled it just out of reach. Taunting us.

"When you came to me for help, at first I thought, 'These kids are playing a prank on me,' but one look at your faces, I knew you were all going to betray our Savior."

"*Hara*..." Sylas said, looking horror-struck. "You watched over me when I was kid. You're my parents' friend. You *know* what they're doing to us here."

I already knew it was a lost cause, even as Sylas tried to reason with her.

"The Convergence is upon us, little one. All of you now serve a higher purpose." As the words left her mouth, the cafeteria doors slid open and several guards marched through it, drawing their batons.

"I fucking knew it. Why can't you guys just trust my gut," Faye spat out.

"The Savior knew about your little plan; did you think it would be this easy?" Ethel let out a cruel laugh. "Thanks to you, I'm not just an expendable lunch lady anymore."

Sylas turned to us, eyes flooding with tears. "I'm sorry," he choked out.

"I'm not." Faye nodded at Lyra and, in one sudden motion, charged at Ethel. Lyra yanked me behind the others, preventing me from bolting after Faye. The guards lit up their batons a moment too late. Faye grabbed onto Ethel's arm and bit down, hard. Ethel screamed and dropped the now-blood-splattered Syncros. Faye moved like a true Ghelcarii, wiry arms shooting through the air to seize the device before it had time to strike the ground.

"Do something you useless golems!" Ethel howled at the wary guards, trying desperately to shake the feral teen from her bleeding arm. Before anyone could come to our traitor's aid, Faye unlocked her jaw and swung the back of her fist at Ethel's stomach, knocking the air out of her lungs. Faye whipped back around, reaching out with the Syncros but the violent triumph in her eyes faded as a baton found its way to her side. Her shrieks pierced the room as she fell to the ground, limbs twitching.

"Fuck you!" Aris snarled and leaped into the fold. The boys didn't hesitate; they jumped in right after him. They threw punches, kicked, and climbed atop the significantly larger guards. They worked like a well oiled machine, trying to topple the men to the ground.

"Stay here!" Lyra barked at me.

"No, I can help!" I snapped, trying to shove my way around her. Lyra grabbed my shoulders, her squeeze tight.

"We chose you," she rasped. The air whooshed from my chest. They knew this plan wasn't going to work. All this time they were preparing for plan B. My hands curled into fists, and I nodded tightly. She then took one deep breath and let me go, screaming as she ran to join the fight.

I watched with gritted teeth as my friends fought, their faces twisted in pain and determination. Aris yelled curses, throwing punches, but the guards stayed standing. I saw the crackle of electricity before it hit them. Lyra managed to snatch the Syncros from Faye's hand but the current struck her before she could make her escape. She cried out, and the device skidded across the floor, far from my reach. One by one, my friends fell, recoiling from the agonizing currents of the batons.

Aurelian, though, stayed on his feet. He took hit after hit but refused to go down. As the guards continued to pour electricity into his system, he locked eyes with me, his face a mix of pain and fierce resolve. With a final burst of strength, he grabbed the Syncros from the floor and hurled it toward me. I caught it just as he collapsed, his body crumpling to the ground.

My heart raced as I slammed the Syncros onto my bracelet. The metal band fell away, clattering to the ground. The guards hesitated, their eyes shifting toward me with new caution. I shoved the Syncros into my back pocket and raised my hands. Two glowing shields appeared on both palms, their edges shimmering with energy.

"Get her!" Brickface shouted. The guards closed in, their batons crackling. I threw one of my shields, and it exploded on impact, sending guards stumbling backward. I hurled the other shield, and another explosion rang out. I moved across the floor on just the balls of my feet—the lighter my steps were, the quicker I was. I charged up a shield to blast the remaining guards away. All those times I was beaten down and kicked to the dirt came rushing in my thoughts.

Pain is temporary... I took a deep breath, trying to calm the chaos inside me. *Read their movements, react quickly, and don't let your defense break.* As I let out a slow breath, everything around me sharpened. I could hear every sound, see every move. My body responded faster, like it knew what to do before I did. I felt Eyre's bond flowing through me, giving me strength.

I dodged the first swing and sent a force field crashing into the guard's chest, knocking him back. Another came at me from the side, but I spun away, blowing him away with a shield that burst like a concussive bubble. The stream of guards kept coming, but I was quicker. I ducked, dodged, and struck back, my force fields slamming into them with bursts of energy. Every time they tried to close in, I pushed them back, my power surging with each hit. Eyre's bond made me feel invincible.

But no matter how many guards I took out, more just kept coming. I was getting tired, and I didn't know how much longer I could keep this up.

"Run!" Aris shouted, his voice breaking through the chaos. My friends joined in, their cries blending with the sounds of battle.

"Run, Jho!" Faye screamed, wincing in pain.

Lyra's words echoed in my mind: *"We chose you."*

I couldn't let their choice be in vain. I was escaping today. With renewed determination, I conjured a massive force field, stretching it to cover the glass walls. The shield rippled and then detonated, shattering the walls and making an opening. I sprinted toward it, just as Abbadon stepped into the room. Our eyes met. I leaped out, creating transparent steps to guide me down to the forest floor.

Behind me, laser guns fired, shots whizzing past me. I made a shield around my back, deflecting their white-hot beams with a shimmering barrier. When I hit the ground, I glanced back to see Abbadon staring down at me from the broken building. I took off through the thick forest, my heart pounding with every step. I ran as fast as I could, the barbed plants slicing my skin as I pushed forward. My breath was ragged, and every cut burned, but I couldn't stop. Suddenly, the sound of warning alarms blared from the facility behind me.

I skidded to a halt, my heart pounding in my chest. The sky above me darkened, and a few drops of rain began to fall. At first, it seemed like normal rain, but then I heard the soft hissing coming from the plants around me. I looked up just as a drop hit my cheek, and I winced in pain—it was acid rain.

Panicking, I quickly pushed out a shield dome around me as the rain started to pour down harder. Any plant life around me began to melt, their leaves and stems dissolving into mush. My force field was holding, but I could see it starting to weaken under the relentless assault of the rain. At this rate, I'd end up just like the plants—melted away into nothing. Abbadon was willing to kill me.

Frantically, I scanned my surroundings for anything that could help, and that's when I saw it—an animal about the size of a leopard, but it looked more like an anteater with its long snout and curved back. Its skin glimmered with a rainbow-like sheen, reflecting the acid rain as if it were nothing.It looked at me before continuing on its way, completely unbothered. A Chrysalorn.

I'd heard about these creatures before—Chrysalorns were known to be extremely adaptive, able to survive almost anything, even the end of the world. Al said they were like Calithoceres—creatures that weren't aggressive unless provoked. Tears welled up in my eyes as I realized what I had to do.

With a heavy heart, I detonated my melting shield, momentarily pushing the rain away, then formed another shield like an umbrella over my head. I conjured the sword Boyko had crafted for me. It bore the sigils of our family, reading "bright forever" in the old tongue. Carved runes coiled their way down its metal—the runes that brought it to me no matter where in the world I was. The Chrysalorn seemed to sense my intent and turned to face me, with a challenge in its eye.

I choked back a sob, and ran at the beast, my heart pounding in my ears. It charged, and just as it was about to reach me, I tensed my body and released a force blast, something I'd learned from all those torturous experiments. The explosion sent the Chrysalorn flying into the air. Without thinking, I gripped the hilt of my sword and sliced through its belly as it came down, killing it instantly. It all happened so fast.

I fell to my knees beside it, plunging my fingers into the fatal wound. Its entrails were hot and slick between my fingers. I forced myself through the nausea churning in my gut as I slid my legs into the emptied cavity of its belly. The shield umbrella above me dissolved just as I ducked my head into its ribcage. The acid rain pattered harmlessly off the Chrysalorn's oil-slick skin. The congealing blood dripped from above and pooled beneath me. I could feel it soaking into my clothes.

I had just killed an innocent animal, a creature that had done nothing to warrant its death, but I had no choice. This was survival, and I was on my own now. Everything I had believed in died with the Chrysalorn. As the blood around me slowly cooled around, something inside me switched on.

I didn't know how long I lay there, huddled inside the Chrysalorn's body, listening to the deadly rain fall. But one thing was clear—I couldn't abandon the people who helped me escape. As soon as this rain ended, I was going back for them, no matter what it took.

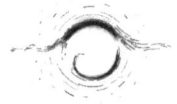

Everything was gone—melted away by the acid rain. For what felt like miles, nothing was left but scorched earth. Some nations had devices to manipulate the weather, though the Space Ring had the greatest need for it—to make people feel like they were back on Ethra. But using it to create acid rain? It proved the suspicions I had all along—the use of poison in Abbadon's experiments.

I walked toward the facility, feeling the rage boiling up inside me. I couldn't hold it back anymore. The alarms were blaring once again, warning them that I'd somehow survived the lethal downpour. This time, I wouldn't run. Guards came rushing out, but instead of batons, they had laser guns. Up in the towers, I saw two more guards with snipers aimed right at me. They wanted a fight. Well, I was going to give them one.

"Dead or alive," one of the guards shouted, and they began to fire. I surrounded myself with a force field, watching as the lasers ricocheted off and sparked against the ground. The snipers were aiming for my head, and I could feel the impact of their shots cracking my shield. I filled my lungs with air, charged my force field, and with one strong push, I blew it outward. The blast slammed my opponents into the walls. I heard bones crack and saw blood splatter. The tower guards were thrown back too, but before they could recover, I swiped my arms in an arc and sent scythed blades of energy crashing into the towers, bludgeoning them to pieces.

I ran into the building, expecting to find scientists or other workers, but the place was empty. *Were they evacuated? Was I too late?* I barely had time to think before another group of guards came marching down the hallway. *How many guards does this place have?!* The red alarm lights made the whole corridor look like it was on fire. There were so many of them—at least thirty. I slowed my breathing, reaching out for Eyre's power.

"*Jhoana...*" I heard Eyre's voice in my head. "*I am here. I lend you my power.*"

I thought back to the hidden cave where I used to visit Eyre. I loved watching her swim, especially when she would shape herself into water. Eyre couldn't fully mimic the water wyrm's abilities—she couldn't turn her head into water. But what if I could borrow that power? What if I could make my entire body flow like water?

I opened my eyes, feeling a bizarre rush through me. My bones felt like they were melding into my flesh. I wasn't sure if I could even move, but the guards were coming at me with everything they had. There was no time to think, so I didn't—I just moved. Somehow, I didn't feel myself come into contact with anything solid. Their bodies buffeted mine, as if I'd merely brushed past them. In my wake, they slipped and fell like bowling pins. I did it—I could shape myself into water.

"Thank you, Eyre," I whispered, gliding past the cursing guards.

When my body solidified again, I turned back to the tangle of guns, batons, and body armor. These were the people who had trapped and tortured an untold number of kids. I couldn't let them keep doing it. I clapped my hands together and weaved the astral weapon spell, conjuring a bow and arrow.

"See you in Hell," I muttered, knowing there was no going back from this. I had become what I never let the Ghelcarii Academy make me—a monster.

I fired, each arrow breaking through their flimsy armor. With each death, a tear fell from my eyes and a piece of my soul crumbled away. When it was over, the hallway was empty, nothing but a trail of corpses and gold dust to mark what I'd done.

"Safe passage," I whispered, the words barely leaving my lips. The motes of glittering dust rose from each lifeless body, carrying the souls of thirty people back to the Ethereal Tree. I knew this was a fact of death here, but I'd never seen it with my own eyes. Until now.

I turned and bolted to the rooms where we'd been locked up, but they were empty. Where could everyone have gone? There was no way they could have moved them while the rain fell. Right? I raced to the security room and took out the door. The screens showed nothing, except for one camera at the back entrance—huge, white transport modules were leaving. If I could get to one, maybe I could find out where they were taking my friends.

I didn't hesitate. I used my force field steps to get to the back entrance faster. Just as I reached it, I saw Faye being shoved into a van with the others. One of the guards slammed the door shut and turned to face me. It was him—Brickface. He smirked at me, but I wasn't going to let him get away. I threw up a force field in front of him and blasted him backward, knocking him away from the van.

I ran to the van and yanked the doors open.

"Jho? What are you doing here? Why'd you come back?" Aurelian shouted, sounding almost angry.

"I'm not losing any of you," I retorted, pulling out the Syncros from my pocket. I quickly disarmed each Stasis Band. My friends flexed their freed wrists. "Where are they taking the rest?" I asked.

"Whose blood is that?" Lyra whispered, but I ignored her.

"We don't know where," Harmon answered, cracking his stiff fingers. "But Abbadon's relocating after our stunt." He shoved his hands toward some bushes just beyond the open garage, and they started expanding. "Powers are back.".

"Plan later. Let's get out of here first," Sylas said.

"Guys!" Lyra shouted. We turned around to see Brickface back on his feet, his finger pressed to his ear.

"You're outnumbered," Aris warned him.

"You don't want to mess with what they've been training us for," Aurelian added, but Brickface showed no fear.

"Understood, sir. No one alive," he said with a devilish grin. "You're all mine to finish." He pulled out a blade from his pocket and sliced his palm, letting the blood drip down as he clapped his hands together. A dark purple aura surrounded his hands, and the blood began to float. I took an involuntary step back.

What kind of magick is this?

"Get ready!" Aurelian yelled. But I wasn't going to wait. I threw a dome around Brickface and, without hesitating, imploded it. Blood splattered everywhere, and his body hit the ground with a hard thud.

I could feel their eyes on me. Fear, horror, disgust, I didn't really care.

I just wanted to go home.

But there was no going back now.

JHOANA

The wind bites at my skin as I step into the village of Glaedhaven. It's always cold here. The air is thick with the scent
of snow and pine, carried down from the icy peaks of the neighboring nation of Verglas. I tighten the worn, red scarf around my
neck—Dustin's gift from all those years ago—seeking warmth from
its familiar comfort. The mountains loom in the distance, their
jagged edges cutting into the gray sky like teeth. The chill seeps into
my bones, but I've long since grown used to it. The cold has a way of
numbing things—feelings, memories, the past. I find it comforting.

The market is nestled in the heart of the village, a cluster of
wooden stalls huddled together against the cold. Smoke rises from
chimneys, mingling with the breath of vendors and buyers alike,
creating a misty haze that hangs over everything. The ground is a
mix of frozen soil and slush, and the air buzzes with the sounds of
trade.

The beings here are as varied as the goods they peddle. A trio of
tall, slender sylren women—ethereal beings from the frozen seas,
known for their control over ice and their ability to commune with
the winds—bartered over furs with a stout dwarven merchant, his
beard streaked with frost. A centaur stands at the edge of the market, his hooves stamping the ground impatiently as he waits for his
turn at the communal blacksmith's forge. A pair of small, winged
sprites flit through the crowd, their laughter like the tinkling of tiny
bells as they weave between the stalls.

I pull my cloak tighter around me, the fur-lined hood shadowing
my face. I've no desire to draw attention, but in a place like this,
anonymity is hard to maintain. Eyes follow me as I pass—some
curious, some wary—but I keep my gaze forward, my pace steady.
The less they see of me, the better.

A vendor catches my eye, his stall piled high with fruits and
vegetables that seem out of place in this frozen landscape. He's

human, tall and broad-shouldered, with a smile that's a little too eager. New blood in Glaedhaven. He doesn't recognize me, which means he hasn't been here long. That's a mistake.

"Morning, miss," he greets me, his voice smooth despite the cold. "Got some of the finest produce in all of Zaltana. Fresh from the southern valleys. How about a taste?"

I glance at the apples stacked neatly in a wooden crate. They're too red, too perfect. I know they won't hold up to scrutiny. "Those apples," I say, my voice, and cutting through the chill like a blade, "look like they've seen better days."

His smile falters, just for a second. "Oh, these? They're just as good as they look, I swear. A bit of a frost nip, nothing more. I'll give you a good price."

I reach out, take one of the apples in hand. The skin is smooth, but it's colder than it should be, and I can feel the softness beneath the surface. It's starting to rot from the inside. I turn it over in my hand, then toss it back into the crate with a disdainful flick of my wrist. "You think I'm an idiot?"

The vendor's smile freezes, and he stammers something about a discount, but I'm already done with him. I grab two and toss a couple of petras, global Ethran coins, onto the counter—exactly what the rotting fruit is worth—and turn on my heel, my boots crunching in the frost as I walk away. His protests fade into the background noise of the market.

I've seen worse than a vendor trying to cheat me. But these small victories—they remind me that I'm still here, still fighting. The cold wind brushes my face, and I welcome it. It keeps me sharp.

The market winds through the village like a frozen river, each stall a little island of temporary warmth. I keep moving, my boots skidding slightly on the slick ground, the cold air filling my lungs with each breath. The crowds thin as I move deeper into the market, away from the more popular stalls. That's when I see it—a small, unassuming stall tucked away in a corner, the wooden sign above it swaying gently in the breeze.

The sign is written in the old Verglasian script, elegant and sharp, like frost patterns on a windowpane. I approach, drawn by a sense of familiarity I haven't felt in years. The stall is cluttered with knick-knacks from all over, but it's the items from Verglas that catch my eye. Carved ice sculptures encased in glass, jewelry made from froststone, and at the center of it all, a mirror.

The mirror is exquisite, its frame crafted from silvery icewood—a material found only in the deepest forests of Verglas. The wood is etched with intricate patterns that shift and shimmer as they catch the light. The glass itself is flawless, reflecting the world with a clarity that feels almost unnatural. It's a piece of home, and it stops me in my tracks.

"Beautiful, isn't it?" The voice is soft, almost reverent. I look up to see the seller, a woman wrapped in heavy furs, her breath visible in the cold air. Her eyes are a pale blue, almost white: a trait common among those from Verglas.

"Where did you get this?" I ask, my voice more controlled than I feel.

"From a trader who passed through Verglas not long ago. You don't see many pieces like this outside the nation. It's rare, one of a kind, even." Her gaze flicks to my hair, which I've braided in the Verglasian style—three tight plaits woven together at the base of my neck. It's a habit I haven't broken, even after all these years.

"Your braids... You're from Verglas, aren't you?" she asks, a note of surprise in her voice.

I nod slightly, unwilling to reveal more. "I was," I say, my tone making it clear the conversation shouldn't go further.

A look of understanding passes over her face. "It's not often we see our own this far from home," she says, a hint of melancholy in her voice. She reaches out, gently lifting the mirror from its stand. "Take it. A gift. Verglasians should hold on to pieces of their past, even if they've left it behind." I start to protest, but she shakes her head, pressing the mirror into my hands. "Please. It's yours."

The weight of the mirror feels heavier than it should. I nod in thanks, unable to find the words, and turn away before the memories can surface. But it's too late. The cold air bites at my face, and suddenly I'm not in Glaedhaven anymore. I'm back in Verglas, crouched behind a boulder near our home's entrance, watching the light dim in my mother's eyes.

I need a drink.

The pub isn't far, a warm glow spilling out from its windows onto the icy street. It's a welcome contrast to the cold that's seeped into my bones. The sign above the door reads, "Monox's Hearth," and as I push the door open, the smell of roasted geluer and the sound of laughter greet me like an old friend.

The interior is a mix of old and new, the walls lined with dark wooden beams that give the place a rustic feel, while the furnishings are sleek and modern. Tables are scattered across the room, most occupied by travelers and locals alike, all seeking refuge from the cold. A fire crackles in the hearth, and the warmth is immediate, chasing away the chill that clings to me.

"Ana!" A deep voice booms from behind the bar, and I look up to see Monox, the cyclops owner, grinning at me, his sapphire eye twinkling. He's massive, even for a cyclops, his head nearly brushing the ceiling. "Your usual?"

"Yeah, thanks," I reply, making my way to the bar. The other patrons barely glance at me, too wrapped up in their own conversations. That's how I like it.

Monox slides a tankard of Frostfire mead across the bar to me. The blue liquid inside swirls with flecks of silver. "On the house," he says with a wink. "That thundertusk boar you took down? It's making me a lot of drin. You've got talent, Ana."

I nod in appreciation, lifting the tankard to my lips. The mead burns as it goes down, a pleasant warmth spreading through my body, melting the ice that's taken root in my chest. I close my eyes, savoring the heat, letting it dull the edges of the memories that won't leave me alone.

When I open them again, the mirror is still there, resting on the bar beside me. My reflection stares back at me, and for a moment, I'm lost in it. I try to see the little girl who first came to Ethra with her best friends, a child full of hope and wonder. But instead, all I see is a woman whose hope died alongside that little girl.

My long, black hair falls well past my shoulders, the same deep shade that Jadis used to wear proudly. I once considered it as a link to my past, but now it feels like a shackle. My hair is braided tight, a habit from home, keeping it hanging between my shoulder blades.

I shake my head, trying to clear away the fog of nostalgia that threatens to overwhelm me. Why am I thinking of them again? Jadis, Rictor, and the others—they're a part of a past that I've left behind. They're a chapter that's been closed, and yet, here I am, haunted by them more than three decades later.

As I lift the tankard to my lips, the sharp taste of the mead jolts me back to the present. The reflection in the mirror is a reminder of the loss I've endured, but it's also a stark realization that today is a day for remembering.

It's the death anniversary of my adoptive parents, Valda and Boyko. They took me in when I had nothing and gave me a family when I was alone. Their deaths were a wound that never quite healed, and every year, I find myself grappling with the weight of their absence all over again.

I take another sip, trying to push away the tide of memories and focus on the present. The fire crackles, the mead burns, and the mirror remains a silent witness to a past that refuses to stay buried.

~ ~ ~

Sylas had determined that we were somewhere in the forests of the Great Eagle Fields.

He suggested we head to the nearest village, Moore View, for help, but Harmon shut him down.

"Too risky," he said. "We don't know how far the O'rians' influence has spread. We can't trust anyone."

The group continued to argue, their voices slicing through the warm air. I felt pulled in a hundred different directions, each one seemingly worse than the last. Suddenly, a thought struck me—*Verglas. My parents.* They were the only ones who could help us, the only ones who could contact the guardians of the Squad.

"We should go to Verglas," I blurted out. My voice sounded more confident than I felt.

Faye nodded eagerly, backing me up.

"Valda and Boyko, my parents, they'd protect us. I'm still a Noble; I have to have some political power left, right?"

Aurelian looked skeptical. "How do we even get there? The nearest Gate is in Islaug, and that's miles away."

"What about the teleportation spell?" Lyra suggested, but everyone else seemed unsure. None of us had ever done such a big spell before. Why would we?

But I remembered Jads teaching me that spell. "It'll work," I forced the words out like I believed them, "but we have to be really exact about where we want to go."

Aris stepped forward. "I can show us what your home looks like if you tell me about it."

I nodded and started describing my home. As I spoke, Aris created an illusion of it—my house, the trees covered in frost, and the sky, all icy blue. With each change to the vision, my homesickness became more intense.

When I was satisfied that everyone could visualize my home clearly, we stood in a circle and clapped our hands together. The air around us began to thrum with energy. The circle glowed bright with a rainbow of colors. It reminded me painfully of the Chrysalorn. I began weaving the signs, telling myself over and over, "Home. Just think of home."

As I completed the spell, the buzzing air clenched tightly around us, like the world was folding into itself. Then, without warning, it all snapped back to normal. We found ourselves standing on the chilly, frost-covered grass of Verglas, our breaths puffing out in the cold air. Despite my calm assurances, I was just as shocked as the others. We did it.

But we didn't feel safe for long. Aurelian saw it at the same time as me; the white transport module from the O'rian facility. *How did it get her so fast?*

"Hide!" Aurelian yelped, and we all rushed to find cover. The others ducked behind houses nearby, while Faye and I squeezed behind a big boulder that was just right to shield us both.

"Is Abbadon here?" Aris's whisper carried through the eerily still air, fear choking his words.

"Where is everyone? Why are the streets empty?" Sylas murmured from behind him. His voice was shaking. With fear or cold, I wasn't sure.

"It's the Iskristall Fest; everyone's at the square celebrating," Faye said softly.

I cautiously peeked from behind the boulder, glancing at the window of my home. Dad stood there, wearing a puzzled expression.

"I'm going in," I said, but Faye seized my arm, holding me back.

"Wait. What if it's Abbadon?" Her voice trembled.

They're all so scared of him. Should I be too? "I don't care! Those are my parents," I snapped back, my heart pounding in my chest.

Before I could move, Harmon's voice cut in, "Why is the clairvoyant from Fleming in your house?"

Chills shot through me as I looked again. There she was—Evanora. She stared out the window, a smug smile curling her lips. I held my breath, praying she hadn't spotted me. Then, something caught her attention, and she turned away, her expression shifting.

"That's her, the witch I warned you about." I said as my heart sank. I leaned back against the boulder, the biting cold barely registering compared to the dread of having the almost-Supreme witch in my home.

"Are we engaging?" Sylas asked nervously.

"No, she's too powerful; we wouldn't stand a chance." Lyra's voice was so small, it could have been a trick of the wind.

"What do we do?" Faye looked to me, as if I was any kind of leader. Just as I was about to respond, the door suddenly burst open. Faye and I both peeked out from behind our rock. Evanora stepped outside, draped in a dramatic, violet, fur-lined cloak, far too extravagant for any Verglasian. Something about her appearance was off. Dark purple veins radiated from her eyes—subtle, yet unmistakable. The color reminded me of something. A brief image played in my mind's eye, of Brickface slicing his palm and conjuring the bruise-colored magick...

Abbadon stepped out of the house in her wake, looking almost like any regular person—charming, even—but there was something unsettling about him too. He could be mistaken for someone's friendly neighbor, yet his eyes were cold, void of warmth or life.

Dad appeared next, his face etched with worry but maintaining a strong stance.

"Please," he implored, "don't harm my daughter."

Evanora responded with a harsh laugh. "Jhoana will be long dead before you can help her."

Dad looked as if she'd struck him. He turned his head towards the boulder where I was hiding. Our eyes met briefly before his gaze snapped back to his unwelcome house guests. Raising his voice, he declared, "Then you clearly underestimate my daughter. She's far braver than you think, and if it's the will of the Tree, she will *hide* from you as long as necessary. I promise you that, witch."

His words were clear—stay hidden.

"Mind your tongue, fool. You're lucky we're letting you and your wife live," Abbadon said, his voice smooth but laced with menace.

Mom and Dad exchanged a glance, then burst into laughter, the sound sharp and mocking.

"You think you're threatening us?" Dad chuckled, shaking his head. "Do you even know where you are? This is our home. You hold no power here."

Mom shot Abaddon a look of disdain. "You barge into our house, demanding information about our daughter, and have the audacity to insult my husband? Get out, and don't come back!" My heart clenched at the sight of her standing tall and defiant.

Abbadon scoffed, unfazed by their words. "Send my regards to the Tree," he said, nodding toward Evanora.

My blood turned to ice. "No," I whispered under my breath, feeling Faye's hand tighten around mine. Her eyes dropped, avoiding what we both knew was coming.

In one smooth motion, Evanora sliced her palm open. Mom and Dad, who had been so sure, tensed immediately, their faces hardening as they braced for a fight. But the sight of the blood spilling from Evanora's hand left them stunned, their disbelief morphing into shock at whatever dark ritual was unfolding before them.

Evanora let her blood drip to the ground, clapping her hands together as a dark purple glow spiraled around her fingers. My parents were already in motion—Dad launched a blast of energy at her before the tendrils even formed, and Mom cast a shield spell around them. They fought with everything they had, trying to sever the dark magick before it could take shape.

But it wasn't enough.

The blood tendrils burst forth, stronger and more vicious than anything they could anticipate. Dad's attacks sliced through a few, but more kept coming. Mom's barrier flickered under the relentless assault, her face tightening with the effort to keep it up.

And then Evanora's spell reached its peak. The tendrils crashed through their defenses with brutal force, latching onto them. The moment they touched, everything changed. Their strength, their life force—it all began to drain away.

I watched in horror as they withered, their bodies growing weak, their faces pale and gaunt.

I wanted to scream, to run to them, but I was frozen, transfixed by the nightmare unfolding before me.

Mom... Dad...

From afar, panicked cries cut through the tension. "Valda! Boyko!" I looked up to see a couple sprinting towards the scene, their faces marked with terror.

"Mom? Mommy?" Faye whispered, her voice thick with dread.

But before her parents could reach us, Abbadon raised his hand. With a mere flick of his wrist, the blood tendrils from Evanora were drawn towards him. He extended his hand towards the approaching couple and, in a horrifying flash, their heads were severed from their bodies.

Tears streamed down Faye's face, her breath hitching in a silent scream. I clamped my hand over her mouth, stifling the cry that threatened to give us away. Our eyes met, sharing a silent agony—our worlds shattered in an instant.

A cold truth settled in my heart. Nowhere was safe anymore. From this day on, our old selves had to die; we had to become something new, something fierce, just to survive.

~ ~ ~

I down the rest of my drink, not to drown the memories, but to honor my parents. Suddenly, the pub becomes a hive of activity; everyone, including Monox, is glued to their Holo-phones.

"Looks like the Nobles might be back," the cyclops murmurs. He shows me a blurry image of a group with glowing eyes but pulls the device away before I can examine it closely. Despite the image's fuzziness, I know without a doubt—it's the Squad.

My hands tremble. *What are they doing back in Ethra? What's happening on Earth?*

Monox adds, "Can't be the Earth Nobles, though. These people look way younger."

His comment catches me; it mirrors my own unexplained youthful appearance despite my true age. Even by Ethran standards, I look far younger than I am.

As I ponder, my pocket buzzes. People always give me strange looks when they see me using such outdated equipment, but I never could bring myself to stop using the phone Rictor gave me all those years back. The Spectra Vision, as it's called, flashes, "Lacey calling." I guess the news has reached her already. Lacey is the only person who truly knows who I am, the one friend I can completely trust.

I thank Monox for the drink and step outside the pub to find some quiet. I answer the call, and Lacey's bright voice bursts through.

"I can't even say if it's them," I admit, though everything in my gut screams it is. I try to rationalize, reminding myself that glowing eyes don't necessarily mean anything.

"But who else has glowing eyes besides Sólel and the Nobles?" Lacey pushes back. "Why are you making excuses? Aren't you excited? This could mean you get to go back home."

"Maybe I don't want to go back," I say softly.

Lacey sighs, letting it go. "Well, when you do decide to go, the picture was taken in Terrene. But see me in Arid first, okay?"

I laugh, feeling a brief lift in my spirits. "*If* I decide anything," I promise.

Lacey grumbles a farewell and I let the phone fall from my ear.

For thirty-two years, my life has been about surviving in Ethra, the world we supposedly crafted. All the pain, the loss, the joy—it's all been real. Am I ready to say goodbye to this life? Then again, am I ready to give up on Earth completely?

I hike up to the hill where Dustin and I once battled Ade', finding comfort under a tree that's become a familiar refuge, overlooking the villages. I set the apples I bought from the new vendor next to the small mirror.

"I miss you every day, Mom and Dad," I whisper with a smile, my words dissolving into the wind. "If only I could have saved you both." The sadness is overtaking me now. I sit with their memory for a while, whispering bits of news about my life and about the world they left behind. When I'm ready, get to my feet and head towards the Gate.

As I walk through the market, my thoughts drift to Maks, Mikal, and Jihyun—my kids, for whom I'd do anything. They're the only ones who witness any remaining softness in me, and even they know it's a rare sight.

Thoughts of my children inevitably lead my mind to the Squad. What would I do when I see them again? Would I confront them with anger for leaving me, or would the overwhelming relief of seeing their faces again drive me to tears? Even as the years began to blend together, I thought of them every day.

With these thoughts spiraling in my mind, I realize that, no matter what happens, I must first prepare the kids for whatever may be coming. It's been a long time since I've felt so torn about anythi ng.This cold heart in my chest is now equally halved between the ghosts of the past and the possibilities of the future.

Fuck.

A tingling sensation courses through me as I step out of the Gate, echoing the familiar thrill of Transcending. I draw in a deep breath of the Space Ring's cool, artificial air. It's nothing like Ethra's, but it carries a comforting semblance of normalcy. This place has been a sanctuary since I escaped with the kids, a refuge far beyond the reach of the O'rians, and over the years, it has remained just that—a safe space.

The customs hall is predictably crowded, the same old scene of travelers and residents shuffling through. Robots move efficiently among them, their sleek forms slipping through the lines with a mundane, practiced ease that I've grown too accustomed to take much notice. The architecture here tries to impress with its clean lines and transparent surfaces that play lazily with the ambient light. Around me, the usual mix of people and leyfolk jostles, each absorbed in the routine of homecoming or departure—a sight so familiar it's almost tedious.

Since the rise of the O'rians over the years, the use of Gate portals has dropped significantly, with most shut tight to block any unwelcome entry. What was once a swift process has become bogged down with additional precautions as the O'rians take over more cities, turning everything frustratingly slow.

I retrieve my passport and hand it over to the agent. My image and alias, Ana Hendricks, display on the glass window. The agent then uses a scanner, designed to detect any traces of blood magick. Those who practice blood magick are marked by a distinct curse—dark veins that wrap around their eyes.

The agent looks up from scanning my passport with a playful glint in his eye. "What was the reason for your visit in Ethra?" he teases. I give him an exasperated look, prompting a chuckle from him. "Just kidding. How was Glaedhaven?"

"Still the same as the last time I was there," I reply, not missing a beat.

He nods, handing back my passport, and clearing me through with a grin. "You've got a bit of snow in your hair," he observes. I casually shake my hair, sending the snowflakes scattering. "See you around, Ana," he says with a wink as I move on.

Despite never entertaining the agent's blatant flirting, it's nice to feel acknowledged every now and then. The thought of dating makes me cringe, however.

Going through customs always sets my nerves on edge, not just because of the process itself, but because it's too close to Quantum Plaza for comfort. The thought of the Huttons spotting me there tightens a knot of anxiety in my stomach. Rictor never did explain why he left the Space Ring or share any details with the Squad. As curious as I am, I can't risk drawing attention. It's safer for all of us to stay under the radar, even if it means being assumed dead.

I hop on a transit bus headed straight for my neighborhood, tapping my phone against the payment sensor before settling into a seat at the back. I slip in a pair of earpieces and dial into the sounds that Ethrans consider music—predominantly instrumentals. Since the infamous incident at Echolyn Grove nearly two decades ago, lyrics have lost their appeal. There, a wizard unleashed an unbreakable spell that caused people to hear the final thoughts of the deceased as haunting lullabies. Many who sought closure found themselves tormented by the somber echoes of their loved ones' last moments, triggering a widespread wave of depression throughout Ethra. Now, as the bus moves quietly along, the strains of orchestral music help me shut out the world.

The journey to Sector 5: Nebula Hollow takes about an hour. While it isn't the most upscale area, my neighborhood, Axion Spire, keeps a low profile, which is exactly what I need. Most importantly, it's the farthest you can get from Sector 1: Helios Core, putting as much distance as possible between myself and the Huttons. As the bus pulls up to my stop, I step off and walk down the street, appreciating the compact layout of the neighborhood.

The tall, slender houses rise like pillars, their reflective surfaces casting a soft, silvery glow. The buildings are stacked vertically with open terraces and gardens, each one blending seamlessly into the next, creating a streamlined, efficient design that I've grown to like.

As I stroll, neighborhood kids run up, eager for stories.

"Just a field day today," I say with a smile before reminding them about curfew. One groans, and they scatter into the narrow paths between the towering homes.

Reaching my house, perched just above another in this vertically stacked neighborhood, I see the lights on, a sure sign that the kids are already home. The morning has stirred a whirlpool of emotions, but now it's time to confront them all. I need to explain everything to my children—the full truth about their heritage and the dangers that still loom.

The sensors catch my movement, and stairs materialize before me, extending down from the porch. I step up, and as soon as I reach the top, the stairs disappear behind me. Pausing for a moment, I grip my scarf, letting the fabric slide through my fingers before unlocking the door.

The second I step inside, I'm hit with a wave of balloons, streamers, and the cheerful shouts of "Surprise!" fill the room. My bag slips from my hand to the floor as I'm immediately engulfed in a tight embrace from all three of my kids. It's hard to believe they're all in their late twenties now, but I pull them in for another hug, needing to feel that connection.

"What's the occasion?" I ask, looking from face to face.

Maks, the youngest and only girl, gives me a shy smile. Her short blonde hair is freshly cut to make her look more approachable, or so she says. "We just wanted to throw you a party, Mom. We've all been so busy these past few months, barely home and... we missed you."

Maks always reminds me of her parents, Aris and Faye—a perfect blend of opposites. She has Aris's quiet, timid nature but carries Faye's gutsy spirit, always ready to protect her brothers.

Before I can say more, Jihyun, Sylas and Aurelian's son and my middle child, sneaks up behind me, covering my eyes with his hands, giggling like he did when he was little. "No peeking! You can't see what we've done with the kitchen yet."

I laugh, letting them guide me blindly down the hall. "Sit down, Mom," Mikal instructs, his voice steady and commanding, like Harmon, but with a hint of Lyra's warmth. He's the oldest, and his tone carries the natural authority of someone used to looking out for others. My hands fumble for the chair before I finally find it and sit.

"Three... two... one!" Jihyun lifts his hands from my eyes.

I'm greeted by a table laden with familiar dishes. The rich aroma of geluer stew hits me first, with its tender chunks of rabbit-like meat and a deep, savory blend of herbs that instantly makes my mouth water. Then there's the Crawdelou sweet meat, its smoky-sweet scent filling the air, glazed to a perfect shine.

But then, my eyes fall on something that takes me completely by surprise—spaghetti. Not just any spaghetti. It looks and smells exactly like Auntie Luna's Filipino spaghetti. The sweet, tangy aroma of the banana ketchup mixed with savory meats and a hint of sweetness fills the room, pulling me back to memories I thought I'd left behind.

I'm speechless. I pick up a fork and twirl it through the noodles, gathering the sauce and bits of meat, then take a bite. A gasp escapes me, and tears prick at my eyes. It tastes exactly like Auntie Luna's spaghetti.

Jihyun beams with pride. "So, I can confirm—bananas don't exist in Ethra. But when I asked about them, the professors at Verdantum Institute didn't think I was crazy. They helped me find something close—the nyrium plant—so I made 'nyrium ketchup.' "

Mikal adds with a grin, "And since hotdogs are off the menu as well, we substituted with Glaeven saus—a Zaltanian specialty."

Maks hesitates, biting her lip before speaking up. "And, um, the ground pork is actually thundertusk boar, and the noodles... We used the ones you made from scratch." She looks at me, clearly anxious about my reaction.

I smile, thinking fondly of Rictor's twelfth birthday. It's funny how food can trigger memories like this. I reach out and squeeze Maks's hand, reassuring her. "You did great," I say, and the relief in her eyes is palpable.

We all sit down together and dig in.

"How's school in Solaris going?" I ask Jihyun.

His face lights up. "It's great! I'm learning so much about our culture and where Sylas grew up. It's fascinating, especially knowing it's where he spent his childhood." His wavy black hair falls into his light brown eyes as he talks, his laughter—so much like Aurelian's—filling the room. With his warm complexion and easy smile, he could easily be mistaken for Filipino. I was happy that Lyra agreed to be his surrogate mother, and passed on her kindness and empathy, making him a blend of all his parents.

At first, I wasn't thrilled with the idea of them leaving the Space Ring, especially with the O'rians on the loose. But Mikal reminded me they're well-trained and cautious, just like I've taught them. I watch Jihyun's animated hands as he shares his research, seeing so much of Sylas in him—not just in looks, but in spirit.

Mikal sits quietly, sturdy and thoughtful, with jade-green eyes like Lyra's and Harmon's steady demeanor. His observant nature is unmistakably Harmon, even down to how he adjusts his glasses.

Today has been a roller coaster of my past, and as much as I've tried to prepare myself, the thought of recounting their parents' deaths unsettles me. But I shove it down—right now, it's about enjoying lunch.

"How's training with the Allied Force going?" I ask Maks.

She perks up, her newly-cropped blonde hair catching the light. "Surprisingly, combat training has been the easiest for me."

I nod, unsurprised. "Faye was an incredibly talented fighter. It's no wonder it comes naturally to you."

Jihyun grins. "Mikal, how's Juno? Are you going to tell Mom about relocating there?"

Mikal flinches, caught off guard.

I raise an eyebrow. "Is that something you want?"

"I'm not sure yet, but... I've been thinking about it."

"You're all adults now." I cover my fear with a shrug. "It's natural to start thinking about leaving home."

They exchange looks, concern in their eyes.

Mikal adds, "I just... enjoy being useful to people."

I smile, a mix of pride and melancholy. I'm happy they're building lives where they no longer need me, but it is achingly bittersweet.

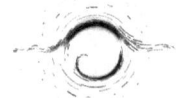

Alone in the kitchen, warm water runs over my hands as I rinse each dish, the soft clatter and splash filling the quiet space. Soap bubbles glide between my fingers, and the lingering aroma of our meal mixes with the soothing sound of running water.

Thoughts of returning to Earth muddy my thoughts—the chance to see my parents and little brother after all this time, to reunite with old friends, and to face the life I left behind. The emotions are almost overwhelming, but then I feel Maks's arms around my waist, her head resting on my shoulder.

"Mom, Mikal said he can feel the sadness in your breathing."

I turn around, wiping my hands on my pants, and pull her into a hug. "My sweet Maks, you know I love you, right?"

"Yes. I love you too." She tightens her embrace. "What's going on, Mom?"

"There's something I need to talk to all of you about." I gently pull away. "Tell your brothers to meet me in the living room. It's important."

Worry flashes across Maks's face, but she nods.

"Give me five minutes," I say, kissing her forehead before she leaves to gather her brothers. As I finish the dishes, my mind races, trying to find the right words to tell them the truth. I've made it known since they were young that their parents were gone, but I've never explained why or the reason we've been hiding all these years. Not that they hadn't questioned it, but I'd put off explaining until they eventually quit asking. I dry my hands and head to the living room, steeling myself for what's about to come.

When I enter, I see them all sitting on the couch, their eyes following me as I take a seat across from them. The room feels heavy with anticipation.

I decide there's no point in dancing around it. "The Nobles have returned," I begin, my voice steady. "My childhood friends from Earth have been spotted in Terrene. They're probably here to bring me back home."

They collectively gasp, eyes wide with shock. I can see the questions forming, but I hold up a hand to stop them. "I need you to listen first, then we can talk."

They nod, falling silent.

"As you know, Earth is where I'm originally from," I continue. "I believe my body there is finally dying, and knowing my friends, they're going to try to prevent that. All these years, I've suspected that we've been sending our consciousness back and forth between here and Earth. If I go back, it could save my body."

I pause, looking at their faces, tears beginning to well up in their eyes. I take a deep breath. "But before we can talk about Earth, I need to tell you about your parents."

They exchange glances, something passing between them that I can't quite read. Then, Mikal speaks up. "We already know, Mom."

"Yeah," Jihyun adds, nodding. "We know about the O'rians and how the Angel of Death kidnapped all of you."

The Angel of Death... That's what Abbadon calls himself now, how fitting for someone so vile.

Maks looks at me with a soft, reassuring smile. "And we know about where you all stayed hiding."

"And what happened to *Tante'* Valda and *Tante'* Boyko," Mikal continues.

"And my grandparents," Maks says quietly.

"How...?"

"Our parents wrote each of us letters," Jihyun explains. "They always knew their time was limited, so they prepared letters for us to read when we were old enough to understand."

"When we turned eighteen, the spell sealing the letters broke," Mikal adds.

"Oh." I let out a sigh of relief, a mixture of surprise and understanding washing over me. "Of course they would do that."

Mikal's expression grows more serious. He looks down at the coffee table before meeting my eyes again. "But Mom..." His voice cracks. "The letters were written before they died. I don't know about these two, but I'd like to know what happened? Why did they have to die?"

Jihyun and Maks move closer to Mikal, who sits in the center, gripping his hands. Their eyes are fixed on me, waiting for the devastating truth about their parents—the friends I loved and lost.

~ ~ ~

I huddled in the closet, trying—and failing—to keep the kids from giggling too much. Three-year-old Maks was the biggest culprit, her tiny voice bubbling out uncontrollably, while four-year-old Jihyun bit his lip, struggling not to join in. Even five-year-old Mikal, trying his hardest to be serious and "in charge," couldn't hold back a smile as their excitement grew.

"Shhh," I whispered, placing a finger to my lips. "We can't surprise your parents if you keep making noises!" Just as I spoke, we heard voices and laughter coming from outside. The kids gasped, clapping their hands over their mouths, eyes wide with excitement. I smiled, gesturing for them to stay quiet as I stepped out of the closet. I glanced back at the door, hearing their muffled attempts to stifle their giggles.

As the front door creaked open, I stood in the middle of the living room, feigning nonchalance. The group walked in—Aurelian, Faye, Aris, Harmon, Lyra, and Sylas. They smiled when they saw me, and I silently motioned toward the closet. They all played along, pretending not to notice the little giggles coming from behind the door.

The kids, eager to carry out their plan, stealthily snuck out from the closet like I'd taught them. They pounced, shouting "Boo!" Their parents pretended to be startled, laughing as they scooped up their kids, smothering them in kisses. The warmth of the moment made my heart swell. It felt like old times, like the days when the Squad was together, embarking on adventures and fighting side by side.

But things had changed. For the last eight years, we'd been on the run from Abbadon. He had underestimated us, just like Evanora had warned him not to. We had mastered hiding from the O'rians, evading their grasp. Instead of chasing adventure, we'd dedicated our lives to protecting the children and stopping the O'rians from spreading their dark use of blood magick. It was a corruption of everything we knew—breaking the rules of the Law of Equivalent Exchange, and slowly destroying the soul of anyone who used it.

We had become the Guardians they trained us to be—moving in stealth, like shadows slipping around every corner. Once the others started having kids, I retired from the fight and stayed home to watch over them. That had been my life since Mikal was born, and it had brought me a peace I hadn't known in years. I'd grieved enough.

Now, it was about building a future. Here in Ethra.

Aurelian gave a subtle nod, and the parents gently put their kids down. "Okay, like we practiced," Aurelian said, and the kids began to sing "Happy Birthday." The house around us faded, and suddenly we were standing in the backyard of my old home on Earth. It wasn't an exact match, but it was close enough to make my throat tighten with emotion. Aris had given me a piece of home—a piece of what I had lost. When they finished singing, Lyra hugged me tightly.

"I know how much you miss Earth," she whispered. "But we'll always be your home."

"I know," I whispered softly, wrapping my arms around her in a tight embrace.

The illusion dissolved, and we were back in the house—our home, woven from the living trees and branches that Sylas had shaped with his powers. It wasn't just a house; it felt like a part of the forest itself, the walls breathing with the pulse of Terrene. The branches and roots intertwined to form walls, floors, and ceilings that, though organic, were as sturdy as any stone-built structure. Everything had been smoothed out by Sylas, giving the natural twists and bends of the wood a sense of purpose and strength. The house was holding us, protecting us in the same way we had come to protect each other.

The kids dashed off to the kitchen, their laughter echoing in the hollowed-out space where the walls seemed to hum quietly with life. Around me, everyone gathered, pulling me into tight hugs, wishing me a happy birthday, the warmth of their affection blending with the earthy scent of the wood.

A moment later, the kids came rushing back, stumbling over each other, giggling and jostling as they fought to be the one holding the lit birthday cake. Watching them, my heart swelled—it was moments like this, seeing them so full of life, that made everything feel worth it. The pure joy on their faces, the way they shared in the simplest of things, brought a sense of peace and contentment that settled deep inside me. I knelt beside them, and the candle-light flickered off the branches above, casting dancing shadows. "Ready?" I whispered to them, and in unison, we blew out the candles. "Astralis," I whispered under my breath. Still, nothing happened.

The kids cheered, their glee filling the space.

In that moment, the house felt like it had a heartbeat, keeping time with ours, wrapping us in a cocoon of love. The happiness on their faces, the sound of my friends' laughter—it made everything else fade into the background, if only for a little while.

I stood up and gently took the cake from the kids' hands. "Let's get this sliced up," I said with a smile, carrying it to the kitchen. The kids eagerly followed, crowding around me as I cut the cake into pieces. I handed them each a plate, and they rushed to distribute the slices to their parents, their little feet pattering across the wooden floor. Once everyone had their slice and the kids finally settled in, I turned to Harmon with a playful smirk.

"So, how did the mission go today?"

Without missing a beat, Harmon struck a pose, as if stepping into the spotlight. "Ah, let me tell you," he began, his voice full of theatrical flair.

The kids giggled as they dug into their cake, captivated as he started reenacting the battle.

"There we were, cornered by one of those Strider-Class Kroloks," he said, eyes cartoonishly wide. "You know, those massive, spidery war machines with energy cores all over."

The kids gasped, leaning forward in their seats.

"And what did I do?" He grinned, pausing for dramatic effect. "I used my vibration powers, of course! Got right under its legs and—boom!" He smacks his hands together, making everyone jump. "Shook it so hard, the thing practically crumbled in on itself."

The kids dissolved into laughter, and the rest of us couldn't help but chuckle, too. Harmon's retelling had everyone in stitches, the tension of the day melting away with every exaggerated move he made.

Everything felt perfect. It was a great birthday. Until a faint hissing broke through the noise. My stomach dropped—I recognized it immediately. Instinct kicked in, and I raised a forcefield just as the wall by the entrance of the house exploded, sending debris flying. The laughter was instantly replaced by screams.

Through the smoke, my heart pounded as I saw them—the five doppelgängers who had haunted my nightmares for years, standing exactly as they had when they attacked us eight years ago. My breath caught in my throat as their cold, familiar faces emerged, unchanged by time, like living specters from my past. But this time, they weren't here to toy with us. Back then, there had been hesitation, a brief uncertainty in their eyes. Now, it was clear as day—they were here to destroy.

Behind them, towering over their unnatural forms, stood Abbadon. He looked worse than I remembered—his presence darker, more sinister. Blood magick had ravaged him. His once-human form now a warped shell, veins crawling across his body like serpents. The sight of him twisted something deep inside me, and for the first time in years, I felt that same panic I did on the day everything fell apart. This time, I knew they were here to finish what they had started. My shields seemed to thicken in response.

Faye's scream tore through the chaos as she whipped around to face Aris. "Did you put up the illusion around the house?!"

Aris froze, his face losing all color. "I... I didn't think we needed it. It's been years. They've never found us!" His voice cracked, panic rising in his throat. "I just wanted Jho to have a good birthday."

Suddenly, Aurelian's face paled, a realization dawning. "It wasn't just the illusion... Aris, you didn't reset the warding spell, did you?"

Aris blinked, confused. "What? No, I—why would I—"

Aurelian shook his head, horror spreading across his features. "The wards we cast years ago—they degrade if they're not renewed. The spell work gets... porous. I should've checked, but after all this time, I thought we were safe."

I felt a knot tightening in my stomach. "So they didn't find us... we've been leaving gaps for them to slip through?"

Aurelian clenched his fists. "Worse. They've been watching us for who knows how long, waiting for the wards to weaken enough to strike. We didn't even notice."

Faye's expression turned dark as she pieced it together. "They baited us. Lured us out with that camp, following us back home—and now, with the wards fading..."

I glanced at Aurelian, fear creeping in. "We played right into their hands."

Fear rippled through the room, thick and suffocating. The kids bolted behind me, their hands clutching at my clothes, shaking in terror. Lyra and Faye rushed to the children's room, scrambling for backpacks and essentials. The rest of us stood frozen, eyes locked on Abbadon as we peered out from behind the forcefield.

Sylas's voice broke the tense silence, low and steady, though his gaze never wavered. "He's weaker. blood magick is destroying him."

But I couldn't focus on that. My hands trembled, the panic rising as the memories of that terrible day came flooding back. The sight of my best friends' unchanged, childlike faces on the other side of my shield, doppelgangers who had torn our lives apart, sent me spiraling into a fear I hadn't felt in years. The kids cried behind me, their sobs piercing the air, but I was paralyzed. I didn't know what to do other than hold the shield in place. So I remained there, frozen.

Faye and Lyra returned, strapping backpacks onto the children with trembling hands. Each parent hugged and kissed their kids tightly, the weight of what was about to happen pressing down on us all.

"Where are we going?" I asked, my voice shaking, barely holding it together.

Faye's eyes locked with mine, "Not we. You and the kids."

Lyra, her face streaked with tears, clung to Mikal before pulling him into one final embrace. "Take them, Jhoana. We'll hold them off as long as we can."

"No!" I cried, tears streaming down my face. "We leave together! We can make it! Aris can use an illusion to hide us." Even as the words left my mouth, I knew the truth. There was no escape for all of us. The only chance was if they stayed behind to give me and these kids a chance to run.

Harmon's voice cut through the chaos. "Wherever you go, we can't know. They'll just peer into our heads."

Sylas, holding Jihyun close, turned to me, his eyes filled with a sorrow I couldn't bear. "We chose you."

Those words had haunted me ever since we escaped and hearing them again left me with no choice. The kids and parents sobbed as they said their goodbyes, and just like that, I took the children's hands, and we slipped out the back. I turned one last time to my friends, my family, tears blurring my vision.

"Survive! That's the wish I'll make this year," I called out, my voice shaking. "I love you all."

No one spoke, but their eyes told me everything—I could see the love, the trust, and the quiet acceptance in their gazes. They were entrusting me with their children, with everything. My heart clenched as I dropped the forcefield, watching my friends step forward, backs straight, ready to face the doppelgangers in what could only be the fight of their lives.

I looked down at the kids. Their eyes were red, cheeks streaked with tears, their small bodies trembling with fear. This was the moment everything changed.

"Okay," I whispered, kneeling in front of them. "We have to keep running. If you get tired, drag your feet. Remember what I taught you. They'll kill us if they find us. You protect each other. Got it?"

They nodded, though their sobs still wracked their bodies. Suddenly, explosions echoed through the forest, followed by a blood-curdling scream—Faye's.

"Mikal, look at me," I said, my voice firm despite the terror gripping me. His face was pale, frozen in fear. "You hold Jihyun's hand and don't let go, do you understand?"

Mikal gasped, his chest heaving as he tried to steady his breathing, then grabbed Jihyun's hand, gripping it tightly.

I scooped Maks up and slung her onto my back. "Hold on tight to me," I whispered, tightening my scarf and clutching the pouch at my waist to make sure everything was still there.

"Go!" I shouted, and we darted into the forest, my feet pounding the carpet of evergreen needles, guiding the children through the maze of trees.

As the sounds of battle faded into the distance, I let out a choked cry, knowing deep down my birthday wish would never be granted.

~ ~ ~

The sobs come uncontrollably, each memory crashing over me like a relentless wave, pulling me under. Maks wraps her arms around me, and the boys follow, holding me tightly. I haven't let myself cry like this since the day I ran with them. Raising three children alone was a challenge, but I was never truly on my own. Every place we lived, every neighborhood, even the one here in the Space Ring—people stepped in to help. I've always thought of it as an extension of my friends' love for their kids.

"I'm sorry," I choke out between sobs. "I'm sorry I didn't go back to save them." I place a hand gently on each of their faces, feeling their tears mix with mine.

"You were just keeping their promise," Jihyun says softly, grabbing my hand. "We've questioned everything our whole lives, but now we can put it to rest. You've been through so much, Mom."

Maks leans into me, resting her head on my shoulder. "Mom..."

Mikal hugs me tighter, his voice soft. "I'm glad you didn't see them go."

Hearing that, I break down even more. The image of the Squad flashes before me—Rictor's horrified face, the sight of them fighting for their lives. We were just kids, and I'm grateful they never came back to this. It was my plan after all. I hope they don't blame themselves.

Without thinking, words slip out, surprising even me. "I'm stuck here. I've been trying to go back to Earth, but now, even with my best friends back, I don't think I can go with them. Every part of me wants to, but... I don't think I can leave you kids. You were your parents' world, and now you're mine." I never thought I'd admit it out loud, but Earth feels like a distant memory now. When Valda and Boyko died, the part that made me a person from Earth died too. How can I return to a life that no longer exists, when I've built one here in Ethra?

The kids exchange glances, soft smiles forming on their faces, then turn their attention back to me.

"Mom, we love you," Maks says quietly. "Let's find your Squad."

Jihyun nods. "If you're stuck here, don't you think you should say your final goodbye?"

"I—I don't know what I'd even say," I murmur.

"It'll come to you the moment you see them," Mikal reassures me.

I sit there, processing the idea of reuniting with them, of saying goodbye forever. My heart feels like it's about to break in two.

"Okay," I finally say. "I'll update you once I find them."

"What? No, we're coming with you," Mikal says, standing up.

"Yeah, Mom." Jihyun smiles. "We've all taken time off. That's why we're home. We missed you."

"We're not letting you do this alone," Maks adds, hugging me again.

I hesitate, knowing the dangers that will follow. But they deserve the truth. I look at them, their faces flashing before me as they were when they were little.

I let out a deep sigh. "The real reason we've stayed hidden is because the three of you are special," I say. "I think your parents knew, but they never told me everything. They only gave me what I needed to protect you. If the O'rians ever captured me, they'd pull the truth from my mind."

I pause, the weight of my next words hanging heavy between us.

"What is it, Mom?" Maks asks, her voice barely above a whisper.

"You were never baptized," I say, my voice low.

"What?" Mikal crosses his arms, disbelief in his tone. "Then how do we have Innate Power?"

"You three were born with it. The first of your kind."

Maks's brow furrows. "But how?"

"I made you believe that you were baptized at birth, even though that never happens," I continue. "Mikal manifested his power when he was seven, and then Jihyun and Maks, you did, too, at the same age. Your powers are a combination of your parents'. Abbadon doesn't know about any of you, or what makes you so rare. Whatever they did to us in that facility... it explains why you exist. But if they ever get their hands on you, they'll experiment on you, just like they did to us. I'll never let that happen."

Mikal's jaw tightens, his eyes narrowing. "Then they're in for one hell of a fight," he says, his voice hard and determined. "If they want any one of us, they'll have to go through all of us."

"He's right," Jihyun adds, cracking his knuckles. "You trained us for this."

Maks nods, resolute. "Let's go find your friends."

I pull them into a tight group hug, my heart swelling with pride. "Your parents would be so proud of you."

"Where are we headed first, Mom?" Maks asks, breaking the moment. "Was the Squad spotted somewhere?"

I let go and check my Spectra Vision, seeing the missed calls from Lacey. "We're making a detour to Arid first. There's someone I need to see."

ARID

The trees sway, their golden leaves shimmering like coins about to drop. My teeth sink into my thumbnail, eyes fixed on those damn branches as if they're hiding answers.

Joven... Of course he works at the Terrerium. I should've put it together. But Albert—he's the surprise. Seeing him again brought everything back: the silence while I waited to be experimented on, and his absence when I needed him the most. He wasn't there during my torture. He wasn't there when it all went to hell.

That's what still eats at me. Not that he didn't agree, not even that he didn't fight for me—but that he didn't care enough to stay. And now he's back, walking into my life like nothing's changed.

But *everything's* changed.

I haven't made up my mind about Miss Delphini or Dr. Wolfgang yet. They're a different kind of monster. But seeing Albert after all these years, after all his promises—yeah, that solidifies it. My anger's justified.

"Ricky." Emierr's voice cuts through my thoughts like a sharp blade. I turn and there he is, standing behind me with that concerned look on his face. "Why did you walk out? It's Al..."

I tighten my fists, feeling the heat rise under my skin. *Why is he pushing this?* My chest boils over with everything I'm holding back, but I swallow it down. I clench my jaw, breathing through the turmoil like Bonnie taught me. *Calm. Control. Don't give in.* "Meer, you—you don't understand what I'm feeling right now," I say, managing to keep my voice steady.

"Ricky, if you just hear him out," Emierr presses. "He has a solid reason."

I snap. "Trillions."

Emierr furrows his brow, confused. "What?"

"There are trillions of stars out there in the universe," I bite out. "I don't have time to be sad or mad because people like me can't afford it. So yeah, I'll keep doing what I've been doing all these years, and keep searching the cosmos for any fucks to give."

Then I see him—Albert. He steps from behind a tree, worn and older than I remember, his face lined with worry and grief.

"Meer" Albert's voice is low, defeated. "Can I get a moment with Ricky?"

I don't want to, but I feel it. The guilt. The sorrow. It radiates off Albert in waves, and I can't stop myself from feeling it. Emierr glances between us, then steps aside, giving Albert space.

"Ricky..." Albert's voice cracks. "I thought... By the Tree, I thought you chose to leave. You and the Squad always talked about exploring Ethra, about going off the grid. I thought you wanted that."

My chest tightens. "You thought I wanted *that*? To nearly die?"

Albert's hands shake. "Ricky, I didn't know. Not until I found out about... the experiments. I should've known. I should've protected you."

I clench my fists, my body trembling. "You didn't. You weren't there when they strapped me down, when they shocked me until I didn't know who I was anymore."

Albert's face crumples. "I know... I failed you. I thought I could fix it... somehow. But I know now—"

"Fix it?" I laugh bitterly. "You think you can fix this?"

Albert shakes his head slowly. "No. I'm not here to apologize for them. I'm here because I wasn't there for you. I thought I was keeping you safe, but I was blind to what was happening..."

His words should feel like a balm, but they sting.

"They don't know you're back, Ricky," he continues, stepping closer. "The Huttons... They think you're dead. They think the whole Squad is dead. And if they knew..." He trails off, and I know what he's not saying. The Huttons would drop everything to see me, to beg for forgiveness. Knowing that makes the weight in my chest heavier.

"You really think they've changed?"

Albert meets my gaze. "I do. And I know you don't have to forgive them... or me. But maybe... give yourself a chance to heal."

Silence stretches between us, and the anger starts to ebb.

"Ricky." Emierr's voice pulls me back. "Borge is here. He's got news on Brunner."

Albert turns to leave, his shoulders slumped.

"Al," Emierr says. "You're leaving already? Say goodbye to every-one."

Albert pauses. "I can't, Meer. I don't think I could say goodbye again." He wipes his eyes. "Please... find Jho. Bring her back home."

I watch him go, a mix of anger and sorrow coiling inside me, unsure which one to let out.

Emierr and I lock eyes, knowing one of us has to explain where Al went. Without missing a beat, I tap my nose. "Not it."

"Not it," Emierr yelps too late, groaning as I grin. "Fine, whatever. Let's save Brunner." He throws an arm around my neck, pulling me into a headlock as we make our way to the front of the house. "How are you feeling?"

I want to say I'm angry, but I can't. Instead, I force a weak smile. "Thanks for saving me from that conversation."

Emierr sighs, but he doesn't push it. "Al left back to the Space Ring," he announces to the group as we rejoin them, all standing by the tree house.

Dustin and Jadis exchange uneasy glances but no one questions it.

"Is everything all right?" Chief Berkarys asks, his gaze sharp on me.

Chieftess Nalani wears a "worried mom" expression, almost enough to make me relent.

"We're good, trust me," Emierr says, flashing two thumbs up.

Borge clears his throat, looking more serious than before. "There's been a sighting near Zaltana. A male fitting Brunner's description... riding a freakishly huge, white bear."

The tension cracks. We all let out a collective sigh of relief.

"A giant bear?" Jadis raises an eyebrow. "Seriously?"

Emierr shakes his head, laughing. "*Why* is he riding a giant bear?"

Borge's expression remains grave.

"What's wrong?" Jae asks.

Borge hesitates. "I got a tip from Arid. They saw a woman—short, with dark, braided hair. They claimed it was Jhoana. No one took it seriously, but they mentioned a red scarf... the same scarf Jhoana was last seen wearing."

Dustin's hand instinctively goes to his neck. "That was my scarf. I gave it to her. It has to be Jho."

The description was vague, but the scarf? That would be quite the coincidence. A knot tightens somewhere in my gut. After all these years... Jhoana. If this is her, I'm bringing her back. No matter what it takes.

"The sightings," Borge says, "were all from three hours ago."

"It's fine. We have a lead. Thank you, Borge," Jadis says.

"Of course... my lady," he adds awkwardly.

"There's no way we can get to both Zaltana and Arid in time," I say. Splitting up is the only answer, but I hate it.

For a moment, no one speaks. The air thickens with worry. After years of finally regrouping, we're splitting up once again.

Jadis is the one to break the silence. "We'll have to split up."

Hesitation ripples through the group.

"I don't like this," Emierr mutters. "Not again."

"Neither do I," I admit. "But we don't have a choice."

Dustin nods, resigned. "I'll head to Zaltana to look for Rune. Meer's coming with me."

Emierr gives Dustin a long look but doesn't argue. He knows it's necessary.

That leaves me and Jadis. Arid... It feels right. It has to be us who bring her back.

Jadis meets my eyes. No words needed.

We're coming, Jho.

"How will we contact each other?" Emierr asks, his brow furrowed.

"We don't, not until we wake up," I sigh. The idea of going no-contact like this feels wrong, but there's no other way.

"You both be safe," Dustin says with a small smile.

Jadis, ever blunt, shakes her head. "If any of you die here, I swear to god I won't attend the funerals."

"Then you better make sure none of us die," I say with a smirk, despite the seriousness pawing at my new empath senses.

A smile cracks across her face. "No promises. I might just kill all of you myself." She pulls us into a tight embrace. The warmth and familiarity ground us, a brief moment where we're just us again. "Stay safe and fight like your life depends on it when the time comes."

I remind them of the mission—our final mission as the Allied Organization Squad. "Extract. Survive. And get the fuck out of here."

Dustin raises his hand, crossing his heart with his finger, the same way Jhoana used to do. Jadis follows the gesture, then Emierr. They all look at me, and I follow suit, crossing my heart.

From a few paces away, Sólel releases Evera from his embrace in alarm. "Wait. No, you guys just got here."

Emierr reaches out, trying to calm him. "Sól, we're coming back. I promise."

But Sólel shakes his head, desperation in his eyes. "I just got my big brother back."

I watch him—a grown man reverting to the kid he used to be. That guilt I've buried for years punches me in the gut, dragging me back to the day Sólel flew off crying when we left him behind to go into Akeurimja.

"I'm coming with you," Sólel declares, his voice unwavering.

"What?" Emierr looks at him in disbelief, shaking his head. "No, you're not coming. It's too dangerous."

"I'm not a child anymore, *kuya*. I make my own decisions, and I say I'm coming."

I can see Emierr scrambling for an argument, trying to find something. Sólel's expression softens, but the determination doesn't leave his face. "I made the mistake of not following you that day. Maybe I could've helped fend off your clones. Maybe *Ate* Jho would've gone home with all of you. Maybe it wouldn't have taken all these years to see you again." He pauses, his voice heavy with regret. "Please, for my conscience, let me make sure you get home safe. All of you."

Emierr exhales, his resistance finally giving way. "Okay," he sighs. "You're coming."

Jae cuts into the conversation. "I'll fly Dustin, Emierr, and Sólel to Zaltana."

"I'll return to the Kingdom of the Forefront and report what I can—without blowing the Nobles' cover," Borge says. "We've been out of contact for too long." He glances at Jae, his face tight with apology. "I'm going to have to use you as an excuse. It's the only way to explain why we went quiet."

Jae rolls his eyes but doesn't argue. We've all got roles to play, and right now, this is the only way to move forward.

"Make sure these two knuckleheads don't mess up the mission," I say, nodding toward Dustin and Emierr.

Jae grins. "Don't worry, I've got them."

"I'll see you next with Brunner and *Ate* Jho," Sól says. Determination lines his face. "The Squad will be complete again."

A faint smile tugs at my lips.

"Jadis, Rictor..." Borge gestures to his vehicle. "I can take you both to Arid. It's on my way to the Kingdom of the Forefront." He gives a quick bow, resulting in little flickers of discomfort from my friends. I see Jadis shrug out of the corner of my eye, deferring to me.

"That works," I say. "Thanks, Borge."

"Of course," he replies, snapping back to attention. "It's no trouble at all, really. I'd be honored."

"Honored?" Jadis smirks, raising an eyebrow. "We're just hitching a ride, Borge."

He stammers slightly, adjusting his posture. "Well, still... I don't mind. Just trying to do my part."

I raise an eyebrow at him, unable to resist. "You know you don't have to bow every time, right, Borge? We're not exactly riding in a golden chariot."

He straightens fully, cheeks flushing slightly. "Just trying to show respect, Rictor."

"Respect noted. But, seriously, relax." I laugh.

Jadis snorts beside me, nudging Borge lightly. "He's right. If you get any stiffer, you'll break."

Borge chuckles nervously, still shuffling in place. Finally, he turns to walk back toward the hovercraft.

"Wait!" Chief Berkarys voice rumbles behind us. He and Chieftess Nalani approach us. The chief speaks first, his voice deep and steady. "Rictor, Jadis," he says, placing a hand on each of our shoulders. "Jhoana is lucky to have friends like you."

I nod, but the words hit harder than they should. It's been years. Too many years.

"May the Ethereal Tree guide you safely back," he adds, his tone softer, like he knows exactly what's on my mind.

Chieftess Nalani, her eyes warm but serious, steps closer. "We've waited too long for this day. Bring back those you love. Do not let doubt cloud your path." Her voice grows gentle as she looks at Jadis and me. "You both carry a piece of this family with you. Be strong, and know we'll be here waiting."

I nod, their words settling over me, lifting some of the burden I've been carrying. Their belief in us makes it feel possible—like we really can bring her home.

"This is for you. It belonged to Astro." Chief Berkarys hands me a metallic silver puffer jacket emblazoned with the emblem of the Space Ring. Outside, under the fading daylight, the jacket catches the light with a subtle sheen, its fabric looking almost like liquid metal. Intricate stitching along the sleeves resembles the delicate lines of circuitry, winding toward the cuffs. "You remind us so much of him. If you had met him, he'd have given this to you himself."

I slip it on, surprised by the fabric—it's soft as cotton but carries an unexpected weight. A cool rush of air flows through the lining, like the jacket has a built-in temperature sensor, adjusting to my body heat.

"Thank you." I smile at them, unable to put the extent of my gratitude into words. Together, Jadis and I leave the reassuring embrace of the treehouse and step into the hovercraft.

The sun sinks, casting the sky in burnt orange and violet. Golden rays pierce through the branches, catching the shimmer of leaves like scattered embers.

As the hovercraft lifts, I watch the landscape shift beneath us. The Ethereal Tree rises in the distance, its branches flickering with a soft, pale glow, swirling dust catching the last rays of light as if drawing the sky's fading colors into itself.

People and leyfolk alike stir, moving through the forest as if the night brings them to life. The air feels charged, like the whole place is waiting for something to happen. It's not the calm of night I knew before—now, it's alive with possibility and danger.

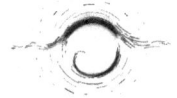

Borge pulls up to a drop-off section just outside what is supposedly Arid's primary port of entry, the hovercraft settling smoothly on the moonlit sand. Borge lifts back into the night sky, leaving us at the edge of a bustling crowd. The line of people and guards before us imply an entrance, but I can't see one.

I take in the desert's beauty. It's even more majestic than the pictures and videos I've seen. The sand stretches in soft, silver waves under the moonlight, the desert glowing faintly blue from strange, twisting plants scattered across the dunes. The stars feel closer here, sharp and vibrant against the endless dark, while the air carries a hint of spice, like warmed stones and desert sage. Jadis grabs my arm, breaking me from my thoughts. She points to the guards at the front, checking for passes.

"That's new," she mutters. "They won't let us in without identification."

I scan the crowd, looking for any advantage we might have. We need a plan, and fast. Then, an idea strikes me. I turn to Jadis, grinning. "We're going in as a couple from the Space Ring," I say, pointing to the small logo on my jacket. "We'll be eccentric enough that they'll be more interested in getting rid of us than stopping us."

Jadis crosses her arms, raising an eyebrow. "You want us to act like Space Ring tourists?"

"Exactly," I say, my smile stretching even wider. She's going to hate this. "Just play along. They'll never see it coming."

She sighs, rolling her eyes. "Fine, but if this backfires, I'm going to remind you of it for the rest of our lives."

"Oh, trust me, darling, you'll love it." I slip into character as we move with the crowd toward the entrance.

"Passports, please," a guard says as we approach, his expression flat.

I glance at Jadis, who stares blankly back at me, then put on my best attempt at a refined British accent. "Oh, dearest, did you not bring the passports?"

Jadis, quick on the uptake, drops into a thick Southern drawl. "Honey, don't you tell me you forgot those darn things again! We spent all our weddin' money on these here tickets to stay in Arid for a month, and you've gone and left our passports in the spaceship!"

I clasp my hands dramatically. "I'm so terribly sorry, love! I was just so swept up in the romance of it all—Arid, our grand honeymoon! Why, it slipped my mind entirely. Can you ever forgive me?"

The guard looks at me, eyes narrowing. "What's wrong with your eye?"

I stammer, caught off guard, but Jadis jumps in, her voice quick and matter-of-fact. "Oh, that?" she says with a drawl. "Poor thing got cursed by a sylren. He got a little too excited when he met one face-to-face, bless his heart."

The guard raises an eyebrow, glancing between the two of us, clearly warring between baffled and intrigued.

I nod along, adding a dramatic sigh. "It's true. I was enchanted by her beauty! I couldn't resist... and, well, this is what I get for being overenthusiastic, apparently."

Jadis huffs, hands on her hips, looking the guard dead in the eye. "Mister, you don't understand. We saved up for months to come here. He just gets so... excited. I don't even think he slept last night, just starin' at all the travel brochures."

The guard blinks, his mouth quirking into a barely restrained smile. "I see, ma'am. I'm afraid I can't let you stay a whole month without your passports, though."

"Oh, but darling!" I say, taking Jadis's hand, my accent growing even more exaggerated. "How will we make memories? I promised you the sands of Arid at sunset, the beauty of the city at night!"

Jadis, taking on a more pleading tone, beseeches the guard. "We can have our passports sent over, can't we? We'll get it all fixed up lickety-split. All we need is a couple days, tops."

The guard chuckles, shaking his head. "All right, I'll give you a temporary pass for two days. That should be enough time for your passports to get here." He hands us two Holo-cards, declaring our permission to enter.

"Oh, you wonderful man!" I declare, seizing his hand in an exaggerated handshake. "You've saved our honeymoon! I don't know what we'd have done without you."

Jadis elbows me. "C'mon, honey, let's get on with it." She nods to the guard, her face a perfect picture of relief. "Thank ya kindly, sir."

He waves us along, laughing, and we move with the crowd toward the entrance. Jadis and I exchange a glance, barely holding back our laughter. I can't believe that actually worked. As we approach, I notice something strange—my reflection ahead of me.

I blink, rubbing my eyes. "Uh, Jads, is it just me, or do I look like I'm already over there? Am I seeing things?"

Jadis smirks, grabbing my hand. "Nope. The entrance to Arid is through the reflection. Just walk forward and try not to think too much."

We step up to the shimmering surface, and I watch as the reflection seems to react to us, the image warping slightly. The shapes of our bodies appear to be carved into the mirror-like surface, stretching and shifting. Then, almost like water parting, the reflection opens up, bending around us as we move forward. It ripples outward in waves, the edges brightening and catching the faint light around us. We step through, and the reflection closes behind us, sealing us inside.

It feels like walking through thick, cool air, almost as if we're passing through the very fabric of the world. The sensation is strange. My skin tingles with tiny pinpricks. Then, with a soft rush, we emerge on the other side, the desert nation of Arid stretching out before us under the glow of a thousand stars.

I look to my left, then my right, taking in the enormous wall that surrounds Arid. It stretches as far as I can see, shimmering in the dusk like a glass fortress. The surface is smooth, almost translucent, with currents of energy running through it—bright, twisting lines that pulse with magick. Runes blinking on the surface, shifting like constellations against the glass, interwoven with threads of technology. This isn't just a wall; it's alive, a seamless blend of science and magick that makes me realize just how far Ethra has come.

I glance at Jadis, and she's mesmerized, staring at the city ahead, like she's seeing it for the first time too. Her emotions hit me like a wave, her wonder coursing through my skin, mingling with a sadness that settles heavy in my bones. I reach for her hand, and she squeezes back, giving me a small smile.

"Welcome to the city of Bayan," she says softly.

Towering solar arrays line the streets, their translucent panels angled to have caught the last dregs of sunlight before nightfall. The air buzzes with an electric charge, not just from magick, but from the people themselves. Massive holographic displays float above us, projecting images of news and entertainment, casting a glow over the crowds below. Robots move gracefully among the people, their movements almost human.

The dry air carries the scent of sun-baked clay and crushed juniper, a smoky tang weaving through with a sharp hint of citrus. Street performers create fiery illusions, sending bursts of light into the sky, while dancers spin under floating lanterns that pulse with changing colors. I catch a familiar scent drifting through the air—something sweet and smoky. Crawdelou sweet meat. My stomach growls, and I realize just how long it's been since I've tasted it.

Jadis tugs on my hand, leading me through the crowd until we reach a glass bridge stretching high above the city. It reminds me of the SkyWalk back on the Space Ring—the kind of place that makes you feel like you're floating. I glance down at the desert below, bathed in the pale glow of moonlight. Beyond the city's edge, a castle rises against the horizon, its towering spires twisting up like ancient, knotted branches. The stones reflect deep shades of red and burnt orange, like coals flickering in the dark. Shadows drift across the castle's surface, giving it the eerie appearance of breathing.

"That's Ambrosia Academy," Jadis says, her voice catching.

I take a breath, feeling something tighten in my chest. I've never been here before, never seen the place where Jadis spent most of her days in Ethra. Seeing it now, it's hard to hold back the emotions rising up. Maybe it's her feelings mixing with mine, but I find myself blinking back tears. I squeeze her hand, grounding us both. "You all right?"

She nods, quickly wiping away a tear. "I'm fine," she says, her voice soft. "It's just... Jho might have been here and we missed her."

I sigh. "Where do we even start?"

"Maybe the Council," she says, but there's hesitation in her voice. "But I don't know how useful they'll be."

"Borge mentioned the Allied Force might have people here. Maybe they're our best shot," I reply.

She nods, but before we can go any further, a voice calls out, "Jadis?"

We both turn to see a woman in a dark green robe, a basket of marigolds tucked under one arm. She pulls back her hood, revealing soft waves of chestnut hair framing a face that Ethran radiation has kept young. Her eyes are sharp, but warm, and filled with disbelief.

"Is it really you?" Her voice wavers, and there's a vulnerability in it that tugs at me.

Jadis lights up, her face breaking into a smile as she steps forward, reaching out as if afraid this is all a dream. "Elyssa?" Her voice cracks, and then she's hugging the woman, holding her tight.

"You're back... I knew it. I knew you weren't gone." Elyssa holds her close, burying her face into Jadis's shoulder.

Jadis pulls back, still holding Elyssa's shoulders. "Ricky, this is Elyssa," she says, pride coloring her voice. "My one true friend in Arid."

Elyssa glances over Jadis's shoulder, giving me a polite nod. "Noble Rictor," she says. "It's an honor." If she's shocked by my reappearance in her world, she does an excellent job of hiding it.

"Honor's all mine," I say, and she returns my smile with one of her own.

Elyssa's attention returns to Jadis. "Since the day you disappeared, I've been coming here every night. This bridge... It was our spot. I never lost hope that you'd come back."

Jadis's glassy eyes flicker to the marigolds in Elyssa's basket. "Who are those for?"

Elyssa sighs, her expression darkening. "They're for Ronan."

I feel a wave of sadness from Jadis, and she just nods, saying nothing. I remember Jadis's retelling of her battle with Ronan. The girl hadn't been much older than Jadis, but she had absolutely been trying to kill her. A fate would have it, she'd lost her life in an effort to revive her dead father.

"Jadis, how long have you been back?" Elyssa asked, turning the subject away from painful memories.

"We just got to Arid," Jadis says.

Elyssa's expression tightens. "They probably already know."

"Who?"

"The Council. I've kept a close eye on things since you left." Elyssa's tone is guarded. "It's... different now. The Council's presence is everywhere." Her voice dips, and for a moment, I see the wary edge to her—someone who's learned to watch her back. "You need to be careful, both of you. This place isn't what it used to be."

I hear the heavy clank of armor. Too late.

"It's them." Elyssa says, her face going pale. She stepped back, her basket of flowers rustling in quaking arms.

Soldiers march toward us from both sides, their brassy metal glinting in the city lights, spears at the ready. One of the guards steps forward, face as hard as stone. "Jadis Salazar, you're under arrest by order of the Council." He raises his spear, and the others close in, surrounding us with sharp, practiced precision. They disregard Elyssa entirely, as if she isn't even there

"Hey, hold on," I say, pulling out the passes from my jacket pocket, holding them up for him to see. "We have passes. There's no need for this."

The guard narrows his eyes and shifts his spear toward me. "You too. Hand over any items and prepare for questioning."

"What?" I blurt out, my eyes darting between him and Jadis. "Then what was the point of these?" My heart is beginning to thunder in my chest. If they know Jadis, have they also identified me? Barely a half hour in Arid and we're already under arrest.

"Don't make us force you."

I raise my hands, keeping my voice steady. "We'll come quietly. No need for the weapons."

Elyssa grabs Jadis's hand, her breathing shallow. "Just do as they say," she says under her breath.

Jadis looks back at Elyssa, suspicion blooming in her eyes. "Elyssa..."

Elyssa gives her a sad smile. "Sororitas."

Jadis's mouth falls open, eyes wide with disbelief. I'm pretty sure she's never told anyone about the coven name she shared with Jhoana. How could Elyssa possibly know? Unless... She spoke to Jhoana herself.

"Step back, civilian," the apparent captain commanded. Elyssa slips backward through a gap between shoulder plates. The guards take hold of our arms, leading us away from the bridge. I catch one last look at Elyssa, standing there with her marigolds, her expression filled with all the things she can't say. As they pull us deeper into the city, I feel her eyes on us, and the weight of what we're walking into settles over me like a shadow.

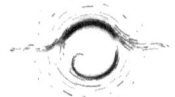

I stand in the foyer—if you could even call it that—of the Council's massive fortress. From the outside, it looks like something out of a dreamscape, towering high into the night, each spire stabbing into a sky washed with starlight and cosmic dust. The building glows faintly, the windows and arches lit from within by a bluish light that pulses like a heartbeat. It's sprawling, ancient, and yet futuristic, with towering turrets manned with automatic laser weaponry and intricate stonework that reminds me of gothic cathedrals back on Earth, only grander and more majestic.

Inside, I'm fairly certain I've stepped into ancient Europe. The ceiling arcs impossibly high above me, covered in gilded carvings that catch the light and throw shadows that seem to shift as I move. Stone pillars rise around me, etched with patterns I can't quite place, like someone tried to mix magick and mathematics in perfect symmetry. The air hits me—thick with old parchment and the metallic bite of relics, history itself clinging to my lungs.

Jadis had told me to wait here. Only she was summoned by the Council member, and she made it clear—if she wasn't back in thirty minutes, I should come looking for her. Oddly enough, the entire garrison went with her, leaving me alone in the terrifyingly silent room. Surely there was some form of security measure in place. I had scanned the rune-laden walls a dozen times already, cursing myself for never learning to read them. Any one of them could say "blow Rictor up if he steps out of line" and I would have no idea.

Anxiety creeps up my spine, wrapping around my chest. I try

to remember what my therapist taught me: ground yourself, focus on what you can see, name it out loud if you have to. *The vaulted ceiling. The stained-glass windows, casting eerie colors across the stone floor. The massive chandelier above my head, crystals dripping like ice.* There's something calming about it, breaking things down, piece by piece. My breathing slows, the anxious knot loosening just a little. But then I realize I've lost track of time—has it been thirty minutes already? Panic crashes back in.

She's been gone too long.

I don't even realize I'm moving until I'm halfway up a sweeping staircase, calling out her name in a harsh whisper. "Jads?" The top of the stairs open into a grand hall, dimly lit by runes and torchlight. No alarms seem to sound and no lights flash. The laser turrets don't whip around and train their barrels on me. I'm not vaporized instantly for my transgression. Maybe the Council just had really shit-for-brains guards.

I push forward, my footsteps muffled by the thick, red carpet that runs the length of the hall. The walls here are marble, cold and smooth, with swirling carvings in perpetual motion.

"Jads?" I call again, but my voice is swallowed by the vast, empty space around me. This is pointless. It's not like I can search the entire castle. I pause, and an idea hits me—something I've never tried before. I can feel emotions nearby, like they bleed into me. But what if I can stretch my awareness, try to catch a trace of her emotions from here? I have no idea if it's possible, but I'm desperate enough to try anything.

I close my eyes, concentrating, willing myself to feel something. I reach out, seeking the familiar tug of her emotions. Usually, I feel her like a warm current pulling me in, grounding me. But now, it's like I'm reaching into fog, my mind fumbling through cold emptiness. There's nothing—no anchor, just a hollow ache where she should be. A chill runs through me. We're further apart than I thought.

The silence tightens around me. Then I hear it: the heavy clanking of armor. My eyes snap open, heart pounding as the overwhelming sound echoes from both ends of the hall. I'm trapped. The guards are coming, and I don't have time to figure this out. I need to find Jadis, and I need to find her now.

The guards circle me, maintaining a cautious distance, their blades drawn and glinting, ready to strike. I swipe at the sweat on my face, forcing myself to stay focused.

"Where is she?" I shout, my voice sharp in the stifling air. It echoes viciously off the marble walls.

"Return to the entrance hall of your own volition, or we will do it for you," one of them snarls. "And you won't like how we're going to do it." He's weaponless at first, but then a golden sword materializes in his grip, symbols glowing down its center. It's hard to tell through the visor, but I think it's the same captain who apprehended us in the city.

It seems like only the captain wields magick. I watch his grip tightening as blue flames erupt along the blade. "This blade will tear through you like you're nothing but air," he says with a ruthless grin, as the flames lick up its length.

Even from this distance, the heat radiates over me, yet the wielder remains unfazed.

I close my eyes, steadying my breathing—*in... out... in... out*—until calm washes over me. I can't afford to die here. I have to be quick, precise. I tap into Aigerim's bond, feeling my senses sharpen. Just like all those years back in Akeurimja, the sounds around me become visible, waving through the cavernous chamber. Something is different, though. Even with my eyes closed, I can see the vibrations pulse around me like ripples in water—sensing every shift, every clink of their armor.

My eyes open.

They charge as one.

I throw my hands up in one, swift motion. Their weapons tear free, fire and steel suspended mid-air. They scramble, hands grasping at empty air. I don't give them a chance to recover.

"He's the Noble from Fleming!" one of the guards shouts, his voice high with alarm.

For a brief heartbeat, everything is perfectly still. I bring my arms in, forcing the blades together in a violent collision. The clashing metal reverberates like a war drum. I clench my fingers, feeling the tingling rush as my mental grip tightens around the crushed heap of steel. With a final thrust, I hurl the mangled mass into the floor, leaving the red carpet torn and smoldering beneath it. Every eye in the room is locked on me.

I lower my hands, tension vibrating in my chest, mind racing. I can see the current that spreads around us, the short-lived fight having left its mark on the space, despite the room appearing untouched.

The air settles, thick with the scent of burned fabric and scorched metal. But then, another smell drifts in—something herbal, sharp like rosemary with a hint of sweetness that cuts through the metallic tang. The flickering flames on the wall shift, their light dancing to an unfamiliar rhythm, casting long, strange shadows. My instincts flare; someone else is here, watching, waiting. I turn, pulse quickening, just as a new voice resounds across the hall, sharp and laced with command.

"Well done, all of you! Now, leave."

The guards march out without question, each casting a seething glare my way. I turn, and there—a woman, standing at the top of a short staircase I hadn't noticed before, dressed in flowing white and gold robes. She's young, could be around my age, but there's a knowing glint in her eye and a smirk that says she's not one to mess with.

"Where the hell is Jadis?" I shout, my voice carrying easily across the hall. I watch the jagged sound waves shudder through the air.

The woman presses her palms together, golden rings glowing on her fingers as her hands radiate a fierce pink light. A witch. She flexes her fingers, thrusting her arms out to conjure four enormous, glowing spears that hover, radiating with energy. With a swift flick of her finger, one of the spears shoots toward me, aimed right for my head.

I feel the ripples before I see them—the sound waves from the speeding weapon shimmer in the air, vivid and unmistakable. My reflexes sharpen, and I step back, swiping my arm just in time to deflect the projectile. It veers into the wall, shattering the marble on impact. The wave reverberates outward, so loud I can see it bouncing off the walls. Runes line the shaft, matching those on the captain's sword. Before I can react, the hallway morphs into a dark cave—she's altering reality.

Two more spears hurtle toward me. I sidestep, knocking one to my left and slamming the other into the ceiling. The impacts ricochet in a flash of vibrating echoes, visible pulses bursting against the stone walls. Another wave, quick and sharp, catches my attention. The final spear comes straight at me, stopping mere inches from my face, held suspended by my hands. The air trembles with tension, sound waves crashing around us. Her smug smile fades as I spin the spear in the air, its tip now aimed at her chest.

A ripple in the air warns me a split second before I hear her voice. My grip tightens, every nerve on edge.

"Enough." The single word, spoken with eerie calm, slices through the chaos. Instantly, the cave fades away, and I'm back in the grand hall. The witch's eyes meet mine, and they hold an unsettling stillness, like she's already calculated every move I could make.

"Ricky, stop!"

I turn around to Jadis, her expression stricken. She steps forward, hands raised, a silent plea in her gaze. Beside her, the robed woman holds her ground, observing us with a sharpness that pierces through the fading echoes of the fight. She has to be a Council member—and that means she's much more dangerous than she seems.

"Ricky..." Jadis's presence pulls me back. She's here, safe, and suddenly, the urge to fight fades.

I lower my hands, releasing the weapon I'd held suspended. Jadis's eyes meet mine, and I feel the terror bleed out of me, replaced by a relief so sharp it hurts. I run to Jadis, pulling her into a tight embrace, my body trembling. "Did they hurt you?" I ask, gripping her hands, searching her face.

She shakes her head gently. "Ricky, I'm fine. Breathe," she whispers, her hand finding my forearm, pulling me closer until our foreheads meet.

Her emotions flood into me—relief, exhaustion, something sharp and tangled underneath. I'm grounding myself in the rhythm of her breath. It's like she's holding my anger, her presence unwinding the tight knot of fury coiled in my chest.

"Good, just like that," she says softly.

"You didn't come back. I thought..." I trail off, pulling back to look at her.

"I know," she says, a hint of guilt in her eyes. "I'm sorry. I found something important—information we need."

"We can't be apart, Jads. We can't die here."

She smiles faintly, her grip tightening. "I know. And we won't."

The spears are gone, but the cracks on the walls and ceiling leave the hallway looking scarred and battle-worn. The witch walks toward us, a bright smile on her face. Instinctively, my hand twitches open, ready to defend again.

"Relax. I wanted to see if you lived up to the stories," she says, tilting her head, a sly grin stretching across her face. "You didn't disappoint."

Relax? You just threw four huge ass spears to my head, bitch!

"Ricky, this is Lady Lâcien, High witch of the Apertus Coven," Jadis says, raising her eyebrows. "A master of Manifestation and Mending magick. Also... Evanora's niece."

"I—Uh—Hello." The words stumble out, awkward and unsteady. Despite her attempt to kill me, I can't ignore just how gorgeous she is. Lâcien's hair flows like a dark river, sleek and reflective, framing her face as it sweeps just past her shoulders. Though petite, maybe 5'2" at most, she radiates a commanding presence that defies her size. Her almond-shaped eyes hold a quiet, lethal focus, and her skin is a warm olive tone.

"You can call me Lacey," she says, a teasing edge in her grin. "Jadis didn't tell me you were brutishly powerful. I guess she likes her secrets."

"Brutish?" My eyebrows pull together, a bit offended, but opting to brush it off. She's got a snarky edge.

Jadis lowers her head slightly, an unusual shift from her typical stance. "I can assure you, there was no secret. It didn't occur to me that you would need to know exactly how... brutishly powerful Ricky is."

"Apologies for my reaction," I say, keeping my voice steady. *Yeah, sorry for reacting like a sane person when faced with attempted murder.*

Lâcien waves her hand. "Ugh, stop that. The Supreme shouldn't be bowing to anyone." She grabs our hands, winking as she holds mine a bit longer. "And you have some strong arms."

Jadis rolls her eyes, and I can almost taste her disgust.

My eyes gravitate to the cracked walls and shattered tiles littering the hallway. Lâcien raises a hand and, with a graceful wave, the damage begins to repair itself. Marble shifts, cracks seal, and the carpet smooths out as if nothing happened. I'm caught between awe and frustration.

"Shall we talk in private?" she says, stepping between Jadis and me, linking her arms with ours and pulling us down another corridor. "It's just me here, the rest of the Council are dealing with matters in the other nations." We walk toward a towering statue of a phoenix at the end of the hall, its wings stretching skyward, detailed with flames that almost seem to flicker.

I glance at Jadis over Lâcien's head. "What did you find out?"

She takes a breath, her excitement barely contained. "Lacey is friends with Jho. She was here to talk with her. She's *alive*, Ricky." Jadis's voice cracks, tears welling in her eyes. It's too late for her to hide it—I'm already feeling it, the waves of hope and relief pouring out of her, sinking into me.

Lâcien looks up at me with interest. "You're an empath," she observes. "How long have you been practicing Divination?"

The question catches me off guard. I open my mouth, but Jadis answers first. "He doesn't," she says. "He developed these empathic abilities when we got back."

Lâcien nods thoughtfully. "I see. I couldn't quite believe you weren't a magick user until now. Watching you fend off those spears... I wanted to test it for myself. The famous 'No magick, non-Keeper.' Nothing but your brute strength and Noble bond."

"Wait," I say, voice tinged with outrage. "You weren't giving me an actual fight? You were testing me?"

She giggles, letting go of our arms as we approach the phoenix statue. She motions for us to step closer, and as soon as we do, the statue begins to rise, carrying us upward. My gaze falls back on Jadis. I can see hope shining from her face, something I haven't seen since our childhood.

"Jhoana was here just a few hours ago," Lâcien says. "She told me to keep an eye out for any of you if you showed up, but she didn't say where she was headed next. We decided to cut contact after. Easy to pry into people's heads these days. But she knows you're all back, and I think she's on her way to find you."

"I mean, does the rest of the Council even know Jho is still around?" I ask, raising a brow.

Jadis interjects, "I told you, Ricky, we can't fully trust the Council. They'll figure it out soon enough when they start digging into Lacey's head during questioning. Things are more complicated than ever in Ethra."

"That's what Elyssa said... Can we trust her?" My voice is sharper than I intended as I jerk my chin at Lâcien .

Lâcien just grins, brushing a finger across my beard. A quiver of *something* slips into my stomach. "You can trust me, handsome," she purrs. Jadis clears her throat loudly. The statue finally halts, revealing a large open room filled with the scent of old books and stardust. In the center stands a golden telescope, glinting under the soft light from above, runes engraved along its sides. A glass dome stretches over the ceiling, the constellations beyond it clear and vibrant, each star shining as though it's been set against velvet.

Lâcien steps off first, gesturing for us to follow. I'm drawn to the telescope, and reach out to touch it, its polished metal cool beneath my fingers. The runes pulse softly, casting a faint glow. The craftsmanship is immaculate. I look up through the eyepiece, and the stars magnify, blazing against the endless night.

A tug of the breeze pulls me from the telescope, and I wander onto the balcony. The capital city of Arid stretches out before me, but from this height, I can see beyond its borders. The desert sprawls beyond the horizon, a vast sea of sand dunes shimmering under the starlight, their pale gold muted to silver in the moon's glow. Tiny pinpricks of light dot the landscape here and there—caravans or perhaps desert outposts—glowing like candles scattered across the dunes. Tall, ancient cacti carve through the sands, capped with magnificent blooms.

Closer to the city, a river cuts through the desert, its waters catching the moonlight, reflecting it like a ribbon of liquid silver winding through the sands. Lush, emerald grasses stand guard along its banks, and beyond them, clusters of date palms sway gently in the night breeze.

Arid feels eternal from up here, the horizon stretching out, blending into the night. There's a quiet stillness in the desert's expanse, a feeling of something ancient, something waiting. Just like it did in Terrene.

Jadis joins me at the railing, and we both take it in, the raw, untamed beauty of the desert under the stars.

"Welcome to Arid," she says softly, her voice almost reverent.

For the first time since we returned, I feel a flicker of hope—of possibility. This place, this night—it's more than a backdrop. It feels like a promise.

Out of nowhere, two hands clamp down on my head, and raw instinct takes over. I telekinetically shove Lâcien back, her feet scraping against the floor as she miraculously manages to stay upright.

"What the hell are you doing?" I shout, keeping my guard up.

"Impressive reflexes," she says, straightening up and running a hand through her hair. "When we fought, I sensed something... different about you. I tried to trap you in an illusion, but it didn't work. Yet you still saw the illusion in the hallway, which made me curious. It seems someone's shielded your mind. I can't read your thoughts at all. Whoever did it is powerful—the barriers are unbreakable."

She glances at Jadis, who shakes her head. "Wasn't me."

I frown, confused. "No one put a spell on me. What are you talking about?"

Lâcien's gaze sharpens as she changes the subject. "Your eye... It's fascinating. Still connected to your Crown Beast, huh? Let me fix that."

She raises a hand toward my eye. Instantly, I take a step back, muscles tightening for an impending strike. "No. Back off!"

"I promise, no more sneak attacks." She holds my gaze, and I don't feel any deceit coming from her—just a wave of sadness. Sadness for me.

Reluctantly, I let my guard down. She probably can't make my ruined eye any *worse*. As she touches the hollow beneath my lower lashes, a strange warmth trickles in—not from her hand, but from something deeper. Her sorrow seeps through, raw and ragged. It's like stepping into a storm—gusts of regret and guilt swirl around me.

I can't shake the sense that she's looking through me, measuring something I don't even know I'm carrying. For the first time in a long time, I wonder if I've finally met someone who's seen the edges of my soul, and isn't the least bit fazed.

Her palm presses lightly against my eye and a flash of bright light floods my vision. She steps back, letting her hand fall.

"Done," she says quietly.

I turn and catch sight of a mirror on the wall. The old scar running from my eyebrow to my cheek has transformed, now etched with rune-like patterns that glimmer faintly. My eye is healed, but my iris—once a light brown—is now the pale color of birch wood, barely a hint of its original brown remaining. Heterochromia. I take in the change, feeling a strange mix of emotions colliding into one another. At least it looks better than Aigerim's decidedly unsettling amber eye.

The face staring back feels like mine, but... worn, somehow. My hair's still short, the sides cut into a burst fade like always, and my beard is just as stubborn as ever, refusing to connect fully to my mustache. But here, in Ethra, I look older. Not in any obvious way, but there's something different in my eyes, a heaviness I didn't have back on Earth.

As I blink, my reflection blurs for a moment, and I swear I see Pa staring back at me. That's when it hits me—I look just like he did the last time I saw him, carrying a weight he couldn't shake off. Shadows hang under my eyes, lines I don't remember earning tugging at the corners. It's like this world took the energy I had and drained it out, leaving this version of me that I barely recognize.

And yet, there's no denying it's me. I'm here, a little more haggard, holding on to whatever's left.

"Now," Lâcien says, standing behind me, "let's talk about the real threat after Jhoana."

I turn to face her, pushing back whatever emotions my appearance dragged to the surface. "What do you mean?"

She looks between Jadis and me, her expression darkening. "Have either of you heard of The Angel of Death?"

DUSTIN

As the hovercraft carrying Rictor and Jadis fades into the horizon, I turn to Emierr, wrapping an arm around his neck and pulling him close. We stand together, watching Sólel share a tender goodbye with his wife.

Sólel's voice reaches us, soft and warm. "Not even a million suns could outshine the way my heart burns for you."

Evera smiles, caressing his face. "Stop being so poetic. It's working, and I don't think I can stand another second away from you. You're my sun, Sólel Jupiter, and I'm your solar system."

Sólel chuckles, voice breaking slightly as he rests a hand on the swell of her belly. "What'll we name him, then?"

Evera shakes her head, eyes shining. "We'll know when he's here."

The way they look at each other—it's like they're caught in a world of their own, and I feel a sudden pang in my chest. I'd give anything to have my Sylvia here, to see my two little girls' sweet smiles. I blink away the sudden moisture in my eyes, leaning in close to Emierr.

"If you don't get a girlfriend by the end of this year, I'm setting you up with Dahlia."

Emierr swats me in the stomach, knocking the wind out of me just a little. "She's not my type," he mutters, his mouth twitching into a smirk as he walks away.

Before we can load up in the hovercraft, Chief Berkarys and Chieftess Nalani step forward. The chief rests a hand on my shoulder, eyes solemn. "Take care of each other," he says. "No matter what awaits you in Zaltana."

The Chieftess touches Emierr's arm, her voice gentle but firm. "Return to us safely, all of you. We will be waiting."

As we step back, Evera moves over, hands on her hips, her gaze pinning Emierr and me to the ground. "And don't you two dare do anything reckless. You'll all come back, understood?"

I raise my hands in mock surrender, flashing her my most charming grin. "Who, us? Reckless? Never."

Emierr rolls his eyes, but I see the corner of his mouth twitching as he tries not to smile. We head into the hovercraft, and I slip into the passenger seat, watching as Sólel buckles in behind me, looking tense.

"What's the matter, Sól?" I tease, throwing an arm over the back of the seat. "Scared of flying?"

He laughs nervously. "Never been in a vehicle before. I could fly myself, but... that would attract attention."

I let out a chuckle as Emierr, seated beside him, leans over and claps him on the shoulder. "He's teasing you, Sól."

Sólel narrows his eyes at me and lifts a middle finger. Emierr bursts out laughing, raising a hand for a high-five.

My grin fades as I turn away, feigning a pout. "I liked you better when you were nine."

Jae conceals his laugh in a cough and powers up the hovercraft. It hums to life beneath us, and as we lift off, the Ethereal Tree's glow shimmers across the villages below, like stars dotting Ethra's surface.

"I'm not Borge," Jae announces, glancing back at us. "I won't be getting us to Zaltana in under thirty minutes. ETA is two hours, so relax and enjoy the view."

As I settle back, a memory of Chief Arun flickers through my mind, his laughter echoing in the night air. Emierr's got it wrong—this trip to Zaltana isn't just for the tribe. It's for Grandpa Arun. I never got to meet any of my grandparents. By the time I spent a few years in Guam, my dad's parents were already gone. But Chief Arun stepped into that role when I first arrived, and I haven't seen him in years. If Ethra gives me one thing, I hope it's the chance to see him again, even just once.

I glance back, watching Sólel and Emierr. It's bittersweet, seeing them reconnect after so many years, knowing this might be the last time they're together like this. I still can't wrap my head around how much older Sólel is now. The kid who used to tag along with us is a man now—mostly. Despite the fact that he and Emierr are currently engaged in a slap fight in the back seat.

Jae glances over. "You all right?"

"My kids and my wife, just miss them," I reply, looking out at the darkness stretching ahead. "I can't believe I used to think this was all a dream..."

Disbelief colors Jae's face. "You think Ethra's a dream?"

"Not anymore," I amend, eyes not leaving the swirl of Ethra's home galaxy, visible despite the golden glow below. "How could all this be a dream?"

Jae chuckles. "You know what everyone here thinks about you 'Earth kids?' The most popular theory is you're all from the future, traveling back in time. That Earth is an evolved version of Ethra."

I finally look away from the starlit horizon. "*Most* popular theory?"

He grins. "Runner-up theory? That you're aliens."

I snort. "Us? You seen the leyfolk?"

Jae just laughs. "So, are you going to debunk all those theories right here, on record?" he asks, flashing a mischievous look.

"Not from the future, and definitely not aliens. Point blank." I shake my head. But before I can get another word out, Emierr cuts me off, pointing. "Look! Aetherwings!"

A group of massive, winged creatures glides alongside us, their wingspans stretching across the length of the hovercraft. Their feathers shimmer in the moonlight, shifting from indigo to deep violet, catching the moving tapestry of stars above. Their eyes glow faintly with an otherworldly gold, and the tips of their feathers trail wisps of luminescent dust, which spiral and linger in the air.

I press my hand to the glass, staring in awe, and I can see Emierr leaning forward, his eyes wide, captivated. The creatures fly with a graceful rhythm, their wings beating in near silence, as if their presence alone is a reverent part of Ethra's night sky.

"They can sense magick," Sólel murmurs, leaning closer to the window as he stares at the creatures gliding beside us. "It must be our presence."

"Let's test that theory," Jae says mischievously. "Everyone, hold on!"

I barely have time to react before he pulls a sharp turn, steering the hovercraft in a wild, looping path. The creatures match every turn, banking left and right alongside the vehicle. All I feel is bliss—the kind that makes you feel alive.

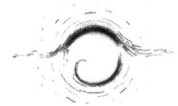

The hovercraft lands softly on the rough, rocky surface of the Zaltanian mountains, its engines humming to a quiet halt. As we step out, the night air hits me like a cold slap, sharp and biting. I take a deep breath, letting the smell of stone and frost fill my lungs. Zaltana rises above us, all towers and lantern-lit shadows, climbing the mountain like it's trying to reach the stars. The place looks like it's been carved right out of the rock—nothing of this mountain has changed, not one bit.

I glance around. The people here move with that same quiet purpose, like they're all part of some ancient rhythm. Leyfolk mix with the humans, their eyes shimmering faintly under the hoods of their cloaks. No one even looks our way.

Emierr wrinkles his nose, glancing around. "This isn't very festive."

I nudge him, grinning. "Everyone minds their business here, Meer."

I take in their clothes. Gone are the bright colors I remember—now it's all dark, muted grays and browns, like they're trying to blend into the mountains.

Kids dart past, laughing as they vanish down the stone paths. Their shadows flicker in the lamplight, but the night swallows up the sound almost as quickly as it comes. I glance up at the towers, feeling that old, heavy weight of this place pressing down on me. Despite the changes in fashion, Zaltana's just as I remember—quiet and unbothered by time.

As we step further into the expanse, Emierr looks around, taking in the scene. "You know, the vibes remind me of Farmington," he says, a wistful look on his face. "I hope Juno's changed a bit, though. I'd like to check out the party scene this time around."

Sólel chuckles, nudging him. "I actually know a club in Juno that would be perfect for you, *kuya*—dark corners, loud music, way too much dancing."

Before Emierr can respond, Jae clears his throat, cutting off their daydreams. "We're here for Brunner, remember? Let's keep our priorities straight."

Emierr and Sólel exchange sheepish looks, and I can't help but laugh. "Hey, maybe we'll get lucky and Rune will be in Juno, too. Then we can really have a reunion party." I give them a wink, but Jae just shakes his head, looking more serious than ever.

"I'm going to talk with the people who reported Brunner's sighting," Jae says, glancing at us. "Stick around, and don't wander too far."

As he heads off, Emierr spots a metal plaque on a nearby stone wall. He reads aloud, "Welcome to Alluvial Plains."

I let out a sigh, shaking my head. "Great, they gave this place a name. Makes it way less cool. Back in the day, being part of Zaltana meant you belonged to all of it. Now they're chopping it up with signs and names. Just feels wrong."

Emierr claps a hand on my shoulder, sensing my disappointment. But I brush it off. It's not about the names; it's about finding Brunner and bringing him back. Sólel has wandered up to a small group of leyfolk, speaking to them in fluent Leymara.

When he turns to come back, I raise an eyebrow, impressed. "Didn't know you could speak Leymara."

Sólel shrugs, his expression turning a little softer. "Evera's leyfolk. I had to learn. I want our son to grow up speaking both languages."

There's a pride in his voice that I haven't heard before, and it makes me smile.

"They haven't seen or heard anything about Brunner nor the bear," Sólel went on with a sigh.

I pause, an idea slowly forming. There's a spot, an old haunt from my younger days. I'd spend hours there, perched on the cliffs, watching over Ethra. A flock of Argentavis had nests nearby—maybe they'd still be there. "I know where we can go," I say, glancing back at Emierr. "The Argentavis. You might be able to talk to them."

Emierr raises his brows, but jerks his shoulders in a compliant shrug. I start walking, muscle memory kicking in as my feet find the old familiar paths. Every turn, every stone, it's all the same. I take a deep breath, the cool mountain air filling my lungs.

The path opens up as we reach the edge, and the view hits us like a punch to the gut. Even I have to pause, taking in the breathtaking expanse before us. Emierr lets out a low whistle, and Sólel's eyes widen as he steps closer to the edge.

From up here, Zaltana's cliffs and ridges stretch out like a stony maze. Just a few peaks over, the neon glow of Juno lights up the rock faces in bursts of electric color, flickering like some wild beacon against the night. The ice caps of Verglas glint in the moonlight, sharp and untouched. Out west, where the land dips and blurs into shadow, I know the sands of Arid are lying in wait, just out of sight.

But the most striking sight is the Space Ring. It hangs low in the sky, a vast structure glinting in the night, its outer edges just beginning to dip below the horizon. Soon, it'll be out of sight, lost to the shadows.

"Holy shit... This is what you saw everyday?" Emierr breathes.

Sólel is silent, his gaze fixed on the horizon. "I forgot how beautiful it all is," he says softly.

I nod in silent agreement. Standing here with Emierr and Sólel at my side—the ache of missing my family eases just a little. I allow myself a few more seconds before pulling myself together. "Okay, Meer, on the right side of this mountain, you'll find a couple of nests," I say, nodding toward the dark slope ahead.

Emierr stares at me, his expression blank, then splutters, "How the fuck am I supposed to get over there, Dust?"

I shrug, a smirk forming. "I don't know, man. I did my part. Now you do yours."

"You both haven't changed," Sólel says fondly. He walks toward the cliff's edge, taking a deep breath.

Emierr leans over, muttering, "Is that a good thing?"

Before I can respond, Sólel's whole body begins to shift. He draws in a deep breath, and his entire form starts to glow, the color intensifying into a deep orange, like molten lava. Heat radiates off him in waves, warming my face even from a few feet away. His features blur slightly, as if he's become more energy than substance. When he turns, his eyes and mouth blaze in a brilliant white light, casting a glow on the surrounding rocks.

I can't move, the sheer intensity of it all holding me in place. Emierr takes a step back, shielding his eyes, but I can't look away. This isn't just a display of power—it's a reminder of what Sólel really is. A damn sun god. He lifts off the ground, hovering in the air like a beacon piercing the quiet night. Turning back, he grins, the light radiating from him. "I'll be back with friends."

Then he soars over the cliffs, his outline a comet against the night sky. His light leaves a faint afterglow on my vision. Emierr and I share a look, both of us speechless, the warmth fading and leaving a chill in its place.

"Holy fuck," I mutter, and Emierr just chuckles, shaking his head. "I can't believe that's baby Sól," I breathe, still processing what we just witnessed. "This is all real, Meer. A superstring universe..."

Emierr nods, his expression a mix of awe and sadness. "I know. It's strange—I believed it for the longest time, and now that we're back... I'm sure I won't give it up, not completely."

A sudden light appears from where Sólel flew off, followed by the unmistakable sound of wings beating against the air. We look up and see Sólel returning, no longer in his solar form but still emitting a soft glow. He's riding a massive bird, its feathers black and white, with wings outstretched and eyes that shine with intelligence.

The bird lands with a loud cry, and Emierr's face lights up, recognition dawning. "North Star!" He steps forward, throwing his arms around the creature's neck, and the bird lets out a happy sound, almost like it's crying. I realize it actually is, faint trails of glistening moisture streaking down its face as Sólel slides back to the ground.

"Dusty, this is North Star," Emierr says, turning to me. "Remember, from the stories? He saved me and Sól."

I nod, feeling a bit nervous under the bird's gaze. I try to smile, but the thought crosses my mind that this creature might have had a part in Brunner's disappearance. North Star stares back, unbothered, but I can't shake the feeling that we're playing with something as dangerous as it is beautiful.

"All right, Meer," I say. "Time to work your magic."

Resting a hand on North Star's head, Emierr's voice is calm as he begins to ask about Brunner and the Argentavis that took him. North Star makes a series of deep, resonant noises in response, his voice carrying a sense of age and authority. Emierr listens intently, chuckling and shaking his head as the bird continues.

I raise an eyebrow, looking between them. "What did he say?"

Emierr turns to me, eyes glinting with amusement. "The one that took Brunner is North's offspring. Apparently, all of his kids are forbidden from eating humans or leyfolk." He pauses, glancing back at the giant bird, his expression turning somber. "But because of the poisoned food supply, they've all been struggling with hunger."

North Star lets out a low croon, turning his gaze to me, and Emierr translates, "He's apologizing, Dust. Says he and his family didn't eat Brunner, but he can't vouch for what else might be out there."

North Star then begins a series of longer, almost melodic sounds, his tone shifting, more serious. Emierr listens, nodding, but then his eyes widen, a hint of surprise on his face. When North Star finishes, Emierr thanks him, then turns to me.

"Rune *was* spotted riding a bear—a huge one. North's kids saw them by the Isle of... *Vereilles?* I think that's a new place but apparently, they disappeared at a certain point there, and North knows exactly where."

"Thank you," I say to the regal bird.

Emierr, smiling, tilts his head toward North Star again. "Where are your old friends, Beak and Snow? You know, the ones from that day?"

North Star lowers his head, glancing at Sólel before making a gentle sound. Emierr raises his brows, turning to Sólel. "North says you'd know."

Sólel sighs heavily, a hint of sadness crossing his face. "I used to visit them all the time. But... they went savage, *Kuya.* Both Beak and Snow tried to take people from Terrene. I had to put them down." He swallows, his voice soft. "Sorry..."

Emierr lets out a quiet breath, his shoulders sinking, and I rest a hand on his shoulder.

North Star lowers his head, rubbing it against Emierr, making a sound almost like a comforting purr.

Emierr smiles, his eyes softening. "He says he'll take us to where we need to go," he translates. "Wants us to enjoy the view the right way." He chuckles.

I feel a surge of excitement. Flying over Ethra with North Star? There's no way I'd pass that up. "Hell yeah. Let's let Jae know where we went first."

Sólel gives North Star a pat, then turns back to us. "I'll call North back when we're ready to go," he says, casting a glance over the cliff. "I kind of want to fly myself, anyway."

I smirk, crossing my arms. "So, you *don't* like flying in cars, huh?"

Emierr lets out a laugh, translating to North Star, who lets out a squawk and takes off, disappearing into the night sky. Just as I'm about to turn back, I notice Sólel staring wide-eyed over my shoulder, his face pale. He bows his head, his voice barely a whisper.

I turn around, my heart nearly stopping. Standing there, with the same quiet strength I remember, is Grandpa Arun. I'm speechless, my breath catching in my throat as all those years without him crash into me like a wave.

He smiles, his voice soft but unmistakable. "Is that really you, my Dustin?"

"Grandpa..." I choke out, barely able to believe it. He looks just as he did then, wearing the same animal print clothing, but time has left its mark. He leans on a wooden walking stick, and his face is etched with deep lines, though his gaze remains warm and familiar.

"You've grown so much, my boy," he says, spreading his arms wide.

And just like that, I'm twelve years old again. I rush forward, falling into his embrace, and all the years of waiting and wondering dissolve. I never expected it to hit this hard, but as he wraps his arms around me, the tears spill over, and I cling to him, letting the emotions pour out. It's the same feeling I had seeing Jhoana again, but somehow deeper, older. Grandpa Arun rubs my back, his voice gentle.

"Welcome home, my boy."

"I'm sorry, Grandpa," I manage through the sobs. "I'm so sorry it took so long."

He pulls back just enough to look me in the eye, his gaze filled with patience and love. "I've waited for you, my boy. Even if it was the last thing I saw, I knew you'd come back."

I can't bring myself to say anything more, so I just squeeze him a little tighter.

Grandpa Arun allows me to cling to him for a few moments longer before taking me gently by the shoulders. "Now, let's go," he says. "Jae is waiting for us." He wraps his arm around mine, his grip surprisingly strong, and starts walking.

As we leave the hidden path and move through the crowd, the citizens bow their heads, parting in quiet respect. Grandpa Arun's presence alone commands a silent reverence that lingers in their lowered gazes as we pass by. Ahead, Jae toggles with the holograms coming from his wrist, his face intense with focus. When he spots us, he runs over. "Thank the Tree! *He* wouldn't let me drop him off to find you guys." Jae shoots Grandpa a look of irritated concern.

"You would've slowed me down," Grandpa Arun retorts, his voice carrying a hint of mischief.

We all chuckle, and I give Grandpa a look of pure admiration. Nothing keeps him down.

"We know where Rune—Brunner—is," Emierr says, glancing at Jae. "Somewhere near the Isle of Vereilles?"

Jae nods, a look of relief crossing his face. "Great, that narrows the search."

Emierr raises an eyebrow. "Care to enlighten us about what the Isle of Vereilles is?"

"Vereilles is the sixth nation," Jae explains, lowering his voice.

"Sixth?" Emierr and I blurt out in unison. Ethra has changed in ways I never imagined since we left it abandoned thirty-two years ago. A sixth nation...

Jae glances around as if someone might overhear. "From what I was briefed on, it's... not like the other nations. Most people don't know much about it, only that it's hidden and extremely selective about who it lets in. They say Vereilles was founded in reverence to the Allied Organization Squad and, well... the Nobles from Earth."

I blink. "Wait, what? A place dedicated to *us*?"

Jae shrugs, looking a bit uncomfortable, "I mean, that's the rumor. They say it's a sanctuary, almost like a secret refuge, for leyfolk and others who seek protection. The people there are dedicated to preserving the ideals they think you all stood for." He pauses, studying my reaction. "It's isolated, shielded by powerful magick. Hardly anyone's even seen it."

"Have you heard about them, Grandpa?" I ask, glancing at his placid face.

"Only that they wear mostly white."

"Oh god," Emierr groans. "Are you telling me we indirectly started a cult?"

I chuckle, but the thought still sends a chill down my spine. "Does that make them Mormon 3.0?" I say, tone light.

Jae's expression is unreadable, a hint of something between curiosity and intrigue. "Maybe. I don't know. I haven't met one to say anything, but some say they believe you'll come back and lead Ethra into some new era. Whether it's true or just a tale, I think it means something to them."

The thought settles over me like a shadow. The sixth nation—it feels like a piece of our story that kept living, even when we left.

"I've also come across some valuable intel." Jae breaks my train of thought. "There's a man named Riven Zykos in Juno who might have a magickal artifact—one that can locate anyone, anywhere, as long as they're in this plane of existence."

Emierr brightens, practically bouncing with enthusiasm. "Perfect! Let's get going!"

But Jae's expression turns uneasy, and I catch the look in his eyes. "And?" I press.

Jae lets out a sigh, looking resigned. "Riven owns a nightclub, and that's where he'll be tonight."

Emierr pumps a fist in the air. "Yes!"

I chuckle, shaking my head, but Jae raises a hand, his expression grave. "Emierr, don't get too excited. Riven isn't someone you want to mess with. His club draws a rough crowd, and he's got connections. People say he deals in rare magickal artifacts—stuff that can get real nasty in the wrong hands. We'll need to stay on our guard."

"Oh." Emierr's hand drops, but the grin doesn't leave his face. "Good thing I'm a people person."

"Oh boy." I let out a heavy sigh.

"By the way, Jae, you can leave your hovercraft, "Emierr says offhandedly. "We're taking an Argentavis to Juno." We begin the walk toward the cliff, Jae choking out protests in our wake. Just before we reach the point where Grandpa Arun will be out of sight, I turn around. He's standing there, watching us with a proud smile on his face. For a brief second, I almost see my younger self standing beside him, reminding me that he was always there, waiting.

We reach the cliff where Sólel, radiating like a fiery comet, has returned with North. "I could just drive, you know," Jae says in a low voice, eyeing the massive raptor.

I smirk, motioning to the cliffside. "Come on, Jae. Live a little. You're a Zaltanian, aren't you?"

"But... can we really trust it?" Jae mutters, glancing around. "I mean, his kind's been known to... I'll just drive, all right?"

Emierr claps him on the shoulder. "Relax, Jae. North Star here is an old friend, and he's strictly on a no-people diet. You're good." He grins, then adds, "And hey, worst case, I can command them. Nothing's gonna eat us on my watch."

Jae blows out a heavy breath, but acquiesces. As I climb onto North Star, I feel a new resolve settle over me, knowing we'll be back—that Zaltana, and Grandpa will still be here. Jae climbs up beside me, grinning despite himself, with Emierr on his other side. North Star lets out a loud cry, and Emierr shouts, "Hold on!" The mighty bird spreads his wings wide. I grip his feathers tightly, bracing myself. Sólel dives toward the cliffs, and North Star follows close behind, the air rushing past us in a dizzying blur.

A rush of tingles courses through my body just as North Star plunges downward. Emierr lets out a loud, "Fuck me!" and I scream, letting the adrenaline take over. The sensation is like nothing else. I feel my body begin to levitate off the bird's back, weightless, as North Star cascades down the mountain cliffs. In that instant, I'm reminded of the time Rictor lifted us all in the meadow; that same freeing feeling, as if there's nothing anchoring us down.

As gravity finds us again, I glance over to see Sólel spiraling in circles, his trail illuminating the night in a glowing path—a vision of pure exhilaration.

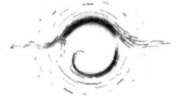

Juno sprawls out in front of us, a futuristic labyrinth carved right into the mountains. The buildings jut from the cliffs, neon lights bouncing off their surfaces with each pulse of the city's heartbeat. It's like a condensed Space Ring, packed with energy and bursting with culture. It's hard to remember that most of this nation is comprised of quiet, peaceful villages. Everything here is loud, sharp, and right up in your face, daring you to keep up.

My eyes leap from place to place, finding a new color, shape, or pattern screaming no matter where I look. No one gives a damn who we are. We catch a few glances here and there—mostly directed at Sólel—but they flick away just as fast, like we're another fixture in the scene.

Sólel mentioned earlier that most Terreneans steer clear of Juno—the place is a full-scale assault on their love for nature—and I can see why. This city is all-consuming, a far cry from the forests and open fields they'd be used to. Jae is ahead of us, scanning the crowd and following some route the rest of us can't see.

"Not much farther," he calls out, his voice barely cutting the rhythm of the city.

Emierr nudges me, flashing that all-too-familiar grin. "C'mon, you gotta take a shot with me tonight."

I give him a withering look. "Really? This is what we're thinking about? Rune's out there somewhere, and Jho—"

He just laughs, throwing an arm around my shoulders. "Exactly, that's *why* it's the best time. Even Sól's game, right, Sól?"

I glance over at Sólel, who's striding alongside us with a rigid, almost military posture, hands clasped behind his back like he's on some kind of guard duty. I let out a low chuckle and nod. "Yeah, looks like he could use it."

Jae's eyes are glued to the holograms flickering over his wrist as he veers into a narrow alley. The air changes in a snap—smells of leaking pipes blend with some unnamed street food scent. As we trail after Jae, and the noise fades a little, replaced by an uneasy silence. The prickle on the back of my neck intensifies as the alley opens up, revealing what is very clearly a red-light district.

Eyes follow us from the shadows, and a few women in sweeping, patterned robes drift over, half their faces hidden. Despite the masks, their stares are anything but shy. They slide their robes open, exposing bare skin traced with bioluminescent lines and metallic implants glinting in the artificial light—a mix of curves and tech, everything carefully designed to make you look. They press in close, fingers trailing over my shoulders and chest. I huff, just about to brush one of them off when Jae spins around, lifting his shirt to reveal a dragon tattoo coiling across his chest, the scales almost shimmering.

"You ladies want a better look?" he says, grinning like he's right at home.

The women's eyes flash, and they hiss as they retreat, melting back into the shadows. Jae drops his shirt and pats my shoulder. "Stick close, or Juno'll eat you alive."

"What the hell was that?" I narrow my eyes at the concealed tattoo.

He pauses, meeting my gaze like he's weighing how much to say. "The reason I didn't end up an Inkweaver," he mutters, then turns back, heading down the alley before I could follow up with more questions.

I keep walking, but his words prod my brain with sharpened sticks. Why would that tattoo keep him from becoming an Inkweaver? And why'd those women back off so fast the second he showed it? Jae suddenly became far more interesting, but I can't shake the feeling there's something important I'm missing here.

Jae moves ahead, cutting through the shadows and back into the main street. I squint as the technicolor gleam hit us again, sharper this time.

We stop in front of a sleek, alien building, its surface dark and polished, curving up like it's primed to rip free from the ground. Purple and blue streaks pulse beneath the glossy finish, throwing sharp, jagged light that slices through the night. The entrance looms—a huge arch, almost like a mouth—and strange symbols flash over it, shifting patterns that draw your eyes in and won't let go. The whole place vibrates with a heavy, pulsing beat, and the crowd outside shuffles impatiently, practically buzzing to get in. This isn't just a club. It's like a gateway to something else, a place that feels like it'll swallow you whole if you're not careful.

Jae jerks his head toward the neon sign overhead, its silver letters flashing in sync with the beat. "Welcome to Lucid Veil," he says. Without another word, he walks right up to the bouncer—an ogre who could pass for Borge if the latter stopped skipping arm day at the gym.

Emierr and Sólel join me at the club's entrance, where we crane our necks in an attempt to peek inside. Emierr casts a glance back toward the street, then leans in close.

"Those were prostitutes, right? I've never seen one back on Earth."

Sólel gives him a curious look, brow furrowing. "Prostitutes? You mean the she-wolves?"

"Hey, let's go!" Jae calls, waving us forward. The bouncer has stepped aside, eying the three of us with some disdain.

I smirk, giving Emierr's face a playful shove before heading toward the door. The bouncer watches me as I approach, then nods me through. Emierr gets a nod too, but as Sólel steps up, the bouncer slams a hand to his chest, stopping him cold. His eyes narrow as he sizes up Sólel.

"Dress code. Sleeves required," he growls, giving Sólel a hard shove back.

Emierr steps up, bristling. "Get your filthy hands off my brother."

My hands curl into fists, ready for trouble, but Jae whips back around, his face darkening. He steps between us and the bouncer, voice dropping.

"They're with me. *All* of them. This is official Serpent Coil business. You want me to bring them down here?"

The bouncer's face tightens, and after a tense moment, he steps aside, giving a begrudging jerk of his head toward the obsidian door.

Inside, the lights resemble glowing coals, bathing everything in a dark red glow. The walls and ceiling are layered with serpent scales—huge, shimmering, reflecting fractured fragments of our faces. The scales pulsate to the beat, twisting the path into a winding, snaking tunnel. With each step, our reflections stretch and warp. I catch Emierr's wide eyes, darting around, his face splitting into a thousand directions as Jae leads us deeper into the belly of the beast.

"What exactly is Serpent Coil?" I ask, keeping my tone low as I glance at Jae, who's already scanning the room with steely focus.

Sólel answers before Jae can speak. "They're a fanatical religious group, worshiping the ancient dragon spirit, Drak'vyr, and trifling with forbidden knowledge to get ahead. They're not at O'rian-level threat, but they're bad news" He gives Jae a hard look. "So, how does someone from the Serpent Coil end up as an Allied Force soldier?"

Jae's face hardens. "I left them a long time ago. Didn't agree with their ways. But tonight... I need to become one again. I'm asking you to trust me."

Sólel nods slowly, voice steady as granite. "We'll trust you—for now. But if you cross us..."

Jae raises his hands in surrender. "Understood." He flashes a quick smile at Sólel's stony face.

"Now, just follow my lead. You're my rookies tonight—nod when spoken to, stay quiet otherwise. We don't need the extra attention."

Emierr grins, nudging me. "Bad guys, huh? This should be fun."

I shoot him a look. "Let's not mess this up, Meer."

He winks. "Relax, Dust. North's just a call away if we need an exit."

Jae's eyes flash in warning. "We avoid fights. We're here for the artifact, then we're out. Everyone clear?"

The music deepens as we approach the inner entrance, the bass humming through our chests. Pushing through the final curtain, we step into a sea of flickering neon lights. The air is thick with smoke, magick, and something else I can't quite place.

Emierr's eyes dart around, wide-eyed. "How the hell are we supposed to find Riven in this mess?"

"He's a halfling," Jae yells over the noise, eyes still sweeping the crowd.

"Fantastic," Emierr groans. "Only about a million halflings in here."

My gaze tracks Jae's, and I spot a halfling on the second floor, shooting bursts of what look like fireworks over the crowd. People below cheer, eyes glued to the show.

"That looks like our guy," I chuckle, nodding toward the second floor.

Jae's eyes lock onto the halfling, his expression sharpening. "Follow me." Without waiting for a response, he weaves through the crowd, leading us toward the staircase. But just as we reach the base, a hulking bouncer with tattoos snaking up his arms steps in, blocking our path.

Without missing a beat, Jae steps up, lifting his shirt to reveal the Serpent Coil tattoo inked across his chest. The bouncer's eyes narrow, but the tattoo apparently takes priority over his suspicions.

I glance back at Emierr and Sólel—Emierr's practically bouncing on his toes, barely restraining himself from breaking into a dance, while Sólel nods to the rhythm, a subtle sway in his movements.

"You two really are brothers," I mutter, shaking my head as we follow Jae up to the second floor.

I instantly spot the halfling lounging in a velvet club chair, arms spread wide, legs propped on the table like he owns the place—which he does. He's wearing a perfectly tailored suit, each piece a crisp black. With a lazy flick of his wrist, the noise from the club fades, like a barrier just slammed down around us.

"Welcome," he says, smooth as anything. "I'm Riven Zykyos, owner of Lucid Veil. It's rare to see a Serpent Coil these days. Please, make yourselves comfortable." He gestures for us to sit, eyes flicking over each of us with a look that lingers too long.

I notice a woman with pink skin I hadn't seen when we first entered, standing nearby. The moment Riven gives her a nod, she disappears into the crowd beyond Riven's VIP section. His eyes return to Jae, waiting expectantly.

Jae clears his throat, sitting up straight. "Vareth seeks an artifact in your possession. It is said to be capable of locating anyone in this plane of existence."

There are plenty of questions waiting for Jae once this whole side quest is over.

"Wait." Riven raises his hand, smiling like we're all part of some inside joke. I count at least one silver ring on each of his fingers. "Let me see the sigil first." His grin widens.

Jae doesn't hesitate. This is the third time he's flashed his abs, showing off that shimmering Serpent Coil tattoo.

Riven's grin spreads, and he leans back, his gaze turning predatory. "Ah, a Scalebearer. Didn't expect that." His eyes flick to the rest of us. "And what about your sigils?" His stare locks onto me, and I shudder involuntarily. There's something about the way he looks at me that makes my skin crawl.

"They're rookies," Jae cuts in smoothly. "I'm bringing them up. They'll be valuable assets to the Serpent Coil."

Before I can react, the pink-skinned woman returns with a tray of angular glasses, seemingly hewn from rough crystal. They're heavier than they look, with sharp edges sanded smooth. They catch the light, casting faint prisms. The liquid inside is deep amber, like whiskey, but streaked with swirling red and purple, as if a sunset has been stirred in. The woman sets the drinks down in front of us, then hands Riven a small device that emits a soft beep as he glances at it.

Emierr fidgets in his seat, his fingers tapping a restless beat on the table as his eyes flick around the room. Sólel leans back, but there's a tension in his shoulders I've come to recognize. Even Jae's unusually quiet. I can feel my pulse in my throat—that low, uneasy hum of waiting for something to tip. Riven hasn't asked enough questions. He's too relaxed.

"You say Vareth is looking for the Locus Aeterna?" Riven's attention is back on us. "Who's he trying to find?" He swirls his drink, smile still hitched into place, but there's a sharpness to it now.

Jae doesn't flinch. "That's not your concern, unless you want Vareth to pay you a personal visit. We both know no one wants that."

Riven smirks, lifting his drink but still watching us closely. "What's in it for me?"

"You get to be in Vareth's good graces," Jae answers, the words steady but feeling more like a challenge than a deal. The silence stretches, and I hear my heartbeat pounding in my ears. Sólel doesn't flinch, but I can feel the heat radiating off him now, like a slow-burning fire on the precipice of exploding.

Riven takes a sip, his eyes never leaving us. "That would be tempting... if you were still a true member of the Serpent Coil, Jae

Navarrosen."

At the sound of his full name, Jae's whole body tightens.

Riven raises a finger, wagging it at us as if we're naughty children. "Ah, ah, ah. Let's not get hasty." Before I can even blink, a group of guards file into the room, laser guns aimed right at us. "Your mistake was bringing him," Riven says, pointing directly at Sólel. "The Sunbringr himself. Quite the honor, really. But Terreneans... They're a problem for me and for the Serpent Coil. Surely, you should've known that."

Jae stays silent, and I feel my muscles tense, my fists curling at my sides.

"Now," Riven's voice drops low, "tell me why you really need the Locus Aeterna. And then I'll decide whether I kill you myself or feed you to the thundertusks."

He's not bluffing. It's written all over his face—he's already decided we're dead. Just as I'm about to reach out to Ade' for help, Emierr leans forward.

"It's us. We need it to find a Noble."

My heart skips. "Meer..." I hiss, but he shoots me a look that says to trust him.

"A Noble?" Riven leans in, intrigued. "The new Nobles have finally been chosen?"

"No. We're looking for Noble Jhoana," Emierr replies, calm as anything.

Riven chuckles darkly. "You and half of Ethra. They're all dead."

"That's where you're wrong." On his next blink, Emierr's eyes shift to Maral's unsettlingly luminescent copper.

Riven shoots up, grinning like a madman. "A Noble! In my club!"

Fuck it. I tap into Ade's energy, and I can feel the power coursing through me. "Two Nobles," I say, my voice low and steady. I know my brown eyes have gone the pale yellow of Ade', snake pupil and all.

Riven's eyes are brimming with the thrill of our revelations. "The rumors were true. You should've started with that. I'm no fan of the Serpent Coils, a bit too ruthless for my taste. But Nobles? That changes everything."

"Can you help us?" Emierr asks, blinking Maral's eyes away. I pull myself away from the stream of Ade's power too, the rush dissipating from my veins.

"Of course," Riven replies, waving a hand. The guards lower their weapons and wordlessly leave the room. "I would be honored to help the Nobles from Earth." He gestures toward the drinks again. "Please, enjoy."

Emierr doesn't hesitate, knocking back his drink with expert precision. "That's... really good."

I take a cautious sip. The liquid is fiery and smooth all at once, with a spiced aftertaste that warms me from the inside out. It spreads through my chest and up through my face, filling me with a lightness I didn't expect.

But then Riven's voice cuts through our relief-wrought euphoria. "Unfortunately, I don't have the Locus Aeterna. That's my supposed twin brother, René Sable, though the family tie has never been confirmed... Anyway, he's completely obsessed with magickal artifacts, a fascination, I never did understand. Last I heard, he made the journey to Vereilles."

"Perfect," Emierr says, his face brightening. "We know someone there. If we find him, we'll find your brother."

Riven's brows furrow. "You know where Vereilles is?"

I shake my head, the drink beginning to buzz in my head. "We'll figure it out."

Riven's face splits in a genuine smile for the first time since our arrival. "Well, then. I have something that might help." He stands and motions for us to follow.

The vibration in my head grows heavier, thoughts drifting as we follow him through the winding, snakeskin hallway. My vision blurs, catching glimpses of people in the other rooms—some are a tangle of lips and tongues, some are doing... other things. My thoughts slip away completely by the time we reach a wall at the end of the hall. What the hell was in that drink?

"I never bring anyone here," Riven says, placing a hand on the obnoxious lime-green surface. It parts like a curtain, revealing a huge room that looks like a cross between a laboratory and an armory. "You're in luck."

Gadgets and weapons line the walls, and in the center, a strange contraption hums with energy—something I couldn't even begin to explain.

"Take what you need," Riven says, waving a hand around the room.

Any thoughts I'd managed to cling onto left me. I stumble over to the weapons, eyes landing on a sleek spear. The metal feels cold in my palm.

"Stormlash spears," Riven explains. "When two or more are near each other, they form arcs of lightning."

I don't even think—I press the spear to my forearm, the green glow sinking into my skin as the spear tattoos itself on my arm. I do the same with a few more. My vision comes back into focus as I feel the drink's effects leeching away from my bloodstream. Apparently it vanishes just as quickly as it comes on.

Then, Riven reveals something I didn't expect: battle knives.

"These were lost by an Inkweaver. I've modified them to extend their heat. I've placed touch biometrics on them," he explained, pride in his tone. It'll be able to recognize you. Just call them, and they'll come right back."

I grip the hilts, a pulse of blue light flickering as it scans my palms. A press of the button heats the blades. A red glow traces along the blade's outline, extending along the tip into a sharp, fiery edge. I swipe through the air, the familiar weight solid in my hands. Another press, and the red light pulses once before fading away. "Sweet," I say, and they sink into tattoos on my palms.

"Dust, check this out!" Emierr calls excitedly across the room. He's pointing to the wall where a set of high-tech laser guns is displayed. I recognize them instantly. Emierr and I share a knowing glance.

"Take them," Emierr says, and I grab the weapon, lifting my shirt, etching the guns along my ribs.

"What did you pick up?" I ask, eyeing Emierr. He doesn't have any weapons strapped on.

He flashes a grin and pulls back his sleeves, revealing some transparent cuffs. "I found these cool bracelets. Maybe I'll store seeds in them and when I need them, grow plants anywhere. Even places without soil." He taps his temple with a grin. "Smart, right?"

I nod. "Ricky would be proud."

We fist bump, and I catch Sólel examining something else—a small, metallic ball that looks like some kind of strange artifact. "What's that?" I ask.

Sólel turns it over in his hand, frowning slightly. "I don't know."

"Be careful with that—it's still in development" Riven's hand shoots out eagerly, like a kid reaching for a toy, his eyes widening just a bit.

Sólel, keeping his usual calm, moves to hand it to him but pulls it back at the last second. "Psych." He smirks, then hands it over to Riven.

Jae, who's been quiet this whole time, stifles a laugh from the corner.

"Thank you." Riven mutters. "It's called the Echo Sphere, a prototype." He raises it to us. "I was inspired by the Inkweavers when I made it. It's like an infinite storage device. I haven't quite nailed the infinite part yet, but it can hold an incredible amount." He looks at the ball for a moment, then back at Sólel. "But I think you'll need this more than I will."

Sólel hesitates. "Are you sure?"

"I can always make more," Riven replies with a casual wave. "Now, are you gentlemen all set?"

"Grab whatever else you need," I say, a little too quickly, as the others start piling things onto my skin like it's Black Friday. Emierr grins like a maniac as he presses more gear onto me, while Jae—now looking more sober—shakes his head at the ridiculousness of it all.

"Okay, enough," I shout, laughing as I tap out. Riven chuckles, seeming unbothered by the near-emptiness of his shelves. He ushers us out, closing the door to the room of wonders behind us.

"Before you leave," Riven says, leading us back toward the main room, "we must drink one more glass of Ignis Elixir."

The thumping bass of the club grows louder as we make our way back into the VIP area. Riven's already pouring more drinks, and before I can protest, he's handing us all another round. And then another.

What happens next is a blur—a chaotic, ridiculous blur. The club begins to feel like a lucid dream. We're dancing like idiots on the dance floor, passing Riven around the crowd like he's a doll, and yelling our thanks over and over again through laughter. I sneak a few more Ignis Elixirs into my tattoos for later. At one point, Jae takes off his shirt, proudly flashing his Serpent Coil tattoo, bragging to anyone who'll listen. Meanwhile, Emierr and Sólel kick off a wild dance battle with a couple of satyrs, spinning and flipping like it's some kind of mythical showdown.

By the time it's over, I'm leaning against a standing table, downing a bottle of water. "Holy shit," I mutter, feeling the buzz slowly wearing off.

Jae stumbles over, shirt back on, but looking no less disheveled. "It's only been ten minutes since we had those drinks," he says, wiping sweat from his face.

"What?" I gape at him. "I thought we were here for hours."

"Guys?" Emierr appears, still panting from his furious dance-off. "Where's Sól?"

We all look around, but he's nowhere in sight.

"There," Jae points, spotting Sólel leaving the club through the front door.

"Where's he going?" I frown, but Emierr's already dashing after him, no hesitation.

"Shit, we shouldn't split up," Jae mumbles as he follows, and I'm right behind them, glancing back at the second floor just in time to see Riven grinning and waving goodbye. I wave back awkwardly and hurry after the others through the tunnel.

I start seeing flashes of my younger self in the reflections, chasing me like some dream I can't shake. "No!" I shout, but no one seems to hear. I bust the doors open and hit the cold night air. Eyes dart my way, and I shake off the hallucinations. I find Jae kneeling by the curb, looking like he's about to puke. "Where's Sól?" I ask, dragging Jae to his feet.

"One second," Jae groans, holding up a finger. I scan the street and spot Emierr turning a corner.

"C'mon, Jae!" I drag him along, half-carrying him as we follow Emierr down the street. Jae grumbles something about how he never drinks on the job. We catch up to Emierr, who's hiding behind a building, and he jumps when we approach. "What are you doing?" I whisper, still slurring a bit. "Where's Sól?"

Emierr points toward the woods. "He went that way. I was too scared to follow—vampires, werewolves..." he trails off, glancing at Jae. "Oh shit, he needs some water."

"Wait, I've got some." A hazy memory hits me, and I pull the cold water bottle from a tattoo on my leg, handing it to Jae. He gulps it down, instantly going from faintly green to his usual color.

"Let's go after Sól," I say. "Just in case he's secretly a werewolf and needs taming."

Jae gives me a sharp look. "You shouldn't say stuff like that. Were-people are actually really friendly."

"So, how exactly are we doing this?" I glance up at the full moon.

"Hey!" Emierr hisses, pulling my attention back. I follow his gaze to Jae, who's stumbling ahead like my dad after too many drinks. Looks like that's the plan. We meander after him into the woods, and the deeper we go, the quieter everything gets—*too* quiet.

"Guys," Jae whispers, his voice steadier now as he comes to a halt. He turns back toward us, the glow of his hologram lighting up his face. "That Ignis Elixir costs two hundred drin a glass. It's basically the equivalent of ten shots."

"Holy shit," Emierr wipes his face. "We took twenty shots?"

A cracking sound echoes from the trees up ahead, and we all freeze, huddling close together.

"Jae, you lead," Emierr whispers.

Jae sighs. "Fine. I got this. Stay behind me." He crouches and starts moving stealthily through the underbrush, the rest of us following awkwardly.

What sounds like a conversation gets louder as we approach. It's definitely Sólel's voice, but there's another—deeper, heavier. That's no werewolf or vampire. Jae peers around a tree, and Emierr and I peek with him.

Sólel is standing there under the moonlight, talking to someone—or something—huge.

"I'm telling you, Gormak, please. You have to talk to the others and let them know what's coming," Sólel says, his voice filled with urgency.

"I told you," The deep voice rumbles. "We won't join the fight."

Sólel steps closer. "You're sure? Because if it comes down to it, your people would tip the balance."

I squint through the moonlight, trying to make out anything in the shadows, but before I can, Jae makes a retching sound, and unable to stop himself, he vomits all over the ground.

"Who's there?" the voice booms, and suddenly, a tree rips out of the ground, floating into the air. Before I can react, Sólel's body lights up, flooding the area with a blinding glow.

It's a fucking giant, towering over us, tree trunk club raised to strike. Emierr and I scream, grabbing Jae. Sólel bursts into his solar form and swoops in, stopping the tree just in time.

"Gormak, they're with me! They're my brother and friends!" Sólel's voice echoes with a strange, warping resonance.

Before the giant can react, Emierr steps forward, shouting as he thrusts his hand toward the tree the giant is gripping. Massive vines suddenly burst from the tree, coiling around the giant's arms and torso, locking him in place.

"Sól?" the giant's voice quivers with panic.

"*Kuya*, stop!" Sólel shouts, spinning around to face Emierr.

"Meer, let him go!" I yell, heart pounding as the vines tighten their grip around the giant.

"Please!" Sólel's voice is pleading now.

Emierr hesitates, then with a shaky breath, releases his hold. The vines immediately loosen, and the giant staggers backward, crashing to the ground and knocking over several trees in the process.

"It's okay, Gormak," Sólel says softly, floating over and dimming his glow as he lands gently. "They were just scared. No one's going to hurt you, and you won't hurt them."

The giant, Gormak, trembles, tears forming in his eyes, his massive hands shaking as he rubs the limp vines away. He blinks, still shaken, but takes a deep, steadying breath.

"I'm so sorry," he says, his voice thick with regret.

Emierr steps forward, looking apologetic. "We're not in the best shape right now, but we're extensions of Sól. If you're his friend, you're ours too." Emierr makes a series of hand movements—leyfolk gestures, I think—something that means "we are one" or something like that.

"Friends," I add, stepping up beside Emierr. "I'm Dustin, and that's Emierr," I point at him, then nod toward Jae, who's slumped against a tree, groaning. "And that's Jae." Embarrassment on Jae's behalf floods my face.

Gormak hesitates, then nods. "I'm Gormak. Forgive me."

The gentle reassurances and introductions are cut off by a loud beeping sound, echoing between the trees.

"What is that?" I ask, looking around.

"What's what?" Sólel asks, looking concerned.

"Dust," Emierr says urgently, drawing my eyes to his. "It's the alarm. We have to go."

"Oh fuck, all right. Sól, keep an eye on Jae. We'll be right back." I nod to Sólel, then turn to Emierr. "On three?"

He breathes out. "If it works this time."

"One. Two. Three."

"Astralis," we say together.

Vereilles

I gasp, jolting upright as the rough fibers of the rug dig into my palms, the cold air of the basement hitting me like a slap. My chest heaves with each breath, like I've been yanked out of deep water. Beside me, Jadis sits up just as fast, her fingers tangling in her hair, eyes wide with confusion. The piercing sound of our alarms cuts through the silence, jarring me further awake. But all I can do is sit there, blinking, trying to make sense of where we are.

Earth. Jhoana's basement.

The ache in my chest is heavy, like the weight of the Ethran air hasn't fully lifted. My hands fumble for my phone, turning off the alarm, and I glance over at the other three still lying there, hands still interlocked. "Should we turn their alarms off?"

Jadis shakes her head. "No, they're going to need them. It'll guide them back."

As if on cue, Emierr and Dustin jolt awake, gasping as they sit up, shaking off the daze. Emierr rubs his temples.

"I still feel drunk," he mutters, turning off his alarm with a groggy swipe. Then he glances around, blinking at the reality of where we are. "I didn't think it'd actually work."

"Same," Dustin adds, shaking his head. "I was sure we'd be stuck for good."

Seems like none of us had actually believed our phone alarm technique would work.

"Drunk?" Jadis raises an eyebrow at him. "Where did you guys end up?"

"Juno," Dustin answers, still shaking his head before turning off his own alarm.

I glance at them. "And Rune?"

They quickly turn their heads to inspect Brunner, the stillness of the room settling in again as worry crawls up my spine.

"He's not back yet?" Emierr's voice hitches, and he crawls over, shaking Brunner. "Come on, man. Wake up."

Jadis gently places a hand on Brunner's arm. "Did you guys find him?"

"No." Dustin's voice is steady, too steady. "But we know where he's at... and that he's maybe alive." As he says it, his breath quickens, and I watch him place a hand on his chest in an effort to calm himself.

"Nose, then mouth, Dust," I remind him, as if we aren't all feeling the same anxiety at the sight of Brunner's nearly lifeless form." Come on, Rune..." I hold my breath, waiting. The alarms have stopped, but the silence presses down on us, heavier than before. *Wake up,* I beg silently. Brunner doesn't move.

I glance at the others—Jadis's hand still resting on Brunner, her face pale, Dustin staring hard at Rune like he can will him awake. Emierr has his hand on Brunner's shoulder, his knuckles white.

The seconds drag on, each one heavier than the last. It feels like the room is holding its breath with us. *Did we just send Rune to his doom?*

Brunner jerks upright, gasping like he's just been dragged back from the dead. The sound of his breath filling his lungs is sharp, a break in the suffocating tension. For a second, no one moves. We're all frozen, staring at him, afraid he might collapse back to the floor again.

Once it's clear he really is here, relief floods through my veins and I take what feels like my first breath in hours. Before I even know it, we have our arms wrapped around him in a stranglehold, making sure he's really here, alive and breathing.

Brunner's head rests against my arm, his body still trembling slightly. "Guys... it's not a dream," he murmurs, his voice shaky.

I close my eyes for a second, letting out a long, tremulous breath of my own. "I never doubted you could do it, but... how the fuck..." I trail off, still trying to wrap my head around everything.

Brunner's voice wavers as he asks, "Did you guys... go after me?"

His question makes my chest tighten. I can feel the rawness in his words, wondering if we had even bothered to look for him. It's a strange thing, this empathy hanging in the air, thick enough that it lingers.

Jadis scans him for injuries, like she's forgotten that nothing from Ethra follows us back here. "At first, yeah. But things got complicated. We had to split up," she says softly, as if afraid her words might shatter the fragile moment of relief.

"We found Jho, Rune." My voice cracks. "Or her last location... thanks to Dusty's scarf. It led Jadis and me to Arid."

"Dusty and I went to Zaltana, looking for you," Emierr adds, gripping Brunner's shoulders tightly. "With Sólel, too."

"You finally saw him." Brunner's eyes glisten, holding onto Emierr. "Your parents too, right?"

Emierr nods, tears filling his eyes.

"And you, Dusty?" Brunner looks up at him, who's standing now, eyes wet. "You saw your grandfather, didn't you?"

Dustin, already standing, nods slowly, a smile breaking through the tears. "Yeah... I did. I really needed that."

It doesn't take long for the room to be filled with quiet sobs, all of us crying for different reasons, but mostly out of relief. Brunner's soft sniffle is the final crack.

"We did it. We found Jho." Brunner closes his eyes and exhales, a deep, relieved breath escaping him.

My stomach growls loudly, shattering the fragile peace of the moment, and everyone bursts into laughter.

"I am pretty hungry," Jadis admits, standing up and pulling me with her. Emierr helps Brunner up, and before long, we're all back in a group hug.

Up until now, we've all probably questioned everything—our existence, our purpose—but right here, together, this is the one answer we all needed.

"You guys love your hugs, huh?" Brunner jokes, squeezing us tighter. "Any idea why we couldn't get back before the alarms?"

"I have a theory," I offer. "We didn't really have enough intention for astralis to work. Our real intention was finding Jho."

Comprehension dawns on everyone's faces.

"I guess the alarms gave us the extra boost," Dustin says with a shrug.

"What's that?" Emierr points to the couch, where five to-go boxes sit in a neat row. A note taped on one of them reads, "*Eat up, drinks in the fridge. – Gordo*"

I turn to them, grinning. "You heard him."

We take the boxes, gathering around on the floor, eating in silence. Mama cooked again for the wake; her famous spaghetti added into the choices. Dustin checks on his family, while I text Bonnie, letting her know what little I can. Everything's fine on her end, for now. The next half hour flies by as we catch up on everything that went down in Ethra, and for the first time in what feels like ages, we're not so lost anymore.

It's a relief to see Brunner talking about his experience, processing everything he's been through in just a few hours. Why didn't I put it together that a freakishly huge bear is a Crown Beast? I still can't wrap my head around how Brunner became a Noble *and* a Keeper just like that. He's got the notebook open on his lap, scribbling down new lore about the shadow creatures and the

Crown Beasts, adding to what we already know. None of us realized our thoughts were connected to our beasts—or that they can borrow our powers. Emierr visibly cringes at the idea of Maral hearing all the silent curses he's hurled at the ancient elk.

Brunner simplifies his Keeper ability, calling it teleporting, or "blinking," as he prefers. Honestly, it sounds more like he's tearing through space itself and stepping into a different point entirely—which, in fairness, does sound a lot like blinking. Then there's the discovery of Vereilles, an entirely new nation that sprouted up seemingly overnight, dedicated to us, which definitely gives off cult vibes.

Dustin and Emierr's discovery of the artifact feels like a major win, boosting our chances of finding Jhoana. Still, something about Riven Zykos doesn't sit right with me, and Jadis feels the same. It's strange how fast he offered to help once he realized they were Nobles. But then again, Borge flipped just as fast. Maybe I'm over-analyzing.

What Dustin and Emierr overheard between Sólel and the giant, Gormak, raises even more questions—especially considering what Jadis and I uncovered in Arid.

"So, Abbadon, this Angel of Death, is at the core of all this." Brunner stares at the notebook, his gaze unfocused, drifting somewhere distant.

"We couldn't get many specifics from Lacey, but from what she told us, it sounds like he's been hunting Jho this whole time." Jadis finishes the last of her water, setting the empty bottle down.

"And he's the one who created our clones," Dustin mutters, almost like he's talking to himself. "What kind of magick can even do that?" He looks over at Jadis, searching for answers.

"I'd guess blood magick," she replies, though her expression tightens. "But it feels too powerful, like there's something more to it."

"Lacey said the O'rians have been building toward this 'Convergence,' but honestly, it's vague what the Convergence even is." I stand, grabbing my empty box to toss it away. Emierr hands me his, and before I know it, I have a tower of empty takeout boxes. I roll my eyes, but cram them all into the trash bag Gordo left by the stairs. As I glance toward the door, it hits me—everyone up there is grieving, and they don't even know we're doing everything we can for the person they're mourning. Perspective.

"Do you think Sól might know?" Dustin asks, turning to Emierr.

"We can ask," Emierr nods. "But I can't stop thinking about what Sól said—about Gormak's kind tipping the balance. Does that mean some kind of conflict is coming?"

"Well, if that happens, it'll complicate everything," Jadis says, folding her arms. "The Convergence, the poison, Abbadon and the O'rians... and now the possibility of conflict on top of it all."

It all feels so much bigger than us, like we've been thrown into the deep end of something ancient and terrible. My mind spins, trying to piece together everything we've learned. But every answer just seems to open up more questions. I wonder if we'll ever have all the pieces, if we'll ever figure it out in time.

What if we don't? What if we're already too late?

I steal a glance at Jadis, who's deep in thought, her brow furrowed. I know she's thinking the same thing. We've been stumbling through Ethra, picking up fragments, but nothing's made the whole picture clearer. Abbadon's been hunting Jho for years—*how are we supposed to stop him when we don't even fully understand what we're dealing with?*

"What the fuck did we walk into?" I mutter, finishing the thought hanging in the air.

"The plan stays the same, right? We find Jho, then we leave," Brunner says bluntly.

Silence hangs between us, tugging at my thoughts. I don't even know what to think anymore. This whole thing has turned into one big clusterfuck. Do we really abandon Ethra when they need us the most?

Dustin's voice breaks the silence. "We need to go back. We left Jae in a really bad state."

"I'll let Amos know you're coming," Brunner says, and there's a new confidence in his voice. "They keep the area hidden, but they'll help you find it." For a moment, I feel a flicker of surprise—maybe even admiration. I'm not used to seeing him like this.

Brunner's always been sharp with his questions, but now it's like he's stepped into a role he's been waiting for. Part of me wonders if it's real confidence or just a front to keep us steady when things are unraveling.

Either way, I'm grateful for it. Because I sure as hell don't have it right now.

"Jads, take a Gate," Brunner continues, sounding more like a leader with every word. "There's one near the shadow forest. Just follow the path. And, Meer... are you guys taking a Gate too?"

"We're flying with Jae," Dustin replies. "Think you can have them drop the barriers, at least from above, so we can spot it?"

"They will for you guys. They'll do anything," Brunner says with a grin.

"Still creepy," I mutter.

"Look, these update meetings are great, but we need to stay longer in Ethra," Emierr says, his eyes shifting between us. "We're going to have to sleep for twelve hours this time."

"*Twelve* hours?" Jadis groans.

"I agree," Dustin chimes in.

Brunner nods. "Same here."

I glance at Jadis, noticing the shift in her expression. "All right then, let's set it for the next twelve hours."

Everyone sets their alarms. I send a quick message to Gordo, thanking him for the food and letting him know we're heading back in, and for much longer this time. We settle down, lying back on the rug, heads resting on pillows, hands intertwined.

"Everyone ready?" I ask, tightening my grip on their hands.

"See you on the other side," Brunner says, excitement in his voice.

"Deep breaths," I guide, listening as our breathing falls into sync. "In three, two, one."

"Astralis." The familiar pull drags us under, but this time... something feels off. There's a weight in my chest that wasn't there before, a nagging sense that when we wake again, everything will be different. And not in a good way.

~ ~ ~

Desert air fills my lungs, and I'm back in Arid. I sit up, my body tingling as the blood rushes back its original position. This didn't happen the first time we transcended here. I shake my head, trying to clear the aftereffects. Jadis's bed is still empty. *She isn't here yet?*

Panic gnaws at me as I rush to where she should be. "Come on, girl. Where are you?" I bite the edge of my fingernail without realizing, spitting out a sliver. My anxiety kicks in hard—there's no escaping limbo if she doesn't make it. "Come on, come on, make it back..." Another shred of nail hits the floor.

A golden glow flickers over her bed. "Thank god," I exhale, relief flooding through me. Her body begins to take shape, veins spreading first—glittering with the rich hue of saffron, outlining her form. I step back, transfixed. I've never actually seen the transcendent body come to life before. I was always the last one to arrive when we were kids, making sure everyone else made it here safely.

Her skeleton materializes next, followed by her organs, muscles, and finally her skin. Watching it unfold is both mesmerizing and unsettling.

The glow gradually fades, and the gold dust particles surrounding her dissolve into the air. Jadis gasps, sitting up with her hands pressed to her chest, catching her breath.

"You all right?" I ask, startling her.

She jumps to her feet, patting herself down quickly. "No, yeah, I'm great. All parts here." She shakes her head and glances at her arms, eyes widening as if she's also feeling the rush of blood. "Whoa."

"I got here first, Jads." I wouldn't even mention it if it didn't mean something: that she hesitated. She acted strange when we agreed to sleep for twelve hours, but why take the risk with limbo?

I stay quiet, letting the awkward silence do the work for me.

She shifts uneasily. "I—"

I still don't say anything.

"Fine! Stop looking at me like that," she snaps, turning her back to me. "I wasn't sure if I wanted to come back, all right? Ricky..." She hesitates, her voice quieter. "After everything we just learned, Ethra's starting to feel like a total shit show."

"Yeah," I nod. What else can I say? Ethra was exciting when we were kids, but now... now everything's so much more complicated.

"I wanted to tell you guys, but I couldn't. And look what happened—just one single thought of regret, and I glitched. It felt like my soul was being pulled away from you all, like I was slipping. Ricky, I'm not cut out for this. None of us are, really."

"Jads," I say softly, taking her hand. "I'm fucking scared. I act like I've got it all figured out, but I'm terrified I'm going to lose one of you again. I get why you hesitated—because I did too."

I can feel her emotions shifting, pulling at me.

"But Jads, Jho needs us. More than ever." I squeeze her hand, grounding us both.

She closes her eyes, nodding, the weight of it all settling between us.

"Let's bring her home," I plead.

"Together," she whispers, her voice cracking as she pulls me into a tight embrace.

This is my third bear hug from Jadis this week, but it's the first time I've ever truly felt her grief. We've all gone through our grieving in different ways, but Jadis... She took it harder than any of us. A memory flashes—back when we were about to graduate high school, and I went to visit Jhoana, knowing it might be a long time before I'd see her again. But when I got to the room, Jadis was already there. I could've gone in, but I didn't. I just stood outside and listened.

"Jho, we're all graduating tomorrow. I wish we could take pictures in our caps and gowns together, do that silly jump shot like in High School Musical.*" Jadis giggled, but there was sadness in it. "The boys? They stopped talking to each other. Dusty left in sophomore year, Meer quit sports, and Ricky... He tries to be here with us, but I know he wants to get away from this place."*

It was the first time I heard someone say out loud what I'd been thinking.

It made me realize I couldn't hide anything from Jadis. Not entirely.

"I'm sorry, Jho..." Jadis sniffled, her voice trembling. "I don't think I can keep my promise. I really wanted to see you wake up, but I have to accept you're not coming back." She paused, her words catching. "Ricky says it's his fault, and Meer blames himself, but I had you... You were holding my hand, and I was about to pull you away, but then it grabbed me by my stupid hair... I got you killed. I'm never going to forgive myself for it." Her quiet tears filled the room.

I wanted to say something, but the words couldn't leave my mouth.

"I'm leaving, Jho. I have to let you go. If I stay here any longer, I'm going to kill myself, and I know you'd hate me for that. I love you, Jhoanalyn, please keep fighting! I want my sister back." Jadis fell quiet, her confession settling heavily between the two girls. Finally, she leaned down and kissed Jhoana's forehead, lingering for a long, heart-wrenching moment.

I never told her I overheard that confession, but I understand her pain. We abandoned Jhoana. How could we ever look her in the eyes again? How could she possibly forgive us after all these years?

Jadis's guilt seeps into me, and for a moment, we just stay in our bubble—silent, but here for each other.

Then, a loud banging shatters the moment, pulling us back to reality.

Lâcien slams the door open. "They're coming; you have to get out of here."

Her urgency coils around me like a snake. "Who?"

"A council member's back," she says, her breath shaky. "They usually announce their return, but—forget it. Do you know where you're going next?" Patches of sweat glisten on Lâcien's forehead.

I'm surprised she even sweats at all.

"V—" Jadis begins.

"No, don't tell me. They'll just read my mind. It's better if I don't know."

"What about you, Lacey?" Jadis asks, her brow furrowed in concern.

"Don't worry about me." Lâcien flashes a soft, reassuring smile. "There's a Gate close by." She peeks out the door, checking for guards. "Let's go."

She darts out of the room, and without hesitation, we follow, sprinting across the courtyard. The Gate sits near the edge, with the vast expanse of the great desert nation stretching before us. Lâcien swiftly weaves the spell signs, the portal shimmering into existence. Jadis and I exchange a glance as the veil appears.

"Hurry, they'll be here soon."

Jadis takes her hand. "Thank you, Lacey. We owe you everything."

"It's been a pleasure meeting two more of Ethra's Nobles. Now go find Jhoana and bring my dear friend home."

Jadis pulls her into a tight embrace.

Lâcien turns to me, her smile warm. "Protect her, okay, handsome?" She winks.

"Always. Stay safe, gorgeous." I wink back with a grin.

"You two are gross," Jadis mutters, rolling her eyes as she steps through the portal.

I pull Lâcien into a hug, and she plants a soft kiss on my cheek, the warmth spreading through me like a blanket.

"Thank you, Lacey," I say quietly.

"Go!" She pushes me toward the portal, and the familiar tingle washes over my body as I'm pulled through.

Towers of trees with green, red, and yellow leaves surround me, their vibrant colors shifting in the breeze. Streaks of sunlight filter through the canopy, casting golden patches across the path. The branches sway gently, almost as if they're welcoming me. I step off the Gate's plinth and walk toward Jadis, the crunch of leaves beneath my feet turning into a soft rustle as they lift into the air, floating back down like delicate feathers.

As I walk, something about this place feels familiar, tugging at the edges of my memory. I glance to my right, and that's when it hits me—the road ends here, just like before. This... This is the entrance we crossed all those years ago.

I stop for a moment, taking it in. The grass beyond the path is overgrown, and the trees stand mostly bare, their branches skeletal and dark. The shadow forest... It's finally claimed its name.

Why does it feel like this place keeps dragging us back? It's like the forest wants to shove every mistake, every loss, right in my face. It's too easy to slip back into that headspace. But then, through the mess of memories and time, I spot it—the sign we fused to that tree. The bark swallowed it up, but our names are still there, worn but holding on. *Not today, Satan.*

"Ricky," Jadis calls out, pulling me from my thoughts.

My gaze lingers on the forest for a few more seconds before I walk over to her. "Straight ahead?" I ask, standing beside her.

"Yeah."

I give her a playful nudge, and she smiles. We start walking, the soft crunch of maroon leaves beneath our feet filling the silence for the next few minutes. *What's going through your head, Jadis?*

"These leaves don't bend to the laws of physics," I say, finally breaking the quiet.

"It's magick, Ricky," she teases, glancing at me. "That's the only explanation—why the leaves float when we touch them, why their colors are off, and why I can cast spells and do all this crazy stuff."

I raise an eyebrow, playing along. "So, you're telling me everything we do here is just magick? No science involved?"

She smirks. "Well, magick is just science we haven't figured out yet, right?"

"I hate that you're always right like me."

Our laughter echoes through the trees before we slide back into a more comfortable silence, the rustling branches and distant sounds of insects and birds filling the air. I glance back, noticing the trail of falling leaves covering our tracks. *That's one less thing to worry about.* Beneath the leaves lies a cracked cement road, overgrown with grass. I've always found it fascinating how nature reclaims its territory from man-made things. I mean, why would this road ever be busy with traffic when it leads to Akeurimja, a place crawling with shadow creatures?

The floating, magick-infused leaves pull me from my thoughts, and I raise my hand, catching a few with my mind. Jadis notices, her eyes widening in awe as I swirl the leaves around us, creating a whirlwind of vibrant colors. She smiles and I can't help but grin as the leaves dance in the air.

"Jads... we haven't talked about Cam. Are you okay?"

She exhales deeply. "It's not that I'm avoiding it. I just don't want him to dictate my life anymore. Not talking about it is my way of taking back control, taking back my narrative. And right now, I'm surrounded by my favorite people in the world, here in Ethra of all places. I'm great. I have you back now."

All I can do is swallow my fears and nod.

"So... You and Lacey?" Jadis's question catches me off guard, and the swirling leaves around us drop to the ground.

"It's nothing," I mutter, cringing.

"She was *this* close to impaling your face with her spears, remember?"

"Yeah, and I almost plunged that spear into her chest, so... I'd say it's the start of a pretty great love story." Our eyes lock for a second before we burst out laughing.

"So, you *do* like her," she teases, grinning.

"Yeah, why not? She's badass. Plus, she thinks I'm handsome, so..."

"Eww." Jadis wrinkles her nose.

"Meanie," I say, putting on a pout.

"But seriously, how would that even work? I mean, dating?"

I shrug. "I don't think it can. Long distance isn't for me, and even if it was, I don't think that term covers inter-dimensional relationships."

She turns to face me, walking backward with a playful smile. "Try it out. You never know. And you deserve that, at least." She spreads her arms wide, tilting her head back and closing her eyes as if soaking in the moment. The fronds sway with her movements, rising and falling as she spreads her arms.

"Where the hell are we even going?" I ask, stretching my arms and interlocking my fingers. "We haven't seen any signs like Brunner said we would, and we've been walking for like an hour now."

"Shouldn't be long. Rune said it's close to the Gate."

"Or we missed the turn. Why don't we just use the teleportation spell?"

Jadis shoots me a pitying look "Is it not your turn with brain cell? How many times do I have to explain this? Teleportation spells aren't a one-person thing. That's why Gates exist—for high-level users to open them on their own. And anyway, you not believing in magick aside, we don't even know where Vereilles is."

"I believe in it to some extent," I argue, pointing an emphatic finger at her.

"That's not enough, dumbo. You have to believe in it completely for advanced spells to work."

"Ugh, give us a sign, dammit!"

Just then, we stop dead in our tracks, face to face with a wooden sign that reads, *This way, Ricky and Jads.*

"Oh my god, he's so stupid," Jadis mutters, shaking her head as she heads for the new path.

"I don't know, Rune seems like a genius to me."

I glance back at the main road, hesitating for a moment before letting out a deep sigh and following her. As we pass, the sign quietly sinks back into the ground. The vibrant, multi-colored foliage gradually fades into shades of green, and soon tire tracks appear, pressed into the grass. The trees pull back, standing farther from the path, and for the first time, the sky opens up above us, bathed in soft hues of dawn—pinks and purples stretching across the horizon.

Jadis' excitement is infectious, wrapping around me like a warm breeze. Even though we just spoke to Brunner in the basement, the thought of seeing him alive again after fearing the worst stirs something in me too.

We come to a towering white wall. The only way through is blocked by a massive, black, metal gate. As we approach, I try to peer through the gaps, searching for any sign of life. Suddenly, small lights flicker to life along the edges of the gate. Sensors—hidden within the walls—scan over us, a thin beam of light sweeping across our bodies. I exchange a glance with Jadis, both of us holding our breath.

Then, with a loud creak, it swings open on its own. Jadis gives me a nod. *Be cautious.*

We step through, moving cautiously over the cobblestone ground. The town unfolds before us, its circular design almost like a sanctuary. "Where is everyone?" I ask, scanning the area for signs of life. Jadis shrugs as we keep walking.

The soft glow of the morning light filters through the air in golden rays, casting everything in a dream-like hue. Dome-shaped houses rise around the circle, their surfaces smooth and gleaming like polished ivory, as if they were carved from single blocks of stone.

A few steps later, the path opens up, and we find ourselves inside a large circle, right in the heart of the town.

As we walk deeper, life begins to stir around us. The hum of distant conversations drifts through the air, and small glowing insects flit lazily above us, their translucent wings glittering. Street performers and buskers put on lively shows, their music blending harmoniously with the sound of a nearby fountain's gentle trickling. The air is thick with the sweet aromas of spiced food from the nearby stalls—meats grilling, sweet pastries baking—instantly transporting me back to the bustling Square Hub on the Fleming Space Ring.

Humans and leyfolk alike mingle together, dressed in flowing white garments that seem to shimmer in the morning light. The fabric of their clothes catches the breeze like sails, giving them the appearance of gliding rather than walking. The entire scene feels surreal—like something out of a forgotten dream.

"This is Mormon 3.0 headquarters," Jadis mutters under her breath, her eyes wide as she takes in the sight.

I can't help but laugh softly. "I don't know, I think it's kinda peaceful."

In the center of the circle sits a grand fountain, its basin etched with intricate runes. Water spills over the edge, glimmering with an iridescent light, casting rainbow hues onto the cobblestones below. Five children's sculptures, lifelike in their artistry, stand at the heart of the fountain—each figure frozen in motion, and I realize who they are with a jolt of recognition; they're supposed to be us. The craftsmanship is flawless, preserving our youthful forms in time, standing watch over this place.

Wooden benches surround the fountain, but they don't touch the ground. They hover at different heights above the cobblestones, gently swaying in the soft breeze. The sight is so surreal it takes me a moment to comprehend it. Every inch of this place has been touched by magick, from the floating benches to the glowing water.

"Ricky! Jads!" Brunner's voice rises above the crowd, cutting through the tranquil atmosphere. I spot him, arms flailing as he waves at us from behind the fountain.

We weave through the crowd, the faces of the townsfolk turning toward us with a mix of awe and wonder. Their eyes track our every movement like we're something sacred—like they've been waiting for this moment their whole lives. The reverence in their gazes sends a shiver down my spine. These aren't just curious looks; these are the eyes of people who believe they're seeing the second coming. There's something unsettling about it—this quiet, expectant awe.

We reach Brunner, and he rushes forward with his arms wide open. Jadis leaps into them, and he stretches out his right arm, beckoning me to join. I wrap my arms around them both, pulling them into a tight hug, squeezing so hard they can barely breathe. When I finally let go, they exhale in unison, laughing through the tension.

"Are you two seriously crying?" Brunner teases, his laughter light, but gravity of it all still lingers. Jadis and I share a glance, wiping our eyes at the same time, before the sound of a whooshing engine cuts through the noise around us. The crowd's attention shifts upward, and I follow their gaze. A red hovercraft circles above us, its windows gradually clearing to reveal Dustin behind the wheel, grinning widely, and Emierr in the passenger seat, pressing a middle finger to the glass. Sólel leans back in the rear, his expression unreadable.

The three of us exchange confused looks.

"Wasn't Jae supposed to be driving?" Jadis asks, raising an eyebrow.

The hovercraft descends smoothly, its turbines humming as it nears the ground. The wheels shift from a horizontal to vertical position, radiating heat that sends a gust of warm air in every direction. Dust and loose leaves are kicked up in swirling patterns as the hovercraft gently touches down in the middle of the town circle.

As the engines power down, the doors of the car open with a soft hiss, rising like the wings of a bird poised for flight. White LED strips run sleekly from the headlights along the roof and all the way to the backlights.

I can't shake the otherworldly feeling as the group steps out of the car. We're surrounded by people who believe in something we barely understand, in a place that feels both peaceful and alien, and yet... here we are, like characters in some storybook, revered as a concept rather than people.

"What happened to Jae?" I ask, my brows furrowed.

"He's needed back at headquarters, but he let us take this," Dustin says, glancing back at the car with a grin. "Felt just like regular driving," he adds, a bit of swagger in his voice.

"We were on autopilot the whole time," Emierr laughs.

"No, we weren't," Dustin protests, playfully shoving Emierr's face.

"You're Brunner?" Sólel asks, eyeing him.

"And you're Sólel," Brunner replies, extending a hand.

Instead of taking the handshake, Sólel reaches for the back of Brunner's head, pulling him in so their foreheads touch. "Thank the Tree you're safe. We were all worried about you." He then pulls him into a hug.

"Oh, uh—thanks," Brunner stammers, awkwardly returning the hug.

"No, thank you, for believing in my *Kuya*."

"Meer, are you crying?" Jadis snickers.

"I never thought I'd see the day my two brothers would finally meet." He chuckles, wiping away his tears.

"All we need now is Jho," I say, and though everyone's smiles linger for a moment, the weight of our missing piece crashes down on us.

"Is René here, Rune?" Dustin asks, quickly changing the subject, steering us away from the rising emotions.

"Yeah," Brunner nods. "We'll see him once we get settled."

"Guys, um... I think we have a problem," Jadis says, her gaze now fixed on the crowd.

The locals are gathering around us, their eyes wide. We instinctively huddle closer together.

"Rune, can you tell your people to back off?" Emierr steps closer to me, his eyes darting through the crowd.

Brunner looks around, bewildered. "I... I don't know what's happening," he mutters, taking a step back.

My hands curl into fists, ready for an attack—but then, the townspeople drop to the ground, prostrating themselves before us.

"Welcome, welcome!" A voice calls out from our left, and we turn to see a man, looking about our age striding toward us, dressed in a white suit with silver accents. His ash-brown hair sticks out in all directions, like he hasn't had a moment to tame it. "It is an honor, truly, to be in the presence of the Nobles of Ethra, again." He bows his head deeply.

"Everyone, this is Amos Zika II," Brunner says.

Even though Brunner has already told us about this man, we stay quiet, still processing the viscerally uncomfortable scene.

Brunner leans toward us and mutters, "His father founded this place. Come on, guys, don't embarrass me."

"Thank you for the humbling introduction, Noble Brunner," Amos says, placing a hand on Brunner's shoulder with a smile.

"My father, he was a simple man—"

"Wait," Jadis interrupts, turning to face Amos. "Please, they don't have to bow to us."

I nod in agreement. "Yeah, really, there's no need for that."

"As you wish." Amos bows his head briefly before raising his voice. "Rise, my brothers and sisters!" His shout echoes through the circle. "Our esteemed guests are finally here. After so many years of praying for their return, they are with us once again. So rise!"

The crowd slowly rises, shock, and tears etched across their faces. There's a palpable energy in the air—a mix of awe and something disconcerting that settles deep in my chest.

I glance at Jadis. Her eyes linger on the faces in the crowd, her usual bravado dimmed by the sheer enormity of what's unfolding. Even she looks shaken, and that worries me. These people... They're looking at us like we're something holy. It's not admiration, it's something else—something stronger. And now we've come back to either disappoint them or save them. I don't know which is worse.

"Continue with the festivities, and let us properly welcome back our Saviors! Let the Day of Awakening commence!" Amos projects his decree throughout the town circle.

A roar of cheers erupts from the crowd. As they disperse, harmonious singing fills the air, the melody eerily sweet. It rises above the hum of daily life, and I feel it in my bones. There's something ancient in it, like a lullaby that speaks to something older than us. The others are swaying slightly, their eyes glazing over. For a second, I catch Dustin humming along, completely lost in it.

"Hey... This—this is a chant for the old gods," Jadis says, snapping out of her trance.

My heart skips a beat. Old gods? That can't be good.

"Yes, precisely, Noble Jadis," Amos's voice is smooth, but there's a knowing glint in his eye. He's enjoying this. "Before magick was gifted to us from the heavens, the old gods protected this world. Mortals knew they had nothing to offer in return, nothing the gods didn't already possess. But they did what they could. They gave the gods protection."

The way he says it, so matter-of-fact, sends a chill down my spine. *Protection? From what? And why does he sound so calm about this?*

"How could mortals possibly protect the gods from anything?" Jadis raises her brow, cutting through the tension with her usual defiance.

Amos looks at her, smiling like a teacher indulging a curious student. "Their faith, Noble Jadis. Their unwavering belief. You see, the chant was more than just a song—it was a form of safeguarding. The people's chanting calmed the gods, kept them from turning on one another. It was the mortals' way of binding them. The stronger their belief, the more powerful the protection became."

I shift uncomfortably. *Binding gods with belief? How does that even make sense? And if it does, what does that say about what we've walked into?*

Jadis stares at Amos, clearly taken aback. She opens her mouth to respond, then closes it, her mind clearly racing. "Just like magick," she finally murmurs, more to herself than anyone else.

I can see it in her eyes—this isn't just some throwaway story. It's real, and it's sinking in. She's realizing just how little we actually understand about Ethra, how much bigger this whole thing is than us.

"What does that mean exactly?" Dustin scratches his head, his voice breaking through terse air between us, but it's clear he's just as unnerved.

Jadis shakes her head slowly, her gaze still fixed on Amos. "It means we really don't know anything about Ethra. If this is true—if what Amos says is real—then we have a much bigger problem than we thought."

REMATCH

J adis's words hit hard. We've been stumbling through this world like blind idiots, thinking we were in control. If people could bind gods with mere belief, what else had we gotten wrong? What other forces are at play here that we can't even see?

Everything feels like it's going to topple—Jhoana's fate, the clones, the Convergence... and now this. I steal a glance at the others. Dustin looks just as shaken as I feel. Even Emierr, who's been so stoic, is fidgeting, his eyes darting nervously between Amos and our newfound cult. And Brunner? He's staring at the ground, a deep furrow in his brow, like he's trying to piece it all together and coming up short.

I turn to Amos. There's something in the way he's standing, stiff, like he's holding something back. His eyes flicker toward us every so often, and I can feel it—he knows more than he's letting on.

The harmonious chant swells again, growing louder, wrapping itself around us. My skin prickles, and for a moment, it feels like the ground beneath us is shifting—like the world itself is responding to the chant. My breath catches, and I wonder if we're about to witness something we can't control.

"Hey," I snap my fingers in front of Dustin's face. His eyes refocus, blinking rapidly as if waking from a dream. "Stay with me, Dust."

"Right... Right," he mutters, shaking his head, though the effect of the chant still lingers in his expression.

I stare at the water spilling from the fountain, trying to piece it all together, but my mind keeps circling the same damn questions.

Jadis, though... She's ahead of me, ahead of all of us. She's standing a few feet away, her eyes fixed on the ground, pacing, thinking, working something out in her head. She stops suddenly, and when she speaks, her voice is quiet but sharp, like she's cutting through the noise.

"Prayers," she says.

I blink, turning toward her. "What?"

She looks up, meeting my eyes, and I can see the weight of realization there. "Abbadon. That's how he's doing all of this. It's prayers. He's using them to gain power."

Dustin scoffs, folding his arms. "Prayers? That doesn't even make sense."

Jadis doesn't flinch. "Think about it. Before spells, before any of the structured magick we know now, people prayed. And those prayers had power—real, tangible power, just like Amos said. People believed with everything they had, and that belief was the first magic. The most primal source of power."

I feel a cold dread wash over me. "You're saying Abbadon is... a god?"

Jadis nods. "Exactly. He's built a cult following—people who worship him, who pray to him as if he *is* a god. That's how he's been doing all these things. The blood magick, the creation of life, everything. The rules don't apply to him because he's bypassing them entirely. He's using belief—pure, unwavering belief."

Amos, who has been silently standing beside the fountain, finally breaks his silence. "The O'rians."

We all turn to him.

"They've been his feeding source," Amos says, his voice dark and steady. "The O'rians promised change, and people flocked to them. But that change wasn't theirs—it was Abbadon's. Hundreds of them, maybe more, have been worshipping him, giving him strength."

"With that many people fueling him, there's no limit to what he can do," Emierr mutters, pacing with a kind of frantic energy. He looks ready to explode.

"Well, think about it—he's only managed to create the clones once. Maybe there's a limit to how many times he can pull it off," Brunner points out, his tone cautious, but hopeful.

"Clones?" Amos's eyebrows knit together in confusion.

"We'll explain later," Emierr assures him quickly.

Jadis's gaze is distant, piecing together the final fragments. "Rune's right. He created those clones of us without the Law of Equivalent Exchange stepping in. The prayers gave him enough power to break through those barriers. But he hasn't done it again... Maybe it's weakened him."

"That's not exactly reassuring," I mutter. "Yeah, he hasn't made more clones, but he can still bypass the Law. And let's not forget—he's still hunting Jho down."

Amos's expression hardens. "It's not just about what he's done. It's what he's planning next. He's after the Arboris Singulos, the meteorite I've been guarding."

My head snaps toward Amos. "The meteorite?"

Amos nods, his expression grim. "Yes, the one that landed here. I'm certain. It's more than just a relic—it's the source of all magick, the same force buried deep within the terra that gave us the Ethereal Tree. If he gets his hands on it, we're finished."

Sólel, who has been quietly observing until now, lets out a frustrated sigh. "So, what do we do? The fate of all Ethra hangs in the balance, and Abbadon's not exactly going to stroll in and ask for it nicely."

"We have to make sure he never gets his hands on it," Amos says, his jaw clenched tightly. "The meteorite is the key to stopping him—or at least slowing him down. Without it, he won't be able to complete whatever he's planning."

Jadis straightens, determination hardening her features. "We need to protect it. We can't let him get anywhere near the source."

Brunner cuts in, his voice tense and urgent. "No, we need to focus on Jho first. Are you all forgetting that back home, it's a ticking time bomb? We can't leave her hanging while we deal with this."

"Yes, I understand the gravity of the situation, Noble Brunner," Amos says, placing a firm hand on his shoulder. "René is preparing the Locus Aeterna for your reunion with Noble Jhoana. But right now, our priority is securing the meteorite."

Brunner's expression shifts, and I can see the same resolve spreading across everyone's faces.

This is it. No more running, no more waiting.

"Let's move," I say, my voice firm and steady. "We don't have any more time to waste."

Amos nods, gesturing for us to follow him.

"I will take you to it," he says quietly. "Its chamber is secure and well-hidden." The soft sound of the fountain fades behind us as we move deeper into Vereilles.

Plan B: save Jho, while saving the rest of Ethra.

Amos leads us through the narrow streets of Vereilles, his steps purposeful. The town looks like any other, with stone houses and winding alleys. Nothing about this place screams that it's protecting a shard of the Arboris Singulos, but that's the point, I guess.

We stop in front of a modest-looking house, nothing special. It blends in perfectly with the rest of the town—if you didn't know what was hidden inside, you'd walk right by it. Amos pushes the door open and the scent of old wood and dust hits me.

Amos looks at us, his expression grim. "When my father chose this area to establish Vereilles, it wasn't by chance," he begins. "He discovered something ancient. The shard. And from the moment he found it, he made sure we would protect it at all costs. That's why

Vereilles remains hidden. The shard had to be guarded."

I glance around at the simple homes, the devout people... the rituals. For a second, I can't help but wonder how far this devotion goes. Do they really believe in what they're doing, or is this all just a way to keep people in line, keep them focused on the "greater good?" My frustration bubbles up, a defense against the gnawing anxiety creeping at the edges of my thoughts.

Before I can stop myself, I blurt out, "So, all of this—" I gesture around, trying to hide my irritation. "The worshiping, the praying... It's just a front?" The words come out harsher than I intended, my accusation hanging in the air. A second of silence stretches between us, and immediately I regret my outburst. But I can't help it. Everything feels like it's slipping out of our hands, and I need something—anything—to make sense.

Amos's eyes widen in shock. "Of course not!" His voice is sharp, almost hurt, as if I've insulted something deeply personal. "The shard is crucial to our protection, but our lives are devoted to all of you." His face flushes with embarrassment at having raised his voice at a Noble.

I can feel the tension thickening, and I know I've misjudged the moment. Trying to diffuse it, I grimace and force a smile. "Of course, my apologies," I say, but even to my own ears, it sounds flat. "Really, we appreciate you and all your... *worship*." The words are clumsy as they leave my mouth, and I cringe inwardly.

Amos doesn't seem entirely convinced, but the embarrassment in his face softens a bit.

"Really?" Jadis mutters, shaking her head as she steps inside the house. Amos gestures for the rest of us to enter first. The house is dimly lit, simple—ordinary, like any other home. But beneath that simplicity, there's something far more powerful lurking.

"It's here?" Jadis asks softly, her voice barely above a whisper.

Amos nods solemnly. "Yes. It's hidden in this very house. My father understood the power it holds. The raw magick from the Arboris Singulos is dangerous—if it falls into the wrong hands, Ethra as we know it is finished."

"We need to move it," I say, the urgency rising in my voice. "Take it somewhere Abbadon can't reach, and won't suspect." I pause, thinking of the only place that might be safe. "The Space Ring. I'm pretty sure his power doesn't extend there."

Brunner crosses his arms, nodding in agreement. "Rictor's right. The Space Ring seems like the only place untouched by Abbadon."

Amos considers it for a moment, then nods. "If the Nobles believe that to be the best course of action, I will support you in any way I can. I don't want my people in harm's way, and if the shard is no longer here, I can't deny that they will be safer."

"Before we go any further, do you have a map?" Jadis asks. "The one we've been using is... outdated."

"Right away, my Noble," Amos says, turning toward the door. "Livia! A map!" Moments later, a beautiful woman with long, brown hair steps in. She passes him a small device, likely containing a Holo-map. Her sharp eyes scan the room, taking in the situation with practiced efficiency before she quietly exits.

"We need a rendezvous point," Jadis says, accepting the device from Amos and activating the hologram. "In case we get separated again, we should have a place to regroup." She pauses, a nostalgic smile crossing her face. She points at a dot of green near Vereilles. "Here. The meadow where we first shared our powers. Jho and I secretly planted purple flowers nearby."

Amos interjects, "That meadow is now called the Isle of Vereilles. The purple flowers are still there—it'll be easy to find."

We exchange glances and nod in agreement. The plan is set.

Amos gestures for us to follow, leading us deeper into the house. He approaches a bookshelf, his hands moving in a practiced rhythm as he murmurs a protection spell. With a soft groan, the bookshelf slides aside, revealing a secret tunnel.

"Let's go," he says, stepping through.

We follow him into the narrow tunnel, dimly illuminated by the glow of crystals embedded in the walls. As we move deeper, I feel soft zephyrs flowing around me, kissing my skin. The breeze grows cooler, carrying a faint hum of energy as we near the end.

The tunnel opens up into a cavern, and there, suspended in the center, is the shard.

It's massive—far larger than I anticipated. The jagged piece of the Arboris Singulos hovers in midair, pulsing slowly with light. Its colors shift from a soft silver to deep violet, then to a brilliant gold, casting eerie, shifting shadows across its vicinity. It feels alive, almost as if it's breathing, and the sheer energy radiating from it is overwhelming.

"Don't get too close," Amos warns, his voice low and serious. "The shard reacts to anyone who touches it—magick overload. It can drive you mad if you try to handle it. And in the worst cases... it absorbs your very essence." His voice falters briefly, the weight of his words heavy. "I've seen it happen once. I won't let it happen again."

We all take a step back, instinctively wary. Our eyes land on Dustin, and he shakes his head immediately.

"Yeah, no way am I carrying that thing," he says firmly.

Sólel speaks up. "The Echo Sphere. I still have it. I think it can hold the shard safely."

Emierr nods, his eyes lighting up. "Good idea. Where is it?"

Sólel grimaces. "It's in the car."

"I'll go grab it—" Brunner starts to say.

"No, I'll get it," I say, cutting him off as I turn toward the door. "Metal ball right? I'll be right back."

Without waiting for a reply, I turn and step out of the cavern, the stale air inside feeling too heavy to breathe. As soon as I step outside of the house, the cool air hits my face. An unseen valve in my skull seems to release the pressure that had been building—but only for a second. The tightness in my chest doesn't go away, and I can feel the edges of panic clawing at me. I need space. Now.

All their emotions were suffocating, their worries and fears choking me. *Just keep walking.* Each step calms me, the tension in my chest loosening bit by bit. I focus on the sound of my feet hitting the cobblestones, letting the rhythm settle my mind.

By the time I reach the hovercraft, I feel more grounded. I pause for a moment, taking in the scene before me, festivities and laughter. It almost feels normal, like none of this—shards, clones, the threat of Abbadon—has happened. But that illusion doesn't last. I pull open the hovercraft's door and rummage through the compartment between the seats. My fingers brush against the cool surface of a metallic sphere. Its weight is comforting in my palm.

I'm about to head back when something strange happens. A sharp ringing goes off in my ears, making the hair on my arms stand up. It's like a warning—something I can't shake. My gaze darts around, searching the crowd. Then I see a figure. A person in a hooded white coat, walking through the circle, moving quickly, like he's trying not to be noticed.

The sensation hits me again, harder this time. Familiarity. It's like a current surging through me, something deep and primal. I freeze, my heart pounding. I know this feeling. I know who they are.

"Hey!" I shout, instinctively bolting after them, my feet carrying me before my brain can catch up. I weave through the crowd, each person I pass allowing their hands to graze me, my chest tightening with every step. I don't even know why I'm running, but something—something powerful—is pulling me toward this person. I have to catch them. I have to see.

"Please!" I shout, my voice cracking as I close the distance.

We're standing in the middle of the street, away from the crowd. My breath comes in ragged gasps, my body running purely on adrenaline.

The person slowly turns to face me, and I take two steps back, my chest heaving.

It's him.

My world tips. My knees feel weak. I stare, frozen, as tears start cascading down my cheeks. It's my Pa. He's standing right in front of me.

"Pa?" I barely choke the word out as I rush to him.

"How are you here? How is this possible?" he gasps.

I grab his face in my hands, feeling his skin, his warmth, everything real. He's aged—deep wrinkles beneath his eyes, streaks of gray running through his once-dark hair, and his beard now speckled with silver. The years have worn him down, but the warmth in his eyes is unmistakable. Tears spill freely, and I weep like a child, my forehead resting against his.

"Papa... I thought—I thought you were gone."

I pull him into a hug, but he resists. He pushes me away gently, his hands firm on my shoulders. There's something distant in his eyes, something not quite right. Before I can question it, a loud scream rips through the air, coming from the direction of the town circle.

I whip around to look, my heart leaping into my throat. Chaos is brewing.

"I have to go," Pa says, his voice low and urgent. "I can't be seen here."

"No—wait, how will I find you again?" My voice cracks, the desperation clawing at my throat. There's now way I'm losing him again, not now.

He reaches into his pocket and presses something into mine. A small, smooth object. "You won't need to. I'll find you," he whispers, holding my face for a brief moment before turning away.

And just like that, he's gone, disappearing into the shadows between the houses.

I stand there, trembling, wiping the tears from my face. The screams from the town grow louder, pulling me back to the present. Seeing Pa again—only to lose him just as quickly—leaves me hollow, like something vital has been ripped from me.

There's no time to process it, no space to let it settle. The urgency crashes back in, a reminder that we're still in the middle of a burgeoning war we can't afford to lose. I swallow the lump in my throat, forcing my legs to move, even though everything inside me feels like it's unraveling.

I run back toward the town circle, the distant chaos swelling in volume. The crowd has erupted into panic, and I can't see what's happening, but I know I need to be there. I have to get this sphere to them.

I break into a sprint, pushing through the crowd until I reach the tunnel. My heart pounds as I rush inside, and when I finally arrive,

I stop dead in my tracks.

Dustin is the only one standing in front of the shard, his face pale but determined. He looks up at me, relief washing over his features. "Thank god, I thought something happened to you." He exhales. "We heard the commotion, and they went to help. Come on, let's do this."

Without thinking, I toss him the Echo Sphere. He catches it, his hands steady despite the tension. He opens the device, and in an instant, the shard is sucked into it, vanishing without a trace.

Dustin presses the ball to his skin, and it merges with him seamlessly. He lets out a breath, his shoulders relaxing. "Let's go. They need our help."

I nod, even though my mind is still reeling, and together we head back to the chaos outside. The frantic crowd still litters the town circle, their shouts and confusion blending into a chaotic hum. I spot Amos in the distance, working with others to push people back, trying to clear the area. Dustin and I weave through the commotion, making our way to the fountain, where the rest of the Squad is already gathered.

But something's off.

As we step beside them, I follow their gazes—and my heart drops. Across from us stand younger versions of me, Jhoana, Jadis, Emierr, and Dustin. They haven't aged. Not a day.

My eyes lock onto my clone, noticing a backpack strapped to his shoulders—no, not a backpack. A jetpack. They all smirk, their faces twisted with a malicious welcome.

Emierr steps forward, squinting at his clone, a deep scar running down the clone's face. "What did you guys do to me?" he asks, turning to us.

Just then, a few citizens pause, looking between the kids and us. Their eyes widen, recognition dawning. The crowd shifts, murmurs rising as more and more people begin to notice.

"They're the real Nobles!" someone cries out.

"The false prophet Brunner brought imposters into our midst!" another shrieks. The crowd surges again, this time aiming for the clones.

"Leave our city, you treacherous traitors," someone else howls.

The chaos from Farmington flashes through my mind—the same condemnation, the same fear, the same hatred. It's happening again.

"No, brothers and sisters!" Amos's voice cuts through the din, trying to reason with the crowd. He points at us, desperation in his voice. "They are the true Nobles! The children are the imposters!"

But it's too late. The crowd doesn't care. The citizens have turned on Amos too, faster than tinder catches flame.

"Guys, they're getting really rowdy," Emierr shouts, panic creeping into his voice.

Amos's eyes dart toward Jadis, pleading. "Noble Jadis, they'll forgive you. Please, get them out of here."

This is what desperation feels like. It makes you do things—things you'd never want done to you. I felt it once, when Jhoana didn't wake up. That helplessness, that frantic need to act. I can feel it in Amos now, the way he's asking Jadis for help. He doesn't want this—whatever it is—but for the sake of his people, he's putting his own feelings aside. He's lost control, and he'll do whatever it takes to get it back.

Jadis gives him a terse nod, her expression hardening. She brings her hands together, and they glow red before golden rings materialize on each of her fingers. Her voice is a low murmur as she weaves a spell, her hands moving in fluid motions. Then, she pushes her hands outward, her voice firm as she utters the incantation. In an instant, the entire crowd, including Amos, freezes in place, their bodies stiff and motionless as if possessed.

"Return to your homes," Jadis commands, her voice calm and unwavering.

The spell takes hold immediately. The crowd begins to walk away, their eyes blank, moving in unison like puppets on strings.

Dustin's gaze locks onto his younger self, and I see the rage flare in his eyes. I step forward, my voice cutting through the moment. "They must be here for the shard. We can't let them get their hands on it." I turn to Brunner. "You're the only one who can outrun them."

Brunner's eyes widen in panic. "I haven't practiced much—I—I don't even know if I can do it—"

But before he can finish, Dustin cuts him off, his voice sharp. "Go long!" He tosses the Echo Sphere high into the air.

"Fuck!" Brunner yells, looking up just as the sphere arcs through the air. In a blink, Brunner vanishes, reappearing midair to grab it before blinking again, this time landing far behind the clones.

"Sól, you know what to do," Emierr says, his eyes burning with the reflection of Sólel's growing flame. "Stick close, protect him."

Sólel doesn't hesitate. He absorbs the energy around him, his body glowing as he transforms into something straight out of a movie—a solar being, light radiating from him as he launches into the air, trailing behind Brunner.

The younger version of me glances at clone Jhoana and motions for her to follow. Without a word, she breaks into a sprint, her force fields propelling her upward, running across the air itself.

Sixteen years. Sixteen years since we've faced this.

Our rematch is finally here.

Dustin steps forward, tearing off his shirt, revealing the tattoos snaking over his body. They look much more acceptable on his adult frame than they did when he was twelve.

"I got my dumb self," he growls, locking eyes with his clone. "He's mine to finish." He raises his hand, twisting his body like he's prepping for a throw. A green glow flashes behind him, and a massive battle ax materializes in his grip. With a sharp bunching of well-trained muscles, he hurls it straight at his clone.

Dustin's clone doesn't flinch. He stretches his hands out and absorbs the ax mid-air, smirking as it rematerializes in his grip. In one fluid motion, he swings it back like a bat, hurling it straight at Dustin.

My bond kicks in, sharp and relentless, pulling everything into focus. The sound waves are everywhere, rippling through the air like threads I can almost touch. But it's overwhelming, and pounds behind my eyes like a drum. The pressure's building, and this time there's pain—something that wasn't there the last time I used it.

I grit my teeth, pushing through the strain. That's when I see it—the sound waves rippling off the ax, distorting the air around it, everything sharpening into clear vibrations. My hand shoots out instinctively, and with a forceful push, I deflect the weapon just in time. The ax slams into Jae's hovercraft with a deafening crash.

"No! Not my car!" Dustin yells, his hands flying to his head.

"Sorry!" I call out, still buzzing from the connection to the bond.

Suddenly, a piercing screech cuts through the air, and my vision blurs. It's Emierr's clone, and I hear an answering cry from the distance. I look up and see four massive birds soaring down toward us, their eyes glowing with something unnatural. Adult Emierr turns and sprints away, the birds hot on his heels, their wings cutting through the air like knives.

Jadis's clone doesn't waste time. She screams an incantation, flinging fireballs at us. But Jadis reacts faster, summoning a force field that absorbs the blasts.

Overhead, the birds circle, diving at Emierr with hooked beaks ready to tear flesh from bone.

Out of nowhere, I feel a hard shove, and I'm thrown backward. My clone is on me, jet pack roaring as he pushes me across the cobblestone street. I grit my teeth, digging my heels in, but I'm sliding. My eyes dart around—I see a barrel near a food stand. I thrust my right hand out, pulling it with my mind and sending the object flying toward my younger self. It strikes him hard, and he hits the ground, rolling with the impact.

I manage to regain my footing, scanning the battlefield. Everyone's fighting their own battles. I see Emierr shouting, "It's North Star!" as the birds attack him. His clone commands them with ease, but Emierr counters, trying to seize control. The birds screech in agony, falling to the ground, caught between his will and the clone's. But then Emierr hesitates—unwilling to harm them. With a grimace, he releases his hold, letting them go.

Dustin swings his glowing blades, the red-hot edges gleaming, and sends them hurtling toward his younger self. His clone yanks a spear from his side, deflecting the attack with ease. The blades spin back to Dustin like boomerangs, both of them locked in a deadly dance of strikes and counters.

Jadis and her clone are trading spells, but I can tell something's off. Jadis is holding back—only casting defensive spells, deflecting every attack. Why isn't she attacking? Her face hardens, and suddenly, she steps back.

"Wait!" Jadis calls out, raising a hand. "They're limited."

"What?" I ask, confusion twisting through me.

Jadis locks eyes with me. "She's only using elemental. No time spells, no shields—she doesn't have access to all five schools like I do."

But I'm only half listening as I see her clone weaving another attack at Jadis's back. "Jads look out!" I scream.

Her clone launches another barrage of fireballs, and Jadis dodges, transforming her hands into fiery wings and soaring into the air.

Another crash to my right—a decorative stone pillar crumbles, adding to the chaos. Dust fills the air, and a nearby statue wobbles on its base, cracks spreading up the stone. Flames from the earlier fireballs have caught onto the wooden stalls, spreading fast, the fire licking up the sides of nearby buildings. The heat builds, smoke rising into the already choking air.

"Damn it, the whole place is coming down!" I shout, barely able to hear my own voice over the destruction.

I hurl the food cart at Jadis's clone, sending it crashing toward her, then launch a barrel at Dustin's. Just as I'm about to throw a wooden bench at Emierr's clone, a ripple of sound hits me. I turn just in time to see Dustin's hovercraft flying straight for me. I drop everything I'm levitating and thrust my hands out, stopping the car inches from impact. My feet skid back from the force, my body trembling under the strain.

The sound of engines whooshes upward, and I see my clone airborne, poles floating behind him, ready to strike. Just as he moves to attack, laser bullets zip past him. I glance over—it's Dustin, guns blazing, forcing my clone to dodge in midair.

But then I spot Dustin's younger self, spear in hand, poised to strike from behind. I react instantly, hurling the mangled hovercraft at him. Just before the car can crush Dustin's clone, a sudden gust of wind knocks him out of the way. It's Jadis's clone, her hand raised, summoning the gust to save him.

Jadis doesn't hesitate, shifting to the offense. She summons giant astral shurikens and hurls them at her clone.

Suddenly, one of the birds swoops down, intercepting the shurikens meant for Jadis's clone. It crashes to the ground in a heap.

"No!" Emierr lets out a guttural scream, a wave of raw grief exploding from him as he thrusts his hands toward his clone. Vines explode from the cobblestone, wrapping around the clone and trapping him. The birds stop their attack. "Leave now, North!" Emierr commands, and with a final screech, they take off, fleeing into the sky.

Without warning, Jadis and Emierr begin to rise into the air, my younger self gripping them tightly. I sprint toward the fountain, ripping my own statue's head clean off, and fling it straight at my clone. The impact knocks him off them, forcing him to release his grip, and Jadis and Emierr fall back to the ground.

I leap forward, reaching out just in time to catch Jadis and Emierr before they hit the ground, placing them them on their feet.

"Ricky!" Dustin's voice cuts through the chaos. I turn to my back just in time to see him cross his arms and spread them wide, as four spears materialize from his forearms. The memory of the fight with Lâcien flashes in my mind. I catch the spears mid-air, suspending them with my mind. Locking onto the targets—Emierr's, Dustin's, and Jadis's clones—I thrust the spears forward. They barely miss, hitting the ground around them.

The spears begin to glow, electricity arcing between them in a violent surge that jolts all three clones. Their bodies convulse under the charge.

But before I can catch my breath, a sudden force slams into me. My clone crashes into my side, grabbing me by the waist, and we're yanked into the sky. The ground falls away beneath me, and my friends grow smaller and smaller as we soar higher.

"Ricky..." Dustin's voice echoes from below, but I'm already too high to respond.

Worst goddamn birthday ever.

Younger Ricky's grip is iron-tight. "Get off me!" I shout, thrashing to break free. Below, Vereilles shrinks in the distance—where the hell is he taking me? I swing at him, but my hand stops midair, caught in invisible chains. He smirks, then twists, hurling me down with crushing force.

The air shrieks around me as I plummet, the ground racing up to meet me. Ruins of an old living area spread out below me—broken walls and rubble. Panic surges through me, but I focus, bracing just before impact. I push against the ground with a telekinetic shove, the force rattling through my bones. It's enough to slow my fall. I hit hard, but I land on my feet.

I glance around, spotting a half-broken pillar nearby. Without a second thought, I dive behind it, my heart racing in my chest. Above me, my clone lands with a heavy thud, hurling debris aside with a telekinetic sweep. I reach for the bond again, but a sharp sting hits me—like a knife slicing through my skull. I groan, gripping my temples as the pain lances through me.

Suddenly, a telekinetic force crashes into the pillar behind me, and it cracks and snaps in two, tumbling toward me. I dive out of the way just in time, skidding across the rubble. My pulse hammers in my chest. As I look up, younger Ricky's eyes lock with mine—blank, soulless, like a shell of myself.

I draw in a deep breath and let it out slowly. *This is it. This is where the nightmares end.*

He grins, jetpack flaring, and tears a chunk from the ground, lifting it into the air. It splinters into shards, and before I can react, they're hurtling toward me. Muscle memory kicks in—I throw my arms up, bracing for the impact. But the shards slam into an invisible barrier, shattering harmlessly. A telekinetic shield. I blink, stunned. *Since when the fuck could I do that?*

He looks just as shocked as I am, but I don't hesitate. Keeping the shield up with my left hand, I levitate a boulder with my right and send it barreling toward him. It makes contact, knocking him flat on his back. The rock strikes the ground with a thud. I rush around to the other side, but he's already back on his feet, jetpack roaring as he hovers above the ruins. My hands curl into fists, and he mirrors my stance, like a twisted reflection.

I step forward, then break into a sprint. My clone rockets toward me, and we swing at the same time. Our fists collide, and a shockwave explodes from the impact, shaking the ground beneath us. The force ripples through me, but I can't even tell if I'm feeling pain anymore—adrenaline's coursing through me too fast.

Each swing reverberates through the ruins, telekinetic bursts erupting with every hit. Fear. I can feel his fear. I mentally shove him with both hands, sending him stumbling back. He quickly boosts into the air to catch himself, but in that instant, something flickers inside me—an emotion I didn't see coming.

Does this thing... have a soul?

I lose focus for a second, but the clone's scream snaps me back. *It has a voice?* Before I can react, he thrusts both hands forward, and I slam into the ground. The impact knocks the wind out of me. Before I can catch my breath, he's on top of me, each punch landing harder than it should, amplified by telekinetic force. My vision blurs, and the ringing in my ears intensifies with every blow.

I want to fight back, but I feel it—the fear radiating from him. Not just fear. Confusion. Like a child who doesn't understand what's happening, or why he's acting out. A knot forms in my chest, twisting tighter with every second. I can't do this. I can't keep fighting him. Not like this.

The punches stop. Younger Ricky pulls back, glancing around like a lost puppy. Pain crashes over me as the adrenaline fades, blood thick on my tongue. Then, he levitates a piece of rebar into his hand, raising it above his head. Our eyes meet again, and the fear drains away, replaced by that cruel smirk—the same twisted smile.

No. I can't die here. Pa is alive and Jhoana needs me.

I tap into the bond one last time, forcing myself to react faster. The rebar hurtles toward my head, but just as it's about to strike, a sound wave slices through the air. Blue energy blurs past my face, and I twist to my right, stunned by the flash of motion.

The scythed energy slams into my clone's chest, exploding on impact and sending him flying away. I shut my eyes as the blast rattles through me, ears ringing again from the force. When I open them, dazed, I turn my head. A woman strides past me, light armor catching the dim light, her braided hair whipping in the wind, the crimson of her scarf trailing behind her like a banner.

I try to push myself up, my elbows trembling against the ground, eyes still locked on her. She finally turns, her gaze catching mine.

"Long time no see, Ricky James," Jhoana says, smiling.

Across The Divide

Arms wrap around me, hauling me off to the side. I feel myself resting on something rough—broken crates, with splintered wood biting into my back.

"Jihyun, fix him up." Jhoana's voice is powerful and commanding, cold and sharp—it's nothing like it once was. She raises her hand and a sword materializes, runes flaring along the blade in sync with her steady breaths. Her grip is solid, practiced, and her gaze locks onto my clone like she's done this a thousand times. Two others close in on her flanks—a blonde woman and a stocky man—moving in, ready to strike.

The blonde woman's eyes are sharp, tracking the clone with focused intent. Her long coat catches in the air behind her, mirroring her movements—tight and calculated. She doesn't charge in; she holds back, steady and watchful, her expression a mix of cool reserve and something keen, like she's reading every move before it even happens.

"Hey," a voice pulls me from the chaos. The man who dragged me here is kneeling beside me, his eyes locking onto mine. The noise, the bells that have been ringing in my head this whole time, suddenly fade away. I can finally hear myself think and everything else seems to slow.

"I'm Jihyun," he says, a calm smile settling on his face as his hand presses gently against the back of my neck. "Don't worry, you're safe." His voice is low. Something instinctively tightens inside me, a reflex honed by years of needing to be ready. For a second, I almost flinch, a flicker of distrust rising with the urge to pull back. It's hard to shake—the habit of bracing for the next blow. But then I really look into his eyes. They're soft, the light catching them in the warmest shade of caramel, and something in them softens that reflex. There's no rush, no expectation, just a steady patience that feels... familiar, like he's seen this reaction before. Gradually, the tension eases, and I feel my grip loosen on the crate, wooden slivers pulling free from my palms.

"You don't have to face it alone anymore," he says, the steadiness in his voice wrapping around me. And with that, I let myself believe him.

At his touch, the crates behind me shift, turning into something softer—foliage. I wince as I'm lowered onto the bed of leaves. They're green but streaked with light aqua variegation I've never seen on leaves before. Must be an Ethra thing. Jihyun's hands press together, glowing with the same light aqua hue as he starts weaving intricate signs in the air, movements fluid and deliberate. He breathes in, pulling his hands toward his chest, and then exhales, pushing them out toward me.

The leaves beneath me begin to glow, wrapping me in a cocoon of soft, soothing light. The pain that was wracking my body mere seconds before ebbs away, like waves pulling back from the shore. Whatever damage my clone did to my face, I feel it knit together and vanish. I take a deep breath, my chest rising and falling as I look up at Jihyun, eyes wide with relief.

"Thank you," I manage, my voice rough. He extends his hand, and I take it, noting the warmth of his grip as he pulls me to my feet. I hold onto his hand a moment longer, trying to press my gratitude into his fingers. "I'm Rictor."

"I know." Jihyun grins, eyes flicking down to where I'm still holding his hand. I quickly let go, feeling the heat creeping up my neck.

I glance toward the battle, having momentarily forgotten the chaos around me. Jhoana's sword glows faintly across her face, and for a second, I catch a flicker of hesitation in my clone's eyes—a flash of fear, just enough to throw him off. Jhoana's sword arcs toward the clone as the stocky man steps forward, grounding himself with a heavy, deliberate stance. The clone's eyes dart between them, trapped, but before he can react, the blonde woman's voice cuts through, sharp and commanding, pulling his focus. Each of them moves in sync, a coordinated advance closing in on my clone from every side. But then, in one quick move, my clone knocks the blade from Jhoana's grip. It flies through the air, embedding itself in a wall with a crackling thud.

I take a step forward, instinctively ready to intervene, but Jihyun places a hand on my chest, stopping me. "Let them handle this," he says firmly.

With a swift clap, the other man sends out a shockwave—a blast of sound that slams into my clone, sending him crashing into a crumbling wall. The blonde's eyes narrow, her whole stance tightening as she takes in the clone's every move. She shouts something from several feet away. Before I catch it, my clone raises his hand, taking control of Jhoana's sword. It hurtles toward the man, but he sidesteps just in time, narrowly avoiding it.

My clone's expression shifts—panic flooding his face as he realizes he's cornered. The blonde woman shouts again, and my clone, in a desperate attempt to escape, flies into the air. His movements are frantic. But the man reacts faster. His hands lift, and in an instant, my clone is suspended midair, trapped in an invisible grip.

How? That's impossible. He's not using a spell.

But the longer I look, the less it seems to be what I initially thought. This isn't telekinesis—not like mine. I would've felt the familiar pull if it were my ability, the subtle shift I always notice when my clone uses it. But his limbs aren't frozen; they're moving, resisting. His hands claw at the empty space around him, searching for something solid, any grip that might ground him again. The blonde yells, but it's cut short. My clone's hand shoots toward her, and suddenly she's gasping, feet lifting off the ground, fighting for breath.

Without hesitation, Jhoana swipes her arms, each motion unleashing scythed force fields that crash into my clone in rapid succession. Explosions erupt around him, smoke billowing through the air as he crashes to the ground, kneeling. His body is covered in soot, fear painted across his face.

I feel it again—that pull toward my clone, his fear seeping into me. But Jhoana's anger flares up, latching onto me just as fiercely. I get it—he's the one who dealt the final blow, trapping her here for all these years. The man and the blonde move closer to Jhoana, all of them towering over my clone. Jhoana throws a force field around him.

The fear that latched onto me spikes and so does the anger. The force field flickers, a telltale sign it's about to explode. Jhoana's not holding back—she's going to blow him up inside the shield.

"Wait!" I shout.

Jhoana's gaze flicks over to me, and just like that, the shimmer of the force field dims.

"Please... don't hurt him," I plead, my voice barely above a whisper.

I look at him—my younger self—and everything inside me twists. This isn't just a fight. This is me, staring at my own reflection, everything I was, everything I hated about myself. The anger, the fear, the mistakes I never forgave.

And he's scared. Just like I was back then. That's what makes this harder. If I hurt him, it's like I'm hurting that version of me—the boy who didn't know any better. A reflection of everything I used to be, all the pieces of myself I never quite forgave. And I'm not sure I can watch him die. Somehow, Jhoana seems to understand too. Without a word, she lets the force field fade, stepping back as if she knows this is no longer a fight I need her help with.

The others hesitate, watching, unsure. I lift my hand toward my younger self, and he flinches—yet the terror in his eyes begins to fade as he meets my stare. I stop, letting the silence hold us, and then I reach out, pulling him into a hug.

At first, he's rigid, tense, but then his resistance breaks, and he sinks into my touch, like he's letting go of something he didn't even realize he'd been clinging to. He feels so small in my arms, more like a frightened boy than an enemy. I feel his confusion spill over, raw and unresolved, along with a sadness that's been buried too deep for too long. I'm not just holding him—I'm holding all the parts of myself I'd once been too afraid to face.

"It's okay," I whisper, tightening my hold. "You don't have to keep fighting anymore."

The feelings swirling around us—the fear, the confusion, the sadness—seem to melt away in the embrace.

"I'm... scared," my clone whispers, the words barely holding together, as if admitting it will break him.

I pull back and see a single tear sliding down his cheek. *They can speak...* Before I can react, he shoves me—hard.

The force isn't just physical; it carries something deeper. I skid across the ground, crashing into Jhoana's arms. For a moment, I catch a glimpse of that sadness and confusion in his eyes, twisting into something deeper—maybe hurt, maybe even betrayal. Whatever it is, it's not aimed at me. It feels like he's fighting himself. Or perhaps I'm imagining it, just another reflection of my own battles. The thought is barely complete when my clone darts up into the sky, and is out of reach.

The man flicks his hand at the clone, but nothing happens. It keeps flying. The blonde steps a little closer to me, eyes fixed upward.

"He's not coming back," she says. But her words barely register. Did I just hear *it* say words?

"They can speak..." I mutter as I watch him go, a bitter taste settling in my mouth as his figure disappears into the sky. *What the fuck is going on?* I stand here, rooted in place, a storm of questions churning in my mind. But then I look at Jhoana, and all of it fades.

My chest tightens as I stare at her, really seeing her for the first time in years. Her face, once soft and full of life, now bears the marks of everything she's been through—lines of weariness etched into her brow, and a faint scar running along her jawline that wasn't there before. But it's her eyes that hit me hardest. Once bright and full of light, they're now clouded with quiet pain, shadows of the battles she's fought alone. And then, there's the red scarf wrapped around her neck, the token of her and Dustin's friendship. She's clung to it like a lifeline, a piece of the past that still holds meaning.

My breaths become uneven as I reach up, placing trembling hands on her face. "Jho..." My voice cracks under the weight of everything I can't say.

"Ricky." She smiles through the tears already streaming down her cheeks. Her voice is what I remember now—soft and gentle.

Without thinking twice, I throw my arms around her, pulling her close. My body trembles, and the choked sobs that escape me—they're not mine. They belong to little Ricky, the boy I used to be. All the years of guilt and regret crash over me, suffocating me in this embrace. But there are two undeniable facts at this moment: Jhoana is alive. And Pa has been here all this time.

I let those truths sink in, consuming me.

"Ricky!" Jhoana's voice shakes, echoing through the haze. The world tilts around me, the air closing in. Jhoana's voice fades into the distance as darkness creeps in at the edges of my vision. Then, everything goes black.

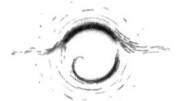

Space. Endless, dark space. That's all I see. *Where am I? Why can't I feel anything?*

"Just jump..." A voice, eerily like mine, echoes through the emptiness.

I look around, but no one's with me.

The voice comes again. "Do it... you coward." Louder this time, mocking, taunting.

Stop... Please...

"Jump!"

My eyes snap open. The dark space is gone, replaced by the canopy of trees above, sunlight filtering through the leaves. My chest heaves as I blink, disoriented. *What the hell was that dream?*

Laughter pulls me out of the haze, and I lift my head. The stocky man from earlier extends his hand toward the blonde woman, and with a soft wave of sound, her hair tangles as if caught by a breeze. They both laugh, apparently playing some kind of game. What else can he do without magick?

"You're awake," a calm voice says. I turn and see Jihyun leaning casually against a tree, his expression as steady as ever.

I sit up too fast, and spots explode in my vision. "Where's Jho?" I manage, blinking away the fog in my head.

"Take it easy," Jihyun moving closer, his brow furrowing with concern. "You took a lot of damage. I couldn't heal everything. Uh— *Jho* went to check if anyone's following us."

I look at him, really taking him in this time. Warm brown skin catches the fading sunlight, like he's blending into the forest. His dark, curly hair is sharply styled, highlighting strong features. His robes—green and white—flow artfully down his body, and his white overcoat drifts in the breeze. He's so composed, like he's in control of everything, even the trees.

All I hear is the wind rustling through the leaves. For a moment, the quiet feels almost nice—until I catch myself drifting and quickly shake it off.

"How long was I out?" I ask, needing to break the silence.

"About four hours. Your body's tired. Maybe you should rest—"

"I'm fine." I stand, using a nearby tree to steady myself. "Thanks again, Jihyun. But I need to find my friends." I try to give him a reassuring smile before stepping out of the shade, squinting as the setting sun hits my eyes.

"You're up?" the other man's voice cuts through. "Thought you'd be out until tomorrow with those injuries." He grins at me.

Sunlight catches on the thin frames of his glasses, a detail almost at odds with the rest of him—stocky, tanned, rough around the edges. But when he smiles, somehow, it all makes sense.

"I'm Mikal," he says, extending his hand.

I reach out, expecting a handshake, but he pulls me in, pressing his forehead against mine. I pause, not quite used to this greeting yet—it always slips my mind. Still, there's something undeniably comforting about it, because Ma always did it to me.

Mikal pulls back. Right next to him is the blonde woman.

She keeps her distance, apparently more reserved than the others. Her hair catches the light, but it's the weariness beneath the surface that stands out. Her sharp eyes hold something she hides well but can't fully mask. Even without knowing her, I can feel the weight she carries, the invisible scars.

"I'm Maks," she says at last. "It's so good to finally meet you." She throws her arms around me, hugging me like we've known each other forever. Evidently she isn't as reserved as she seems.

"Hi..." I stammer. "I'm Rictor." Slowly, I return the hug, an unexpected wave of grief rising up inside me. Who is this for?

Then, out of nowhere, the images hit me—flashes of burning city buildings, an underwater tunnel collapsing, blood-stained ground, and the sky raining fire. I pull away from Maks, gasping, my heart racing. She looks at me, equally shaken.

"Did you see that?" Maks breathes, her eyes wide.

"I did." My voice is steadier than I feel. I don't know what the hell I just saw, but I saw it.

"Good, you've all officially met." Jhoana's voice pulls us out of the moment. I spin around to see her walking toward us.

"Mom," Jihyun says casually.

"Jho..." I don't hesitate. I rush to her, grabbing her shoulders. "Is it really you?" My voice trembles, thick with disbelief.

"Yes, Ricky. I'm really here."

"Oh my god," I mutter, pulling her into an embrace. "Oh my god, oh my god." My arms tighten around her, like she might disappear if I let go. "Wait." I pull back, turning to Maks. "Did you say *Mom?*"

Jhoana steps forward, a smile spreading across her face. "Ricky, meet my kids."

I blink. *Kids? Jho had kids? Three?*

"I think you broke him, Mom," Mikal laughs, his voice booming.

Jhoana's expression softens as her eyes meet mine. "The others, Ricky—where are they?" she asks.

"Uh... We were at Vereilles, and they attacked us." The words tumble out, my mind still reeling from the bombshell.

"See! I knew it!" Mikal whoops, punching the air, while Maks and Jihyun sigh in unison, not the least bit surprised.

"You were there?" Jhoana asks, her eyes wide.

"Yeah, but not for long." I glance around, still trying to shake off the shock. "Obviously."

"We've been circling the forest for hours trying to find Vereilles," Mikal says, placing both hands behind his head.

"We got intel in Juno that someone there could help us," Jihyun adds.

"Riven Zykos?" I ask, my brow furrowing.

"Yeah." Jhoana nods. "He told us his 'brother' has the Locus Aeterna. I figured, with Dusty's scarf, I could use it to track you down."

"We were planning to do the same for you." I let out a breath.

"Then we heard the commotion by the ruins and found you... and your clone," Maks adds.

"Do you know how to get back to Vereilles?" Jhoana asks, her eyes searching mine.

I shake my head. "No, but we had a place to meet if we got separated. Somewhere called the Isle of Vereilles?"

Mikal's expression hardens, and he exhales sharply. "We're already *at* the Isle."

"The meadow with the purple flowers," I mutter, meeting Jhoana's gaze. Her face brightens with recognition.

"I know where they're going." She nods, turning toward the path. "Prepare to head out."

As she steps forward, I reach out, gently taking her hand. She glances down, but I don't look at her, heat creeping up my cheeks as my grip tightens.

"I'm not going anywhere, Ricky," she reassures me, her voice soft.

"I know," I breathe out. "I won't ever let you leave me again."

Her grip tightens in return. "They're my adopted kids," she finally says.

A wave of relief floods me. "Oh, thank god," I mutter, unable to hold back the small smile that tugs at my lips.

The sun hangs low, drenching the sky in brilliant strokes of purple, orange, and pink, as if the heavens themselves were painted in soft pastels. The wind moves through the meadow in gentle waves, rustling the purple lilacs stretching endlessly across the landscape. Jhoana stands at the edge, her long, dark hair cascading down her back. Her purple armor catches the fading light, hints of silver glinting. Each piece hugs her, merging with her stance—strong and unbreakable, just like her. Dustin's red scarf is wrapped around her waist, its color flickering in the dying light, like embers from a fading fire.

Ahead of us, in the distance, the Ethereal Tree looms, tall and otherworldly, its massive branches and golden leaves shimmering faintly as it watches over us. I feel a strange familiarity, an eerie déjà vu. This moment... It's like stepping into a dream I thought I'd forgotten. Wait... I *did* dream this. I remember now, the morning Pa woke me up. I'd thought it was me standing there, looking out over the world. But no—it was Jhoana all along. How is that possible?

"You look just like Uncle James," she murmurs. She doesn't turn to me; her gaze remains on the horizon. I move to stand beside her, the tears threatening to spill over.

"Jho..." My voice is thick with emotion, and I try to steady it.

She faces me, her soft features bathed in golden light.

The words slip from my mouth almost without thought, each one feeling foreign and unreal. "My Pa... He's here."

Her brows knit in confusion. "What? That's impossible."

"I saw him. In Vereilles," I manage, wiping at tears that insist on falling. "He's been here all this time." I choke back a sob. I've been holding it together since finding out he's alive, forcing everything down so I could keep moving. But now, standing here with her, it all starts to crack open, spilling out faster than I can catch it.

"You're absolutely sure?"

I cross my heart.

"Oh shit." The words escape her, and somehow, hearing her swear fits this new version of Jhoana. "Oh *shit!*" Her eyes widen, a mix of shock and disbelief. She reaches out, drawing me into a tight, clinking embrace, her armor pressing solidly against me. "Wait, let me put this away." She steps back, spreads her arms, and her armor dissolves in a cascade of shining particles, like stardust vanishing into the breeze. Free of the metal, she leaps back into my arms, and I hold her as tightly as I dare.

Her voice trembles, determination lacing her words. "After all this time... We'll find him, Ricky."

I pull away, wiping my eyes, feeling the warmth of her relief wash over me. "Don't you miss those Farmington sunsets, Jho?" I say, glancing at the painted sky, steering the conversation to a safer topic, before I break down completely.

"Always," she answers, her voice softening. "But I miss my family the most." She pauses, and the silence grows heavy between us. "Why didn't you come back for me?"

The question cuts through me. I blink, fumbling for an answer.

"You can be honest, Ricky," she says, stable and calm.

Swallowing, I search my heart for an answer I can bear to say, but nothing comes. My gaze stays fixed on the sky, avoiding her eyes. Why didn't I? Was it fear? Weakness? Or something I've buried so deeply I can't bring it to the surface?

"I—I have no answer, Jho... But I should have come back... I— I don't know."

Jhoana reaches out, taking my hand in hers. "I forgive you, Ricky," she whispers.

I stare at her hand, warmth radiating through my skin. "No." I pull away, shaking my head. "I was too weak to save you, Jho. And I'm weak, even now." My voice trembles, and the ache in my chest intensifies.

"That's not true," she counters, her gaze unwavering. "You know that's not true. We were kids, Ricky."

"I watched you *die*." The words spill out, raw and jagged.

She grips my hand once more, grounding me. "I'm here," she insists, her voice cracking. "You found me."

At last, I manage to meet her gaze—those dark brown eyes, warm and kind, achingly familiar.

This is my Jho. My best friend. My soulmate.

She smiles, soft and sweet, and pulls me close again. This embrace feels different—the reunion I've been longing for since the day we lost each other.

"Mom, there are people coming," Mikal says, his voice cutting through the quiet. The three of them tense, readying themselves. Jhoana and I release each other, turning to see figures in the distance. Across the endless wave of flowers, I see them. The Squad. They stop, faces frozen in disbelief. Then, all at once, they burst forward, closing the distance with each step.

Jhoana grips my arm, her face lit with shock and joy. I give her a nod, urging her forward. She doesn't need more than that—she's off, sprinting through the flowers, tears spilling down her cheeks as she goes. I can't help but notice the warmth in the air, tinged with the faint scent of wildflowers and the earthy loam of the meadow.

As I watch the scene unfold, an arm slips through mine, and I feel a weight on my shoulder—Maks. She leans on my shoulder, grounding me. Another hand finds my right shoulder; I turn slightly and see Jihyun, wiping his eyes, nodding like he's saying, *"We did it."* I don't pull away; the same calm I felt near him before blankets me. And I like it. Mikal stands close by, beaming, his smile as wide as mine, and his eyes glistening.

Up ahead, Jadis is the first to reach Jhoana, throwing herself into her arms, holding tight as her sobs echo across the field. She clings to Jhoana like she's terrified to let go, shoulders shaking as she mutters something I can't hear, broken words spilling out between sobs. Just for a second, she pulls back, her wide, tear-filled eyes searching Jho's face, like she's trying to take in every detail, fill every gap in herself that's been empty since she thought she lost her.

Dustin takes his turn, cupping Jhoana's face in his big hands, eyes brimming with something raw. He just stares for a second. Then he pulls her close, one of his trademark bear hugs that lifts her off her feet, crushing her with every ounce of strength he has. Her laugh breaks through, and she clings to him, tears slipping free even as she tries to hold them back.

Then Sólel reaches out, his face streaked with fresh tears, the kind only years of pent-up sorrow can bring. His arms wrap around her, his grip hesitant at first. But as she pulls him closer, the dam breaks—he lets out a shuddering breath, the hurt and guilt melting into relief. For the first time since he was a child, he's finally surrounded by *all* his brothers and sisters.

Brunner is next to approach, disbelief shadowing every step. Jhoana straightens, her shoulders bracing for something unseen. But as he reaches her, they fall into each other's arms, clutching one another tight. Their embrace is fierce, both of them holding onto a lifeline in a moment they never truly expected to come.

Emierr lingers a few steps back, hesitation etched into every line of his face. He's the one who set this all in motion, yet now he looks too afraid to close the distance. Jhoana, however, doesn't hesitate; she stretches out an arm, placing her hand on his cheek. His resolve crumbles, and he bows his head as the tears he can no longer hold back fall.

I've faced monsters, clones, and endless staircases—but put me in a room with a hug or a heartfelt moment, and suddenly I'm back to square one. My own tears resume their cascade—no longer from pain, but from everything else: love, relief, the end of years of waiting. Every step, every scar, every choice led us to this, and for once, it feels like enough.

Jadis turns to me, her face breaking into a smile. "Ricky!" she cries. Then the others start stampeding toward me.

Maks gives my arm one last squeeze. "Go on," she says, smiling. "It's your turn."

I release Maks and Jihyun, then break into a sprint.

The warmth of my friends' love surrounds me, filling my heart. Jadis reaches me first, pulling me into her arms, and then the others pile on—a tangle of arms, laughter, and choked sobs.

I reach out, touching each of them, still checking, still making sure. "Are you all okay? Anyone hurt?" The words stick in my throat.

"You got taken," Jadis whispers against my shoulder. "We thought..."

I pull back, blinking through the tears, glancing around at each of them. "I found Jho, guys," I say, a laugh escaping. They laugh too, brushing away their own tears, the weight of it all finally lifting. "What happened with our twins?" I ask. "Mine took off after Jho saved me."

"They got away too," Emierr replies.

I pause, frowning. "Wait—if you guys thought I was a goner, how'd you know to come here?"

"We used this." Jadis pulls a small, ornate object from her pocket, my necklace chain wrapped tightly around it. My hand instinctively goes to my neck—empty.

"It fell when your clone took you," Dustin explains. "Lucky for us. We needed something of yours to make the Locus work."

This is it—the artifact we've risked so much to get.

Brunner's voice breaks through, raw and full of disbelief. "Guys, that's really Jho, right? I'm not dreaming?"

We all look at Jho, her hands pressed against her chest, a sight we know by heart.

She steps forward, her voice trembling. "I'm right here, Rune. I've been here all along." Her words falter, heavy with the years we lost. She takes Emierr's hand, setting off a ripple—one by one, we all reach for each other, hands interlocking, holding on like we never want to let go.

The Allied Organization Squad is whole again at last.

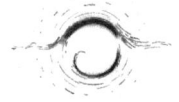

The bonfire crackles, casting flickering light over their faces as we sit in a circle. Across from me is Jihyun, with his siblings beside him, each of them looking a bit uneasy, like they're not used to this many eyes on them. An awkward silence settles in, with everyone glancing around, clearly waiting for someone to break it.

"What happened in the forest?" Jadis finally asks Jhoana.

At the same time, Dustin leans forward, eyes shifting to the new faces. "Do you guys have powers too?"

Jhoana chuckles, nodding to her kids. "Go ahead, you can answer first."

Mikal clears his throat. "I can manipulate sound waves," he says, extending a hand toward the pile of chopped wood. A ripple of sound moves through the air, brushing past Maks's hair like a breeze, setting it into soft waves. One of the logs rises from the pile, hovering, wobbling slightly as if caught in an invisible current. I watch, struck by the effortless grace of it—the way he shapes the air so naturally, like it's part of him. There's a finesse in his power, a subtle and measured contrast to mine. Where my powers push and pull with brute force, his are like watching someone sketch in midair, each movement precise and featherlight.

For a moment, I wonder how he views his power compared to

mine. All eyes are glued to the log until it drifts back down, settling with a soft thud. I feel everyone glance my way, as if they're thinking the same thing I just did.

"It's not telekinesis," I explain, catching their gazes before looking back at Mikal.

"I can also sense emotions through the soundwaves people give off," he adds with a grin. "Comes in handy when I need to fish out the truth."

"Can read emotions too, huh?" Dustin laughs. "Smells the same to me."

I scoff playfully. *State the obvious, Dusticle.* Different abilities, sure, but I can't deny the odd overlap in how they work. Who knows—maybe I could pick up a thing or two from Mikal.

"I'm a Transmutare," Jihyun cuts in, offering me a break from the attention. "I can turn any non-living thing into a pile of leaves." He gives a crooked smile.

"Just leaves?" Emierr raises a brow.

"Yeah," Jihyun nods. "But I can also alter the density of a leaf to make it razor-sharp."

"Like Bulbasaur?" Brunner snorts, stifling a laugh.

"Who?" Jihyun glances at his siblings, a little lost.

"Think fast." Dustin tosses a rock at Jihyun, who reflexively blocks it with his hand. The instant it touches him, the rock transforms into a flurry of leaves, each streaked with the same light aqua variegation I saw earlier. Everyone stares, a mix of awe and fascination, though Emierr seems especially taken—he can't turn objects into plants.

"I call it 'foliar manipulation,' " Jihyun explains, holding his hand over the fallen leaves. They lift, floating around his arm in a graceful spiral. He hardens them, their edges glinting in the firelight. With a flick of his wrist, he sends the razor-sharp leaves flying toward a nearby tree. Each one hits with a solid thud, like the edge of a blade.

"Can you control *all* leaves?" Emierr asks, eyes bright with curiosity.

"No," Jihyun says. "Only the ones I create."

"Interesting." Emierr nods thoughtfully, thumb pressed to his chin.

"What about you, Maks?" Jadis asks, all eyes shifting to the blonde woman.

A wave of tension passes over her, and she lowers her head, staring at the flames.

"Sorry," Mikal interjects. "Maks isn't big on talking to groups. But she can send her consciousness back in time—twelve minutes, max."

"A clairvoyant?" Jadis lifts both her brows.

"Not quite," Jhoana explains. "Clairvoyants see glimpses of uncertain futures. Maks experiences her present and then sends herself back to warn us of any immediate danger."

I glance over at Maks, sitting with her knees drawn up, her head resting on them. Now I understand—she's the reason they were able to dodge my clone's attacks. But how many times has she seen them get hurt, or worse, die? That weight... it must be crushing.

Sólel speaks up, breaking the silence. "I'm sorry, little one." His voice is solemn as he looks at Maks, catching her off guard. "It doesn't take magick to see how much grief you carry. But your strength has kept your siblings—and your mother—safe. Without you, we wouldn't have Jhoana back."

Maks's cheeks flush. "Mom, tell them your story."

Jhoana looks around at us, takes a deep breath, and sighs, a faint smile tugging at her lips. "Where do I even begin?" Jhoana's voice is low, each word pulling us deeper into the story.

She describes the facility, the brutal torture from Abbadon, and Evanora's role in all of it—how the witch killed Valda and Boyko before her eyes. Her gaze is unwavering, holding nothing back—not the pain, not the years that took everything from her.

I can feel it all hit the Squad, each of us swallowing down our own guilt. My chest feels immobile, my stomach hollow. They're mirroring what's twisting inside me: the regret, the disbelief, the shame that we couldn't be there for her. Despite our failures, some weight lifted just knowing Jhoana wasn't entirely alone. She found a sister in Lâcien, someone to help shoulder the loneliness we left her in.

And yet, this quiet dread wraps around me, settling in as I listen. She built a life here—she's a mother, a protector, even happy in a way I never thought possible after what happened to her. She found her place, and became everything those kids needed.

How can we ask her to leave all of this? Ethra isn't just some place she's been trapped in. It's her home now. And going back to Earth? It's starting to feel like a prison sentence.

"You were cursed," Jadis breathes out, breaking the silence.

Dustin, brows knitted, leans forward. "I know this might be a dumb question, but... what exactly does it mean to curse someone?"

"It's a binding contract, forced on someone without consent. The caster controls every term, every consequence," Jadis explains. "Once it's set, there's no breaking it—not unless the caster dies. That's the only way out."

"Unbreakable?" Brunner asks, searching for some loophole. "Nothing to break it?"

"None," Jadis answers grimly. "Back then, people abused it—casting curses over petty grudges. Murders became rampant, all traced back to untraceable curses. It was... a horror show." She pauses, her voice thick. "That's why curses are forbidden now. If you're caught casting one, they strip your magick from you—literally. No worse punishment."

Sólel shakes his head slowly. "It's a death sentence," he murmurs.

"Yes," Jadis agrees. "Here, having your magick stripped away... is worse than death."

"Abbadon—it had to be him who cast the curse," Emierr suggests.

Jhoana and the trio fall silent, like they already know who's responsible. Of course—who else could it be?

"It was Evanora," I say, meeting Jho's gaze.

"Isn't she dead?" Dustin asks, brow furrowed.

"Astralis," Jhoana murmurs. Nothing happens.

"I knew it was too easy," Jadis hisses, anger simmering beneath her words. "Of course she'd be at the heart of this."

Jhoana's gaze moves over each of us, her voice carrying a haunted edge. "I can still feel her... Like phantom chains latched to me. I've spent years searching, but I might as well have been chasing a ghost."

Emierr clenches his fist, a fierce grin gleaming in the fire's glow. "Good thing we've got the Locus Aeterna. She won't stay hidden for long."

Jhoana nods, her gaze sweeping around the circle. I can see a ferocity growing in her face—a ferocity built on the life she never asked for.

"Then we train," she says. "Abbadon, Evanora, the O'rians... even our clones—they're all out there, and they won't hold back. We can't go in unprepared. This could be the fight of our lives."

Jhoana's right. We're out of practice; barely held our own against our clones, and they're just reflections of us. Twelve-year-old reflections. The ones who wield magick beyond our understanding—they're still out there. But the real enemy is time. Can we train, fight, and get Jhoana back before they pull the plug? Doubts needle my mind, but I push them down. This will take everything we have.

"I agree," Jihyun says, standing up. "But training can wait until tomorrow. The night's still young—we should celebrate." His grin spreads wide, lighting up his face.

Mikal claps his hands, a glint of mischief sparking in his eyes. "Couldn't agree more. You all finally found each other again."

"And it's technically still Ricky's birthday on Earth," Dustin points out.

"Happy birthday," the trio echo, one after the other.

"Happy birthday, *Kuya*." Sólel smiles at me.

"Thank you guys."

"Twenty-nine?" Jhoana smiles softly.

I nod, feeling the tension lift, replaced by something lighter, almost easy. "All right then, what's the plan?" I clap my hands and stand up, finally finding purpose in celebrating my birthday.

Jihyun reaches into his coat and pulls out a small, round container. "This." He twists the lid, revealing a glowing, cream-like substance inside.

The Squad and I rise from the logs, leaning in for a closer look.

Dustin's eyes widen, his face lit with curiosity. "What is it?"

"Spirit Bloom," Sólel says, a touch of nostalgia coloring his voice. "I haven't seen that in ages."

"It's safe, right?" Jadis asks, skepticism in her tone.

Mikal chuckles. "Completely harmless. Spirit Bloom helps us feel connected—to each other, to Ethra itself. Think of it as magick's way of reminding us to celebrate life."

"But be careful," Sólel warns, his voice serious. "It's addictive if you're not cautious."

"Intense," Emierr mutters, eyeing the shimmering cream with intrigue. "What are we waiting for?"

Jihyun scoops a bit of the cream onto his finger, tapping Mikal, Maks, then Jhoana's foreheads, moving around the circle until he reaches me. I hesitate, but with everyone else now glowing faintly, I give a nod. He dabs it onto my forehead. The substance is cool at first, then warming, a subtle glow barely visible in my peripheral vision.

Almost instantly, there's a sensation under my skin—a deep, rhythmic pulse that feels as if it's resonating from within. The fire crackles deeper, laughter feels warmer, and there's a heightened awareness weaving through us all, a connection that feels practically tangible.

"Whoa," Jadis murmurs, her eyes widening as she takes in the gleam surrounding her. "It's like... I can feel everyone."

"Exactly," Jihyun replies, looking serene. "This is what ties us to Ethra. The magick, the land... and each other."

Jhoana leans forward, her gaze soft as she takes each of us in. "It's been so long since I felt this," she says, her voice thick with emotion. "I've missed this—I've missed all of you."

Brunner places a steady hand on her shoulder, his own glow intensifying. "We're not letting you go again, Jho. Not this time."

This is what we've been fighting for—a love that defies universes, a bond that knows no limits. The battles and dangers blur into the background, leaving only this moment, solid and unbreakable.

Mikal claps his hands, both palms glowing with a deep magenta light that flows between his fingers as he weaves the spell. A lute shimmers into existence, resting easily in his grip. He strums the first few notes, the chords ringing out with a familiarity that stirs something deep in me. Jhoana grabs Maks, and the two spin together, laughing so hard they can barely stand.

"Come on!" Jihyun shouts, taking Jadis's hand, pulling her into the rhythm next to them. The rest of us exchange glances, and one by one, we join in, dancing wildly, our steps as offbeat as Mikal's playful strumming.

I let myself go, letting the laughter, the music, and the night carry me, feeling something break free inside me—something I've kept locked away. Tears run down my cheeks, happy ones, as I laugh and lose myself in the moment. Sólel even joins in, creating a dazzling light show with bursts of colors that arc and spiral around us. Dustin takes over the lute at one point, and Jhoana leads us in songs she remembers from years ago.

When the night finally begins to wind down, we all collapse back around the bonfire, a warm, satisfied quiet settling over us. Out of the corner of my eye, I see Jhoana standing at the cliff's edge, her silhouette against the star-filled sky. I get up and walk over, the cool air a welcome embrace after the dancing.

"It looks just like the skies on Earth," I say softly, gazing up.

Jhoana turns to me, a question in her eyes. "Ricky... are you going to tell them about your dad?"

I look away. "No. He said he'll find me, and I trust him." My hand grips the locator in my jacket pocket, and my thoughts drift to the others, especially Dustin. Why do I get my dad back, but he doesn't get his mom? The thought digs in, guilt twisting deeper alongside something darker I can't shake. It feels unfair, like I'm holding onto something that should be his too, a piece of happiness he'll never get. I try to brush it away, turning back to Jhoana, hoping the sensation will ease if I focus on her instead. Maybe it's my turn for some answers. The question that's been pressing at the edges of my mind slips out before I can stop it.

"Do you... like me, Jho?" I blurt out, the Spirit Bloom clearly still playing with my inhibitions.

She chuckles, brushing a strand of hair back. "I did. When we were kids, I had the biggest crush on you." She half-smiles, a little wistful.

"Oh," I say, honestly surprised. "I wish I'd known." *Would I have liked her back?*

She shakes her head, looking away, her voice quiet. "Actually... I was lying. I was in love with you, Ricky. I think it's what kept me fighting all this time." She meets my eyes. "But... I don't know anymore. Fighting for and loving—they're not the same thing."

On impulse, I lean in, and she meets me halfway. We kiss, a soft, lingering touch that carries years of emotion. When we finally pull back, a little breathless, I meet her eyes. "So... what did you feel from that?"

She sighs. "Nothing."

"Same." I smile, feeling lighter, both of us understanding something unspoken. "But you're still my soulmate," I say, taking her hand, and we both turn our eyes to the cosmos. In another universe, I'd be with her. But here—and on Earth—she's my sister.

"Happy birthday, Ricky James." She leans her head on my shoulder.

"Mind if we join?" Brunner's voice comes from behind. *Bitch, I hope he didn't see us kiss!* He and the rest of the Squad walk up, forming a line beside us.

"Come on over," I say, glancing toward the bonfire where Jhoana's trio lingers. I turn to my best friends. "How's everyone feeling?"

Dustin gives a lazy grin, his voice slow and a bit hazy. "I feel high." Laughter ripples through the group.

"Hey, should we hold hands?" Emierr suggests, catching us all off guard. "Feels like a hand-holding moment."

Jadis chuckles. "Never thought I'd hear *you* say that, Meerina."

"Yes, please!" A light, excited tingle stirs in my stomach as I reach for Jadis's hand, linking us all together as we gaze up at the sky.

"All right, now *this* is a view," Brunner mutters, almost to himself, the wonder just a flicker in his voice.

As the quiet settles around us, a faint, buzzing hum fills my ears—almost like music, rising and falling in waves. It's subtle at first, but the melody builds, weaving into the silence, as if it's been waiting for us to listen.

"Do you hear that?" I ask, casting my eyes over the others.

"Hear what?" Emierr replies, still gazing up.

As I lift my eyes, the stars sharpen, colors deepening, galaxies and planets swirling together in a breathtaking cosmic dance. The hum rises, unfurling into a full symphony, as if the universe itself is an incomprehensible orchestra. I choke back a surge of emotion, my voice unsteady. "The universe... It sings for us."

Gasps ripple around me.

"I hear it," Sólel murmurs, his voice tinged with quiet awe.

"What... What is this?" Jadis whispers, her voice caught between disbelief and marvel, fully wrapped in the universe's melody.

I take in their faces, softly lit by the colors above, mouths gape.

At this moment, we're kids again, gazing out a window on the Space Ring and discovering the secrets of the universe.

Training

October 5

I'm halfway through the burrito, chewing with determination, when Gordo's eyes alight on mine. There's a gleam in them I've only seen since we got back from Ethra—hope mixed with that unspoken, constant fear.

"Can you tell her that I've been practicing my singing." he says, voice low, barely holding steady.

"Gordo, let the man eat in peace," Jadis scolds, though there's a teasing edge to it. "Your *ate* has been running him ragged in training."

I give a half-hearted eye roll. "Please," I mutter through a mouthful, the burrito my only comfort since Jhoana's thrown me into a full course of sprints and drills. "She's torturing me with this marathon stuff. I bench press 300—let me use my arms, forget the legs."

Dustin snorts, cheeks distorted by what some would call an unholy amount of beans and cheese. "Dicktor, you were always last running laps. Jho knows what she's doing." He and Emierr laugh, and for a second, it feels like old times—getting bullied by these two idiots.

Gordo leans back on the couch, and I catch him discreetly wiping a tear. "I just want her to know I'm okay and I've grown into a man she'd be proud of."

I swallow down the ache his words leave in my chest. Brunner settles beside him, arm wrapped around his shoulder.

"We've told her everything you wanted her to know since we last woke up," he says quietly. "But you should tell her yourself—when we bring her back."

"Thanks... *kuya*," Gordo exhales, his jaw tightening like he's holding something back. Then, from his pocket, he pulls out a small hairpin—a delicate white and gold piece shaped like a crescent moon. He holds it out to me, his hand steady but his voice softer than I've ever heard it. "She loved her hairpins," he says, almost wistfully. "Used to wear them all the time before we lost her. I found her shard after she went into the coma and had it made into this while I was stationed in Japan. I've kept it safe ever since." He hesitates for a breath, then meets my gaze. "Will you give it back to her when you see her?"

I take the hairpin; its smooth edges cool against my palm. The shard embedded in it glints faintly. It's heavier than I expected—heavier because I know exactly what it means to him.

"You should give it to her yourself," I say, but he shakes his head.

"When she's back, maybe," he replies, voice steady but filled with a quiet kind of determination. "Right now... I need you to make sure she knows we've never stopped fighting for her."

I nod, tucking the pin carefully into my pocket. Around me, the Squad has gone quiet, their expressions solemn.

Gordo clears his throat, a new seriousness hardening his expression. "You all better get back soon. Ms. Santiago's risking everything to give you more time; she's doing her best to stall the unplugging. This has to work. She's putting her job on the line—my *ate*, too." He glances at Emierr. "You know my mom will raise hell if things go wrong."

"No pressure, cousin," Emierr teases, raising his hands in mock surrender, but I can see the tension under the humor.

"Sorry. I'm just scared." Gordo stands, running a hand over his face. "I want my sister back more than anything, but... Just be careful out there, please. I can't lose all of you too."

His words settle over us, making the stakes feel higher. Gordo's been fighting his own battles on Earth, keeping us safe and making sure no one catches on. And he's been holding his breath all this time, hoping with each return, his sister is back with us.

"Then send our thanks to Ms. Santiago," I say, nodding at him. "We'll head back now. Let's get Jhoana home."

I walk up to Gordo, and he stiffens, bracing himself. But I just pull him into a tight embrace. He hesitates, then finally gives in, shoulders shaking as he lets out a flood of tears he's probably been holding back for a long time. The Squad exchanges looks, our faces shifting from empathy to determination. I hold him steady until his breaths start to even, then he pulls away, wiping at his face.

"Thanks, *kuya*," he murmurs and casts his gaze over everyone one last time before heading upstairs, leaving us in silence.

One by one, we lie down on the rug, closing our eyes as we settle into place. With a final look around, we begin the countdown together.

"Astralis."

~ ~ ~

I open my eyes to clear skies, back in the training area of Vereilles. My legs immediately remind me of all the running I've been doing since yesterday, and I push myself up from the seating step of the Observer's Circle, groaning.

"Hey," Jihyun's voice cuts in as he sits beside me, looking at me with that calm, steady gaze. "Everything good back on Earth?"

"Yeah," I say, rubbing my stomach. "Twelve hours with no food really hits when you're bouncing between realities." I try to make it sound like a joke, but my stomach isn't laughing.

His eyes flick down to my legs. "They're sore?"

"A little. Your mom's training is no joke." I manage a grin.

He smirks, standing up. "Here, let me help."

Before I can protest, he's already weaving a spell, his hands glowing with a familiar warmth. He hovers them over my legs, close enough that I feel the soothing heat radiate through my muscles, blanketing the soreness and exhaustion. It's like someone hit pause on the pain.

"Thanks," I say, flexing my legs as the ache fades away.

"Don't mention it," he replies, giving me that crooked smile.

"You two," Jhoana calls out. I turn with Jihyun and spot the rest of the Squad huddled together. We walk over to join them, where Amos stands with a halfling who I can only guess is Riven's supposed twin, though I still have no clue what that's supposed to mean. I catch the glint of respect in Amos's eyes as he gestures toward the halfling.

"Noble Rictor, Noble Jhoana, and honored guests, this is René Sable, our Warden of Lost magicks."

"It's an honor to finally meet the rest of the Nobles from Earth," René says, extending a hand for Jhoana and me to shake.

Amos clears his throat, addressing us all. "My Nobles, since the conflict has reached our grounds, Vereilles is no longer a safe haven. I've spoken with my council, and they agree—we need to evacuate and request aid from the other nations before more O'rian reinforcements return. I wanted your blessing before making it official."

"Absolutely," Jadis says without hesitation. "Get your people to safety." The rest of us nod in agreement, a silent, united front.

"Thank you, Nobles." Amos blows out a sigh. "Vereilles will join the cause to preserve the sanctity of Ethra. And René here will be a valuable asset moving forward."

René removes his glasses to clean them before he speaks. "Since making Vereilles my home, I've done everything I can to strengthen its defenses. But what happened here with your—those things..." He trails off, his expression darkening. "The reach of blood magick has spread far and wide, casting a shadow of uncertainty on everyone. Still, we have a chance—you were able to use my potential brother's device to contain the Arboris Singulos."

"The what?" I tilt my head.

"The meteorite," Amos says.

So that's what it's called.

"Yes, I have it here," Dustin says, lifting his forearm to show the tattoo of the Echo Sphere.

"Good," René says, looking at it with a wary eye. "Keep it safe but heed my warning—my 'brother' cannot be trusted. Power and corruption consume many these days. There's a reason I left his side." He pauses, his gaze hardening. "He wants dominion, places where he can reign untouchable, without opposition. I've seen what he'll do to get there, how far he'll go to hurt others to stay on top. That's not something I'll ever be a part of." René glances at each of us, his voice resolute now. "But knowledge belongs to all of us, and that's why I'm sharing this."

He squeezes his eyes shut for a moment. "As a Warden of relics, I've discovered many forgotten magicks. One in particular—the Heart of the Leyline—was hidden from history itself. It's rumored to be forged directly from the source, buried deep within the terra, containing a fragment of every soul that has returned to the Tree. In the wrong hands, its power could bring ruin to Ethra—and perhaps even beyond."

My stomach tightens at the thought. "So... in theory, this *heart* is like a mini Ethereal Tree?"

René's grave eyes meet mine. "Exactly that. Riven wanted to find it, to wipe out his competition—the Serpent Coil."

Emierr frowns, scratching his head. "*That's* why he let us go so easily."

"But what's more, if the O'rians were to get their hands on it... their blood magick would grow far beyond anything we've seen. With such raw, foundational power, they could twist the Heart's natural magick to fuel their own rituals, amplifying their hold on the lands. Imagine them wielding something that birthed magick itself—nothing would be safe from their influence."

"I'm sure you've kept this information close for good reasons. Why tell us now?" Jadis narrows her eyes at him.

René's gaze sweeps over each of us. "Protection."

Amos chimes in. "We have worked together for many years to ensure the safety of Ethra, by safekeeping objects of great power. It has become René's life's work. In exchange for his aid, we humbly ask that you find a way to bring the leadership of each nation together. What has happened in our home has proven to us that one nation alone cannot preserve the sacred balance of Ethra and its magick."

"A council of all nations' leaders would be wise. The connection between lands is stronger than it's ever been—they'll listen," Sólel says, his expression resolute.

"We could get Jae involved, too," Dustin adds. "He could bring it to the Allied Force."

I look between Jhoana's trio, making sure I have their attention. "You three get a vote now, too. You're part of the Allied Organization Squad."

They exchange glances, and Mikal nods. "We're all in agreement."

René gives a short bow. "Thank you. We'll begin preparations." He reaches into his bag and pulls out a set of metallic bracelets, handing one to each of us. "I noticed you don't seem to have a way to communicate between yourselves or with others across distances." "These are encrypted communication devices, connected exclusively to each other. No one outside your team can intercept the signal."

I examine mine, running a finger over the engraved sigils.

Beside me, Emierr's already strapping his on, holding up his wrist with a grin. "Any earpieces to go with these?"

"You won't need those here," Jhoana says, and the rest of us strap them on.

"To see your or your friends' location, just swipe over it," René says, demonstrating as his bracelet lights up, projecting a hologram of his location.

"Thanks, René," I say. "These will help a lot."

"There's one more thing." René reaches into his bag and pulls out a golden cylinder—a handle, its surface detailed with symbols of the elements, glinting in the sunlight. "This is the Vambrace. It absorbs elemental energies and forms a spear of the chosen element." He holds it out, looking at each of us. "I don't have any relics specifically designed for combat to give you right now, but I hope this can aid you on your journey."

I glance around, waiting to see if anyone else will step forward, but they all seem to look back at me. After a brief pause, I reach for the device. A small smile tugs at my lips. "I'll take it." Finally—a weapon of my own.

René returns the smile. "We're counting on all of you." With a respectful bow, he turns and leaves with Amos.

As they disappear into the distance, Jhoana gives us a look befitting of a commanding officer. "Update your bracelet names so we know who's who." I set mine to *Ricky* and tuck the Vambrace into my jacket pocket, feeling the weight of it bounce against my hip.

"All right," Jhoana says, already moving. "Next stop: the Isle."

"For what?" Dustin asks, scrambling after her.

She doesn't look back. "It's time we spar with each other."

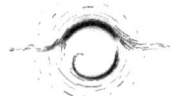

Lasers slice through the air as tendrils of vines erupt from the ground, intercepting each shot. Dustin versus Emierr. Neither of them would admit it, but there's still tension simmering between them.

I lean toward Jadis, smirking. "My money's on Dusty."

"You're on." Jadis grins, and we shake on it.

We're standing at the edge of the woods, right where the meadow meets the forest—a safe enough distance to let them go all out without risking damage to Vereilles, but still close enough for us to re-enter the protection of the border.

"You have to anticipate your opponent's next move!" Jhoana shouts, her voice sharp. "Stay two steps ahead, and you'll win faster." This is the Jhoana Ethra's turned her into—tough, focused, and unyielding.

As I watch the match, the intensity hits me. This isn't the casual training we used to do back in the Space Ring or even on Earth. Ethra's changed all of us, hardened us. Jhoana's right—if we don't push ourselves here, we'll crumble when it really counts. If we're going to get through this alive, it's going to be because of her.

Emierr and Dustin going at it is like seeing an old argument turned physical—only this time, their powers do the talking. They've always had this thing, pushing each other's buttons, testing limits, never quite knowing when to back down. Their fight now isn't just a clash of power; it's decades of rivalry, of friendship, of trying to prove who's better. The air practically vibrates with their energy, and I can't help but shake my head. Some things never change.

"All right, that's enough," Jhoana says, stepping in. "Dusty's the winner."

"Told you," I say, nudging Jadis with a grin.

She scoffs. "I put too much faith in that idiot." We both laugh, following Jhoana as the rest of the Squad gathers around.

"I need to react faster," Emierr mutters, catching his breath.

"Maybe I should tap into the Bond."

"We need to avoid relying on the Crown Beast's powers too much," Jhoana warns him. "Overusing it can take a toll on your body."

"She's right," I add, rubbing my temples. "My eyes started aching the longer I used Aigerim's sight."

Jadis just crosses her arms, grinning. "I don't know about you guys, but Tana and I have a strong Bond. I could fly for hours with her wings and not feel a thing."

"Me too," Jhoana mouths to her, and they both chuckle. I can't help thinking maybe men just aren't as in sync with their Crown Beasts.

"Has anyone heard from them?" Emierr asks, his voice tight with worry.

"It's been years since Eyre spoke to me," Jhoana says softly, her gaze distant.

Jadis shakes her head, frowning. "Tana hasn't responded to me at all."

"Same with Oberon. He just... went silent," Brunner says, running a hand through his hair. "I really hope he found the rest of them like he said he would."

Dustin tries to sound reassuring, though the uncertainty creeps into his voice. "The Bond still works. That means they're okay... for now, at least."

I glance up at the Space Ring, the glimmering expanse above seeming impossibly far away. I've never spoken to Aigerim, not even once, but right now, I can't help but hope he's okay.

"*Kuya*," Sólel catches our attention. "Your power is drawn from the breath of nature—let it guide you. Feel the life around you, sense where your opponent will strike next."

Sólel's advice hits home, and I can't help but smile, proud of how much he's grown. It feels like just yesterday he was tagging along quietly, absorbing everything we said, for better or worse. Now, here he is, guiding his older brother like he's been doing it all his life.

"Thanks, little one." Emierr wipes sweat from his forehead.

"Nice job, Dusty," Brunner says, giving him a high-five. "Looks like the new clothes are doing the job—no more taking your shirt off before every fight." Brunner laughs.

Dustin shrugs, frowning. "I actually prefer taking my shirt off."

The group breaks into laughter.

"All right, let's switch it up," Jhoana says, pointing at Maks and Jadis. "You two next."

"Oof, good luck, Maks," Emierr says, leaning toward Brunner with a hint of amusement. "Going up against the Supreme? Not a chance."

Mikal arches an eyebrow, flashing a daring look. "Wanna bet?"

Emierr steps up, extending a hand, and Mikal clasps it with a smirk to seal the deal. "Bring it on."

"Jadis won't land a single hit on Maks—guaranteed," Mikal says confidently.

I glance between them. "You guys know we're on the same side, right?"

Jihyun suppresses a smile. "I'm betting on my sister."

"Jadis is winning," I say without hesitation, crossing my arms with a confident smile.

"Remember, this isn't about showing off—it's about understanding how you react to whoever you're up against," Jhoana says, positioning herself between Maks and Jadis. "We've all seen what the O'rians are capable of. Every sparring session from here on out is about survival—yours and each other's. Fight like your lives depend on it. Are you ready?"

"Ready!" they reply in unison, each settling into their stance.

Jhoana steps back from between them, joining us as the sparring match kicks off. "Begin."

They circle each other, Maks crouches low, eyes locked on Jadis. Jadis keeps her posture straight and steady. Then they're off. Jadis raises her hands, shouting an incantation, and meteor-like fireballs appear, streaking right at Maks. She dodges each one with flawless precision. Jadis throws spell after spell, but Maks moves one step ahead, evading every strike.

As I watch, I feel a twinge of nerves, resisting the urge to jump in. It's just training, but every strike and dodge reminds me how close we are to fighting for real, where these skills are going to mean life or death.

"Maks moves just like you, Jho," Dustin comments.

Jhoana smiles. "No, she moves just like her mother."

I can't help but think back to those images Maks and I saw when we hugged. I haven't told the others yet, but it happened again. When I was staring up at the universe with the Squad, I thought it was just the Spirit Bloom's effects—but it felt like more than that. A memory, vivid and real. Did direct contact with Maks unlock something new in my abilities?

Jhoana's kids are nothing short of miracles—powers not from the Ethereal Waters but born into them. I know what it's like to have something different about you, to feel like everyone's watching, waiting to see what you'll do.

This was the first time Jadis and Maks had faced each other in combat, but you'd think they've been sparring partners for years.

Jadis's phoenix wings flare with every strike, and she moves with relentless energy, while Maks counters each blow with fluid accuracy, as she anticipates every move. They don't know each other, not really, but their rhythm feels almost instinctual—Jadis's fire meeting Maks's calm in a way that's mesmerizing.

Dustin, Emierr, and Brunner watch on, wide eyes following each maneuver. But between the two, Maks is still the more seasoned fighter. She catches Jadis off guard, clamping her in a firm headlock.

"It's over," Maks says, but Jadis grins, pointing up. Seven astral spears hover above Maks's head, shimmering and ready.

"Nicely done! You turned each other's weaknesses into your own advantage. Great work, both of you," Jhoana says, looking satisfied.

Emierr and Mikal exchange a glance, both conceding with a smile.

Beside me, Jihyun lets out a low whistle. "Guess I was wrong about my sister winning."

I shrug, smirking. "Looks like a draw to me."

"Who's up next? Ricky and Mikal," Jhoana calls, and Mikal and I size each other up. He strolls to the center of the sparring ground, entirely unbothered.

I dig into both jacket pockets, feeling for the Vambrace and the locator Pa gave me. *Where is he?* I pull the jacket off. The cool air trapped in the fabric is replaced by the sticky humidity of the meadow. Jihyun wishes me luck as I move to face Mikal.

"Remember, anticipate!" Jhoana shouts as she steps back. "Begin!"

"Let's go, Ricky!" Dustin cheers.

"Go, brother!" Jihyun hoots.

Mikal weaves a spell. Astral weapons carve through the air, glowing with an energy that hums against my senses. He fights with creativity, weaving his soundwave manipulation into each strike, while I rely on instinct, every move sharpening the edge of my control. The Squad's cheers blur into the clash of power and the rhythm of magick echoing around us. When Mikal falls back, I don't feel triumph—just the familiar burden of what we've become. Survivors, locked in this cycle of testing and preparing, as if fighting is the only language we've ever truly known.

If he's sticking with weapons, I'll match him. My hand extends toward where my jacket lies, my focus zeroing in on the artifact inside. *There.* The Vambrace slips free, soaring into my grip. I tighten my hold on it, my eyes flicking back to Mikal as he pushes himself off the ground.

"How do I use this thing?" I shout.

"The elements! Just smash it on the ground!" Jadis yells back.

Mikal's already on his feet, summoning an astral staff. I slam the

Vambrace into the ground, and it's instantly alight, forming a spear of solid rock at each end.

"Whoa," I mutter, feeling a wild grin split my face.

Mikal slices through the air, amplifying the waves of sound he sends crashing my way. Each pulse, every vibration, forces me to counter with my Vambrace and telekinesis. Every clash feels less like a fight and more like a test—not just of strength, but of understanding. The way he moves feels like he's already decided what I'm capable of. And maybe he's right, because with each strike, I start to see it too—that strange, unsettling sense of being measured, pushed to prove I can endure. I refuse to be the one to falter.

I push out my arms, sending a surge of raw energy that tears through the ground, ripping up dirt and grass in a path that barrels straight for him. Its power pulses against my skin, sending a shockwave through the field. Just in time, a force field flickers to life around Mikal, but the ground shudders underfoot as cracks splinter across his shield.

My hands tremble as a deep ache begins to radiate through my arms.

Jhoana drops the force field, and Mikal beams. "Rictor, you're a beast!" he says, giving me a thumbs-up. But my hands won't stop shaking. I don't know where that surge came from, but it feels just like when I escaped the Space Ring.

"Ricky, you okay?" Jhoana asks, walking over. That's right; she doesn't know what happened to me up there.

"I got him," Dustin says, wrapping an arm around my shoulders. "You're okay," he reminds me, and I nod. He pulls a chilled bottle of water from the tattoo on his arm and hands it to me. "Here, cool off and catch your breath." He gives me a reassuring smile, and I look over at the rest of the Squad, all watching me with concern. I manage a half-smile and sit down on the boulder, next to my jacket.

Jhoana calls Brunner and Jihyun up next. As they head to the sparring grounds, Mikal walks over and holds out the Vambrace. "If you were on the O'rians' side, we'd be in real trouble," he says with a chuckle.

I take the Vambrace and sip my water. "I don't even fully understand my power yet. Sorry if I went a little overboard."

Mikal laughs. "I'm the one who hurled sharp objects at you. If anyone went overboard, it's me." He glances at the sparring grounds, then back at me. "Mom—Jho—says you're on tally duty. You don't want to miss this one." With a nod toward Brunner and Jihyun, he heads back to watch the match.

The sounds of the match grow faint for a moment, fading behind the gravity that pulls me toward Jihyun—a feeling I can't quite explain, but one that's there, unshakable. It's something quiet yet powerful, and I feel it whenever he's close.

There's a sense of tranquility he brings, something familiar—like Bonnie's presence. After nearly ten years by my side, being apart from her now brings up all these feelings I've barely faced. Funny how it's the same with both of them—Jihyun and Bonnie. They have this strange ability to quiet the infinite noise, bringing peace just by being near.

But maybe peace is a luxury I can't afford right now, not when there's so much riding on what we're doing.

The cheers pull me back to the match, and I refocus on Brunner. He moves like he's always been a part of Ethra, his teleportation sharper, his speed relentless, while Jihyun plants himself firmly, unshaken even as exhaustion claws at him. Brunner's tenacious attacks crash into Jihyun's defenses, his momentum so fierce it feels like he's weaponized the air around him. Jihyun counters with serene efficiency, reshaping astral weapons into a storm of razor-edged leaves that orbit him in perfect rhythm. For someone who seems like a pacifist, Jihyun fights just as aggressively as Brunner, though with much more subtlety.

Brunner stumbles, tripping over his own momentum. Before Jihyun's final strike can land, Jhoana's force field flares to life, halting the barrage.

Winner: Jihyun.

Brunner lies winded on the ground as Jihyun , composed as ever, offers him a hand. So far, the score stands:

Dustin - 1, Emierr - 0
Maks - 1, Jadis – 1
Mikal - 0, Rictor - 1
Jihyun - 1, Brunner - 0

Jihyun walks over, wiping the sweat from his forehead, his steps a little unsteady. Admiration sparks in me, laced with another feeling I can't quite place.

"Here," I say, holding out my bottle of water. He takes it with a nod of thanks and chugs down the rest, sinking onto the grass beside me.

"Didn't think it would work," he says, catching his breath. "Turning astral weapons into leaves."

"It makes sense," I reply, trying my best to still my suddenly racing heart. "Astral weapons are tangible and non-living—that was clever."

He glances at me, eyes bright and a smile dancing across his lips. "I'd have been a goner if I hadn't thought of it."

"Jho's force fields would've saved you," I retort with a grin.

He give me a playful shove, and we both laugh.

Jhoana's voice draws our attention. "That just leaves Sólel and me." She turns to him, as he moves into the sparring grounds, now scattered with overturned dirt and debris.

I shoot a glance at Jihyun, who's beaming with pride. "Come on—my mom's one of the best fighters I know," he says, jerking his chin toward the field. "And if even half of what they say about the Sunbringr is true, this should be something."

I take his offered hand, letting him pull me up, and feel a thrill of excitement. Out of everyone here, those two have been in Ethra the longest—they've mastered things the rest of us are still learning. I have no idea who's going to take this one, but it reminds me of watching a mecha suit face off against a witch or wizard. I settle in beside Dustin and Emierr, both wearing those eager expressions I remember from way back. Just like old times.

Sólel and Jhoana face each other from a distance.

"Go, Mom!" Jhoana's kids cheer.

"You got this, little brother!" Emierr yells over them. The two opponents hold each other's gazes for a moment before Jhoana readies her stance. Sólel spreads his arms, drawing solar energy into himself.

Jhoana strikes first, sweeping a dozen scythed force fields toward him. Sólel leaps into the air, shifting into his sun god form, just as the barrage sweeps past. But Jhoana's already on the move, positioning herself directly beneath him, her sword ignited in blue flames. With a swift motion, she summons a force field under her feet, detonates it, and launches herself skyward, twisting midair as her sword inches past Sólel, who spins backward to dodge.

Sólel dives at her, but Jhoana extends her limbs, and suddenly, pieces of armor materialize out of thin air, scattering in all directions. Some strike Sólel, knocking him off course and sending him crashing to the ground, skidding through the grass and tearing it up in his wake. The armor pieces then snap back toward Jhoana, finding their places on her body like magnets to iron. Standing firm on a force field , she tosses her sword. It vanishes, replaced by her astral bow, already drawn and aimed directly at her opponent.

Sólel notices her aim and immediately takes to the air, darting in a tight, snake-like path to evade each arrow she fires. His movements are sharp and fluid, cutting through the air with precision. He streaks upward like a comet, then dives straight at her, both arms extended. Searing beams of light burst from his palms, aimed directly at Jhoana. She crosses her arms just in time, and the energy strikes her armor. Refracted light scatters violently under the impact but it holds strong, resisting any sign of melting or breaking.

"Chrysalorn Armor," Mikal mutters to the group. "Toughest stuff there is. These bracelets are made out of it too." He raises his hand, admiring them. "He's not getting through that."

Sólel swoops in close, his fist knocking Jhoana off her platform. She reacts instantly, forming a protective bubble around herself as she bounces off the ground. The shield explodes on impact, sending ripples through the grass. She lands lightly on her feet, her hands igniting with glowing shields. With a swift motion, she hurls them at Sólel. He darts to the side, narrowly avoiding the blasts, but the explosions detonate close enough to send shockwaves shuddering through the air, forcing him down to the ground.

"I can use magick too," he says, his voice sharper than I've ever heard it. He claps his hands together, and solar energy fuses with an earthy, green glow that deepens into a shade like aged wood. Slowly, he opens his hands like a book, then crosses them downward, his thumbs meeting at the center as he takes a deep, steady breath. When he exhales, his arms sweep wide, and all at once, dozens of identical sun gods splinter away from his body, forming an entire army of himself. It's almost like Jadis's mirage spell, but it feels... heavier. Tangible.

"What is that?" I mutter under my breath, glancing at Jadis.

She narrows her eyes, studying the doppelgangers as they close in. "It's not a mirage—it's something else entirely."

"Could it be a forgotten magick?" I wonder aloud, the thought unsettling. The idea that Sólel's discovered or tapped into something outside our grasp makes me uneasy.

"Get her," he commands, and the doppelgangers swarm toward Jhoana. She quickly raises a glowing dome around herself just as they slam into it—these clones aren't illusions. They're solid, hammering against her shield, determined to break through.

The clones converge on a single spot on her barrier, their hands pressing hard, melting through its surface. With a fierce battle cry, Jhoana detonates the field, the explosion sending them flying in all directions. Wasting no time, she summons her astral bow and draws back, the arrow glowing white-hot as she charges her shot. When she releases it, the arrow splits midair, scattering into a hundred glowing shards, each one finding a target.

"Sól!" Emierr calls out.

Two of Sólel's clones leap in front of him, their backs absorbing the incoming arrows. They collapse to the ground, dissolving like mirages. Sólel steps forward, his palms outstretched, and beams of light extend from his hands, slicing through the air and cleaving Jhoana cleanly in half.

For a heartbeat, the field falls silent, the tension thick. Did he just...? No, he didn't. But something's off—Jhoana's body ripples like water, shimmering fluidly under the light, no longer solid flesh. Her eyes glow red—she's tapping into Eyre. The two opponents lock eyes, white heat with fierce scarlet, then charge at each other again. Sólel's fist is pulled back, ready to strike, while Jhoana glides toward him in her water form. Just as they are inches apart, she solidifies, her hand raised, force field ready to detonate.

My chest tightens as I watch them. Every strike feels too real, every blow too close to harm. This isn't how sparring is supposed to look.

Just as they're about to collide, I lunge forward, raising my hands. With a sharp motion, I grip them both midair, freezing them in place.

"What's gotten into you two?" I snap, my voice sharp with frustration.

Sólel shifts back into his human form as Jhoana disperses her force field. The tension that had me holding them in place ebbs away, and I let go, my grip easing. Jhoana places a gentle hand on Sólel's cheek. She smiles, her voice filled with pride. "Little one, you might not be a Noble by name, but you're more of a Noble than any of us will ever be." Her eyes shimmer with unshed tears, and Sólel exhales a shaky breath, releasing not just his exhaustion but the years of unspoken longing to belong. Tears well in his eyes as he finally lets himself feel the pride and acceptance he's craved.

Guilt twists in my chest. All he ever wanted was to join us on our adventures, but we always told him, "Next time," none of us willing to admit we didn't want to be stuck babysitting. And yet, here he is—stronger than we ever imagined. Hearing those words from Jhoana—it must be everything to him. He pulls her into a hug, his shoulders trembling as the tears finally come. As the others cluster around Jhoana and Sólel, a familiar pull tugs at me from the edge of the woods, stopping me in my tracks.

I turn, and there, partially hidden behind a tree, someone is watching us. The Squad is still caught up in the moment, their cheers and laughter filling the air, so I slip away quietly, drawn toward that unmistakable feeling. Each step brings me closer, and there's no denying it.

My breath catches, and for a moment, the world around me blurs. It's him. It's really him. "Pa..." I whisper, my voice breaking.

He steps out from the shadows, his face warm with that familiar smile—the same one that greeted me on the morning of my twelfth birthday.

"Come on, Pa," I murmur. "They'll be glad to see you." I offer him a smile, trying to ease his hesitation.

"I'm not sure I'm ready," he mutters, voice low. His eyes drop to the ground.

"I'm here," I say. "You don't have to do this alone."

He glances toward the Squad, his uncertainty still plain. "Okay." He places a hand on my shoulder, and the world tilts. A flash hits me—sharp and vivid—but it's not mine. It's his.

I see him approaching Vereilles, walking toward the Gate. Is this from the first day I saw him? The scanner sweeps over him, and I brace for alarms, for warnings—but nothing happens. The Gate lets him through, welcoming him in.

And just like that, the vision ends, severed as he pulls his hand away.

What the hell was that?

"Take me to them," he says, and I nod, pushing the strange moment to the back of my mind. We head toward the Squad, and my chest tightens with anticipation. How's Dustin going to react? What will everyone say? My thoughts spiral, but I keep my focus on guiding Pa forward. Sólel is the first to notice us. His head tilts, curiosity flickering across his face before his eyes narrow. One by one, the others follow his gaze.

"Hold up—everyone, stay back." Jhoana steps forward cautiously, her eyes sharp and scanning Pa like she's trying to place him. "Ricky, who's this?"

I glance at him, unsure of what she's seeing. Pa looks exactly like he did back on Earth—just a little older, greyer, like time softened him without erasing the man he was.

"Ina?" Pa's voice is soft, almost reverent, as his gaze settles on Jhoana. His expression shifts, fragile and uncertain—recognition, maybe hope. He turns to Emierr. "Chris." Then to Jadis. "Dana..."Finally, his eyes rest on Dustin. "Josh." His voice cracks, the name catching in his throat. His shoulders slump as he whispers, "It's been so long."

The pain in his words, and his confusion, sink into me. Something's off—deeply off—but I can't bring myself to say anything. Not yet.

"Who *is* this?" Emierr's voice is sharp, his eyes narrowing as he locks onto me. "And how the hell does he know our parents' names?"

Before I can say anything, Dustin moves closer, staring hard at Pa's face. His breath catches, and his eyes fill with tears. "Is it really you?" he whispers, his hand trembling as it reaches for Pa.

Jadis's voice breaks the moment, sharp and probing. "You know him?"

"It's me, Josh," Pa says softly, taking Dustin's hand in his. He squeezes it, a bittersweet smile flickering across his face.

"Uncle James... You're alive." Dustin's lips quiver as the words spill out.

Pa's name sinks into the rest, like a slow, heavy wave. Jhoana's gaze meets mine, a quiet understanding in her eyes. She already knows, but there's no smugness—only a kind of unspoken support, like she's bracing me for what's to come.

The others are frozen, confusion and disbelief written all over their faces.

Dustin pulls Pa into a fierce hug, and before I know it, tears are streaming down my face. I don't even know who I'm crying for—Pa, finally seeing the Squad, or Dustin, who's probably wondering where his mom is.

"Masking spell," Jadis murmurs, her voice clipped, eyes narrowing as she analyzes him.

"What are you talking about?" I ask, my voice unsteady as I wipe my face.

"We're not seeing what you're seeing," Jadis says. "That means there's a spell on him—something making us see a different face. I might be able to dispel it."

"But why can they see him?" Emierr cuts in, gesturing to me and Dustin with a raised brow.

Dustin pulls away and he looks at me, eyes asking the same question I can't shake: Why *can* we see through it?

"Ina, Chris, there's no spell on me," Pa says. Something about his tone makes my skin crawl. I stare at him, my thoughts a chaotic blur. Why does he keep calling them by their parents' names? I can't shake the feeling that there's a thread unraveling right in front of me, and I can't stop it.

Jadis approaches Pa, breaking the silence, her hands already moving as she weaves a spell. When nothing happens, her jaw tightens. "This is stronger than I expected," she mutters, her frustration barely contained. "I'll need help."

"I'm here," Jhoana says without hesitation. Jadis nods and quickly teaches her the weave, their hands moving in synchronization.

"You're wasting your time," Pa mutters, shaking his head. *What has Ethra done to him? Is this even still my Papa?*

Jhoana and Jadis move closer, positioning themselves on either side of Pa. Dustin and I step back, giving them space. Together, the two of them begin weaving the spell, their movements like clockwork.

The air around Pa ripples, like heat waves bending reality.

Simultaneous gasps fill the air.

Jadis, Emierr, Jhoana, and Brunner don't hesitate a moment

longer. They leap forward, wrapping him in an embrace.

My eyes drift to Dustin. I can't tell if he's happy, sad, or somewhere in between. But I remain rooted in place as Dustin's quiet acceptance washes over me.

We're only meeting one dead parent today.

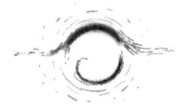

"He still hasn't explained how he's been here all this time, has he?" Jhoana asks under her breath, settling beside me on one of the Observer's Circle steps.

"No," I say, shaking my head. "It's like he's got amnesia or something. Or maybe something *did* go wrong when he Transcended here." My eyes drift across the circle to where Pa is sitting with Emierr, Mikal, and Jihyun. He looks so... normal. Almost like the man I remember, like the years haven't touched him.

My thoughts circle back to Amos, who had blindsided us all by greeting Pa like family. Turns out, Pa was friends with his dad and practically watched Amos grow up. It makes sense now—almost too much sense. From what I've seen of Amos these past few days, he doesn't do anything on a whim; every move he makes has a purpose.

He was the one who cast the Masking Spell on Pa all those years ago, and it wasn't just strategy—it was loyalty, plain and simple. I can still feel it. He respected Pa, trusted him, maybe even admired him in his own quiet way. And of course, Pa earned that. He always does, without even trying. But knowing this about Amos shifts something in me. That kind of trust is rare, and it changes the way I see them both.

"At least those three can talk to him without looking completely lost," Jadis says, settling onto the step beside me. Maks follows, stretching out after their training session.

Across the way, Emierr laughs, and for a moment, Pa looks like his old self again—relaxed, at ease. What I wouldn't give to call Ma and tell her husband is alive in Ethra. But I know the moment I say the words, she'll forget them. The thought lingers, pressing down on me. Another question surfaces before I can stop it: What if someone *made* him this way?

"Where are the other boys?" Jhoana asks, glancing at Maks and Jadis with a raised brow.

"Dusty's with René, working on intel about the Heart," Jadis says shortly.

"I hope he's okay," I murmur, letting out a slow sigh. I felt it—the glimmer of hope in Dustin's eyes fading the longer we talked to Pa. He wanted to believe his mom might be here on Ethra, too. But she's not. We need to figure out what happened that day on my birthday—why Auntie Via didn't make it through. And maybe we'd all get the closure we need.

"Yeah... Let him distract himself if that's what he needs," Jhoana says softly.

"Sól's with Rune, helping him work on his *blinking*," Jadis scoffs.

"Brunner's trying to teleport through walls," Maks says with a slight shrug. "He's managed it twice so far."

"Yeah, and almost left his leg inside of one," Jadis says with a wry smile. "Good thing, the wall wasn't as thick as his skull."

"What?" I look over at her, startled.

"I thought he had more brains than you boys combined, but nope—he's just as bad as you idiots."

My gaze drifts back to Pa. "What if... What if it's a spell?"

"I've tried, Ricky," Jadis says, exasperated. "Whatever's happening to him isn't magick—at least not the kind we know. Blood magick or old magick, maybe, but I can't say for sure."

If it's not magick, then... what? I dig through the haze of old memories, trying to recall anything unusual about Pa from my childhood. He was always forgetful, sure, but it never seemed strange. Then there was the occasional slip—calling Mama *Aluna* instead of *Luna*. I always chalked it up to a mistake, but now? Maybe it meant something more.

"Maks," I say, eyes flicking to her. She jumps a bit. "At the meadow—what do you think we saw?"

Jhoana tilts her head, curiosity lighting her face.

"What are you talking about?" Jadis crosses her arms, her eyes narrowing. "You never brought this up."

"I'm getting there," I reply. "Bear with me."

Maks hesitates, her brow furrowing in thought. "I've been wondering the same thing," she admits quietly. "It felt like... key moments, but I couldn't tell whose eyes we were looking through."

That stops me cold. I hadn't even considered that. *Whose memories were those?*

"Okay," I say, swallowing hard. "Maybe I can do something to help him remember."

"I'm still not getting it," Jhoana says, her arms moving to mirror Jadis's. Oh god, both of them have their arms folded. I feel like a kid caught in a lie, with two of my moms demanding the truth.

I hesitate, uncertain if testing my theory will even work. "I haven't told anyone about this—it's just been a lot to process—but I think I can see people's memories… or something like that. It started with Maks, when we touched. I think it unlocked something in me. Then it happened again that night, looking at the stars—I saw us as kids, doing the same thing back on the Space Ring. And just earlier, with Pa… I saw him entering Vereilles. I think it was the same day as the clone attack."

"I still can't wrap my head around it," Jhoana says, her voice low. "Amos and Uncle James… They knew each other this whole time? It just doesn't make sense."

"More than the fact that he's the one who cast the masking spell *on* Uncle James?" Jadis shoots back, one brow arching in challenge.

"Guys," I say, cutting in. "Amos was sincere. He only wanted to help his friend—I could feel that." I pause, trying to find the right words. "Whatever his reasons were, they came from respect and loyalty to my Pa. If we're going to get answers, we need to help him get his memories back."

Maks speaks up, her voice curious but cautious. "And how do you plan to do that?"

I let out a deep sigh. "My best guess is that maybe I can get into his mind, help him piece things together. But…" I pause, glancing at them. "I should test it out first—figure out how this works before I try it on him. Any volunteers?"

Jadis and Jhoana exchange a look, and without a word, Jhoana lifts her finger to her nose. Jadis mimics her a second later.

"Really?" I say, face deadpan.

"What's that supposed to mean?" Maks asks, glancing between her mom and Jadis.

"It means you're up," I say, glancing at her with a wry smile.

Jhoana and Jadis burst into laughter, sounding for all the world like two sisters ganging up on a younger sibling. Some things truly never change.

Maks goes quiet, her eyes momentarily seeming lost in thought. Then she blinks, refocusing. "Fine. I'll do it."

"Did you just… zone out or come back from the future?" I say, frowning.

"Just making sure my brain doesn't end up rewired." Maks says, shrugging.

"Come on! A little faith—*that's* all I'm asking for," I say, throwing up my hands in mock exasperation.

Maks switches spots with Jadis, sitting beside me while Jadis stands on a lower step with Jhoana. I glance at Maks, then down at her hand. My own hand hovers near hers, hesitating. *How am I even supposed to do this?*

"You have to want to make a connection," Maks says, her tone calm, like she's read my mind.

"That's a neat trick," I say, a small smile tugging at my lips.

"Good for skipping all the dragging moments," she jokes, a hint of lightness breaking through the tension.

I let out a quiet laugh and focus. My mind drifts to the moments I've made connections before—those strange, inexplicable flashes of memory. I concentrate on the feeling, the tingling awareness that came with them. Slowly, I reach for her hand, my fingers brushing against hers.

The moment we touch, a tingle races through my body, like static electricity buzzing just beneath my skin. The world around me shifts, blurring at the edges before completely warping. I blink, and suddenly, I'm standing in what looks like outer space.

Stars shimmer all around me, brilliant and endless, scattered across an infinite canvas. Some glow faintly, while others pulse with brighter light—the first stages of a supernova. Hourglasses float in the void, their sands moving in mesmerizing patterns—some flowing smoothly, others stopping and starting erratically. The ground beneath me isn't solid; it's reflective, like I'm standing on a mirror that reflects not me, but a swirling collage of memories. Images flash and ripple across the surface—faces I don't recognize, moments frozen in time.

Rivers of glowing colors snake through the space, carrying fragments of these memories like currents. Shards of glass hover and spin in the air, occasionally clicking together to form fleeting, incomplete pictures before scattering again. In the distance, a massive pendulum swings, its motion slow and deliberate. Each swing sends a faint ripple through the space, as if time itself is anchored here.

This is what Maks's mind looks like. Her subconscious... Her connection to time. It's beautiful, but there's an underlying fragility, like a machine that's constantly on the verge of breaking down.

The stars lower to my level, and one—a shimmering red—floats down and lands in my palm. As soon as it touches me, the memory begins to play inside the star. At first, it's just flashes—moments flickering past too fast to grasp. But the more I focus, the clearer they become. I realize what I'm seeing: moments from before Maks sent herself back in time.

The images sharpen. Each memory shows her family dying in front of her. Jihyun. Mikal. Even Jhoana. Not just once. Over and over again. I want to look away, but I can't. Jhoana died so many times in so many different ways. Maks has been carrying this with her, all this time. No wonder she's closed off. How do you live with that? How do you grieve over and over without losing your mind?

I glance around at the stars surrounding me. Each one is a memory, a piece of her. Together, they make up who Maks is. As I walk among them, they all play in endless loops, fragments of her life laid bare. Ahead, near the pendulum, I see a star glowing brighter than the rest. It's blue, slightly larger, and seems to pull me toward it. As I step closer, the memory inside starts to unfold.

I see Maks, younger, hiding in a closet with Jihyun and Mikal. They're giggling, barely able to contain themselves as they peek through the crack in the door. Jhoana barges into the room, completely unaware, and sits down hard on the bed. She looks so young—barely eighteen. Reaching under the bed, she pulls out a small box and rummages through it. She finds what she's looking for—a picture. Her shoulders start to shake as she stares at it, and then she breaks down, sobbing.

"I can't do this without you guys..." she whispers, her voice cracking.

The closet door creaks open, spilling light over the kids. Maks steps out first, followed by Jihyun and Mikal. Jhoana freezes, quickly wiping her tears and trying to hide the picture. But the kids rush her, wrapping her in a hug before she can build her walls back up. She crumbles, crying openly as they hold her. Jhoana pulls the picture out again and shows it to them. It's a group photo—her new Squad, her family, with the kids standing in front.

The memory tugs at me, hard. For the first time, I truly understand how much Ethra means to Jhoana. And just as clearly, I see how much Jhoana means to her children.

She's not coming back with us.

The memory fades, and I pull my hand away from Maks, the tingle still running through me. She looks at me, confused.

"Did it work?" she asks.

"How long was I gone?" My voice is shaky.

"Barely a second," she says, tilting her head.

I take a deep breath and reach for Jhoana's hand. She stares at it for a moment, then slowly takes it.

"I saw everything," I tell her, my throat tight. Then I look at Maks. "Your memories. All that grief you've been carrying... You don't have to keep it locked up. You can tell them what you feel. What you see."

Maks's breathing hitches. Her eyes fill with tears as she glances at Jhoana and her brothers. She reaches for her mom's hand.

"I saw..." My voice lowers as I turn to Jhoana. "Your life here... It means so much to you, doesn't it, Jho?" I try to smile, but the words are too full of sorrow.

Jhoana holds my gaze, her silence speaking volumes.

I let go of her hand and stand up, releasing a heavy breath. "Okay,"

I say, steeling myself. "I can do this."

I look at Pa. Emierr, Jihyun, and Mikal all turn to me, one by one, until finally—Pa's eyes lock with mine.

THE VERMILLION TWILIGHT

"**A**re you sure this is safe?" Dustin's jaw is clenched, a muscle ticking in his cheek.

I ignore him, my focus entirely on Pa. The Squad forms a loose circle around us, in a smooth gradient of fascination to anxiety.

"Are you ready, Pa?"

He gives me a nearly imperceptible smile, and extends his hand toward me.

I take a breath to steady myself. *Here we go.* I take hold of his hand, focusing all my intent on making the connection. Instantly, the world shifts, and I'm transported into a strange, fragmented space.

Mirrors surround me, their surfaces catching shards of light with no visible origin. The floor beneath me is made of glass—solid where I stand but splintered and fractured farther out, the pieces broken and floating in irregular separation. Slivers of glass litter the space, as though pieces of reality have been scattered here.

Okay, something definitely happened. Something bad.

I take a cautious step. Images begin to surface in the glass beneath my feet—Pa's memories. To my left, one of the mirrors snags my attention. A memory flickers across its surface, growing clearer with each step I take. Pa's walking through the streets of Vereilles, keeping to the shadows, ducking behind houses. I watch our clones appear, moving toward the town circle.

"*Anak*, you're here." Pa's voice echoes from the mirror, cracking as he moves to follow them.

The scene shifts. He's in the town circle now, but he's lost sight of the clones. His gaze lifts—and there I am. He freezes, his face unreadable.

"How am I here?" Pa mutters, confusion and disbelief threaded through his words.

What does he mean by that?

The memory moves quickly. Pa is running, and I see myself chasing after him. He moves like he knows exactly where to lose me, ducking through alleyways and around corners. But then, he slows.

"No," he says to himself, his voice trembling. "I have to face myself."

He stops in the middle of the street and rotates, waiting for me. I hear his thoughts now, ringing out raw and unfiltered: *It's me—How can it be me?*

His mouth resumes its movement. "How are you here? How is this possible?"

My stomach drops. *Does Pa think I'm him?*

I shove the glass aside and look around, taking in the shards and fragmented memories scattered like the broken pieces of a puzzle. The forgetfulness I remember growing up with. But the way he calls the Squad by the names of his old friends, that's where it gets weird. It's all making sense now. *If it's not magick, then... Pa has dementia.*

How long has he been like this? Did Ethra do this to him? Was it something else? The questions spiral without end, but there's no time to dwell.

I know one thing: I have to try to help him.

I reach out for one of the fragments of glass. To my surprise, it floats toward me, almost as if it knows what I want. I grab it, and it hums faintly in my hand. My powers work here, too, I guess.

Carefully, I begin working. I gather pieces of glass and fit them together, matching cracks and edges like a puzzle. Memory after memory.

I don't know how long I've been here—minutes, hours, maybe longer—but I don't stop until every fragment is in place.

Finally, the last shard clicks into position. It's done.

The world shifts again, and I feel the connection break. My hand rips out of Pa's, and he lets out a sharp gasp. When our eyes lock, I see it—recognition sparking in his gaze, lighting him up from the inside. He places both hands on my face, his touch trembling.

"Rictor James? Is it really you?" His voice cracks, tears brimming.

"Pa..." My voice is tight, barely holding back my own tears. "It's me. It's really me." The longing I've carried for so long—the need to be seen, to be known by him—lifts off my shoulders.

"*Anak...* I finally got back to you," he whispers, tears falling freely as he pulls me into a crushing hug. It's so tight I can barely breathe, but I don't care. None of that matters.

I have my Pa back.

He pulls back, eyes sweeping over the group. "Jhoanalyn. Emierr. Jadis. Even you, Brunner. You're all here." His gaze lands on Dustin, and the smile fades. "And Dustin." Pa's lips tremble.

Dustin's struggling. I can see it all over his face—the way he's trying to keep it together but failing. "My... My mom? Did she... come here with you, Uncle James?"

"Oh, my boy." Pa gets up and rests his hands gently on Dustin's arms. "I'm so sorry, *balong*."

Dustin crumples, falling into Pa's arms, letting out a broken sob. Dustin's grief radiates from him, overwhelming, all-consuming. All the hope that blossomed when he first saw Pa . Pa holds him tightly. But I can see it's settling over him too—all of it. Everything he's missed. Everything he's realizing.

I stand, wrapping my arms around both of them. *I'm so sorry, Dusty.* Pa tenderly wipes Dustin's tear-streaked face, then lifts his gaze to take us all in. "I can't believe it's come to this," he says softly, shaking his head in disbelief.

His eyes shift to the others standing a little farther away. His gaze lands on Sólel, familiarity shaping his expression. "You look so much like your father," he says warmly. "How are Berkarys and Nalani?"

Sólel freezes, mouth parting slightly in shock. The rest of us stand equally stunned.

Pa knows them too?

"T—They're good, sir. Strong as ever," Sólel stammers.

"How do you know them, Uncle?" Emierr interjects, his tone edged with suspicion.

Pa's lips curve into a faint smile, his eyes distant, as though caught in a memory. "They're some of my oldest friends here," he says softly. His gaze shifts back to me, his expression warm. "I'm glad my jacket suits you."

I glance down at the metallic fabric, the realization hitting me like a bolt. "You're Astro."

Pa lets out a quiet chuckle, almost as if the name pulls him back in time. "Astro..." he murmurs, more to himself than anyone else. "I haven't been called that in years." His demeanor shifts. "All right, all of you—gather around. That includes you three, whoever you are" he adds, gesturing toward Jihyun, Mikal, and Maks.

Once we've taken up places on the surrounding steps, Pa takes a deep breath.

"It's time you all knew the truth," he says.

This is it. The answers we've been waiting for. Our closure.

"My mind is finally whole again," Pa begins, sounding stronger with each word. "Whatever you did, *anak*, it freed me from..." He pauses, searching for the right words before shaking his head. "No point beating around the bush. Abbadon is on the move, and we need to stop him before the Convergence happens."

"The Convergence," Jhoana says, voice thick with emotion, as her children press close to her for comfort. "My friends died because of it, and we never even knew what it really was."

"The Convergence," Pa explains, his tone unsettlingly calm. "It's the phenomenon where two universes merge into one."

The silence is deafening.

"Holy shit," Brunner mutters under his breath, breaking the spell.

What does this mean for our universe? Are we on a collision course with Ethra?

"Meer was right," Jadis says, glancing his way.

"I'm never right," Emierr retorts, earning a few faint smiles despite the horrifying revelation.

I lean forward, heart pounding. "Pa... Is Ethra a superstring?"

"Yes, exactly that," Pa replies. "Ethra is one of infinite multiverses. And so is our own. I thought you would've figured that out the first time you arrived here." He arches a brow at me, like he'd expected it to be obvious to my twelve-year-old self.

"Things weren't easy after you died," I say quietly, voice barely maintaining an even keel. "It was hard—for all of us.

Pa's face softens. "I understand. There's so much we need to work through together, but for now, let me get this all out. No interruptions, no questions—just try to process everything, all right?"

I nod alongside the others, but inside, I'm not sure what I'm feeling. A slurry of confusion, anger, and hope.

"Both your moms," Pa begins, his gaze shifting between me and Dustin. "They're Ethran. Sisters. Their real names are Aluna and Fulvia. I met them when I went on my white hole expedition in 1989, only to find myself careening through a black hole and landing in Ethra. Chief Arun is your grandfather."

The revelation lands like a thunderclap. Not one of us could have predicted any of what just left Pa's lips—not even Jhoana's kids, who look just as stunned as the rest of us.

1989... That's way before any of us were born. Everything is falling into place now. Ma could never tell me where she was from because the spell that held them would force her to forget—she's Ethran. She can't even say it without triggering the spell. That also explains the meteor shards—they reacted to me; my blood carries the radiation, the connection to this place.

And Dustin... Dustin is my cousin. I can't help the swell of warmth that thought brings. I already think of him as my brother; now it's official. Blood. Dustin catches my eyes, and there's a fragment of joy in his expression. I give him a small smile back, and for a moment, everything feels just a little lighter.

"Dustin, you met your grandfather, didn't you?" Pa asks. I can tell he's trying to cushion the shock, but there's a note of lingering heaviness in his voice.

"Yes, I did." Dustin appears to be calm, but I can tell he's still reeling.

"That's wonderful to hear. He's a good man—a man I admire deeply," Pa says, the corners of his eyes crinkling. Then, his gaze shifts back to the rest of us, and his expression grows more serious. "I was diagnosed with early-onset Alzheimer's. That's why my memories were so scattered. But your mama, *anak*—she slowed it down, gave me time to think clearly again. She was supposed to be the High Priestess, even higher than the Supreme. Old magick came to her like breathing." He pauses, his smile bittersweet. "We fell in love, though it wasn't easy for everyone to accept. But my being here—my particles from another universe—set the Convergence in motion, though I didn't realize it at the time. Ethra's matter started reacting to mine. For seven years, I stayed. That was enough for the universes to start bleeding into each other, for anomalies to appear—things that don't belong, manifesting in Ethra."

Pa shifts his gaze my way. "That's why I sent Albert to the southern pole, to Islaug, months after you all arrived. I needed someone I trusted to investigate the changes. Anomalies were becoming more frequent, I had to know what I'd set in motion, even if I didn't fully understand it at the time."

Albert's name makes us all exchange looks. Then it hits me—he's the reason Albert wasn't there for me when everything went to hell. And old magick? My thoughts are spinning so fast I can barely keep up. I'm not entirely sure I can handle any more life-altering information.

"But yes," Pa continues, like he's plucked the thought straight out of my head. "I was there, on the Space Ring when all of you began to appear. It was me who came up with the plan to let you explore Ethra. I told Wolfgang and Delphini that each of you was the key to answering the questions Ethra had been asking for years. I sent Albert to speak with specific people in each nation, making sure only those I trusted would watch over you before I completely forgot about all of you." He pauses, his expression clouding over.

"But, why didn't you just *talk* to us?" The words leave my mouth before I even think.

"I began confusing you all as myself and my friends, in child form. I thought I was being haunted... I'm going off track," he mutters, shaking his head before continuing. "The night of your birthday, *anak*—Abbadon found me. I still don't know how, but he did. He managed to take over the body of our neighbor... Mr. Dawson. He'd probably been in there for years."

A collective gasp escapes from the Squad. Abbadon was—*is*—Starseed89. All this time, we've known him. And worse, he's known us.

"It's starting to add up now," Jhoana says, nodding slowly. "When I first met Abbadon, he greeted me like we were old friends. I could never figure out why he felt so familiar." Her gaze drops. "Poor Mr. Dawson."

Either everyone's remarkably good at holding their questions, or they're just as baffled as I am.

"Abbadon only wants one thing: a particle accelerator." Papa's tone is grim. "He was a friend, back in '89. He believed in the idea of a multiverse way before we even met, and I became his proof. He talked about colliding charged particles at high speeds, using raw magick as a power source to create a controlled black hole—a portal between universes. He described a particle accelerator perfectly."

He pauses, his gaze distant. "That kind of science doesn't exist here, but I managed to help him build one. It's how I made it back to Earth after those seven years. I rigged it to explode after I left, because by then, Abbadon wasn't the same. I knew he'd use it for something catastrophic." His voice drops, quieter now. "I never thought I'd see him on Earth. When I made it home, no time had passed. No one knew I was even gone. I just picked up where I left off. That final night, he showed up in the lab, threatening me with magick, telling me to open the portal. I wanted to show him his threats didn't work on me, but the accelerator malfunctioned—it exploded. It took Via... and Mr. Dawson. It should've taken me too, but at the last second, Abbadon pulled my essence back here and forced me into this body."

Total silence fills the air around us. Decades of unanswered questions are being laid bare. That morning—the last time I saw Pa—has replayed in my mind countless times, each one haunted by the thought: *What could I have done differently?*

But now, in this moment, a different thought rises to the surface. The way my shard reacted to my touch... and how Pa took it from me. "I..." My voice wavers as I try to speak. "I don't know what Abbadon did, but I think I know how you got here." Everything is painfully obvious now. "The meteor piece I touched," I say, meeting Pa's eyes. "You grabbed it from me. Its properties must've transferred to you." I swallow hard, guilt tightening in my chest. "I'm sorry, Pa. I didn't mean for this to happen."

"You had no way of knowing," Pa says, his voice heavy with regret.

"None of you were prepared for any of this. Maybe... Maybe it was a mistake. We shouldn't have hidden any of it from you." His words seem more directed at himself than at us.

We?

Emierr picks up on it instantly. "Who's 'we?' "

"All of your parents," Pa admits, glancing around at us. "They knew about Ethra. They knew about Aluna and Fulvia. They wanted to come back with me, to see the world I made a life in. But..." He hesitates, his expression darkening. "It was too dangerous. Things spiraled out of control, and Cadence got hurt."

"Cadence?" Jadis's eyes widen. "She's part of this too?"

"Just how far does this go?" I mutter, shaking my head.

"This is too much." Dustin stands abruptly, his voice tight with frustration. "I can't take this." He turns and starts to walk away, his shoulders stiff with anger.

"A memory spell," Papa says, his voice loud enough to stop Dustin in his tracks. "That's what's protecting your mind. It was your mother's request."

Dustin slowly turns back, his face a mix of shock and disbelief.

"You too, *anak*," Pa says, his voice steady but low. "Your mama—she's the one who placed the spell on you. When magick from Ethra started seeping into Earth, old magick found its form there, and she could tap into it. She made Cadence forget. And when you kids came, she put all your parents under a memory spell. The moment Ethra was mentioned, it was triggered. She was trying to keep you safe—scared of what the Exiled might do if they found you on Earth. The people forced out of Ethra and to another plane of existence," he added, noting the confusion on our faces. "Shielding your minds, yours and Dustin's, was the only way to hide your true heritage. She then erased Ethra from her own memory and from Fulvia's too. But before that, she tried to make me forget." He pauses, regret tightening his features. "But it didn't work. Something went wrong. Instead of erasing my memories, she unbound the spell holding back my Alzheimer's. And when I tried to tell her about Ethra, she'd forget again. I was the only one left. The only one who remembered everything."

To carry the weight of all those memories alone, for everyone, all this time—it must have been unbearable. Emierr and Jhoana glance downward, their silence heavy. Right—they've both been through this kind of pain too. I'm not sure I want to hear any more.

The Squad is reeling, each of us processing the truth in our own way. But the one thing we all share is the same sinking feeling: the bleakness of it all.

Pa turns to Jhoana, his tone gentle. "Jhoana, how are Valda and

Boyko? I stayed with them before I went to the Space Ring."

Jhoana hesitates, her lips pressing into a thin line. "They're gone, Uncle. Abbadon got to them."

Pa's face crumples. "I'm so sorry, Jhoana. I... I saw you at the Space Ring once. I tried to reach you, but my mind—" He stops, shaking his head. "I thought you were Ina. I'm sorry you ended up stuck here, too."

"I'm not," Jhoana murmurs, glancing at her kids. "I gained something here."

"We have so many questions, Pa."

"I'll answer them," he assures me. "But first, we need to get you all back to Earth before Abbadon strikes."

"But Jho's cursed," I counter.

That gave him pause.

"That's why she's been stuck here."

Pa's gaze cuts through me. "Then we kill the bitch who cursed her."

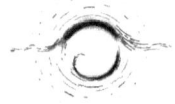

I pace outside Amos's house, my nerves stretched thin. Inside, Pa is still talking to him, and every second is dragging through the primordial ooze at an agonizing pace.

"Hey." Dustin's voice distracts me.

"Hey," I reply, stealing a glance at him. The tension rolling off him is palpable—we're both barely keeping it together.

We should probably talk about everything—being cousins, being half Ethran. But where do you even start when your whole reality has been turned on its head? Pa unloaded all of this on us at once, rapid-fire, like a storm we never saw coming. How are we supposed to just move past that?

"So, Grandpa Arun... He's really our grandpa," Dustin says slowly, like he's still trying to wrap his head around it.

"Yeah," I say. "And we're cousins."

A small smile forms on his face. "I was right."

"About what?"

"Choosing you as my brother."

That lands harder than I expect, and I blink quickly, fighting to keep the tears from falling.

"Uh," he mumbles. "There's so much we have to ask your mom,

but just know I always got your back. Okay?"

"Me too." I don't give him the chance to hesitate—I pull him into a hug, holding on tightly.

He lets out a sigh of relief and after a moment we let go.

"Is everyone ready?"

"Yeah." He nods. "A little shaken, but it would be kind of weird if they weren't. The Allied Force should be on their way."

"Good," I say, letting out a deep breath. "We can't stick around anyways. My original idea was we split into two groups—one to deliver the shard to the Space Ring and the other to find Evanora. But now that my Pa's here... maybe he can take the meteor up instead. I don't want us to split up again."

"That's a solid plan." He hesitates. "But... are you sure you're okay with saying goodbye so soon? You just got him back."

"No," I admit, my voice catching for a moment. "But he's here now, and I can always come back when the time's right. For now, Jho has to come first."

Dustin watches me for a moment, then pulls the Echo Sphere from his forearm and hands it to me. "I'll check on the others," he says, shaking his head. "Jho's kids are full of questions—nonstop."

I scoff. "They're going to love Rune."

He chuckles and walks off. The sphere vibrates in my hand. A tingling sensation spreads through my fingers, like the shard inside is calling out to me.

"*Anak.*" Pa's voice cuts through my thoughts.

I look up to see him stepping out of the house.

"Amos says the whole nation is ready. They're just waiting for the Allied Force. Terrene will take the Vereillic in. Berkarys will keep them safe."

"That's good to hear, Pa." I force a small smile.

His frown deepens. "What's wrong?"

I hesitate, turning the Echo Sphere over. "I have something I need you to do."

Pa's brows furrow as he watches the metallic orb between my fingers.

"We'll be the ones to find Evanora."

"No. I'm coming with you."

"Pa..." I say, exasperated, holding out the sphere to him. "You need to take this to the Space Ring."

Pa glances at it, a flicker of confusion crossing his face. "What is it?""

"Abbadon's after another shard, like the one connected to the Ethereal Tree," I explain. "It landed here, and Amos has been keeping it hidden, but it's not safe anymore. If you take it to the Space

Ring, where Abbadon has no power, it'll be out of his reach for good."

Pa takes the sphere, studying it intently—almost too intently.

"In the wrong hands," he murmurs, "this could destroy everything."

"Exactly. That's why you have to keep it safe until we come up with a plan."

Just then, a familiar sound cuts through the air—a ringtone.

"Do you hear that?" I look around.

"Hear what?"

"It's Bonnie's ringtone," I say, a sinking feeling growing in my gut. "I told her only to call me as an emergency."

Pa's lips curl into a sly grin. "Is she your girlfriend?"

"No!" I blurt out, heat rushing to my face. I shake my head quickly, trying to dismiss the trivial thought. "I'll be right back." I turn away, but a nagging sense of unease creeps over me. Something feels... off.

"Astralis," I say aloud, glancing back to Pa, his gaze locked on the sphere. But it's not the look of someone holding a precious artifact. It's something darker, something wrong. His grin stretches unnaturally wide, sharp and twisted—belonging to someone I don't recognize.

~ ~ ~

I gasp for air, sitting up so fast my head spins. My chest feels like it's caving in. To my right, my phone buzzes against the floor and I snatch it up.

"Bonnie?"

"Rick... are you okay?" I can hear the muffled stress in her tone.

"I... I need to tell you something," I stammer. "It's about my dad—"

"Ricky," she cuts me off, her tone urgent now. "I'm so sorry. I really tried."

"What's going on, Bon?" My stomach knots so tightly it feels like I might collapse in on myself.

"Oscar did it," she says, her voice breaking. "He launched. As of today, Superposition is live."

The words hit like a sledgehammer. My mind blanks for a moment before the information crashes in. It's out there. Oscar launched it without me. Without us.

"Ricky?" Bonnie's voice pulls me back. "Are you there?"

"I'm here," I say, though it feels like a lie. My voice sounds hollow, like it belongs to someone else.

"What do we do?" she asks, the desperation bleeding through her words.

"I..." My throat tightens, and I can barely force the words out. "I don't know, Bon. I don't know anymore." Three hundred souls will enter Ethra today—and it's on me. Every decision, every failure to stop this, has led to this moment. And now it's happening, whether I'm ready or not. "I have to go, Bon," I whisper.

"Ricky," she says with urgency. "No matter what happens next, I'm staying by your side. Okay? I'll do my best here."

Her words cut through the fog of panic, a fleeting moment of solace.

"Thanks, Bon," I say, holding back the breakdown threatening to overtake me. "Thank you for everything." The call ends, and I let the phone slip from my hand. A strangled cry escapes me, raw and helpless. I bury my face in my hands, every ounce of strength draining out of me.

What was I thinking? That I could do this? That I could fix it?

I glance over at my best friends, all of them sleeping peacefully, unaware of the chaos that's just detonated. My resolve hardens, even if it feels paper-thin. All I can do now is get them back home. That's the only thing that matters. I lie back down. My hands instinctively find Jadis's and Dustin's, their warmth anchoring me. I take a deep, steadying breath, forcing the panic to recede, even just a little.

"Astralis," I whisper, and let the world dissolve around me.

~ ~ ~

The air floods my lungs, gasping for breath. My eyes dart around, searching frantically for Pa, but he's nowhere to be found.

Fuck!

I force myself to move, but my legs tremble with each step before I freeze. My thoughts spiral into oblivion. I inhale deeply, focusing on measured breaths, desperate to push back the rising tide of panic. *Your training, Ricky. Feel for the emotion.* I close my eyes and draw in a shaky breath, letting the chaotic pull of emotions wash over me—thousands of threads tugging in every direction. It's almost too much, but I push through the noise, honing in.

Dustin's emotions flash vividly—steady, familiar, grounding. For a moment, the urge to run to him and unload everything about Earth overwhelms me. But I shove it aside. I need to focus.

Find Pa.

I feel it—a presence, heavy with something I can't quite name, like pain and determination tangled together. When I open my eyes, an amber trail of smoky energy weaves through the streets. It pulls at me, and I don't waste any time. My feet move on their own, carrying my numbly along the path until I see him. Pa stands at the edge of a cliff, staring out at the horizon. An uneasy feeling grabs at me—maybe it's just my fear of heights.

My bracelet dings, snapping me out if it—Dustin's sent a location request. I swipe to accept it, then make my way toward Pa, the way one might approach a wild animal.

"Pa," I say cautiously, stepping closer. "What are you doing out here?"

"You shouldn't have restored my memories," he replies, his back still to me.

"What? Why would you say that?"

"I was better off not remembering the pain," he says bitterly. "Do you have any idea what it feels like to yearn for a life you've lost?"

"I do," I say, the words tumbling out, all jagged edges and sharp spines. "Ever since you died, I've been stuck wondering what life would've been like if I convinced you to stay. Maybe... Maybe I wouldn't be so broken."

The confession settles between us. Saying it out loud doesn't ease the weight—it's been with me for so long, I don't know how to exist without it.

Pa finally turns, and his eyes are like ice—cold and unfamiliar. "You're not my son," he spits, voice detached. "My son just turned twelve. He's at home with his friends, celebrating his birthday. And my wife... she's waiting for me to come back." His gaze drops to the Echo Sphere in his hands, cradling it like it's the only thing that matters.

Why is he saying this to me? I thought I fixed his memories. Papa would never say something so cruel—this isn't him. I scramble for something logical, anything to avoid triggering another lapse. "Wouldn't you cause a Convergence by going back home?" I ask, voice trembling, barely keeping it together.

"Do you think I care?" Pa snaps, his voice sharp and laced with a bitterness. "Riven was right—getting your trust was almost too easy. You handed me exactly what I needed to start the particle accelerator."

My breath catches. *No. No, no, no.* "Pa..."

"Don't call me that!" He roars, voice thundering in a way I've never heard before. "Abbadon thinks he broke me. Riven thinks I'm on his side. And you? You think I'm your father." He steps closer, face twisted into something I no longer recognize. "All I am is a man trying to get back to his real son and wife. And I will." His glare pins me in place as my vision blurs with tears. "You're nothing like my son," he continues, his voice growing more unhinged. "If you were, you'd have figured out that I was here by now. You'd have saved me from this hell and brought me home. You're a disgrace to my name."

He brushes past me without hesitation, his steps firm and final.

Something inside me shatters. The pain, the frustration I've buried deep—it all surges to the surface like a dam breaking. "Hey!" I yell, as I whip around. "Don't walk away from me!"

Pa doesn't stop, doesn't even flinch.

"I said stop!" My hand lashes out on reflex, and suddenly, Pa freezes in his tracks, his body stiff and motionless. "Pa!" My voice cracks, desperation clawing at my throat. "Please... don't make me do this." My grip tightens, and Pa lets out a strained groan. The sound cuts through me, but I can't let go. This is too much—Ethra, the Squad, my failures stacking higher and higher. I'm at my breaking point, and there's no stopping it now.

A memory then floods my mind, sharp and vivid. Pa, crouched down on the hill the Squad and I biked to in the middle of the night, pointing out at the streetlights scattered like a galaxy across the dark expanse.

"You see, anak?" he said, his voice warm, wrapping me in his arms. "This is just like the ISS. The street lights—they shine like stars, guiding us." He pulled me closer, his words soft and certain. "Someday, the universe will sing to you. And when it does, you'll know—it's always going to be there for you. Just like your friends are. And just like I always will be."

I snap back to the present, my grip faltering as the memory fades. I release him, and Pa stumbles forward.

He turns, gaze meeting mine for a fleeting moment before he bolts.

That memory... It came to me without even touching him. Pa has to still be in there somehow. He has to be.

I stop, realizing I've almost walked off the edge of the cliff. When did I start making my way here? Something had just happened... Hadn't it? I stare out at the sprawling view before me. Breathtaking. It's everything I wanted—a place to call mine. But... Ethra's never been mine.

It's a mistake.

"Do it," a dark, familiar voice whispers in my mind.

The noose flashes in my mind—the sensation—Jadis's screams.

"You can do it," my voice taunts. *"Just jump."*

My breath catches as I stare down the at endless drop beneath me.

"Jump!" it hisses, louder this time.

"Ricky!" Dustin's voice slices through the haze.

I whirl around, too quickly, sending loose rocks tumbling over the edge. Standing there—Dustin, Emierr, Jadis, Brunner, Sólel, Jhoana—they're all here.

"Come on," Jadis says softly, stepping closer, her hand outstretched. "Let's talk, Ricky. Let's get out of here."

"Stay back!" I scream, my voice cracking. "Please, just stay away!"

"What happened?" Jhoana asks, panic threading through her voice, her eyes wide.

"Everything! Everything is so fucked!"

"Just talk to us," Brunner says, fighting to keep his voice gentle, like he's afraid I'll shatter.

"Why?" I shout, my voice breaking. *Why does it always end like this? Why does the universe seem hellbent on tearing apart everything I've tried to hold together?* "Why does this keep happening to me? I've tried so hard—I've been good, haven't I? I've done everything I can, I've put everyone first, but it's never enough! It's never fucking enough!"

"Ricky, please," Emierr's voice trembles.

"My Pa betrayed us!" I choke out. "He took the Echo Sphere. And Oscar—he fucking launched the game! Three hundred people are going to be trapped here because of me!" My voice falters. "It's not fair. I wish I'd died that day, Jads. I wish you hadn't saved me."

"No!" Jadis cries, tears now streaming down her face. "Don't say that!"

"*Kuya...*" Sólel begins, a fragment of the boy he was shadowing his face.

"It's too much!" I scream. "I'm tired of hurting! I'm tired of feeling!" I turn back to the cliff, the sunset painting the sky in colors too beautiful for a moment like this.

I'm done. My feet lift off the ground and I hover in place.

"Ricky!" Dustin begs.

A raw, guttural scream tears out of me, pain exploding in every direction. Energy ripples outward, knocking everyone to the ground, uprooting trees like they're nothing. Gravity takes hold, pulling me toward the abyss below, and I let it. I'm not going back to Earth—not this time.

Then, a sudden jolt stops me mid-fall. My jacket is caught. Dustin's hand gripping it tightly, knuckles white. His face is streaked with tears, eyes locked onto mine.

"You fucking idiot!" Dustin cries, his voice breaking as he struggles to pull me up. "You promised me!"

"Dusty?" I murmur. The agony, the rage, the sorrow... They're melting down into numbing confusion. What am I doing?

"Help me!" he shouts.

The others rush forward, grabbing onto me and working together to hoist me back up. As they pull, a shimmering force field materializes under my feet. A blinding glow cuts through my daze—Sólel, flying close, his light anchoring me.

Panic floods my chest as I grasp what I almost did. My friends pull me onto solid ground, and I collapse into their arms.

"I'm sorry." I grip onto them like a lifeline.

"If you even think for one second that our lives would be better without you," Jadis pauses to catch her breath. "You're so fucking wrong."

"Oh god…" My throat aches and I can hear myself sobbing. "What was I thinking?"

"We've got you." Dustin's hold tightens.

"Mom?" Jihyun's voice statics through our ears, distant but urgent. "Hello? Can you hear me?"

"Jihyun?" Jhoana stands up. "What's happening?"

"Vermillion Sages—they're here!" Jihyun's panic is unmistakable. "They're attacking the town!"

Blood magick users?

The connection cuts off abruptly.

"Jih? Son?" Jhoana's voice wavers.

A deafening rumble splits the air, and we all freeze. My gaze snaps upward as the protective dome around Vereilles begins to fracture, cracks spreading like spiderwebs. Golden light seeps through the fissures, and then, like fire devouring paper, the entire structure starts to disintegrate.

Of course. I never catch a break.

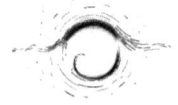

Screams pierce the air, and chaos erupt all around me. People dart, panicked, in every direction. "Let's move!" I shout to the Squad. "Evacuate everyone! Rune, you're the fastest—tell them to head to the rendezvous point!"

Brunner nods sharply and blinks into the fray. The rest of us fan out, weaving through the panic to help however we can.

I push toward the edge of town. An eardrum-battering blast erupts to the building on my right, the ground trembling. "Look out!" My heart skips as a massive chunk of rubble plummets toward a woman below. I thrust my hands out, and with a burst of telekinetic energy, I yank her toward me, catching her in my arms just as the debris crashes behind her.

"Are you okay?" I ask, shoulders heaving.

A familiar face looks up at me. "You saved me, my Noble," she chokes.

"Livia," I gasp. "Go. Find your dad and help him get everyone to safety."

She nods, slipping from my arms, and dashing toward the rendezvous point.

With a flick of my hand, I shift the debris to the side, clearing the street as best I can. *Just how many blood magick users did Abbadon send?*

"Sir!" A tiny voice pulls me from my thoughts.

I glance to my right and spot a little boy—blond-haired, chubby-cheeked, and barely five years old. He's clutching his arm, a streak of blood running down his forehead.

"Please help us," he pleads.

"Oh god," I mutter, crouching down to his level.

"I'm fine!" he blurts, grabbing my hand with surprising strength and pulling me forward. "The adults said they'd come back, but everyone's still trapped inside. You have to help them!" He tugs me toward a crumbling chapel, its entrance buried under rubble. "I saw what you did," he says, his wide, tear-filled eyes locking onto mine. "Please, you can save them, right?"

I take a steadying breath. "Of course. Stay back," I say, guiding him behind me. Stretching out both hands, I focus. The mountain of crumbled rock and brick groans as it rises, shifting and sliding away. The path clears.

The boy dashes to the door, throwing it open. Inside, dozens of human and leyfolk children are huddled together, their cries echoing in the empty space. They're so small, so vulnerable.

"It's okay," the blond boy says, his voice shaky. "He's here to save us."

The cries don't stop. Their fear is palpable, and eyes filled with terror meet mine, searching for a reason to believe him, but finding none.

I think of Jhoana—her voice, soft and steady, grounding me when I was their age. I clear my throat and begin to sing quietly.

> *Hush now, little one, don't you fear,*
> *I'm always near.*
> *In the whisper of the wind,*
> *Feel my heart under your chin.*

Their cries begin to quiet, all eyes turning to me.

> *In the quiet of the night,*
> *Where the stars are shining bright,*
> *Close your eyes and let your dreams take flight.*

The words flow out of me, and the room begins to quiet. One by one, the kids edge closer, their fear melting away.

"You're all so brave," I tell them. "You have each other—that's your strength. Stay close, look after one another. I'm going to look for help, but don't open this door unless it's my voice you hear. Can you promise me that?"

"No one's coming back," An older boy mutters, his tone hardened. He's leaning against the back wall, arms tightly crossed. "None of us have any parents. The *righteous* people of Vereilles won't miss us."

My gaze meets his. " I care," I say firmly. "And right now, these kids need someone strong to protect them. That's you. Can you do that?"

He scoffs, glancing away, his face guarded.

"Mister?" The little blond boy tugs on my jacket, his wide eyes filled with worry. "You will come back, won't you?"

I crouch down to his level. "I will. But I need you to be brave again. Watch over them, okay?"

He stands a little taller, his small chest puffed out as he gives me a sharp salute. "Yes, sir!"

A faint smile tugs at my lips as I rise. "Good man." I step out, pulling the door closed behind me. I sprint through the empty streets, my voice echoing as I shout for help, but this part of town has clearly been evacuated. Swiping my bracelet, I activate the comm.

"Is anyone there? Can you hear me?" The explosions grow louder, shaking the ground beneath me. My bracelet buzzes, and Dustin's voice crackles through the static.

"I hear you, everything okay there?"

"Dusty, I need your help," I say between ragged breaths.

"What? You're cutting out."

"I found kids—they need to be moved. I can't do it alone."

"Got it," he says. "I'm on my way. The others are all here."

"Good. See you soon." I cut the line and push forward.

As I turn back toward the chapel, rounding the corner, I freeze in place.

The chapel is gone. A direct hit has obliterated it, leaving only smoke and rubble where it once stood.

"Bitch" I whisper, my voice barely audible. My legs move on their own, carrying me toward the devastation. "Oh god, no." I force the broken door open. The sight that greets me knocks the air out of my lungs and my legs threaten to give out. Small, fragile bodies lie crushed beneath fallen stone and splintered timber. Blood seeps across the floor, pooling in the cracks. My breath catches as gold dust begins to trickle from their broken bodies. "No..." The word falls from my lips, hollow and weak. They're gone. All of them.

"Ricky, I'm here!" Dustin's voice rings out, but it falters as he comes up behind me. "Where are the—" His words cut off, swallowed by the horror before us.

"I... I told them to stay," I whisper, my voice cracking. "I told them they'd be safe."

"Help..." A faint voice calls out from the back of the chapel.

Dustin and I exchange a look before moving together, stepping cautiously through the carnage. It's the older boy, pinned under the rubble. His face is pale, but he's alive.

The rocks levitate and move to the side. Dustin weaves a healing spell, his focus razor-sharp.

The boy's eyes flutter open, and he breaks down, sobbing uncontrollably. "I tried to save them," he cries, his fingers digging into my skin. "I really tried!"

"It's okay," I say, my voice wavering. "You did your best. You're going to make it."

Dustin clenches his fists, heat radiating from his palms as frustration overtakes him. A faint shimmer dances along his skin—so faint I almost miss it.

"Come out, come out, wherever you are!" a mocking voice calls.

The voice of the one who did this.

Dustin steadies the boy, and leans down to him. "Go. Find the other Nobles—they'll protect you."

The boy nods, tears streaking his face as he stumbles out of the rubble, glancing back only once before disappearing into the chaos.

Dustin turns to me, his eyes blazing with a fury that mirrors the storm brewing in my chest.

"They're going to pay," he growls. There's a dangerous look in his eye.

I clench my fists, my jaw set. "Together. Let's end this."

We step into the street, the smoke swirling around us, screams echoing faintly in the distance. Two figures wait ahead, draped in blood-red robes. The younger one leans casually against a crumbled wall, a smug grin carved into his face. The older man stands still, his icy demeanor unnerving. Dark, unnatural veins creep from the corners of their eyes like cracks in porcelain.

"Hand over the Arboris Singulos," the younger one demands, his tone laced with derision. "We know it's in your possession."

"Woden, where are your manners? Introduce yourself properly to the Nobles," the older one says, his tone thick with condescension.

The younger man scoffs but dips into a shallow bow, his smirk firmly in place. "Woden, at your service, Nobles," he says dramatically.

"I am Tholric," the older one adds, inclining his head just enough to feign respect. "An honor, truly."

Dustin steps forward, his voice sharp and guttural. "We don't give a shit who you are. You're going to pay for what you did."

I glance at Dustin and do a double-take. A cocoon of white energy pulses around him, taking the shape of a massive tiger. It moves with him, superimposed over his body. His eyes glow with a fierce intensity, and sharp fangs glint where his teeth were. When he speaks, his voice carries a second tone—deep, ancient, and primal.

Is this the Bond?

I glance down at my own arms, now encased in swirling black energy. My nails have morphed into razor-sharp claws, and power pulses through me. It's almost too much to contain—but I embrace it, letting the rage fuel me.

"Oh, the kids?" Woden says with a mock pout, barely suppressing a laugh. "Not our fault they were in there when I blew it up. Tragic, really."

My hands curl into fists as my vision blurs with rage.

Tholric's tone is infuriatingly calm. "An army of O'rians is already on its way here," he says, extending a hand like he's offering mercy. "Surrender the Arboris now, and we can avoid unnecessary bloodshed. Well. *More* unnecessary bloodshed."

"Go to hell, bitch," I snarl, the sound ripping from my throat, too feral to be human.

Tholric's expression hardens as he lowers his hand. "Pity," he mutters. "Though it will be an honor to kill you both."

"You had your chance—"

I don't give Woden the chance to finish. Before I can process what I'm doing, I find myself in front of him, moving faster than I ever thought possible. He throws up an arm to block, but my punch still sends him rocketing into the side of a house. The wall explodes on impact, rubble raining down around him.

I whip around to Tholric, who's already weaving a spell. His hands glow with dark purple energy, the air crackling ominously around him. I can see his movements, but I know I won't make it in time.

Dustin matches my speed, charging in like a bull, slamming both fists into Tholric and sending him hurtling backward. Before Tholric can recover, I seize him midair and yank him back toward Dustin like a slingshot.

I whip around to Woden, who's struggling to regain his footing. I lunge toward him, ready to strike, but he spits out an incantation, shoving his hands to the side. A powerful gust of wind erupts from his palms, propelling him away just as my fist slams into the house. The wall crumbles under the impact, stone fragments exploding outward, but I feel nothing under Aigerim's protection.

I glance back—Tholric's shield bubble is barely holding under Dustin's relentless strikes. My attention snaps back to Woden, who's watching me with wide eyes, the hunter cornered by the hunted. He bites down on his thumb, and blood wells from the wound. Before he can act, I stretch out my hands, lifting him into the air. With a flick of my wrists, his arms are wrenched wide apart. He groans in pain, thrashing as I tighten my grip, the power coursing through me daring me to tear him apart.

A sharp, piercing sound slices through the chaos, making my ears ring. I raise my hand instinctively, and a mental shield flickers to life just in time. Blood spears slam into the barrier, splattering like liquid knives. The impact sends tremors through me, and I release Woden, spinning toward the source of the attack. With a burst of power, I fling Tholric upward, his body sailing high across the street before crashing into a distant wall.

"You good?" I shout at Dustin, coughing as I steady myself.

"Look out!"

I spin just in time to catch Woden hovering midair, blood swirling menacingly around his arms. His hands blaze with cursed indigo energy as his blood shapes itself into jagged, corrupted spears. They float in a deadly circle, ready to strike.

With a motion of his hands, the spears shoot toward me. I raise my forearms to summon my shield, but a sharp pain jolts through my body, slowing me down. The spears close in—until something slices through the air from my left. Glowing green weapons streak past, colliding with the spears mid-flight, shattering them in bursts of sparks.

Dustin charges at Woden, laser guns blazing, forcing him to switch focus.

I leap into the air, searching for Tholric. My leap carries me farther than it should, momentum propelling me as I hover just above the ground. I'm not flying—I can feel gravity tugging at me—but the glide feels smooth, almost natural, as though the air is holding me up for just a moment longer.

A blood spear whistles past me from below, but when I glance down, the street is empty. The air shifts, and I look up just as Tholric strikes—his arm extended, blood tendrils twisting into a blade. They slash through the air, aimed straight for my head.

I throw up my shield just in time. It holds, but the impact hurls me downward, slamming me into the ground. Dust billows around me, and pain radiates through my body as I struggle to catch my breath. Groaning, I blink the haze from my eyes. Tholric is gone—vanished into thin air

"Ricky," Dustin shouts, sprinting toward me. He grabs my arm, hauling me to my feet. "You okay?"

"I'm fine," I snap. "This ends now."

Woden staggers out from the shadows, his face smeared with blood, a twisted grin stretching across his lips. "Pathetic," he jeers. "You really think this is over?"

A portal unfurls behind Woden, swirling with bloodstained violet energy. Tholric steps through, his cold gaze locking onto Woden as their hands catch hold of each other. He can create Gates effortlessly. Blood magick—it's a power beyond anything I can fully grasp.

"Enough," Tholric commands, his tone sharp and unyielding. "We're leaving."

"What?" Woden snarls, his bloodied face twisting in defiance. "We can take them!"

"No, boy," Tholric snaps, his voice as steady as it is final. "It will take an army to defeat them. Now, into the portal."

"You promised—"

My power surges, and with a flick of my hand, I yank Tholric toward me. His body jerks violently through the air, but in a calculated motion, he grips Woden and hurls him into the portal. The swirling energy seals shut with a sharp crack, leaving Tholric in my grasp.

Tholric crosses his arms over his chest, then claws violently down his torso, tearing his shirt, and splattering blood in every direction. The droplets twist and writhe, forming tendrils that whip toward me.

I step back, raising my hand instinctively. Tholric freezes midair, his body locked in place, but the blood tendrils continue to lash out relentlessly.

A blur of motion catches my eye—Dustin, heat blades igniting in his hands. With a sharp yell, he slices clean through the tendrils, severed blood splashing harmlessly to the ground. He's fully human again, but his focus hasn't faltered.

Without hesitation, I twist my wrist in a smooth arc, carving an infinity symbol in the air. Tholric's body jerks violently, slamming into the ground once—then again—before I hurl him down with a final, bone-crushing crash.

He lies gasping, bloodied and battered, but it's not enough. Not yet.

I leap into the air, my hands surging with telekinetic energy. As I slam into him, the impact cracks through the air like a thunderclap. The chaos around me, the screams, even Dustin's voice—it all fades.

I don't stop. I can't stop.

Slash after slash, my claws tear through him, each strike more feral than the last. Blood sprays across the ground, painting it with my rage. Every ounce of pain, every shard of anger, ignites the fire in me. I carve an "X" into his face, ripping through flesh with unrelenting fury.

"Ricky!" Dustin's voice cuts through the fervor, sharp and horrified.

I stop, glancing at him. His face is frozen in shock, his eyes wide with something I can't bring myself to name. When I turn back, Tholric's body is already releasing a steady stream of golden dust. It drifts toward the Ethereal Tree, carrying my anger with it, leaving me hollow.

Dustin's hand lands on my shoulder, and I flinch. His fear is obvious, but I don't look at him. All I can see is Tholric's sightless eyes staring into the vermillion twilight sky.

"Let's go," I shrug Dustin off.

The rage is gone, but something else remains, hidden beneath the emptiness.

This power—it feels good. Too good. And that scares me.

Whose Bright Idea?

The rendezvous point is a whirlwind of chaos. leyfolk and townspeople scramble to gather what little they can carry, their faces etched with fear and sorrow. Some clutch their meager belongings, others hold tightly to their children, and some only grasp for fragments of hope that threaten to slip through their fingers. Just like that, they're forced to abandon their homes—all because of us.

"Where's the kid?" I ask the Squad, my gaze darting across the disordered.

"He told us what happened," Jhoana says gently, dropping a hand on my shoulder, and nodding toward a carriage where the boy sits, staring into the distance, his face hollow. "The Vermillion Sages—what happened to them?" she asks, her eyes darkened with grief. She already knows the answer.

"We took care of it, all right?" My voice comes out sharper than I mean.

Amos approaches with Livia close at his side. "The O'rians are closing in, my Nobles," he warns, his voice calm despite the whirlwind around us.

His composure grates against the rawness of everything we've just lost. "Did you know?" I demand, grabbing his collar, my voice rising. "Did you know my dad would betray us? Did you see this coming and say nothing?"

"He *what*? James? He would never." Amos's shock is genuine, the disbelief plain in his eyes. He's just another pawn in this mess. I let go of his collar, but the images won't leave me—those children, their limp bodies, lifeless—dust.

"Those kids..." My voice cracks, trembling under the weight of it. "They were waiting for someone to save them."

Amos's expression shifts, his voice faltering. "What kids? What are you talking about?"

"They were just kids!" I shout, the words ragged and unraveling. "And your people abandoned them!" The sobs bubble up, but no tears come—I have none left to cry.

A deep, echoing boom rolls across the darkened skies.

I catch Jihyun's worried gaze fixed on me, but I can't hold onto his warmth—my emotions are slipping out of control.

Dustin places his hand firm on the back of my head as he pulls me close, our foreheads pressing together. "Breathe," he says, his breaths loud and deliberate, a rhythm for me to follow.

I mimic him, my pulse slowly syncing to his pace. The storm within me begins to settle.

"These people need us," he says, low but resolute. He pulls back just enough to meet my eyes. "Let's just get through the storm."

I nod, a flicker of clarity returning, though the tension still simmers beneath the surface. My gaze hardens as it lands on Amos.

"All right, everyone," Dustin says, shifting the group's focus to him. "The trail's too narrow. So now what?"

Sólel doesn't hesitate. "Then we head for the Isle. More space to fight."

Amos nods, his gaze flicking toward me one last time before he rushes to the front to lead the way.

"We'll cover all sides." I scan the group. "No matter what happens, we protect them."

We're running now, the entire nation surging forward as one. Behind us, the O'rians' battle cries pierce the air, growing louder, closer with every heartbeat.

"Move! Keep going!" I yell, urging everyone to press on.

The sky churns above, dark clouds rolling in like an ominous warning.

Then the ground beneath us begins to shimmer. Water rises suddenly, pooling around our ankles, spreading across the meadow like a mirror. I glance down, my breath hitching. What is this?

The O'rians are too fast—they're closing the gap with terrifying speed.

I hold my ground, turning to face them. I have to buy everyone some time. For the first time, I see them clearly: dozens of leyfolk, their forms twisted and corrupted, alongside humans with faces contorted in bloodlust. They charge like feral beasts, their eyes filled with the promise of violence.

I glance up at the roiling clouds above. *Could it work?* There's no time to think. Raising my arms, I reach for the storm, calling it to me. Electricity crackles to life, surging through my fingers with a searing intensity. The familiar agony of it tears through me—electrocution, the Huttons. The pain is almost unbearable, but I force myself to endure it, letting it fuel my scream.

The O'rians are nearly upon me.

I clench my fists and yank my arms down, then thrust them forward with everything I have. Lightning rips through the sky, a blinding streak that tears into the O'rians, illuminating the mayhem. The blast cascades across the water, leaving shimmering pools of sparks in its wake.

Pain flares in my left hand, building to an agonizing peak. I cry out as one of the bolts of lightning surges from my hand, striking the ground and igniting another wave of sparks. When I glance down, I see it—a lightning scar branching out from the tip of my middle finger, spreading across the back of my hand in fiery veins, glowing like molten fire.

The smoke begins to clear, but it's still too thick to see through. *Did I... kill them?*

I turn and run, my legs leaden, the others motioning frantically for me to hurry.

"Come on!" Dustin shouts.

But then, a sharp, searing pain shoots through my back, stopping me cold. My body feels like it's reached its limit. I drop to my knees, hands braced against them as I struggle to catch my breath. My reflection shimmers in the water below, distorted and unfamiliar. I stare at it, trying to recognize the person looking back, but I can't.

Something catches my eye on the water's surface. Slowly, I twist, craning to see what's reflected behind my back.

An astral arrow.

Lodged in me.

I twist toward the thinning smoke, and there he is—Woden. Bow in hand, a faint smirk playing on his lips, but behind it, I catch a flicker of something else. Grief? Regret?

"Oh, fuck!" Dustin charges toward me, water splashing violently with every step.

My legs buckle, and I collapse, rolling onto my back. The arrow has vanished, but my body feels impossibly heavy, my vision swimming in and out of focus.

"Ricky!" Jhoana screams. I can hear the panic in her voice, but it feels distant, like it's coming from another world.

The Squad surrounds me, their faces blurring together. Jadis kneels beside me, her hands tugging at my jacket before carefully repositioning me on my side. Half my face dips into the water, the cold a shock against my skin. Her sharp gasp cuts through the air. "It's blood magick," she whispers, voice trembling.

Their voices grow muffled, fading into an indistinct hum, as if I'm slipping beneath the surface of deep water. Jihyun's delicate leaves drift down around me, their edges shimmering with an ethereal aqua glow.

Suddenly, pain lances through my back, wrenching a final scream from my throat.

And then... nothing.

The world fades as I feel myself slipping, the darkness wrapping around me, pulling me under.

Finally. Rest.

"Transcend, Ricky!" a voice cries, distant but insistent.

Okay.

I summon the last shred of my strength, forcing the word past my lips.

"Astra—"

~ ~ ~

I open my eyes to an endless expanse of stars and galaxies, a universe stretching far beyond what I can comprehend. I'm weightless, floating in the stillness, the cold seeping into my skin. This isn't right—this isn't how Transcendence is supposed to feel. We're aware, but there's never this... sensation. Never this *presence*. So why the hell am I here?

"Guys?" I call out, my voice breaking the stillness and echoing back, distorted. "Wake me up!" The words ricochet through the void, but there's no reply. Just the hollow sound of my own desperation fading into nothing. I try to piece together what I was doing before this, but my thoughts slip away, hazy and unreachable, like trying to hold onto air. Instead, a strange calm washes over me. The stars, the galaxies, the endless unknown—they feel comforting, like a lullaby cradling me in their glow. For the first time in what feels like forever, I think I could finally sleep.

Maybe when I wake up, things will be better. Maybe I'll remember who I am or what happened. But right now, all I feel is this dull, aching sadness lodged in my chest. I don't even know why—it's just there, heavy and hollow, pulling at me, making it harder to keep my eyes open. As I blink, something stirs in the distance. A black hole, its edges glinting with a strange, eerie light. I turn and spot another behind me, a little smaller, slowly spiraling toward the first. They move together in perfect, steady rhythm, like some inevitable cosmic dance.

For some reason, I smile. It's beautiful, in a way that feels beyond explanation. I think, for a fleeting moment, that I'm lucky to see this—whatever *this* is.

I close my eyes, surrendering to the cold as it seeps into me. Maybe it's finally time to rest.

"You're not done yet!" Jihyun's voice rings out, shattering the stillness around me. Before I can process it, a violent force grips me, yanking me toward the black hole ahead. The pull is chaotic, wild, dragging me relentlessly forward. In an instant, it consumes me, and my whole being slams back into my body.

~ ~ ~

The air sears my lungs as I lurch upright. My ears buzz with a piercing ring, chest rising and falling in frantic heaves. Before I can gather my thoughts, Jihyun throws his arms around me, his sobs muffled against my shoulder.

"What—" The words stick in my throat as I turn my head to my right. The water is now streaked with a dark purple substance, swirling and mingling with ribbons of blood, curling upward like smoke. The surface ripples, shattering any illusion of tranquility.

Was that a dream? "How long was I out?" I rasp, my voice hoarse.

They don't answer. Instead, a wave of something darker crashes over me. Grief. It's not theirs—it's coming from somewhere else. I hear faint weeping and pull myself free from their grip, my legs unsteady as I rise. The scene before me freezes me in place.

Amos kneels on the damp ground, cradling Livia in his arms. Her lifeless eyes remain fixed on the sky, empty and unseeing. As the water drains away, revealing the grass beneath, the tragedy stays frozen in place. Amos's tears streaking down onto her pale, motionless skin.

"What... What happened?" The words catch in my throat.

Amos lifts his gaze to meet mine, eyes red and swollen. His voice trembles as he looks back down at Livia, brushing her hair from her face. "She said you saved her," he chokes out, "So, she did the most honorable thing she could think of... She gave her life for yours." His composure fractures as his voice drops to a whisper. "She always believed in you... In all of you." For a moment, his grief overwhelms him, his shoulders shaking as he presses his forehead to hers.

I... died?

Amos smooths her hair back one final time, his hand trembling as he closes her eyes. His lips moving in silent prayer, body wracked with silent sobs. Slowly, flecks of Livia's spirit rise from her lifeless body.

Amos stays still, watching as the remnants of his daughter drift upward, carried by an unseen force, returning to the Tree.

"We've lost so much—our home, our families. And now my daughter. She was the best of us. You need to make it count, my Noble. You need to make her sacrifice mean something."

I glance back at the Squad, their faces heavy with grief. Brunner looks utterly broken. He knew her longer than the rest of us.

Amos sinks to his knees, bowing low before me. "I won't let this be for nothing. For her. For all of us."

I look past him and see them—the entire nation, leyfolk and townspeople alike, standing motionless, their eyes locked on me. Slowly, one by one, they lower themselves to the ground, bowing deeply, their heads pressed to the earth.

They should've just let me rest.

The moon's bright tonight, full, and lighting everything in the reflection of the sun's glow—it's mocking me. I've been staring at it for... who knows how long. My brain just won't shut off. Today's been one of those days where the world flips on its head over and over. I almost threw myself off a cliff. And then, somehow, I actually *did* die.

I still can't wrap my head around it—Livia gave her life for mine. No hesitation, no second thought. She just handed over her life force, like she owed me. There's barely a moment to breathe, let alone process it. Everything's just... completely fucked. Pa has the shard, and he might be working with Abbadon, Riven—or worse, both. We're nowhere near finding Evanora. And Jhoana? Time's almost up. One day. That's all we've got left in Ethra before they pull the plug on her.

I'm starting to worry about Gordo. He's running out of excuses to keep our parents off us. We've decided to let him drop Ethra into the conversation if he needs to buy time—but even that feels desperate as fuck.

"Hey." A voice comes from my right.

"Jesus!" I mutter, my heart nearly jumping out of my chest. I turn to see Jae standing there. "You scared the hell out of me."

He chuckles. "Sorry. I know you wanted to be alone, but—"

"You don't have to worry about me," I cut him off. "Thanks, though."

"Your friends are really worried," he says softly. "Especially Ji-hyun." He hesitates, like he's trying to find the right words. "You've been through a lot since the last time I saw you."

I let out a heavy sigh. "They told you, huh."

He moves around the tree and leans against it, eyes fixed on the moon. "We're all worried about you," he murmurs. "I know we haven't talked much, but... I get how you feel."

I scoff, crossing my arms. "This isn't a contest, but I doubt you do."

He doesn't flinch, doesn't even look at me, just keeps staring up. "I've made some really bad calls too, Rictor. Got people I care about hurt. Two of them even had their magick bound because they took the fall for a mistake I made. I've caused more pain than I thought I was capable of. And it took me to a dark place—so dark I didn't think I'd find a way out. At one point, I was ready to end it all."

I wasn't expecting this from him, but I stay silent, letting him continue.

"But then I realized," he says, his voice steady, "there are people who'd hurt even more if I went through with it. People who still cared about me, no matter how much I'd messed up. You're allowed to break down, Rictor. You're human. But don't let yourself fall too far. Take the hand that's reaching out to you."

I don't know what to say. His words hit me differently than I expect, breaking through the numbness. Something inside me has cracked open It all makes sense now—I don't have to carry all of this alone. I should be able to talk to the Squad, to let them in. They've been my anchor through all of this. I wipe at my eyes quickly, hoping he doesn't notice. "Thanks, Jae. I needed that. I just... I don't know what to say to them when I get like this."

"Well," he says, walking over and activating his watch, "I'm starting to like having you guys around. If you ever need someone to talk to—or just need me to show you around when things calm down—I'm here."

"Yeah," I reply, a faint smile tugging at the corners of my mouth. "Thanks. I'd like that."

I tap my bracelet, and Jae connects our devices with a quick swipe.

"Now I'm just one call away," he says with a grin.

"Thanks, Jae," I say again, this time the word carrying more weight.

He nods toward the camp. "There's a kid looking for you. Should we head back?"

"Yeah," I say, rolling my neck with a wince. "My neck's killing me from dramatically staring at the moon anyway."

He laughs and claps me on the shoulder as we fall into step together, heading back to camp.

We set up camp on the outskirts of the Isle as soon as the Allied Force found us. Borge insisted we stop to rest, his concern clearly for the people of Vereilles. He wanted them to have time to grieve their losses and regain their strength. Allied guards patrol the camp's perimeter, and for now, it seems enough to hold the fragile sense of safety together.

Jae leads me to a small tent and motions toward it. "The kid's inside," he whispers before stepping back.

I clear my throat, trying to steady my voice. "Hey, it's Rictor. Can I come in?"

The tent flap opens, and the kid bolts out, throwing himself into my arms. He's trembling.

"You're okay," I say, wrapping him in a firm hug. "You're safe, just like I promised."

"They said you died," he chokes out, his voice breaking with a sob. "I didn't even get to thank you."

"I'm right here," I reassure him, pulling back slightly to check him over. "You're not hurt, are you?"

"Mister Jihyun healed me," he says, wiping his eyes with the back of his hand.

"That's good," I say, relief flooding through me. "I'm glad you're safe."

"His name was Tumble," he says suddenly, his voice small and hesitant.

"Who?"

"The little blonde boy," he replies, looking up at me. "He was always tumbling on things."

I nod slowly, not sure how to respond. The anger I unleashed on Tholric flashes in my mind, raw and ugly. I don't want to feel that again—even if, for a moment, it felt good. "What's your name?" I ask gently, steering the conversation away.

"I don't have one," he says, shaking his head.

"Not even a nickname?"

"No," he replies quietly. "My parents died when I was really young. The man who brought me to Vereilles said I could pick my own name, but... nothing ever felt right."

I study him for a moment—jet black hair, fair skin, scars scattered across his arms and a few around his chin. His deep blue eyes catch the firelight, shimmering like ripples in water, holding a depth that no kid his age should have. He's seen too much, endured too much.

"How about River?" I suggest, the name slipping out before I can think twice.

"River…" he murmurs, testing it out. Slowly, a bright smile spreads across his face. "I like it."

The moment's warmth shatters as a woman's piercing scream slices through the camp. River flinches, his grip tightening on my sleeve.

"Stay here," I say, placing a firm hand on his shoulder. "I'll be right back." As I move toward the sound, the commotion grows louder. I see a human woman on her knees, clutching Amos's arm like her life depends on it. She's sobbing uncontrollably, her voice breaking as she begs.

"Please, my child! You have to go back and find him!"

Around her, more people step forward, their voices rising in desperation.

"My husband's still back there!" someone shouts.

"My sister—she might still be alive!" another cries out.

Amos tries to hold it together, raising his hands and speaking calmly, but his words are drowned out. The crowd swells around him, fear and frustration bubbling into uproar. Children cry, clinging to strangers, their tear-streaked faces searching for parents who might never return.

I spot Borge and Jae nearby, caught in a storm of questions they clearly don't have answers for. Both of them look strained, barely keeping things from spiraling further. The Squad arrives at my side, and it's like striking a match in a room full of gas. The moment someone spots us, the fragile balance snaps. The floodgates burst open.

"Please, help us!" someone cries from the crowd, their voice crackling with desperation.

"My son is missing—he might still be in Vereilles!"

"You're our Nobles! You're supposed to protect us!"

The shouts grow louder, overlapping into a deafening wave of panic and pleading. Their thick, cloying emotions are suffocating me.

There's no calming them. Not like this.

Jhoana steps forward, clapping her hands together as she begins to weave a spell. A soft, pulsing wave ripples outward from her hands, spreading over the crowd. The effect is immediate—soothing, like a gentle touch that eases the bedlam in their hearts.

The commotion dies down. Grief-stricken keening fades into quiet murmurs as broken, frightened eyes turn to Jhoana. Her voice is a beacon of hope in the silence.

Hush now, little one, don't you fear,
I'm always near

The words wrap around the crowd with a warmth that pulls everyone towards some semblance of calm. I freeze. The words stir something deep, something I can't ignore. When I glance at the Squad, I see it in their eyes—they know it too. Jhoana keeps singing, her voice steady and unwavering.

In the whisper of the wind,
Feel my heart under your chin

Jadis moves beside her, taking her hand without a second thought, and begins to sing along.

In the quiet of the night,
Where the stars are shining bright

Brunner and Emierr join in next, taking the girls' hands, their voices blending seamlessly into the song.

Close your eyes and let your dreams, take flight

Dustin and Sólel arrive, closing the circle as their voices join the harmony.

Hush now, little one, don't you fear,
I'm always near
In the whisper of the wind,
Feel my heart under your chin

Without hesitation, I move into the center, taking Jhoana's and Jadis's hands. The words flow from me, as if they've been waiting for this exact moment. My thoughts drift to the kids I couldn't save.

In a world beyond our sight, where our dreams weave through the night,
I will guide you to the light

Jhoana and Jadis exchange a glance, something unspoken passing between them. They fall silent, letting the rest of us take up the next line.

Even when it's pouring rain

Then, all of us together.

When the sun is out again

It feels natural, instinctive, like we've done this countless times before. The air around us hums with a power both ancient and alive. Jhoana takes the final verse on her own, her voice rising as she holds the last note.

And when the night goes on,
I'll be by your side.

The lullaby weaves around each soul standing in our midst. The crowd remains silent, their faces softer, breaths steadying. I feel it—a pulse, steadfast and rhythmic, like a heartbeat echoing through the space. This isn't just a song. It's something deeper. Something primal.

This is old magick.

Jhoana places her hands over her chest, her gaze sweeping across the crowd. She takes a slow breath, her voice soothing yet strong—the voice of a mother. "I know it's terrifying. Confusing. Devastating. You've had to leave everything behind, and along the way... you've lost people you love." She pauses, her voice catching slightly before she presses on. "I've been there. I know what that feels like."

The crowd watches her in silence.

She takes a step closer, her voice quieter now but no less certain. "But even when the light feels gone, it isn't. You saved Vereilles. You saved each other." Her words linger, offering the crowd just enough to hold on to.

The citizens glance at one another, unsure at first. Slowly, some begin to reach out, clasping hands, drawing comfort from their shared pain.

"Be there for each other," Jhoana urges. "Mourn properly. Tonight, we grieve for those we've lost."

Her words pierce the silence, and anguished cries slowly rise into the nigh sky. Grief spills from the crowd, unrestrained. They weep openly, no longer holding back the fullness of their sorrow.

I feel it too—the despair. It clings to me, pressing against my chest until every breath feels heavy. It's overwhelming, but I let it in.

Not Emierr.

I glance at him, and his face is carved from stone. His jaw is tight, his hands clenched into fists at his sides. I can see it—the way he's swallowing it all, shoving it down before it can surface.

The Squad shuffles back, obviously feeling that this shared loss was not something they should encroach upon, but my focus stays on Emierr. Without a word, he turns sharply and disappears into his tent.

What's got him so angry? I follow him, pushing through the flaps just in time to catch him muttering curses under his breath. His back is to me, shoulders tense, hands gripping the edge of a table as if it's the only thing keeping him standing.

"Meer," I say quietly.

He doesn't respond, but his head dips slightly, a subtle crack in his armor.

"Meer," I say again, this time more firmly.

He turns to face me, his expression heavy with something I can't fully read.

"I can't take this, Ricky," he says, voice low. "All those people are depending on us, and all we've done is fail them."

"I know," I admit, the words bitter on my tongue. "I'm starting to not know what to do anymore."

His eyes finally meet mine, and he takes a few sharp breaths, like he's searching for the words. But instead, he closes the distance and pulls me into a tight embrace.

I hesitate, Jae's words echoing in my mind. Then I let out a breath and accept it, wrapping my arms around him.

"Ricky," he says, his voice cracking. "I should've known what you were going through. You were..." He trails off, his grip tightening around me.

"I'll learn how to speak up, I promise." I let out a soft chuckle.

His eyes light up as he looks at me, placing both hands on my cheeks, his touch unshakeable, even as his voice trembles. "Good. Try pulling that silent shit again, and I swear I'll hurt you myself." A choked laugh escapes him.

"Deal," I murmur. "But what are you planning?"

Emierr pulls back, his expression set. "I'm done waiting. We can take him. Fuck Abbadon."

Reckless doesn't even begin to describe it. Emierr's always been impulsive, but this? This is a whole new level. Abbadon isn't just some shadowy figure in the distance—he's the root of so much pain and destruction. We don't even know what he looks like, let alone the full extent of what he's capable of in person.

My brain screams at me to stop this, to shut it down, but there's a darker part of me that agrees. We've made no progress. No victories. Nothing. If Emierr and I bring the fight to Abbadon—if we can actually end this—maybe we can stop more suffering before it spreads.

"We don't bring the others," I say, my voice low and steady. "No one else gets hurt."

Emierr smirks faintly. "I was planning to do this solo anyway." He pulls the Locus Aeterna from his pocket, the faint glow catching the light in his determined eyes. "Let's get the motherfucker."

"Meet me in the back in ten minutes. I'm going to say goodbye to the kid," I say, heading toward the tent flaps.

"Don't get attached," Emierr says, his tone oddly serious. "Less heartache."

I barely glance back, giving him a quick nod before leaving. *Don't get attached? What the hell is he talking about?* I'm not like him—and this kid isn't Sólel.

As I make my way to River's tent, my gaze flashes to Jihyun's tent. I pause. It's probably not a good idea to speak to Jihyun, or any of the Squad, but I'm surprised I haven't run into any of them yet. My legs betray me, and I end up in front of Jihyun's tent. I call out, just to be sure.

"Jihyun? It's Ricky. Can I come in?"

"Yeah," he answers.

I step through and freeze. Jihyun's sitting on his bed, but he's not alone. Maks and Mikal are here too. It throws me off for a second. They all look at me, and then Maks moves first, wrapping her arms around me in a hug. Maks has become like a little sister to me, and I didn't realize how much I needed this until now. Mikal gets up next, holding out a hand. I take it, and he pulls me in, pressing his forehead to mine. A heavy sigh slips out of me, easing the load just a little.

"I know we don't know each other that well," Mikal says quietly as he pulls back, "but you mean a lot to our mom. So, you mean a lot to us too."

I wasn't expecting that. "Thank you," I say, a genuine smile breaking through. "That really means a lot. I feel the same." I turn to Jihyun. "Can I talk to you outside?"

Maks and Mikal glance at him, concern flickering in their eyes. Jihyun nods, offering them a reassuring smile. "I'll be right back." He follows me out of the tent.

There's a pause.

"I—"

Jihyun leaps into a tight embrace. "We lost you... you..." His voice breaks, the words trailing off into silence.

"Thanks for helping save me," I say, returning the hug.

"All thanks goes to Livia," he replies, his voice heavy with regret the second the words leave his mouth. "I'm sorry—"

"No, you're good," I interrupt gently. "Actually, I need your help."

"Yeah, anything," he says with a crooked smile, though worry still clouds his face.

"I'm going somewhere," I begin carefully. "And no one knows."

His brow furrows. "Do you need me to come with you?"

"No," I say, shaking my head. "I need you to make sure the kid Dustin and I saved gets to Terrene safely."

He nods slowly, still unsure. "Okay, but where are you going?"

"Just promise me, please?" My voice hitches slightly, betraying more than I intend.

Jihyun studies me, his gaze steady, before nodding. "Alright. Just be safe." He squeezes my arm, the sensation of his fingers digging into my skin somehow comforting.

"His name is River. Just let him know I'll see him when I can. I'll keep you updated, okay?"

"Okay."

I give him a small smile, before walking away.

"Ricky," Jihyun calls after me, his voice stopping me in my tracks. I glance back at him.

"Please," he says. "Be safe."

I give him a small wave and turn away. That was harder than I expected.

I'll miss you, Jihyun. I move through the camp, keeping to the shadows and stepping as quietly as possible, doing everything I can to avoid drawing attention. Finally, I spot Emierr, crouched behind a tree, waiting for me. Without a word, we slip onto the trail, the dense woods swallowing us as we disappear into the night.

"And where are you two dumbasses sneaking off to?" Jadis's voice cuts through the quiet. She steps out from behind a tree, arms crossed, her expression unimpressed.

"What the hell? How long have you been there?" Emierr yelps.

"Long enough to hear you take a piss," Dustin answers, stepping out with a smirk.

Brunner, Sólel, and Jhoana emerge from the shadows, surrounding us like they've been planning this all night.

"How did you guys—"

"You were just going to leave?" Jhoana cuts me off.

"No one else needs to get hurt," I say, my voice hard. "No one else has to sacrifice their life for me. I can end this."

"Ricky, you're going through a lot right now," Dustin says, tone softer, trying to reason with me. "Let's figure this out tomorrow."

"There's not enough time," I argue.

"He's right," Emierr interjects. "We bring the fight to Abbadon."

"And how exactly do you plan to do that?" Jadis asks, one brow raised in skeptical amusement.

"With this." Emierr pulls out the Locus Aeterna.

Jadis narrows her eyes at it. "And what do you have that belongs to Abbadon to track him?"

Emierr freezes, his confidence faltering as he glances at me, like I might have the answer.

My stomach drops. *Damn it. Why didn't I think of that either?*

The others burst out laughing, the tension breaking for just a moment.

I shove Emierr's shoulder. "You didn't think that part through?"

Embarrassment colors his face, and he rubs the back of his neck. "I... Well... Not exactly."

"And that's why we're coming with you," Brunner says, grinning like it's the most obvious thing in the world.

"No, please—" I start to say.

"It's not up for discussion," Jadis says, brushing past me and taking the lead "We're coming."

I glance at Emierr, who just shrugs like it's out of his hands.

"What about the other three?" I ask, looking at Jhoana.

"They're staying put," she says firmly. "I'm not letting them anywhere near Abbadon." She starts walking, motioning for me to follow. "Come on, Ricky."

I exchange a look with Emierr, who sighs and moves after everyone.

I love them. I really do.

Taking a deep breath, I fall into step with the group. Sólel emits a soft, warm light, lighting the path ahead like a walking lantern. I make a mental note to call Jae and let him know what we're about to do.

"So," I say, breaking the silence. "Does anyone have anything that belongs to Abbadon?"

Emierr winces, and for a moment, I think we're out of luck. Then Jhoana speaks up.

"I have this," she says, pulling a bracelet from her backpack. "It's a Stasis Band from the facility he kept me in."

I stare at the bracelet. It looks so basic, but it's one of the worst things to happen to Ethra. "Why do you still have it?"

"I wanted to study it," she explains. "To see if there's a way to negate its effects. But it's way beyond anything this world can comprehend." She shifts her gaze to Emierr. "Can I have the Locus, cousin?"

Without a word, Emierr stretches out his hand, passing it to her.

"May I say something, *kuyas* and *ates*?" Sólel's voice drifts back to us, breaking the quiet.

"Yeah, buddy, what is it?" Dustin replies.

Sólel glances over his shoulder, the glow from his light catching in his eyes. "Now that our journey is nearing its end, I'm really happy I got to have you all around me again."

His words settle over us, bittersweet and pulling at something deep inside.

"I almost convinced myself I made all of you up at one point," he admits. "But deep down, I knew. What we had—what you all meant to me—I knew I'd see my brothers and sisters again." His voice cracks, and he hesitates before finishing. "I really do love you all. I'm sorry I didn't say it before."

"We love you, too, Sól," I say, my throat tight.

"What the fuck," Jhoana whispers from behind us.

We all spin around to look at her. Jhoana is frozen, her eyes fixed on the artifact in her hands. It shimmers, casting a pale, flickering image into the air.

Jhoana's face is fully drained of color. "No... He's back at the facility."

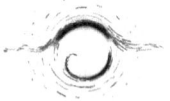

The jungle closes in around us as we circle the deteriorating, gray structure. Thick vines snake up skeletal trees, their branches clawing at the dense fog that blankets the air. The ground is uneven, littered with roots and jagged rocks, while the sounds of nocturnal creatures echo around us. This place looks like a forgotten ruin, its structure decayed and sagging. The walls are streaked with grime, and what little light the moon provides filters through cracks and broken windows, while chunks of concrete dangle precariously from above.

"Looks abandoned," Emierr mutters, squinting up at the crumbling exterior.

Jhoana glances at the Locus Aeterna in her hand. Its light pulses steadily, casting a faint glow over her features. "He's here," she says, her voice clipped.

Dustin scans the area, hand on the hilt of his blade. "Then where are the people? This doesn't feel right."

"Stay sharp," I say. "If anything happens, we move together."

Jhoana leads the way, stepping cautiously through the entrance. The remnants of a battle linger—charred scorch marks on the walls, broken weapons discarded on the floor. Dust floats in the air, disturbed only by our steps. The others fan out slightly, keeping their guard up, but Jhoana doesn't stop. The hallway stretches ahead, cracked and crumbling. Debris are scattered everywhere, and cobwebs cling to the edges of broken doors. Jhoana raises a force field in her hand, the soft glow illuminating the path as we follow behind her.

She halts abruptly, her gaze fixed down a branching corridor. The air feels heavier here.

"That's where he kept you," Jadis says quietly, her voice barely above a whisper.

Jhoana nods but doesn't look back. Instead, she refocuses on the Locus, which pulses more rapidly now. "He's just a few turns away," she says. "I've never been that far in." She glances back at us.

My lips press into a thin line. "I definitely think this is a bad idea, but let's get this bitch."

"Lead the way, cuz," Emierr says, cracking his knuckles. The rest of us ready ourselves, weapons drawn, spells at the edge of Jadis's fingertips.

We press on, the atmosphere suffocating as we near the end of the path. The Locus pulses furiously now, its glow so bright it almost hurts to look at. Finally, we reach a corridor that leads to a set of double egress doors.

"He's right in there," Jhoana says, her voice tight.

Anticipation coils in my chest like a spring ready to snap. The same tension hangs over the Squad, every emotion palpable—fear, adrenaline, determination. Is this where it ends? Jhoana pushes the doors open, the bang echoing down the empty halls. The room beyond is massive—a cafeteria, judging by the scattered remnants of tables and chairs. Moonlight streams through the broken ceiling, illuminating the space with an unsettling glow. In the center of the room sits a wooden throne-like chair, facing away from us.

The Locus Aeterna falters, its image flickering before disappearing entirely.

"That's not creepy," Brunner mutters.

The chair creaks, the sound deafening in the stillness. A chuckle echoes through the room, low and mocking. "Finally." The voice is round, deep, laced with scorn. "I almost thought you wouldn't come back here, Jhoanalyn." A hand rises from the side of the chair, waving lazily. Then the figure stands, stepping into the moonlight.

Abbadon.

His face is grotesque—purple veins web out from his hollow eyes, and his skin is sickly pale, almost translucent. It's like he's aged decades beyond what he should have. His movements are confident despite the apparent decay of his body, and it's clear he's enjoying every moment of this.

"Your parents kept their promise, after all," he sneers at Jhoana. "We never found you... until now."

Energies crackle to life around us, everyone poised to attack.

"It's been so long, Allied Organization Squad." His voice echoes through the cavernous space. "You've all grown up... exactly as I remember it." He coughs, the sound wet and grating.

What does he mean by that?

"It's rude not to greet an old friend," he chastises us mockingly. "I did watch over all of you. Well... five of you."

"Fuck this," Emierr snarls as thorny vines slither from his cuffs.

I grab his arm. "Wait. He's taunting us. He wants us to fight him."

"Good," Emierr snaps, wrenching free. "I'll give him one hell of a fight."

Abbadon smirks, his eyes briefly darting to the shadows above before settling back on Emierr. "Are you just going to stand there, or are we going to do this?"

Before I can stop him, Emierr charges, and the rest of us prepare to follow. But something catches my eye—a flicker of movement on the second-floor railing above. Shadows shift and take shape.

"Wait!" I shout, but it's too late.

Blood spears tear through the air, pinning Emierr upright with brutal force. His pained cry echoes, then abruptly cuts off.

"No!" I scream, reaching out, but the world around me bends and distorts, folding in on itself. My vision warps, and in an instant, I'm pulled back—to the moment I grabbed Emierr's arm.

What just happened?

"Good," Emierr says again, his voice repeating the words like an echo. "I'll give him one hell of a fight."

Déjà vu crashes over me, the same events playing out before my eyes. "This happened already!" I whisper under my breath.

Emierr dashes, and the vision floods back—the blood spears. Acting on instinct, I lunge forward, deflecting them before they can pierce him. They ricochet, slamming into the walls.

Abbadon grins wide.

"Just as you said," a woman's voice calls from the shadows. "He and his Scream will be a problem." A ghastly cloud begins to descend, swirling as it drifts toward where Abbadon stands. As the dark smoke dissipates, the voice is given a face—a sharp, haunting beauty framed by shadow.

Jadis's breath catches. "It's her," she whispers, the words barely audible. "It's Evanora."

Jhoana's face pales, her expression frozen in disbelief.

Evanora steps fully into view, her appearance mirroring Abbadon's—dark, web-like marks stretch across her skin, but she doesn't look as ravaged as he does. Still, there's something chilling about her. They both barely look human, and it's more terrifying than I could've imagined

"Ah, little duck," Evanora smiles at Jadis, showing far too many teeth. "The Supreme herself graces us with her presence. Tell me, have you lived up to the title you stole?" Her eyes slide over to the Squad, lingering just long enough to make everyone tense.

"And Jhoana," she says, her voice softening into something far more dangerous. "How are Mom and Dad? Still keeping the family proud?"

And just like that, it's as if the air is ripped from the room. I don't need to look at everyone—I feel it. The rage, burning like an old friend, consuming the Squad. The energies cocoon around them and me. It's the same overwhelming force I felt when I fought the Vermillion Sages.

Sólel bursts into solar light, the room flaring briefly as the Squad surges forward. But something shifts. My gaze darts to the corners—figures shrouded in a color like blood in water, soundwaves rippling outward from their palms.

I spot the projectiles too late. They launch from every direction, metal bands latching onto the Squad's hands. I shove the ones heading to me with a burst of force, but they recoil, faster than I expect. Cold, unyielding metal wraps around my palms, locking tight. The moment they snap shut, I feel the severance—a clean break between me and Aigerim. The others are already looking at their hands, panic etched into their faces.

"I can't use my powers," Dustin says, his voice tight with panic. The Squad each tries again, desperation now fueling their movements, but there's no luck. The bands on our hands jerk, pulling us toward each other until they snap into place, locking tight.

I pull at the bands, expecting nothing—but resistance pushes back. The bands tremble slightly against the magnetic pull locking them in place. My telekinesis still works. Somehow, it's not suppressed. The realization sends a thrill through me, but I force my expression to stay neutral. Better to play along, and wait for the right moment to act.

The masked figures step closer, as Abbadon and Evanora's laughter echoes through the room. The Squad shifts collectively, their backs pressing against mine as we form a tight defensive semi-circle, with me at the center.

"Whose bright idea was this again?" Jadis hisses, her voice biting.

"See? What did I tell you?" Abbadon says, derision dripping from each syllable, casting a glance at Evanora, who leers at Jadis with smug satisfaction. "Predictable as ever. Always playing into my hands. Just like before."

"We have them, Abbadon. Let's prepare for the Convergence," Evanora says, cutting off his supervillain monologue in her cold, commanding voice.

"You're always in such a hurry, aren't you?" Abbadon laughs, the sound echoing off the broken walls, wild and unrestrained. "Can't we enjoy the moment? I do love playing with my food." His gaze sweeps over us, pausing on each of us like we're mere pawns in his game. "It can't hurt for them to know. After all, they'll be dead by daylight."

"I'll make you pay, Evanora!" Jhoana shouts, her voice shaking with fury. "For my parents—for everything!"

"Enough of that!" Abbadon's voice booms, filling every corner of the room like thunder. He strides closer, his presence pressing down on us. We huddle closer together. My focus darts between the masked figures around us and Abaddon.

"You all look the same," he says, his gaze cutting through us like a blade. "All those years ago, you just didn't know when to quit. And now, here we are. I thought bringing you to Ethra would change things—give you a chance to rewrite your fate. But no. Seven pieces on the board, each of you playing your part. And yet, the end never changes, does it? The collapse... inevitable, no matter how you fight it."

"All this time, I was terrified of you," I say, my voice steady despite the fire in my chest. "All I knew of you was fear and destruction. But now that I'm looking at you?" I scoff, the laugh bitter in my throat. "I don't know if I should laugh or pity you. You're just a badly drawn anime antagonist who probably needs to get laid."

"Ricky!" Jadis hisses, snapping her head toward me. "What the hell are you doing?."

Abbadon smirks. "There's the Rictor I remember," he says, his tone patronizing but pleased. "I was starting to think you'd gone soft. Your *Pa* dying wasn't part of the plan, but you're welcome. He didn't die completely, as you know."

He's baiting me, trying to get under my skin. *Not today.*

I edge closer to Jhoana, keeping it casual, almost absent. A quick flick of her eyes meets mine—barely a glance—and she shifts just enough for me to telekinetically unzip her backpack. Smooth, quiet, no room for mistakes.

Abbadon continues, "Your *Pa*... Now there was a man who understood the value of sacrifice. You're a lot like him, Rictor—willing to give everything, even when it's not yours to give."

His words catch me for a second. *Don't let him get to your head.*

Focus, Ricky. I nudge Jhoana's bag with my mind, coaxing the contents to lift and float just enough to peek out. A coin, a broken necklace, and a folded piece of paper. Finally, I find the Stasis Band and carefully slide the other items back, keeping every movement subtle.

"I'm going to enjoy killing your dad first," Abbadon says, his words slashing through my concentration. "Then I'll deal with the rest of you."

The Stasis Band hovers just within reach.

The masked figures close in, their movements swift and synchronized. I focus on the bands restraining me, willing my power into them. I push, straining against their grip until, with a crackling surge of energy, I tear them apart. My hands splay open as a force explodes outward, slamming the masked figures into the walls. They crumple to the ground like broken marionettes.

Without missing a beat, I seize Abbadon with my telekinesis, freezing him mid-step. Before Evanora can react, I snap my right hand toward her, sending a crushing invisible force that hurls her backward. She slams into the wall with a sickening thud and slumps to the concrete floor, unconscious.

I glance at the floating Stasis Band, then flick my head toward Abbadon. It zips through the air, wrapping tightly around Abbadon's wrist, locking into place. His eyes widen, the smirk wiped clean off his face.

"All I need is to touch him," I say, turning to the Squad. "And we'll get all our answers."

The masked figures recover quicker than I anticipate, lunging toward us again—but not with blood magick. Why not?

The Squad moves as one, kicking, shoving, and blocking their attacks, giving me the opening I need. Abbadon struggles against my telekinetic grip, but it's useless. I reach for him, my fingers trembling as they near his forehead. His eyes lock with mine, a flicker of amusement dancing across his face.

My hand makes contact.

The world twists and collapses around me, my vision snapping into chaos.

I'm standing somewhere unfamiliar. The skies above are torn open, jagged cracks bleeding light and shadow. The air reeks of death and despair. My shirt and arms are soaked in blood—too much blood. Around me, crimson splatters stain the ground. Just ahead lie mangled bodies, torn limbs scattered among the carnage, unrecognizable at first glance. But as I stare, their faces come into focus—eyes wide, mouths agape.

It's the Squad.

No.

My knees give out, and I stumble back into reality, yanking my hand away from Abbadon. I hit the ground hard. The vision lingers, vivid and searing, clawing at my sanity. I look around my surroundings. It's over. The Squad is floating in the air, unconscious, their arms stretched above their heads like puppets on a string.

Abbadon's voice pierces through my disorientation. "You wanted a peek inside my head, but instead, you saw the truth—what you did to your precious Squad." He waves toward the masked figures. "Take her too," he says with a nod toward Evanora before turning his attention back to me. One by one, the Squad is dragged out of the room, leaving me alone with Abbadon.

He glances down at the Stasis Band on his wrist and sneers. "Figures. Your powers aren't bound by magick." His words are laced with disdain. "Do you get it now? You're nothing but a parasite."

His words fester inside me like poison. I crawl back, still shaken, the image of my friends' butchered bodies imprinted into my mind.

"Do you ever wonder, Rictor, what it would feel like to stop? To let it all go? You could. Right now." Abbadon says softly, his tone almost... kind. "No more pain. No more guilt. No more running. Just quiet."

I blink, thrown off balance. Is this a trick? A distraction? But he sounds so... sincere. Like he understands something no one else could. The words settle uncomfortably in my chest, stirring something I can't quite name.

"I know how much it hurts, Rictor. I've seen it. You don't have to fight anymore."

For a moment, the fight drains out of me. The anger, the determination—it's all swallowed by the exhaustion. The temptation to give in, to let go, tugs at me, pulling me closer to the edge. But then I see it—that flicker in his eyes. Not pity. Not kindness. Satisfaction. He's savoring this, watching me unravel. My chest constricts, anger sparking back to life. He wants me to give up. He wants me to break.

I grit my teeth, forcing the words out. "I'm not done yet."

The bands tighten around my wrists, lifting me into the air. They force my arms apart as if trying to tear me in half. Pain lances through me, white-hot and excruciating, ripping a scream from my throat. And for a fleeting moment, it feels disturbingly familiar—the agony, the pull—like I've been here before, like I've already lived this.

Then, suddenly, the pressure on my left hand vanishes. My body sags, my weight now pulling against the remaining band. Blinking through the haze, I look down and spot Jihyun below. His hands glow softly, radiating a calming light as leaves swirl around him in a vibrant, living halo.

Relief washes over me in a crashing wave. "Jihyun," I rasp, my voice barely audible.

He doesn't hesitate, launching razor-edged leaves at Abbadon, who evades them with an unsettling, almost inhuman grace.

Come on, Ricky! Fight! Electricity surges to my fingertips, crackling with intensity. A scream rends my throat as I thrust my free hand forward, unleashing a bolt of lightning that arcs straight for Abbadon. Just before it connects, a shimmering force field materializes, absorbing the attack. My eyes dart to the back of the room, where raised hands glow with a sinister purple light. Evanora. She's back.

I glance at the band still clasped around my right hand. Gritting my teeth, I clench my fist, channeling the electric current coursing through me. Sparks flare and crackle, growing brighter until, with a sharp burst, the band shatters into fragments. Gravity takes hold, but I manage to levitate. I try to move, to fly, but I remain suspended, stuck in place. Why can't I control this?

"Ricky!" Jihyun shouts.

Amethyst fireballs streak toward me, their brilliance piercing the darkness like molten gemstones. Panic surges, and instinct takes over. I force my hands downward, lightning crackles out in a ragged burst. The force propels me toward the ceiling, flames erupting below in a cascade of light and heat.

Duh dumbass, the Law of Inertia.

I hover above the chaos, catching sight of Jihyun battling Abbadon and Evanora. They dodge and block his attacks with ease. He's holding his own, but it won't last.

I dive toward them, unleashing a burst of energy that blows Abbadon and Evanora away. Without hesitation, I grab Jihyun's arm, hoisting him onto my back.

"Hold on!" I yell.

He locks his arms tightly around me as I propel us toward the solid metal wall, my hands positioned like I'm diving. Lightning wraps around my fingers, humming with sharp, electric chirps. Its energy slices through the barrier, blowing open a hole as we burst through. Fire erupts behind us, molten metal dripping and sparking in our wake.

"Oh shit!" I shriek as momentum hurls us through the jungle canopy. Branches crack, leaves shred, and we tumble, slamming into the ground with a bone-jarring crash.

Groaning, I try to shift, but a red hot pain rips through my leg. My breath catches as I look down—*oh fuck, is that my femur?* My head drops back to the ground, a wave of nausea churning in my stomach.

Jihyun crawls toward me, his right arm twisted at an unnatural angle. His face tightens in pain, but the injury doesn't slow him down. His left hand begins to glow, that familiar aqua hue radiating around it as he mends his broken arm. The bones realign with a sickening pop, his arm twisting back to normal.

"Your leg," Jihyun says, his voice trembling as his eyes dart to the gruesome injury. He begins weaving a spell, intricate and advanced—far beyond anything I've learned from Jadis and Jhoana. The bone shifts, knitting itself back together. I bite down hard on my hand, the pain ripping through me like nothing I can put into words. It's excruciating, clawing at every nerve. "There," he says softly, his voice steadier now. "You're good."

I take a shaky breath, grabbing his shirt and pulling him into a tight hug. My chest heaves, overwhelmed by relief and gratitude. "Bitch," I mutter, my voice barely steady. "I'm so damn glad you're here."

He chuckles weakly, wrapping his arms around me. "Lucky for you, I don't know how to quit."

Run, Run, Run!

The tunnel stretches ahead, flickering lights splitting the darkness, my shoes echoing against the metallic floor.

"Okay," I gasp, throwing a glance at Jihyun as we round a sharp corner. "Maybe going with 'What would Emierr do?' wasn't our brightest idea."

"Bright? Try suicidal," Jihyun mutters, barely dodging a low-hanging pipe. The scrape of metal against his skin makes my spine tingle. "Next time, let's not channel the guy who has literally used himself as bait."

We reach a fork in the tunnel—left or right? No time to think. I shut my eyes and force myself to focus. I push the noise out—shouts, boots, the clang of distant footsteps. The connection comes faintly at first, like a whisper in the wind. Then stronger. Warmer. Assuring. *Them.*

My eyes open. Faint trails of smoke twist through the air, each hue alive with its own rhythm—soft blue for Jhoana, fiery red for Jadis, pure white for Dustin, glowing orange for Brunner, and two shades of green, earthy and luminous, for Sólel and Emierr—guiding us left. I glance at Jihyun. His own aura shimmers around his head—a soft, light aqua glow, radiating like heat. *The colors of their auras... They're the same as their magick.*

I jerk my head to the left.

Jihyun doesn't question it. He runs his hand along the wall, transforming the metal into a barrier of cascading foliage that hardens into razor-sharp blades, sealing off the tunnel behind us. He dams the right path just as quickly.

We take off down the left path. Through labored breaths, I say, "God, I love your power."

"Tell me that when we're not running for our lives," he snaps, but there's the faintest edge of a smile.

"Ric—" Dustin's voice crackles through the comms, barely audible over the static. "You—hear— Ricky, are you there?"

I skid to a stop. "Dusty, I hear you!"

"Fuck yeah, it still works." There's a pause, then his voice booms, "I got him, guys! I got him!"

"Jihyun's here—he saved me," I say, glancing back at him, but he's busy scanning for our next move.

"He's *what?*" Jhoana's voice cuts through, furious.

"We're coming. Hang tight," I say, brushing past her question, locked on the task ahead.

"No pressure," Dustin says, his tone light. "But I did overhear them saying they're taking us somewhere else soon."

Before I can respond to his poorly timed joke, a sudden gust of wind slams into us, cutting me off and throwing us both backward. My feet scrape against the metal floor as I fight to stay upright. Ahead, a satyr steps into view, his arms outstretched, spirals of blood swirling around them like crimson ribbons. The wind is suffocating, howling in our ears as we struggle to push forward, but it's too strong.

Then, another figure appears—a second Sage. I don't know what type of leyfolk she is, but with unnerving calm, she drags a blade across her palm, the blood pooling and taking on a dim glow. She presses her hand to the ground, and red spreads in dark, rippling patterns that crawl up the walls and floor. My stomach knots as I watch it snake toward Jihyun.

"Move!" I yell, but it's too late. From the sticky spirals, something sharp bursts out and latches onto his wrists like shackles. His eyes widen in shock, a gasp ripping from his throat. He's yanked off his feet, his boots scraping against the blood-slicked metal floor as he's dragged backward. The shadows swallow him whole. He's gone.

"No!" My voice cracks as I raise a hand after him, but the wind surges again, pinning me in place.

I grit my teeth, focusing on the satyr. *Enough of this.* With a sharp jerk of my head, I shove a wave of energy straight at him. He stumbles, the wind faltering for just a second—enough for me to throw my arms back and hurl them forward, sending a crackling wave of force down the tunnel. The blood recoils, splattering against the walls, and the Sage stumbles, her footing briefly lost.

"Please, stop! I don't want to hurt anyone!" I beg, my hands sparking with electricity. It reflects in the dim glow of the crimson on the walls.

The Sages exchange a glance, their expressions unreadable. A surge of raw emotion—confusion, loathing, despair—slams into me like a physical blow. I stagger, groaning as my knees give out, collapsing onto the cold floor. Panic claws at my chest, but it's not mine—it's theirs.

The noise swells as two more Sages step forward, their masks smooth and unreadable. Their emotions collide, overwhelming my senses, turning my mind into a warzone.

"Ricky! What's going on?" Dustin's frantic voice breaks through the static, pulling me back from the edge.

"It's... It's too much," I gasp, clutching my head as my ears start to ring. "I can't, Dust... I can't take in all their—!"

"Breathe." Jhoana's voice glides in. "Slow and steady."

I can't. My breaths come in quick, shallow bursts as a chilling thought claws its way into my mind. Of course, Abbadon knows. He knows too much about us—about *me*. My powers, my weaknesses, everything. He's turning my own abilities against me, using them to tear me apart from the inside.

And then, through the noise, something unexpected cuts through—a melody.

Dustin's voice, singing.

It slices through the chaos like a ray of light, pulling me back to solid ground. I stifle a laugh. It's like I've been dropped into one of those musical episodes from a TV show. As his voice swells, pitchy and confident, the panic starts to fade, giving way to something steady and assuring. It's the song I clung to in seventh grade, the one I listened to on repeat until the words were practically etched into my brain.

"What the hell are you doing?" Jadis enters the chat, teetering between disbelief and mirth.

"Music calms him down," Dustin says. "I thought his favorite song might snap him out of it." Without missing a beat, he starts singing again.

To my surprise, Emierr joins in as a harmony.

"Oh, for fuck's sake," Jadis scoffs.

When the chorus hits, Dustin belts it out with the intensity of someone singing for their life. "Loooove!"

Before I even realize it, the word rips from my own lips. The noise splinters, the pile of the emotions shifting. They're still there, but they're no longer drowning me—they're fuel. I push myself to my feet, the world snapping into focus.

"Loooove!" I shout, the word pouring out of me like a battle cry.

The Sages falter, their masks tilting slightly, confusion rippling through their stances as I half-yell the rest of the song. It's the opening I need. The energy surging through me erupts, and with a sharp flick of my hands, they're hurled backward like ragdolls. They slam into the walls, pinned in place as if ensnared in an invisible web.

Get the Squad first.

I push forward through the tunnel, keeping my eyes locked on the faint smoke trails of the Squad's auras. Dustin, Emierr, and Brunner's voices carry alongside me, but I don't let myself slow. Every step brings me closer to them. Closer to getting us out of here.

Every masked figure or O'rian that crosses my path falls—some struck by force, others by the lightning now crackling through my veins. The thud of bodies hitting the ground and the distant echoes of impact meld with the melody in my ears, forming a rhythm I can't ignore.

When I reach the chamber where the trail ends, a group of masked figures bars my way, blood spiraling like serpents around their arms. I don't waste any time. With a sharp thrust of my arms, the force blasts them back against the massive metal doors. They hit the ground in a heap, unconscious.

Electricity crackles in my hands, lightning twisting around my fingers like living threads. I slam my palms against the door, the metal shrieking under the pressure as it bends and warps. With a final surge of energy, I rip through it, tearing a jagged hole. I spread my hands wide, and the edges groan in protest as the opening pulls apart, creating a gap large enough to step through.

I walk into the room, the bright white walls glaring under the harsh lights. It's spacious, sterile, and disturbingly familiar—almost identical to the lab where they tortured me on the Space Ring. My chest tightens, memories clawing at the edges of my mind, but I shove them back. Not now.

The Squad is on me in seconds, pulling me into a tangle of arms and relief. For a brief moment, I let myself breathe, grounding in their presence.

Jhoana steps back, brow furrowed. "Where's Jihyun?" Her eyes dart to the doorway behind me, searching like she expects him to appear any second.

"They took him," I say, the words like ash in my mouth. The relief in the room evaporates.

Jhoana's face hardens, but she doesn't press me. I take her hand, the Stasis Bands around her palms unnervingly cold. "This might hurt a bit," I warn, tightening my grip.

She nods once, jaw set. I charge the bands with a surge of electricity, feeling sparks jolt between us. She winces, a sharp intake of breath escaping her, but the bands crack and release, clattering to the floor. I turn to free the others, each of them cringing and yelping through the jolts of electricity.

"Electrokinesis?" Jadis asks, a flicker of intrigue in her voice as she tests her magick.

"Looks like the near-death experience came with a free upgrade," I say, trying to lighten the mood, even though my chest feels like it's being crushed.

Jhoana flexes her hands, her expression unreadable, then suddenly grips my arm, her fingers digging in. Her voice is low, but filled with steel. "Where'd they take him?"

I glance at my friends' faces, each one of them ready, trusting me to lead. But all I can see is the image burned into my mind—their bodies, twisted and lifeless, piled like garbage. It's not real, not yet, but it could be. I saw it in *his* memories. My stomach churns. My hands shake.

"Ricky?" Jadis's voice snaps me back. She's gripping my arm, her jaw clenched. "What happened with Abbadon?"

I shake my head, swallowing hard. "Nothing. I almost had him, but Evanora saved his sorry ass," I lie, my voice steady enough to sell it. Before she can press further, I turn my back on her, closing my eyes and reaching out for Jihyun's safety net. There—faint but present—the aqua trail tugs at me, guiding me forward. There's no way I'm telling them what I saw. Not now. Not ever, if I can help it.

"Let's get Jihyun and get the fuck out of here." My voice edges out with more bite than I intended. No one argues.

The trail pulls us into a tight tunnel ending in a curved steel door. Before I can even reach for it, Jhoana charges ahead, her force field slamming into the metal like a wrecking ball. The door bursts open, revealing a cluster of scientists hovering around Jihyun, who is strapped to an operating table. His body lies motionless, his face pale—like they've already stolen the fight from him.

Jhoana doesn't give them the chance to react. Her hands fly up, and glowing force fields streak across the room, slamming into the scientists with explosive force. The air vibrates with the impact. No one's getting up from that.

"Oh my god," Jadis whispers, her hand flying to her mouth. The others stand frozen, their eyes wide with horror. The only sign that Jihyun isn't dead is the meager rise and fall of his chest. It isn't until this moment that I understand what the void of stolen magick feels like. His body no longer emits those beams of calm, sun, and love. Instead, I can feel the smallest echo of the vacuum of space—magick's death rattle, clawing for salvation.

"Ricky, help me!" Jhoana calls, already at Jihyun's side. I rush over, my heart pounding as I see the straps biting into his wrists, leaving deep red marks. Electricity snaps at my fingertips as I grab the Stasis Band locked around him, sending a sharp jolt through the device. It emits a metallic pop, and clatters to the floor. Jihyun groans softly, his eyes fluttering open. He's dazed, but alive.

"They used some device. They—" Jihyun starts, but his voice trails off. "I'm sorry, Mom."

"I've got him." Sólel gently lifts Jihyun, wrapping an arm around his shoulders. Solar energy radiates from him, seeping into Jihyun. The color begins to return to his face, and his breathing steadies.

Jihyun exhales a deep, relieved sigh.

"How did you do that?" Emierr asks, his gaze fixed on his brother.

"The energy of the sun flows through all living things," Sólel replies with quiet modesty. "I can share it, which enhances the energy of those around me."

"What about taking energy away?" Dustin asks, his curiosity sparking a ripple of interest through the group. The idea of draining someone's energy... It sounds almost like blood magick.

"Emergency lockdown," a calm, mechanical voice announces, the words echoing ominously through the room. A second later, shrill alarms blare, the building itself preparing for battle.

"That's definitely not good," Brunner mutters, glancing around.

"Do we even know the way out?" Emierr's voice wavers, the edge of panic creeping in.

"We'll make one," Jihyun says. He pushes himself off the table, and the fire in his eyes is unmistakable. He's pissed.

We tear through the tunnels, running like our lives depend on it—because they do. Jihyun shoves his hands forward, pushing against the metal walls as we go. The smooth surfaces ripple and burst apart, transforming into pathways lined with crumbling leaves that crunch under our feet. My focus sharpens into three vital thoughts: Break through. Find a hallway. Get to the sunlight.

As we pile into a corridor, my eyes immediately catch the metal door on the left. It's slowly grinding down, threatening to trap us inside.

"There!" I shout, adrenaline surging through me as I push us forward. But before we can reach it, a figure sprints into view from our right. My blood runs cold.

Abbadon.

His arms swirl with blood, the liquid twisting and hardening into long, razor-sharp spears.

"Run, run, run!" I yell.

Brunner takes the lead, shooting a look over his shoulder at us. "Hold onto each other!" he shouts.

We grab hands, forming a chain. Abbadon's rust-hued spears shoot forward, closing the gap between us. I can feel the heat of the air splitting around them. Brunner screams, and in a blink, everything ripples. The hallway stretches and folds like warped glass, pulling us out of one space and slamming us into another.

We land on the other side of the door, just as the spears crash into it, their impact a revoltingly wet splatter. I stagger, catching my breath, and look around. We stand on a narrow ledge, still holding hands, at the top of a spiral staircase that winds down and out of sight.

We're in a cave? The cavern below us is massive, and its entrance sealed by a towering, white gate whose surface streaked with pale grooves that reflect the dim light.

"Hold on," Brunner says. Before anyone can question him, the world ripples again, and suddenly we're on the ground, at the base of the stairs. Through the gate's partially translucent surface, Abbadon's piercing gaze locks onto us.

Then, as if by some unspoken agreement, we all raise our middle fingers in perfect unison.

Abbadon smirks, a flicker of amusement crossing his face, before shaking his head and turning away, disappearing from view.

Jihyun reaches out for the gate's odd, wood-grain texture, and presses his hands against it, but nothing happens. His fingers trail along the strange, organic patterns, his expression tightening with frustration. "This..." he murmurs, glancing around the cavern. "What is this place?"

Without so much as a gesture, we all move, like a single, unspoken instinct pulling us forward. The Squad's in sync, just like me—tapped in, no hesitation. Electricity crackles between my fingers as I charge my hands. If touching it won't work, maybe this will. I slam them against the door, timing my strike with the others. The instant we make contact, an invisible force erupts outward, throwing us back. I hit the ground hard, pain shooting through my shoulder. I grit my teeth, swallowing a groan.

"That didn't fucking work," Jadis mutters, shaking it off.

"They're going to send more O'rians to attack us," Jhoana warns, her eyes scanning the area. "Everyone, get ready—"

"No," Sólel interrupts, his gaze locked up on the door we came through. "I can sense their life energy. They're fleeing this place." His golden eyes snap back down just as the PA system comes to life.

"Warning! Warning! All personnel evacuate the building immediately. Facility eradication will proceed in two minutes." And, with maddening, robotic calm, the countdown begins.

"Shit," Emierr snarls. "He's fucking blowing us up!"

My fists clench, fury rising through my blood. *Abbadon.* The bastard's gone past unhinged—he's willing to destroy this entire place just to rid himself of us.

"Rune, you need to blink us out of here!" Jhoana says, voice laced with urgency.

Brunner glares at the gate, jaw clenched. He narrows his eyes, weighing his options, before shaking his head. "It's too thick," he mutters, frustration creeping in. "I'm not sure I can even get through it myself, let alone bring all of us. We'd be stuck in there—I'm not risking it."

"Then the Teleportation Spell!" Jihyun suggests, his usual calm slipping.

"Ricky doesn't—" Jadis begins.

"He has to," Jhoana bites out.

It's magick or cremation.

"Form a circle!" Jadis commands, clapping her hands together as she begins weaving the spell.

I hesitate for a heartbeat, doubt clawing at my mind, but there's no time for it. We gather in a tight circle, the air around us growing dense.

"Think of the Great Eagle Fields," Jadis says, her voice steady as her fingers weave the signs in the air. "Where we used to play. Picture it clearly in your mind and clap your hands together once you have the image."

Jhoana turns to Jihyun. "I brought you and your siblings there—you know this place."

Jihyun nods, closing his eyes. His expression softens as he pulls the memory forward. One by one, they clap their hands, their auras glowing brightly, their energy swirling together like threads of light.

I squeeze my eyes shut, willing the image of the fields into my mind. But the only memory I have is from watching them play on a screen in my room on the Space Ring, their laughter echoing like it belonged to another world.

I clap my hands.

Nothing.

I try again.

Still nothing.

"One minute to facility eradication..."

"Ricky!" they all shout, the terror in their voices growing with each lethal second that ticks by.

"I don't know!" I yell, my hands trembling. "I can't do it!"

"A moment," Jihyun says suddenly, his voice calm. "A moment that felt like magick. That's all you need." He smiles, and the noise around me quiets.

I close my eyes, searching. The smell of Ma's spaghetti fills my senses—sweet, tangy, a taste of home. Pa's there too, grinning, his voice warm.

"Try it, anak." A tear slips down my cheek, and I can't help but smile.

"Three... two..." The countdown echoes through the cavern, each number landing like a punch to the gut.

I smash my palms together, and this time, they glow with a radiant gold. The air around us compresses, pulling inward like we're being swallowed by a black hole. The noise, the light—everything warps and disappears.

My feet hit soft grass, and I stumble back, gasping for air. I open my eyes and find myself staring up at the Space Ring, towering above, its metal gleaming against the teal sky.

The break of dawn stretches over the horizon, casting a muted glow across the fields. Distant rumblings echo through the air, jolting me upright. My heart pounds as I spot the explosion in the distance, smoke rising in a twisting column.

"Bitch, I did it. I used magick," I pant, wiping the sweat from my brow. My hand swipes over my bracelet, activating the comms. "Guys? Are you safe?"

"Hello?" Jihyun's voice crackles through, staticky but still clear enough.

"Jihyun," I say, relief flooding me.

"I'm sorry. My mind was racing, and I thought of Maks and Mikal. I'm back on the trail where the camp was," he says, voice tight with exhaustion.

"Thank the Tree," Jhoana sighs. "Just get to safety."

"I'll catch up with them and let them know where you are," Jihyun says. I can hear the note of suppressed anxiety in his voice. "Stay safe, all of you." The line cuts off.

"Ricky, where are you?" Dustin's voice crackles.

"I'm at the fields, I think," I reply, scanning my surroundings.

"We see you," Brunner says. "Turn around."

I whip around and spot all six of them in the near distance. Relief crashes over me and I dash toward them. "Holy shit, that was close!" I gasp, throwing my arms around Jhoana.

"You did it," Jhoana says, her smile warm and proud. "You used magick."

Jadis lets out a laugh of pure relief. "What memory did it for you?"

"My mama's spaghetti," I admit, feeling my face heat up.

"That *is* magickal," Brunner says seriously.

"Ricky?" Jae's voice crackles through the static. "Can you hear me?"

"Jae. We made it out. We're all okay," I say, exhaling as I glance at the Squad for reassurance.

"Did—ny—te—you?"

"What?" I frown, eyebrows furrowing as I glance back at the Squad. "Guys, I can't understand him. Help me out." I swipe down on my bracelet, linking the Squad to the call.

Jae's voice is still garbled, words lost in the static.

"Jae, you're cutting out," I say, trying to keep the note of frustration from my voice.

Then his voice comes through, sharp and clear: "Fleming has been compromised. The O'rians have overtaken them."

I freeze as the words sink in. My gaze snaps upward as the Space Ring lurches, its massive structure beginning to spin the wrong direction.

What in the actual fuck.

"They've announced the Convergence," Jae says, his voice hollow, as if all hope has drained from him. "A part of me was hoping you all were just talking crazy, but it's real. They're waging war on the six nations, Ricky."

Did Papa give them the shard? Did he really mean what he said?

"What about the citizens in Fleming?" Jhoana asks sharply.

"We don't know what's happening up there anymore," Jae admits. "The Fleming Allied Force is gone. Our last contact reported that Dr. Hutton is calling for a surrender."

"Wolfgang?" I blurt out, surprised. "He's leading? He hated everyone in leadership, from what I remember."

"Yes," Jae replies curtly. "Guys, there isn't much we can do. The Allied Force is stretched too thin across every nation. We won't make it to Fleming in time."

"We have to help them!" Jhoana says, turning to all of us, her eyes blazing.

"Noble Jhoana, trust me, I'd be there in a heartbeat if I could," Jae says. "But the whole world is in chaos right now. We have to protect what we can down here."

"And who protects the people up there?" Jhoana fires back.

As much as I don't want to go back to the Space Ring and face all the trauma waiting for me up there, I can't stand here and do nothing. There are so many innocent people, people who didn't ask for this. They don't deserve what's coming for them.

"We do," Sólel agrees. "We're the front lines now, and we can help by evacuating the citizens. How many escape pods are there, *Kuya* Ricky?"

"They made sure there are enough for every citizen to flee, if it ever came to that," I reply, mind already working in tandem with his.

"Then that's our plan," Sólel says, conviction ringing in each syllable. For so long, it felt like we had our little brother back, but in this moment, I see the man Sólel has become.

"If you can evacuate the citizens, I can convince Captain Kaelor to agree to move them to safety. I'll head to the Great Eagle Fields with an armada of transportation once everything's in place," Jae says, the barest trace of hope reemerging.

"What about the nations? Aren't they going to help?" Emierr asks.

"Zaltana would help—the Space Ring is their sister nation," Dustin offers.

"I'm sorry," Jae says, his voice heavy. "The nations are choosing to protect their own. They're opening their borders for any refugees but the Allied Force is all you have right now. I have to go. Good luck, my Nobles."

"Thanks, Jae," I say as the line cuts off.

"Okay, so we go in, save the people, and get out. Simple enough, right?" Brunner's tone betrays his nerves.

"Not quite." Jhoana's eyes move to meet his. "There are nine sectors and only seven of us."

Jadis closes her eyes. "We'll have to split up. It's the fastest way to get everyone out."

"I can cover two sectors," Sólel offers without hesitation.

Dustin, Emierr, and Brunner exchange worried looks. Splitting up again—it feels like a death sentence. My mind races, and I know what has to be done.

"And how exactly are we stopping the Convergence?" Brunner's brows draw together in a tight knot.

I don't need to dig into their emotions for this—I know. We all know. It's been sitting in the air between us, unspoken, for a while now.

"There's only one way now," Emierr says grimly, breaking the silence.

My jaw clenches as I give a tight nod.

"But," Jadis hesitates, her voice faltering. "That means..."

"Are we seriously blowing up the Space Ring?" Dustin's voice rises, a mix of disbelief and anger, as his gaze locks on mine.

"Is *that* what we're thinking?" Brunner cuts in, his expression tightening as he rubs his forehead. "Blow up the Space Ring *we're going to be inside of?*"

I meet Dustin's gaze, ignoring the waves of Brunner's panic lapping at the edges of my mind. "We both know what happens when the accelerator goes—our parents' work made that clear. It'll take the whole Space Ring with it."

"That's your home, Ricky. Jho's too." Dustin eyes flick between the two of us.

Jhoana exhales, her shoulders stiffening. "A place doesn't make a home, Dusty. It's the people in it. Right now, that means getting everyone out alive."

"It's Vereilles all over again," Brunner mumbles.

"Look, I never wanted any of you here to begin with. The risks were always too high. If you want out, I understand." My voice is steady, but inside, I'm bracing myself. They've already sacrificed so much. If someone has to stay, it has to be me. Livia gave me this second chance—I won't waste it.

"You're a smart guy, Ricky," Jadis snaps, her voice dripping with exasperation, "but you've been saying some really stupid shit lately."

The bluntness silences everyone, and even the tension in the air falters.

"You really don't get it?" Jadis plants both hands firmly on my cheeks, forcing me to meet her gaze. "We're not leaving without you. We get home together—that's the promise we made. To our families, to Gordo. It means *all* of us."

"Do you need us to hug you again?" Brunner quips, trying in vain to lighten the mood. .

Tears sting my eyes. These stubborn assholes. "All right, then," I manage, a small smile breaking through. "Let's get to work." But before we can move, I notice Sólel's gaze is fixed on the sky, his expression dark and unreadable. "Sól, what's wrong?" I ask, the knot in my stomach twisting tighter.

His voice is low, almost hollow. "Has the Fleming Space Ring always looked like that?"

We all look up. My stomach churns, and the sight knocks the air out of me. An unmistakable structure—a cannon of sci-fi proportions, its massive eye rolling in our direction.

I was just a kid, sitting with the Huttons, joking about building something like the Death Star from *Star Wars*—a planet-sized world destroyer. Only this version wouldn't destroy worlds; it would sit on the Space Ring, protecting Ethra from deadly asteroid impacts. It was a joke—a stupid, childish fantasy. I even laughed at the thought, imagining a giant eye on the Space Ring, ready to obliterate asteroids.

But now...

This isn't my imagination. Somewhere along the line, in our thirty-two year absence, they'd actually built it. "That's... an asteroid destroyer," I rasp.

LIKE STARS ON ETHRA

"**D**estroyer? Let's get the fuck out of here, *now!*" Brunner shouts, panic lacing his voice.

"No!" I yell, shaking my head. "If that thing hits Ethra, it'll tear the world apart. The energy from something that massive is too powerful. We have to stop it."

"How do we stop a blast that can destroy asteroids?" Dustin asks, disbelief thick in his voice.

"Me," Sólel says.

"What? No." Emierr steps in front of him, blocking his path. "It's too dangerous."

"I'm the only one who can handle it. Trust me." Sólel replies, his voice firm, and walks past him. He's not wrong—he might be the only one who can face a force like that head-on. But he has a family, a kid on the way. I'm not sure I can let him sacrifice that. Not because of my mistakes. He lowers himself into a cross-legged position, pressing his fists together. "I need to recharge." Solar energy flickers faintly, seeping into his skin, each pulse growing stronger as it builds.

Above us, the cannon begins to glow. We're out of time. "Fuck, I think they're going to fire it," I shout, unable to tear my eyes from the emerald light shattering the sky.

Jadis and Jhoana exchange a look, a silent understanding passing between them.

"We'll hold it off as long as we can," Jadis nods. She weaves the shield spell, pushing her hands forward. A massive barrier forms around us, shimmering like molten glass. Jhoana steps beside her, cracking her neck before adding her own force field. The barrier thickens, glowing brighter as it expands.

"I need more," Sólel mutters, his voice strained. "It's not enough."

"There's no more time!" Dustin looks up, terror distorting his features.

"Gather around Sól!" I snap, moving into action. The boys move without hesitation, forming a tight circle around Sólel. "All living things have energy," I repeat Sólel's words from a few moments ago. "The Healing Spell. We can transfer our energy to him."

"Like charging a battery—genius." Brunner grins.

"Then I'll borrow a trick from Jihyun," Emierr says, placing his hands on the ground. Roots begin to snake from the earth, curling themselves around Sólel.

"Let's fucking do this," Dustin mutters, rolling his shoulders

Please work! Filipino spaghetti! Filipino spaghetti!

We clap our hands in unison, weaving the Healing Spell. Our energy floods into Sólel, and Emierr's roots begin to glimmer, amplifying the flow of power. Sólel's body flickers, his form glowing brighter as he begins shifting into his light-forged state.

A piercing whistle cuts through the air, and in an instant, the laser collides with the shield around us, sending tremors through the ground, splintering cracks streak across the barrier.

"How the fuck do they know exactly where we are?" Brunner shouts.

No... he wouldn't. But all that time—could he have hacked my bracelet? Pa wouldn't betray us... betray *me*, right?

"It's too much, it's not gonna hold!" Jhoana screams.

I feel the heat of the blast pushing against the shield, threatening to rip it apart.

Sólel transforms fully, just as the force field explodes.

Time stretches, the world around me slowing as Aigerim's energy rolls across me again. I see it—Brunner yanking Emierr and Dustin out of the way, Sólel pushing himself off the ground, and the girls dangerously close to the blast.

Then, everything snaps back into motion. Brunner blinks out with Emierr and Dustin. In one swift move, I'm behind Sólel, spreading my arms to rip the girls out of the way. Before I can grab hold of them, Jhoana turns her body into water, slithering to safety. Jadis snaps her wings open, and she propels herself upwards, her body arching gracefully against the force of the blast.

The laser's green light floods my vision, searing everything in its path, and for a split second, I wonder what it will feel like when it consumes us. Sólel rockets forward, his arms outstretched, solar beams roaring to meet the oncoming blast.

A pair of arms locks around me, and the world distorts, glass bending like elastic. In a heartbeat, we're a few meters from the blast zone, safe for now.

Sólel is actually fighting the Space Ring, pushing against the laser—and winning. He soars skyward, his energy slicing through the beam.

But he doesn't stop there. The pillar of golden light keeps pushing back against lethal green, relentlessly pursuing the source.

"No!" I scream as Sólel's light tears through the eye of the destroyer.

"Oh shit!" Dustin shouts, his voice echoing in my ears.

The explosion blossoms across the sky like a second sun, igniting the heavens. I stumble, watching fragments of the Space Ring tear through the atmosphere. They blaze like stars on Ethra, leaving fiery trails across the horizon.

"Ricky." Jae's voice chokes over the comms. "Tell me that wasn't you."

"What have I done?" The static of Sólel's voice is barely audible. "I couldn't stop it."

I watch the Squad, their eyes fixed on the Space Ring, faces weighted with the same grim realization. What the fuck did we just do?

"Jae.… They fired the laser directly at us—it would've destroyed Ethra if we didn't stop it." My eyes stay locked on the debris streaking down, dying embers scattering through sparse clouds.

"The whole world is watching, Ricky."

The Squad turns to me, silence stretching between us. They're bruised and bloodied, but still standing. Their eyes hold the same fire I feel—we've still got some fight left in us. I cling to that spark and let it take over.

"We're going up," I say, my voice resolute. "We're stopping the Convergence."

No one hesitates. No one says a word. We're ready to face what's coming.

"The Allied Force is with you," Jae says, his voice steady now. "My dad would be proud of his heroes. Good luck, brother."

"So, teleportation spell?" Brunner suggests.

"Not this time." Sólel shakes his head. "I've never been up there. If I try, we could all end up splintered."

"Splintered?" Brunner tilts his head.

"If I can't envision the destination clearly, the spell tears us apart—literally. Rips flesh and bone until it forces us into a location. I've seen it happen once, and I'm not risking it."

"Yeah… maybe not," Brunner mutters, hesitating. "Then how are we getting up there?"

"We fly."

Jadis folds her arms, raising an eyebrow at me. "Okay, that works. But, uh, what about the no oxygen part?"

Emierr's face lights up. "I can plant seedlings on you guys—create a pocket of oxygen for you to breathe in."

"That's actually... not a bad idea." Jadis squints at him.

"Then I'll bubble us," Jhoana chimes in. "Keep the oxygen contained."

"Now we just need a way to move the bubble through space," Brunner says, wrinkling his nose.

"I guess that's where I come in," Sólel volunteers without hesitation.

"Okay." I pause, glancing at each of them. This is it—no turning back. "We stick together." I launch myself forward, each step propelled by bursts of telekinetic force, lifting me off the ground and driving me against the whims of gravity. Beside me, Jhoana glides along the terrain in her liquid form flowing like a seamless stream. The grass rising beneath Emierr's feet carries him in a singular, smooth motion while Brunner and Dustin charge ahead, their eyes alight with the strength of their bonds, movements perfectly in sync. Above us, Sólel streaks through the sky, radiant energy trailing behind, shadowed by Jadis's flaming wings, shimmering in the morning light.

It's just like when we were kids—running through the meadow with the sun on our backs—but this time, it isn't laughter carried on the wind. It's a promise.

"We rule Ethra!" I scream, the words echoing like they did all those years ago. "And nothing crushes us!"

Emierr tosses a fistful of seeds over his back, and they erupt into life, sprouting branches that coil around his torso. The vines extend outward, forming wings as leaves unfurl along them like feathers. With a single powerful flap, he ascends into the air, his figure silhouetted against the blazing horizon. Emierr's hand stretches down just as Brunner takes a running leap, grasping his hands midair, soaring toward the decimated cannon's eye.

Jhoana conjures stepping stones from thin air, each platform glinting as she leaps higher and higher into the sky. Jadis and Sólel streak past like shooting stars. Lightning crackles at my fingertips, and with a push, I propel myself upward, the static charge lifting me off the ground.

Dustin leaps and I reach out with my mind, catching him mid-fall, and pulling him above me with a precise mental tug. The cold wind lashes at my face as we ascend. Around us, debris cascades in a deadly rain, jagged pieces spinning and whistling through the air, narrowly missing their mark.

I feel it—the air tightening around us. The pressure shifts abruptly, a sharp reminder we're climbing too high. My breath grows shallow.

"Come to me!" Jhoana calls, standing on a glowing platform thousands of feet in the air. One by one, we converge around her. As Jadis and Emierr land, their wings dissolve into nothingness.

"Okay... That's really fucking high," I mutter, glancing down as my knees threaten to give out.

Emierr moves quickly, placing a small handful of seeds on my shoulders. The seeds sink into the fabric of my jacket, taking root as if they've found fertile soil. Within seconds, tiny sprouts emerge, curling upward and releasing a soft, shimmering mist. The air around me feels lighter, fresher, and I catch the faint scent of leaves after a storm. A small cluster of translucent petals blooms near the base of the sprout, pulsing gently as it emits oxygen. One by one, he works his way through the Squad, the subtle glow of his power fading as the plants settle into place, their rhythmic motions matching the rise and fall of our breaths.

"Ricky, hold us together," Jhoana shouts, fighting against the wind.

I reach out, my mind tethering to each of my friends, pulling us into a single orbit. Together, we levitate, and a massive force field erupts around us, its surface rippling like molten, scaly glass.

"Where's Sól?" Emierr glances around frantically as the bubble hovers in midair. A sudden surge beneath us answers his question. Sólel ascends, pressing firmly against the bubble's base. We break through the stratosphere, the blue dissolving into the infinite black of outer space.

I glance at Sól, his face shadowed with grief, but unwavering in focus. "Sól, can you breathe?" My voice feels muffled, distorted in the strange stillness of space.

"Somehow, yes," he replies evenly, his energy rippling as he pushes us toward the blast site.

The eye of the Space Ring looms ahead, pulsating with the energy that almost destroyed us. This is it—where we either stop the Convergence or lose everything.

Our bubble drifts along a steady path, guided by Sólel through the debris-cluttered void of the Space Ring. Fragments of metal and glass strike Jhoana's force field, each impact sending faint vibrations rippling through the barrier. Around us, flecks of golden dust float, eerily still. Sólel's jaw clenches, eyes wide as he scans the wreckage.

"All these souls," Sólel murmurs over the comms, his voice barely above a whisper.

Jhoana's gaze softens, a flicker of shared understanding in her eyes. "Sól, grieve later. We have a job to do," she says, though the faint tremor in her voice betrays her unwavering demeanor.

"Little brother," Emierr calls gently.

Sólel glances back at us, his expression torn. After a moment, he nods, his resolve hardening. He floats back toward us and resumes pushing the bubble forward, navigating through the obliterated remains of the Space Ring's center. Twisted beams and shattered panels line the corridor ahead, a graveyard of destruction. Everything and everyone here—gone.

We reach a sealed door, its sleek metal surface unmarred by the chaos outside. It scans us, a green sensor flashing at the top, and with a hiss, the door opens. We're pulled inside by a sudden rush of air, the door sealing shut behind us with a resounding slam. Sólel lands gently on the ground, shifting back to his human form.

He exhales, shoulders sinking. "The air's fine," he says, relief thick in his voice.

Jhoana drops the force field, and we all take slow, measured breaths. The air tastes sterile, metallic. It's the first moment of stillness we've had since the laser fired. I glance around at them, their faces etched with exhaustion but still holding a fierce determination.

"We're in Sector 3," I say, glancing at the number on the wall.

"Sector 1 isn't far," Jhoana says softly. She doesn't need to say it aloud—I know who's in Section 1. Albert. The Huttons. I don't want to face them—Not like this.

"You guys hear that?" Brunner asks, tilting his head toward a nearly inaudible noise. At first, it's just a whisper of sound, but then it swells—distant cries and screams. He strides to the far end of the corridor, his hand hesitating over the panel. With a sharp press, the door slides open, and mayhem rushes in.

People and leyfolk—hundreds, maybe thousands—flood in, their faces pale, their voices rising in desperate cries. The streets churn like a frantic river, fear spilling in every direction.

How the hell are we supposed to get everyone out of here?

I let out a sharp breath. "Stay in constant communication. The O'rians are here, so don't drop your guard. I'll handle this sector. Now go!" My voice comes out steady, but doubt twists in my gut like a knife.

They exchange glances, a knowing look passing between them.

"Go," Jhoana says with a small smile. "Save the Huttons and Al."

"We've got the rest," Jadis adds.

"We're right behind you," Dustin says with quiet reassurance.

I nod, though uncertainty gnaws at me. Am I ready to face them? Their faces flash through my mind. I don't know what I'll say, but one thing is clear: I won't let them get hurt. If I can do one good thing today, it'll be this.

Without another word, I turn and sprint toward Sector 1. I leap into the air, electricity snapping between my fingers. *I'm coming.*

As I soar above the pandemonium, the devastation unfolds beneath me with gut-wrenching clarity. The Space Ring groans under its own weight—metal beams buckling, entire structures collapsing into jagged heaps. The Quantum Plaza lies in ruins, its once-brilliant lights flickering weakly through clouds of rising smoke. Among the wreckage, flashes of crimson catch my eye. *Vermillion Sages.*

A booming voice reverberates through the Space Ring, halting me mid-air.

"Attention, fellow citizens," Dr. Wolfgang's voice echoes, softer than I remember, yet commanding enough to give everyone pause. "We've done everything we can to hold the intruders back, but now you must evacuate immediately. Escape pods are ready. Leave everything behind and go! Help one another as your neighbor, protect each other. This is not the end. We can always rebuild. *We are the fifth nation,* and we're not going out without a fight."

The announcement cuts out, replaced by a chilling countdown.

"Warning: Self-destruct sequence initiated. Detonation in 1 hour. Evacuate immediately. Repeat—1 hour to self-destruct."

Did I hear that correctly? Dr. Wolfgang is the one sacrificing the Space Ring? The Huttons practically built this place—it's their legacy, their obsession. They've always been about science above all else, even if it meant torturing a child under their care like I was just another experiment. And now they're ready to blow it all up? I don't know... I don't know how to feel about this. Maybe Albert was right. Maybe they've changed. Maybe, for once, they're actually putting people first.

Citizens scatter like startled birds, their panic threatening to drown me. I mentally hum my middle school favorite song—it's a ridiculous habit, but it works.

"You guys hear that?" I call through the comms, dodging a falling beam.

"Goddammit, we really can't catch a break!" Brunner snaps, frustration bleeding through the static.

"Listen, once your sector is clear, get out," I bark, weaving around a crumbling wall. "Do not stick around, you hear me?"

"Got it," Jadis replies.

"I'll clear faster if Ricky stops yelling at us," Dustin mutters, his tone half-joking.

"Dusty, I forgot how bad you are at being serious," Jhoana says, letting out a breathy chuckle despite the tension.

"Hey, stress relief is my magick," Dustin fires back.

"We should all definitely take a shot after this," Emierr adds with impeccable timing.

A chorus of groans reverberates in my ears.

"We seriously need to talk about your commitment to booze," Brunner says.

A laugh escapes me despite myself. "Just keep moving, idiots."

I land firmly, steadying myself. "This way!" I yell, guiding the frantic crowd toward the sector's docking station. My voice cuts through the chaos as I lift debris, pull people to their feet, and clear paths for the injured, every motion fueled by urgency.

As my eyes sweep over the turmoil, they land on a corridor at the far end of the plaza—the way to the Terrarium. *Al.* Without hesitation, I take off, dodging and weaving through the citizens. My heart pounds wildly as I push through the shattered entrance, his name already spilling from my lips.

But it's not Albert I find.

"Miss Delphini?" Her name barely escapes past the lump in my throat as I catch sight of her in the dim light, surrounded by toppled biome pods. She turns sharply at the sound of my voice, soot streaking her face, her expression softening the moment recognition dawns. Time has worn on her, just like it did with Mama. Without a word, she rushes forward and wraps me in a tight embrace. It's brief but heavy, like it's been waiting for decades.

"I knew it," she says, her voice trembling. "I knew you would come back. I knew you weren't dead. I'm so sorry. I'm so sorry for all of it."

Before I can respond, the sound of footsteps behind us pulls me out of the moment, and I instinctively step back from her. Dr. Wolfgang emerges, his face pale, his eyes bloodshot.

"My love, it's time to go," he murmurs, but then his gaze lands on me. His entire demeanor shifts. His lips tremble, and wide, tear-filled eyes hold mine. He takes a few unsteady steps forward before collapsing to his knees.

Miss Delphini rushes out of the room, with a quiet, "I'll be right back." The sharp click of her heels fades as she leaves us alone.

"I'm sorry," he whispers, his voice raw and broken. "I'm so sorry for what I did to you, Rictor. I let science blind me. I can never undo the pain I caused." His shoulders shudder, and he buries his face in his hands, choking on his words. "I never should have let it happen. Never."

I glare at him, anger flaring in my chest, but as I study his trembling form, I see it—the regret etched into every line of his face, the unfettered truth in his broken posture. Against all odds, I understand. I let out a slow breath, the crackle of lightning in my veins quieting.

"I forgive you," I say, my voice low, even surprising myself. "But forgiveness doesn't erase what you did."

He lifts his tear-streaked face, his eyes swimming with a bittersweet mix of gratitude and sorrow. He collapses into another wave of sobs, his words tumbling out between gasps— insisting he doesn't deserve it. After a tense pause, I reach out, pulling him to his feet.

"I forgive you," I say, my voice firm, final.

He wraps his arms around me, tight but warm, his trembling grip carrying a lifetime of guilt and relief.

I embrace him.

Miss Delphini reappears, wiping her eyes, clutching a sleek black case to her chest. "We built this for you," she says, her voice soft. "Before the experiments, before everything went so wrong."

"You always wanted to be with them, your friends. Maybe this can atone for even a fraction of what we've done." Dr. Wolfgang squeezes my hand, then places the case into my grasp.

I hesitate before accepting it. "Get to the escape pods," I say. "Leave this place."

Miss Delphini's face clouds with concern. "What about Al?" she asks, her voice trembling.

"Where is he?"

"He went to retrieve all our research, everything about the Space Ring," Dr. Wolfgang explains. "It's in the safest place we could think of—Aigerim's chamber."

I exhale a heavy sigh. Of course, it had to be in Aigerim's domain. The last time I saw him, he bonded with me, and now, with the revelation that Crown Beasts can hear our thoughts, one question gnaws at me: *How much does he hate me?* God knows I'd hate having a one way radio tuned to my cesspool of emotions.

"I'll get him. Go. Now."

They don't think twice before obeying this time.

I open the case, staring down at its contents, uncertain of what I'm seeing—a chip? Or something that only vaguely resembles one. Tentatively, I reach for it, and the instant my fingers brush its surface, it activates. A surge of energy courses through me as the material spreads rapidly, encasing my body in a seamless flow. It shifts, morphing into sleek, advanced armor—nothing like the bulky mech suits used in the matches. This is something else entirely... nano tech body armor?

My thoughts scramble to catch up as the armor hardens, yet remains weightless, like I'm not wearing anything at all. I glance down at my hands, shimmering in gold and silver, the intricate designs casting a slight glow.

Badass.

"Squad, listen up. Get to the escape pods. Leave. I'm right behind you—I just need to grab Al, then we're out."

Jhoana's voice comes through, tight with concern. "Ricky, don't do anything stupid."

"Just go," I reply, cutting the line before anyone can protest.

The tunnel to Aigerim's chamber is eerily quiet, the destruction muffled, almost like a distant memory in this part of the Ring. Nothing's changed—not the oppressive stillness, not the faint stench of the pipelines that clings to the air. I reach the end of the tunnel, where the same massive black metal door looms, etched with glowing rune symbols. It groans open at my touch, the sound echoing through the darkness. Inside, the room is pitch black, save for a faint light flickering at the far right. It draws my eyes to Albert, hunched over a console, his hands moving frantically as he loads data onto a hard drive.

"Al!" I call out, my voice cutting through the dark. He doesn't respond. "We have to go. Now."

"I got it!" he shouts, holding up the hard drive triumphantly before turning, his face suddenly twisting in alarm. "Who are you?"

I raise my left hand, sparks of electricity crackling to life, illuminating the room in sharp flashes.

"Ricky!" His eyes widen in recognition as he sprints toward me, throwing his arms around me in a tight embrace. "You came! Have you seen—"

"Already handled," I interrupt. "They're on their way to an escape pod."

He pulls back, scanning the suit I'm wearing. "They gave you the suit." His eyes light up with awe. "It's the only one of its kind. It's also a fully functional space suit."

"Great. You can explain all its features after we're far away from this detonating death trap."

Before we can take another step, a voice cuts through my mind—a low, guttural growl that freezes me in place.

"Rictor."

I freeze. *Aigerim.*

"What is it?" Albert's voice wavers.

"The Crown Beast," I say, my tone clipped. "Give me a sec." I start moving through the dark room, each step instinctive, like I already know exactly where to go.

"You are never quiet. Always thinking, always moving. Do you know how exhausting that is?" The primal voice resonates in my mind.

I stop, turning slowly, holding my ball of lightning aloft. And there he is—caged but commanding, his glowing eyes locked on me. The faint luminescence of his black fur gives him an almost spectral quality.

"I'm sorry," I whisper, my voice shaky. "I'd get tired of listening to me too."

He growls, low and deep, a sound that vibrates through me. *"On the contrary. I understand your pain. Your anger. Your loneliness."*

My throat tightens, a raw ache rising with the weight of yearning. He's been trapped here for so long, carrying a pain that would have destroyed me. I take a step closer, my hand instinctively reaching toward the cage. The air hums with a sharp current—I can feel it, the cage is electrified. Without hesitation, I grip the bars. The jolt surges through me, but I don't pull away. Instead, I focus, drawing the electricity into me, letting the charge dissipate until the air stills.

"You can use my powers. Why didn't you just break yourself out?" I ask, my voice tinged with confusion.

Aigerim's gaze is piercing. *"Your kind has always believed I belong in this cage."*

"That's not true, not for me. No one deserves to be trapped." I take a breath, my guilt pressing down. "I'm sorry I didn't save you before. But I'm here now." I step back, extending my telekinetic grip to the bars. With a sharp, decisive pull, the cage shrieks and bends, metal warping and twisting as I carve a path to freedom. "Come on. Your brothers and sisters are looking for you."

Aigerim's eyes widen, and for the first time, I catch a flicker of gratitude. He steps out, his towering presence radiating power. It's overwhelming, but I stand firm, unshaken by the fear his form inspires.

"Get on," he growls, his tone leaving no room for argument.

Before I can respond, I feel myself lifted into the air, landing firmly on his back. He moves with startling grace, charging through the room. Albert comes into view, his eyes wide as he shouts in alarm, but Aigerim effortlessly scoops him up, placing him behind me.

"I got us a way out," I tell Albert, glancing over my shoulder.

He doesn't reply, just clings to my shoulders, grip tight.

The world blurs around us as Aigerim races through the shattered remains of the Space Ring, his powerful strides carrying us through the destruction.

"Let's feel the wind, together," He echoes in my head.

As we hurtle through the wreckage, a sharp whistle slices through the air. A sudden gust of wind strikes, throwing Albert off Aigerim's back. He tumbles to the ground, landing with a choked gasp.

"Al!" I spin around, my eyes locking on a figure emerging from the debris—blood coiling menacingly around their arms. I leap off Aigerim, ready to face the scum, but a chunk of the ceiling breaks loose, hurtling toward Albert. I'm too late—there's no way I can stop it.

Aigerim springs forward, shielding Albert with his body as the rubble crashes down.

"No!" I cry out.

"We're fine," Aigerim's voice echoes back. *"On your left."*

The Sage strikes, crimson spikes protrude from the ground, directly at me. The mecha suit responds instantly to my rage. Its nanotech ripples across my body, the armor lifts from my hands, forming massive fists that crackle with latent energy. I punch my fists at the Sage, the nano fists shadowing the movement, breaking through the attack and unleashing a telekinetic force that sends the Sage staggering back. The suit shifts and twists with my movements, creating extensions—blades, shields, even a massive hammer-like construct that smashes through their defenses. *Where the fuck was this when I was twelve?*

Just as the Sage unleashes a flurry of blood tendrils from their back, an explosion shatters the ground beneath us. The deafening blast robs the air from my lungs, and the entire structure collapses into the void, sucking all sound into its vacuum.

In an instant, the suit reacts, encasing my body completely and forming a helmet over my head. I gasp and realize—I can breathe. I steady myself amidst the chaos whirling around me, and frantically scan the void for Albert.

My heart lurches. There he is, drifting farther away, his face contorted in silent terror.

"Al!" I scream, my voice raw as I reach out with everything I have. The suit senses my desperation, its surface rippling and snaking outward like liquid metal. With a sharp mental command, I will it to envelop Albert, molding around him, forming a protective cocoon that seals him from the lethal conditions outside the Space Ring.

I feel the shift immediately—the suit's oxygen redirects to him. My chest tightens, my breath vanishing as the air drains away.

My jacket fights to keep me warm, its heating systems working overtime, but the relentless cold of space is winning.

Third strike. Is this really where it all ends for me?

Albert stirs, taking jagged, panicked breaths before his eyes lock onto mine. "Ricky, no! You'll—this suit—it has to be you!" His muffled voice carries weakly within the warped suit, but I can't respond. I can't move.

My vision blurs, darkness creeping in at the edges. Just as the cold overtakes me, a brilliant, sparking light erupts below. Aigerim.

Lightning sparking beneath his legs.

"Ricky, I'm here," Albert shouts, his voice trembling as he grabs onto me, clutching the fur along Aigerim's neck. With the last ounce of strength I have, I latch onto Albert. The suit snaps back to me in an instant, and I gasp sharply, filling my lungs with precious air.

"Al..." I breathe, meeting his eyes. He smiles softly, his grip tightening around me.

Aigerim's voice rumbles through my mind. *"Hold on, Rictor. I have you both."* With a surge of power, he propels us forward, his massive form weaving through the debris as we descend toward Ethra.

The atmosphere embraces us in a fiery cradle. Fragments of the Space Ring streak past, glowing trails against the morning sky, accompanied by hundreds of escape pods drifting toward Ethra.

I watch as Albert gasps, air flooding back into his lungs. Above us, the place we once called home burns, reduced to ruins. I glance at Albert again—his eyes fixed on the Space Ring, silent tears streaming down his face.

"Aigerim," I rasp. "The fields—land there."

"I know," Aigerim replies, a flicker of amusement lacing his calm tone. *"Your thoughts are never quiet."* Lightning snaps under his paws as he moves with unmatched swiftness, weaving through falling debris. The sunlight glances off his sleek fur, its warmth a stark contrast to the exhaustion pulling at my body. *"Appreciate the upgrades,"* Aigerim rumbles, his voice surprising me with its dry humor.

As we near the ground, his movements slow, his descent measured. He hovers briefly, then lands lightly in the ground. Around us, citizens recoil in fear, their steps hesitant as they take in Aigerim's towering form.

I slide off his back, my knees buckling as I hit the grass. My comm statics to life, and I clutch at it, my voice hoarse but steady. "Guys? Did you make it?"

One by one, their voices filter through, each reply flooding me with relief.

"The pods are landing all over the nations," Emierr reports. "Some here, some in Zaltana, Verglas—thousands of them. Ethra's about to get real crowded."

My body shakes with relief as I take in the scene around us. Space Ring citizens huddle together, their faces etched with confusion, fear, and uncertainty. There are so many of them. Their emotions roar like an unstoppable current, dragging everything in their path.

"Absorb it all, Rictor," Aigerim's calm, steady voice rumbles in my mind. *"Do not suppress what you feel. Embrace it, but do not let it consume you. Become the observer, not the receiver."*

My eyes close and I do as he says. I focus inward, separating myself from the flood of emotions. The noise gnaws at me, but I pull back, detaching myself. I imagine the emotions swirling around me like a gentle breeze—not touching, not consuming. They're close, yet they no longer dictate my mind. For the first time, I sense my own aura—a protective bubble, broken but resilient, shielding me from the tidal wave of pain surrounding us.

Then, something shifts, cutting through my focus.

A deep rumble pulls my eyes upward. One end of the Space Ring erupts in a blinding explosion, shockwaves rippling through the sky. Cries and screams erupt from the crowd, a chorus of fear that cuts straight to my core.

"The Huttons," I breathe, my chest tightening. My gaze snaps to Albert as he slides off Aigerim, his face mirroring my panic. "Al, can you see them?"

Without hesitation, I launch into the air, scanning the sea of faces below. I hover, eyes darting frantically from one person to the next, desperate to find them. But the crowd is vast, a blur, and I can't pick them out.

"Ricky, we see you," Jadis's voice breaks through, but I barely register it.

I drop back to the ground, legs buckling. "What if they're still up there," I choke out, tears streaking my face. "I couldn't save them—"

"Ricky!" Albert's voice cuts through my spiraling despair.

I turn toward him, confusion giving way to disbelief as I see the wide smile on his face. He's staring past me. Before I can process it, familiar arms wrap around me, their warmth pulling me back from the edge.

"Ricky. You made it." Dr. Wolfgang's voice, full of relief, registers in my ears.

"Thank the Tree, you're safe." Miss Delphini's voice trembles as her embrace tightens.

Relief pours out of me. As I sink into their arms, memories flood my mind. Miss Delphini and me laughing under the sweeping lights of the Skywalk. Another flashes through—Dr. Wolfgang and me, shouting ourselves hoarse during the cyber boxing match of the year. The last one lingers the longest—the three of us crammed into that tiny restaurant, plates piled high with unlimited Crawdelou sweet meat, our laughter rising above the clatter of dishes.

The moments were fleeting, but I can feel it now—the depth of their affection for me. Not just past tense. They truly care for me. My heart softens, ready to let them back in.

Al hands over the hard drive. "Everything is in there."

"Thank you, Al, for everything." Dr. Wolfgang takes the device with a fragile smile.

"The storage on that thing must be massive," I joke, swiping at the tears streaking my face.

"It's what's inside that really matters," Miss Delphini replies softly, taking my hand.

"It's not just our life's work—all of our happiest moments with you are here," Dr. Wolfgang's voice trembles. "We couldn't bear to lose them—or you."

Just as I'm about to respond, Papa's voice cuts through, clear, as if he's standing right next to me. "Rictor James? Can you hear me?"

"Pa?" My breath catches. I scan the crowd even though I know I won't find him. "Where are you? Are you okay?"

"I'm right here, watching the world below," he replies, his tone calm, though it sends a knot twisting in my gut. "I've really left Wolfgang with no choice, haven't I? They don't even know who I truly was but they were good to you weren't they?"

"Pa." My voice cracks, panic rising. "Get yourself out of there, now."

"It's not worth it, to sacrifice a world for another. I'm doing the right thing," he says, but more to himself than to me. "Since the day I was pulled into Ethra. It was all about coming back to your mama and you. The Convergence was the answer. I thought—" His voice falters, cracking in a way I've never heard before. "I thought it was my way home. But now I see what I've done, and this... this is the only way to stop it. Abbadon will never reach Earth."

"No! I'm coming!" My voice breaks as I leap into the air, lightning sparking along my hands, pushing me higher and higher. "You don't have to do this, Pa! We can get out of here together. We can go home. Mama's waiting for us!"

For a moment, only the sound of rushing wind fills the silence. Then his voice returns, softer now, like he's smiling. "You're so much braver than I ever was, *Anak*. I'm proud of you—for being everything I couldn't be."

The air thins, and the helmet snaps into place around my head. "Please... Don't say that. You're my hero, Pa. We can fix this. Just—"

"I'm proud to have a son like you," he interrupts gently. "A good kid. And a loyal friend. I'm sorry I wasn't there for long enough... That I couldn't be better for you. I wish... I had more time." His voice wavers. "I love you, *Anak*."

"Say it to my face, Pa!" I scream, my voice cracking under the strain. "Don't leave me—please!" The Space Ring looms above, broken and teetering on the edge of oblivion. The entire structure trembles, seconds away from tearing itself apart.

I'm almost there. I can save him. I have to.

"The O'rians are bringing an army. You have to get everyone to safety," his voice trembles, but it doesn't break. "I'm sorry, *Anak*. Sorry for the things I never said, for the answers you deserved but never got. I never wanted to fail you, but I did. I left something for you, under the table in the basement—it's my last gift. I hope it gives you what I couldn't." His breath hitches, and I feel it—his pain, his regret. "Goodbye, *Anak*. You've always made me proud. Take care of your mama for me. Astralis."

The air stills. And then, my world shatters.

"Papa!"

The explosion engulfs the Space Ring in a blinding flash, and the deafening silence tears through the air like the universe itself is splitting apart. The shockwave slams into me, ripping the air from my lungs. I'm spinning, hurtling uncontrollably, my body weightless as the utter silence begins to suffocate me.

I stabilize myself with telekinesis, stopping the chaotic tumble long enough to lock onto the Space Ring. I reach out, as if Papa's hands will appear out of nowhere to take mine—but only the void reaches back. My heart breaks all over again, this time for good.

The Space Ring convulses in a blaze of fury. I watch it collapse—space folding inward, pulling the entire structure into a singularity. The Ring implodes, vanishing into nothingness.

Then, darkness.

When I come to, there are arms wrapped around me. I'm on my back, cradled like a child. I manage a soft smile. *Papa saved me.*

My vision sharpens, and Brunner's face comes into focus, his eyes red-rimmed. He doesn't say anything, just holds me tighter.

Above us, the sky is clear. The Space Ring—the place I called home—lost to the infinite darkness.

"It's gone," I whisper, my voice hollow. "He's gone."

ONE LAST MISSION

I force myself to stand.

My body feels heavier than ever, but my legs obey with Brunner's steady support. The Squad are a few paces away, all huddled together in frozen shock. Sólel lingers just behind them, his head bowed in quiet reverence. Maks, Mikal, and Jihyun are wrapped around their mother like a shield. Their hollow eyes meet mine briefly before looking away.

Jae and Borge stand a little off to the side, heads bowed, while Amos grips his chest, his gaze fixed squarely on me. Understanding my pain, even if I can't feel it right now.

Albert and the Huttons approach cautiously, like I'm made of glass, like one wrong word or step will shatter me. But I don't feel fragile.

I don't feel anything.

It's all a blur, a mess of screams, chaos, and death.

The words I need come out of nowhere, automatic. "My Pa told me one thing before he..." My voice cracks, but I push through. "The rest of the O'rians are on their way. With an army."

That snaps everyone back into motion.

"Jae, Borge," I say. "Get the Allied Force. Start relocation procedures immediately. Every squad we have to spare needs to get these people out of here—now."

They nod sharply, no questions asked, and start barking orders. The hum of urgency spreads through the air, a buzzing I can feel in my chest cavity.

Turning to Albert and the Huttons, I speak quickly. "You'll be safer in Terrene. It's where I was kept safe when I... ran away." The words stick in my throat, but I swallow them down. "Find the chief and chieftess. They'll protect you." I flag down an Allied Force member to serve as their escort.

"What about you?" Albert's voice shakes.

"I'm done running. Just... trust me." They pull me into one final hug before the soldier shepherds them away. Time feels both too fast and too slow, like I'm running in place. My head spins as I try to keep up, but then another overwhelming fragment of reality hits me.

Today is the day they pull the plug on Jhoana.

A hand grabs mine, pulling me back. It's her. Jhoana. And behind her is the Squad. Their faces drawn tight with exhaustion and defeat.

"Ricky... you can cry. Even just for a second. *Feel.*" Jhoana's voice is soft, almost pleading.

I pull my hand away. "There's no time to grieve. Just like you said to Sól."

She looks away, her composure slipping.

"You need to choose, Jho. Now. Stay, or come back with us?" *Stop talking dumbass!*

The Squad stares at her, wide-eyed.

"You're staying?" Jadis's voice breaks.

"Jho..." Brunner breathes, his voice edged with disbelief.

"She hasn't decided yet," Maks says, trying to diffuse the situation. "She thought... At first, she thought she didn't want to. But now..." She looks at her mother, unsure if she should continue.

"I don't know anymore," Jhoana sighs. "Being with all of you again... I don't know. I have a life here. I have my kids. What would I even be going back to? Gordo? My parents? A world I don't recognize anymore? A body that's probably too atrophied to even function anymore?" Her voice falters, and she glances at her children, taking in the way Maks clings to Mikal like a lifeline, while Jihyun stands a little apart, his eyes red but steadfast. They're her world now—her reason for staying.

I take her hand on instinct and her memories of Earth creep in, Uncle Kit and Auntie Ina laughing as they baked together, Gordo's hand on her shoulder when everything felt too much, the Squad standing by her side, always. The warmth of those moments feels so distant now, like they belong to someone else. She blinks quickly, trying to shove them away.

"Tell me, Ricky," she says, turning to me. "Can you honestly say Earth is better than Ethra?" Her voice wavers, a quiet plea for clarity she knows I can't give. "I have to make the right choice—for them," she whispers, gesturing toward her kids. "And for me."

I don't give her an answer. I don't like either choices right now.

Sólel steps back, quietly joining the other three Ethrans as the rest of the Squad erupts. Voices overlap, rising in a hectic blur as everyone talks over each other, desperate to convince Jhoana to come back home.

What the hell is wrong with me? Before I can step in, Aigerim's voice booms through the noise, calling my name. I turn to see his yellow eyes locked on me.

"I'm staying with you," Aigerim says simply. *"I'll fight with you for your cause."*

"No," I reply firmly, my voice silencing the Squad as they look around at the monstrous wolf. "This war isn't your concern. You're free from it. From all of it. Go find your siblings, Aigerim. You don't owe me anything."

Aigerim hesitates, his gaze heavy, before bowing his head deeply. *"Out of all I have bonded with."* He pauses. *"You are the first to show me compassion. My gratitude is boundless, Rictor."* Without another word, he turns and walks away. It's only then that I notice a second tail waving behind him.

A Crown Beast's aid could shift the tide in our favor when the O'rians arrive, but Aigerim has spent a lifetime in confinement. He deserves freedom, not another set of shackles.

The Squad looks to me like I have the answers, like I know what comes next. But my mind is fracturing, splintering under the pressure. There's no time to process, no time to grieve. I can't stop—not now. Not when so much is at stake. Not when everyone is counting on me.

My hands curl into fists, nails digging into my palms. The pain anchors me, keeps me here, keeps it all from spilling out. If I let go—if I start crying now—I'm terrified I won't be able to stop.

"Leave," I blurt out, the words sharp and final. "From now on, your only mission is to use the Locus and find Evanora. I'll stay here and make sure the rest of the Space Ring citizens get out."

The silence that follows rings in my ears, stretching between us like a canyon I can't cross.

Emierr sighs through his nose. "And what if Evanora shows up with the army, huh? What then, Ricky?"

"It doesn't matter!" I snap. I'm shaking now, and I hate it—the loss, the despair, I can't handle it. I've *never* been able to handle it. "Just fucking go, okay! It has to be me. It—"

"Shut the fuck up, Ricky!" Dustin's voice snaps like a whip, stopping me cold. He's never yelled at me like this before. I'm really pushing it, and I know it. He shakes his head, his jaw tight, his expression a mix of anger and something else I can't quite place. Disappointment? Concern? Maybe both.

"All this time," he says, his words sharp but controlled, "we've been following your orders—not because we agree with them, but because we're tiptoeing around you. We're scared, Ricky. Scared you'll crack. Scared you'll fall off the edge again. After everything you've been through—*especially* in the last day." He swallows hard, lips quivering. "But this?" He gestures around us, sweeping a hand at the havoc, the aftermath, the ghosts we can't shake. "This isn't about you anymore. It's bigger than that. It's bigger than *any* of us. This is about fixing what *we* broke. About making things right for Ethra."

His words hit harder than any punch to my gut could. It's the undeniable truth. I try to argue, but the words don't come.

Papa's gone... He's really gone this time.

"Dammit, Ricky, stop trying to carry everything by yourself! We've *always* been here. You're not alone, so stop acting like you are!" Dustin says, pleading now. "We all made promises too. Promises we need to keep."

Please... just let me be... It's so much easier to take the blame for everything. All my life, that's what I've done—bear the blame, shoulder the guilt, carry the burden so no one else has to. But here they are, still fighting, despite everything I've done. I don't deserve them, yet somehow, I've been lucky enough to have them stand by me.

"I can't lose any of you." My hands shake as I think of what's ahead, of the damage I know I'll cause, of futures I can't escape. "You mean everything to me." My voice is barely a whisper now. "All of you. And I'll do whatever it takes to keep you safe."

Dustin exhales a heavy, tired sigh, and pulls me into an embrace.

I don't resist. They all just hug me. "I don't want to fail," I say, almost inaudibly.

Jhoana's eyes meet mine. "If it comes to it, we do that together too."

My mind goes still. My chest loosens. "I love you guys," I say, the only thing I know to be true.

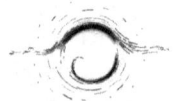

I gnaw at my nails, anxiety kicking into overdrive. In the few moments just we'd spent back on Earth, everything had proven to be just as complicated as ever. Auntie Ina had unexpectedly come back home from work early which means the dramatics are slated to start sooner than we planned. It was noon when we woke up in the basement. Jhoana's life support is set to be turned off at 4 p.m. Now that we're back in Ethra, that leaves us with roughly seven hours to pull this off.

Ms. Santiago and Gordo are going to do everything they can to prolong the unplugging while we're in Ethra. We'd set our alarms for 3:30. If they go off and stop, it means Gordo somehow pulled off a miracle and bought us a little more time. He'd reset the alarms after that.

A sharp sting jolts me back into place. Bitch—I bit too deep. Blood beads along the edge of my nail, dark red against my skin. I shove my finger into my mouth, the metallic tang of iron coating my tongue.

"Noble Rictor."

My head lifts, meeting the gaze of Kaelor, the Silver Sentinel of Ethra and Captain of the Allied Force. His gray skin has a silver tint to it, a subtle mark of his feyborn heritage. Sunlight streams through the ceiling of the makeshift war tent, catching on his polished armor. From inside, the tent is translucent, but outside, it blends seamlessly into its surroundings. Looking at the immaculate state of Kaelor's armor, I can't help but wonder if he's ever had to dirty his hands in battle.

Kaelor had come as a stand-in for Allied Force President, Ceryn Vestra—someone I had yet to actually meet. What she was dealing with that was more important than the brink of war was beyond me.

"The floor is yours," Kaelor says, motioning with a gloved hand.

I gaze around the space, every eye fixed on me. To my left sit the official members of the Allied Organization Squad, the Nobles of each nation, and Sólel—who officially earned his place amongst the leadership during the years we were away.

To my right, the leaders of the six nations are gathered—most appearing in hologram form. The rest, I was introduced to just minutes ago.

Amos nods in my direction. Finally, his people have a voice at the table. Beside me, projected in hologram form, is Dr. Wolfgang—proudly representing the Fleming Space Ring, securely under Terrene's protection. Both of them are a solid presence after everything their nations have endured.

Chief Berkarys's image flickers, smiling proudly at his two sons.

"Right." I clear my throat, knowing I should probably start by thanking them for being here. I stumble over my words at first, but a quick glance at my friends steadies me. With their silent support, I find my footing.

"The O'rians will attack," I say, my voice stronger now, "and they'll throw everything they have at us. The Convergence has been stopped—my father made sure of that—but it'll only make Abbadon more desperate. He'll resort to whatever drastic measures he must to start it again." I pause to meet the eyes of each leader. Rorik Styrn, a glacien acting as High Warden of Verglas, returns my gaze with his unnervingly pale eyes. He reminds me of a frozen corpse. I hastily break eye contact and continue. "With the aid of the six nations and the Allied Force, we believe that taking the O'rians head-on, here in Great Eagle Fields, will not only diminish their numbers but also keep blood magick far from civilians. The Nobles have all agreed that drawing the brunt of their attack is the best option we have. If we succeed, we can end the conflict before it spreads further. And if we bring down Abbadon..." I let the words hang in the air for a moment before continuing. "The O'rians fall with him."

Emirah Valcoris, Sovereign of Arid, furrows her brows. She is the first duneclad to be elevated to her position, and for good reason. She commands respect with her mere presence and I feel increasingly inadequate the longer I look at her. Her golden veins pulse beneath sun-kissed skin and intricate braids twine around her shoulders.

Emirah turns to exchange a glance with Amaya Calder, Zaltana's new chieftess. Delicate tattoos paint the young Inkweaver's skin. I can't tell what they're feeling, but Amos's emotions are as clear as day.

"Vereilles will aid the Nobles. We may be a small nation, but many of us are ready to fight."

Dr. Wolfgang inclines his head in agreement. "The Fleming Space Ring stands united with you. We will deploy every weapon and mecha suit we've managed to salvage for this cause." He turns to address the other leaders. "To the four nations that gave refuge to my people—you have my deepest gratitude. Fleming owes you a debt beyond measure."

Amos dips his head in acknowledgment. "To each of you, my deepest thanks for the profound kindness you've shown my people."

The other nations' leaders incline their heads slightly.

Captain Kaelor interjects, his tone self-assured and authoritative. "We owe you our gratitude, Noble Rictor, for the intelligence regarding the incoming army." He glances toward the assembled leaders. "All Fleming citizens have been safely evacuated, and under President Vestra's directive, the Allied Force will align with the Allied Organization Squad in this conflict."

He pauses briefly before gesturing toward the table. A holographic map materializes, casting vague rainbows across the translucent space. "Surveillance has confirmed a legion of O'rians advancing toward us," he continues, as the map zooms in on the mountain ranges. "Their trajectory leads to the Great Eagle Fields, with an estimated arrival within the hour. It seems the sole focus of the O'rians is to destroy the Nobles before taking further action." Kaelor's gaze sweeps the council. "What we resolve to do in this moment will shape the course of this inevitable war."

Sovereign Emirah tilts her head, her expression unreadable. "What exactly do you expect will come of our presence here? It seems clear that our priority must be to keep our nations safe from the threats of the Vermillion Sages and the O'rians. After the decimation of the Fleming Space Ring and the relocation of Vereilles, each nation is barely managing to stay afloat."

Amos and Dr. Wolfgang exchange uneasy glances. Amos places both hands on the table, voice filled with grief. "It's because of those struggles that we *must* act. Vereilles has already lost so much—countless parents, children. My daughter, Livia." He pauses, his voice catching. "All gone."

Dr. Wolfgang picks up where Amos falters, his tone solemn. "The Fleming Space Ring has paid an unbearable price. Too many of our people have returned to the Tree. If we don't act now, the losses will only grow."

Sovereign Emirah's gaze sharpens. "And that is precisely why I will not send my forces into battle. If war is inevitable, my soldiers will remain in Arid to defend our people. I refuse to risk more lives for a cause that offers no guarantee of survival."

High Warden Rorik shoots Captain Kaelor a disdainful glare. "Verglas has endured enough. The Ghelcarii population in my homeland has dwindled, and yet the Allied Force continues to draw our warriors away. Protecting our people is the only viable strategy now—not sending them into a battle we're not equipped to win."

Dr. Wolfgang and Amos falter. Their arguments fall flat in comparison to the harsh reality each leader is bound by. As much as I hate to admit it, Rorik has a point—protecting people caught in the crossfire is what matters most.

Chief Berkarys clears his throat. "I agree with Rorik and Emirah. Our priority must be the safety of our people, especially with the influx of refugees."

I didn't see that coming; even Sólel and Emierr share the same expression of worry and shock.

"However," Chief Berkarys continues, "solidarity is just as vital as strategy. Even if we cannot send our forces to the battle, we can stand united. People are scared, and morale is fragile. Let us give them something to believe in. Hope is how we turn the tide."

High Warden Rorik scoffs, his laugh sharp and void of humor. "Are we really going to ignore the thundertusk in the room?" His piercing gaze zeroes in on the Squad. On me.

I stay silent. We all do. Deep down, I know the truth—we don't belong here. Not really. We haven't lived their struggles, haven't walked even a step in their shoes. Only Jhoana and Sólel can truly claim that right.

"The moment you returned, you brought nothing but misfortune," High Warden Rorik shakes his head. "Because of you, two nations have lost their homes. If you just leave us in peace, perhaps things will go back to normal. It's you. It's always been you."

Sólel slams his fist on the table, the sharp crack silencing the room. His usual calm is gone, replaced by barely restrained anger as he glares at the High Warden. "It's so easy to blame someone else for your failures," he spits.

"Excuse me?" The High Warden snaps. "Mind your tone when addressing me."

Sólel doesn't flinch. "I've traveled the world, High Warden. I've seen the devastation blood magick leaves behind, the lives it's destroyed. While you've stayed hidden behind your glaciers, the world is only now beginning to uncover the truth about the Convergence. Tell me, isn't Verglas responsible for overseeing anomalies? Islaug has been a hotspot for years, and yet you've kept your research hidden."

High Warden Rorik's composure cracks. Sólel's words strike a nerve—turns out the Squad's little brother knows more than he lets on, and right now, he's laying bare the High Warden's hypocrisies.

Sólel shifts his accusatory gaze to Sovereign Emirah. "The O'rians' deadliest ally, Evanora, is one of your own. You declared her dead. So tell me, Sovereign, what's really going on here?"

The room falls into a stunned silence. Sólel's accusations linger in the air, weighty and indisputable.

Watching them squirm—appalled, embarrassed—I want to shove two middle fingers in their direction and yell, "Suck on that!" But I hold back, knowing that it would be a poor decision for a leader on the precipice of devastating war to tell his prospective allies to "suck on that."

Chieftess Amaya finally breaks the silence. "Forgive my intrusion, but these conflicts you've raised didn't begin with the return of the Nobles," she says, voice calm. "I may be new to my position, but I am not blind to the realities around us. Ethra is facing a threat far beyond anything we can comprehend. While the Allied Organization Squad has a role to play, the blame cannot rest solely on their shoulders. As leaders, we bear responsibility as well. We've allowed the O'rians to act unchecked, driven by fear, and now we are paying the price for our inaction."

Sovereign Emirah lowers her gaze, nodding slowly. "You're right, Chieftess," she says, her voice quieter now. "I've let fear cloud my judgment." She takes a few moments to work her thoughts into speech. "But if we come together, as Chief Berkarys suggested, the O'rians won't stand a chance." She turns to Sólel, her expression now resolute. "And let me be clear—I watched Evanora return to the Tree with my own eyes. I've been deceived, just like the rest of you." Emirah's gaze shifts to the High Warden, silently urging him to respond.

But he doesn't look at her. Instead, his gaze lands squarely on Jhoana. "Noble Jhoana," he says, pointedly ignoring the Aridian Sovereign. "All this time, you've been alive, hiding here in Ethra. You could have stopped the Allied Force from taking the Ghelcarii, but instead, you cowered in the shadows. Boyko and Valda would be ashamed of you."

I'm on my feet before I even realize it. "Say one more word," I growl, my fists clenching at my sides, "and I'll fly to Verglas myself and relieve you of the burden of having a tongue."

The room erupts, voices rising in a cacophony of outrage and confusion. But Jhoana raises her hand, a glowing force field rippling into existence. The hum fills the air, silencing everyone instantly.

"I don't owe you an explanation. I don't owe anyone an explanation. But in honor of my parents, I'll give you one." Jhoana's cold eyes lock on the High Warden. "Don't you ever speak their names again. Boyko and Valda fought valiantly to protect me and Verglas. They were honest, ordinary people, but they showed more honor in their lives than you've ever known." She pauses, turning her gaze to the other leaders, her shoulders squared. "I was cursed by Evanora. I've been on the run, because wherever I go, Abbadon follows—with death. If I'd stayed, I would have risked every life in Verglas." Her voice drops. "Fleming was the only place that felt safe from the O'rians. It was home." She takes a measured breath. "Maybe staying away was a mistake, but I have so much more to lose now—and I won't apologize for that."

The leaders exchange glances, their uncertainty written across their faces.

"There's clearly more to address," Captain Kaelor says, his tone steady, "but for now, we need to focus on the immediate threat."

Chieftess Amaya places a fist to her chest without hesitation. "I support the open alliance with the Allied Organization Squad."

Chief Berkarys, Amos, and Dr. Wolfgang follow suit, their fists rising to their chests in silent agreement.

Sovereign Emirah hesitates, her gaze flickering between the others. After a moment, she mirrors the others, her knuckles thumping just below her collarbone.

High Warden Rorik exhales, the tension in his shoulders evident.

He lingers for what feels like an eternity before finally touching his hand to his chest in agreement. "May the Tree guide you," he says, bowing his head before his hologram fades out.

As the remaining leaders flicker out of existence, I glance at the Squad. None of us need to say anything. The thought of war—actual *war*— settles over us like a thick fog.

"Now," Captain Kaelor says, "who here has experience fighting Vermillion Sages?"

I stare out onto the field, where glistening blades of grass sway and dance with the wind. The Allied Force stands assembled in tight rows, their numbers only a fraction of the hundreds the O'rians are bringing. Aside from the soldiers in their armor, any Vereillics or Space Ring citizens who volunteered for the war effort have been given Allied Force insignia patches to mark them as allies. Even we have to wear them.

Mecha suits and salvaged Space Ring tech are scattered among them, gleaming under the sun like relics of another era.

I think about something I once said to Albert about Earth—about its endless wars and violence. I told him that my hopes and dreams were for Ethra to be different, a place where technology wasn't used to destroy but to make lives better. But standing here, looking at all this... That dream feels so far away. An echo from a time that barely existed.

"Hey."

Jihyun is at my side, his expression soft but searching.

"Hey," I say. "How are you feeling?"

"Much better, considering they sucked the life out of me," he jokes, a small chuckle breaking through the undercurrent of concern "I'm more worried about you."

"I'm..." I hesitate. "I'm worried about myself too." It's not something I'd ever say out loud, but Jihyun's the kind of person who makes you want to be honest. "There's this bookstore near my job in New York—on Earth." My voice is quieter. "It's small, kinda dusty, but I go there a lot. So often that they made a spot for me in the back. Whenever I feel like giving up, I end up there. Stepping into worlds, walking in the shoes of characters who don't even know they're just characters in a story. It helps. Even if it's just for a while, it matters to me." I glance his way, a faint smile painting his face. "I wish I could bring you to that bookstore."

Jihyun looks down, then takes my hand. I don't flinch. Instead, I hold his tighter. "I have a garden in Solaris," he says, looking up at the clear skies. "My father was from there. I never got to know him, but he loved plants. I tend to that garden all on my own—no magick. It's my quiet place. When I'm watering or pruning, it makes me feel closer to him. I'd like for you to see it someday. I use the vegetables to make one hell of a great Filipino spaghetti. My mom says so." He shrugs modestly.

"I'd love that."

"I wanna hold hands too," Emierr cuts in with the Squad behind him, and Jihyun and I immediately let go.

Without missing a beat, I grab Emierr's face. "Here, let me give you a kiss instead."

He pulls back, but Dustin traps him in place. I plant a big, exaggerated kiss on Emierr's cheek.

The Squad bursts into laughter, the sound a brief, fleeting moment of relief. Emierr wipes his face dramatically, groaning like I've mortally wounded him.

"Can you believe it?" Emierr says, throwing his hands in the air. "Just a few days ago, we were all living our own lives. And now? Here we are, saving the world."

I shake my head, a smile tugging at my lips. "My therapist's going to check me into the psych ward when I tell him about this." I chuckle.

"Ricky," Dustin says, his voice more serious now. The tone makes my stomach twist. He's about to drop something heavy on me, isn't he? "We all talked," he continues. "And we've decided we need to split up—a team to stay here and one to go after Evanora."

"What?" My brows knit together. "But... what if she's with the O'rians, like Meer said?"

"She's not," Jadis cuts in. She pulls out the Locus Aeterna, a handkerchief tied around it. The artifact glows faintly, projecting an image of what looks like a temple.

"Lacey mentioned this belonged to Evanora," Jadis explains. "So I stole it before we left Arid."

"Ricky," Jhoana says, her tone leaving no room for argument, "you're coming with me and Jads."

I open my mouth to object—I want to stay and fight—but I know she's right. If Evanora's out there, I might be the best chance we have to stop her.

"We'll hold the line until you get back," Dustin says, grinning as he gives Emierr a fist bump.

"I..." The word catches in my throat.

"Like Dustin said," Jihyun adds, his smile warm and steady, "we'll be right here waiting for you."

"And we have the Sunbringr," Emierr says, reassuring me. "We'll be fine."

"Let's end this, Ricky," Jadis says, her hand landing on my shoulder. "Let's bring Jho home."

"Wait," Brunner says, his voice trembling and drawing all of our attention. "Jho, I—We haven't had a chance to talk, not really, but..." He lowers his head, taking a shaky breath.

Oh no. Is this where he confesses his undying love for her? My eyes flick toward the others, and sure enough, they're all fighting to keep their smirks in check.

Brunner looks up, his gaze locked on Jhoana. "Jho... I don't know what's going to happen next, but there's something I need to say." He pauses, his voice thick with emotion. "My life—since the day you left us—has been nothing but uncertainty. I never knew where I fit in without you. Over the years, I watched the Squad grow stronger, more resilient without you, ready to defend your name at every turn. Even when the town... and I... turned against them and blamed them for what happened to you, they became their own community. And me?" He swallows hard. "I was stuck in this strange place of longing and bitterness for years. But seeing you again, having you back..." His voice cracks, and he fights to steady it. "It made me realize just how much I was my true self when I'm around you."

Oh shit, that was a good confession.

Brunner takes a deep breath, his next words coming out as a plea. "Come home, Jho. I don't know what's left for you there, but I know one person who desperately needs his best friend back."

Jhoana's face softens, her eyes glistening as she reaches for his hand. "Rune," she says quietly. "Thank you. For standing by me all these years. I can't even begin to imagine the pain I've caused all of you—the guilt I've left behind." Her voice falters as she glances at her children. "But how can I say goodbye to my kids?"

Mikal holds tightly to his crying siblings. His voice is resolute, though his eyes are red. "We're going to be okay, Mom."

Jhoana's grip on Brunner's hands tightens as tears spill freely down her face.

I look at all of them, taking in their faces, their determination. My chest deepens, but this time it's not from fear. A smile breaks across my face. "One last mission," I say, letting the moment settle before I allow a cold smile to creep over my face. "Let's get this bitch."

My feet hit the ground hard as the teleportation spell spits us out in front of the temple depicted by the Locus.

The building looms ahead, its towering obsidian columns etched with intricate, glowing runes that pulsate faintly. Twin statues of a cloaked woman with three faces flank the entrance, their shadowed gazes fixed on us as if in judgment.

Jadis, Jhoana, and I ready our stances—we're not giving Evanora a chance. Echoing footsteps reverberate from the temple, and my fingers spark with lightning. Just as we brace to unleash everything we've got, the figure steps into the light.

It's Lâcien. She greets us with a casual smile. "It's about time. My hair was starting to frizz."

"Lacey?" Jhoana gasps, dropping her force fields before rushing to embrace her.

"Sister, I'm so glad you're okay," Lâcien says.

Jadis stands frozen, her expression twisted with confusion as she clutches the handkerchief tightly in her hand. "Why are you here? Where's Evanora?"

"You took the wrong one." Lâcien answers, jerking her chin at the handkerchief.

Jadis stares at it, realization dawning on her. "You didn't say which one..."

"I had a vision. I knew you'd end up locating me instead of her, so I decided to at least do my part." Lâcien swallows hard, her expression shifting. "I swear to all of you, I didn't know she was alive. But it all makes sense now." She takes Jhoana's hand gently. "The reason you couldn't leave. You were cursed, weren't you? And you came here to kill her, to break the curse." Her gaze flickers between us, searching for confirmation.

The air grows still, the tension between Jadis and me thick enough to cut. At this point, anything could happen. I don't know where Lâcien's loyalty lies.

"Lacey—" Jhoana begins.

"I wouldn't stop you," Lâcien says, cutting Jhoana off. Her mouth thins. "The Council told me everything—about the atrocities she's committed. What she's done to those children..." Her voice wavers for just a moment before she steadies herself, her expression turning to stone.

"Do what you have to do. My aunt made her choices. There's nothing left for me to defend. Even my family lost faith a long time ago. She has to answer for what she's done. And stopped from doing any more damage"

Lâcien's words hit like a quiet storm. I can feel the sorrow beneath her composed exterior, a sadness so deep it feels endless. But she holds herself together, her back straight and her face dry. Not one tear falls, even as the ache in her voice lingers.

"What is this place?" I ask, steering the conversation away from the inevitable death of her family member.

"This is a temple to one of the old gods," Lâcien answers, her voice almost reverent. "The name of the god is long gone, but the knowledge left behind was too valuable to lose."

"What knowledge?" I glance up at the myriad of nonsensical runes, mentally berating myself once again for not knowing how to read them.

"We call it the Temple of Volentes—the Temple of Wishing," Lâcien says, eying Jadis. "Maybe you've heard of it?"

Jadis's mouth hangs open as she scrutinizes the runes. "The wish spell... I thought it was lost or forbidden or—"

"In a way," Lâcien agrees. "It's outlawed for most people because it's too powerful and too deadly for the average witch. If everyone on Ethra knew there was a spell that could grant any wish, how many people do you think would want to try it? Even knowing the cost of failure is pain akin to death?"

"And the cost of success?" Jadis asks harshly.

Lâcien hesitates, then turns to her. "The wish is granted at the cost of your magick."

Jadis freezes, her fingers clenching tightly around the handkerchief. "And you want me to attempt it. You want me to save Jho—to lose my magick."

Lâcien's true purpose in bringing us here... was to sacrifice Jadis. The words slam into me, leaving my thoughts scattered. My throat tightens, and for a moment, I can't find the words to respond. A wish spell—something so rare and monumental it feels almost mythical. Could this actually work?

Jadis didn't speak. Instead, she took small, tremulous steps backward, eyes fixed on the floor. Without a word, she whipped around and bolted from the dim light of the temple.

"Just give us a minute," I mutter to Lâcien before following her. Jhoana falls in step beside me. We catch up to Jadis a few steps away, where she paces in short, angry strides, her frustration boiling over.

"I won't do it!" Jadis snaps. "I can't be the one responsible for whether Jho lives or dies. You can't put this on me. What if I fail? Then what? And what if I somehow manage to do it? I'll be useless against Abbadon."

"Jads," Jhoana says, her voice cracking as the words tumble out. Her composure is gone, stripped away completely. "If you can't do it, I would never blame you. I'm just asking you to at least try. We've all been breaking our own rules lately, and I get it. I know how important it is to stay true to yourself, to not lose who you are. But what's one more? Just this once, so I can come home. That's all I'm asking, sis."

Jhoana's mind's made up—I can see it in her eyes. She's coming back. I feel the terror radiating off Jadis—the absolute fear of being the reason Jhoana never wakes up.

"You're not alone, Jads," I say gently. "We'll be right there with you. Succeed or fail, all that matters is you tried. We'll find a way no matter what happens."

Jadis stops pacing, her uneven breaths finally spilling out in a shaky exhale as her head drops in reluctant acceptance. But before she can say a word, her hands shoot to her throat, her eyes widening in panic. She gasps, choking, her body trembling violently.

"Jadis!" Jhoana and I rush to her side, but she collapses to her knees, the handkerchief slipping from her fingers.

She collapses to the ground, her body convulsing violently. I drop beside her, trying to steady her, but her form starts to shimmer, edges flickering like static before she begins to dematerialize right in front of us.

"What's happening to her?" Jhoana cries, panic rising in her voice as she crouches down beside me.

Lâcien rushes over, her face pale and drawn. "What's going on?"

The sounds around me blur—overlapping voices, Jhoana's panicked questions, Lâcien's sharp demands—but it's not just them. There's something else.

"Wait, wait!" I shout. They both go quiet as I close my eyes and focus, straining to hear past the frantic voices. There—it's faint but unmistakable. Jadis. Her screams echo somewhere distant, wrapped in another sound. A voice—desperate and strained.

"Let go of her!" Gordo's voice rings out, clear but distant.

"She's in trouble," I say, snapping my eyes open. "I'm going after her."

"Ricky, wait—" Jhoana starts, grabbing my arm, but I pull away.

"Astralis," I whisper, and the world around me tears away.

As I soar through the cosmos, the voices grow louder, sharper. A man's voice, cold and taunting, resounding in my ears.

"Did you really think you could hide from me?" a man's voice sneers. "That stupid letter didn't even have a return address, but it wasn't hard to dig up some articles about your friend. Too bad she's dying."

My jaw tightens, anger flaring hot in my chest. *Who the fuck is that?*

"I knew you and your so-called 'friends' were close, but lying on the ground with all these men? You're nothing but a slut. You're better off dead."

I slam back into my body with a jolt, gasping as air floods my lungs. My vision sharpens, and the scene comes into brutal clarity—a man, towering over Jadis, his hands clamped around her throat, squeezing the life out of her.

For a split second, I freeze. The rage surges, but my mind snaps into focus. Gordo's on the ground, blood streaking his face as he struggles to rise. Cam—twice Jadis's size—leans his full weight onto her, his grip tightening. Her face is pale, her lips trembling as she claws weakly at his wrists.

This is it. If I don't act now, I'll lose her.

"Get your hands off her!" I roar, the words ripping from my throat as I propel myself forward. My fist crashes into his jaw, and he staggers back, his grip on Jadis slipping.

Without hesitation, Gordo lunges at Cam—wrapping his arms around his neck in a chokehold.

My eyes dart to the stairs, light spilling from the upper floor. The door. I bolt for it, taking the stairs two at a time. Auntie Ina's voice drifts through the house, sharp with concern.

"Gordo? What's happening down there? You know people are on their way here." She stops cold at the top of the stairs, her eyes widening when she sees me. "Rictor? What are you—"

"Ethra!" I shout. The spell triggers immediately. Auntie Ina freezes, her eyes glazing over as the magic takes hold. I slam the door shut, locking it tight before racing back down.

Jadis is still on the ground, one hand clutching her throat, her face pale but fierce. Gordo's grip is tight, and Cam's face is red, slowly turning a dangerous shade of purple.

"When I say so," Jadis rasps. "Let him go."

Gordo hesitates but nods, his grip holding steady.

"Three... two... one... now."

On her command, Gordo releases him. Cam wheezes and gasps for air. Before he can compose himself, Jadis moves. Her fist swings hard, landing with precision. The breath whooshes out of Cam as he collapses to the ground, unconscious.

We all pause, the room falling silent except for the sound of Jadis's ragged breaths, as if her lungs are fighting for each inhale.

"I should call the cops," Gordo pants, wiping the blood from his face.

"No," Jadis croaks, her voice strained. "We have to finish this."

Gordo shifts his gaze between Cam and us, his expression torn, his thoughts clearly racing.

"Then I'll tie him up for now." He places a hand against his head, wincing. "Who the hell is this guy?"

Jadis lets out a heavy, shuddering breath. "My ex-fiancé."

Fiancé? She's never called him that before. Not once. Then again, if I'd been engaged to a psychopath, I wouldn't be broadcasting it either.

Cam lies crumpled on the ground, unmoving. My heartbeat pounds in my ears, drowning out Gordo's muttered curses as he wraps duct tape around Cam's wrists.

"Ricky..." Jadis's voice is a whisper, her fingers brushing against my sleeve. I meet her eyes, and everything crashes into me at once. "You alright?"

"I'm fine." I breathe out and look at the blood smeared across Gordo's forehead. "Are you sure you're okay, Gordo?"

He gives a weak chuckle, wiping at the wound with the back of his hand. "I've taken worse blows to the head in combat. This? This is nothing." He leans back, catching his breath. "You guys need to go. Time's up here. I'll be fine," he says.

I lower myself onto the rug beside her, the fibers pressing into my palms as I brace myself. Her hand finds mine, and it's shaking—whether from pain or fear, I don't know. Maybe both. Probably both. My thumb brushes over her knuckles, trying to steady her. Or steady myself.

My eyes drop to her neck, bruises already darkening against her skin. It's rage-inducing. No. It's soul-crushing. Because I wasn't fast enough—again.

"You okay?" The words feel useless, hollow. Of course she's not okay.

She doesn't answer at first, just turns her head slightly toward me, eyes fluttering shut as her chest rises and falls. "Ready," she murmurs hoarsely through her mangled throat.

My head begins to thump—the war, Cam, the fact that every second feels like the last one we'll get. It's unbearable. But I have to bear it.

The concrete floor under the rug is hard, grounding. It's as if it's trying to remind me that I'm still here. That Jadis is still here. That we're still here. For now.

I tighten my grip on her hand. Holding on to her feels like holding everything else together, as if this one fragile connection can keep us from falling apart.

"Let's end this," I whisper to myself.

Together, we say, "Astralis."

~ ~ ~

My eyes snap open to find Jadis crumpled on the ground, her eyes shimmering with unshed tears.

"What happened? You were both gone for a while." Jhoana leans down, her hand steady on Jadis's arm, guiding her up with careful movements. As soon as Jadis is on her feet, she falls into me, gripping me tightly. Her shoulders shake, and a choked cry escapes her.

For a moment, I believed she hadn't let it affect her. But I knew that couldn't be it. No one walks away emotionally unscathed after nearly being killed, especially when it's at the hands of someone they once trusted and loved. Guilt pools in my chest. I should've been there sooner. Now, holding her trembling form, I feel helpless—no matter what I do, it's never enough.

Jhoana and Lâcien stare at me for answers, but all I can do is hold her. Jadis is better than me—I know I would've seriously hurt Cam if I were in her shoes. Hell, maybe I would've killed him.

Jhoana edges closer. "Jads?" she says softly.

Jadis breaks away from my embrace, her hands trembling as she wipes at her face. Her voice breaking between words. "My ex... He found me." She swallows hard, her eyes darting briefly to the floor before meeting Jhoana's. "I ran away because he's been hurting me for the last year. He... He was about to kill me." Her breath hitches, and she grips her arms tightly as if holding herself together. "If Ricky and Gordo hadn't been around, I—I don't think I'd be here right now."

"Oh my god." Jhoana immediately pulls Jadis into a protective hug. Her arms tighten around her as if shielding her from any lingering pain. "He's never going to hurt you again. I'll make sure of it when I see him."

"I'm sorry," Lâcien says, breaking through the moment. Her eyes flick between us, her posture rigid. "There isn't much time."

"The O'rians made it to the Eagle Fields, didn't they?" I ask, already dreading the confirmation.

"Yes," Jhoana answers, voice low and tense. "Abbadon isn't there, and neither is Evanora."

A wave of unease grips me; the two people we need to find are still missing. Dread threatens to take hold—the boys are out there, in the thick of the battle, and I'm not beside them to fight.

"Ricky, go," Jhoana says, as if reading my mind.

"What? No." I shake my head. "What about Evanora and the wish?"

"I've got Jads," Jhoana says "Trust me, Ricky, I won't leave her side.".

If anyone can do this, it's her.

I hesitate, torn. Should I be helping to face the O'rians or staying to protect Jadis and ensure Jhoana breaks her curse? I grapple with the decision, each option feeling like a gamble I can't afford to lose.

Jadis decides for me. "Go, Ricky. They need you out there. We'll take care of things here and catch up with you soon." Her voice quivers, but determination burns in her eyes. "You've got this."

My breathing comes in short, shallow bursts. I trust them, but fear lashes at me, whispering every possible way this could go wrong. "Are you sure?" My voice feels small, uncertain.

"Sororitas," Lâcien says with a wan smile. "We stand for each other, no matter what. Trust us, Ricky." Her hand brushes my arm briefly, a grounding touch settling through my hesitation.

Jhoana motions for me to go. "We'll be fine," she says. "You need to be there for the boys. We'll catch up soon."

I nod, swallowing the lump in my throat. "Keep us updated. Whatever it takes, we all go home together," I say. "I love you guys."

"We love you," Jhoana replies, her smile faint but warm.

With one last glance back, I leap into the air, lightning sparking from my fingertips, propelling me toward the battlefield.

"Good luck," I whisper, my words lost to the wind.

Ashes To Ashes

"Guys, I'm en route. How's it looking out there?"

"Ricky," Emierr's strained voice bursts through the static. "Did you guys take care of Evanora?"

"No. Jads and Jho found another way to deal with the curse."

"Alright, well, it's a mess over here. These guys just keep coming." Battle noise muffles Emierr's words, the clash of metal and distant shouting bleeding through the connection.

Below, my shadow glides over the treetops, a black dot drifting over a sea of green. Then it hits me just how high I am. On Earth, the height would have turned my legs to jelly. But here in Ethra, it feels instinctual—like I was meant to be soaring with the wind.

"Ricky, get your ass here!" Dustin's voice booms through the comms, almost deafening me.

"I'm on my way!" I shout back, pushing myself faster toward the battle ahead, and wishing desperately that the damn teleportation spell could be done solo.

The world below unfolds in breathtaking detail—emerald hills stretch into amber fields, rivers carving shimmering paths through the land. It's serene, a now-rare glimpse of Ethra's beauty untouched by conflict. If only it could stay this way, free from the scars of war and fear. The reality of what lies ahead sharpens around me. The sky above reflects hues of violet and gold, an ethereal contrast to the turmoil ahead. For a moment, I breathe it in, not as a battlefield but as the place we swore to protect.

Ahead, a dust bowl encircles the fields, a churning, unrelenting vortex. Flashes of different-colored lights flicker through the dust, casting fleeting glimmers that burn through the haze. The instant I enter, the sound of war blazes around me—shouts, clashing weapons, and the unmistakable hum of magick. Hundreds of O'rians swarm the Allied Force's defenses. This is far worse than I expected.

I was expecting their numbers to be maybe a hundred more than our own force of three hundred, but it looks like Abbadon sent his entire army to wipe us out.

The thought grips me for a moment—how can we hold out against this? I know how this ends—either we survive, or they do. There's no middle ground, no mercy in this fight.

"*Kuya*," Sólel calls out as he swoops beside me. He's calm, even as he incinerates a volley of arrows with a sweep of light beams. "I have the skies. Help them below."

I nod, scanning the raging battlefield. Focusing on the Squad's auras, I let their energy guide me. My vision hones in as colored streams of smoke rise from the dust—distinct markers of my friends amidst the fray. They're far from me—good. I dive toward the ground, landing with a thunderous quake that booms outward. O'rians near the impact are thrown into the air, and the battlefield stills momentarily as eyes snap toward me.

The Huttons' armor shudders to life around me, the circuits rippling like liquid light across its surface. leyfolk and humans with weapons begin to circle, their intent clear. Thirty, maybe more—it's not good, but I've faced worse. Still, the odds are not in our favor, and doubt snakes its way in.

Then, a shadow descends behind me, and I feel the familiar shift of air. "I got you," Mikal says, landing at my back. A smirk cracks my face as we fall into position, covering each other's blind spots.

"I think this is yours." Mikal pulls the Vambrace from his pocket and tosses it to me.

Before I can respond, a human woman charges, the signal for the rest to attack. Mikal and I brace ourselves as the clash begins. I let the Vambrace float beside me. Crossing my arms, I send a pulse outward, a massive surge that flings incoming O'rians like leaves in a storm. A quick glance behind me confirms it—Mikal's wave hits with the same force, scattering the enemy like shredded paper.

"Thanks, Maks," he calls into his comm, flashing a grin at me. I snatch the Vambrace out of the air, and tap into Aigerim's bond. Instantly, the world sharpens; Mikal's soundwaves ripple like threads in a vast web, carrying him through the air.

A sharp hum shreds through the clarity. I whip my head around to see a spear hurtling toward me, its deadly edge flashing as it closes in. My body stills, and with a mental strain, the spear freezes midair, its tip mere inches from my face. I redirect the spear, guiding it above my left hand. It locks on its source.

The woman who threw it freezes, terror etched into her wide eyes as if she knows what's coming. I thought I could fight this war without hurting anyone else, but cruel satisfaction creeps through me—the same feeling that clung to me when Tholric turned to dust. The spear thrower spins on her heel, desperate to escape, but it's already too late. Her own weapon arcs back with ruthless precision, burying itself in her spine. Her scream cuts off abruptly as her body collapses and flecks of gold begin to rise, spiraling toward the Tree.

It's come to this. Survival demands we become something darker, something ruthless. Clenching my jaw, I tighten my grip on the Vambrace, and force electricity through it, reshaping it into a lightning spear. If I'm going to make it out alive, I have to lock away the part of me that cares—the part that's still human.

"Ricky, on your right!" Maks's voice snaps me back. Four O'rian soldiers charge, their weapons catching the dim light filtering through the dust-choked air. I release the Vambrace, letting it whirl into a deadly cyclone. Sparks burst as their weapons crash against the Vambrace, failing to even scratch its surface. The screech of metal grates through the air, scattering molten shavings in every direction. I tilt the Vambrace upward. A sharp hum bursts from the weapon, and lightning surging through their weapons, electrocuting the wielders. The soldiers cry out as their grips slip, and the blades ricochet, spinning high into the air.

They barely have time to register the shift. I raise the rotating Vambrace with deadly precision, carving through the air. Their gasps break into strained, wet gurgles, their bodies swaying unsteadily. I watch as the light fades from their eyes. Then, with a brutal finality, their heads fall, blood spraying in jagged arcs across the ground. The Vambrace returns to me, halting mid-spin in my grasp. I stare at their lifeless forms, their fear frozen in wide, unseeing stares. None of them have those dark veins around their eyes. Are these just regular people? Were they even O'rians at all?

A bitter scoff escapes me, as I watch their bodies begin to emit glittering dust, carrying their souls back to the Tree. This isn't who I wanted to become, but the reflection staring back at me through the blood and ashes says otherwise. Abbadon's nightmare wasn't just a warning—it was a prophecy, a mirror to what I am now. I'm not standing at the edge anymore; I'm one step away from plunging into it.

"Ricky, duck!" Maks shouts again, but her voice reaches me a fraction too late. Two arrows streak toward me. *Move, damn it, move!* But my feet stay nailed to the ground. In a split second, forceful waves crash into the arrows, intercepting mid-flight. The shafts wobble, their deadly trajectory shifted just enough to miss me by inches. I glance up to see Mikal hovering, his astral staff glowing as he sends more waves my way.

"Snap out of it!" he yells as twin vibration blasts slam into a pair of O'rians behind me, sending them sprawling. I let out a wordless shout of frustration. I can't afford to lower my guard for even a heartbeat. Whether they're O'rians or not, their intent is clear—they want me dead.

"They're breaking through my side!" Jihyun's voice crackles through the comms, urgency spiking every word. Heat prickles along my skin as adrenaline surges through my nerves. My eyes sweep across the battlefield, searching desperately for his aura. The familiar aqua smoke weaves through the haze, twisting and curling without a discernable pattern.

The soundwaves ripple all around me, drawing my vision as they cascade through the battlefield. They don't just echo—they uncover. Every vibration reveals a shape, peeling back layers of matter as though unveiling a hidden world. The ripples pass through people, structures, and dust alike, painting a living map of the chaos around me.

I blink, and my focus narrows further. Through the shifting shapes, I see him—Jihyun. He's on his back, crawling frantically away as a massive figure looms over him, blade poised to strike.

The creature is humanoid yet alien—a leyfolk with foxlike ears and a tail that lashes like a whip. Its sharp, angular features gleam with a deadly cunning, each calculated movement bringing it closer to Jihyun. It's quick, fluid, and deliberate.

But so am I.

"A fenrix is on Jih!" Maks shouts.

That's what it is. Not that its name matters much.

"Anyone near him?" Mikal hollers, his voice strained as he fends off a dozen O'rians.

I never imagined my vision could function like this. The ripples of soundwaves bring clarity, exposing the Allied Force insignia patches on some and the absence of them on others. The people in my line of sight are unmistakably enemies, their intent as clear as the weapons in their hands. I hurl the Vambrace like a thunderbolt, its lightning-infused edge tearing through human soldiers and leyfolk alike. It carves a path of destruction, leaving a shimmering trail of floating dust that lingers in the air, faintly outlining the forms of the bodies it once belonged to.

The fenrix lunges at Jihyun, but the Vambrace intercepts with a lethal strike. It skewers into the creature's skull, sending cracks splintering across its angular features. The force crumples its body mid-attack, and it stumbles, collapsing lifeless into the dirt. Dust rises in swirling clouds around Jihyun.

"I got you Jihyun." I say and he looks at my direction. For a moment, I hesitate. Is the fear in his eyes aimed at the fenrix that nearly killed him, or at the reflection of the monster I've become?

A soundwave pelts my right side, and I raise my hand reflexively, halting an arrow mid-flight. It hovers inches away before clattering harmlessly to the ground. I don't break Jihyun's gaze. He nods, his lips pursed tight, a silent understanding passing between us. Does he truly grasp what's at stake? I hope so.

I surge into the air, lightning propelling me upward as the battlefield sprawls beneath me. From above, the conflict unfolds—each ally fighting with relentless determination, pouring everything they have into our last stand.

Dustin fights alongside Jae and Borge. His body is vaguely backlit by his tattoos—living ink across his skin. With each move, he absorbs weapons and debris into swirling patterns. The tattoos pulsate with green light as he unleashes the weapons in controlled bursts, scattering O'rians into vulnerability. Jae's blasters fire beams of laser energy. At the same time, his hands weave intricate spells, summoning bursts of magick that explode around him. Both Jae and Dustin have their Zaltanian training on full display, their movements a deadly rhythm that tears through enemy lines.

Borge moves with swift expertise at odds with his size, disarming foes in close combat with, brutal efficiency. Then, something extraordinary happens—a cascade of shimmering crystal shards materializes around him, radiating in a mesmerizing array of colors. With a flick of his hands, the shards dart through the air like guided missiles, cutting through enemy lines with deadly accuracy. He hasn't weaved any spells. He's not using magick.

I watch him decimate those unfortunate enough to be standing in range. He's been a damn Keeper this whole entire time. But the shock and questions will have to wait.

To the east, Emierr towers atop a colossal tree, its sprawling roots tangling around enemy lines with relentless force. He lets out a primal scream, his glowing eyes radiating power as he taps into Maral's bond. Woodland creatures surge to the tree, their ferocity unmatched, tearing through O'rians with unrelenting precision. The tree itself seems alive, its branches lashing out like whips, flinging enemies aside as if they weigh nothing.

"Meer, can you command the nonhumans to stop?" I yell.

"You don't think I tried? Only about five of them listened," he shouts back, shooting wooden needles from his cuffs and letting the tree sprout vines, whipping, wrapping, and flinging enemies away. "Fuck you!" he screeches at the O'rians.

I scan the ground and spot Brunner, flickering in and out of sight like a phantom. Each reappearance is marked by a concussive force that erupts outward, sending O'rians flying like debris caught in a storm. His grin is wide, almost wild, as he weaves through the terrain.

"I don't see Abbadon anywhere," I say through the comms, my eyes scanning the battlefield. The thought gnaws at me—he's really not coming, is he?

"He looked rough when we saw him," Emierr points out. "Probably licking his wounds somewhere."

"Okay, but why aren't any of these people using magick or blood magick?" Dustin taps in, only slightly winded, like he's doing burpees rather than in mid-combat.

"I was thinking the same thing," I say. "It doesn't add up."

"Maybe they all blew up in the Space Ring," Brunner suggests, static distorting his voice. Behind him, faint screams echo through the connection.

"I have a bad feeling about this," Sólel says, his voice carrying a rare edge of unease. "Don't these people seem completely out of their depth to you?" From across the sky, I see him gliding effortlessly, beams of light streaming from his hands as he disintegrates arrows in mid-air.

I think back to the woman who threw the spear, when I first landed on the battlefield—her sheer terror etched into every frantic movement as she turned and ran. Why didn't she fight back? Why didn't she try to stand her ground? The more I dwell on it, the more off it feels.

"Then, this is easier than I thought," Emierr scoffs, his sarcasm failing to conceal his fear. "Let's get 'er done."

The comms go silent.

In the back lines, Captain Kaelor and Amos move like twin forces of nature, their magick intertwining in a mesmerizing display of power. They're the leaders for a reason. Captain Kaelor's sword blazes with golden flames, every sweep sending arcs of searing heat toward the enemy. Amos, clad in his battle-worn white suit, moves with focused intensity. His hands swirl with lavender energy, casting a luminous glow as he summons spectral spears. The weapons materialize above him, hovering like a deadly constellation before raining down on the foes. I take back what I said about Captain Kaelor ever getting dirty, but Amos sure as hell can fight.

"Vermillion Sages," Maks shouts over the comms. "They're throwing a wall of fireballs. Brace yourselves!"

"Do you see them, Sól?" I ask.

"Not yet, kuya," he replies, eyes darting across the horizon, scanning every shadow for movement.

I don't see the Vermillion Sages yet either, but I spot the trio of siblings' auras blazing through the commotion. They move as one, their coordination seamless. Mikal wields a massive astral battle axe, cleaving through O'rians, each swing accompanied by a burst of vibrations. Jihyun supports by turning weapons into a pile of leaves and intercepting bullets and lasers alike, the petals dancing around him. Maks darts between them, her twin daggers flashing as she strikes with deadly efficiency, her speed a blur. Together, they form an unbreakable wall.

"They're here," Sólel's voice cuts in, but laced with an edge of tension. "The clones... They've entered the battlefield.

I follow his gaze and my stomach knots. "What? Why the hell would he send them here instead of having them guard him?"

The clones march at the forefront of the O'rians, their movements eerily synchronized, each step perfectly in tune. A second wave. Behind them, figures in maroon robes raise their hands, exactly as Maks predicted, preparing to unleash a barrage of fireballs in our direction.

Sólel's eyes meet mine but there's a flicker of hesitation, a hesitation so brief I almost miss it. His jaw tightens, his fingers twitch slightly, and then—without a word—he launches into the sky, vanishing into the heavens.

"Sól!" I shout, confusion and panic spiking through me. But he doesn't look back. He just... leaves.

"Did something happen to Sól?" Emierr demands.

"He just left us," I say, still stunned. *What the hell is he doing?*

"What? He wouldn't." Emierr's voice wavers. "Sól! Little bro, where'd you go?" But the comms stay silent.

A surge of violet energy flares beneath me, yanking my focus downward. My breath hitches as colossal orbs of indigo fire coalesce above the Vermillion Sages' heads. Then, like vengeful stars falling from the heavens, they streak toward us, leaving searing trails of destruction in their wake.

"Oh bitch!" I yell, veering back toward the Allied Force lines. The heat from the fireballs licks at my heels as I twist and weave through their deadly arc.

I barely make it past the protective shield held aloft by Captain Kaelor and Amos.

The moment my feet hit the ground, the first fireball crashes into the shield, sending waves of energy rippling outward. Each impact slams against it like a battering ram, shaking the earth beneath us. I exhale sharply, glancing at the fractured shield.

"Do I need to weld myself to you?" Jihyun appears beside me. "You're pushing it."

I exhale sharply, chest still heaving. "Yeah, I know. That was way too fucking close."

"We can take them. There aren't many Vermillion Sages," Mikal says, approaching us with Maks beside him.

"Appreciate the warning," I tell Maks.

"Don't thank me yet." A small smile ghosts her lips. "I'm used to warning my family—not a whole battlefield."

Emierr's next breath comes out in a hiss, his eyes locked on the incoming wave. "The real problem is the kid Squad." He frowns, lifting his comm. "Sól, come in. Where the hell did you go?" Silence. His jaw tightens.

"He really just left?" Brunner mutters, eyes planted on the clones. "It's like looking at ghosts."

The shield drops, and we stand frozen as the clones march forward—behind them, a handful of Vermillion Sages.

"Mecha suits, you're our best line of defense against those Sages," Captain Kaelor says across the comms, and the seven mecha pilots advance with heavy, measured strides. Their armor gleams under the dust-choked light, massive, exoskeletal frames powered by pulsing energy cores embedded in their chests. Inside, the pilots remain focused, their visors glowing with data streams as they prepare for the oncoming assault. Dustin catches my eye, and we share a thin smile. The mechas were our favorite—despite losing most wrestling matches, they shredded through spells like paper. These ones look upgraded. If Dr. Wolfgang took Dustin's childhood idea of infusing defensive spells into the suits; they should be even more effective at countering magick.

As the mechas take position at the front, My gaze locks onto my clone, moving toward us with the same, hollow expression I'd see before. After our last fight, I couldn't shake the question—do they have souls? Do they feel anything at all? I hadn't given up hope, but that was days ago. Abbadon could have reset him, wiped him clean.

My clone suddenly halts, raising a hand. The Sages and clones stop in perfect sync. To my surprise, my clone breaks away from the formation, striding toward us. The Squad's clones exchange glances, hesitation flickering across their faces.

"What the hell is it doing?" Brunner mutters.

"Prepare yourselves!" Emierr calls. The tension tightens like a wire about to snap.

The clone stops just short of us, staring at me. I notice something—thin wisps of red smoke curling from his head. My pulse kicks up. He's forming an aura. He's feeling something.

"Friend," he says, his voice soft but unfamiliar in its sincerity.

Dustin gasps, eyes darting around to see if anyone else just heard that. "Did it just speak?"

I force myself to take a slow step forward. My nod is tight, cautious. "Friend."

A smile twitches on his face. He turns away, walking back toward the other clones. They watch him, studying him. And then—something shifts.

Without warning, they rush him.

The Squad tenses. Weapons raised. Shields up. But they're not coming for us.

The clones collide in a storm of force and energy, their movements bordering on the uncanny valley. My clone stands alone, telekinesis warping the battlefield around him—debris twisting midair, the ground buckling beneath his will. Every strike from the others is met with a ruthless counter, their attacks deflected as if he's always a step ahead.

"Holy fuck, is your clone fighting them?" Dustin's mouth hangs open.

The Meer clone seizes control of one of the leyfolk Sages, forcing it to cast a spell. Kid Ricky reacts instantly, shoving him back hard, severing the connection before it can fully take hold. The Jads clone's spectral wolves charge, but Ricky pivots, unleashing a force wave that disperses them before they can reach him. Kid Jho's force fields flicker as Ricky hurls chunks of earth at them, each impact splintering the barriers until they finally shatter. The Dusty doppelganger summons weapons, but with a flick of Ricky's wrist, they wrench from his grasp and scatter uselessly across the battlefield.

They close in from every direction, overwhelming my clone with sheer numbers. He's putting one hell of a fight—but it's not enough. The clones are forcing him to give ground. I have to help.

"Fight off the Sages, the clones are mine!" I shout, barrelling forward.

The Vermillion Sages hesitate for a split second before launching into action, hands swirling with blood, weaving their corrupted spells. Behind me, Captain Kaelor's war cry rallies the Allied Force.

"I have his back." Jihyun moves in sync with me, his swirling leaves slicing through the dust around us, cutting off the clones' approach.

"Don't hurt them!" I bark, skidding to a halt. The leaves shift, wrapping around my clone, halting the kid Squad in place.

"I know." Jihyun channels a healing spell, the leaves flaring the aqua color of his aura "I can still heal. I can help this way."

The clone Squad hesitates, their eyes locked on the storm of fronds. Little Ricky meets my gaze, and for a moment, we both understand—we're on the same side this time.

Jihyun and I move to flank Ricky, forming a defensive circle as the clones watch the wind carry the leaves high, a brief calm before the inevitable storm. They blink, their rigid coordination breaking as they process what they're seeing—my clone standing with me, fighting against them. Uncertainty flashes across their faces, their once-flawless synchronization unraveling like a glitch in their system.

"What's wrong with them?" Jihyun whispers.

"We're about to find out." I say as Dusty locks eyes with me. But his confidence wavers. He frantically scans his clone friends, his movements turning erratic. With a sudden burst of panic, he flings a barrage of weapons straight at Ricky. I react reflexively, throwing up my right arm, and my mental shield absorbs the impact. The weapons ricochet off, scattering across the battlefield. Ricky doesn't hesitate—his hands thrust forward, and little Dusty is blasted backward, hitting the ground hard.

The rest of them charge, but something's changed—I can feel their their confusion. It's bleeding into their movements.

Jihyun intercepts attacks, twisting the weapons midair into bursts of leaves before reforging them into a solid metal shield to block incoming strikes at Ricky. They're not attacking us—they're only after him. I press forward, weaving through their attacks, parrying and countering, pushing them back step by step.

Jihyun, my younger self, and I move as one—blades colliding, spells erupting, the air thick with the scent of scorched earth.

"They're not going down! How the hell are we supposed to beat these guys?" Emierr's voice bursts through the comms, frustration lancing through every word.

The Vermillion Sages unleash devastation, turning Allied Force soldiers to dust. Panic spreads like wildfire, gripping not just the soldiers, but the clones as well. I can hear it now—the clones' frantic breathing. They don't know what to do.

"Stop!" Ricky's scream cuts through the mayhem, freezing the clones, Jihyun, and me in place. The only sound left is our ragged breathing. He lifts both hands, voice filled with desperation. "We family," he pleads. "Not bad, family."

"Family?" Little Jho echoes, her brows knitting together with uncertainty.

I feel my jaw drop. Of all the things I expected from this battle, this is not one of them.

"Yes. Family, no hurt," Ricky says.

"Them?" Dusty's gaze flicks to Jihyun and me, suspicion clouding his face. "Bad?"

"Friends." Ricky interlocks his fingers, reinforcing the word. "Friends," he repeats, firmer this time.

"M—Master..." The Jads clone hesitates.

"No." Ricky glances at me for a brief moment before turning back. "Master wrong. Master bad."

Jads doesn't argue. The conflict is already there, buried beneath her carefully controlled exterior. I can feel it.

"Family..." The younger Meer says, his voice barely above a whisper. He stares at his hands for a moment before slowly interlocking his fingers, mirroring Ricky's gesture. The word ripples through the clones, and one by one, they follow suit, threading their fingers together. The tension in the air shifts. Ricky steps forward cautiously as their hostility begins to dissolve.

They're more than echoes—they have souls.

One by one, they exchange looks, silent understanding passing between them. Then, with steady resolve, the five clones form a barrier, our people to their backs, facing the O'rians. Ricky cracks his knuckles, and the clones square their shoulders.

Jihyun glances at me, amusement flickering in his eyes as a smirk tugs at his lips.

"Rictor." Ricky calls out to me. "We friends... right?" His gaze is fixed on the battlefield. Hearing my own twelve-year-old voice say those words makes my stomach twist.

How did it come to this? How many have I hurt? Is this what I've become?

The Vermillion Sages regroup, their eyes locking onto us with renewed fury.

"Traitors!" one of them spits, venom laced in every syllable. The Allied Force regathers, catching their breath, bracing for another round.

"How in the Tree did you turn them?" Amos's voice is sharp, his gaze darting to the clones, distrust still blatant in his expression. I almost forgot—these clones nearly destroyed Vereilles. His fear is justified.

"I didn't." I shake my head. "They made the choice themselves."

Before Amos can respond, the Squad joins us, their younger selves standing side by side with their older versions for the first time—not as enemies, but as something else. No lingering malice—just an unspoken understanding. The moment hangs, fragile and fleeting—the line between past and present blurring.

"Amos!" Captain Kaelor barks, turning to him as they both weave a shield spell, their hands moving in swift, practiced motions. Before they can complete it, the mecha suits surge forward, intercepting the Vermillion Sages' attack.

The air distorts as the blood-infused spell slams against the mechas' reinforced plating, sending sprays of crimson energy searching for a target, but the mechas absorb the impact, their energy cores pulsing violently as they nullify the corruptive force. They stand strong, an unbreakable barrier between us and the enemy.

The Sages' attacks intensify, their energy refusing to dissipate. It latches onto the mechas, dark tendrils of magick weaving through the metal, corrupting them from the inside.

"Get out of there now! It won't hold!" Captain Kaelor's command crackles over the comms, but it's too late.

"For Ethra!" One of the pilots screams, his voice distorting in our comm links as a blinding light erupts from the mechas. Agonized screams pierce the air, and for a moment, the battlefield is nothing but searing brilliance and devastation.

Then, silence.

The Sages' spell dissipates, leaving the mechas still. Gold dust begins to drift from them, scattering into the wind.

I suck in a breath, my feet moving before I even register it. A guttural scream tears from my throat. Around me, the others follow, our battle cry rising in unison as we charge. Ricky keeps pace as we dive into the mayhem. Emierr and Dustin stay on my heels, their clones mirroring their every move. Kid Jho and Jads stay back with Brunner, fortifying our defenses.

The battlefield blurs into a hurricane of clashing steel and magick of every kind.

My armor shivers to life, nanotech shifting and reforming as I summon spears into existence. I hurl them toward Ricky, and he catches them midair without missing a beat. We move in sync—every strike, every counter, an echo of the other.

Around us, the Squad battles alongside their clones, the once-enemies now turning the tide in our favor. Blades clash, spells ignite, and the O'rians struggle to hold their ground.

Brunner, Jho, and Jads' combined efforts reinforce weak points in our lines, sealing gaps before they can be exploited.

The O'rians falter, their formations unraveling as their forces crumble. A glimmer of hope cuts through the blood-soaked landscape.

We might actually end this war.

"Ricky." Jhoana's voice cuts through the comms, uneven and shaken.

"Jho? Tell me it worked! It's crazy out here."

"Ricky... Jads tried, but the wish—it didn't break the curse."

My chest tightens. "What? That was our only shot. If the wish can't break the curse, then what the hell are we supposed to do? Abbadon and Evanora aren't even here. Is Jads okay?"

"I—I have to try again!" Jadis's voice cracks through Jhoana's comms with frustration and panic.

"Jho, the clones are here and—"

"The clones are with them!" Jhoana interrupts, urgency spiking in her voice before the signal distorts into static and vanishes completely.

"Hello? Jho!" I yell into the comms, but static is my only answer.

Ricky moves—fast, deflecting magick missiles just before they slam into me. He flashes me a small, reassuring smile—but then his expression falters, face crumpling. Ricky's movements stutter, as if something unseen just reached out and touched them.

"What's happening to them?" Brunner's voice rips through the comms.

My clone—Ricky—locks eyes with me, his gaze filled with something human. Tears well at the corners of his eyes as he takes an unsteady step forward. He reaches for me, desperation in his outstretched fingers—but before I can grasp his hands, his body begins to glow. A brilliant light surges from within him. I whip my head around, panic flooding my chest. The other clones are glowing too, their forms shimmering like dying stars.

Ricky's lips part, barely above a whisper. "I'm scared."

I lunge, fingers brushing empty air as Ricky vanishes into the radiance.

The light swallows them whole.

My hands snap shut on nothing.

"No." The word escapes me, barely a breath, as I stare at my trembling hands. *Abbadon.* It has to be him. Because they turned on him, he erased them? Rip them from existence? Can he even do that?

"Where did little Meer go? He was just here." Emierr is staring blankly at the spot his younger self occupied mere seconds before.

With no warning, the air around me ignites. The Vermillion Sages unleash a barrage of fire, streaks of molten energy crashing down like meteor showers. My hands curl into fists and I leap into the fray, lightning crackling at my fingertips as I charge forward, meeting the inferno head-on.

I no longer have control of my body.

My clone was changing—he had changed. The clones were finally on our side, fighting with us, and just like that, they were wiped out. Reduced to nothing. They never even had a chance to live, to start over.

I weave through the onslaught, heat searing against my armor as I push through to the back lines. Every breath is fire in my lungs. I slam my fists into the ground, sending a raging bolt of lightning through the earth, launching a group of Sages off their feet. My armor shifts, forming into weapons that hum with electricity. I lash out, unable to contain my anger, but they deflect each of my attacks.

"Ricky, get out of there!" Dustin's voice rings in my ear.

But it's too late. I'm in too deep.

Dozens of Vermillion Sages turn to me at once. They close in, hands already dripping crimson. I launch into the air, barely dodging the barrage of attacks that crash into the ground below. One second slower, and I'd be dust.

Just as the Sages ready another assault, one drops. Then another.

It's Jae, cutting through the enemy line, laser guns blazing, his shots reducing a few to ashes.

I thunder toward him, twisting through spells and hurling bolts of lightning in return. "Behind you!" I shout, mentally shoving the Sage away as I dive in beside him.

Jae exhales sharply, recharging his guns in a well-practiced motion. "You really don't care if you live, do you?"

I steal a quick glance back. Reckless. Emotional. What the hell was I thinking, taking them all on alone?

Jae presses both palms against the grips of his laser guns, and a maroon glow pulses from them. In a single, fluid movement, he swings his arms downward, summoning metallic orbs that hover in a perfect circle before him. With another flick of his wrists, the orbs spiral behind his back, floating in formation.

"Where's Abbadon?" Jae's roar snaps me out of my daze. "Talk, you bastards!"

"He dares speak his name!" one hisses, their eyes burning with fury.

A strange sensation trickles down my body. My armor is wearing thin, the nanotech struggling to keep up as more of my body is exposed with every weapon I summon. *Shit.* The Vambrace—it's gone. *When did I lose it?*

"Doesn't matter," another sneers, blood pooling in their palms, twisting into a whip. "The Angel of Death will reward us for eliminating this scum!"

The Sages' blood shifts, twisting together into the same whip, their intent unmistakable—kill.

I create a double-edged spear of raw lightning, electricity surging through my hands as I grip it tight.

"Die!" a Sage howls as her blood whip snaps straight for Jae.

Jae reacts instantly, flicking his wrist. One of his metallic spheres shoots forward, intercepting the whip mid-strike. Without missing a beat, he fires a precise shot, piercing through the Sage's head, turning her into dust before they even hit the ground.

I tighten my grip on the spear, its hum vibrating in my palm. The sages move in unison, sending whips lashing toward us from every direction. I mentally spin the spear at high speed, arcs of lightning sparking from the blade as I push its momentum outward. Electric currents surge around Jae and me, carving through the incoming whips before they can reach us. Severed blood spatters across the battlefield, hissing as it meets the scorched ground.

We move together—Jae dodging and firing, his metallic spheres forming a shifting barrier around him, deflecting attacks before they can reach him. I guide my spear, impaling enemy after enemy, like a conductor leading an orchestra. A bloody symphony.

Sparks and embers dance through the air as the battlefield becomes a blur of movement. A Sage lunges at Jae from behind. My armor reacts before I do, nanotech forming razor-sharp hands that shred through the Sage, cutting their attack short.

"Look out!" Jae's eyes flick behind me. I spin just in time to see crimson tendrils lash toward us. Jae slams his hands onto the ground, his voice ringing with an incantation. The terra erupts beneath the sages, rippling outward in jagged waves. They stumble, thrown off balance, but I don't give them time to recover. I launch myself into the air, lightning coiling around my arms before I send a crackling bolt crashing down into the throng. Screams tear through the air.

I land beside Jae, both of us staring at the mountain of limp bodies, smoke and gold dust curling from their blackened forms. We exchange a glance, neither of us speaking—until Borge's desperate voice breaks through the comms.

"They're flanking me, I need help!"

Jae doesn't pause to think; he sprints off into the thick of the battle. I'm right behind him, barely registering the chaos around us as I yank Allied Force soldiers out of harm's way with telekinesis, shoving them aside before an attack can land. The battlefield is a blur—steel clashing, spells detonating, bodies falling. The Squad is fighting with everything they have. The Vermillion Sages' numbers are thinning, but so are ours.

Then I see them—three Sages closing in on Borge. He's crouched behind a crystalline barrier, barely keeping up as blood spears and spells hammer against his shield.

Jae wastes no time. He flicks his wrist, sending a barrage of ice shards at the sages. Two cry out as the shards pierce their arms and legs, staggering them. But instead of retreating, they turn to face him, summoning astral bows out of thin air, arrows already nocked and aimed.

I brace myself to deflect—but something slams into me first. A gust of wind, sharp and sudden, knocks me off my feet. I hit the ground hard, dust choking my lungs. When I push myself up, a Sage looms over me, blood tendrils writhing, reaching—

Lightning surges from my palm before I even think, blasting the Sage backward. I scramble to my feet, whipping around just in time to see the Sages loose their arrows.

"No!" The word rips from my throat, but before the arrows can reach Jae, a crystalline wall materializes in front of him. The arrows shatter harmlessly against it.

Borge saved him. But—

My breath catches. I lunge forward, but I'm too late.

A spear of crimson light plunges into his chest.

Borge's body jolts. A sharp, strangled grunt escapes him as he stares down at the wound, his hands instinctively reaching for the pulsing glow in his torso. Even as agony twists his face, he forces his trembling arms upward, conjuring one last crystalline wall to shield Jae from another attack. The barrier solidifies—

Then Borge collapses.

"Borge!" Jae's scream cuts through the battlefield.

Before the Sages can press on, thick roots erupt from the ground, lashing around them like constricting serpents. Their arms snap to their sides, mouths silenced by creeping vines. Then the needles sprout. A muffled gasp escapes them all—in an instant, they disintegrate into bloody pulp and specks of dust. I follow the tendrils to their source—

Emierr. He strides forward, his expression grim.

The rest of the battlefield stills. We've cleared the wave. But the cost?

Too high.

Everyone regroups in the fleeting lull. Jae drops to his knees beside Borge, his hands shaking as he picks up one of Borge's crystal shards. His grip tightens around it, knuckles white, grief etched into every movement.

"You broke our rule, dumbass! You're supposed to save yourself first!" Jae chokes out, his jaw clenched so tight it trembles. He grips Borge's hand, pressing it against his forehead before leaning his head onto his chest.

"Listen..." Borge's voice is barely a whisper, his eyes fluttering, struggling to stay open. "Tell my kids I love them. Jae, you are my fav—" His breath hitches, the words dying with him.

Jae doesn't hold back. Borge's glittering ashes scatter in the wake of Jae's grief, joining the countless souls lost to this war.

My head hangs low, I know it all too well.

"May the Tree guide him home safely. May they all find peace." Captain Kaelor bows his head. "Mourn, brothers and sisters. Let your hearts carry the weight of our fallen."

Loss and emptiness engulfs the battlefield. I want to mourn the clones, the lives I stole, this crumbling world. But I can't. The tears won't come. I'm empty.

"Ricky—*Ricky,* do you copy?" Jadis's frantic voice comes through. "Jads?"

The Squad snaps to attention at her name.

"Evanora showed up. She ambushed us. Lacey's hurt, and Jho went after her."

"Shit. Where are you now?"

"What's happening? Did it work?" Brunner's eyes search mine for any kind of answer.

I have no idea how to explain any of this to them. My throat tightens, but before I can even try, Jadis speaks first.

"Ricky, it's worse than we thought. The O'rians... They took children from every nation. They forced the parents to fight in this war, for their kids' freedom."

The words hit me like a physical blow, knocking the air from my lungs. My mind reels, piecing it together. The first wave—Sólel was right. Those people, the ones we turned to dust... They weren't O'rians. My stomach twists violently. The image of the woman fleeing from me sears itself into my mind—the terror in her eyes as she watched me hurl the spear back at her.

She wasn't a soldier. She wasn't a threat. She was just a mother trying to get her child back. And I was the danger she was running from. *What have we done?* A wave of nausea crashes over me, and for a moment, I think I might throw up.

"Are they okay? Tap us in." Dustin pulls me back.

"The O'rians..." I choke. The Squad's faces mirror the same mix of exhaustion and confusion. Everyone around us has suffered enough. I won't tell them about the parents, about the truth of the first wave. Not now. Maybe not ever. Instead, I steady my voice. "They took children from every nation." I swipe on the bracelet, connecting the others into the call.

"The kids—They're being held at an abandoned O'rian hideout."

Emierr exhales sharply, relief cutting through the tension. "Jads, it's damn good to hear your voice."

"Guys, we don't have much time. Evanora said the kids are where Jho abandoned her friends—whatever that—" Jadis's voice warps into static and cuts out.

"Jads? Jads!" I shout, frustration clamping down on my chest.

The rest attempt to reach Jhoana and Jadis, but the sputtering comms offer nothing.

Emierr tries again, reaching out to Sólel this time. Silence.

"I..." Mikal starts, but he takes a steadying breath. "I know where the kids are." His eyes flick to Jihyun and Maks, a silent understanding passing between them.

"That place... It's where our parents died," Jihyun mutters.

Maks clenches her fists, shaking her head. "And now they're making who knows how many kids suffer there too?" Her voice wavers, anger laced with something deeper—grief, resentment. "They're monsters, all of them."

"Someone else can go—"

"It has to be us." Mikal cuts Brunner off. "We'll get the kids."

"Wait. How far is it? You guys shouldn't go alone." This could be a trap for all I know, and they'll be out there with no backup.

"They won't be alone," Jae says, rising to his feet. "I'll go with them."

"Are you sure? You can sit this out." Dustin places a hand on his shoulder.

"We don't have time. By the time reinforcements arrive, the children could already be gone. They need us now—We're the only ones who can reach them in time." He pauses, taking in the Squad. He's still hurting. All of them are. "It's been an honor serving with you, my Nobles. Stay alive."

"Jae... Thank you." I try to pour every ounce of gratitude I can into those three words. He meets my gaze with a small smile before turning to the siblings.

"Teleportation's our best shot," Jae says as they gather in a tight circle. Mikal projects an image of their destination, his hands steady, while Jae begins weaving the spell, energy crackling between his fingers.

"Remember, no matter what it takes, get our mom back home." Maks's gaze lingers on us, fierce and unwavering. Jihyun meets my eyes, a small, knowing smile flickering across his face—then, in an instant, they're gone.

Captain Kaelor strides through the battlefield, his expression grim. Blood soaks the ground, and the air is thick with the metallic scent of death.

So much carnage.

And most of the blood spilled wasn't even our enemies'.

Amos scans the battlefield around him. "What now?" His voice is laced with uncertainty, exhaustion, or maybe both.

"There aren't many of us left. We've held out long enough. We need to retreat while we still can," Captain Kaelor says. He's a husk of the captain who entered this battlefield.

One look around, and it's clear—we can't take much more of this.

"It's for the best." Dustin exhales. "Jho's already dealing with

Evanora. Let's just find Jads, get her, and get the hell out of here."

Captain Kaelor nods at Dustin, then looks over the weary faces around him. "You've given everything. What happened here will not be forgotten. Let's prepare to move."

Everyone stirs into motion—some tending to the wounded, others combing through the wreckage, their hands brushing over bodies, discarded weapons, and tattered insignias, searching for remnants of those they lost.

Dustin and Emierr approach, their expressions tight with concern, their eyes scanning me like they're bracing for the worst.

"The clones…" Emierr starts, his voice hesitant. "Did they—"

"I think so," I breathe.

"Borge…" Dustin's voice wavers as he shakes his head. "Your dad… All of them…"

"They did what they had to." I cut him off before he can say more. There's no time to mourn—not now. "We find Jho, get Evanora, and get out. We're this close."

They both nod.

"Wait, where's Rune?" Emierr asks, scanning the area. A few feet away, Brunner stands still, his head twisting around as if searching for something. "Rune, we need to move!" Emierr calls out.

"Where the hell did they go?" Brunner shouts, his voice tight with panic.

"What are you talking about?" Dustin's brows furrow.

"The people I fought… I left them right here. I—I thought I knocked them out. So where the hell did they go? They didn't… Oh, god."

Dustin and I exchange a look. "What do you mean?" I ask, voice edged with unease.

Emierr places a hand on his shoulder, grounding him. "Rune, we—"

"They're gone. I—" His breath stutters, his chest rising and falling unevenly as realization crashes over him. "Did I… kill all of them?"

The others try to reason with him, to justify it.

"They were trying to kill us too, Rune. They killed Borge, Uncle James, and so many others," Dustin says, but Brunner's expression doesn't waver.

"That's not what I signed up for," Brunner mutters, stepping back, his hands shaking. "I'm not a killer! You all—" He cuts himself off, blinking rapidly, rubbing his face as if trying to wipe away the horror settling in. "I'm not a monster. I'm not—" His breath quickens, his chest rising and falling unevenly.

A cold weight sinks into my chest. All this time, Brunner had been holding back, fighting differently—while the rest of us struck to survive, he fought to spare. I can't let him know the truth, it'll break him.

"Rune, it's okay. You didn't mean to. None of us ever do." Dustin says. "We were just trying to survive."

"Weren't they just trying to protect themselves too? From us?" Brunner's voice cracks.

"Everyone!" Captain Kaelor's voice cuts through the tense air. The battlefield stills as all eyes snap to him. His face has gone pale. "They're coming! Bigger, stronger, and in greater numbers than before! The five nations are sending reinforcements, and we must stand our ground until they arrive."

Exhaustion and fear casts a heavy fog over the survivors.

"I know you're exhausted. I know this is more than anyone should have to give. If you need to leave, no one will fault you. But if any of you still have the strength to stand, to hold just a little longer, it would be my honor to fight beside you."

"For Ethra!" Amos yells.

The remaining Vereillic follow their leader, their voices rising in unified chants. The Allied Force hesitates for only a moment before joining in, their resolve hardening as they prepare for the fight ahead.

"I've got one fight left in me." I turn to the boys.

Emierr and Dustin nod.

Brunner hesitates, conflict flickering in his eyes, but he doesn't back away.

The Allied Force soldiers snap to attention, forming a solid front, shields locking, weapons raised. We brace ourselves as the winds of war fly toward us.

"We hold the line! This is our last stand—no one gets through!" Captain Kaelor's voice carries over the battlefield.

Then, the horizon darkens.

Hundreds of massive figures appear through the swirling dust, their forms clad in ancient battle-worn armor, their faces twisted and fearsome.

Captain Kaelor takes a sharp step back. "Impossible. Orcs haven't been seen in hundreds of years... They were thought to have perished in the Great War."

Another ripple distorts the battlefield. Four ghostly figures with flowing, ethereal tails flicker in and out of sight. Dustin squeezes my shoulder.

"Are those... gumiho? They're mythical beings, only in stories," Amos breathes. "What is going on here?" He tightens his grips on his astral long sword.

One of the gumiho emerges from the formation, weaving a spell with its delicate, clawed fingers. The air hums, static dancing over my skin. A device materializes before them—a spiraling construct of darkened metal and polished glass, its core thrumming with an ominous violet glow. Strange runes flicker across its surface, shifting like living ink, morphing and contorting as if whispering secrets to the air. Ripples of energy coil outward, warping the space around it, distorting light and sound. The sheer force it emits presses against my skull, setting my teeth on edge.

The hum grows into a piercing frequency. It takes half a second to realize what's about to happen.

Then, everything tilts.

The soundwave detonates across the battlefield, ripping through the Allied Force like an invisible blade. Soldiers drop where they stand, their bodies crumpling to the ground in an instant. The entire army—leyfolk, humans, warriors—all unconscious before they even realize what hit them.

A searing pain explodes in my skull, and the world around me twists and bends. Reality fractures—then suddenly, I'm back, Dustin's grip firm on my shoulder, anchoring me to the present.

"Are those... gumiho? They're mythical beings, only in stories," Amos breathes, just as he had in my vision. "What is going on here?"

A thrill of horror washes through me. "Squad! Cover your ears!" I bark.

"What?" Emierr's eyebrows shoot up.

"Just do it!" I snap, clamping my hands over my ears. "Now! Everyone!"

The machine hums, its vibration creeping into my bones. Confusion ripples through the crowd—some hesitate, unsure, while others ready their weapons. The Squad's hands fly over their ears just as the device reaches its peak. Then, with a sudden, violent pulse, it unleashes its full power. The air fractures, the frequency splitting through reality itself.

One by one, bodies drop to the ground. The battlefield falls silent in mere seconds. I watch Captain Kaelor and Amos hit the muddied ground below. For one, tense moment, I think this is it. The faintest rise of their chests sends a fleeting rush of relief through my limbs. No golden glimmer rising from the field. Unconscious, but alive.

Only the four of us remain standing.

My ears ring, but I push past the disorientation.

Enough.

Power rush through me, untamed, my nails sharpening as a dark aura cocoons around me like second skin. It's happening again—just like when I fought Tholric in Vereilles, and when we took on Abbadon at the abandoned facility. That power. The one that felt good. My senses heighten, every detail searing into my mind. I glance at the Squad—Brunner takes a few steps back, but Emierr and Dustin feel it too, the shift, the surge. And I let it fully consume me.

"We hold the line, no matter what!" I shout, my voice distorted.

The gumiho begins to charge the device again, but I don't let it. My hands raise, and the creature is yanked into the air, limbs spread wide as its body convulses. The device slips from its grasp, shattering against the ground. The gumiho writhes, its cries piercing, but I don't release my hold.

"Why aren't the rest attacking?" Brunner asks, perplexed.

I glance at the Orcs. What are they waiting for?

The remaining three gumiho dash in my direction, desperation flashing in their glowing eyes. Before they can reach me, the ground shudders, and thick roots surge upward, snaring them mid-stride. Vines coil around their limbs, tightening like iron shackles, choking their cries into strangled gasps. Their bodies thrash, but it's useless. The one suspended in my grasp trembles violently—I don't hesitate. I twist its limbs one by one, sharp cracks punctuating the mayhem, before flinging it skyward, its form vanishing into beyond the dust clouds.

"Finish them," I order Emierr, my voice a hollow echo of itself.

Emierr flinches, his face twisting with horror as the gumiho cry out, their voices raw with desperation. His hands tremble, fingers twitching, but he can't move. He can't do it.

"It's okay, Meer. I'll handle it," Dustin mutters. A green glow ignites from his wrist, and his blades carve through the air in deadly arcs. The gumiho's cries are abruptly silenced as the strikes land—final. Their forms slump against Emierr's vines and a trickle of dust begins to fall. The blades snap back into Dustin's grip. I catch the flicker in his eyes. He despises this as much as I do. But still, he does what must be done.

Brunner stands frozen, his face contorted with disbelief. His breath catches, but then his expression steels, resolve settling beneath the tears streaking down his cheeks.

"Rune, if you don't—"

"No," he cuts me off, voice hoarse. "Whatever it takes, right?"

A bone-rattling screech rips through the battlefield. Then, like a tidal wave of muscle and steel, the Orc horde surges forward, their battle cry rolling over us like a thunderclap, shaking the very ground beneath our feet.

Brunner is the first to move, blinking through the chaos, each step detonating in a concussive blast that hurls Orcs through the air.

I move on instinct, flanking the enemy, lightning crackling at my fists as I strike. Dustin blurs through the battlefield like a shadow, Ade' amplifying his every move, his blows breaking through entire flanks with terrifying ease. Emierr flows like the wind, his needles finding their marks without fail. Vines burst from the ground at his command, spearing through enemy ranks, releasing thick, toxic fumes that spread through the battlefield, suffocating anything in their path.

I unleash a telekinetic wave, bodies flinging through the air like weightless debris. My armor pulses—deflecting, countering, adjusting to every strike. Lightning hisses and snaps at my fingertips, each blow sending seismic tremors through the ground.

Enemies fall, but they keep coming.,

A sharp sting pierces my skull—my first warning. The familiar agony of pushing the bond too far shreds through my senses like shattered glass, snapping my connection to Aigerim. My vision falters, my limbs dragging as if weighed down by lead.

Dustin stumbles, his movements growing sluggish, Ade's aura completely drained. Emierr doubles over, gripping his knees, each breath a sharp, ragged gasp. Heat radiates from our bodies, steam curling into the air—we're running on fumes, pushing past the edge.

Still, none of our people stir.

We won't last much longer like this.

"All of you, get these people out of here!" I order, knowing full well my plan is futile. We should have just left the moment Captain Kaelor suggested. I know what needs to be done. "I'll hold them off. I'll buy us enough time and be right behind you." I hope I'm not lying.

The boys don't bother trying to argue. They sprint toward the blanket of unconscious bodies.

"Sól, can you hear me?" Emierr urgently tries the comms again. "We need you—now!"

Something in the air shifts. Instinct screams at me, and I turn just in time to see a Stasis Band snapping toward my wrist. My armor reacts before I do, adjusting at the last second, causing the band to latch onto a loose plate instead. It clatters to the ground, useless.

A second band hurtles toward me—I snatch it midair, lightning crackling from my fingertips as I reduce it to dust. I pivot to warn the others, but I'm too late. The Stasis Bands snap onto their wrists with a metallic hiss, yanking them off the ground. Electricity surges through their bodies, locking their muscles in rigid, agonized convulsions. Their limbs jerk violently, and then—like magnets—they slam together before being dragged toward the enemy.

My mind races. Jae's metallic spheres—I remember the way he

wielded them. Drawing from the last remnants of my arm armor, I forge three orbs, their surfaces rippling like liquid metal. I propel myself forward, reaching for the boys, mentally pulling at their bodies. They lurch toward me, but an unseen force yanks them back with equal strength—a brutal deadlock.

Orcs close in from all sides, their snarls drowning out the turmoil around me. My orbs react instantly, shifting into spears that fire outward, impaling anything that dares get too close. The battlefield turns into a savage push-and-pull, my armor stripping away piece by piece to shield me. My focus sharpens on the ones holding the boys. I unleash a searing barrage of lightning, dropping them where they stand. The resistance weakens. With one final yank, I tear the boys free and drag them behind me.

The last of my orbs streaks over my shoulder. I pivot just in time to see a massive orc, larger than the others, swat the attack aside with a sweep of its colossal club. It bellows, muscles rippling as it barrels toward me. I brace myself, but it's too fast. My leg armor snakes upward in a desperate attempt to reinforce my ribs.

Impact.

Agony erupts in my side, a sharp, splintering shock that hurls me across the battlefield. I tumble through dust and debris, my body skidding to a brutal stop. A crack ripples through me—something inside gives way. My breath stutters, each inhale a struggle. If my armor hadn't reacted, I'd be dead.

Through the haze of pain, I see the orc striding toward me, its massive club poised for the killing blow. My pulse hammers as I scan for a weapon—anything. My gaze locks onto a fallen battle-ax. I reach out with my power, yanking it through the air with a desperate pull. The weapon spins end over end, a lethal blur of steel. The orc barely has time to react before the blade buries deep into its skull. It shudders, then collapses to the dirt, its Ethereal ashes already slithering free.

I clutch my ribs, pain radiating in sharp waves through my torso. More orcs are closing in. I press my hands together, willing magick to mend me—but nothing. No warmth, no glow. Just empty silence where power should be.

Now is really not the time to lose my faith in magick.

Sólel The Sunbringr

"*L* *ittle one, when the day comes, what kind of person will you be?*" *Father asked as he carried me on his shoulders. Shafts of sunlight filtered through the trees overhead, illuminating our path. Villagers greeted us with waves of their hands, hooves, and other less identifiable limbs, as we made our way toward the Ethereal Lake.*

"*Does it matter, Dad?*" *I leaned my arms on top of his head. I haven't called him Dad since I was very young. When he became chief, he also became Father. I never knew the reason why.*

"*It always matters who you ultimately become. Especially you, little one. Someday, you will lead our people when I become one with the Tree.*"

"*Do I need to know now?*" *A soft breeze blew through us as leaves from the vines cascaded around, twirling and dancing with the wind.*

"*No, no, sorry.*" *He let out a chuckle.* "*I shouldn't trouble you with such questions, not for several more years at least.*" *He paused, shaking his head.* "*I apologize, let's just forget I even asked.*" *For the remainder of the walk, Father stayed silent, steadily carrying me on his shoulders.*

That was the only time he ever asked me that question, not even when I was old enough to begin my training as chief. It always left me wondering why he'd asked it at all, knowing he'd never bring it up again. Did he have doubts about my path? Or maybe he wasn't sure if I was truly meant to succeed him?

A sudden surge of energy snaps me back to the present. *Almost there—just a little more.*

I've never ventured this close to the sun before. I'm not exactly sure how it's possible for me to breathe in outer space, but I concentrate on filling my lungs as deeply as possible. Absorbing more and more solar energy into my being, the radiance intensifies, ready to erupt from within me. Pressure mounts as every muscle in my body tightens to its limit.

"*What kind of person will you be?*" Father's question reverberates in my mind. I let out a primal scream as the energy bursts from my skin, transcending the body I'd always known into something beyond. *Kuya* Ricky had once told me, in our childhood, that the true hue of the sun is white. As I inhabit my new form, my solar essence flickers, blending hues of orange, red, and the white I'd only ever heard of.

I feel unstoppable.

"Sól—can—" Meer's voice statics through the communication.

"*Kuya?*"

"We—now!" The connection dissolves into a meaningless drone.

"I'm coming!" I soar through the skies at a velocity beyond any I've ever known myself to be capable of. The rush of pulling solar energy straight from the sun floods me, propelling me forward like a comet streaking through the cosmos. In mere moments, I locate the battlefield and descend with the force of a falling star. Debris scatters in my wake, sending O'rian soldiers sprawling in all directions. Some are already cinders in my wake.

Terror welds me in place as I take in the extent of the carnage before me. The once proud ranks of the Allied Force lay broken and scattered across the battlefield, their banners torn and trampled beneath the relentless advance of the O'rian forces. Then I realize—these are not people.

Are those... orcs? The creatures' eyes widen with fear at my catastrophic appearance, their advance faltering for a moment as they assess. But it's only a fleeting pause before they regroup and converge upon me with savage determination.

An unending throng of opposing forces form a ring around me, their leathery skin taking the brunt of my heat. Their weapons gleam in the harsh light of the sun as they close in from all sides. In one final effort, I attempt to reach my *ates* and *kuyas* through the comms once more, but I'm met with static.

Then, a voice cuts through the chaos, sharp and clear in my ears. "Sól... you came back." It's Ricky.

"*Kuya*, where are the others?"

"They're down, but still breathing. It's just me left." He coughs. "I think I broke a rib. I'm not sure how much longer I can hold out." There's a beat of silence. "We're the last stand, Sól."

"What about the clones?"

"Gone."

An invisible hand crushes my heart in its iron grip. I spot Ricky amidst the wave of enemies, struggling to rise. "Conserve your strength, *kuya*. I'll take it from here."

The orc soldiers charge at me, a stampede from every side. I ascend into the air, out of reach of their crude weapons, a nimbus of solar energy. Every fiber of my being pulses with power as I unleash the full extent of my newfound strength. Flares of solar heat lash at the army below, leaving charred flesh and ash in their wake.

"Do you vow to cherish and protect all life, with every breath you take, until the Tree calls you home?"

"I swear it."

With a gasp, I reign my power in, staring down in revulsion at what I'd done. Fatal wounds, cauterized too late. Scorched limbs crumpled into heaps in the dust. I'd killed them. And I'd done it with ease.

"Sól, there's more coming. Hundreds more. The nations are next if they get through to us." Ricky's voice is a thread in the roar of fire and gut-wrenching shame. Before I can respond, the sky above becomes a canvas of shadows as countless astral arrows blot out the sun's light. "Oh god," he whispers.

I raise my arms skyward, summoning the power of the sun from within me. Brilliant radiance bursts forth from my outstretched fingertips, weaving a shimmering barrier of light that encircles me and our fallen comrades like a protective canopy. The astral arrows rain down upon us in a relentless storm, but the barrier holds firm, dissipating each deadly projectile as it makes contact.

I drop the shield of light and propel myself forward. Now is not the time to fall apart. The incoming enemy reinforcements loom on the horizon, their ranks swelling with each passing moment. A primal roar shreds through my vocal chords, and I unleash torrents of enhanced solar beams, each beam slicing through the enemy ranks with unparalleled precision.

I am not a killer. But Abbadon has made me one—and I'm not going down without a fight. This is not just for us anymore, but for the countless lives that hang in the balance. Even if it means I lose my soul or die trying.

"Sól!" Ricky's urgent cry pierces through my ears, drawing my attention back to him. Several enemy soldiers have breached our defenses.

"*Kuya!*" I shout, my warning reaching his ears just as a battle axe descends from above, wielded by a heavily-scarred orc. I barely reach Ricky in time, seizing the orc's arm in a vice-like grip before the blade can strike him. "Forgive me," I murmur, nausea welling within my gut as I embrace the snarling orc. My aura pulses. The orc's life energy pours into me like blood from a severed artery. The creature withers, its form reduced to little more than a skeletal husk.

Ricky gapes at me, but there's no time for explanations. I kneel beside him, placing my hands over his broken ribs, channeling his attacker's life energy into the torn cartilage and shattered bone.

"Are you all right?" I cautiously help him to his feet as the warmth of healing energy courses through his body, dispelling pain.

He stares at me with wide, shocked eyes. "You just broke your oath," he murmurs softly.

I ignore him and extend my left arm toward him. "Power up."

"I'm not going to burn am I?"

"I choose who I burn."

He nods and reaches out. Relief washes over his features as his demeanor shifts as a fresh surge of energy courses through him.

"I really thought you left us." His eyes scan me. "New look?"

"Upgrade." I force a laugh. "Where are the others?"

The orc's soul returns to the Tree, gold dust wafting into the air. His withered body remains—evidence of my sins.

"They're unconscious," Ricky says. "I don't know where Jho and Jads are, but I don't think these bitches intend to kill us. They were trying to take Dusty, Meer and Rune. Jihyun, Maks, and Mikal are with Jae on a mission." With a weary sigh, he removes the shattered pieces of his armor. "The nations are sending more forces. They should be here soon. I hope."

"Then we hold the line until they get here." I cast a glance toward the oncoming wave. "You ready?"

"For Ethra." Electricity crackles to life in his hands.

"For Ethra," I echo. As one, we drive ourselves forward to meet the enemy—Ricky's lightning holding him aloft with renewed strength and my own blinding beams of sunlight striking the golden mist below. For a fleeting moment, a surreal stillness descends upon us, as if time itself hesitates in anticipation. Then, with a deafening roar, we unleash an onslaught of our own upon the enemy ranks.

The hissing snap of Ricky's lightning intertwines with the radiant beams of my solar energy, erupting from our outstretched hands. The sky seems to split apart as our combined assault tears through the wave of attackers, transforming countless bodies into shadowy smears of ash.

But even as the dust settles and screams fade into the distance, a sinister aura emerges from the chaos below. A familiar dark purple glows amidst the swirling clouds of smoke and dust.

"More Vermillion Sages." Ricky's tone is grim. "Of course. They wouldn't send their strongest assholes all at once."

"Ready for a second round, *kuya*?" I glance over at him. Rage, pain, grief, and lethal determination are etched into every line of his face.

With one last, deep breath, we plunge headfirst into death. The orchestra of battle surrounds us as spells and projectiles rain down from all directions.

As I weave through the barrage of attacks, my senses heightened to their limits, I catch sight of Ricky narrowly evading a deadly dragon's breath spell. His lightning-imbued levitation propels him with superhuman reflexes as the searing green flames lick at the air where he had just been moments before.

Meanwhile, my solar-enhanced form acts as a shield, incinerating any attack that dares approach me. I unleash a flurry of obliterating flame into the heart of the Vermillion Sages. But with each opponent I incapacitate, echoes of Ricky's words haunt my mind, reminding me of the oath I've broken beyond repair. With every strike, a pang of remorse thrums through my conscience, and the burden growing heavier and heavier

"Life is sacred, little one. Down to the ants that build their community. Remember, every life is a part of you. You are the Sunbringr, that means you are life itself."

Rays of solar devastation carve through each red-cloaked figure below. *Not anymore, Father.*

Ricky flings both arms to either side. I can see the tendons in his neck strain as he curls them skyward. A host of orc soldiers leave the ground. Their terrified, furious roars do nothing to prevent their fate. Ricky rotates his palms down and, with a decisive motion, he sends them plummeting to the terra, their cries cut short by the thud of bodies shattering against the pitiless soil. Once more, Ricky ascends into the sky, hands engulfed in crackling tendrils of lightning. Without hesitation, he curls his hands into fists, intensifying the power. With a roar, he releases a tempest upon the broken bodies of his foes. The momentary survivors' shrieks of pain are deafening. I've only ever seen the true level of his pain and anger once, by the cliff where he tried to end his life, but this—I'm afraid Ricky harbors more than I could have imagined.

A second wave of distant dark purple catches my attention. I rocket toward the aura, building a fistful of blinding light in my palm. But before I can reach it, the sound of arrows slicing through the air fills my ears.

I hurl the beam from my hand, dispatching the archer, but my efforts are in vain. A second barrage of astral spears and arrows arc towards Ricky. Despite his valiant attempts to deflect them, one spear finds its mark, piercing his right forearm perilously close to his head, while an arrow embeds itself in his left leg. A pained shout escapes his lips as he crashes to the ground, his defenses shattered.

"*Kuya!*" I yell, but he remains motionless. Faint, monstrous noises emanate from the billowing smoke I've left behind, replacing the temporary silence. I sense an incoming surge of life energy pulsating just beyond the battlefield. No such life exists in the air around me—the Vermillion Sages have been neutralized. Yet, the distant sound of enemy reinforcements looms ever closer. Something doesn't feel right.

The smoke begins to clear. I falter, dropping a few feet in the air. The army marching to meet me in my final stand is neither human nor orc. It is a nightmare—monsters from stories told to Ethran children to keep them inside at night. Beings that had fallen into myth following the great war. Harpies cut though the air above as trolls' footfalls shake the ground below. Minotaurs snort and bellow, their cloven hooves marching alongside slithering naga. There are creatures whose names I do not know and creatures whose names I wish I didn't.

The ancestors of the Commisceo Tribe—the tribe of the ley-folk—marching on the side of the O'rians. On the side of those who would poison the magick which birthed them.

How is any of this possible?

My lungs are frozen, unwilling to draw breath. I am alone, facing unspeakable horrors, and I am going to lose.

Calm yourself, just like Ate *Jho taught you.* I take a deep breath, willing my racing heart to calm. It isn't over yet—I haven't played all my cards. I didn't think it'd come to this. I clap my hands together and my shaking fingers weave a spell of my own creation. Eight versions of myself materialize, each standing tall in their godly form. Without a glance back at me, they spring into action, igniting into minute suns and turning the front lines into a blaze of destruction.

As my other selves hold back the tide of ancient beings, a sudden sting shoots through my body. "Shit." I grimace, hitting the terra on all fours. I can't fly. I've been in this form for too long.

Think outside the box, just like Ate Jads. With a gentle touch, I infuse solar energy into the grass beneath me, guiding it to where Ricky lies unconscious. The grass grows lush, cushioning his limp body. I use the final strands of my magick to weave a healing spell into the verdant blades, imbuing them with the power to heal his wounds and restore him to strength.

A wave of exhaustion washes over me, causing my vision to blur momentarily. The strain of maintaining my godlike form is taking its toll on my body, and I can feel the white hues of power fading. Panic sets in as my concentration breaks and my doppelgangers flicker out of existence.

Wincing in pain, I struggle to rise to my feet. I've never pushed myself so far beyond my limits. As the remnants of the nightmare horde turn their attention towards me, I take a deep breath and exhale, calming my abused body. I glance towards Ricky, who is still unconscious on the ground.

"Protect them, *kuya*," I murmur before launching into the sky.

I soar away from Ricky, murmuring quiet prayers to the Tree that I can buy him enough time. Fear roils in my stomach as I near the mythical army. Rage simmers in the eyes I meet, and teeth gnash, longing for my flesh.

But they don't attack. Instead, a minotaur unleashes a deep low, shaking his massive horns from side to side. "Traitor!" he snarls. His fur is a sickly blend of grays and blacks that seem to swallow all light. His eyes burn with a dark red hue, and his twisted horns are like gnarled branches of a dead tree, protruding from his skull. "You dare consort with filth that has no right to our world."

The horde erupts in shrieks, bellows, and roars of anger. I can see them clearly now—beings long thought to be mere myths, standing before me. The harpies circle overhead, their raucous cackles echoing one after another as they await the opportunity to feast upon the injured. Their talons gleam like razors, ready to rend flesh from bone.

Some of the creatures I have no name for display exhibit animal-human hybrid traits, like the lion with a woman's head, or a man with the head of a slender dog.

The ancient relatives of the fenrix are here too—the gumiho.

They weave through the ranks of the O'rians, their silver-white fur shimmering like ghosts in the dim light. Multiple tails flick behind them, restless, calculated—like they're already envisioning their next kill.

Legends say the gumiho don't just hunt; they toy with their prey, luring victims into a false sense of security before striking. When I was a kid, Father used to scare me, saying if I wasn't home by sundown, a gumiho would find me, drain me dry, and leave nothing but hollow skin behind.

Now, staring at their bared fangs and gleaming, predatory eyes, I realize the stories weren't just meant to scare me. They were warnings.

The mass appearance of these ancient beings only deepens the mystery. Where the hell have they been all this time? And why now—why Abbadon? I allow myself to descend to the terra, maintaining a cautious distance from the horde.

A hiss escapes one of the naga. "The Earth children have no concern for us." Her black hair flows unnaturally, as if stirred by an unseen hand, and patches of scales mar her once-human face. Her torso seamlessly merges with a silvery-red, serpent's body, its sinuous coils undulating with a hypnotic grace. Her pale yellow, slitted eyes gleam with a sinister intelligence, and her nails are razor-sharp, capable of carving through flesh with ease. "They're the same as every other human in this world. They would prefer our kind diminished. Action is imperative!" Her glare pierces through me, and her sisters hiss in agreement.

That's when it hits me—we're communicating. These ancient beings shouldn't be able to understand me, but somehow, they do. "You speak the tongue of the first," I manage, grasping for time.

A cacophony of mismatched crows and screeches of laughter ripples through the ranks before me.

"You thought us animals, incapable of human speech?" A troll's voice grates against my eardrums. He thumps his wooden club against his hand, thick, gnarled muscles rippling with every movement. His skin, rough and mottled like the bark of a twisted tree, is scored with jagged scars and boils oozing with pus. He grins, revealing a jutting jaw lined with rows of razor-sharp teeth.

"Why Abbadon?" Even I can hear the desperation in my words. "He is the cause of magick's poisoning. Soon, it will reach the Ethereal Tree, and the magick flowing through all of us will die. What will become of you then?" It's a fool's hope, but I search for any sign of uncertainty in each pair of burning eyes.

"You don't think we know that, Sunbringr?" The red-eyed minotaur's powerful jaw is set, without a whisper of empathy on his inhuman face. "Abbadon's atrocities are no concern of ours."

"Don't be fooled!" I can feel the panic clenching my ribs. "Abbadon is merely using us all for his own gain. He's the true enemy to our way of life. Let's put an end to this madness."

My pleas are met with nothing but laughter.

"You are the fool," the naga hisses. "We've been watching from the shadows, witnessing how your kind destroys our home."

"That's not true. The world has united since the Great War. We've made improvements, we—"

The minotaur spits, cutting me off. "Even with the power of a god, you're as blind as the rest of them, Sunbringr." His hoof strikes the terra, sending tiny shock waves through my legs. "Do you know why we have not shown ourselves all this time? After the Great War, all the nations discarded us like the bodies wasted in that foolish conflict, each of us labeled as monsters, when we're born from the same magick that you wield. We don't choose our forms, nor do we feel ashamed. We embrace what we're given. And Abbadon is giving us what we rightfully deserve—a place in this new world."

"This is not the way," I plead. "Things have changed. We will make a place for you, as you deserve, as we have done for your descendants. Destroying the source of our magick will accomplish nothing. You must believe me." It's becoming difficult to draw breath. I cannot fend off this army. I don't want to. These beings have been wronged, and their rage transformed into a tool. They deserve this no more than we do.

"Hypocrite!" the harpies screech from above.

"Do you comprehend the side you have chosen?" the minotaur snaps. "Your Nobles are the true abominations. Their existence alone disrupts the balance of ours! Beings capable of such feats don't even exist. And when their betrayal comes, as it inevitably will, you alone will bear the condemnation of our downfall."

"What are you talking about?" I demand, my voice finding an edge though its tremors.

"You are blind to the truth," the naga retorts, averting her reptilian gaze and addressing the red-eyed minotaur. "Abbadon will soon know of our interference. We must seize them now."

The minotaur grunts and jerks his head in my direction. A chill creeps through my body as I hear the harpies strike the ground behind me. I'm surrounded.

"Please... don't do this," I gasp. For a split second, the beautiful face of my wife fills my mind. Our unborn child—the son I will never meet. "Forgive me, Evera," I whisper.

"The Convergence is upon us!" The minotaur's roar incites savage cries of victory, spreading across the seemingly endless horde.

A distant rumble reverberates through the air, and to my disbelief, the colossal silhouette of a giant emerges on the horizon. The terra shudders beneath my feet with each ponderous step. Giants shun conflict, and their involvement always signals grave consequences. The last time they intervened was during the Great War, ending it decisively. And now, one has come to the aid of the O'rians. I gather my remaining strength and force myself back into the air.

Where in the world are our reinforcements?

"We will claim our rightful dominion over Ethra, emerging from the shadows to reign supreme," the minotaur bellows in a rallying cry. "Not even death can halt our ascension. Today, Ethra bows to us!" The crowd's fervor reaches a fever pitch.

Before I can find the power to flee, a crushing weight smashes me back into the ground, talons piercing through my weakened solar form. The harpy crows triumphantly, and whatever force that held the horde at bay breaks. They descend upon me, biting, clawing, pounding, and tearing into me without mercy.

I turn my focus inward, away from the barrage of pain. A feeble burst of radiance sears those around me, and their cries are accompanied by the scent of burning flesh. With every ounce of strength, I curl up, unable to anything except endure. Slowly, the agony of my body fades into the background, allowing my mind to take me to a happier place.

The tranquil waters of the lake rippled as I wiggled my feet just beneath the surface. Father's wise, baritone voice broke the silence. "Little one," he began. "Our people have sworn an oath to cherish and protect life until our dying breath. But... you're more than just a Tellus now. You're a Keeper of Terrene, and that comes with its own set of challenges. There will be those who don't have your best interests at heart." The words piled like stones.

I turned to look up at him, trying to comprehend the lesson.

"Your mother and I cannot protect you from those who would use you or wish you harm, nor can we shield you from the world. There may come a time when you must make a difficult decision. If you find yourself in a position where you cannot escape unscathed..." Father paused, seeming to search for the right words. "What I'm saying is... protect yourself, son. Always protect yourself first."

This wasn't one of his usual lectures—not a lesson from a chief to his heir. At that time, Father was talking to me as a parent rather than a mentor. I never knew if he realized the impact his words had. They helped shape each decision I'd been forced to make in this life. And every decision I would make in whatever was beyond.

Though I hadn't been able to understand fully as a child, at this moment, I fully understand.

A primal scream tears from my lips as a second solar flare lashes out from my blinding form. I shove myself to my feet, whipping my head around at the ring of shrieking assailants. Smoke rises from flesh and feather alike, but this is not the end of my reckoning.

I can see them—the thin trails of life energy curling off each creature surrounding me. As I begin winding each tendril into myself, I slam a stone door on my heart. There would be no return from this mutilation of my soul, yet there could be no return from death either. And here, now, forced to choose between a life sculpted from sin and a death carried by cowardice, there was only one true option.

The roar of my solar form returning to full strength erased the howls and shrieks of terror. I draw innumerable threads of life force into myself, fanning my flames to levels I've never dreamed of reaching. One by one, the creatures collapse, empty, withered husks. The golden shimmer of death trickles from each corpse, carrying their souls back to the Tree.

The sound of rumbling terra yanks my gaze from the swathe of destruction around me. The giant is going for Ricky. Without thought, I launch into the air and soar across the ashen battlefield. The giant takes a lethal swipe at me, the slipstream of his massive hand sending me tumbling through the air. His strikes are immeasurably powerful, but lack speed.

I right myself and weave between each swing of his arms. He roars in frustration and pain as I crash into the nape of his neck. The giant's life energy is so massive it nearly blinds me as I start to siphon. A palm descends from above, ready to crush me like a stinging fly.

I gather my focus and send a powerful beam directly up and into the falling hand. The giant's wail is painful in my ringing ears, though I suspect the cauterized hole in his hand is worse.

He drops to his knees as the seemingly endless life force flows into me. I can feel his skin beginning to wither away beneath my grasp. I clench my teeth, willing the door on my heart to remain sealed. It takes several long seconds for the giant to finally fall. I rise amidst the golden shimmer of his passing, thrumming with energy and plagued by what I've become.

But my respite is short-lived as two more giants thunder over the horizon, running full-speed at their fallen brother and his murderer. Unable to take any more energy into myself, I release the siphon and prepare to face them head-on. As I charge my radiant beams, another set of ground-quaking footsteps reverberates up my legs from behind. I whirl around just in time to see a third giant pelt past me and meet his brethren with a mighty punch.

It's Gormak. I spare a moment to shoot me a grim smile before winding up to pummel the second giant.

"Gormak, what are you doing here?" I yell, the relief so strong I feel my eyes burning with tears.

"I'm not hiding anymore, Sól," he rumbles. "This is my home, too." The ground shakes beneath us as Gormak and the giants clash, each blow echoing like thunder in the air.

Leaving Gormak to his battle, I spin on my heel and bolt for Ricky's prone form. I stumble across the lush greenery that surrounds him and drop to my knees.

"*Kuya?*" A sharp pain pierces my shoulder—a dagger, barely breaking the skin. Instinctively, I whip around and melt the weapon away, only to find a young man hovering in midair behind me, trembling with fear. The shallow wound burns beneath my skin. I can feel something slithering through my veins. I grit my teeth against the pain and look over my shoulder.

Ricky, on his knees, turns the levitating man towards him. A spark of recognition flashes across his face and his expression twists into a snarl. This man had wronged him somehow. And wronged him deeply. What will Ricky choose: vengeance or mercy? Before I can fathom the answer, he sends the young man hurtling into the distance. Perhaps he will survive the fall, perhaps not.

Ricky doubles over, hands braced on his knees, and struggling for breath. "Are you all right, *kuya?*" I rest a cautious hand on his shoulder.

"I'm fine, thanks for pulling me back," he wheezes.

"Who was that man?"

Ricky sucks in a few more gulps of air and straightens. "The man who killed me."

The memory floods my mind—his final moments on the Isle and Livia's sacrifice to revive him.

He gazes out at the three dueling shapes in the distance. "Is that Gormak?"

I look over at Gormak, bloodied and battered, still fending off the two giants. My heart sinks.

"We need to help—oh, shit." Ricky's voice is devoid of life. Even the energy rolling off of him feels like defeat.

In the distance, a horde of ancient Commisceo charge towards our direction. The minotaur's words were true after all—we cannot stop them at this rate. *Is this the end?*

"This is it, Sól. I'm sorry I let you down," Ricky murmurs. He sinks down to his knees, watching his fate catch up with him.

I take a deep breath and exhale, calming my heart rate.

I'm going to die trying if that's what it takes.

I plant my hands on my *kuya's* shoulders, and channel a fierce cascade of energy into his body. His familiar essence mingles with my own. Our connection shifts into a two-way street, with Ricky's energy tumbling up against the tide of my offering. I'm inundated with a flood of emotions—not my own, but Ricky's. His battles, camaraderie, and sacrifice become tangible, breathing life into his existence. But of these feelings, I know which ones I must tap into.

I've already tarnished my soul beyond recognition, but I fear neither Ricky nor I will make it out of this intact. Silent apologies clamor behind my lips as I pour everything I have into Ricky's fear and his pain. I have to avert my gaze when his face begins to twist.

The patchwork of corpses and unconscious forms litter the field. I can see who we have lost as a kaleidoscope of colors shimmer over those who still breathe. Is this what he sees all the time? I feel the last of the energy leave my hands, and patches of solar glow retreat, leaving my hands their familiar shade of rich brown.

Beneath my touch, I feel Ricky's shoulders bunch as his arms slowly rise from his sides. With them come the limp forms of the survivors. I watch in awe as dozens of our wounded drift overhead, coming to rest safely behind us. His hand fall back to the ground, curling into the soil.

"*Kuya...*" I murmur. "You need to let it out. Let go like you did on the cliffside."

With the ebb of my own energy current, Ricky's flows back into me, full force. Time slows around me and memories that are not my own cloud my mind's eye. I'm in a bedroom where a young Ricky embraces a man who looks just like him, and a woman with a streak of silver in her hair. The vision shifts, and he sits alongside the Huttons in the Space Ring, eating what looks like plate upon plate of Crawdelou sweet meat. Deep love radiates from these memories, but there is also immeasurable grief. The scene vanishes and *Ate* Jho stands beside him, gazing out at the Isle meadows with skies painted in hues of purple and fiery gold.

Just as his and a*te* Jho's eyes meet, I'm in a classroom with another woman , a stranger to me, with curly hair, soft eyes, and a smile that warms both him and myself.

A faint smile ghosts across my lips as a new memory surfaces. This one I'm familiar with—a day I also cherish. The Squad's laughter fills the air as we take turns flaunting our hard-earned magickal prowess and Keeper abilities. An undercurrent of sadness gnaws at my heart in the aftermath of this memory.

I understand now, kuya. You've been through more than most people can endure, yet your heart is as mighty as the sun. You can let it out now, let them hear your rage.

I jolt back to the present and recoil—the ancient Commisceo are upon us. A naga lunges for Ricky's snarling face.

"Let go, Ricky!" I shout, my fingers digging into his skin through fragmented armor, forcing myself to maintain the connection, to keep his spiritual wounds from closing.

With a deafening blast, a raw scream erupts from Ricky's throat, ripping through the naga's flesh. Her shrieks blur into the wails of the horde, a crescendo of agony as the battleground fractures beneath us. Gormak braces himself but is untouched by the force, while the other giants are decimated.

Ricky's soul floods into me, carrying with it years of grief and pain.

Another surge erupts from his vocal chords, engulfing everything in its path. The world around us shatters into fragments, consumed by the power of Ricky's unfettered rage and pain. Only Gormak remains, a solitary figure amidst the destruction.

A haunting silence fills the air.

No wind.

No sound.

Absolute silence.

There's no one left to destroy.

DUST TO DUST

Each breath is a lance through my lungs, but I can't get enough oxygen to my racing heart. Dust settles back to the earth as a sea of shimmering gold rises from the battlefield. A mass graveyard of my own making.

My chest feels like it's trapped within an iron band as I desperately search for any aura amongst the dead—any sign of life. There's nothing. Even the ground beneath my palms is lifeless. Something hot streaks down my face. I'm crying. Sobbing.

"I killed them all, Sól," I choke out. "I fucking killed them all."

Sólel falls to his knees beside me, his solar form patchy and broken. Even as tears fall from his dimming eyes into the dust, he can't seem to look away from the carnage we've wrought.

How did it come to this? My mind is numbed, like wading through glacial waters. I barely acknowledge the whirring sound of crafts approaching.

"They came, *kuya*," Sólel whispers, pushing himself unsteadily to his feet.

I don't move—I can't move— but I hear people rushing to the aid of the few I managed to save. New emotions cling to me as our would-be saviors continue to land and pour out. I can feel them realizing what I've done. Little jolts of victory, and flecks of relief trickle onto me, but one emotion is the most prominent.

Fear.

One by one, the fallen rise as they are healed awake. Whispers surround me, and I don't have to hear them to know what they're saying.

A hand finds my left shoulder, and I turn to see Dustin. Emierr grips my right, his face crumpling. Brunner gets behind me before falling to his knees, wrapping his arms around me in a tight embrace. Through threads of grief, shock, and horror, we gaze out at the field, trying to remember when it was a place of flowers and joy.

I try to recall the sound of my friends' laughter echoing through the fields—only fragments now, distorted through video calls from the Space Ring. The memory was tainted now, by the blood of hundreds, and there was no getting it back.

"Guys, can you hear me?" Jadis' voice comes through the comms.

Brunner releases me, and helps pull me to my feet.

"Jads, you're not hurt, are you?" My voice is little more than a rasp.

"I'm safe, and I'm following Jho. Sending location now."

Robotically, I glance down at the hologram that appears on my bracelet.

"Hurry," Jadis whispers, and the comms go silent.

I feel everyone's eyes on me, waiting to see what I'm going to do next. I finally turn to look behind me, where the Huttons are gazing at me with broken expressions. I see Jae, huddled with Mikal, Maks, and Jihyun. A vague sensation of surprise ripples through me at the sight of Evera, cradling Sólel, in her arms. Chief Berkarys and Chieftess Nalani hover nearby, clearly torn between the desire to comfort their son and allowing him time with his wife.

I can't bear the weight of all these eyes. I see pity, reverence, and gratitude where I should see disgust, horror, and accusation. I want to flee—to run somewhere no one will be forced to bear witness to my shame.

I'm so tired.

I want to rest.

But this isn't over yet. *Keep moving, Ricky.*

"I'm going to get Jho and Jads," I say hoarsely. Without waiting for acknowledgement, I turn to stride away.

"Wait," Dustin calls out. Three sets of boots scuffle after me.

"We're coming," Emierr protests.

"No, I'm going alone. Help everyone here. They need you." I quicken my pace, willing them to just let me go.

"Ricky." Brunner catches hold of my arm, and brings me to a stop.

A hot, almost painful wave of tears blurs my vision. "Please, just let me do this."

Brunner's fingers go limp and his hand slides away.

"It's all my fault," I whisper, turning to face them. "I brought all of you into this world. Let me be the one to get us home." Words fail me as my shoulders shiver with contained sobs.

"You don't have to be alone," Dustin says softly.

"I need to be for this one." I press the heels of my palms into my eyes, trying to stem the flow of tears. . "If I need you guys, I'll call. I promise."

Emierr, for once, doesn't fight. "Please be safe."

Dustin's hesitation is brief, but his worry needles at me as he speaks. "If anything goes wrong, we're there—got it?"

Brunner shakes his head. "But—"

"Just let him go, Rune. He's gonna be fine. We have to trust him." Emierr squeezes Brunner's arm.

It takes a few moments, but finally, Brunner sighs. "Bring them back."

I drop my hands, and blink my vision back into focus. "Thanks, guys."

Dustin gives me a short nod and tugs Brunner back toward the makeshift medical tent being set up.

I catch Miss Delphini giving me *that* look—the one I'd seen on Ma's face before. The kind that hopes, somehow, to take away all the pain, all the sadness—a silent prayer only a mother can make. My lips twitch into the faintest smile, but it doesn't last. Her tears fall, as if they could heal me—maybe once, they could have. But I let the moment pass, let the smile fade, and turn away, allowing my legs to carry me toward Jadis's location.

"Ricky, wait!" Jihyun calls out, grabbing my hand. "I'm coming with you."

A bubble of frustration snaps inside me, and I pull my hand away. "No. Stay here. They need you more than I do. So, please—stay." I avoid his searching gaze.

Since I met him, Jihyun has had this way of quieting my thoughts, steadying my emotions in a way I can't explain. Even now, with him so close, I feel a calm settling over me. But it's not enough. The weight of what I've just done—of all those lives lost—crushes everything else.

"Okay." Jihyun folds his arms tight to his body. "But don't be reckless. Come back to me."

I glance back at him. His hands are clenched into fists, worry carved into every line of his face. *Back to him...*

"Okay." I don't give myself time to dwell on his words. Instead, I summon the sharp sting of lightning and take off into the sky.

The faces of everyone I care about flood my mind—self-loathing twisting their sympathy into accusation. I chose to save them, to protect them at any cost. That meant eliminating those who stood in the way. But I never anticipated the soul-cleaving repercussions of what that meant.

I killed people.

Even if they weren't innocent, the truth is a bitter pill to swallow. All I wanted was to stop the harm, to protect—but in the end, I only added more pain.

One hand propels me forward, the other flicking over my bracelet as I track the hologram's display. Jadis's location shifts across the map, moving toward the village of Moore View. Then—she stops.

"Jads, you there?" I call through the comms.

"Ricky?" Her voice comes through in a whisper, breathless and strained. "Are you guys on your way?"

"It's just me. The boys are helping whoever they can..." My words die in my throat.

"Is everything okay? Did everyone make it out?"

I swallow hard. "Borge is gone... But it's over, Jads. I ended it." My voice is flat, hollow.

Jadis doesn't respond.

"I'm here." I descend into the heart of the forest, where the air hangs heavy with the remnants of battle. Scorched earth, shattered branches, and the faint sting of smoke lingers. It looks like the war reached here too. I spy her, hidden behind a sprawling bush. I land a few feet away, keeping to the shadows.

"Jads," I whisper, crouching beside her.

Her head snaps up. "Oh my god, Ricky." She cups my face, eyes searching mine. "What happened back there?" She looks exhausted. Dark circles smudge beneath her eyes, her skin paler than before, as if something vital has been drained from her.

The failed wish—it's taken a toll on her.

I pull away, ignoring the question. "What happened here?"

She swallows hard, her gaze flickering over my battered state. "I followed the destruction after helping Lacey—I tracked them here."

I peer cautiously over the bush—and there they are, standing in a clearing, surrounded by dense foliage and towering trees. Jhoana lingers just behind Evanora.

"Let's get in there, three is better than one," I whisper.

"Ricky..." Jadis trails off. "My magick is gone."

I whip around and gape at her. "What—"

"I wished our clones didn't exist." Her eyes glittered with tears.

The memory of our clones disappearing into dust clouds my mind's eye. "It was you."

"It was the only way I could think to get rid of them. I had to find some way to help you guys. "

My lips press together. Telling her the truth now might break her. But she'll find out sooner or later. I'm spared from having to choose when Jadis reads my expression.

"Ricky, what happened?" she asks slowly.

"They switched sides," I mumble. "We were about to win against the wave of O'rians because they turned traitor."

"Oh fuck... I... I fucked up." She presses her hands to her mouth. I can see her arms beginning to tremble.

"No." I shake quickly, resting a hand on her shoulder. "You were doing what you thought was right." On some level, I was talking to myself, not Jadis.

Evanora's voice splits the air with a cold laugh. Jadis and I strain to see between the bare bush's limbs.

"I should've gotten rid of you the day I first laid eyes on you," she jeers at Jhoana. "If I had known what you'd become—this *warrior*—I would've never cursed you. You should have been chased off with your friends. Here I thought you would be the least of my worries."

"Then why did you?" Jhoana's voice quakes with fury. "You could've just let me die. That would've been better than *this*. You condemned me to a life I never wanted."

Evanora scoffs. "Don't lie to yourself—it's not very noble of you. I don't need a spell to see how much you love this world. You don't *want* to go back to your pathetic, mundane Earth. You *thrive* here. That's why you were the true threat to this entire plan." Evanora's eyes gleam with wicked amusement. "Abbadon was reckless, just like the rest of you. The day he made those children, I told him it wasn't the right time. You and your little friends weren't even at your prime. But no—'desperate times call for desperate measures,' he said." She waves a dismissive hand. "Those mindless brats were supposed to bring me *Jadis Salazar*—not you. You were just leverage. I was so sure your 'Squad' would come back for you... but I never expected them to abandon you instead." Evanora's thin lips are curved in a cruel smile, her words sharpened to cut, digging where it hurts most.

Jhoana exhales. "I'll admit there's some truth in the bullshit you're spewing."

Jadis and I exchange a glance. We *know* Jhoana loves us—but we also know she loves Ethra more. She'd never say it outright, but I knew the moment I saw her. She's never felt more like herself than she does here.

This time, she might actually admit it.

"Ethra means everything to me." Jhoana maintains her composure, though I can feel the intensity of her emotions like a bed of nails. "It was our sanctuary. Every corner of this place holds memories—moments I cherished with them. Here, I learned to embrace who I really am. But my best friends never got that chance. And you kept me from them." Her brows knit together, resentment breaking through her stoic mask. "That was your mistake."

"Fuck this," I mutter, pushing to my feet. "Enough!"

Both women's heads snap toward me.

"You!" Evanora snarls, eyes pinned on Jadis.

Jadis doesn't respond. Her being here without magick is too dangerous, and if I have to kill one more person to protect the people I love, I won't hesitate.

"I got this!" Jhoana shouts, her hands igniting with force fields.

"It's over, Evanora. Give it up," I say, my voice edged with warning. "Abbadon abandoned you. The O'rians are dead. You're all that's left."

Jadis and Jhoana stare at me, unmoving. I avoid meeting their eyes—I know if I do, I'll break.

"That means nothing to me." Evanora leers at Jadis. "Once I'm done with *her*, you're next, little duck."

The blood magick has consumed her completely. I can't even sense an aura—her soul is beyond saving.

"No," Jhoana says, drawing the witch's attention. "I've spent my whole life a few steps behind my friends—hiding, blending in. But not anymore." Jhoana steadies herself, eyes blazing. "You can't knock me down. Not when I'm finally *living*."

"If you insist." Evanora lifts an arm and slices through her wrist. Blood oozes from the wound, but she only laughs—low and manic. She claps her hands together, releasing a surge of dark purple light. The blood lifts, dancing around her fingers in twisting ribbons. Her veins darken, bulging beneath her skin, pulsing with energy as she rises into the air.

I take a step toward Jhoana, but Jadis places a hand on my chest. "It has to be Jho to break her curse."

"But we can still help her," I argue, keeping my eyes fixed on Evanora.

The look in Jadis's eyes says it all—she wants to be the one to take down the old witch herself. But only the cursed can break the bind that holds them. Her grip tightens on my shirt, a silent plea I don't refuse. Without a word, we turn to watch the battle unfold.

Evanora's blood morphs into something unnatural—shifting, writhing masses of dark matter, almost in the appearance of shadow creatures. The air stirs as zephyrs whip around us.

Jhoana lets out a wordless shout, her arms swinging forward as scythed force fields slice through the air.

But Evanora is faster. With a swift motion, she whirls her right hand above her head, and the force fields detonate against an invisible barrier.

This is more than blood magick.

"Cute, but useless. I'm not just a witch anymore. You can't even fathom what I have become." Evanora's harsh laugh rings through the air, accompanied by the sharp crack of her hands slamming together. Dark matter seeps out of her in every direction, twisting and curling like ink in water.

Jhoana summons her astral bow, drawing an arrow and aiming

high into the sky. She releases, and the arrow tears through the air at breakneck speed. It splits in mid-flight, creating a torrent of projectiles to rain down on Evanora.

My grip tightens around Jadis's hand. The memory of an arrow piercing my leg, and a spear buried in my forearm floats to the surface.

But Evanora's shield doesn't waver. It deflects every one of Jhoana's arrows without so much as a single crack.

"Screw it." I raise my left arm out to Evanora, trying to take hold of her, but my mind bumps up against a solid wall. Telekinesis can't get past it either. How is this possible?

Evanora spreads her arms wide, tilting her head back as the dark matter begins pulling back into her body, absorbing like a tide retreating into the sea. The sight is eerily familiar—like Sólel drawing solar energy into himself.

The realization of what's about to happen knocks the wind out of me. "She's gonna blow everything up!" I gasp. "A mass of dark matter thrown out at that velocity—"

"Jho, get out of there!" Jadis screams. We simultaneously make a move toward Jhoana, a forcefield snaps into place around us.

"What the hell." I press my hand against its surface. "Jho!" My eyes lock with hers. "What are you doing?"

"It ends here," Jhoana says, turning back to Evanora.

No... No. Jhoana has sacrificed more than enough. She can't leave us again. I'm not losing her, not again. *Please, Jho, I need you.*

Jhoana pushes both her arms forward, conjuring another dome around Evanora.

Evanora freezes, her eyes wild. "What are you doing? Release me."

"If I can't hurt you, you'll just have to hurt yourself." Jhoana's voice is lethally calm.

"Release me!" Evanora shrieks. "I can't—I can't stop it!" Her body begins to shudder. The spell is too much; it's going to consume them both.

"The blast will break your field," Jadis shouts. "Let's just get out of here, Jho."

"No, I can't. If this kind of magick unleashes, it might take hold of this area too. There's a village—families and children nearby. I can contain it. I'll implode the blast on itself. That should lessen the impact on the shield around you both."

"What about you? Shield yourself too," I plead, knowing it's pointless. She can't conjure that many shields—not if she wants them to withstand the explosion.

Jhoana's stare lingers on us both. A nameless emotion sweeps over me—the feeling of oxygen after holding your break for too long. The feeling of freedom. A ringing floods my ears, and everything else becomes background noise. Jads and I bang on the field, but I can't hear it. I can't hear our desperate cries for Jho to save herself.

Evanora's body seems to rip apart in slow motion. The initial boom of the explosion is muffled by Jhoana's shields just before they shatter, blowing jet smoke in every direction. Jhoana's feet skid on the grass as the force shoves her back. She flings a second shield around the smoke as the spell gathers itself for a second detonation.

"Jho!" I scream, but I can't even hear my own voice. Jhoana is holding her ground, but her force field won't hold much longer.

She turns our way, an agonizingly beautiful smile spreading across her face as she mouths, "I love you, guys."

"Jho!" And before I can comprehend what I'm about to see, the dome breaks, and Jhoana implodes it with everything she's got. The sound hits us first, before all the dark matter crashes onto the field around us.

"No!" Jadis cries. I spin and fling my arms around her, shielding her with my body. Our own shield splinters, threatening to collapse.

Then, all the noise stops.

"Jho..." Jadis sobs.

"Why did she do it?" I whisper. "She could have saved herself."

Jadis stays buried in my chest, and I fight to keep myself from falling apart. We came here with one singular purpose—save Jhoana. And we failed.

The force field around us looses another cracking sound. I whip my head around at the weakening dome. *How is it still standing?*

"I told you—it all ends here." Jhoana's voice rings out from behind me, strong and *alive*.

Jadis and I break apart with a unified gasp—Jhoana stands just beyond the force field walls, completely unscathed, with Brunner at her side.

She drops the shield, freeing us to crush her in our arms.

In those few seconds I believed she was gone, some part of me had begun making plans to give up. Losing Jhoana wasn't something I could live with.

I'm never letting her go again.

"How?" Jadis's voice cracks.

"Rune," Jhoana says with a wobbly grin.

"I followed you," he admitted. "Never been great at following rules."

I let go of Jhoana and leap at Brunner, welding my arms around him. "Thank you, Rune." I murmur. "Thank you for saving her."

He pauses but returns the hug, resting his chin on my shoulder. "I'd do it for any one of you."

"I'm free." Jhoana stares into the distance. "I can go home."

I drop my arms and allow Brunner to take a step back.

"Everyone is waiting for you." Jadis grabs her hand, smiling through a trickle of crystalline tears.

"I can't believe Ev—"

"Hello, can you hear me?" Dustin's voice interrupts me.

"Dust?" Brunner acknowledges, touching a finger to the comm bracelet.

"Rune... Did you find them?"

"We're here, Dusty," Jho says. "We did it."

Dustin doesn't respond for a moment.

We all look at one another, anxiety prickling the air between us.

"Guys..." Dustin exhales deeply. "You need to come back here now. It's... bad, real bad. Hurry." The line cuts.

"When I left, everything seemed fine." Brunner looks over at me, eyes wide with fresh fear.

"Nobody's hurt, right?" Jhoana asks, looking between us. I don't even know how to answer. Who *didn't* I hurt is the real question.

"Nobody we're close to, at least," Brunner speaks for me. "Um, should we use the teleportation spell?"

"I—I lost my magick." Jadis mutters, her guilt and sorrow flooding through me. It must be like losing a limb for her.

"What?" Brunner's voice hitches.

"I'll explain later." She clenches her jaw. "But no magick."

Brunner extends his arms out to us. "Then you guys better hold on tight."

"I'll keep us together," I say.

We latch onto Brunner—gripping his arms, his shoulders—and onto each other. With a steady pull of telekinesis, I anchor us in place.

We brace ourselves, and in an instant, our surroundings fracture like shattered glass, stretching and distorting before snapping upward into the sky. The broken pieces realign, forming a single image—we're no longer on the ground.

We've teleported midair, high above the forest.

"Fuck." I dig my fingers into Brunner's arm just as we blink again—this time, even farther, still suspended in the air. Another blink. Then another. The fractured mirrors shift downward, pulling us closer to the earth.

I squeeze my eyes shut, bracing for impact—

But solid ground appears beneath my feet. My eyes snap open. We're back at the Great Eagle Fields.

"Woah." Jadis breathes out. "It must've been one hell of a fight."

We look out into the aftermath. My hands begin to tremble.

Gormak kneels, his massive frame looming over the ground as he bows his head. A crowd has gathered around him, their silent grief washing over me. We push through the crowd.

There is no victory today. Not after all the lives lost.

"Mom!" Maks calls out, darting over and wrapping Jhoana in an embrace, Jihyun and Mikal close behind.

"Is it done? You get to go home?" Mikal's voice is a blend of fear, excitement, and sorrow. His eyes keep darting toward mine. There's something he's not saying.

Their mother is finally going back to Earth, just as they always wished for her. But beneath, the grief is unmistakable. Tears slip down their faces, lips trembling as they struggle to hold themselves together. Anyone can see it—how much this breaks them.

Jhoana has to leave them.

But this isn't the end. She *will* see them again. *We* will see Ethra again.

We just have to get Jhoana home.

"Dusty!" Jadis yells, startling me from my reverie.

Dustin lifts his head, and the look on his face guts me—a hollow, haunted expression. The kind you only wear when you've lost someone.

Who the fuck is hurt?

"What's going on?" Jadis asks, her voice wavering. Her walls are cracking, and I can feel her fear creeping in. We half-run to Dustin's side.

"Dust?" Brunner's tone is uneasy. "Where's Meer?"

A crushing wave of panic grips me, and I push through the sea of people, the others close behind. Past the suffocating sorrow, we see him—Emierr, on the ground, wracked with sobs as he cradles Sólel's limp body.

I stop dead, my legs no longer willing to carry me closer.

What happened? He was fine when I left. Did one of the O'rians survive?

A few steps away, Evera kneels, motionless. Chief Berkarys and Chieftess Nalani hold onto her, their eyes heavy—not just with sadness, but mourning. They believe he won't make it.

My focus snaps back to Sólel.

His skin is ashen, dark tendrils of poison snaking through his veins in a sinister web, spreading outward from the wound. *How could anything pierce his solar armor?*

His breath is ragged, his half-open eyes barely clinging to awareness. Emierr's face is twisted in agony, tears carving silent paths down his cheeks as he whispers soothing words, desperate to comfort his brother.

Sólel's fingers twitch weakly, grasping at Emierr's shirt, a frail attempt to hold onto life.

The acrid stench of poison mixes with the sharp metallic scent of blood, turning my stomach.

The world around me blurs, shrinking to the heartbreaking scene before me—the cruel, slow theft of life from our little brother.

"How? When?" I drop to my knees beside him.

Sólel's voice is barely a whisper. "*Kuya...* Your killer—he got me."

The moment replays in my head like a distorted reel.

I had just regained consciousness, and the first thing I saw was Woden—his blade poised, ready to strike Sólel. But I caught him... Didn't I? I remember the weapon slipping from his grasp as soon as I had him in my telekinetic hold. But was it before or after he struck? I was too weak, too out of it to know if I held him tight enough. Did he—

"It's not your fault," Sólel whispers, cutting off my unraveling.

I clutch Sólel's hand, and his memories flood into me—every single one. Moments frozen in time, flickering like stills in a film. Every adventure, every laugh, every tear. Every time he felt at home.

He *loves* us. Truly, deeply. As if we were his real brothers and sisters.

Oh, Sól... You saved us all.

It's not fair.

He gives me a weak smile and squeezes my hand three times. "*Ate...* Jho?"

"I'm right here, little one." Jhoana kneels down next to me.

"Thank the Tree." He smiles weakly. "Ready..." He wheezes as he tries to take in air and winces. "To go... home?"

Jhoana nods. "Thank you, Sól." She leans forward and presses her forehead onto his.

"Jads, do what you did with Ricky." Emierr looks up to her. "Please... Save him."

"Meer..." Jadis's voice cracks. "I lost my magick. But... the poison. It's blood magick, and it's spread too far... I—I'm sorry."

"No, look!" Emierr reaches up and grips her wrist. "If this is blood magick, then why is he still alive? It took Ricky down faster than it's taking him."

Jadis's mind is racing—she *has* to know how to save him. She *will* know.

"His powers... They might be fighting it off," she mutters. "That's why it's taking longer."

My heart drops. *She doesn't have a solution.*

"Then bring in the Menders, teach them how you did it." Emierr's words are desperate. He scans the crowd, but no one steps forward. "*Anyone?*"

All at once, a familiar ringing starts to resound in my ears. The Squad all look at each other. Our alarms on Earth.

"No!" Emierr shouts. "We can't leave him like this. We can't let him die!"

"If we don't go now, they'll pull the plug on Jho," Jadis says shakily. "I'm sorry, Sól."

"Go..." Sólel coughs. "All of you."

Evera rises to her feet, cradling her swollen belly. "We have him. Let us send him to the Tree."

"It's okay, my son," Chief Berkarys has never sounded so fragile. "You'll be okay."

The alarm is blaring now, tugging at my consciousness.

Fucking bitch! What do I do? It's always the same—we come here, do what we want, and leave them to pick up the pieces of the mess we made.

"Ricky!" Jadis snaps.

"Transcendence," I blurt out, the word tumbling from my mouth before I can think.

"What?" Emierr stares up at me, the faintest thread of hope in his eyes.

"We bring Sól back with us." I'm practically tripping over the words. "It's the only way to save him." It sounds completely insane but—Ma did it. Auntie Via did it. It's possible. It *has* to work.

"Let's do it." Emierr doesn't hesitate, clenching his fingers around Sólel's hand.

"Transcendence..." Chieftess Nalani whispers. "You're taking him to Earth?"

"Our son will live..." Chief Berkarys says, holding his wife to his chest. "Little one, go. Your brothers and sisters will protect you."

"We will bring him back," I vow. "We will find a way to bring him back to you."

"Guys, I don't think Gordo bought us enough time," Jadis warns, tension snapping off her body.

"Then you have to go with Jho, Jads." I glance between them. "Get her home."

"What about you?" Jadis shoots back.

"I'm not leaving until I see all of you Transcend back. No one's getting stuck here again."

"No." Jadis' breath comes fast and uneven. "We go back *together.* That's what you said."

"I'll go with Jho." Brunner steps in. "I'll guide her back."

I give him a short nod of thanks. The alarm blares louder, unbearable now. *Fight it. Don't wake up yet.*

Jhoana's kids hold onto her one last time, trying to stay brave in the face of their family's impending fracture.

Jhoana unties her scarf and wraps it around Maks. "I love you three," she whispers through tears. "Just look up at the sky—I'm never too far away. I'll be back. This isn't goodbye."

Brunner takes her hand, and together, they inhale deeply. "Astralis."

It's working. Their bodies shimmer, golden outlines flickering before they fade into nothing.

We did it.

"Dust." I scan the crowd for him.

"I'm here." He appears beside me.

"Go with Meer. Help him guide Sól back to Earth."

"I'm on it." He kneels behind Emierr, gripping his shoulders in quiet support.

"Rictor."

Miss Delphini takes one of my hands. Dr. Wolfgang interlocks his fingers with the other, and Al rests both hands on my shoulders. No words are spoken. They don't need to be.

Memories flood my mind—Miss Delphini watching me with quiet amusement as I ramble about Earth on the Space Walk. Dr. Wolfgang pulling me into a tight hug as I strut around in his oversized lab coat, pretending to be him. Albert soaring through Ethra's skies with me in his spaceship, laughter echoing between us.

All of it. Every moment. Every piece of love they've given me.

No family is perfect, but I'm grateful I had them. That I still *have* them.

"I love you guys," I say, releasing the last of the pain they left behind.

"Please... say your goodbyes," Emierr chokes out, his voice breaking as he looks at Sólel's family.

Chieftess Nalani clutches her son, her quiet sobs muffled as she presses her forehead gently against his.

I tighten my grip on the Huttons' hands, and they lean their heads against my shoulders, grounding me in their silent grief.

"Mom..." Sólel's voice trembles, small and fragile. He's nine again. "I'm scared, Mom."

"It's all right, little one," she whispers, her voice thick. "I will always be right beside you. *Always.* I will sing to you every night—just listen to the winds. And you will hear my heart, okay?"

Sólel nods. "I'll come home, Mom. I promise."

"Your *Kuya* Meer will take care of you until then, just as he always has," Chieftess Nalani murmurs, pressing a gentle kiss to his forehead.

"My son..." Chief Berkarys murmurs. His voice trembles. "My beautiful son." Tears spill down his face.

"Father..." Sólel's breathing is labored now. "I'm sorry I didn't become chief like you wanted."

"That never mattered." Chief Berkarys grips his son's hand tightly. "The reason I never pushed you to take the title is because I realized—I didn't want that for you. I just wanted you to be *my son*. And you've given your mother and me the greatest honor—we are so proud to be your parents. Ethra is proud to have you as its Noble." His voice breaks, but he holds firm. "I don't want you to go. But if this means you get to breathe a little longer, then take it. Take it, my son. And I will see you again."

He presses his forehead against Sólel's, a silent goodbye.

"I love you, Mom. I love you, Dad," Sólel whispers, his voice barely audible.

Chief Berkarys's face crumples at the sound of his son calling him "Dad." A name he hadn't heard since he became chief. A name he might never hear again.

My tears betray me.

"My heart," Sólel murmurs, a fragile smile trembling on his lips as he reaches for Evera.

"Hello, my love." She gently takes his hand, guiding it to her belly.

"I love you both," he breathes. "With everything I have."

Evera's resilience finally cracks and tears trace her cheeks. "Solén. His name will be Solén."

Sólel's hand moves weakly to her cheek, his touch feather-light.

"He will know his father," she whispers. "He will know the stories of the Sunbringr. Until you come home."

"I'm sorry, my dearest," Sólel's chokes.

"No, my love. You've done your duty," Evera whispers. "You won't be gone—you are everywhere we are. You are the energy of the sun, the flowers in our garden, the winds that rattle the trees. And now... you will be infinite." She presses her forehead to his, holding his hand tightly. "We will miss you, but you will never be far from us. And I know you will come back to me. I love you, Sólel Jupiter." She leans in, kissing him one last time.

"The Sunbringr..." Chief Berkarys' voice carries across the crowd, strong and unwavering. "Has fulfilled his duty. Let us honor Ethra's Noble. We sing him the *Passage of Life* so he may breathe anew."

The people of Terrene lift their hands, and a melody rises—a song I have never heard, yet its tone is achingly familiar. A song of loss.

Harmonies intertwine, voices trembling with grief, and in one breath, Dustin and Emierr whisper, "Astralis."

Sólel's voice is barely a whisper. *"Per stellas iter facere."*

Dustin and Emierr begin to dematerialize as Evera cradles Sólel in her arms. He exhales one final breath, and the light in his eyes dims—fading into nothing.

His parents kneel beside Evera, holding onto him, cherishing their last moments together. Then, gently, quietly, golden dust rises from his body, carried away by the winds, guiding him back to the Ethereal Tree.

Please work.

"Ricky." Jadis steps in front of me, her voice steady. "It's time." She glances toward the Huttons and Al. "I'll give you a minute."

Miss Delphini releases my hand, Dr. Wolfgang following suit.

"Take care of yourself, okay?" Dr. Wolfgang's voice wavers, thick with unspoken emotion as he fights back tears.

"Okay." I give him a small smile.

Miss Delphini clasps my arms, her eyes scanning me as if memorizing every detail. She brushes off my jacket, fussing over me like she always did. "Make sure you eat three full meals a day, and..." Her grip tightens. "Just be you. Never change."

I press my lips together and nod.

Albert grins, though his eyes glisten with unshed tears. "I'm so proud of you," he says, voice full of warmth. "You really are the little brother I never had."

We fall together into a tight embrace. I kiss both the Huttons on the cheek, and Albert rests his forehead against mine. It's not goodbye. I know that now.

Miss Delphini pulls back first, glancing over her shoulder. "Say goodbye to him," she says softly.

I follow her gaze.

Jihyun stands with Maks and Mikal, waiting.

"One more goodbye," I murmur, looking at Jadis before stepping toward him. I never thought I could hate the sound of my alarm more than I do at this moment.

Maks offers me a small, bittersweet smile. "Take care, Ricky. And please... keep my mom safe."

"Always." I smile back and pull her into a tight hug.

"Don't forget us," Mikal says, gripping my shoulder firmly.

"How could I?" I extend a hand, but he brushes it aside, pulling me into an embrace.

"I leave it to you," he whispers. "Make her happy."

"I promise."

We let go, and they step over to Jadis, who's now quietly crying. They pull her into a gentle hug before the Huttons and Albert wrap her tightly in their arms, their voices low as they whisper their goodbyes. Sólel's parents and Evera join them, surrounding Jadis in quiet comfort.

"Ricky." Jae's voice crackles through the comms.

"Jae…"

"I couldn't stay, but take care. It was nice meeting you—you're exactly what my dad said."

A lump forms in my throat. "I'll see you again, brother."

"Till next time. See you around."

The line cuts out, and the alarm fades into the background, drowned out by the pounding in my ears—beating in sync with my racing heart.

"Ricky! We gotta go!" Jadis yells.

I don't look at her—I can't. My eyes are locked on Jihyun, just a few feet away.

Every step toward him feels like running a marathon, like I'll never reach him fast enough.

There was something about him I couldn't quite place when he first held me in his arms. Now, I understand—our connection is stronger than I ever imagined.

And that smile—the soft, half-smile he only wears in moments of quiet—makes me feel safe in a way nothing else does.

We're barely a foot apart now. My legs feel unsteady.

"Just say it," he breathes.

My throat tightens, and I swallow hard. I *can't.*

"I…" The words catch, and before I can force them out, he speaks first.

"Ricky… I'll miss you," he says, his voice warm, yet aching.

In a single breath, I close the distance, pulling him into an embrace. His arms wrap around my waist, our cheeks brushing as we hold on tighter. The weight of everything—every unsaid word, every moment between us—settles into that single touch.

"I'm glad I met you," I whisper against his ear.

"The gardens, remember," he murmurs back.

"Ricky!" Jadis shouts. A deep ache roots itself in my chest.

This is goodbye for now. I don't know when I'll be back. Years could pass until I see him again.

"Now!" she snaps, planting a hand on my back.

I pull back just slightly—my lips hovering inches from his.

"Astralis," Jadis and I say in unison.

The last thing I see is Jihyun's face before I'm wrenched from his arms, hurtling into the abyss of the cosmos.

We spiral wildly, our essences flung through endless universes, racing back toward our bodies.

"Ricky!" Jadis reaches for me amidst the chaos of space.

"Jads!" My fingers stretch toward hers, brushing just out of reach—until finally, we grab hold, anchoring each other.

"You gave up your magick!" I yell.

"And you never told Jihyun how you feel!" she fires back.

We burst into wild laughter, our voices echoing through the void. Our arms pin our bodies to one another—the only solid presence keeping us grounded.

We close our eyes, the pull back to Earth growing stronger. A familiar tingling spreads through me, and suddenly—I feel it. My toes. My fingers. The weight of my body.

I inhale sharply, stale basement air filling my lungs.

Jadis and I exchange a look before turning to the couch—where Cam sits, tied up and waiting.

It takes everything in me *not* to punch this scum in the face.

"*Ate* Jads—*Kuya* Ricky." Sólel's voice rings out from behind us.

We jolt, spinning around.

"Sól?" My brows furrow.

Emierr and Dustin sit beside him, looking just as stunned. This *is* Sólel, but he's younger—our age, maybe, clad in the same dusty clothes he'd worn on the battlefield. I blink hard, trying to make sense of it, but right now, none of that matters.

"It worked!"

Jadis and I pile onto him, fighting tears of relief.

"How are you feeling?" I ask, cupping his face.

He blows out a breath. "I feel like… me," he says, then pauses before adding, "but I feel lighter here."

"Time dilation?" Jadis muses.

I shrug, scanning the room. "Where's Rune?"

"He wasn't here when we got in," Emierr answers.

Jadis's eyes widen. "Jho!"

We jump to our feet, but Sólel staggers, caught in a sudden wave of dizziness. Dustin and Emierr steady him, and we waste no time rushing up the stairs.

As we reach the living room, we freeze. Strangers fill the space, their faces unreadable. The front door stands wide open, and beyond it—the entire town gathered outside, anticipating.

We push forward toward Jhoana's room, but the movement feels wrong. It's like teleporting with Brunner, except instead of getting closer, the distance stretches, warping as if we're being pulled away from the steps.

Did she come back in time? Or are we about to say goodbye?

My feet feel impossibly heavy, each step up the stairs making my legs wobble.

We're here, Jho. We're all here.

We burst into the room, and all our parents are gathered around Jhoana's bed. Auntie Ina's weeping echoes off the walls.

"Jho!" I shout, my voice cracking.

Everyone turns toward us. Their eyes shimmer with tears, yet their faces are alight with relief—joy. Auntie Ina steps away from the bed, still crying, and suddenly pulls me into a crushing hug.

I don't know how to handle *this* side of her.

The parents step aside, revealing Jhoana at last. She's *awake*—a radiant smile lighting up her face. The tubes that once tethered her to the machines are gone, and the sickly pallor she wore for years has been replaced with warm, healthy color.

Dustin, Emierr, Jadis, and Sólel rush to her, their joy spilling over as they wrap her in fierce hugs. Jhoana's eyes widen, a mix of shock and relief washing over her as she takes in the sight of Sólel standing in *our* world.

The parents glance at him, a flicker of confusion in their eyes—but no one questions it for now.

Tears spill down their faces, soaking into Jhoana's clothes. Brunner stands at her bedside, where the monitors once hummed, his own tears falling freely as he mouths a silent *thank you* to me.

I wipe at my face, ready to join them—

Then, a scream pierces the air outside.

Everyone freezes. Another scream follows. Then more, joining in a panicked cry.

I move to the window, heart hammering. My eyes widen at the sight.

"Bitch," I mutter, bolting for the stairs.

"Ricky, what is it?" Dustin shouts. Footsteps echo behind me, and as I reach the living room, police officers are swarming into the basement, guided by Miss Santiago. The living room is deserted; the commotion outside has drawn everyone's attention. As I step into the fresh air, a cacophony of screams and shouts assaults my ears, the smell of burning wood stinging my nostrils. The crowd is a chaotic mass of bodies, their faces twisted with fear and confusion. I shove through the throng, my heart pounding in my chest, feeling the rough push of shoulders and elbows as I force my way forward.

The heat from the flames reaches me before I see the source. I finally break free from the crowd and stand in the middle of the road. My breath catches in my throat as I take in the sight of Mr. Dawson's house, engulfed in roaring flames, the fiery tongues licking the sky. The structure is collapsing, burning into oblivion, the wood cracking and splintering with explosive force.

Dustin, Jadis, and Emierr join me, their faces pale and eyes wide with horror. Just beyond the flames, standing on the other side of the burning home, I see a handful of people who look like Mormon missionaries—the Mormon 2.0. They ignored us for once, gazing at the devastation.

Together, we stare, rooted to the spot, as the inferno consumes all the evidence we needed, leaving behind nothing but ashes and smoke.

ACKNOWLEDGEMENTS

I want to preface this by saying that becoming an author has been my lifelong dream. As I write this, I find myself in tears, forever grateful. Thank you all for making me an author.

First and foremost, I want to thank my Papa and Mom, the greatest inspirations in my life, for giving me the freedom and support to choose my own path. I will spend the rest of my life making sure they reap the rewards of my success. I love you both more than the world itself. To my family and relatives back in the motherland, the Philippines—thank you for your endless love and support.

To my siblings—Jun, Ling, and Raven—thank you for not only helping me fund this passion project, but for always taking care of me. And to Shawn and Roshelle, thank you for always believing in me. I love you butt faces.

Jesruel Segovia, my ultimate best friend—thank you for creating the BEST book cover EVER, for listening to me ramble about plotlines and plot holes, and for everything else in between. You stuck with me through *Superstring* from its inception to its completion. Every time I lost hope, your friendship, wisdom, and love reminded me to take it one step at a time. I couldn't ask for anyone better to wake up in the middle of the night just to hear my latest idea. *Wumbo.*

To my best friends, thank you for believing in me since the first grade—I love you bitches. And to the friends who supported me through it all, this is for all of you. My friendships with each of you are why I can do this. It's why I *do* this—to share just how grateful I am to have you in my life.

To my editor and co-author Regan Westergard—*we fucking did it!!!* I'm so happy my desperation led me to join those Facebook writing groups, because meeting you changed everything. I promised you a lifelong partnership and friendship, and I meant it. I hope the universe showers you with all the blessings you deserve. I love you so much. *We in this for life, bitch! Love you!*

Sorry, got a little unprofessional there—where were we?

To the writers I met along this journey—thank you for being part of this monumental milestone in my life.

To Kallie Wassem, author of *The Wingless King*—thank you for being a light during the early stages of *Superstring*. Your drive and passion kept me going, and I'm so grateful to have you as a friend.

To Emily Bellman, author of *The 11th Code* (Parts 1 & 2)—you have been such a huge influence and a rock during the most crucial stages of *Superstring*. You are my writing soulmate. I love you, I love you, I love you!

To my writing communities: *Authors Alliance*—my very first writing group, love you all. *Beautiful Talented Creatures*—thank you for giving me a space where I feel wanted and appreciated. You are some of my favorite people in the world. Ten years from now, we'll all be bestselling authors—I just know it. *Up, Down, Left, Write*—you just recently accepted me, but the sheer talent and inspiration in this group are *unsurmountable*. Thank you. And to all the incredible writers out there cheering for me—right back at you!

Lastly, to the people I grew up with—Justin, Kierr, Junior, Gladys, and Rhoana—you don't know what it meant to me to have all of you choose me as your friend.

Junior, you were my very first friend in Guam. I'll never forget you calming me down on my first day of school. You showed me what kindness is.

Kierr, I don't even remember how we met, but you taught me how to laugh at life and enjoy the moment in all its glory. You may not know it but, a lot of my happiest memories are laughing with you. I loved being your ride-or-die.

Gladys, you were the one friend who reveled in my weirdness. You taught me how to live unapologetically. Thanks for always running beside me.

Justin, you are unequivocally my brother. You taught me that family isn't just blood. The day you called me your brother changed my life. I love you, man—you'll always have a home with me, like we promised.

Rhoana, my soulmate—thank you. Words aren't enough, so I wrote you a book instead. You taught me that nothing is ever impossible when you're *finally living*. I love you, in every universe.

Thank you, weirdos, for living in my world with me.

About The Authors

Photographed by Rhoana Lynn Hendrix

Victor Cabinta is a Filipino author based in Guam. He holds an MA in Creative Writing and aspires to pursue a PhD in the same field. His debut work, *Infinite Vol. 1*, is a short story collection, and *Superstring* marks his first full-length novel.

Cabinta's mission is to share his Filipino heritage and culture with the world while also representing Guåhan's rich traditions and lifestyle in every story he creates. When he's not building worlds, he can be found dancing—whether in his room or on the dance floor.

His dream is to one day own a dance studio with a library.

To stay connected and support his work, follow him on Instagram **@victorcabinta** for updates, or visit **www.victorcabinta.com**.

About The Authors

Regan Westergard is an American author living in South Korea and the co-author/editor of Superstring. When she's not violently crocheting, she's wrangling ferrets, and boldly assuming she can do DIY home improvement.

Regan has been writing fantasy since she was eleven years old, first foisting a half-baked werewolf novel on her extended family. She likes to think she has somewhat improved since then, though she did receive rave reviews. From there, she became the kind of essay writer Idaho public school teachers loved, then graduated to a freelance content writer after graduating magna cum laude in bullshitting.

Beyond her writing career, Regan is also an independent editor and loves nothing more than discovering the hidden gems that independent writers have to offer. Of course, she is also willing to polish a turd for the right price.

To stay connected and support her work, follow her on Instagram **@regan.westergard** for updates, or her editing page **@eyebright.e diting**

www.ingramcontent.com/pod-product-compliance
Lightning Source LLC
Chambersburg PA
CBHW051052030726
47504CB00006B/1591